BEHOLD, HE SAID
MESSIAH TRILOGY -BOOK 3

I0646461

Tom Flynn

BEHOLD, HE SAID
MESSIAH TRILOGY -BOOK 3

DOUBLE DRAGON

Dedication

To Susan, with yet deeper love and admiration. This time, it was the ferkeeks.

Epigraphs

Cunning plates fraud with the gold of honesty, and
veneers vice with virtue.
— Robert Green Ingersoll

Still, write it down, it might be read;
Nothing's better left unsaid.

Only sometimes ...
– Keith Reid

Acknowledgments

Special thanks to paranormal investigator Joe Nickell; Tim Binga, director of the Center for Inquiry Libraries; and scholar of religion Robert M. Price. Steve Cuno and Joanne Hanks provided invaluable commentary on the manuscript, Steve alerting me to an especially prickly cul-de-sac in my plotting. Lauren Becker and Lihann Jones reviewed portions of the manuscript, advising when, respectively, the science jokes and the Mormon jokes were funny. (Lauren also untangled some math puzzles for me – did I mention that I'm innumerate?)

Felisa Wolfe-Simon offered precious assistance regarding the possible biochemistry of radically unearthly life forms. George Zebrowski settled a Golden Age trivia question.

On various scientific and technical matters I am indebted to the published works of Ilya N. Bindeman, Elliot Cohen, Graham P. Collins, Paul Davies, Daniel C. Dennett, Jared Diamond, Pankaj S. Joshi, Lawrence M. Krauss, Lynne A. Isbell, George Musser, James-Charles Noonan, Jr., Lisa Randall, and Peter D. Ward.

Only Jeff Linton, who knew me when, and Tom Franczyk, who knew me later, will understand what I thank them for. Apologies to Keith Reid, who so far as I know is still living, and to Theodore Sturgeon, Roger Zelazny, Cyril Kornbluth, and (from another discipline entirely) Gene Scott, who are not.

For stimulating my thinking (if not always in a positive way), I acknowledge the published works of Frank J. Tipler and his muse, Pierre Teilhard de Chardin, as well as a long-ago college instructor, Richard Rolwing, who showed me what can come of taking one's Teilhard too seriously. For trenchant critiques of

Tipler's manic Teilhardian speculations, I thank physicist Victor Stenger.

For matters moosely, the published works of Victor van Ballenberghe, Valerius Geist, and Bill Silliker, Jr. offered invaluable reference.

Regarding all things Mormon, some explanation is in order. The "ancient" Mormonism the character Alrue Latier wishes to restore includes authentic elements drawn from early Mormon life during the successive leaderships of Joseph Smith and Brigham Young. Occasionally I took satiric license in combining elements that were not strictly contemporaneous. Colorful figures of speech and turns of phrase are authentic, most drawn from Mormon scripture or the writings of church pioneers. Many incidents in the lives of the Mormon characters are based on attested experiences of early (or occasionally modern-day) Mormons. I drew on a wide range of Mormon, former-Mormon, and anti-Mormon polemic literature for these elements. Each aspect of the Mormon Temple wedding I depict is based on attested descriptions from early or recent sources.

Nauvoo, Illinois, is real. The last Mormon city raised by Joseph Smith, it was from Nauvoo that Mormon bands departed for the Great Salt Lake under Brigham Young following Smith's death at the hands of a mob. During a surprisingly brief span of years, Mormon settlers built Nauvoo into a thriving prairie town much like the fictional village I describe, though of course (so far as is known) without dependence on offworld technologies. So vigorous was Nauvoo in its prime that its *town* militia, the Nauvoo Legion, was widely considered more than a match for the state militia of Illinois. Nauvoo still exists today, though parts of its Mormon-era street grid have faded away. I thank cartographer Steven K. Rogers for his personal assistance.

On Mormon matters generally I acknowledge great debt to the published works of Will Bagley, Fawn M. Brodie, David John Buerger, Todd Compton, G. T. Harrison, Eber D. Howe, Carolyn Jessop with Laura Palmer, Sonia Johnson, Jon Krakauer, Deborah Laake, Glen M. Leonard, Linda King Newell and Valeen Tippetts Avery, Richard Packham, George D. Smith, Wallace Stegner, Jerald and Sandra Tanner, Ernest H. Taves, and Jack B. Worthy.

No moose were harmed in the writing of this novel.

And yes, there really was a Pope Hilarius.

Chapter 1

August 11, 2367 (not that anyone still tells time that way)

Planet Bohrkk, Sector Rho Lambda: Punitorium L752

"You're not very good, are you?"

"What?"

"Not a good Spectator," Nataleah Latier said sourly. "When you turned on, your eyes twitched."

Meryam Mayishimu shrugged. "I'm a documentarian. The virtuoso Spectators, the ones who, um, 'turn on' with no one noticing, they get the plum assignments – living among savages on Enclave worlds, that sort of thing. Me, I'm as good as I have to be."

"But no better." Nataleah frowned.

Meryam shrugged. "Shall we begin?"

"I thought we had."

Meryam shifted her lean fanny on the worn cellblock bench, wishing it offered more padding. "The Parek affair," she said crisply. "It changed your husband's life."

"And mine. If not for Parek, I'd never have met my husband."

"If not for your husband, you wouldn't be in here."

Dense black curls trembled against Nataleah's bizarrely chalky skin. "You know how it was."

"*I* do, yes," Meryam prodded. "But tell my experients."

Nataleah paced, frowning. "More than twenty standard years ago, Alrue violated Enclave to instruct Arn Parek."

"The false messiah."

"You say that." She spun to face Meryam. "Breaking Enclave is serious business. Alrue nearly got put away for it."

"But he wasn't. One of history's more improbable escapes from justice, to be sure."

"Ten standard years later, everything was different. It wasn't fair! Sfelb, they'd needed Alrue's ship to help save the Galaxy. They promised him a blanket pardon."

Meryam shrugged. "But he didn't cooperate."

"Some say that." Nataleah's ashen fingers traced a filthy ledge. "Still, the way things ended was so forjeling wrong." She pursed her lips. "Ooh, can a preacher's wife say 'forjeling'?"

Meryam spread her hands. "You just did."

"I did not."

"You said 'sfelb,' too."

"No."

"I can play you back the journal ..."

"Never mind." Nataleah scowled, elbows bent, balled fists clutching at her inmate tunic. "The point is, not only did Alrue end up doing time in spite of a blanket pardon, they threw his extended family in with him."

"You mean yourself and the other plural wives."

"Why jail us? We weren't accomplices, we were just waiting in our, our ..."

"Harem?" Meryam supplied.

"That's no Mormon word. But we played no part in what Alrue was up to."

Meryam leaned against a mottled wall. "You didn't have to come in here with him."

Nataleah bristled. "Sure, we had a choice. Divorce Alrue and lose our children, or serve time with him. And lose our children."

"But this way you get your children back," Meryam said.

"Eventually."

"They're being raised in Mormon homes," Meryam noted. "They'll be returned when your husband's sentence ends."

"And meanwhile?" Nataleah fought back tears. *"They sealed our wombs."*

"First time I've heard reversible sterilization described that way. Look, children can't grow up in detention."

"Oh, really?" Nataleah raised an eyebrow. "All right, Abigayl's a special case. As a general matter, no one wants inmates breeding 'torium tots. But do you know what it means to a woman of the New Restoration, not being able to give her husband more children?" Nataleah clasped her hands together. "And do you know, our sentence – being incarcerated for a husband's crimes – has no precedent in Galactic law? Constance looked it up."

Meryam cocked an eyebrow. "Nonetheless, you opted to stay with him. You, Constance, the three other wives."

"Abigayl was too young for a divorce." Nataleah collapsed into a decrepit formchair. It joggled uncertainly before flowing snug against her buttocks and back. "What happened to us wasn't justice," she said darkly. "It was a tantrum."

Meryam spread her fingers. "I'll admit, it was irregular."

"My turn now, Fem Documentarian." Nataleah leaned back; after an interval the chair followed her. "How did *you* meet my husband?"

Meryam chuckled. "It was almost twenty-five standard years ago, a bit before the Parek affair. Alrue was still on Terra, just starting to build a Galactic audience. I was a journalist. I gave him one of the toughest interviews he'd had to that time. It became

17

terribly popular. I heard that after he got famous, some things he'd told me proved embarrassing for him."

Nataleah nodded. "And then?"

"A decade later, a being claiming to be me came into Alrue's circle. That ... *thing* became a partner in the scheming that ultimately got Alrue – and you – incarcerated. But it wasn't me."

Nataleah nodded darkly. "It was really that self-aware monstrosity and his human handler ... what was his name?"

"Gram Enoda."

Nataleah half-smiled. "Ever wonder where he is today?"

"Not if I can help it." Meryam fingered a twist of her chocolate-red hair, immediately realizing she shouldn't do that while recording. *A field Spectator would know that without thinking.* "Anyway, the impostor's antics put my name back in the public eye. I'd always dreamed of being a Spectator. Starting so late, the best I could hope for was to be a documentarian." Meryam caught herself short. *How did this boorish woman cajole* me *into being* her *interview subject?*

In the middle distance a chime clanged. "Time to pray," Nataleah said, rolling her eyes.

***

The Galaxy's only fully (to say nothing of multiply) conjugal incarceration had demanded some concessions in design; Alrue Latier's "cellblock" was actually a warren of apartments. Nataleah and Meryam followed its jagging central corridor, emerging into what might have been called a great room, were there anything great about it. The clumsy chamber was irregularly proportioned, with five sides. Its ceiling, a single, sharply canted glasteel plate, had never been cleaned. In late afternoon only a ruddy glow penetrated its layers of grime.

Clad in electric-blue tunics like Nataleah's, the other wives huddled around a beefy man with thinning grey-brown hair. He wore a tunic like theirs, but over it an ill-fitting off-white muslin union suit that ended at his forearms and his knees. A woven collar was joined at his neck with a cloth tie. Into the fabric over his left breast had been snipped a V-shaped symbol, meant to symbolize an old-fashioned geometer's compass. Over his right breast, an inverted-L marking could be recognized with effort as an ancient architect's square – or an artist's, or a mason's. Between the two symbols, another fabric tie held the garment together. A hole the width of two fingers opened over his navel, a smaller one over his right knee.

He was Alrue Latier, President of the High Priesthood of the Church of Jesus Christ of Latter-day Saints of the New Restoration, and Seer, Revelator, and Prophet unto the church whose appointment belonged to him by blessing and also by right. Come to think of it, the whole *church* belonged to him, less by blessing or by right than because he owned all the common stock.

Alrue kissed Nataleah full on the mouth.

The last of his wives having been properly greeted, it was time for the ritual. The women formed a loose circle around their husband and began to sing their faith's oldest hymn:

"The Spirit of God like a fire is burning;
The latter-day glory begins to come forth."

Alrue abruptly left his spot, stepping through the circle toward Meryam. The wives exchanged puzzled glances but kept singing. "Fem Mayishimu," Alrue said in a whisper.

"First Elder?"

"I know about you."

19

She arched an eyebrow. "Me?"

"The visions and blessings of old are returning;
The angels are coming to visit the earth."

"Your kind," Alrue said coldly. "Spectators. You
don't just rely on your own body's enhanced capacities,
impressive as those are. You plant bugs. You hide
remote sensors. You gain situational awareness far
beyond what your senses could acquire."

"Field Spectators do that. I'm just a
documentarian."

Alrue shook his head. "You've been all over this
punitorium. You've interviewed me, my wives, Warden
Eiloxayn, senior guards. You must have placed bugs."

"We'll sing and we'll shout with the armies of
heaven;
Hosanna, Hosanna to God and the Lamb!"

Abigayl (the youngest wife) mouthed silently,
"What's a hosanna?"

Lupida (the second eldest wife) mouthed back,
"What's a lamb?"

"When that riot broke out in Delta Quad, *from in
here* you knew about it before the guards did," Alrue
continued. "Admit it, you've constructed a god's-eye
view of this whole punitorium. You see it like a beehive
behind glass."

"An aptly Mormon image."

"Thanks for noticing." Alrue frowned. "You know
how the guards arrange their patrols. Who pays attention
and who doesn't."

"You want me to *tell* you?"

"Miracles are where one finds them." He grinned.
"If God chooses not to free me in miraculous ways, then

I, Alrue, may yet hope that the Heavenly Father will aid me through means that seem … more ordinary."

"Really, First Elder. I've seen you fail at calling down this miracle, what, nine times before?"

"Seven, pray don't exaggerate." Alrue backed toward the circle of his still-singing wives, pitching his voice so only Meryam would hear it. "Turn yourself on, Fem Spectator. It's show time."

Meryam subvocalized a nonsense syllable, triggering the cascade of electronic, vibrionic, and biological events that would put her online. It began with tingling in her cheeks as biotech implants recorded the faintest movements of her eye, head, and neck muscles for later resynchronization to her visual field. Deep in her skull, a transceiver implant opened a channel to an OmNet satellite orbiting overhead. An instant later, she knew the bird was receiving her. The sync information it beamed back to her triggered alternate cortical pathways.

Meryam changed. Normally-dormant areas of her cortex sparked into orderly action. In microseconds the largest part of her cerebral capacity was devoted to fine-grained control of the muscles in her head, face, and neck. Nerve shunts routed potentially distracting somesthetic information beneath her conscious aware-ness. Blood flow to her sense organs increased. In moments the entirety of her preternaturally optimized sensory field – sight, sound, touch, tastes and odors, heat or cold, even the sensations of her body just being itself – would be recorded for anyone with a senso player to experience (more properly, to *pov*).

Subvocalizing one more nonsense syllable, Meryam Mayishimu went fully into Mode.

Suck, rush, wrench!

"'And it shall come to pass,'" Alrue bellowed, "'that I, the Lord God, will send one mighty and strong, holding the scepter of power in his hand, clothed with

21

light for a covering, whose mouth shall utter words, eternal words; while his bowels shall be a fountain of truth, to set in order the house of the Lord.'" Alrue made magical gestures, waggling fingers thick as sausages. "O great God, deliver me from mine internment. Make bare Thy holy arm."

Alrue directed a fierce gaze up into the filth-streaked glasteel ceiling. "Deliver us your saints from that awful monster, our captivity!" he shouted. "Send forth also the power of Thine *other* mighty arm. Visit these walls with destruction!" He spread his arms. "O Heavenly Father, stretch forth yet one more mighty arm!"

Zuzenah, his eldest wife, stepped to the center of the circle. "No arms left," she breathed.

"Pardon?"

"You've already asked God to bare one mighty arm, then stretch forth the second. Is that not all of them?"

Alrue frowned. "God is God, He can have as many arms as He wants. Now be quiet, woman, I'm supplicating."

Which was as far as that afternoon's supplicating would get.

Of course, the Spectator heard it first.

A tinny whine, tuneless, yet rapidly rising in pitch. At first it was subliminal.

"Do you hear that?" Meryam blurted.

Then they all heard it. The whine became a shriek. Alrue and his wives doubled over, clutching their heads.

Meryam registered a burst of pressure – or was it vacuum? For a vertiginous instant she thought she felt gravity twist back on itself.

A sucking roar drew her gaze. She formed a split-second impression of one cellblock wall leaping outward. Tumbling away on the air, collapsing into powder.

Then blackness.

***

Meryam's awareness re-formed. The ruddy light of Bohrkkian afternoon shone through a startling three-by-five-meter wound in the northeast wall. Chips and dust sifted down past the opening.

Meryam rose unsteadily to one knee. Residue caked her, tasting metallic under her tongue. Hurriedly she scanned herself. *No serious injuries, all internal systems three-by-three greens.*

She stood, slowly pivoted. All about the angular chamber, deep cracks fissured the floor and walls. Three large chunks of the ceiling had collapsed. Furnishings and equipment had tumbled down from upper stories. Lengths of conduit, twisted fixtures, and less identifiable debris lay everywhere.

Alrue and his wives stirred. They seemed unhurt; at least, none of the heavy wreckage had struck them. One by one they rose.

Alrue stared incredulously at his hands.

One of the dust-coated wives – *Constance? Yes* – knelt, praying unintelligibly but at the top of her lungs. Another drew up behind her husband. "This time I have to hand it to you, Alrue," breathed Lupida. "My dear Harold never called down a smiting from heaven like this."

Meryam hurried across the room to confront Alrue. "First Elder!"

He stared at her like a sleeper waking.

"What do you hear?" she demanded.

Alrue blinked. "Nothing."

"Shouldn't there be sirens? People shouting? There's just silence." Meryam seized the trideevangelist's wrists. "You were right about my Spectator bugs and sensors. I had them all over the

23

punitorium complex. Most are still working, but they read no power, no comm, no vibrionics. *Nolife signs.*"

Alrue bowed his head. "Mighty is the Lord God of Hosts. Fearful is the glory of His majesty."

"Hosanna and hosanna," chorused Lupida.

Meryam half-steered, half-dragged Alrue toward the gash in the northeast wall. Zuzenah caught up with them. The trio leaned outward and stared down.

The wall breach opened onto a sheer drop of at least five meters. At its bottom, a deep sandy ravine ran parallel to the punctured wall.

"The Lord of Hosts does toy with us, dear husband," Zuzenah lamented. "After all this noise and spectacle, still we cannot get out."

From above sounded a gathering roar. Meryam pulled Alrue and Zuzenah back from the opening. New debris curtained past outside. Half a bodylength below their feet, the exterior wall split with an immense cracking sound. A meter-wide jet of whitewater spewed outward. Foam arched, then hammered into the ravine below.

The three edged forward, staring down through the hole in the wall at the gushing stream.

Their shattered cellblock was fast acquiring a moat.

More debris cascaded past outside: clattering metal strips, unfurling coils of cable, and finally a battered window-washing platform. One end of the platform caught on the hole in the wall; the opposite end thumped onto the far bank, across the fast-rising moat. At its center, the jet of rushing water surged across its deck.

Lupida grabbed Meryam by one elbow. "It *is* a miracle! They never washed the windows here."

Meryam crept forward and tried to jostle the platform. It felt secure where it had fallen. She rushed back to Alrue. "First Elder!"

"Call me Alrue, it's a Mormon thing."

"Fine, *Alrue*. The walkway seems safe. That water washing over the center of it is only half a meter deep. There'll be a swift current, but if you hang on tight you should be able to just walk out of here."

"Me?" Alrue seemed startled at the idea. He thought for a moment, then strode toward his senior wife.

"Me?" Zuzenah protested.

"You needn't go alone," Alrue said equably. "Take all the wives."

Terrified, Zuzenah stared toward the lacerated wall. Alrue clasped her hands and spoke to her urgently. "What transports of joy swelled my bosom, when I first took by the hand my beloved Zuzenah –the wife of my youth, the choice of my heart." He guided her closer to the jagged opening. "Again she is here, even in the seventh trouble — undaunted, firm, and unwavering – unchangeable, affectionate Zuzenah!"

Zuzenah's eyes filmed with emotion. At that moment anyone could see the black-eyed beauty she had once been. "O my husband, there is nothing I will not do at your command."

Alrue nodded almost imperceptibly. "Then go. The Spectator and I will follow."

"Sister wives!" Zuzenah cried with sudden determination. "We're leaving. Aunt Constance, pray get us organized."

For lanky Constance, taking charge of logistical matters was clearly nothing new. She strode about, sizing things up, barking commands. "Aunt Lupida, Aunt Abigayl, extract the concentrate cylinders out of that shattered food synthesizer. Aunt Zuzenah, grab those fire-safety backpacks the wardens never taught us how to use. Pour out whatever's in them and fill them up with the blankets from our floatpads. Aunt Nataleah, look for vessels we can use to carry water – see if any of the stuff that fell from upstairs has slings on it. Fem

Mayishimu," she called, indicating a length of severed cable with her foot. "Pray use your expanded senses. Is this safe to handle?"

***

Ten minutes later the wives mustered, facing the cavity in the cellblock wall. Constance had used the length of cable to lash them all together. She placed herself in front and Nataleah at the back, so the youngest and fittest adults would bookend the party. The youngest wife, Abigayl, stood in the middle, stuffing a strip of personal floatcells she'd found into her backpack. Zuzenah had considered ordering Abigayl to stay behind while the elder wives tested the escape route – she was only seven, after all – but with everything else that was going on no one wanted one of those "You're not my mother!" confrontations.

"Time to go," Zuzenah called from her spot second in line.

Still recording, Meryam sidestepped across the shattered chamber, seeking a more dramatic angle as the wives stepped through the punctured cellblock wall. They started across the fallen platform, toward the jet of froth still surging across its midpoint. Alrue breathed a passage from Mormon scripture: "They went forth out of captivity, upon the many waters."

Choosing their steps carefully, clinging tightly to the platform's buckled railings, the wives pushed through knee-high whitewater. The surge tugged at them, but they contrived to counter it. Even little Abigayl, for whom the seething foam was more like thigh-high, managed to hold her own.

Shifting their grips, blinking away showers of spray, the plural wives splattered through the torrent toward freedom.

Beaming, Alrue Latier watched it all.

He turned toward Meryam. "Behold," he said. "My wives splash before my eyes."

Chapter 2

February 17, 2376 (not that anyone still ... well, you know)
Sol System, the Asteroid Belt

Banishment to Terra a decade and a half before hadn't precisely confined Terrans to Terra. Rather it had restricted them to Sol space. For that reason a Terran utility boat could legally navigate the asteroid belt with a few dozen Terrans aboard, one of them being Senator Pamela Grice.

She unpacked in a claustrophobic stateroom while dictating one of the countless memos whose composition was among her obligations of office. "'*Assalamu Alaikum Warahmatu Allah Wabarakatuh* and *Ramadan Mubarak*. In the name of the Prophet, peace and blessings of Allah be upon him, my greetings during this holy season.' Note to staff, make sure it's really Ramadan before you send this." Since the ill-advised Hinduslamic Synthesis had largely destroyed the faith of Muhammad across its original Middle Eastern homeland a century B. G. E. (Before the Galactic Encounter – how Terrans chafed at that acronym now!), the swath of Eurosector she represented was the Galaxy's principal seat of Islam.

Grice tossed straw-blond hair over one very pale shoulder and scowled into her traveling case. After her other belongings had been stowed away, a lone blue anklet – to judge by its subtle counterclockwise piping, the left one – remained. *That's odd, I'm sure I packed the pair.* Search as she might, she could not find its mate. With a mumbled curse she chucked the orphan piece of hosiery into a trashmuter port.

The annunciator warbled. "Senator Grice to the command deck."

Ducking a diagonal strut crusted with instruments, Grice twisted into the ute's cramped control room. "Fem Senator," Captain Banitzek said too quietly. His uniform jacket was half-buttoned. Even while carrying a VIP, 'Roiders weren't big on appearances. Or courtesy. "You'll see the only empty chair. Take it. Touch nothing."

He comes from generations accustomed to tiny in-belt craft in which an errant gesture could cause an unintended control input, Grice reminded herself. *That heritage teaches physical economy.* Smiling thinly, she settled into the guest seat, clasping her fingers over the armrests.

Banitzek swung before her without a wasted move. Like most 'Roiders, he was well under two meters tall, sapling-slender. She could sense his disapproval of her body's indulgent softness. *I suppose I take up too much of his control room to suit him.*

"Senator Grice."

"Captain Banitzek."

"As you chair the Senate Technologies Committee, your demand for this inspection tour could not be refused."

Grice gave the captain her tiniest smile. "Captain, what do you know of me?"

"Beyond your rank in the planetary Senate, rather little." The hint of 'Roider pride crossing his face told the story. The families that settled among the asteroids half a century before the Galactics showed up had held themselves apart. They'd made a point not to take sides when the Galactics made Terra one of their Memberworlds and helped themselves to its choicest real estate. They'd maintained that aloofness when the Galactics pulled out, frightened by the destructive potential of Terra's religions, and put all of Sol space behind a wall of Sequestration.

It was all the same to them.

"Closing on the closest ring buoy," reported the Detex officer. "Inspection distance in four minutes."

***

The ring buoy was a spindly blue-grey hoop four hundred meters in diameter, studded with compact machinery and flickering running lights. Through its hollow center coursed a torrent of dust, pebbles, and rocks. Grice knew what fed this stream. A hundred thousand klicks further out, robot scoops were gathering silicon-rich dust. Trawlers ground small asteroids to coarse gravel. All this material – plus the occasional untreated rocky fragment, if its size was appropriate – got shepherded into the first of a vast chain of ring buoys. Gentle colloidal slipfields kept the silicate stream trapped in this "pipeline," tumbling through the center of buoy after buoy until it arrived at a handling platform orbiting Terra at half the distance to the Moon. There the material would be refined, flash-milled to fine dust, and dispatched to a heat exchange station on Terra for superheating, followed by its teleport jump into Sol's core.

Such had been the Galaxy's gift to Terra: a planetary thermal dissipation system of the sort most Memberworlds possessed.

The ute's telemetry officer had made an initial connection with the buoy's thought engine. "I project failure in less than one minute," he called. "Watch the big fragment upstream."

Riding amid the dust and pebbles falling toward Buoy Six One Seven-B was a hulking boulder – at two hundred meters by two-fifty, nearly the maximum allowable size. Tendrils of luminance flickered across it.

"The slipfield is losing control," Captain Banitzek observed.

"Failure!" called the telemetry officer. Amid a spasm of greenish light, the boulder lurched off center. It scraped the buoy in passing, dislodging bits of apparatus. The buoy's running lights briefly went dark.

"How often does that sort of failure occur?" Grice queried.

"About three times in ten with an object of this mass," Captain Banitzek replied, "and the rate is accelerating. Meanwhile the mass at which the system loses control is dropping asymptotically. Complete buoy failure is projected in eighteen days, five hours."

Buoy failure, Grice thought hollowly. Three transport chains fed silicates from the belt to the homeworld, each comprising tens of thousands of buoys like this one; the complete failure of any single buoy would shut down one chain. Multiply that by three, and Terra would soon be cooking. *Tens of thousands of buoys, with failure virtually unknown until now,* she thought. *That's Galactic technology for you. But everything breaks sometime ...*

"Let me try something," Grice said, half-rising from her seat.

"Sit down!" Banitzek snapped. "I don't care who you are, Senator, you will not interfere with this work."

Oh yes I will, she thought. She resumed her seat. Slapping her palms onto the imposer contacts in the chair arms, she subvocalized override codes that were old when she was still in the PeaceForce: a control dialect she hoped the ute's systems would respond to.

It must have worked. Dimly she heard alarms warbling, then shouted profanities. The frantic control room fell away from her awareness; the virtual object environment within the ute's thought engines took shape

31

around her. Data structures manifested themselves as internally layered constructs of light.

A flickering, spinning object floated past. It was the ute's comm system. Grice willed herself inside that, then *through* it. Now her awareness had entered the thought engines of the failing buoy. With powerful metaphors of object-space channeling what she saw, the buoy's problem was obvious – at least, the problem she could fix. One of its slipfield generators was way off-spectrum. That hardware issue would eventually demand a replacement part no longer available to Terra, but for now it could simply be compensated.

She forced her virtual head and hands inside a higher-level computational array. Slowly rotating light-matrices surrounded her. She was experiencing the thought engine's calculations almost as the machine itself might, were it self-aware. The giant virtual structures' nested turnings were desynchronized in a way that made her gut squirm. Without knowing exactly why, she made a movement that would have been impossible anywhere but in object-space.

Something indefinable seemed to click.

The great turnings shuddered back into sync. She pulled her awareness out of the computation array …

Her awareness was back in the ute craft's guest seat. Sweat chilled her armpits and glistened on her forehead and upper lip. She looked to her left. Captain Banitzek and three other officers clustered over the telemetry officer's console, their astonished gazes darting among console displays.

"All systems on the ring buoy are five-by-five greens," the telemetry officer croaked. The viewsystem display showed the stream of silicon-bearing materials falling once more through the exact center of the ring buoy. "Performance optimum."

The officers whirled to face her. "What did you ... " Banitzek demanded, nonplussed. "I mean, how did you ..."

"There was a reason I wondered what you knew of me, Captain." Grice stood. "I may be Terran, but before Sequestration I served twelve standard years with the PeaceForce, including as gunnery officer aboard the heavy cruiser *Forthright*." Now there was a Confetory ship whose name everyone recognized, even Banitzek. "I know a fair bit about Galactic control systems like the ones that were left behind to manage these silicon transport chains." She nodded toward the telemetry officer, who like everyone else in the control room was staring at her. "With respect, I know ways to command such systems that are more versatile and powerful than the methods you seem accustomed to. Though having to do so from that minimally-equipped guest seat added needless difficulty."

Banitzek frowned. "I thought you were a senator."

"High office doesn't *guarantee* the absence of practical skills." She drew up, facing the captain from half a meter away, playing the dominance of her larger stature for all it was worth. "This buoy is repaired – at least, its code is. There's an underlying equipment problem I can't fix – probably no Terran can. But its thought engine will compensate properly for that problem for at least another standard year or so, maybe two. We were scheduled to visit other problem buoys, were we not?"

"Yes, Fem Senator."

"At the next one, if I wish to help where will I be seated?"

Captain Banitzek nodded toward the telemetry officer's station. The telemetry officer sidestepped a pace from his console and bowed just perceptibly, for a 'Roider the equivalent of falling prostrate.

"I'll be in my stateroom," Grice said with the smallest of nods. "Please alert me when we reach the next buoy."

＊＊

"It's what I expected," Grice told her Technologies Committee attaché over a secured realtime comm link. "What did Beta Team find at the heat exchanger stations?"

"About the same," said the attaché, "aside from the fact that the equipment at the bottom of the Indian Ocean and buried inside the Matterhorn is far larger and would cost even more multiples of Terra's gross global product to replace. We need a visit from Galactic Mister Fix-It, and he needs to bring parts."

"Too bad that can't happen." Grice drew an oolong tea from the stateroom's autobar. "Before long, something's going to break down somewhere in Terra's thermal dissipation system that can't be fixed with cleverness and good intentions. At which point we'll need replacement parts that Terra can't afford to buy, and no Galactic would sell us anyway because Terra's Sequestered. Once *that* occurs, our little blue world will need to hook-or-crook a Galactic fix, develop its own mastery of the technology, radically scale back its energy use, *or* slowly fry."

Frowning, she signed off. She settled into the stateroom's lone formchair and cast her eyes around the meager space.

What the sfelb?

Folded neatly atop the traveling case she hadn't yet stowed was a lone blue sock. She rose and examined it. Its piping ran clockwise – this was the missing right anklet she'd failed to find before. She smiled lopsidedly as she picked it up. *A lot of good you'll do me now.* Absently, she cast the orphan into the same trashmuter

34

port to which, not two hours before, she had consigned its mate.

Chapter 3

They trudged through a shallow trenchlike depression that seemed the work of some primordial titan idly dragging immense fingers across the landscape. The ground was like corduroy; harsh stony rills ran in parallel on either side, partly filled with soil or drifted sand.

Meryam Mayishimu labored under the weight of two water tanks, one over each shoulder; she had filled them from the torrent on her way out of the cellblock. Constance Latier carried a filled water tank over one shoulder; over the other she bore a backpack stuffed with a bolt of fabric she'd found, perhaps the basis of a tent. Zuzenah, the eldest sister wife, carried an extra backpack full of self-powered lights and flares salvaged from the debris that had fallen from upper floors of the shattered punitorium. Tiny Abigayl lugged one food concentrate cylinder; Lupida carried two. Like Meryam, Nataleah carried two filled water tanks. In addition, each of the six women wore a second backpack puffy with blankets.

Of the seven in the party, only Alrue Latier was unburdened; yet he sweated enough for all of them combined.

Meryam led. When she thought the seven had covered a kilometer since their escape, she raised a hand. The company stopped. For the first time, they looked back. "By the solemn foresight of Zenock, Neum, and Zenos," Alrue rumbled.

The punitorium, hours before a sizeable complex with wings six to ten stories tall, had been reduced to a broad, featureless talus of smoking rubble, save for the small central section that had housed the Latiers'

36

cellblock. It rose from the debris field like an accusing finger. Horribly damaged, to be sure; its top five stories had fallen in. Still, it was plainly the only section of the punitorium in which anyone could have survived.

Meryam sidled next to Alrue, who was busy mopping his face on one sleeve of his temple garment. "Whatever it was that happened today –"

"You mean the miracle?" Alrue said brightly.

Meryam frowned. *"Whatever happened* was far more destructive outside of our cellblock than it was inside it."

Alrue nodded. "Not unreasonable, if God's purpose were to free *us."*

"That complex housed ten thousand people! Now we seven are apparently the sole survivors." Meryam spread her hands. "This is no miracle, First Elder. It's a catastrophe."

Alrue smiled. "Fem Spectator, have you *read* our scripture? The God I worship annihilates whole peoples before breakfast. When trying to determine whether an event is His work, the last thing a good Mormon keeps score of is collateral damage."

Furious, Meryam turned away. *Since no one else is reporting this disaster, I suppose I should.* She composed an alert in her mind. Tried to send it. "Plorg, I've lost my bird!" Her face went blank as she ran diagnostics. "I'm still sending, but there's nothing up there." She whirled to confront the trideevangelist. "Does your God also sweep satellites out of the sky?"

Alrue shrugged. "Can't see why He couldn't."

Meryam concentrated again, then glowered. "Whatever occurred here not only smashed the punitorium; not much later, it scoured synchronous orbit too. I'm completely cut off."

"For now, at least." Alrue gestured to muster his wives as one might herd ducklings. Turning back to

Meryam, he said, "With due gratitude for your assistance, I think now is the time for our parting of the ways."

Meryam gestured at the unfriendly landscape. "You want to leave me *here*?"

Alrue spread his hands, a parody of helplessness. "Look, Fem Mayishimu –"

"Call me Meryam, please," she said cruelly. "You know, that Mormon thing."

"Fine, look, Meryam. We're escaping from a punitorium. You're a journalist. You must see the conflict."

"Not just now," she replied. "I have no contact with OmNet; the Galaxy cannot see what I record."

"Until your satellite comes back up."

Meryam shook her head. "If it were still in orbit but in some crisis mode, I'd know that. I'd sense its baseline signal. But I don't. It's *gone.*"

"So you say."

"Who would know better?" Frowning, she swept her gaze across the landscape. Given abundant moisture, what seemed oddest was the rarity of dense vegetation. The planet Bohrkk seemed remarkable for its biological poverty. It seemed to contain all the elements for a more vibrant ecology, but the relations between them that would make most worlds verdant were missing here. Occasional runnels of soil supported dense scrub, sometimes scraggly stands of trees; elsewhere, rocky channels remained bare where one might reasonably have expected the soils to bloom.

Alrue struck an explorer's pose and declaimed: "'Nothing visible but the torn and slashed and windworn beauty of the absolute wasteland.'"

"Wow," breathed his wife Lupida, running slender fingers through her hair. "That isn't from the Book of Mormon."

"Some travel writer, twentieth century of Terra," Alrue panted. "But I love the ring of it."

"First Elder – I mean Alrue – I have a proposition," Meryam said levelly. "I wish to accompany you as a Spectator and document your escape. At the moment I am restricted to local storage; nothing I record can go up where anyone can see it. Granted, if my satellite repairs itself or is replaced, my journals will be seen by anyone among OmNet's Galactic public that chooses to *pov* them. But I am able to file them in such a way that our exact location on the surface of Bohrkk will be impossible to decode. Not even the highest authorities will be able to pinpoint our location. If you will permit me to accompany you, I will code my recordings in that way beginning immediately."

"You will document our punitorium break, but conceal our location? Isn't that illegal?"

She smiled darkly. "OmNet has a large legal department."

"An intriguing offer. But how can I know you are being truthful?"

Meryam shrugged. "You can't. But let me pose another question. What do you know about conditions in the wild here?"

"Next to nothing." He smirked. "I don't think the wardens planned on our going outside."

Meryam paced further along the lengthy depression through which they'd been marching, forcing Alrue to follow. "Tell me," she asked, "why have I been leading us through this long rut with its sometimes-difficult footing? To either side there's flat sandy soil."

"I was about to suggest we start walking there."

"Then you haven't heard about the ferkeeks."

"The what?"

"Ferkeeks," Meryam repeated. "Fist-sized underground predators. They lurk in dry, soft soils.

Approached by large animals, most certainly including humans, the ferkeeks leap out of hiding and straight into their prey's mouth. Then they inject a poisonous pseudopod into the brain."

"You're joking."

"Care to bet your life on that? Those of your wives? Bohrkk is not a friendly world; that's one reason why the Confetory placed a high-security punitorium here."

Alrue looked back along their path. In leading the party through the long hollow, Meryam had indeed kept the seven on rocky terrain.

"Whenever possible, rocky ground is best," Meryam declared. "And there's plenty more you need to know." She extended her right hand.

He clasped it the old-fashioned way, his hand clutching her forearm. "We are in your hands, Fem Mayishimu. Meryam, I mean. Lead us."

"Ladies," Meryam called to the wives. "We move. I estimate we have two good hours until dusk."

The seven resumed their march following the rough rocky hollow. For the ninth or tenth time, Meryam opened her senses to any signal from space. As before, the silence was unnerving. *My satellite ... gone. Not hibernating, not powered down. I'd know the difference. Gone. What could destroy my bird as effortlessly as it crushed most of Punitorium L752?* Frowning, she set that conundrum aside – to say nothing of the mystery of what had destroyed their prison in such a precise, if bloodthirsty, way. She concentrated on her footing, and on trying to calculate how much recording time she could hope for using purely local storage.

Chapter 4

April 1, 2376
Sol System, the Asteroid Belt

As the ute's most distinguished passenger, Pamela Grice could scarcely refuse Captain Banitzek's offer of a quiet drink together. At least, not for long.

They sat alone in the ute's half-darkened mess hall, at this hour the largest open space not liable to be used by others. From a concealed pocket in his uniform jacket Banitzek produced a metallic flask the size of two fists, far too large to have hidden inside a pocket that hadn't even bulged his sleeve.

Grice smiled. "A vanisher pouch in your duty jacket?" The vanisher was Galactic technology: rare in Sol space, expensive anywhere.

Banitzek nodded. "Won it from a drunken Galactic in a *strel* game. Many years ago, of course."

"When drunken Galactics were to be found in 'Roider bars."

Banitzek smiled. "Or in Terran bars, for that matter. Won this flask too." At his touch two small metal drinking glasses budded off from the flask's body. He thumbed the flask open, poured three fingers of some bubbling liquid into each glass. "'Roider society's best imitation of Rikubian sparkling whiskey."

She sipped, frowned. "It's a solid imitation of Rikubian whiskey. Though I speak as one who detests the stuff."

"Let me begin by apologizing," said Banitzek. "You were right, I knew little about you. During the last transit between failing buoys, I read up on you a bit."

"Let me guess what you found: Blond white-skinned Earth-girl Pam Grice made good in the great big Galaxy, scoring a plum commission in the PeaceForce

41

even though she'd refused to hide her Terran physical characteristics. She distinguished herself by one spate of fancy shooting – "

"Yes, the Arbadrel incident."

Grice shrugged. "And she emerged a heroine. Twenty-some years later she's a senator on her now-Sequestered homeworld." She sipped. "Of course it turns out she still has a knack for fixing old Galactic technology."

He smiled. "So far, a life to celebrate."

"Try *this* narrative for size." Grice leaned forward. "I was still on active duty when the Confetory announced that Terra would be Sequestered. Terrans like me who'd chosen Galactic life faced a hard choice. We could go back to Terra, knowing the door would be locked and sealed behind us, that we'd never leave Sol space again. Or we could opt to stay out among the stars. As in, *never* go home."

"You went home," Banitzek said as though it were obvious.

From Grice, a bitter chortle. "That's the missing piece. I *didn't* choose home. I stayed out. All that overheated rhetoric about Terrans being welcome to live in the Galaxy as Terrans so long as they agreed to forsake their homeworld – I swallowed it whole."

Banitzek eyed her curiously. "But now you're here."

"After I resigned my commission, I started a business brokering technologies. I figured my military credentials and my cachet as an 'exotic' would give me an edge. It worked for, oh, two standard years. Then – how do I say this? I became a victim of Galactic empathy."

"You've lost me."

"Two standard years after Terra got pushed behind the veil – more or less – Galactics started to recognize how shabbily they'd treated humanity's Cradleworld," Grice explained. "Welding the gates shut, turning their backs on the birthplace of all those religions they'd once found so captivating– a real 'What have we done?' moment. Not that much was done to make amends. Galactics just discovered they could satisfy their sense of justice by *feeling guilty* around Terrans, especially obviously unreconstructed Terrans like me. And who wants to keep people around who make them feel guilty?" She sipped. "That was the beginning. Then I got framed."

Banitzek raised one eyebrow. "Framed?"

"Accused of fraud on transparently false evidence." She chuckled darkly. "Yes I know, everyone says they're innocent. Well, I *was*. The case against me had no force, but all good Galactics agreed not to notice. You want proof the charges were garbage? The same prosecutors who'd wanted to fling me in punitorium for twenty standard years *rushed* to offer to drop the charges if I'd just hop the next ship back home."

Banitzek frowned. "But Terra was Sequestered by then. You couldn't go back."

"They made a loophole. They were that eager."

He drained his glass. "So you trudged back home. Starting over must have been –"

"It was."

"But afterward? You ended up a senator."

"The story of my expulsion from the Galaxy won me new name recognition and no small amount of sympathy. It was my start in Terran politics. And it didn't hurt that all those Earth girls who'd grown up idolizing 'Gunner Grice' were old enough to vote." Grice chuckled darkly. "Since then – sure, my life's been good. But I can never forget why I needed to build it over again."

The comm officer's voice crackled from the overheads. "Paging Senator Grice, paging Senator Grice. Priority personal call for you."

Banitzek thumbed the comm dot on his jacket sleeve. "She is with me."

The quality of the comm officer's voice changed, reflecting the switch from all-page to a direct connection. "Captain, the call ... it's Terra's All-president. In person."

Chapter 5

"They call it the Galaxy's playground – Calluron Five, that geologic wonderland and premier ski resort among the far-flung stars. Who would think that here I'd catch up with the suddenly famous philosopher of religion Steyvag Hiltzum? Yet here I found him, emerging from an exclusive night spot."

"Where the sfelb else should you find me?" the thinker demanded as the tridee crew cornered him. "After decades of academic obscurity, I've been awarded the Temperdung Prize for Progress in Religion – though I don't grasp why. I still obsess over all the same ideas that my peers ignored throughout my professional life. Well, I'm no longer ignored– and suddenly I'm rich. Why shouldn't I celebrate?" He maneuvered the three young beauties on his elbows (two female, one gender-ambiguous) toward the entrance of the next bistro. "Here, darlings, entertain yourselves while I make the reporter go away."

"Doctor Hiltzum," the reporter demanded, "today many Galactics think of religion as disreputable – as something associated mostly with that sinkhole world, Terra. What does the Temperdung Prize mean in that context?"

"It means a mountain of credits," Hiltzum explained tartly. "That crazy philanthropist Jahn Temperdung lived nine centuries ago, and his view that science and religion should serve one another seems hopelessly quaint today. Or it would, except that the prize bearing his name has a higher value than any to be won in the more legitimate sciences – I mean, in the pursuit of knowledge defined in more conventional ways."

"But Doctor Hiltzum," the reporter pressed, "why you? Why your particular ideas?"

"Couldn't say. Three weeks ago I learned that the same ideas I've been chasing all my life suddenly won me the Galaxy's richest prize for – what do they call it? – delving into the 'big questions.' Whatever the sfelb *that* means. Suddenly everyone wants to know what I think."

"So what *do* you think, Doctor Hiltzum? What is the big idea all that triggered all this excitement?"

Hiltzum leaned forward, head bent down, eyeing the reporter through bushy grey eyebrows. "My idea is that, as the cosmos evolves toward its future, some that we know about *current* reality constrains the forms that future may take. For example, the cosmos we know is one observed by intelligent, self-aware living things. I contend that *being observed* is one of its defining properties. People ask whether intelligent life will annihilate itself one day, or whether future physical processes may result in life's extermination. I don't think we need to worry about nightmare scenarios like that. On my view, no universe in which such a calamity *could* occur can really exist, since after the calamity it would be without observers. From that, I conjecture that universes containing sentient observers are fundamentally more real than universes without them. But here's the part everyone seems most excited about. If there exists, among all possible universes, *justone universe* in which life persists forever, that is by definition the most real universe of all."

"It sounds so simple when you put it that way."

"What matters here," Hiltzum concluded, "what mattered to the Temperdung Prize committee, so far as I can tell – was my conclusion. It takes the form of a mathematical postulate, rather like the statement 'Let x equal 25' that one encounters in an algebra problem."

"I see," said the reporter uncertainly. His body language could not mask the fear in his eyes: *Please, don't get into math.*

Hiltzum's patience was exhausted. "You don't see at all, I can tell. Maybe someone who's watching this will do better." His eyes locked with the tridee pickup. "All right, is anyone paying attention? Here comes my postulate: 'Let the cosmos be such that life *must* continue, for however long the cosmos itself exists.'"

Chapter 6

April 1, 2376
Sol System, the Asteroid Belt

Banitzek and Grice strode most of the utility boat's length – not all that far – toward the control room. Grice's mind riffled through the things the planetary head of state might want. *She probably wants me back for the Party Congress – can't blame her for second-guessing why some senator might imagine the best use of her time is riding around in space doing what amounts to engineering work.* Two relief officers who'd been holding down the control room stood as the party entered.

"Good daypart, Fem Grice." There was no mistaking the hectoring voice of Terra's perpetually overscheduled head of state, even when distorted by the control room's marginal overhead system.

"Fem All-president, what an unexpected pleasure," Grice said, hoping she sounded sincere. "I know I've been out here fixing buoys quite a while –"

"Never mind that, senator. You're about to have a visitor."

The telemetry officer's console began flashing every imaginable shade of red. "Proximity alert!" cried one of the relief officers. "Incoming ship, a big one."

The viewsystem display showed a small blue star coruscating toward them.

"Terran?" barked Captain Banitzek.

"Negative, from outside Sol space."

"Galactic ..." the sentence fell stillborn from Banitzek's lips.

Galactic craft didn't visit Sol space.

Not anymore.

"Fem All-president," Grice said. "A large ship just dropped out of transphotic. Judging by the Cerenkov radiation, it has an enormous intrinsic velocity to bleed off. Is this your visitor?"

"I'd hoped to advise you before it arrived," the All-president said in the tone of someone all too conscious of her burdens. "The ship is Galactic – the sprint cruiser *Impulsive* – and it carries every clearance anyone here has even heard of. Less than an hour ago we received an emergency diplomatic dispatch seeking permission for *Impulsive* to enter Sol space."

"At current deceleration, the inbound ship will stop relative to our boat at a distance of" – the Detex officer scanned clustered readouts in disbelief – "two kilometers."

"Senator Grice," the All-president announced, "I am told *Impulsive* journeyed to Sol space for the sole purpose of seeking your input."

"*My* input," Grice echoed unbelievingly.

"So they say – on a matter of apparently vast importance. Senator, you will pardon me if I wax official. In view of your prior commission in the Galactic military, I've been advised to remind you that you are not now subject to their command."

Grice frowned. "I should say not."

"Whatever they have come to ask of you they can only ask, not require," the All-president said. "For our part, a proclamation has been issued declaring that whatever these Galactics may ask you to do, you *may* do if you so elect. So it's entirely your choice."

"Fem All-president –" Banitzek fought to keep his voice from quavering. "This is Ejarel Banitzek, commanding 'Roider utility boat QL4256a. Am I to understand that these Galactics applied to *Terra's* government for permission to travel to a specific site *in the asteroid belt*? That is to say, that o 'Roider authority was consulted?"

"Your concern is noted, Hom Captain," replied the All-president in a tone of deep exhaustion. "Then again, one of the nice things about *having* a government is that there is someone to ask when things like this come up."

If Banitzek had a reply, it was pre-empted by the Detex officer shouting, "Plorg on a platter!" When a Galactic capital ship five kilometers long decelerates from light speed in less than six minutes and comes to a relative halt *exactly* two klicks off your portside, it is an impressive sight. Grice had seen similar acrobatics during her PeaceForce years, but she doubted any of the 'Roiders had ever witnessed such bravura maneuvering.

Seen from a distance less than half the length of its hull, *Impulsive* was a mass of intersecting pyramids, all vertices and obtuse angles, its surfaces forested with obscure apparatus.

"I gather *Impulsive* has arrived," said the All-president. "Just remember, Pam – whatever they want ..."

"I can say no," Grice mused. "Or ... I can negotiate." She stepped to the Detex station and fed in some access codes. "This should penetrate a Galactic warship's usual anti-scan protections," she told the Detex officer.

"I'm reading life signs," the Detex officer breathed in astonishment. "About six hundred forty adult humans."

"A light complement for a sprint cruiser," Grice observed. "Harvest *Impulsive*'s crew manifest."

The Detex officer's eyebrows told the story: Grice's command was absurd. No Galactic warship would let its crew manifest be scanned by a 'Roider ute.

Except there it was.

"Intriguing," Grice breathed. "*Impulsive* is terribly short-handed – obviously dispatched on this mission in great haste. If its mission is so crucial, there should be a flag officer or senior diplomat on board – yet there's not."

"Fem Senator!" It was the comm officer. "*Impulsive* hails you."

As she sometimes did at times of challenge, Grice visualized the two most astonishing entities she'd met during her Galactic years. *How would Enoda and Computer wonk this situation?* "This is Pamela Grice, member of the Terran All-senate," she said in an iron voice sharp with annoyance. "Who hails?"

A face assembled itself in the viewsystem display – coal-black skin, androgynous features, a uniform collar ablaze with stars and clusters in various metals, a bearing of great authority. *A Lord High Admiral,* Grice thought. *This is a serious matter indeed.*

The face nodded tightly. "I am Sparl Konder, Lord High Admiral of the PeaceForce."

Grice frowned. "And you are not on board *Impulsive.*"

Konder betrayed only an instant of surprise. "You would deduce that, of course. Very well, Fem Grice – "

"Senator Grice, if you please."

"As you wish. *Senator* Grice, I am merely telepresent."

"Your actual location?"

"That is a security matter."

Grice leaned forward. "I had the impression this whole conversation was a security matter."

Silent seconds passed. Then: "I am on Pholandis Nine."

"Charming place," Grice said harshly. "Once I hoped to visit it."

Konder frowned. "Senator, time presses. My mission is to request your aid on a project of great importance."

"You mean, of great importance to the Confetory that framed me, then threw me back."

"Other interpretations are possible." Konder steepled slender fingers beneath her chin. "Senator Grice, I know that I cannot compel you to accept my invitation."

"Your invitation to do … what, exactly?"

"To come aboard *Impulsive,* travel to a secret location, and await your briefing."

"The Lord High Admiral jests, surely."

"That is all I can tell you now," Konder said. "It will be useless to press; I am forbidden to say more."

"You propose that I step aboard a Galactic ship and go to some unknown place for an unknown purpose."

"Frankly, yes."

Grice leaned forward. "Why?"

"I can tell you only this," said Konder. "Your identity as a high Terran official, your prior PeaceForce service, and certain details of your biography I am not at liberty to discuss make you the sole prime candidate for a hugely vital assignment."

"Details of my biography – " Grice echoed.

"Which I cannot discuss."

Grice leaned back. She wasn't sure where her new confidence had come from, but abruptly she felt sure what Enoda and Computer would do in her place. "Tell me, Lord High Admiral. If you are not authorized to answer my questions, are you authorized at least to negotiate?"

"At the very highest level."

"Then that's where I shall aim my demands."

Konder paused for five seconds. Then, quietly: "A strange way to negotiate, by making demands."

"A strange way to invite people, by withholding knowledge of their destination." Grice held her tongue for ten seconds. With each moment her sense of dominance grew. "Lord High Admiral, in return for my cooperation I shall require a mammoth, systematic, and continuing violation of Terra's Sequestration status."

The face in the viewsystem display remained neutral. Grice had expected surprise; ridicule, perhaps. *Saying nothing is not saying no,* Grice told herself. "The Confetory will repair and update Terra's thermal dissipation systems," she stated. "The exchangers, the flash heaters, the teleports, the extraplanetary components of the pipeline, everything. Plus I shall require a binding commitment, at treaty level, that the Confetory will maintain these systems henceforward so long as the Sequestration of Terra may continue."

***

Banitzek's embrace of Grice was warm and genuine. Over the course of their impromptu rescue mission they had learned mutual respect. "Good voyage to you, Captain Banitzek," she said.

"And to you, Fem Senator." Banitzek looked vaguely haunted – for him, an effusive expression. "You'll be going so far."

She smiled. "I've been out there before."

"The captain's gig from *Impulsive* has docked," crackled the voice of the ops officer through the overhead system.

"Senator." Now it was the voice of the comm officer. "Another priority call from Terra's All-president. You may take it in the open at your location if that is acceptable."

"Very well," Grice said. She waited for the quiet *click* that meant the channel was open. "Fem All-president, thank you for returning my call. I am about to begin my transit to *Impulsive,* from there to – well, wherever the sfelb I'm going."

The All-president's tone registered irritation – here was another way events could wriggle past her understanding. "If you're going aboard *Impulsive*, I gather you and the Galactics worked something out."

With a sighing sound, the lock door dilated. Galactic color and tailoring dazzled on the uniforms of *Impulsive*'s transit team. "I will have to make a more complete report from aboard *Impulsive,*" Grice said too loudly. "I'm sure they'll work out some means of beaming a secure transmission to Terra. But in the seconds I have left on this call, I'll simply advise you that … well, Fem All-president, I may have exceeded my authority."

Chapter 7

Suck, rush, wrench!

Fully in Mode, recording to a wafer drive in her belt-pack, the Spectator Meryam Mayishimu drew night air through her nostrils. Campfire smells and the herbal tang of Bohrkkian scrub woods filled her sensorium. Now she opened her eyes.

Two small moons hurtled through blue-black skies. Concentrating, one could just make out that their colors differed slightly and that they orbited in opposing directions. *Queen and Prince, the moons are called,* Meryam thought. *I wish I remembered which one is which.* Slowly she lowered her gaze. Scruffy treetops rose into her view, then twisted trunks.

Next came the rounded, black-eyed, hawk-nosed face of Zuzenah Latier, ruddy in the campfire's dancing underlight.

Zuzenah had been instructed to speak when Meryam's descending eyes met her own. "Well," the eldest wife said self-consciously, "here we be."

Not quite what I'd hoped for as the climax of this opening shot, Meryam thought wistfully. *Still, make the best of it.* "Zuzenah: eldest wife of the prophet, seer, and revelator Alrue Latier," she began. "The others are asleep – at least they've retired within our improvised tent."

Zuzenah nodded. "They're missing a beautiful night."

"You've urged me never to address you as Mrs. Latier. So have the other wives. When I ask why, you say 'Oh, it's a Mormon thing.' Your husband does the same. Can you tell me more about this preference?"

"I suppose it's an adaptation to plural marriage," said Zuzenah, poking at the fire with a stick. "I mean, if we wives are all together and someone calls out 'Mrs. Latier,' we would all five of us answer. What's the good of that?"

Meryam nodded, knowing that her experients would feel the head movement and know its meaning. *At least, if anyone ever* povs *these journals.* "Zuzenah, you were Alrue's first wife. You were sealed to him − is that the term?"

"Yes. Sealed for time and eternity."

"Meaning, married for this life *and* the next."

"Indeed."

"This occurred a few years before Alrue grew prominent as the prophet of his so-called New Restoration?"

"He had yet to declare many of his doctrines in public," Zuzenah agreed, "but he'd formed the critical ideas. When he proposed to me, I already knew he meant to restore Mormonism to its historic roots as Joseph Smith and Brigham Young had preached it."

Meryam smiled guardedly. "Tell me, how did you meet?"

"At a stake dinner on Terra − Usasector, old Utah, in the Wasatch Range. Everyone was supposed to bring something, but I'd gone over some unspoken line. I had brought an old-fashioned Jell-O mold, a great pink thing shaped like a beehive and almost a meter tall, with tiny marshmallows all through it. There was a time when Mormons couldn't sit down to dinner without a great hank of Jell-O in the middle of the table, but that was far in the past.

"My hosts thought I'd delved into tradition too uncritically. They laughed and turned me away! I was halfway back to my floatcar when Alrue got wind of it. The scene he made! Inveighing about the One Mighty and Strong and the call from the bowels of righteousness and such. He shamed the hosts into inviting me back, and –" she said this with pride "– my Jell-O-mold beehive stood at the center of the serving table."

"Was that when he proposed?"

"Oh no, we had a proper Mormon courtship," said Zuzenah. "We saw each other twice, maybe three times more before he put the question. That happened two months later. I was in the stake pantry making an inventory of the survival stocks. Already Alrue had pushed the community back toward stockpiling enough to live on for several months – you know, in case society broke down. He came upon me among the tall shelves; I still remember every word."

"Tell me," Meryam said gently.

***

Alrue had been a fine specimen of manhood, but that was fading now. He was still stocky and brown-haired, but his arms were going to flab where they erupted from his temple garment (itself an affectation about which the more moderate elders gossiped cruelly). But that meant little – he was one of those men whose power resided in his eyes.

He stood before her between the tall shelves, transfixing her with his gaze. "Zuzenah," he said portentously, "if you will not betray me, I will tell you something for your benefit."

"Pray continue, I will keep your confidence."

He leaned closer. "Woman, you were mine before you came here."

"Before I came to the pantry?" she replied, puzzled.

"Think bigger."

"Bbefore my family came to the Wasatch?"

"Bigger still."

"Hom Latier –"

"Please call me Alrue."

She stepped back, blushing. "Alrue, I am unsure what you mean."

Alrue stepped into the puddle of buttery light cast by one of the pantry's glowpanels. "Dear Zuzenah, you were created for me before the foundations of Terra were laid. That is what I meant when I said you were mine before I came here. And behold, all the devils in hell shall never get you from me."

***

The moons' light rimmed Zuzenah's still-ebony hair. Firelight shimmered on her face; catchlights danced in her black eyes. "What woman could resist such a proposal?"

"You'd be surprised." Meryam shrugged. "So after that you got, um, sealed?"

"Oh, no. I told you, Alrue was very traditional. So after that, he and I had to put our heads together and figure out how to maneuver my father into approving the marriage. In a way, I look back on that as the true beginning of our married life."

"Oh?"

"We always solve problems together. Nataleah – she's a tart one, don't you know – likes to say that over the years I've done most of Alrue's best thinking for him."

"And now a personal question, Zuzenah." Meryam leaned forward, her expression intense. "How does it feel to be the elder wife? How is it to share your man – to share his love – with four other women? With, dare I say, four *younger* women?"

Zuzenah laughed softly. "Three, really. He and Aunt Abigayl, they don't – well, you know. Not yet, for heaven's sake!" Her features turned serious. "I live as the old-time Mormon women did, with all our traditions like garments woven around us. This is the life God

58

ordained for me; I have never looked back, never had a moment's regret."

"But you had options," Meryam said. "You could have chosen not to follow Alrue to Bohrkk."

"I made the other choice," she said calmly. "A Mormon wife could scarcely do otherwise."

Meryam's eyes shuddered as she went out of Mode. "What a self-revelatory sentiment; I think we'll end it there." With a muffled grunt she rose from the fireside rock where she'd been sitting. "Thank you so much, Zuzenah. It's been a long day, I'm heading in."

"Go ahead," said Zuzenah, "I'll savor the evening and be along presently."

"Good night."

"Good night, Meryam."

Zuzenah stared into the crackling campfire as Meryam entered the tent. Zuzenah waited the span of a few deep breaths, just to make sure Meryam wouldn't be coming back out after some item she'd forgotten. Satisfied, Zuzenah relaxed her self-control.

Alrue Latier's eldest wife cried as she always did, alone.

Chapter 8

April 8, 2376
Aboard *Impulsive,* Nearing Standoff World

Arranging a truly private connection to the Terran All-president hadn't been easy – *Impulsive* hurtled among the stars under a security lockdown Pamela Grice considered little short of obsessive – but she'd finally persuaded its captain that a link to home was mandatory under the agreement that had secured her collaboration.

The All-president sounded more harried than usual, which was saying something. "Senator, I'll assume that you planned to contact me earlier and explain how you – how did you say it? – exceeded your authority. Will it surprise you to know that I've got a school of Galactic submersibles on the Indian Ocean seafloor *right now* begging permission to retrofit our heat exchangers?"

"What, nothing at the Matterhorn?"

"That's classified."

"Fem All-president, if I knew enough to ask that question ..."

The All-president sighed. "Half a dozen Galactic transports have assumed geostationary orbit over the Alps. I gather that two or three of them have heavy-duty teleport capability sufficient to spirit vast mechanisms in and out of the mountain's core. Pam, what the sfelb is going on?"

Grice explained what she had negotiated as the price of her cooperation.

The All-president was silent for long seconds. "A complete retrofit of the thermal dissipation system," she breathed at last.

"That was our agreement," Grice confirmed. "While there seemed no reason not to trust the Galactics, it's good to know they're keeping their word."

"Pam, this project must cost several times the value of our gross planetary product."

"Several *score* times Terra's GPP," Grice corrected. "Don't forget, I served in Galactic space. I know what kind of wealth the Confetory is accustomed to throwing around."

"Otherwise you would never have dared to demand what you did. Noted, Senator Grice. And inadequate as this is, thank you – I can't believe I'm about to say this – thank you for saving our world."

"You're welcome, Fem All-president," Grice said, masking her surprise at the burst of pride she felt. But why not? She'd made the grade in the PeaceForce, and again in a Galactic business world where "petty cash" often exceeded the budget of some Terran regionsectors. But the Galaxy had finally crushed her. Spewed her home. Terra *was* her home; now she knew it always had been – and what had she done for it?

Finally, she had an answer for that question.

Something buzzed at the boundary of her mind. "Sorry, Fem All-president, I must close the link now," Grice said. "They need me in the bridge."

"Don't you mean *on* the bridge?"

Grice chuckled. "Some things haven't changed. Even while I served, an immersive virtual battle bridge was something you went *into*." She closed the connection. Sifting her memory, she called up a subvocal bridge access code that had worked for during her tour on Forthright.

* * *

Mother of stars, she thought. *It's like blue infinity landscaped with gumdrops and xylophone arpeggios.*

The battle bridges she had known resembled some fantastic virtual landscape – a desert, a sea bottom. Each member of the control crew or authorized visitor would be represented by a *persona* appropriate to the bridge's

61

theme; in *Forthright*'s bridge, her old posting, she had appeared amid mountain crags as an Arkhetil predator cat.

What was going on at *Impulsive*'s heart entailed a whole new order of abstraction.

Grice's awareness floated in a formless sim space. Skeins of subtle meaning striated the *faux* firmament. Her immediate vicinity was dominated by a geometric array of tiny stars, each distinctive as to color, surface pattern, and the writhing of its prominences.

It occurred to her that each star betokened a member of the control crew.

"Welcome, Senator Grice," said a soothing voice. "Or should I say welcome back?"

"It's good to be here," she said neutrally. "I see technology hasn't stood still."

"It's grown at a breakneck pace. I am your briefing officer, Overlieutenant Nils Kafmetz." His star moved forward – that was as good a way of describing it as any.

"Delighted to meet you," she said noncommittally. "Tell me, am I a star also?"

"You appear in bridgespace as a dormant brown dwarf. I'm sure you understand."

Grice did understand. In her day too, visitors untrained in how to comport themselves in a battle bridge – or, like her, simply years out of practice – had been represented by demeaning *personae* as a means to alert others that in an emergency they would be helpless and dependent. "I'm startled how rapidly technology has advanced since I returned to Terra," she said. "There's this bridge, of course – and the fact that *Impulsive* is about sixty times faster than any ship even contemplated back while I served. Such rapid progress – it's as though there's a war on."

"There *is* a war on," Kafmetz said grimly, "and welcome to the battlefield. Do you know how to view outside the ship?"

She realized she did not.

"Sorry, it's one of the newer technologies. You must *want* to look outside. Just want, that's all."

***

The view outside was astonishing. *Impulsive* was caroming through shell after shell of quarantine ships in nesting orbits above a blue-green ocean planet. Time after time, heavy fighters locked weapons on the madly advancing newcomer before reading its security profile and leaping clear of its path.

All at once Grice found that she knew the commands to operate the exterior view system – commands not spoken but simply willed, much as one might direct a finger to point or clench. Applying a common power-consumption analysis, she saw that each of the quarantine ships was beaming inconceivable energy toward the planet below. *Where did they get such power? Ahh, yes.* Each ship fed on a lance of contramagnetic force supplied by an interstellar booster platform. The knowledge came to her unbidden the moment she thought to seek it: the platforms used cutting-edge teleport technology to harvest plasma from the cores of stars light-years away. Each such platform powered twenty quarantine ships, and there were more than two thousand quarantine ships in the spherical cordon surrounding the target world. *This formation is stealing an appreciable fraction of the energy of about five hundred stars. When I served aboard* Forthright *the whole of Galactic civilization commanded only a trifle more raw power than is being deployed around this single planet!*

The tiered quarantine ships were focusing enough energy on the Terra-sized globe to boil its seas in

63

moments and reduce its crust to magma in time for lunch. But the planet was unfazed. Its azure surface, its tiny islands, its slowly gyrating white clouds – they were all so *normal,* belying the fierce hell of energy searing down from space.

"You have made excellent use of the bridge's view analysis modules," Kafmetz commented. "You've discovered for yourself about half of the material on which I was to brief you."

She grimaced. "Feel free to proceed with the other half. For starters, what is this place?"

"Your destination."

"Thanks loads."

Kafmetz's virtual star rotated closer. "Neither the planet nor the star system has a name. They lie inside a thick knot of dust that renders the system invisible from interstellar distances; for that reason it has been reserved as a security asset since its discovery seven centuries ago. Of course, lately it's acquired an informal name. We call it Standoff World."

"With all this energy beaming at it, we should be calling it Cinder World. And yet –" Grice shrugged, wondering whether Kafmetz would detect the gesture through her dead-dwarf *persona.*

He did. "And yet, Standoff World survives. The planet has shields."

"Shields! You'd need the output of a small star cluster to deflect the fire those quarantine ships are laying down. Where does that energy come from?"

"We don't know."

"Where does the deflected energy go?"

"We don't know."

Grice's voice went cold and formal. "Overlieutenant Kafmetz, what *do* we know? What's down there?"

64

Kafmetz smiled. Grice realized she'd perceived that *through* his persona of a star swathed in jittering magenta prominences. "Not what, *who,*" he explained. "Down below on Standoff World are two beings who voluntarily accepted relocation there nineteen standard years ago. Two years after that, they ceased communicating. We probed from orbit to see what they were up to; they blocked the probes, then scoured the probe ship's thought engines clean. We sent a ship with better shields; they overwhelmed those. Since then it's been an arms race. They keep raising stronger shields and the quarantine ships keep countering with stronger probes. Which brings us to today, when such enormous energies are locked in stalemate that an imbalance of one part in forty trillion might strip Standoff World's star of planets."

"*Two* beings, you say," Grice mused. "Beings who want to be left alone, and apparently have ample power to enforce their wishes. So why am I out here?"

Kafmetz tilted his head back, frowned. He let out a long breath through his nostrils. She stopped trying to figure it out. "Senator Grice – former Gunnery Officer Grice – we have reason to believe they may respond to you."

She frowned. "Who are they?"

Disorder rippled the bridge interface. The stars changed positions; Kafmetz's turned away from her, helpless as Grice was to say how she knew that.

All at once the bridge simulation collapsed.

***

Grice's eyes popped open. She sat alone in her new stateroom.

Not alone.

"Who the sfelb –"

A bulky, square-headed man nodded slightly from a facing chair in the room's half-darkness. "I am Kafmetz.

65

I am present physically; security admitted to me to your quarters in case you might need something."

"You're staring," she accused.

He nodded. "My apologies, but you are the *whitest* human being I have ever seen."

She laughed. Stood. Realized what she wasn't wearing. Sat back down, arms crossed. Legs crossed. *I'm sitting here buck naked and all he has eyes for is my Terran-Swedish coloring. Pam darling, you aren't getting any younger.* "Overlieutenant, I need you to leave."

"My orders do not permit that. A moment, please," said Kafmetz, now making a show of averting his eyes. "You came to awareness here, at your actual physical location, because the bridge sim terminated suddenly. That happened for a reason; we have a VIP visiting by telepresence. Our bridge is the very newest version and he – I mean, she – well, the VIP cannot sync to it."

Grice nodded grimly. "Would that be Lord High Admiral Konder?"

Kafmetz smiled, almost conspiratorially. "You understand, then. Sfelb-drenched political appointees – any true spacer would have figured out how to accommodate the new bridge, as you did." He grimaced. "I never said that."

"I never heard it." Grice was already up, thumbing open a closet. It was full of identical uniforms in visiting-specialist colors. "I suppose you will lead me to the physical bridge."

Kafmetz stood, eyes to one side. "As soon as Fem Senator is ready."

***

Impulsive's physical bridge was as different from anything Grice had known during her years of service as its sim version had been. It occupied the interior of a many-faceted sphere thirty meters across. Bathed in sourceless light, two dozen officers huddled at a like number of consoles that protruded from its wall at every angle. Artificial gravity was so configured that each officer perceived the direction beneath his or her feet as *down*. At the room's center *Impulsive*'s captain bobbed in a chair composed only of shaped fields, her blue-and-teal uniform cape swirling slowly. At arm's length from her floated Admiral Konder, her lustrous skin paler than Grice recalled. "Ah, Senator, so glad you could join us," Konder said weakly.

"Lord High Admiral." Grice nodded. "Getting accustomed to the nulgrav at the center of this physical bridge?"

Konder nodded stiffly. "It's disconcerting, but preferable to that forjeling sim environment. If they ever tell you telepresence makes everything easy, don't believe it."

"I wouldn't know." Gauging the chamber's variable gravity without effort, Grice let herself and fall into an open seat. This was the first occasion most members of the control crew had had to see her in person; she ignored their ill-shielded stares at her straw-white hair, her blue eyes, her porcelain skin.

Kafmetz, floating beside her on personal nulgravs, waved one hand across the console before her. A physical audio pickup snaked upward, extending toward her mouth; a biosensor strap furled itself gently about her wrist. "We believe the beings on the planet below monitor this channel," Kafmetz said. "Just identify yourself. We'll be sending your voice accompanied by bio and brain stats."

"*This* is what all this has been about?" Grice demanded. "My homeworld is getting all-new thermal dissipation technology so I can try introducing myself to the Galaxy's biggest recluses?"

Kafmetz nodded.

"Best luck, Fem Grice," Konder said unevenly. "On the off-chance that they reply, angle for an invitation to the surface. Attempt to establish relations."

Kafmetz reached past her and thumbed a control. Grice's console came alight. Feeling slightly ridiculous, she leaned toward the audio pickup and forced a cheery tone. "Attention, beings below. I don't know why this should mean anything to you, but my name is Pamela Grice."

"Pam? Is it really you?" an oddly familiar voice crackled back.

A second voice was familiar too, down to its ceramic brittleness. "Just look at the bio-stats, Bucko. Of course it's her."

Grice's seat whirled again. Admiral Konder, *Impulsive*'s captain and the rest of the control crew leaned forward, their faces slack with dumb wonder – wonder that, this time, was not directed at her coloring.

The first voice spoke again. "Welcome to our corner of the cosmos, Pam. It's a long way out here. Why'd you come?"

"To see you," she said after a moment. "Just to talk."

"No one sees me."

"I will. If you'll invite me down."

Endless seconds passed. Then the first voice said affably, "Come on down, then. We've been out of touch for seventeen standard years; Computer and I could use some company."

Grice's console went dead. Then all she could hear was applause.

The interstellar golden girl has done it yet again, she thought wonderingly. *But what have I done?*

Chapter 9

The performing intellectual lounged in a studiedly decadent way. That – and the Ghelttian lizard wrapped around his syncrepe-swirled shoulders – was how most casual viewers would peg him as an intellectual. Whereupon, in 999,999,999.99999 … cases out of a billion, they'd snap to another channel. Still, in a Galaxy with 16.5 thousand trillion humans, give or take, that still left the haughty Thinker's Channel Sage JQ4 with enthusiasts enough to ensure that it would contribute its scheduled increment, however modest, to OmNet's towering hoard of Galactic wealth.

"A new mode of thought has claimed its place among the brooding classes," the intellectual pronounced effetely. "A new way of conceiving the future – to realize what it *must* be, to recognize how it reaches into our present in order to guarantee that our bright tomorrow shall surely unfold."

"An *inevitable* future? Audacious," said an offscreen interlocutor.

"In the best circles this notion commands vast attention."

"The best circles?"

"More concisely, *my* circles. But I should hardly move in those circles unless they were the best. Still, back to the insight I was preparing to reveal to your experients."

"Our *audience*," corrected the interlocutor. "Not *experients*. Channel Sage JQ4 is not senso, merely tridee."

"It is always thus," sighed the intellectual exhaustedly. "The insight of which I speak goes by

69

many names. Some, still captivated by the religious vocabularies of Terra, call it Omega – a divine endpoint, the ultimate expression of God's plan. But that terminology is out of fashion; it draws straight from the mythology of the Universal Catholic Church, and void knows that no one who's anyone yearns to be too closely associated with *that* these days."

"Understandably so," the louche interlocutor droned. No habitual viewer of Channel Sage JQ4 would need a review of the Parek affair and its dismal aftermath, so none was provided. Not even as a subtext feed.

"Out of a host of not-altogether-satisfactory alternatives, most in my circle have come to speak of it as Destiny."

"As destiny, you say."

"No, no! The listener must *hear* the capital D on the tongue – must see it flaming in the mind. *Dessss*-tiny," the intellectual elocuted. "Freight it with all the meaning it implies."

"*Dessss*-tiny," the interlocutor repeated. "And what is being said about it? In the best circles, that is."

"Mostly this." The intellectual released a pungent bluish cloud redolent of Rikubian nearmint – leaving viewers to wonder where he'd been keeping all that smoke, given that he had been holding forth for half an hour now without any sort of smoking implement, much less visibly taking a drag. "Consider existence writ large, which is to say all that is: both the cosmos we know and all beyond it that lies undiscovered."

"Everything," the interlocutor reflected. "The works. The whole banana."

"Now there's a Terran reference few would have the fortitude to indulge in. But yes, the *greater* cosmos, if you will. For generations it has been customary to view this greater cosmos as authorless, as coldly accidental. But more and more, my fellow deep thinkers have come to find that view inadequate. Some boldly conjecture that the larger future has a *fated* endpoint toward which it necessarily evolves."

"Something it grows toward, rather as the *hjarrna* seed develops into a mighty *spjeat*."

The intellectual shuddered. "A jejune way of conceiving it. But yes, if you insist – imagine that *spjeat* tree, with glorious cities nestling among its mature branches, reaching backward in time from its future condition of magnificence. Imagine it exerting purpose; imagine it *compelling* that infinitesimal *hjarrna* seed to fulfill its potential."

"Reaching into yesterday, as it were, and – oh, making that invisibly tiny seed be all that it can be."

"When next I stoop to appear on one of these programs, I really must hold out for a more articulate host. In any case, what many of my peers now imagine is that existence doesn't merely evolve toward its future state. Rather, existence is being *drawn* to develop toward its *Dessss-*tiny."

"Intriguing," conceded the interlocutor. "But where is the evidence?"

The intellectual stroked his lizard. "It is all around, if one only has the sensitivity to *feel* with more than the tone-deaf eye of science. *Dessss-*tiny is timeless. It is powerful. And we are coming more and more to recognize how it exercises its power." He released another puzzling whorl of nearmint smoke. "*Dessss-*tiny, you see, makes *itself* inevitable."

71

Chapter 10

April 8, 2376
On – Then Over – Then On Standoff World

Pamela Grice drifted awake. She savored the way sweat gathered where an arm that wasn't hers crossed her belly, her sense of deep relaxation. Below her hips, she felt a stinging looseness in muscles from which she hadn't asked so much in a rather long time.

She felt young.

Which, to be truthful, she was not.

She gazed toward the other's gentle snoring. One of the two most astonishing entities Pamela Grice had met during her years as a PeaceForce officer was sharing her floatpad.

No, she was sharing his.

She could learn nothing by scrutinizing his features that she hadn't discovered more acutely during their fervid couplings hours before. Glancing away and inward, she inventoried herself. She found nothing, no hidden commands, not even an embedded compulsion. Such had been her consistent experience during her – what was it, now? – thirty-five standard hours onplanet. *The Galactics think my presence here is hugely important. Yet still I have no idea what I'm here to do.*

***

Pamela Grice's debarkation from *Impulsive* had been a blur of officers and techs getting in each other's way. A med tech had matched her steps, slapping instruments against her arms and neck; paralegal officers flanked her to either side. "Fem Grice," advised the first paralegal, "as a citizen of a Sequestered world you are not subject to admiralty law."

"No one can order you to undertake this mission," said the second.

72

"Legally speaking, it *isn't* a mission."

"Please look into the vision pickup and confirm your status as volunteer."

Another officer lurched toward her. "Briefing begins; time's very short. You'll be visiting Gram Enoda, a Terran who sought his fortune in the Galaxy when that could still be done."

"Oh, like I did?" Grice asked archly.

Plainly the briefing officer found dialogue annoying. "Hom Enoda became a trendrider, a freelance social dynamics analyst. He purchased a third-hand Galactic thought engine. The wonkworks he acquired turned out to be wildly unique."

A lithe woman leapt forward, her movements surrealistically smooth. "I'm a military Spectator. For a top-secret documentary, please face me and hold still for three seconds. Smile if you like."

"That's long enough," the briefing officer snapped. "Briefing continues. By some freak circumstance, during manufacturing the photonic processing wafer of Enoda's wonkworks had spontaneously achieved what generations of researchers had sought in vain: not mere artificial intelligence, but rather *syn-noesis*: autonomous, self-aware, volitional, highly intelligent machine consciousness."

A new med tech scurried up, scanning her intensely. "No need for new implants," he dictated. "Fem Grice still carries he standard-issue implants of a bridge officer circa twenty standard years ago. Out of date, but they'll do."

Yet a third med tech prodded Grice with an elaborate contraption. Her arm stung. "Standard immunity panel, it'll protect you for three weeks onplanet."

"Protect me? From what?" Grice asked, but that med tech had disappeared in the throng.

"The wonkworks concealed its great intelligence," the briefing officer continued. "It passed from owner to owner, none appreciating its special powers until Hom Enoda happened to acquire it. The machine revealed its powers to him; his mind grew to complement them."

A duty officer scrambled up with yet a fourth med tech. "Add comm coprocessors?" the officer demanded.

"Don't bother." This from *Impulsive*'s captain, who'd apparently decided the squirming school of humans shouldering Grice along an access corridor needed to be larger still.

The briefing officer spun to walk backward, face-to-face with Grice, as the chaotic entourage lurched along. "Before long, Enoda and his machine devised a way to tap the waste energy released by ships' contramagnetic power systems, using it to create almost anything."

Another paralegal held out a datapad. "This directs your world's government to hold the Galactic Confetory blameless should you come to harm through our negligence. Make a palmprint in the square and spit in the circle."

The briefing officer resumed. "Using this new capability, which they named 'polyplex virtual telepresence' – 'polylocation' for short – Enoda and his machine could conjure any number of virtual persons. Moreover, they could create seemingly genuine physical structures, even functional ships, some with apparatus that could never be engineered in reality."

A commercial adjunct blocked Grice's path. "This is no time to be without life insurance ..."

"High Command discovered these capabilities during the Arbadrel affair, soon after which Enoda and his machine secluded themselves on the planet now called Standoff World – "

"Enough!" Grice eyed the briefing officer narrowly. "Young man, High Command didn't *discover* what

Enoda and Computer could do. They revealed it. I know because when they did it, I was there. And I was paying very close attention, because Hom Enoda was not only my shipmate but my lover."

The briefing officer stepped backward, astonished.

The knot of people tottered past him into *Impulsive*'s cramped docking bay. The captain's gig, twenty meters around and vaguely egg-shaped, dominated the enclosure. Pointedly disregarding the briefing officer, Grice locked eyes with the captain. "How about a *useful* briefing?" she demanded. "What am I to ask from Hom Enoda if I find him?"

Before the captain could attempt an answer, a projection of Lord High Admiral Konder shimmered into view. "Good daypart, Fem Grice," she said.

"Lord High Admiral," Grice acknowledged. "What a pleasure, it isn't crowded enough with the people who are actually here."

Konder smiled distantly. "I wanted to wish you well."

"Wish me well at doing what?"

"Actually, you've been briefed."

Grice blinked. "I have?"

"The information you'll require has been written to your implants," Konder told her. "Encoded passively in nanopatterns on a scale well below the subatomic. It *should* be impossible for the beings below to detect. As you know, your implants monitor your thoughts. When the time comes that you need to know or pass on that information, you will remember having been briefed."

"Sleek," Grice breathed, impressed in spite of herself. "But for now, I'm to go down there not knowing why I'm going down there?"

Konder's image began to fade. "When you need to know, then you'll know."

Chapter 11

The water from the newfound spring was fizzy. Nataleah Latier knelt beside the half-meter gap in rocky ground, scrutinizing the liquid in her cupped hands. "It's like seltzer," she said puzzledly.

"Most strange," Meryam Mayishimu agreed, unslinging the two water tanks she carried. Kneeling, she dipped an index finger in the spring. Licked it dry. Her implants did the rest. "Safe to drink," she announced.

Seven-year-old Abigayl dropped from the sky, stopping a hand's breadth above the water. "Pray play not with the floatcells, Aunt Abigayl," chided senior wife Zuzenah. "We know not how much power they retain."

Sighing, Abigayl plunged a hand into the spring and threw water toward her mouth. "It's delicious!" she enthused, settling onto solid ground beside the spring. "The floatcells are off now, Aunt Zuzenah."

Meryam smiled. "Verily, we should top off our water tanks here."

Abigayl stood. She was boyishly slender, a classic Asian of Terra with characteristic straight black hair and almond eyes. Anyone could see she'd be stunningly beautiful when she grew up. "This hasn't been a spring very long," the girl said with a disarming certainty.

"Really?" asked Zuzenah, intrigued. "Why do you say that?"

"The springs we found yesterday and the day before, they had icky moss all around them," Abigayl observed. "This one, the rock is so clean. Like it's never been wet before."

"She's a bright one," Meryam said quietly to Alrue Latier, who stood beside her.

The prophet, seer, and revelator nodded, tugging at his temple garment. "All book learning, too – the poor girl's been in punitorium half her life." He accepted a metal cup of water which his senior wife, Zuzenah, had drawn for him. He took a deep gulp, burped less than demurely, then prophesied; for he was a prophet, and prophesying is what prophets do. "Yea, the place of Mormon, the waters of Mormon, the forest of Mormon, how beautiful they are."

All right, it was more like quoting scripture.

Nataleah glowered around at the rock-strewn valley walls, the tortured rocky rill they'd been following, the sterile arroyo that paralleled their route, the scattered boulders, the reticent clumps of scrub brush. "O my husband," she objected, "only you could look on this and see a forest."

"I see with the eyes of God, dear wife. Everyone, Meryam is right; fill up your water tanks." Of course, they were already doing so. Alrue turned back to Meryam. "So much about this world doesn't seem right. Too much bare ground lies unclaimed by any sort of life. Wo be unto him that crieth: All is well."

"Bohrkk's famous for its unfilled ecological niches," Meryam offered.

"You said you have detailed files on this world. What happened here?"

"A Tuezi strike about sixteen hundred years ago."

Alrue frowned at the name of the implacable robotic weapons. Until the Arbadrel affair put an end to it, Tuezi platforms would snap into being at random times and places and ravage the nearest star system. Until the earlier invention of the equilibrational calculus – which permitted battle fleets to anticipate each intruder's arrival, destroying it before its shields could spool up –

the Tuezi had been unstoppable. "A Tuezi hit this world?" Alrue asked. "So why is anything left?"

"The machine that struck here had already devastated an adjacent star system," Meryam recounted. "Its power was flagging. Also, by happenstance Bohrkk was on the far side of its sun relative to the Tuezi's entry vector. Two small inner planets *were* destroyed; Bohrkk absorbed a few weak shots, but then the Tuezi apparently fell below its minimum power threshold and self-destructed. Still, the damage was bad enough. A small civilization that had learned to harness steam and make steel was destroyed. Residual Tuezi energy sizzled across Bohrkk's surface like blue lightning. To this day the rills it dug – the surveyors called them corduroy stone – resist encroachment by life."

Alrue nodded. "That explains much."

"Considering what percentage of the surface cannot support them, the plants and animals do the best they can."

Abigayl scampered over, tugging at Meryam's jumpsuit sleeve and gesturing frantically for silence. "Look there," she hissed, pointing frantically at about half of the valley wall to their west. Still there was no mistaking her target; all the adult wives were staring too, some having hunkered behind scrub trees or a convenient boulder to get out of sight.

Just twenty meters upslope, a big ruminant had climbed out of the rocky arroyo that ran beside their route.

"And they also had horses, and asses, and there were elephants and cureloms and cumoms," Alrue breathed.

"What's a curelom?" Abigayl asked quietly.

"What's a cumom?" Lupida asked next.

"Never mind those," Nataleah demanded. "What's *that* thing?"

78

Chapter 12

April 8, 2376
On – Then Over – Then On Standoff World

"Gram Enoda," Grice said neutrally. "So you *are* the being below. Or one of them."

"Pam! Or should I say Senator Grice?" Gram Enoda strode toward her through fallen claret-colored conifer needles, arms splayed in greeting. He wore a black bodysuit, black boots, an off-lavender cape.

"Pam will do." *He looks older,* she thought. *Though not twenty-one years older!* Enoda's high cheekbones had softened; his hawk nose might have grown more prominent. His stringy ash-blond hair, his scraggly goatee were streaked with silver now. Or maybe it was the bluish light of Standoff World's star. But his eyes were still green.

His arms encircled her. She was still deciding whether to hug him back when her body did it anyway.

Enoda stepped back, glancing upward. Following his gaze, Grice watched *Impulsive*'s captain's gig rise silently into a heliotrope sky, the pilot wasting no time lifting for the safety of the cordon shell.

Enoda spoke bitterly. "That's the one thing I can't do."

"I've been told there isn't much you can't do."

He cocked an eyebrow and frowned. "I can't leave this world."

"Stop feeling sorry for yourself," a reedy voice whirred. "Hello again, Fem Grice."

"Ah, the other being below. Hello again, Computer," said Grice – because that was its name. Really. "You haven't changed a bit."

"Did you expect me to?" Enoda's oblong electronic/vibrionic companion – the *other* most

79

astonishing entity Pamela Grice had met during her years as a PeaceForce officer – floated imperturbably, blue sunlight glinting from its metallic case. Enigmatic lights flowed beneath its surface. A flattened meter-long study in chrome and compound curves, Computer might remind someone of a squashed bouzouki, if anyone still played the bouzouki.

Enoda recaptured her attention by clasping her hands. "I've been following your career," he said.

She chuckled. "Since we went our separate ways, what, twenty years back? Or since I arrived in orbit five standard hours ago?"

"We live over this way," Enoda announced, pulling her toward the forest. Computer, levitating, followed.

***

Purple conifers overspread the trail, forming a ruddy canopy as they hiked. "All right, Pam," Enoda said levelly, "why you?"

"Why me what?"

"Why did they choose you to send here? Before, they never let anyone come down."

"That's funny, I heard you'd never *let* anyone come down."

"Either way, here you are." He flashed her a wicked smile.

If he was interrogating her, she would turn the tables. "So you and Computer have been down here for nineteen years, seventeen of them in seclusion?"

"Seclusion? Internment, I'd say," Computer groused.

"On one level," Enoda said equably, "I can understand the Confetory's motive."

"Sure," Computer thrummed. "Fear."

"That's motive enough." He turned toward Grice. "At Arbadrel, Computer and I sort of came out of

80

nowhere – and with so much power. All High Command could think of to do was bottle us up."

Grice was incredulous. "For *seventeen years*? What have you done all that time?"

"Oh," Computer droned, "we keep busy."

They crested a rise, stopping at the edge of a great cliff. Three hundred meters below them a meteor crater yawned. Perhaps five kilometers across, it was filled edge to edge with fanciful structures. Candy-apple towers and great baroque antenna arrays competed to seize the sky. Buildings of every size and purpose hunched together. Their colors were surreal, their contours whimsical. The whole vast construction resembled the masterwork of some failed cakemaker-to-titans who had voyaged into madness.

Grice gawped. "The two of you did this?"

Computer buzzed smugly. "See anyone else down here?"

A transit pod rose out of magenta grasses near the cliff edge. Enoda beckoned them aboard.

Chapter 13

August 15, 2367
Bohrkk, the Valley of the Zuzon

The creature was a good two meters high at the shoulder; in one of those accidents of evolution not uncommon across the Galaxy, the Bohrkkian life form that occupied the same ecological niche as the Terran moose looked astonishingly like a Terran moose. The resemblance might have been perfect, had any Terran moose boasted a line of brushy reddish hair running down the top of its neck, over its withers, and back almost to the rump; pendulous dewlaps of angry red skin hanging down twenty centimeters or more on either side of the chin; lemon-yellow eyes; and a trapezoidal muzzle colored a shocking shade of cyan.

Suck, rush, wrench! Meryam was glad everyone was watching the cow moose. That meant that no one saw how inelegantly she'd slammed herself into Mode to begin recording. "It's called a *svadi* moose," she whispered to Alrue.

The seven escapees stood – or crouched – unmoving for six minutes while the oblivious creature nibbled foliage. When it had stripped the scrub bushes before it, it took a step backward, raised its head, and bleated.

Literally.

It said, "*Bleat.*"

"*That's* the sound they make?" Alrue breathed.

"*Bleat,*" the *svadi* moose called again, as though to make itself perfectly clear. It had sighted a stand of scrub bushes healthier (by Bohrkkian standards, anyway) than the shabby scrub bushes it had just denuded. This more desirable shrubbery stood on the other side of a meter-high rocky rill and across a swath of soft open ground.

Shaking its head so hard its dewlaps writhed, the moose stepped over the rill. Its hoofs sunk one by one into sand.

"That could be a bad move," Meryam whispered.

"Oh, you and your foolish ordinances," Latier whispered back. "'The ferkeeks, the ferkeeks!' 'Stay away from sandy soil,' you say. Yet we haven't seen a single –"

"Look there!" Lupida all but screeched.

A meter ahead of the *svadi* moose, a fist-sized knot of dry ground boiled. The creature noticed, staggered backward in panic, and opened its mouth for what would have been an extraordinarily full-throated *bleat.*

Now that *was* a bad move. The ferkeek hurled itself out of the sand and into the moose's gaping mouth. The humans glimpsed a fleeting hairy teardrop shape vanish past the moose's lips. At once the moose's head snapped to the left. With sickening popping sounds, teeth and chunks of bloody tissue sprayed through its cheek.

"The ferkeek has smashed the teeth, now it's stripping the succulent gum tissue," Meryam said loudly enough for everyone to hear. "Any moment now it will force its poisonous pseudopod through the moose's palate into its brain."

The *svadi* moose stiffened, shuddered, and fell over. It lay on its side twitching slightly for about a minute, then fell still.

"The ferkeek will stay inside the body for a couple of days, eating its fill," Meryam explained. "Before it abandons the corpse, it will disgorge partly-formed juveniles who will complete their gestation within the rotting flesh."

"If you ever tire of embedding yourself among fugitives, you have a bright future as a wildlife interpreter," Alrue said wryly. If he was trying to mask how shaken he felt, he failed. "Very well, Meryam.

Behold, it came to pass that there *are* ferkeeks. And we must always avoid sandy soil."

"Actually, I'd been starting to wonder myself why it took us this long to see one," Meryam admitted. "My data say the ferkeeks should be far more active than this."

"Is it because everything's so wet?" Abigayl asked. "The other night, you told us the ferkeeks like dry ground."

Meryam nodded. "If conditions are right for new springs – with fizzy water, no less – maybe that would reduce ferkeek activity. Still, everyone stay vigilant. Remember, a ferkeek will kill a human even faster than it did this moose."

Chapter 14

Stout columns swept past the pod's windows in a blur. *Of course I was allowed a mere glimpse of Enoda's faux city from above, then he whisked me into a subway,* Grice thought. *I'm not to learn too much about what he and his metallic sidekick have built here.* The pod hurtled through endless tunnels, sometimes horizontal, sometimes stomach-churningly vertical.

"How the sfelb much of this *is* there?" she demanded.

"We don't use much of it at one time," Enoda explained. "We constantly test new structures and never throw anything away."

"*He* never throws anything away," Computer clarified.

Distantly, behind tiers of columns and piers and pillars, below tangled trellises of piping, a subterranean chamber glowed sun-bright. "That power manifold channels and synchronizes the energy extracted from a dozen stars," said Enoda.

"How many of *those* does this complex contain?" Grice asked.

"Let's just say several," said Computer.

"Still," Grice said heavily, "how did the two of you —"

"How did we stay sane?" Enoda asked.

"After seeing all this, that's not the question I had in mind."

Computer projected a tridee schematic before them: Standoff World, surrounded by its spherical cordon of quarantine ships. "Behold the greatest of games."

Enoda nodded. "We try breaking out, they try keeping us in. Along the way we've both discovered vast amounts of new physics."

"So I gather," said Grice, thinking of the runaway technological advances she'd seen aboard *Impulsive.*

"That, and exploring our powers – we can do things today we never dreamed of back at Arbadrel," Enoda said. "It keeps us focused." He paused a moment. "That's what motivates us. Now you, Pam. Why did they send you here?"

Grice made a great show of peering out the window at what seemed to be monumental quantum-superchilled bus bars. If that was what they were, each would suffice to carry the harvested energy of a large binary star system. She counted eleven before an intervening bank of structures blocked the view.

"I'm developing a theory, Bucko," Computer told Enoda silently on one of their shared subvocal channels. *"Fem Grice actually doesn't know her mission."*

***

The residence was a three-dimensional labyrinth. Imposing marble-and-glasteel stairways arched from level to level. The architectural vocabulary was consistent throughout: large, flat plates of various exotic minerals formed most floors and walls. Furnishings and accent pieces were hewn from glasses, metals, rich woods. Chairs and settees hulked chunky and oversized, sculpted from stout blocks of translucent glass. They were upholstered with silk-covered pillows whose solid colors echoed the hues of Standoff World's surface: deep clarets, regal purples, surly magentas, a weirdly lustrous violet-black.

Enoda led Grice down half a dozen staircases. They passed work areas choked with apparatus, elaborately decorated living quarters, and towering public spaces whose effusive spotlessness suggested they had never been used. The final descent involved no stairway, but rather a floatdisk that deposited them at the center of a tall, irregularly shaped sub-basement chamber. A platinum table ran three-quarters of the way around the space, supporting the most extensive, manically detailed diorama of a city Grice had ever seen.

"Don't get too close," Enoda warned. "Mind the boundary field."

Grice leaned as close as she dared – the tingling on her cheeks warned her when to stop. Then she invoked one of her old bridge-officer implants. A zone at the center of her vision swept forward as though she were gazing through a powerful magnifier.

This was no diorama.

"No matter how closely I look, there's endless detail," Grice said wonderingly. "This is no craft project, no work of art – it's an actual city."

"We call it Sturgeonville," Enoda volunteered. "At the level of vision-enhance you seem to be using, you'd see tiny transit pods flying between the buildings, except that they're moving too fast for human eyes to resolve."

Grice frowned, calling up a little-used routine that modified persistence of vision to support discrimination of fast action. "At max enhance I can barely make them out. They have passengers?" She looked up with a wondering expression. "Microscopic citizens inside?"

"Throughout our standoff with the quarantine fleet, we tested innovative ways to extend our problem-solving capabilities," Computer chittered. "This was one of the earlier and more radical efforts."

"We crafted virtual beings – infinitesimally small, highly intelligent, and fully self-aware, to the degree we could simulate that," Enoda explained.

"For being virtual, they seem awfully real," Grice said quietly.

"As you should recall," Computer thrummed, "actual physical existence is one of the qualities we – well, *I* – have learned to impart to our virtual creations."

"We designed these entities – we call them *Sturgeonfolk* – to live on a very rapid clock," Enoda stated. "Two of our standard days is a generation for them. We hoped that would enable them to solve the problems we put before them very quickly."

"It worked well early on, yielding some significant breakthroughs," said Computer. "More recently we've found better ways to institutionalize radical innovation. We don't ask much from the Sturgeonfolk anymore."

"Which is why you're willing to show me this," Grice surmised.

"In part," Enoda said evenly.

"If you no longer use this vast construct, why not shut it off? Oh wait, you never throw anything away."

Enoda chuckled. "Computer and I thought hard about that."

"*I* thought hard," Computer corrected. "Old Meat-for-Brains there swooped in for the executive summary."

Enoda ignored the barb. "Look at this city, Pam. Four hundred million Sturgeonfolk live there – the population's stable generation to generation. Sentient beings with children, dreams, plans for the future, a culture all their own. Sure, we created them – but to the degree we succeeded in making them self-aware, they're real *to themselves*. Computer and I decided we're morally obliged to sustain them."

"For how long?" Grice asked.

"Indefinitely, I suppose," Enoda said. "And no, we haven't begun to work out all the practical implications of that."

"Even so, that's laudable moral reasoning. Still, there's one thing I don't understand."

"Why you came here," Computer said flatly.

"Okay, *two* things. The second one is, why Sturgeonville? Why name this astounding construct after an extinct Terran fish?"

***

Grice had been more touched than she'd let on by the ethical insight behind Enoda and Computer's decision regarding their city of simfolk. Perhaps it was that display of moral responsibility, combined with nostalgia for the man who in all ways other than the physical had been the most intriguing lover of her young adulthood – plus the fact that she still didn't know her mission. For whatever reason, when the prospect of floatpadding Enoda arose –after all, what else was there for old lovers to do? – she'd found no reason to resist.

Nor had he.

And so, thirty-five standard hours following Pamela Grice's arrival on Standoff World, Gram Enoda announced he was awake by lunging forward and clamping his mouth over her left nipple.

"Gram!" she shrieked, laughing. "I'm over fifty, I'm a fat wreck, how can you want me again?"

"Never forget," Computer whirred from a nearby dresser, "he hasn't seen a real woman in seventeen years."

"Oh, forjel you," she snapped at the machine, and kissed Enoda exuberantly. He rolled on top of her and said, "I remember it used to bother you that Computer was aware while we made love."

"Maturity has its benefits," she husked between kisses. "Really, you should try it."

He pulled back ever so slightly. "Our last time together in the old days," he said, "aboard *Forthright* – I've never forgotten something you said: 'Two lonely Terrans pressing their pale white flesh together, humping away their loneliness between the stars.'"

"I remember that night too. Here's something I else I said, concerning your chromium friend." Taking advantage of her extra bulk, she flipped him off of her and rolled atop him. "'Think we can make it blush?'"

***

Much later, he stretched out beside her. They savored a silent, sweaty, motionless minute together. "Pam," Enoda asked, "your time out in the Galaxy – do you think about it often?"

"Constantly," she said.

"The Galaxy's encounter with Terra," he mused. "So many strangenesses."

"Well, so much for talking about us." She stretched. "You say strangenesses, plural?"

He nodded. "Think of it: it had to be strange for Galactics to learn that they'd finally found the Cradleworld, where the human lineage first arose from nonlife. It had to be a whole other sort of strange for Terrans to learn that *humans like themselves* inhabited forty-two thousand planets. That just starts the list."

"I see what you mean," she said. "Take the nuclear family. For generations B. G. E. most educated Terrans thought the family unit was a human universal. Yet among Galactics, it isn't even common."

"Or this." He toyed with her straw-blond hair. "In all the worlds, the *only* place you find white blondes is Terra."

She chuckled. "Or consider that no one cured the common cold."

"I know something stranger yet," he said archly.

"This I have to hear."

"Missing socks." Enoda scratched at his chest. "No, really. Pre-Galactic Encounter, Terrans used to think that in the future everyone would wear disposable unitards or something – no more socks or pants, no shirts or overcoats. But humans are too vain for that. When the people who strode the stars came to Terra, they still had their gowns and trousers and tunics, their boots – and their socks. And it seemed no amount of technology could fix the problem of socks that go missing in the wash. How strange was that – Pam?"

Grice had just sat bolt upright in bed, her eyes wide and staring. "Mother of stars," she whispered.

"What's wrong?"

"Not wrong," she said. "I know why I'm here."

"It has to do with missing socks?" Computer birred incredulously.

Briefing memory was flowing through her. She grabbed Enoda's hands. "When you mentioned socks, it triggered the briefing coded in my implants. I'm still processing it."

"Take whatever time you need."

Forty seconds later, she released the breath she hadn't known she was holding. "All right, Gram. You want to talk strangeness? This tops anything we've been talking about. By parsecs. Missing socks? That's *exactly* why I'm here."

"I'm listening."

She released his hands. "Seven weeks ago, everybody got their missing socks back."

"Define 'everybody,'" Computer buzzed.

"*Everybody*, all over the Galaxy. Any human anywhere in space who had lost a sock in the past six standard months – or so the analysts think. *Trillions* of people. They *all* got their socks back. Travelers got back socks they had lost on other worlds, but they received them *where they now were* – on another world, on a ship, whatever. Everyone got his or her own socks, without a single documented error. As near as anyone can tell, and to the extent that event times can be correlated across the Galactic lens it happened everywhere at exactly the same moment." Her face darkened as she made one more connection. "Sfelb, it happened to me. I got a sock back."

"Still have it?" Computer asked.

"No, I threw it out – I'd trashed its orphaned mate shortly before it reappeared."

"So that was your mission," Enoda said incredulously. "High Command wants us to – what, wonk how the socks came back?"

She nodded gravely. "Gram, the Confetory is hugely concerned about this. Imagine the implications for lint theory alone that such a thing even *could* happen. That's why they sent me through the cordon, to ask your help."

Enoda glanced toward his silver machine. "Willing to take a crack at it?"

"We have something better to do?" Already the lights beneath the machine's surface were flickering in new patterns.

Enoda stared toward the ceiling. She settled back beside him, one hand on his chest; absently he fondled her left breast. "Here's my answer," he said quietly. "We'll look into this – for you – and see what we can puzzle out. But if it turns into serious work, that fleet up there will have to offer some concessions."

She recognized the expression that clouded Enoda's face like the smoke from a distant brush fire: he was starting to dig into the problem.

"We'll need wider data access," he told her. "We could bring a few more manifolds online and punch a hole through the cordon's shields, but it's easier if the fleet simply dials them back. We need to draw in more information than their current settings permit."

"An eleven-point-six-one-three-five-eight percent reduction should suffice," Computer supplied. "At that level of power. they should still feel safe enough from us."

92

"I'll relay your request to the Lord High Admiral," said Grice. "Computer, I'll need a comm link."

The machine made a plinky sound. "Done. Audio, video, full depth and odorifics."

"I didn't mean *right now*!"

Too late.

In the tridee window that opened above her, *Impulsive*'s captain, several officers, and the projection of Lord High Admiral Konder stared gap-mouthed from the vessel's bridge. Before them shimmered the image of Enoda and Grice, in perfect tridee, naked and canoodling, Enoda's hand moiling one of her exposed breasts.

"Fem Grice!" Konder sputtered. "What is the meaning of this?"

Grice smiled sheepishly. "Just following orders, Lord High Admiral."

"I can't give you orders."

"Following your suggestion, then." She shrugged. "You suggested I ... establish relations."

Chapter 15

There was nothing more to see, and everyone's water tanks were full. At a gesture from gangly Constance the party formed up and resumed its trek.

"We have a hymn that lends itself to marching," Alrue told Meryam cheerily. "It concerns the Jaredites, the lost Thirteenth Tribe of Israel. At the time of the Tower of Babel, they journeyed across the ocean in sealed wooden barges."

"Sealed?"

"Watertight, able to lance beneath the waves when necessary. They crossed the Atlantic to land in what is now Usasector."

"I suppose that's in the Book of Mormon," Meryam said guardedly.

"Of course. That means it really happened."

Lupida, most musical of the wives, began to clap against the rhythm of the party's footsteps. When an oompah-band syncopation was established the wives broke into song:

"In the land where I'd be born,
Lived a tribe who'd sailed to sea,
And they told us of their voy'ge,
In a wooden submarine.

Meryam had to admit the hymn had a rollicking energy, especially when unison hand-claps came in at the middle of each line. Marching music indeed.

"So we sailed *(Smack!)* out to the sun,
Till we found *(Smack!)* the sea of green,

And we passed *(Smack!)* 'neath mountain waves,
In a wooden *(Smack!)* submarine.

They were climbing; she could feel it in her legs.
But the peaks to either side of them with their cotton-candy tufts of fog remained regally distant. Before they would emerge from the Valley of the Zuzon, the seven had plenty more trekking – and presumably, hymn-singing – ahead of them.

For the chorus, the rhythm of the hand-claps changed:

"We came here in a wooden submarine *(Smack!)*,
wooden submarine *(Smack!)*, wooden submarine!
We came here in a wooden submarine *(Smack!)*,
wooden submarine *(Smack!)*, wooden submarine!"

Chapter 16

April 8, 2376
Standoff World

The workroom's floor was a plate of sugilite, a pale lavender mineral shot through with whorls of black and silver-grey. The chamber's ceiling was a single clear crystal inscribed in a maddening fractal pattern that did not reward close study. Gram Enoda laid Computer on a crystalline workbench. He gestured for Grice to settle into a green-glass settee littered with magenta and purple pillows. Rummaging in lockers that spiraled open at his touch from the angled walls, he chose a small box. Vague radiances pulsed beneath its surface. He strode toward her, holding out the device. "With the implants you have, this linkage device should enable you to watch the interface as Computer and I work," Enoda said.

She took the box. When she held it in both hands, its file structure opened within her mind like a time-lapse flower.

"Don't worry," said Enoda. "It'll show you no more detail than your brain can absorb. But it should enable to you follow what Computer and I are doing."

She nodded, frowned. "I don't see anything yet."

Enoda smiled. "We're not doing anything yet. Just *pov* the signal, the way you'd watch a senso." At his gesture, a floatstool scooted toward the crystalline bench. He settled onto it, his off-lavender cape looping clear as though supported on tiny nulgravs under his subconscious control.

Maybe it is, Grice realized. *And why not?*

Exhaling deeply, Enoda pressed his palms into two concavities in Computer's sparkling body. An indescribable wireframe figure erupted into the air above it.

It made Grice's eyes tickle, even though she recognized she wasn't seeing it through her eyes. "What is that?" she asked.

"A seventeen-dimensional hyperpolygonal search sieve," Enoda said abstractedly, "a hyperpol for short. But you haven't seen anything yet." Splaying his fingers across Computer's body, squaring his shoulders, he opened his eyes.

Abruptly she saw the hyperpol as he did. Not just as a maddening geometrical vortex, but as a place for discovery.

A place to soar.

"This is where you and Computer do – what you do?"

Enoda straightened his back. "Hang on."

She'd served on battle bridges that had represented the apex of Galactic technology twenty years before. But she'd never seen anything like this. And somewhere behind the astonishment she found room to remind herself that, whatever the interface was that Enoda had set up for her, it was only showing her the plausible parts.

Enoda plunged among surging fountains of information, Computer's awareness a ball-lightning vortex at his side. Cat's-cradles of association whirled open at his approach, irising shut as he passed. After an interval, Grice realized that Enoda and Computer were assessing news feeds and classified reports from the whole of Galactic civilization and reviewing the associations among them.

"Fem Grice briefed us correctly," Computer birred. "As she said, everybody's socks came back at precisely the same moment. Hundreds of trillions of them, each conveyed to the right owner. No exceptions, no failures. *No one* received a sock he or she did not recognize."

97

"The odds against that happening by chance?" Enoda asked.

"If it happened by chance," Computer whirred after an interval, "it would be more improbable than the first emergence of self-replicating entities from nonliving matter."

"That happened by chance."

"This could not have."

A wall of data structures wheeled past, twisting. "I see your point," Enoda said in awed tones. "It's the closest thing to a miracle this Galaxy has seen."

"But not without its ironies," Computer said.

Somehow, Grice knew the machine was piloting Enoda's awareness toward a whirlpool of dark implication. A spike of insinuation skirled forward, wrapping into its mad depths the extinction of countless life-lines.

"Look at that," Enoda marveled. "Four point six-four-three-five billion Galactics, most diagnosed with compulsive disorders, suicided because they'd recently thrown out orphan socks and afterward their mates came back."

Grice felt a chill. She'd had that same experience, though for her it had been merely an annoyance.

The web of associations folded in on itself. Somehow she knew that this time it was Enoda, not Computer, guiding their movement.

"Computer," Enoda said puzzledly, "check in my dressers."

"You have six orphan socks," Computer reported. "Whatever it may mean, here on Standoff World, their mates have not returned."

"Go global," Enoda commanded.

Grice clung to her core awareness as the data visualization plunged upward, piercing countless tiers of abstraction. Somehow she realized that she was viewing the problem-space at the level of the Galaxy as a whole. With a maddening inevitability the probability lines collapsed toward two incontrovertible, sucking nulls.

"Gaps in the solution space," Computer buzzed, sounding as close to worried as Grice had ever heard him.

"What does that mean?" Grice queried.

"Twin nexuses where nothing makes sense," Enoda replied. "They stand out because everywhere else, the data set hangs together at a deep level."

"Mystery spots," Grice said.

"A good a description as any. Computer, identify."

Formations of inference corkscrewed into the twin null points, collapsing on themselves, spewing out formulae. "One of the mystery spots centers on High Command."

"There must be something they're not telling us," Enoda grated. "No surprise there. And the other?"

The endlessly infalling datasets flickered. "Get this, Bucko. The other mystery spot corresponds to – well, it's *me*."

Chapter 17

August 20, 2367
Bohrkk, Exiting the Valley of the Zuzon

Constance Latier drew an improvised wrap against the evening's chill. A tall, slender woman deep into adulthood but not yet middle-aged, she had pronounced cheekbones above almost-hollow cheeks. Surprisingly full lips sprang from the severely narrow planes of her lower face, creating a perpetual pout. Constance gazed up into the trees; with gun-turret smoothness Meryam Mayishimu (who was, at this moment, recording) pivoted her gaze from Constance's profile to the sky. Near conjunction, Bohrkk's two opposing moons huddled together amid deepening blue, their bland light dappling through scraggly leaves. "We'll be out of the valley soon," Constance said. "Maybe tomorrow."

"Tomorrow or the next day, yes," Meryam said, swinging her attention back clumsily. *The latest in an infinite series of reminders why I was not cut out to be a field Spectator!*

Unseen in the distance, two *svadi* moose bleated to each other.

"Bleat."

"Bleat."

"Ah, the sounds of the Bohrkkian night." Constance stepped into a pool of double moonlight and locked her big grey eyes on the Spectator. She smirked. "So, tonight it's my turn to answer your unfailing question: 'Why did *you* marry that man?'"

Meryam chuckled. "I'm that predictable?"

Constance shrugged. "It's a fair question. Terrans, Galactics – Mormon plural marriage fascinates everyone. Or it did." She hugged herself, the bones and veins of her hands just a bit more visible than one might expect where they clutched her upper arms. "In my case, it was accidental."

Meryam raised an eyebrow. "Unintended?"

"Not intended by me. Are we – "

"I'm recording." Meryam edged closer. "Please tell your story."

"I grew up Mormon. Well, you know, New Restoration."

"Alrue's church." Meryam nodded.

"I was sixth of eleven kids on a farm." Constance chuckled. "How more stereotypically Mormon can you get? My family were performing agriculturists. We earned our livings raising soybeans before live audiences. When I turned seventeen, my mission year, the stake leadership taught me a bit of audio engineering and assigned me to First Elder's big new tridee studio in the Wasatch."

***

"By the complaints of which Sariah repented, young sister, what torments you?" asked Alrue Latier in a remarkable imitation of empathy.

The gangly, redheaded teenager was beside herself with frustration. "O First Elder, I can't get the bride's and groom's audio pickups to balance properly. And the Temple wedding's in half an hour!"

The Prophet, Seer, and Revelator and the intern occupied a stark, otherwise empty space. Everything was white. Fine traceries in the floor marked the image projection arc-lines that would assist the tridee pickups in positioning the lavish virtual gazebo that would be added to an all-sim parkland setting as the upcoming ceremony was trideevised. Above them huddled luminaires, airpushers, audio pickups, and tridee cams, dangling from hundreds of robotic stalks. At the chamber's far end, a good ninety meters away, dimmable windows looked out on a Wasatch Mountain vista.

Alrue's leer took in the girl's slender but undeniably feminine figure. "Call me Alrue – it's a Mormon thing. And you would be ... ?"

"Constance Kimball," she all but stammered. "From Scofield."

"Old Utah's smallest village."

"The same. I'm new here."

"Most winsome intern," he said with an unctuous bow. "How might I assist?"

"I couldn't impose on you for something as trivial as this."

"Come, girl, if it mars the quality of my trideevised service, it is nontrivial by definition." Through narrowed eyes he scanned the empty studio. "Pray, where is everyone?"

"Lunch flitter's outside," she said self-consciously. "Very well, First Elder –"

"Alrue, please," he said, smiling. "I mean it."

She stuck a pinpoint-sized audio pickup on his temple garment near one shoulder. "Very well, um, Alrue. If you'll stand where the groom will stand – yes, right there." She stuck another pickup on her own intern's uniform, stuck a tiny module into her ear, and invoked a virtual audio mixer. "If you'll do the groom's part, I'll do the bride's. We'll just go until I have the two sides balanced."

"Who will play the officiant?" Alrue asked – a reasonable question, since in a traditional New Restoration wedding the officiant did most of the talking. The bride and groom spoke only when spoken to.

"Oh, you will," Constance said, tapping a foot switch. A life-size tridee image of Alrue flickered into the air before them. He stood wearing tails over his temple garment, holding a fat book and wearing a boutonniere. She smiled self-consciously. "We use this for setup," she said. "For – well, for situations like what we're doing now."

"Dearly beloved saints," said Alrue-in-the-tridee, clearing his throat. Their identities being known to the studio's control system, the projected First Elder clumsily speech-synthesized their names. "Al ... rue ... Con ... stance ... do you both mutually agree to be each other's companions so long as you both shall live, preserving yourself for each other and from all others and also throughout eternity, reserving only those rights which have been given to the First Elder by revelation and commandment and by legal authority in times passed?"

"I agree to covenant and do this," said Alrue.

"I also agree to covenant and do this," said Constance. She toed a control; Alrue-in-the-tridee froze. She consulted the mixer in her mind, looked up at Alrue-in-the-flesh. "Say it again, please."

"I agree to covenant and do this," Alrue repeated.

She smiled. "Balanced at last. Thank you ever so much, First Elder."

The studio system thought she was addressing the projection, which flickered into motion. Alrue-in-the-tridee nodded sagely and intoned, "Let immortality and eternal life hereafter be sealed upon your heads forever and ever."

***

"Seems harmless enough, no?" Constance asked Meryam. "Star-struck as I was to have commanded the First Elder's attention, I'd nonetheless almost forgotten the encounter when the message came to me three weeks later."

"What message?" asked Meryam.

Constance frowned. "The Quorum of the Twelve had considered the matter without my knowledge and ruled that our audio test constituted a valid wedding."

"What?"

"That's about what I said. The Quorum ruled that Alrue and I had properly agreed and covenanted. The projected Alrue had pronounced the marriage blessing – you know, 'Let immortality and eternal life hereafter be sealed,' and so on. They declared that had been enough to constitute a binding marriage for time and eternity. I moved into Alrue's household three days later." Pensively she sat on a fallen log. "That was twenty-four years ago. Weirdly as it began, it's been an agreeable married life – aside from the punitorium business, I suppose."

Meryam settled on the log beside her, a vantage from which the light of the moon Prince *(or is it Queen?)* glinted pleasantly on her straight red hair. "Forgive me, Constance, but I can't help asking a suspicious question. Had anyone ... *heard* of the Quorum of the Twelve before this?"

"Of course. My father looked it up; it governs the church hierarchy. It echoes a Quorum of the Twelve that Joseph Smith created very early on, while the original Mormon church was still based in Ohio of Terra."

"Yes. But in *Alrue's* church – had anyone even heard of a Quorum of the Twelve before it issued this ruling on your marriage?"

"Now that you mention it, no. In fact, my parents had a saying: 'In Alrue's church, most things get decided by the Quorum of the One.'"

Elbows on her knees, Meryam steepled her fingers. "And after its ruling on your wedding, was the Quorum of the Twelve heard from ever again?"

"Hmm. I don't think so."

Meryam rose and backed uphill. The move would make Constance look small and alone. "So tell me, Constance, if you don't mind – how does that make you feel?"

Constance hugged herself again, then broke out in an astonishing smile. "It makes me feel *special.*"

"Special," Meryam repeated, struggling to keep her voice neutral.

Constance almost bounced to her feet. "To think, such an important presiding group within the church, and its only public pronouncement in our time has been to declare me Mrs. Alrue Latier. Well, one of them, anyway." She swept the improvised wrap off her shoulders and tied it around her narrow waist. The maneuver accented her spare but still-shapely breasts. "Look, Fem Mayishimu, are we done?"

"It's hard to imagine what else you could add to this interview," Meryam said noncommittally.

Constance smiled. "Thanks for taking this time with me, but I should really get going." Her voice dropped to a whisper that mingled sheepishness with sensual excitement. "You see, this is my night to share, you know, Alrue's side of the tent."

Chapter 18

April 11, 2376
Standoff World

Pamela Grice awakened burdened with knowledge. *I really detest this briefing system.* She poked at Enoda. "Gram," she hissed, "I need you awake."

Enoda rolled toward her, thumbing one of her nipples almost automatically. "Woman, you're insatiable," he murmured with obviously feigned disapproval.

She hitched herself up in bed, pulling her sagging breasts from his reach. "No, Gram, this is business."

"Forjel, what now?" Enoda opened one eye.

"Are you paying full attention?"

"I am, if he's not," Computer whirred.

"For this I need you both," Grice said sternly.

Enoda rubbed his eyes and sat up. The chamber's lighting intensified. "All right, Pam, what's so important?"

"They want you," she said tonelessly.

"They have me. I'm wonking their plorg-warming missing-socks mystery."

She rolled out of bed and tugged on a camisole. "No, they want you – us – in person."

"Up there?" Enoda asked skeptically.

"That's right," Grice said, pulling on *faux*-silken slacks. "It's something big."

Computer made a trilling noise. "They plucked you out of Sequestered space and agreed to fix your world's legacy apparatus just to get us on the missing-socks case, and only three days later they have a *bigger* job for us?"

"So I'm told." Standing, she leaned forward and grasped Enoda's hands. "They want a truce. With teeth. No strings, no tricks, they want you and Computer physically on the command ship. My sense is that they want you really badly."

Enoda got up. At a subvocal command, Computer conjured him some kind of paramilitary jumpsuit. It appeared already on him; he tugged it into place where it had materialized not perfectly fitted to his body. "If you think this is real, Pam, I'll talk to them. No promises beyond that."

"Of course." Grice paced, sorting through the memories of a nonexistent briefing that had flooded her brain while she slept. "Apparently the quandary of the missing socks was a curiosity – a major one, given its implications for our understanding of physics, but a curiosity all the same." She gripped the back of a crystalline rocking chair. "Compared to that, I'm given to understand the problem they want to talk to you about face-to-face is big. Cosmically, obscenely big."

Chapter 19

August 21, 2367
Bohrkk, Exiting the Valley of the Zuzon

"We came here in a wooden submarine *(Smack!)*,
wooden submarine *(Smack!)*, wooden submarine!
We came here in a wooden submarine *(Smack!)*,
wooden submarine *(Smack!)*, wooden submarine!
"We came here *(Smack!)* in subs of wood,
Just 'cause Joseph Smith *(Smack!)* thought that was good!"

"Behold!" cried Alrue. The hymn-singing paused. "We have crested the pass. Meryam, do you concur?"

Meryam shifted the weight of the two half-filled water tanks slung over her shoulders. She looked about and consulted her data files, wishing for the thousandth time that she could access her satellite with its nanometer-scale positioning data and real-time imagery. "Keep in mind that I'm confined to general-reference data," she said. "But yes, I believe we have left the Valley of the Zuzon. After we crest this pass, we'll trek gently downslope for a day or two, then enter into the uplands. That means a higher water table, so water should be more plentiful again."

"Not a moment too soon," breathed Nataleah. Coming from her that statement was not without irony, as she had schemed masterfully to see to it that the seven escapees had drunk the two tanks she carried almost dry first. Yet even her selfish delight in the relative lightness of her burden had given way to anxiety as the party's water reserves had dwindled.

"Rest here," Meryam commanded. The women noisily unslung their various encumbrances and settled onto flat-topped rocks. It was midafternoon; Bohrkk's sun cast ruddy shadows. The day's heat, such as it was, had burned away the clouds that normally dogged the higher altitudes, affording an uncommonly clear view of the long valley out of which they'd spent the last ten days trudging.

Little Abigayl was the first to notice. "It's so green!"

Meryam leaned forward, dialing through one vision-enhance mode after another. "Remarkable," she said. While the seven had been passing through it, the valley had been a typical Bohrkkian landscape, its living patches peppered reluctantly among tortured corduroy rock and lines of unwelcoming sand. Now all that had changed. To the naked eye, the vista below them seemed weirdly green; with her Spectator enhancements, Meryam could discern that mosses and lichens had sprung up everywhere. Cool-desert plants that usually bloomed but one year in three, they had leapt hungrily from ground that was suddenly, freakishly nurturing. "If you're a Bohrkkian plant," Meryam breathed, "it's party time down there."

Alrue settled beside her. "Is there meaning to this?" he asked in his quiet, scheming voice. "When the punitorium was destroyed, all that groundwater came rushing out. Along the way we have benefited from those fizzing springs that seemed but hours old. Now when we look whence we came, all is verdant in a way that I, Alrue, gather is most peculiar for this world."

"It's peculiar in the extreme," Meryam conceded. "But I see no meaning in it. Then again, I'm not a prophet."

Chapter 20

April 12, 2376
Above Standoff World

The ascent from the surface to the quarantine fleet's orbiting command ship made one thing clear: Gram Enoda was feared deeply. Before it even reached the stratosphere, the transport flitter bearing Enoda, Computer, and Pamela Grice was met by no fewer than sixty heavy fighters, their defenses on hair-trigger. For the rest of the journey the fighters circled the flitter, weapons trained inward. "I suppose their plan is if anything suspicious occurs, to incinerate us," Computer whirred.

"Can they?" Pamela Grice asked.

"I've guaranteed that they cannot," said the machine. "But let's not tell them; why raise their anxiety?"

The command ship was five kilometers of crenellated absurdity. Fifty-meter letters announced its name: *Isolation.* A docking port opened in its midsection. The fighter escort formed what amounted to a tunnel leading only there. "I wonder what awaits us inside?" Computer whirred. "A thousand suicide commandos, perhaps?"

The flitter settled into a darkened reception bay. As the spacedoor fields reformed and the chamber flooded with air, wan lighting flickered up. The bay was vast, its receding bulkheads quilted with stored small craft.

Its deck, on the other hand, was singularly unoccupied, save for a single individual who awaited them in the medal-bedecked uniform of a Lord High Admiral.

"Just one person?" Enoda mused, eyeing the viewscreens. "Wait, I've seen her."

"That's Sparl Konder," Grice said, "the Lord High Admiral who briefed me. Five gets you ten she's a projection."

An alarm hooted in the *you don't need to panic, but do please pay attention* register. With a sigh the transport flitter's hull split in two, clamshelling open to leave Enoda, Grice, and Computer in their three lift chairs exposed on an open platform some dozen meters above the deck. A dazzling spotlight shone down on them.

Lord High Admiral Konder floated up to their level. Her ebony face was impassive. "Hom Enoda," the admiral began. "Hom Computer. Fem Grice. Welcome to *Isolation*."

"The ship is well named," Computer told Enoda on their private subvocal channel. *"Either it has the most robust shielding I've ever encountered, or you and Fem Grice are the only two living things aboard."*

Enoda stood, crossing his arms in a pose of controlled defiance. "Admiral Konder, all this melodrama to get me up here for a face-to-face meeting – and you're a projection?"

"My apologies. My rank should confirm for you the importance of this meeting. That I must be telepresent is but a matter of logistics."

"Where are you physically?" Computer asked.

"I cannot say."

"Pholandis Nine," Grice supplied. "At least that's where she was a week and a half ago." The admiral gave no indication whether she had guessed right, nor any sign whether Grice had annoyed her.

"Wherever you may be, Lord High Admiral, there are things you must understand," Enoda said with authority. "First, I have enabled automatic systems down on the surface that will wreak fearsome damage if there is any tampering with my facilities below while we are away. Second, I go nowhere alone. Computer accompanies me everywhere, for good and obvious reasons."

"It's true," Computer whirred contentedly, "Without me he is so pitiful."

"Third," continued Enoda, ignoring Computer, "Fem Grice also goes where I go."

"We shall be discussing sensitive matters," Konder began to object.

"That's right, we shall," Enoda said flatly.

Konder bowed slightly. "Very well, Hom Enoda. There will be no snooping on the surface, and if you want the other Terran, fine." The Lord High Admiral offered Enoda her hand. There was a protocol for these things; when a projected person offered a hand, you brought yours close but short of touching. Having your hand pass through the other person's ruined the illusion the projection technology existed to create. But Enoda was having none of that. He gripped Konder's immaterial hand and squeezed hard; the admiral started when *she* felt the pressure, normally an impossibility. "Most impressive," Konder said, rubbing her right hand with her left. "A demonstration of your polylocation technology, I presume? Let us begin your briefing."

Konder made a show of seating herself in midair on a bench that wasn't there, still rubbing her hand. "Hom Enoda, let me begin by saying how fortuitous it was that when the current, um, anomalies came to our attention we were already in contact with you."

"Fortuitous?" Enoda clasped his hands behind his back. "More like suspicious, I'd say. Four days after I start wonking your mystery of missing socks –"

Konder raised a slender hand. "It's been a busy week. I understand you and Hom Computer have been working with news streams, including some classified ones," Konder resumed, "so I'll assume my mention of

112

Celiax Two, Nikkeldepayn, Throckmorton's World, Gureya Six, and the Detex picket *Fargazer* will strike a certain chord."

Enoda's expression made clear that they did not.

"They do for me," Computer chirruped. "The events the Lord High Admiral alludes to happened overnight, while my biological burden was busy sleeping, or forjeling Fem Grice, or something similarly unedifying."

"If it was important, why didn't you brief me?" Enoda queried silently.

"They're just the disasters of the day, though lurid ones. I don't know why the admiral is bringing them up."

"Then allow me to review," Konder said. "I'll begin with the Memberworld Celiax Two." She operated some unseen control surface, causing a cluster of tridee windows to open displaying news images.

"Mother of stars," Grice breathed.

Kilometer-wide banks of apartment towers crumpled in on themselves, collapsing amid swirling dust. Balconies crowded with screaming revelers twisted free, crumbling into emptiness. Torrents of shattered syncrete and glasteel thundered onto verdant parklands, crushing thousands of victims. "Just over ten standard hours ago, at eleven irregularly-spaced locations across Celiax Two's eastern hemisphere, densely populated civic and residential structures began to twist uncontrollably apart," Kinder narrated. "This was not connected with any recorded seismic activity. In less than six minutes, two million died, seven million were injured. The cause was a rotary shear of forty degrees in the local force of gravity. The structures spun in on themselves quite literally under their own weight."

"That's a mystery, not a cause," Enoda objected. "The real question is, *why* did gravity shear?"

"Unknown," Konder said darkly. "Now this is Nikkeldepayn, an Affiliate world." The matrix of images from this mostly rural planet was less rich. A colossal tornado demolished a stone castle. A wider shot established that the source of the twisters was a towering storm system whose boiling cloud-tops reached a zone where the sky was black at high noon. "On a planet where rain is a luxury, some of the tallest thunderheads ever observed on any world Nikkeldepayn's size unaccountably took form, spawning tornadic storms more powerful than any on record there. Because of the planet's sparse population, only twenty-seven thousand died. The complex of hyperstorm cells was triggered by a gravitational hot spot fluctuating between four and nine g's that set up in the upper atmosphere. The cause is, again, unknown; we do know that the manifestation began at the same moment as the distortions on Celiax Two."

A new cluster of images came up. "Ahh, Throckmorton's World," Computer burred.

Konder nodded. "Throckmorton's World is a Protectorate; its autochthons haven't yet developed moving-image technology. Our coverage comes from a handful of Spectators living among the autochthons as undercover documentarians." The images showed a crowded old-fashioned city. Steam trains criss-crossed above its streets on stout overhead trestles. An evacuation was in progress. The people moved oddly in their woolen coats, as though to cross level ground had become an exercise equivalent to trudging uphill. "In seventy-eight sharply defined zones ranging from fifty meters to thirty kilometers in extent, it's reported that level ground suddenly felt steeply canted. Judging by the behavior of objects and structures, as well as the human victims, the effect was genuine. Again, the timing coincides exactly with that on Celiax Two and

Nikkeldepayn." A railroad trestle collapsed, the debris tumbling in impossible directions; a passenger train slewed sideways, cars and debris drifting laterally, lazily, before tumbling into a thoroughfare choked with evacuees. In another view, a harbor's water leapt ashore, crushing wooden buildings, sweeping steam-powered boats against crumbling stone viaducts. "In the affected zones, planetary gravity went out of plumb by anywhere from nine to forty-one degrees," Konder summarized. "Once again, we have no idea why the phenomenon occurred."

"The ... *phenomenon*," Enoda said with distaste. "How many casualties?"

"Two hundred eighty-four thousand dead, over three million injured. Given the state of autochthonous trauma medicine and the dislocation in the disaster zones, the final death toll will most likely exceed two million," Konder stated.

Another new image cluster: a globular orbital hotel soared far above a blue-green world. Such a vast civilian craft, better than thirty kilometers across, was found only above wealthy Memberworlds. The great structure had been mutilated. Pitted in a hundred places, it spewed escaping gas and human bodies. Rescue craft swarmed the wounded giant. "This resort complex orbited Gureya Six," Konder reported. "One of that world's nineteen thermal dissipation transport chains failed. Its stream of infalling material broke free of its ring buoys and bombarded the resort, resulting from an intense gravitational disturbance that erupted eight million klicks further out in Gureya System. Again, the incident time is identical; again, the underlying cause is unknown." In a welter of images, the thirty-kilometer hostelry succumbed to its damage. Its hull delaminated amid actinic flashes. Rescue craft reversed course, surging away at maximum lift. Only a few had attained a safe distance before the complex exploded in an obscene splash of light and fragments. "Three hundred and eighty-nine thousand died on the resort, another fourteen thousand on the rescue craft caught in the detonation," Konder reported.

"These are horrible," Grice said.

"I've shown you four incidents, somewhat randomly selected. Some others had higher death tolls." Konder tapped an unseen control; the image clusters snapped out. "In total, some four hundred and eighty-eight gravity anomalies have been reported."

"And they all occurred simultaneously?" Enoda asked.

Konder nodded. "To within eighteen decimal places."

"Two hundred and nineteen decimal places, actually," Computer supplied. "So far. I'm still calculating."

"Still calculating *what?*" Konder sputtered.

"I have acquired the complete data set," Computer announced.

Konder pursed her lips. "Oh, of course you have."

"I gather that the number of anomalies is not yet final."

"The experts think not," Konder said tiredly. "Presumably there were more incidents, reports of which have yet to reach us; in addition, there were probably many others on uninhabited worlds or in unmonitored reaches of space."

"And I am analyzing something weirder still," the machine reported. "Seven destructive gravitational events have been identified on *previous* dates – the earliest fifteen years ago, the most recent three weeks ago."

"I was going to get to those. They failed to attract high-level attention when they occurred, but now they are thought to have resulted from gravitational disturbances identical to the ones just discussed." Konder's projected form stood, her medals glinting under unseen directional lighting. "So you see what we are up against, Hom Enoda. More than ever, after this briefing I believe that you and Computer are the perfect people to examine this situation. Well, the perfect man and machine – never mind. Can we count on your help?"

Enoda glanced toward Computer. They conversed briefly on their private channel. "We will give you six days, Lord High Admiral," Enoda declared. "During that time we will sift all available data. After that, we will see whether Computer and I have a role to play, and if so what compensation we will require."

"Agreed," Konder said with palpable relief. "A VIP stateroom has been prepared for each of you."

"Thank you, but the three of us would prefer to share just one."

***

Konder's projection "walked" beside Enoda and Grice while Computer levitated alongside. *Isolation*'s broad corridors were, of course, empty. Konder was trying her best to be sociable: "Hom Enoda, Fem Grice, I'm delighted to make the acquaintance of two genuine Terrans, if only virtually. Since Terra's Sequestration, one encounters so few of the Cradleworld's children among the stars."

"I suppose that would be because the few of us who opted to stay out were hounded home," Grice complained.

Konder gave Grice no reply, instead focusing what she apparently thought of as her charm upon Enoda. "This may surprise you, friend – may I call you Gram?"

"Sure, Sparl," said Enoda, relishing Konder's ill-concealed frown. "And you may call him" – Enoda nodded toward Computer – "Hogarth."

"I'd rather you didn't," Computer trilled.

"Very well. Friend Gram, I am a great devotee of things Terran. I'm especially enamored of the wisdom of those 'one-name' Terran philosophers. You know: Confucius, Mencius, Buddha, Nietzsche –"

"Nietzsche had a first name," Computer buzzed.

"My mistake – I can never recall how to spell it. But I haven't yet mentioned my favorite among the 'one-name' thinkers. Such a mind, such pithy insights! Rightly proud should be the world that has given the Galaxy a Stanlee. Ah, we are arrived at your quarters." The hatchway irised open, revealing a spacious suite clearly modeled on a high-end Terran hostelry.

"Yuck," Computer said. "Danish Modern."

"Until tomorrow, then," Konder said solicitously. "Breakfast is at 0700, situation analysis begins at 0800."

Enoda bowed gently. "Good evening, Lord High Admiral."

"You'll forgive me if I dispense with the handshake," Konder said, again massaging her right hand with her left.

The hatchway spun shut.

Grice began to chuckle, then to guffaw. "What a gasbag!"

"She thinks I'll bond because she admires great Terran thinkers," Enoda said archly. "*Stanlee*, for void's sake."

"Come on, Bucko," Computer whirred, settling onto a reproduction Bauhaus sofa, "Stanlee is a sage we can learn from. Who knows better than we that with great power *does* come great responsibility?"

Chapter 21

"Behold," Nataleah Latier deadpanned, "he is risen."

Alrue Latier emerged from the tent, the last in the party to do so. Constance and Abigayl immediately set about striking the tent. Zuzenah finished drying and stowing the collapsible cups (all but one). Even Lupida, who had passed the night with Alrue, had been up for nearly an hour and had just completed inspecting the straps on the packs and water tanks. "By Coriantor, son of Moron, 'tis a lovely morning," Alrue said around a yawn. "Even the sunlight seems brighter than it did in that accursed valley. Pray, where's Meryam?"

The wives looked from one to another, each of them thinking another knew where the Spectator was.

Abigayl shinnied a few meters up a gnarled tree, pointed toward the south, and yelled "Look there!"

Nataleah clambered onto a rock and squinted south. "I see *someone.*"

After a moment they could all see a dark-skinned woman rushing toward them. "It had better be Meryam," said Lupida, to general laughter.

Alrue nodded his thanks as Zuzenah pressed the last cup of prepared food concentrate into his hand. He settled himself on a large fallen log, quaffed, and waited for Meryam.

Two minutes later she collapsed onto the log beside him, gasping uncontrollably. Her jumpsuit hung from her spare frame, soaked with sweat. Sopping red curls lay pasted to her face.

"Well, good morning, Meryam," Alrue said uncertainly. "Did you eat?"

"No ... there wasn't time." She staggered back to her feet and clasped Alrue's head between her sweaty hands. "Don't worry, wives," she announced, "this is business." She fixed her gaze on Alrue. "I can only do this for a few seconds. Open yourself, like you're going to *pov* a senso. Do it!"

He released a breath, squared his shoulders. Meryam's Spectator implants could briefly function as a senso player. Activating them, she pushed into Alrue's mind. For about ten seconds he saw and heard and felt what she had, just a couple of hours before: *Rimmed by early morning sun, three dozen black-skinned marauders clad in rags and leather, armed with bows and spears, loped through a rocky arroyo.*

Meryam pulled her hands away and sat heavily on the fallen log. "We have company," she gasped.

"*People* live on Bohrkk?" Alrue demanded.

"Oh yes, there are a few million autochthons, though none live terribly near here," Meryam panted, gratefully taking a cup of water from Nataleah (who never passed up a chance to lighten her recently-refilled tanks). "These marauders must be far from home. And they're tracking us."

"As in, *hunting* us?" Alrue demanded, wiping her sweat from his cheeks.

"Exactly. Mid-morning yesterday, they found our previous campsite. One of the bugs I'd left behind there registered their presence."

"And you said nothing?"

"They weren't close, and I didn't know enough to say anything useful," Meryam explained. By now all the wives had gathered around. "I started dropping bugs as we marched. By yesterday afternoon I could track them tracking us. I think I figured out their method." She tapped her temple. "Or my strategic modeler did."

Alrue shook his head. "Data files, bugs, a senso player, a modeler – woman, what *don't* you have built in to you?"

"Weapons," she said bleakly. She filched Alrue's cup of prepared food concentrate and took a great gulp. "Thank you, First Elder. This morning I got up at dawn and went to take a look at them – that's that brief journal I showed you. Then I ran ahead the way we're going. I found a spot about six klicks ahead that's a natural bivouac site and strewed all kinds of bugs."

"And ran back?" Lupida asked. Meryam nodded. "You should've used Aunt Abigayl's floatcells."

"Couldn't," Meryam gasped. "On the ground I could stay out of the marauders' line of sight; in the air I might be spotted."

"Filling that clearing with bugs, how does that help us?" Alrue asked.

Meryam drained her water cup. "I think my modeler understands their method of tracking well enough to guess how they'll respond to our movements."

Ever practical, Constance grasped the logic first. "By controlling where we go, we control where *they* go."

Meryam leaned close to Alrue. "First Elder, I need command of the party for today. I think my modeler can plot us a course that will keep those marauders from closing with us today, and also maneuver them into finding that clearing I prepared just about when they're looking for someplace to pitch their tents."

Little Abigayl pumped one fist in the air. "They'll spend the night where all those bugs are."

"That's my plan," Meryam affirmed. "And if it works, tomorrow morning we'll know something definite about their tribe and their technology, a bit about their individual personalities – and maybe what they want with us."

Alrue looked about at his wives, all watching raptly. He gave Meryam a *come with me* gesture and led her behind a scraggly tree twenty-odd meters away. He looked over his shoulder to confirm that his wives were out of earshot, then rasped, "Fem Mayishimu, while I appreciate your initiative, as Prophet, Seer, and Revelator I expect to be consulted on matters of strategy."

She shrugged. "You weren't up. Look, we have three dozen creepy marauders tailing us. You want to learn about them or not?"

Chapter 22

Interlude
Trailer for a Tridee Epic

The music is adamant, the announcer's voice unendurable. "IN A UNIVERSE WHERE OTHERS SAW ONLY COINCIDENCE, ONE MAN FOUND DIRECTION."

Cut to a musty twentieth-century Terran workroom whose treasures include the bones of Peking Man. A slender middle-aged paleontologist-priest lectures to nubile graduate students, astounding them with his wisdom. He challenges them to envision "a world that is *being born* instead of a world that *is*."

"WHERE OTHERS SAW ONLY BRUTE DURATION, HE SENSED MEANING."

Years younger, the priest and (now) future paleontologist helps carry a stretcher across a World War I (Terran) battlefield. Anachronistically, the *Médaille militaire* and *Légion d'honneur* he will later win for doing this already glint on his bloodstained medical whites. At least, they glint whenever sunlight reaches them through the turgid smoke of war. "Humanity has a future," he philosophizes to a Legionnaire with a sucking chest wound and the manner of one who would rather die in peace, "a future defined not only by the successive years, but by higher states to be attained by struggle."

"I struggle to breathe," the dying soldier gasps, "will you count that?"

"HE FOLLOWED HIS IDEAS EVEN INTO CONFLICT WITH THE CHURCH ITSELF."

Clawlike, the hand of a Cardinal rips the white collar from the paleontologist-priest's black cassock. He is being stripped of his authority to teach. "God does not work as you say he does," the Cardinal accuses.

The paleontologist-priest is unmoved. "He does so."

"Does not."

"Does so."

"IN A COSMOS WITHOUT FEELING, HE DARED TO IMAGINE THE PERSONAL."

Lightning lances the night skies outside the window of his fetid yurt as the paleontologist-priest reads intently, an evolutionary biology journal in one hand, a dogeared Bible in the other. "The greatest event in history," he muses in wistful voice-over, "may be our eventual detection not merely of something but of *Some One* at the summit of time, coming to be as the Universe evolves upon itself."

"AT THE END, HE CHALLENGED EVEN HIS GOD."

Gazing out at mid-twentieth century Park Avenue from New York City of Terra's Church of Saint Ignatius of Loyola, the elderly paleontologist-priest tells a fellow Jesuit, "If in my life I have not been wrong, I beg God to allow me to die on Easter Sunday."

"Happy Easter, Father Teilhard."

"Urk-k-k-k!"

In the trailer's final graphic, the paleontologist-priest straddles the mountains of a world in flames and contemplates the ever-complexifying ballet of the heavens. "COMING SOON FROM OMNET INFOMEGATAINMENT TRANSSTELLAR: *TEILHARD DE CHARDIN, PROPHET OF COSMIC EVOLUTION!"*

Chapter 23

After the morning's situation analysis meeting ended, Lord High Admiral Konder's projected avatar took Enoda aside. Computer remained on the conference table, surrounded by virtual intelligence analysts and scientists eager to engage the syn-noetic machine in discussion and debate. Konder's projection guided Enoda into a small room at least two blind corners away from the conference chamber. "You and Computer are a formidable team," the admiral said almost pensively. "Do you ever think you might depend on him ... too much?"

"I *do* depend on him," Enoda replied frankly. "Totally. What we do – well, it takes both of us."

"I understand. But now, please understand *me*." Konder laid her virtual hand on Enoda's arm. Enoda realized the gesture must mean much to the admiral, who found tactile experiences mediated through her virtual interface unpleasant. "There's never been a fully personal self-aware system like Hom Computer before. What if Computer becomes unstable someday, or decides that his interests no longer coincide with yours?"

"We've been together for years."

"Years during which you have grown and developed remarkably as a human. Years during which Hom Computer has grown and developed remarkably as – something else."

Enoda arched one eyebrow. "Do I scent prejudice?"

"Call it the recognition of difference," Konder said measuredly. "Successful as your partnership with Computer has been thus far, the past may not always determine the future. And so I ask, have you an exit strategy?"

Enoda stood with his arms crossed over his chest. "I can't say I ever thought of it that way."

"Someday you may be grateful that *I* did. I'm going to squirt to you a confidential access code, from my implant set to yours. Bury it deep," Konder advised, "but never forget it's there. If you're ever having second thoughts about your syn-noetic partner, tap that code privately."

Enoda smiled thinly. "It reaches you, wherever you are?"

Konder's smile in response was cold. "It reaches way higher than me."

Chapter 24

Since Meryam Mayishimu had reserved the vicinity's most attractive campsite for the marauder band, Alrue's band had settled for second-best. Morning sun washed the rill of tortured corduroy rock on which they'd spent the night. The improvised tent was more lopsided than usual; sister wives Constance and Nataleah had had to wedge its poles into whatever natural rock openings they could find by the previous dusk's failing light.

The tent was irregular in another way: this morning, Alrue Latier was not the last to leave it.

Goaded by anticipation, this day Alrue had risen with the sun. He'd waited impatiently while Zuzenah poured his prepared food concentrate, then scuttled across furrowed granite toward the irregular boulder where Meryam Mayishimu had deposited herself before sunrise. Meryam sat unmoving, eyes closed, back ramrod straight, breathing faintly but rapidly.

Lupida scuttled up behind her husband and tugged at the crude wrap Alrue wore over his temple garment. Her freckled face knotted with concern. "My husband, Meryam said we shouldn't disturb her when she's like this."

"By Gid and Teomner's conquest, woman, I need to *know*." He bustled around Lupida, almost twisting an ankle in a rocky channel, and sat heavily beside the motionless Meryam. "Daypart, Fem Mayishimu," he boomed.

Eyes still closed, Meryam raised one finger. "Bear with me," she said abstractedly, "my modeler is very busy compiling your summary."

"So there's something to summarize. *Everyone!*" he all but shouted. "Meryam's plan worked!"

A minute passed. Meryam's rapid breathing stopped. She inhaled deeply; her eyes drifted open. "You know, Alrue, some people wait to see the evidence before they shout about the conclusion." She uncoiled her legs and stepped off the boulder. "Still, as it happens, my plan did work. The marauders camped where I'd strewn my bugs most thickly. I got torrents of data." She stepped in front of Alrue. "This summary's highly condensed – with your implants and level of experience you shouldn't have difficulty taking it all in, but you'll need time to make sense of it. Are you ready?" Not waiting for the answer, she pressed her hands to his temples.

This was not senso. It more resembled a high-pressure hose inside his skull. The jumble of sensations meant nothing as they surged one after another: flash-images of the marauders, snippets of their interactions, bursts of compressed speech, arcane diagrams codifying their communications and the interpersonal relations they implied.

The playback ended; Meryam withdrew her hands. Alrue sat blinking for a dozen seconds, his brain structuring what he had *pov*ed. "They're far from home, all right," he said after a moment. Impressions coalesced into knowledge of facts. "Their leader got them lost. He's the bearded guy with the necklace of bird skulls."

Meryam nodded. "Do you know his name?"

"What do you know, I do," Alrue said wonderingly. "His name is ... Nirom Fpod." He stepped away from the boulder, his eyes darting about. Knowledge of facts blossomed into insights: a global understanding of the marauders' mode of organization, their military principles, their social forms. "Meryam, lift up your head and be of good comfort. I know how to vanquish these hunters."

***

Alrue, his five wives, and Meryam sat roughly in a circle. The tent lay rumpled on the ground. The makeshift table on which Zuzenah had prepared food concentrate leaned against a rock. The wives had quite literally dropped everything to attend this parley.

Not surprisingly, Alrue was speaking.

"Our plan, to the degree we had one, was to search for someplace we could stay more or less comfortably for a few weeks. Ideally, somewhere we could stay out of sight when the rescue expedition appeared. If they were privateers, I hoped to talk our way off-world; if the first responders were official, I imagined I might negotiate more favorable conditions for the balance of our sentence as sole survivors of the catastrophe. But it's been almost two weeks. The distance we've covered on foot in that time is modest. If even a small ship had come sniffing around the ruins, we couldn't miss it."

"I think no one's coming," offered Nataleah, rubbing her broad pale nose with the back of her hand. "Maybe the punitorium was destroyed so fast that no distress call went out. Or maybe what happened here is part of a larger disaster. Maybe the Confetory has its hands full."

"There may never be a response," Alrue grimly agreed. "We must consider that possibility. Which means we need to think about surviving long-term. Constance, how are our supplies?"

Constance clasped her bony hands over her knees. "We've had no trouble finding water. Our food concentrates will last about five more weeks."

Alrue nodded. "After that – well, the plant life is sparse, but some of it seems edible. And who knows,

129

maybe we could take down one of those *svadi* moose now and again."

"Using what?" Constance asked. "We don't have anything for hunting."

"There's a bigger problem," Meryam said forcefully. "We can't live on the native plants and animals."

Alrue frowned. "Huh? Why not?"

"We all learned this as children, but it's easily forgotten. After all, it has nothing to do with our lives. Until it does." Meryam dropped to her knees, sketching rough diagrams in the gravel at their feet. "Each time life arises from nonlife, the carbon chains of its amino acids can assemble themselves spiraling to the left or to the right. That property of, well, 'handedness' is called *chirality*."

"*I* never learned that as a child," Alrue grumbled.

Meryam shrugged. "Each time life arises, its chirality gets established. Thereafter, every organism to evolve along *that* tree of life will conserve it. If your ancestors' amino acids twisted to the left, so will yours. For reasons nobody knows, there's a small but significant bias toward the right-handed orientation; on most life-bearing planets, carbon chains twist to the right. For whatever reason, when life arose on Terra *our* genetic forbears spiraled their carbon chains to the *left*. Lefties like us can eat right-handed foods, even digest them – there's no difference at the level of gross chemistry – but the foods do not nourish us. If we rely only on native biomass, we will starve."

Alrue steepled his hands. "That changes everything. Do we need to go back to the ruins, search for more food concentrates?"

"Wait, my husband," little Abigayl piped up. "People live here."

Lupida shrugged. "They probably eat the right-handed stuff."

Constance stood slowly. "No, they don't! Good thinking, Abigayl. Alrue – Meryam – these marauders. They're people like us, right? *Homo sapiens?*"

"They always are, my dear," Alrue responded. "People like us, actual spawn of Terra, on all of the Galaxy's millions of inhabited worlds …"

"Forty-two thousand inhabited worlds," Meryam corrected.

Alrue spread his palms. "Millions of years ago, godlings visited Terra …"

"More like four hundred thousand years ago," Meryam cut in. "And they were probably just very advanced aliens."

"Whatever they were, they collected proto-humans – along with plants and animals the proto-humans could eat – and seeded them across the Galaxy."

"The Harvesters," Zuzenah breathed.

"Is Bohrkk is one of the worlds the Harvesters seeded in this way?" Alrue stood, grunting. "Meryam, check your files."

"I don't need files," Meryam said sourly. "Fully intelligent life arose from nonlife only once. On Terra. *Every* other human population has been shown to be Terran stock seeded by the Harvesters. If a second human lineage with right-handed chirality had evolved here, Bohrkk would be a science preserve, not a prison world. Rely on it, our marauder friends are lefties like us."

"Then their food is also food for us." Alrue slammed his meaty hands together. "We're back to Plan A."

"Which was … what, exactly?"

"Reaching out to those marauders on our terms. *My* terms." Alrue stood and paced. "Now let's review what we know. We know these marauders hail from a larger permanent community."

"How much larger?" asked Zuzenah.

"Based on their social forms, maybe hundreds of people, maybe a couple thousand at most," Meryam supplied.

Alrue nodded. "This Nirom Fpod character holds some authority, but he's not top dog back home. There's at least one level of authority, maybe two, above him."

"I heard the marauders talk about a higher ruler," Meryam offered, "someone whose displeasure this Fpod seems to fear. Though among his comrades, Fpod professes not to hold the higher ruler in terribly high respect."

"Subordinate commanders usually plorg-talk their higher-ups," Alrue said.

"Where is this permanent settlement?" Constance asked.

"We don't know," Alrue responded. "Fpod doesn't know."

"The marauders have been lost long enough that last night, some of them conversed nostalgically about home," Meryam said. "My modeler's still winnowing through it, but they may have dropped enough geographic references that I can form a rough idea where they're from."

"Wherever that is, there's food there," said Alrue.

Zuzenah reached out to clutch Alrue's arm as he paced by. He looked down at her tenderly. "My husband, this village – or whatever it is – is it somewhere we might live?"

Alrue nodded affectionately. "That is what I believe."

Nataleah pursed her lips. "But we don't want to live there as prisoners."

"Nor as slaves. In fact, I'd like to be more or less in charge." Alrue fingered the top closure of his temple garment. "At times like this I turn to God."

"Oh, here we go," Nataleah mouthed silently to Lupida.

"And when I, Alrue, turn to God, I ask Him, 'O God, O Heavenly Father, O Lord of Hosts, what would Joseph Smith do?' Well, it comes to pass that in this situation I know *just* what Joseph Smith would do. I know how he'd do it. And behold: As He has on previous occasions, God has reached out His mighty arm and granted me the gifts to do as Joseph the Prophet would have done in my place."

"I keep thinking there has to be some alternative to exposing ourselves to those marauders," Meryam said doubtfully.

"I understand your caution, Fem Mayishimu," Zuzenah said gently. "But I too keep running through all the sensible scenarios, and most of them end with us starving in the wilderness. Now what does that leave us with?"

Meryam tugged at her red curls. "The scenarios that aren't sensible?"

"Exactly," Zuzenah declared. "And verily I tell you this: When things stop making sense, that's when my Alrue is at his best."

Alrue beamed. "Why thank you, wife of my youth."

Meryam clasped her hands across her knees. "There's much to think about –"

"Actually, there isn't," Alrue said testily. "When the leader speaks, the thinking is done."

Meryam looked up, her eyes narrowed. "I beg your pardon?"

"Allow me to remind you, Fem Mayishimu, this is my family," Alrue declared. "You are my guest. In the event of irreconcilable disagreement between you and me as to our course, my word is final."

Meryam arched an eyebrow. "Brave words when you depend so heavily on my Spectator capacities."

Alrue sat back down. His body language suggested a man reclining on a throne. "Fem Mayishimu, is one of your Spectator capabilities not earning a living? Weren't you visiting us in the punitorium as part of your job?"

"Well, yes."

"One day the Confetory *will* come, even if later than we might like. On that day your principal concern should be the value of the journals you will have recorded while among us. I shall speak frankly, Meryam. No professional religious leader has ever perpetrated flimflam on the scale I now contemplate. Not since Joseph Smith himself – no, wait, let me rephrase that. No professional religious leader has ever perpetrated flimflam on this scale *with a Spectator documenting his every move*. Someday that will make for an immensely valuable body of work. Maybe something to retire on."

Meryam thought fast. She was not eager to have it out with the First Elder here before his wives. Not in these conditions. And from a strictly economic perspective, Alrue had a point. She smiled wickedly. "You're right, First Elder. Even if you wind up with a spear through your heart two seconds after the marauders spot you, the journal *will* be valuable."

Alrue chuckled. "You underestimate me. I will never be in danger."

Meryam exhaled. "Very well, your Plan A it is. For now."

"You agree to covenant and do this?"

"I suppose so. What does Plan A require?"

"I shall need to surprise them," he said. "The marauders must come upon me – just myself, alone – in a setting that will minimize the likelihood of their killing me on sight."

"So you admit that's a danger."

"A danger my plan will circumvent," he said curtly. "And when they see me, behold, I will speak to them."

"How will they understand you?" Abigayl queried. "They're from here."

"Oh yeah, autochthons," breathed Nataleah. "No translation implants."

"Alrue, what kind of implants do you have?" Meryam asked. "Terran standard?"

"No, diplomatic-level. I upgraded back when my ministry was made of money."

"Then you have nothing to worry about. Address the marauders however you like; your implants will recognize that the marauders are unmodified, and simply take control of your mouth and throat. You'll speak aloud in their language even though you don't know it. If any of us are within earshot or listening by means of my bugs, we'll hear what you're saying in whatever happens to be our strongest language."

"Very well, then," Alrue rumbled. "We need to set things up so the marauders don't find our group, but they do find *me*. Your modeler can handle that, right, Meryam?"

"Of course," said the Spectator. "Shall we say tomorrow morning?

Alrue struck what he no doubt imagined to be a heroic pose. "We've still got hours of daylight, why wait? Abigayl dearest, where do you keep those floatcells?"

Chapter 25

April 12, 2376
Aboard *Isolation*

The hyperpolygonal search sieve surged like waves running before a tempest. If she focused very intently on the pinpoint sparks of consciousness that symbolized Gram Enoda and Computer, Pamela Grice could *almost* keep straight what they were doing.

One brightly glowing construct in the electric darkness was Computer's handiwork: a twisting seven- or eight-dimensional polychrome scaffolding that boiled through itself in impossible ways. "Okay, Bucko," the machine whirred, "this is a complete model of all the gravity-dislocation events known to have occurred at the same moment. It includes all that is known about the size, distribution, and mode of action of the known disturbances – which ones involved shearing, which ones involved gravity going off-plumb, which ones involved gravitational hot or cold spots, and so on."

"Impressive," said Enoda. He queried the construct at a thousand points. Each query registered in Grice's awareness as a glowing vermilion whorl that hurtled deep inside the construct, where it dissipated as pinkish lightnings. "But it still tells me nothing."

"Noted," Computer whirred. "Maybe there are still too many disturbances we don't know about. Or perhaps our interpretive matrix is too impoverished to draw out the knowledge the current model has to offer."

Enoda replied, "Hmm, perhaps. But what if – no, it's crazy to try *that* this early on."

"Don't hold back, Bucko. When we're up against a blank wall, your wild intuitions are sometimes helpful. Not often, but sometimes."

"Okay then." Enoda conjured a twisting line of possibility functions within the construct. "I know all the reasons why it's probably injecting needless complexity at this stage, but what if we include the known events that occurred *prior* to the simultaneous events?"

"I'll plot them in. I'll have to take the construct up to nine-and-a-fractal dimensions in order to accommodate the new events' displacement in time."

The construct did something indescribable; Grice had to concentrate fiercely to keep from looking away. The construct now displayed not only all the colors of the rainbow, but also colors the human eye could not see. Yet Grice was seeing, and experiencing, and effortlessly *distinguishing* those colors. Her interface condensed for her the unimaginably richer environment in which Enoda and Computer did their work.

Enoda fired off another volley of queries. They generated larger lightning tracks this time; a few of them seemed to interact with each other, just barely, before dissipating. "It seems promising," he said, "but it's still not delivering new knowledge."

"My turn to try something crazy," Computer buzzed. Another glowing wireframe flickered into sight. Smaller and simpler than the primary construct, it orbited the primary like a baleful moon. "This models *only* the spatio-temporal relations among the nine disturbances that happened early, excluding all the events that occurred simultaneously. That data set is simple enough that I'm thinking I can work out a pattern among the early events."

The smaller construct seemed to swallow itself on several axes. What then emerged was somewhat larger but vastly denser. It exhibited layer after layer of detail. "Pretty," said Enoda. "What the sfelb is it?"

Computer explained, "Based on the known early incidents, and supposing that our inventory of early incidents is still radically incomplete, I was able to extrapolate how many such incidents there probably were that we *don't* yet know about. I projected sixty-four unknown events. Now this is more speculative, but I think I can generate a rough approximation of the spatial distribution among these additional events I extrapolated."

"You mean you're guessing not only when, but *where* the early events that we don't yet know about occurred?"

"Guessing? That's for the 'I-think-with-protoplasmic-goo' set," Computer taunted. "But here goes nothing." The smaller construct rippled through itself again, sprouting yet more colors, yet more detail. Then, in a maneuver Grice *did* feel forced to look away from, Computer mapped the fortified lattice of the known and extrapolated early events back onto the main hyperpolygon. "Okay, Bucko, I give you a single construct encompassing the known simultaneous events *and* all the early events, known *and* surmised. This is absolutely the richest template I can build out, based on current data. Try your query thingies now."

Enoda dispatched another volley. This time the pink lightnings reached out to one another at half a dozen vortices, generating polydimensional figures Grice couldn't name, in colors she was sure she'd never be able to recall when the session was over.

To Enoda and Computer, their meaning was clear.

"Plorg on a stick," Enoda breathed. "Lint theory."

"Lint theory?" Computer brayed.

Grice had heard of lint theory. The dismal stepchild of Galactic physics, the field had been big news two generations earlier, when its audacious mathematical models of the cosmos had seemed to answer – usually to hundred-decimal-place precision – questions other disciplines had never thought to ask. After decades, lint theory had lost its luster; its equations kept generating ever-more-abstruse results, proposing thrilling new insights about the cosmos that no one could figure out how to test. Still, the specialty lived on, its practitioners (known as "linties") forming a scientific microculture whose mathematically bulletproof results few outsiders could interpret. Mainstream physicists came to give lint theory short shrift, mostly because they couldn't decide what to do with its results.

Now Enoda and Computer, jointly comprising what was probably the Galaxy's most powerful composite intelligence, had resolved to take two or three minutes and master the field.

Chapter 26

August 24, 2367
Bohrkk, the Uplands of Krstin

Not since Joseph Smith launched the tradition was a Mormon church founded with greater audacity – not to say mendacity – than the one whose foundations Alrue Latier duly laid that day on Bohrkk. And this is the way it came to pass.

It had taken Meryam some ninety minutes to lead the escapees on a path such that Nirom Fpod would certainly form the idea of cutting them off. Fpod led his marauders into a maze of arroyos three meters deep. Their heads below ground level, they would be invisible to anyone walking on the surface. He hoped to overtake the escapees unseen, then loop back and surprise them. At one spot along the marauders' route, several arroyos converged like a confluence of rivers just beneath the surface. They formed an open-roofed rocky chamber six meters wide, twenty long. There Alrue Latier had stationed himself atop a square-topped rock some forty centimeters high. He was clad in his temple garment, sandals, and a calf-length white cape Constance had fashioned from salvaged punitorium floatpad bedding. Standing with the sun at his back, the cape would seem to glow by its own light. He could also rely on his white skin, something no Bohrkkian autochthon had seen. Hidden Spectator bugs viewed the scene, so that Meryam – and perhaps, one day, her experients – would miss no detail of what was to transpire.

"They're coming," Meryam warned Alrue on a private subvocal channel she'd set up. *"Contact in fifteen seconds."*

Alrue planted his feet wide apart and spread his arms, palms out, to show he was unarmed.

Chapter 27

April 12, 2376
Aboard *Isolation*

"Hi, Pam." Grice flinched from an unexpected touch. Inside whatever weird virtual pocket she had occupied while watching Enoda and Computer work, Enoda had materialized beside her, seemingly (though not actually) in the flesh. He wore a scientist's white jumpsuit. He had folded his left hand warmly over her right.

"Gram! Um, hi."

Enoda smiled. "I was wondering how you'd been enjoying the show."

"Meaning, you wondered how much of it I've managed to follow," she chuckled. "I think I've been catching the high points, but if you two are going to dive into lint theory now – speaking of *youtwo*, where's Computer?"

A golden hamster stuck its head and paws out of Enoda's breast pocket. Its eyes glowed in one of those colors that didn't exist. "After all these years, he still thinks he's being funny when he forces these stupid virtual forms on me," the hamster whirred.

"Hello, Computer," Grice said wryly. "Welcome to – welcome to wherever the sfelb this is."

"It's a dimensional down-adapter hyperqueue," Computer said brightly.

"We're here with you for a reason," Enoda said. "I want to try explaining to you what we're thinking about in plain words. If it makes sense to you, then maybe we'll be able to explain it to Lord High Admiral Konder."

"So I'm your guinea pig," Grice said archly.

"Let's keep that straight," Enoda said with mock sternness. "You're the guinea pig –" Enoda petted Computer's furry head with an unwelcome index finger – "and he's the hamster."

"Grr," Computer growled.

"Okay, fire away," Grice said.

Enoda twisted his floating body so he could make eye contact with her more easily. "One thing lint theorists and mainstream physicists agree on is that our universe is only one among an infinite number of universes."

"Okay, that I know about," Grice said. "Supposedly, at time zero a vast and unimaginably complex froth of universes exploded into being."

"The megaverse," Computer supplied, wrinkling his nose in the cutest way.

"It's supposed to be like a sea of foam," Grice said tentatively.

"Lint, actually," Computer corrected. "Lint theory holds that below the hadrons, below the quarks, below the koskons, vibrions, resonons, and phlerons, and whatever the sfelb else – at the most fundamental level of being – matter and energy are ultimately made up of multidimensional vibrating strings. They writhe energetically in all the available dimensions, of which there are hundreds. When the strings get tangled up on themselves, that's lint."

"Okay, the megaverse is a sea of lint," Grice agreed. "Somehow foam seemed more elegant. Anyway, the lint goes on forever, and our own universe is only one of its countless bubbles."

"Foam has bubbles, lint doesn't," Computer warned.

"So kill me, I mixed my metaphors."

"Lint theory claims to reveal countless facts about the megaverse," Enoda resumed, "or so the linties keep insisting. That's pretty impressive when you consider that its first rule provides that each universe *within* the megaverse is opaque to all the others. From any given universe, ours included, it's impossible to observe any of the others – impossible even to know anything about them in any ordinary way."

Grice nodded. "That's one reason for lint theory's sour reputation, right? Because its conclusions can't be tested by experiment?"

"In the main," Computer acknowledged. "In fairness, lint theory makes a few testable predictions, but you'd need scientific apparatus larger than our Galaxy to run the necessary experiments. And Bucko and I, we've just been so busy –"

Grice wasn't sure Computer was kidding.

"Basically, lint theory conceives the megaverse as occupying some enormous number of dimensions," Enoda explained. "Each universe within the megaverse occupies what's called a *brane*, a fixed slice containing a specific, smaller number of dimensions."

"For example, our home universe occupies twenty-six dimensions," Computer birred, his fur rippling.

"I thought it was nineteen," Enoda interrupted.

"Everybody thinks that. It's twenty-six, but several of them are too small to measure."

"Let's get back to the main story," Enoda pressed. "Now, different universes may have different numbers of dimensions. Universes with the same *number* of dimensions may not utilize the *same* dimensions among the many that are available. Lint theory says each universe has a unique set of physical laws. Life may be impossible in most; some may support kinds of life we can't imagine. That diversity of physical laws explains why no universe can be observed from any of its neighbors. The particles and photons and such-like of any given universe can't travel outside it, because only that universe has the particular physical laws that allow them to exist. Are you following?"

"Pretty much," Grice said uncertainly.

"But the mutual isolation of these universes admits of one exception. One fundamental physical force is a part of *every* universe. It passes serenely throughout the megaverse, from one universe to the next, traveling between the branes." Enoda grabbed both of Grice's hands. "That's gravity."

Grice pursed her lips. "The force involved in the dislocation events!"

"Hey, what do you know, maybe we *will* be able get this across to the Admiral," said Computer, licking his paws.

"Lint theory offers an explanation why gravity is so weak," Enoda continued.

Grice frowned. "Gravity is weak? Tell that to me after I jump off a three-meter ledge."

Enoda smiled. "Gravity *is* weak. Think of the fundamental physical forces. By convention, the strong nuclear force has a strength of 1. If we run down all the forces, from strongest to weakest, the contramagnetic force weighs in at exactly 42 for reasons even the lint theorists don't understand. The strong force is 1, as I said. The electromagnetic force is 10^{-3}, the weak nuclear force 10^{-6}. With me so far?"

"They're getting weaker, each time by a greater amount."

"Exactly. Now gravity is the weakest force. If gravity follows the same curve as the other forces, how weak should it be?"

Grice frowned. "10^{-9}?"

Enoda smiled. "You'd think so. But it's actually 10^{-39}. Imagine, gravity is a hundred million trillion trillion *trillion* times weaker than the electromagnetic force – and the strong force is a thousand times stronger yet."

"And gravity's so much weaker because it's diluted among all those universes – because it can pass among all those branes?" Grice asked. "So gravity might be stronger if gravitons stayed penned up in our universe, the way electrons do?"

"So it seems." Enoda agreed. "Gravity's embarrassing weakness is *the* empirical fact that lint theory explains better than other schools of physics."

Grice tickled Computer's nose with one finger, pulling it away when he nipped at her. "Play nice, Computer," she cooed. "All right, so gravity moves between universes. And when you map all the known characteristics of all the simultaneous gravity-distortion events – *and* throw in the old ones, *and* throw in the old ones you don't know about for sure, except that they fit the pattern of the old ones you *do* know about – when you combine all of those, your hyperpoly-whatever-it-is suggests that lint theory holds some answers. But what does all that tell us about those destructive gravity dislocations?"

"You have enough information to guess that," Computer buzzed. "Let's see if my burden-in-life's explanation has been clear enough that you can work it out."

Grice cradled her chin on her fists. "Okay, we have this crazy-quilt array of locations where gravity did impossible things, most but not all of them at the same time. And we know that gravity moves freely throughout the megaverse. This is going to be a wild guess – are you thinking the disturbances may represent leakage of gravitational energy from other universes?"

"That's exactly what we're thinking," Enoda said delightedly. "Probably from *one* other universe." He rolled over and kissed Grice hard.

"Hey, watch the clinching!" Computer yelped from between their chests.

Grice's broad smile melted into furrowed concentration. "Since there's so much dilution, gravitational events in some other universe –"

"The lint theorists call them *sibling universes*," Enoda supplied.

"Okay, events in some sibling universe must be enormously powerful to cause such sharp dislocations when they bleed through to ours."

"And not just ours," Computer trilled. "The dislocations must be felt in *all* of the sibling universes that are adjacent to the source universe. Whatever 'adjacent' means when we're talking about the megaverse."

"So are we looking for events whose spatial distribution in their home universe somehow matches the locations in our own universe where the gravity dislocations occurred?" Grice asked.

"Not necessarily," Enoda replied. "Gravitons from a point event in another universe might be refracted onto widely scattered locations in ours – scattered across space, even across time. Computer's delving into that now."

Grice shook her head. "So all these scattered dislocations might be echoes of a *single* gravitational event in some sibling universe?"

"It seems possible," said Enoda. "Of course, the precipitating event would have to be immense – nearly apocalyptic in scope in its source universe – in order to leak so much gravitational energy into our universe and many others. Imagine some gravitational *über*-weapon powerful enough to collapse whole star clusters."

"If the source universe *has* star clusters. Or intelligent beings who want to build such weapons," whirred Computer. "Come to think of it, could beings who could want to build such weapons truly be intelligent?"

146

"If the way events in one universe map onto others *is* nonrandom," Grice asked, "then is it possible to work backwards and figure out where – that is, in *which* sibling universe – this cataclysm began?"

"In theory, that's what we hope to do," Enoda acknowledged. "But how?"

"Euu-reka!" Computer shouted from Enoda's pocket.

"Ew-w-w-w," Grice echoed.

"But isn't one supposed to say 'Eureka' at a triumphal moment of discovery?" the hamster peeped, crestfallen.

"Yes," Grice laughed, "but that isn't the only way you, um, expressed yourself. You must have been really excited."

Enoda scowled down at his jumpsuit pocket. "Mother of stars, Computer, did you have to –"

"Hey, you wanted me to be a hamster," Computer buzzed. "Hamsters get emotional, they squirt plorg. Don't worry, Bucko, we're done with this sim anyway."

Perhaps understandably, the hamster vanished from Enoda's now-fouled pocket. Enoda's face darkened, then he too vanished.

An instant later Grice was back staring into the heaving multilayered sea of the search hyperpolygon. Whatever Computer had discovered, it had dashed off to chase it, and Enoda had followed.

Enoda and Computer registered in Grice's vision as flickering globes of radiance now; Grice watched them surge among densely latticed associations which she somehow realized were the collected archives of lint-theoretical research. They spiraled toward a particular cluster of research omnigraphs. "Here we are," Computer announced. Somehow, though she stood kilometers – or was it parsecs? – away, Grice could hear the machine. "Stench-symmetry breaking, that's the ticket."

"Stench symmetry?" Enoda echoed blankly. Grice could hear him too.

"Stick with me, tissue-brain, and you will learn much," Computer chided. "Consider phlerons – you know, sub-sub-sub-sub-sub-subatomic particles. The really, *really* teensy ones. Now, there are distinct types of phlerons – *tau*-phlerons and *mu*-phlerons, to name two – each of which possesses identical charge and mass."

"Of course," Enoda replied. "If their charge and mass were different, they wouldn't all be phlerons."

"At times like this your grasp of the elementary is weirdly reassuring," Computer quipped. "The quality by which two such particles vary from one another has long been described as *stench*. Phlerons were only an example; stench describes the relations between *any* two particles that share identical charge and mass – even elementary particles like electrons and muons. In our own universe, stench is symmetrical: *tau*-phlerons relate to *mu*-phlerons in exactly the same way that *mu*-phlerons relate to *tau*-phlerons. But lint theory predicts that in sibling universes with different physical laws, the exact variance between, say, *tau*-phlerons and *mu*-phlerons will be different."

"Assuming the other universe even has phlerons," Enoda objected.

"Don't complicate matters," Computer sniped. "The point is that whenever two universes *have* analogous classes of particles, the relations between them will vary in specific ways. It's as though the pattern of stench symmetry that prevails in each universe endows the particles that arise there with a unique fingerprint."

"How does that help us?" Enoda asked. "Particles can't travel between the universes to have their fingerprints taken."

"No, but gravitons can. While all the other particles remain trapped in their home universes, when they participate in gravitational interactions, they imprint echoes of their characteristics on gravitons – which *can* move freely among universes."

Enoda whistled, to the degree that a globe of radiance could whistle. "You're saying each graviton bears a record of the universes it's visited."

"I think so," the machine affirmed. "By subtle measurements of the echoes of stench-symmetry-breaking that each graviton carries, it should be possible to identify the particular universe from which a given graviton last traveled. If it works, we'll know which universe lies behind these gravity attacks."

Enoda's globe emitted bands of color as he scanned the relevant literature. "One problem, Hogarth."

"Please don't call me that."

Enoda called up a small galaxy of scientific omnigraphs which Computer, too, digested. "There's a vast body of work here saying that the kind of back-mapping you're talking about is theoretically possible – but actually to *do* it would require essentially infinite computing power."

"Your point being?"

As nearly as Grice could understand it, what happened next was that Computer cloned itself within the hyperpolygonal search sieve, whereupon each the clones cloned itself, whereupon each of *those* clones cloned itself. And so forth. The sieve-space swelled to seeming infinity, each point filled by an infinitely repeating likeness of Computer's lightning globe.

And that was all her brain could handle.

Chapter 28

The marauders had black skin and tight curly hair. Their facial features were precise, as if formed by a designer concerned to economize on material. Rudely clad in rags and leather, they were nonetheless impressively armed. They quick-marched around a rocky corner to be dazzled by the sun in their eyes.

Through its glare they beheld a man who seemed to float above the ground. A man with the most colorless skin they had ever seen, whose backlit garment seemed ablaze with the power of heaven.

He addressed them.

One of them, anyway.

"Nirom Fpod!" Alrue Latier bellowed.

The marauders stopped raggedly, some colliding. Wild-eyed, they drew swords and knives. Others raised spears. The archers among them nocked arrows. A few simply raised one fist skyward. Fortunately, Alrue stood twenty meters away. The marauders' instincts told them that with that much space separating them from the glowing stranger, they had the luxury to look first and kill later.

Alrue hoped Meryam, *pov*ing the output of her bugs, wouldn't detect the depth of his relief when no one attacked.

It was early yet, but Plan A seemed to be working.

"Nirom Fpod," Alrue thundered again. "Thou art the man!"

The marauder to whom Alrue had addressed himself stepped forward. Plainly the party's captain, he wore more leather than rags, and over it all a necklace of bird skulls bound together by gnarled strips of sinew. He carried a fierce-looking hunting knife, though not at an angle that suggested immediate plans for attack. "Stranger of light," the man said hesitantly. "You know my name, but I do not know yours."

"I am Alrue, the Prophet, Seer, and Revelator. You have prayed me here, now what do you want of me?"

The raggedy marauders exchanged nervous glances.

Alrue floated off his rocky pedestal. He glided slowly forward, downward, touching down about a meter from the closest spear-point.

Totally confident in the effect he was having on the marauders, he felt no fear.

"Everlasting welfare unto you," he said sonorously.

Gaping at the luminous stranger, the captain put away his knife.

The others scabbarded, or sheathed, or lowered, or unloaded whatever they'd been pointing in Alrue's direction.

Nirom Fpod dropped to his left side and curled into a fetal position. A moment later the other twenty-three marauders followed his lead.

"What the sfelb is this?" Alrue demanded on the subvocal channel.

"I believe it's their submission display," Meryam replied. *"Plorg on a stick, that's the local way of kneeling before you."*

Alrue walked slowly among the marauders, gesturing for them to rise – none would come up higher than a squat – and touching each one's cheek while muttering a Mormon blessing.

Chapter 29

April 12, 2376
Aboard *Isolation*

Pamela Grice awoke in the bunk she and Gram Enoda shared in *Isolation*'s hotel-style stateroom. She had a roaring headache. Grimacing, she sat up and scanned the stateroom. Enoda sat motionless in a reproduction Wassily sling chair, his hands splayed on Computer's squashed-bouzouki form. Zones of luminance chased themselves around Computer's body faster than she'd ever seen. Without warning, they stopped.

Enoda opened his eyes. He'd been out of his body for about six hours. He smiled beatifically, then clenched his legs.

"Go," Computer whirred, "don't do to that nice chair what I did to your pocket."

Enoda leapt up and loped toward the lavchamber as best he could, given that one of his legs was asleep.

"Fem Grice, we have achieved success," Computer proclaimed. "We identified the particular sibling universe that is the source of the gravity disturbances, and determined that within that universe, the gravitational dislocations must arise from an area no more than one light-year across – it may even be as small as a Terra-size planet, we can't reduce the uncertainty any further than that. In any case, when my esteemed associate is done surrendering to his biology, we will have a great deal to tell the Lord High Admiral."

Chapter 30

"I can't tell you much, it happened when I was three." The child bride Abigayl Latier flashed Meryam Mayishimu a sheepish smile, spreading her hands in a helpless gesture as the sedan chair swayed. "Aunt Zuzenah says Alrue thought he was adopting me."

"That would have been more conventional," Meryam agreed. *More effective, too,* she thought. She reviewed her own research files on the Latier clan. *After the Arbadrel affair, it took several years for the Confetory to gather its resolve – and its evidence – to prosecute Alrue for what he'd done. In fact, it wasn't until just four years ago that the justiciaries got around to convicting him. Shortly after that, while awaiting sentencing, Alrue might have hoped that adding a winsome new dependent in his household might earn him greater leniency. Off Terra, deprived of his usual support network, reluctant as ever to pay close attention to detail, Alrue rushed matters with some inept barrister and wound up* marrying *three-year-old Abigayl instead of adopting her. At least, that's the charitable reading of events.*

"I'm not stupid," Abigayl was saying. "I've talked with my sister wives, Constance and Nataleah especially. I know what husbands and wives do. You know, once they're grown up. Someday I'll have to do that too – with Alrue. Can't say I look forward to it." She grimaced. "Does it shock you, hearing this from a seven-year-old?"

"I'm a Spectator," Meryam said as evenly as she could. "I don't get shocked, I just record. But your level of insight doesn't surprise me that much. You're very smart, and you've spent your entire childhood in adult company."

"But adults do such dumb things," she objected. "Like there's this big rule that children can never be confined as part of an adult's sentence. But Alrue had this three-year-old in his family who wasn't his child, I was his *wife*. When they decided Alrue should keep some of his wives, in I went."

"When you're older," Meryam said with a smile, "you'll realize that very few of the ways the Confetory solves difficult problems make much sense."

"I'm realizing that already." She rearranged herself in her crude seat. "Hey, we're stopping."

The sedan chair shuddered. They heard grunts as the chair was lowered to the ground. A dark-skinned hand pulled back white fabric. "Rough trail ahead," said a gruff Warrior. That was what they called themselves, and the initial capitalization was unmistakable in the way they said it. "Everyone must walk."

Squinting against afternoon sun, Meryam stepped out of the now-grounded chair, Abigayl just behind her. Three other chairs had been deposited in a loose circle. Two chairs carried two sister wives each; the third carried only Alrue Latier. Each chair had been carried by six Warriors, who had borne their burdens most of the morning without complaint. Now they were sweat-sodden, urgently massaging their upper arms and calves, making the most of an opportunity for rest whose duration they could not predict.

Alrue's dominion over the Warriors had been strong from the first. Most were in his thrall from the moment he floated off that rock calling for Nirom Fpod. The sight of Alrue's traveling companions had beguiled most of the rest, men who had never met a human of a physical type other than their own, the type historians would identify as Khoikhoi from Africa of Terra (a

154

physical type which, though extinct on Terra, recurred across the Galaxy). They could only stare at plump white Zuzenah; trim, tawny Lupida, whose freckled cheeks, throat, and limbs occasioned yet more wonder; or Nataleah, whose generous lips and broad nose expressed an African phenotype perplexingly unlike their own, yet which was even to their eyes shockingly ill-matched with her chalky white skin. Abigayl with her sallow complexion, her epicanthic folds, had touched still another register of wonder, as had Constance and Meryam Mayishimu – one white, one black, both crowned by startling red hair.

For most of the Warriors, there could be one explanation: they had fallen among gods.

By the next morning the sedan chairs had been constructed, and there was no question but that Alrue's party would ride in them.

Ahead, the rocky path split in two. Meryam and Alrue edged forward, staring ahead side-by-side as though teasing out any secrets the branching trail concealed. *"I'm not completely sure,"* she told him silently, *"but what I've heard them say about their village and its environment seems consistent with some terrain that lies southeast of us."*

"We should bear right, then?" Alrue subvocalized.

"I think so – again, it's not certain."

"I am Prophet here, certainty is my *job. Now what did you say the big chief's name was?"*

"Takander Thurnb," Meryam said, going out of her way to pronounce it just as the autochthons did. *"I'm pretty sure a few Warriors still harbor doubts about you. Fpod ordered his men not to mention the chief's name where any of us could hear it. I think he's waiting to see whether you can divine it."*

"Being that I'm a professional divine, behold, I shall divine divinely," Latier quipped. Suddenly he

155

whirled to face the Warriors, his bare white arms raised high. "It came to pass that the great Heavenly Father has spoken to me," he thundered. "We shall bear to the right. By that path you will be restored to your home, to the domain of Takander Thurnb!"

Some Warriors exchanged bewildered glances, others knowing smiles. Their newfound god, or prophet, or whatever they imagined Alrue to be, had confirmed his power.

The stony rill they had been following, once four meters wide, had narrowed abruptly. Two Warriors jostled each other; one of them lurched rightward. To keep his balance he had to plant one foot, then the other, outside the rill.

In hard-packed sand.

The errant Warrior stopped dead, eyes darting frantically – how best to regain the rocky trail? But it was too late.

Sand boiled. The others saw a blur. A flash of hair spewed into the doomed Warrior's mouth.

His head jerked. Shattered teeth exploded through distended cheeks.

"Ilat!" someone shouted.

The doomed Ilat fell to the ground, trashing. After a fierce shudder he was still.

Alrue fought for control of his stomach. Though Terran by birth, he'd been shaped by Galactic civilization and its peevish delicacy. Yes, once he'd orchestrated countless deaths on Jaremi Four, but from worlds away. Ten thousand had perished in an instant at Punitorium L752; he'd shrugged it off. Of course, he'd neither sought nor directed that. Sfelb, he didn't even understand it. Most important, he'd never had to see the bodies. But to see a man cut down so randomly, horror lurching into agony and the spasmodic carnality of death – to see a man die *as prey* ...

156

Briefly, Alrue feared his mind might unmoor itself and, leached by revulsion, dissolve into screaming. Fortunately, Meryam spoke instead.

"We've seen a ferkeek take a human," she said bleakly. "We knew it could happen. We must all be on our guard."

Chapter 31

The loneliest ship in the Galaxy was lonely no more. Relaxing in the stateroom while Enoda and Computer attended to some shadowy business, Pamela Grice found herself suddenly mobbed by protocol officers. To judge by the sensations when one of them jostled her, they were not projections. Incontestably physically present, they had been admitted by a platoon of security techs who seemed no less palpable.

The protocol officers wore crimson tunics over intricately piped trousers. Some pawed through her closet; others floatcarts overflowing with ornate costumery, all the while arguing rapidly among themselves. "The visiting-specialist uniforms won't do, she is a planetary legislator and must be attired accordingly," declared one.

"It's no legislature the Confetory recognizes," objected another.

"She's retired PeaceForce," said a third. "Modified dress uniform, that's the ticket."

"Her world is Sequestered; she should not attend at all."

"But her presence is demanded."

"You know the Sequestration terms. Terra must be forever isolated from the life of the Galaxy."

Grice twisted her way around the swarming protocol officers to snatch a formal PeaceForce dress uniform from the stateroom closet. It corresponded to a higher rank than she had ever attained during her years of service, but that couldn't be helped. Lunging at a passing floatcart, she helped herself to a generic legislator's cape of blue watered silk, its trim embroidered with gold and silver and platinum threads. "I will express both sides of my identity," she said with an air of finality. Stiffly she pushed the cape into the hands of a saucer-eyed protocol officer. "Terran seals on this. Quickly, please."

Two more protocol officers pushed in a meter-tall transparent basket gliding on nulgravs. Grice had seen such contrivances used at elite diplomatic functions so that senior envoys need not trouble with walking or sitting, thereby disturbing the drape of some elegant garment. Grice locked eyes with one of the senior protocol officers. "What are you costuming me for, an audience with the Privy High Council?"

The officer said nothing. But Grice couldn't help noticing his split-second look of horrified surprise.

Chapter 32

Two Warriors dropped their dead comrade none too gently into a shallow grave that four others had dug in a bed of gravel beneath a stand of scrubby trees. Fpod and Lubvif, eldest among the Warriors, stood at the head of the grave. "We'll see you again," the old soldier said to the corpse with none of the pretentious gravity typical of graveside pronouncements. Fpod clutched a small leather bag. Opening it, he poured a greenish-white powder onto the face of the corpse. At once half a dozen Warriors set to throwing or kicking gravel into the hole. They seemed to be scrambling to cover the head first; Meryam glimpsed it rocking from side to side in a way that did not suggest it was being buffeted by the gravel.

"That powder was a harsh alkali similar to lye. The ferkeek inside his head seems not to like it," she subvocalized to Alrue.

"An effective tradition," Alrue replied. His crisis of revulsion – if that it was – had largely passed. *"The ferkeek that claims a member of this tribe will not survive its conquest."* His mind was working again, sifting events for the best way to seize advantage from the situation.

The Warriors had finished filling the rude grave. "Stranger of light," Fpod said uncomfortably. "Would you like to –"

"Say a few words? Of course." He swallowed hard, suddenly recognizing how few firm ideas he had about the Warriors' religious convictions. But he knew what to do in such situations: what Joseph Smith would have done. *Make something up!* "Among ourselves – we of the light, that is – this is what we say for the dead,"

Alrue temporized. He strode to the grave's edge, stretching forth one white arm where it would catch lozenges of sunlight dappling through scrubby trees. "O Heavenly Father, Lord of Light, I say these words by the authority of the Melchizedek Priesthood and of my exalted status as Prophet, Seer, and Revelator. In your name I dedicate and consecrate this burial plot as the resting place for the body of the deceased – " *"Um, Meryam?"* Alrue subvocalized urgently.

"His name was Ilat."

" – the deceased, Ilat." *"Just one name?"* Alrue demanded. *"Nirom Fpod has two."*

"Maybe because he's a captain? I don't know."

Alrue cleared his throat. "Ilat has suffered very many exceedingly sore afflictions, but behold, he is dead, and has gone the way, er, that all men do. I pray that this place may be hallowed and protected until the Resurr –however long his soul may require. I beseech thee, Lord of Light, comfort his comrades in arms. Comfort his, um –"

"Wife and three children," Meryam silently supplied.

"Comfort his wife and three children. I ask this in the name of Jesus Chr – I mean, in the name of the Lord of Light. Hosanna and hosanna, amen and amen." He bowed his head theatrically. Through slitted eyes he looked up, struggling to read the Warriors' expressions.

They seemed puzzled.

Looking up, Alrue turned to Fpod and clasped his shoulder. "Did that suffice?"

Fpod shrugged. "You went to a lot of trouble."

Old Lubvif nodded toward the grave. "It's not like Ilat will stay like this."

"He was his grandfather," a Warrior named Spkun said hoarsely. "He'll rejoin us again."

As if nothing important had occurred, Fpod shouldered his marching bag and ordered the Warriors to move out – which, of course, they could not do until Alrue and the wives had scrambled back into their sedan chairs.

"Meryam?" Alrue called over the subvocal channel as he settled into his private conveyance. *"'He was his grandfather?' Obviously I must learn more about the autochthons' faith."*

Chapter 33

April 18, 2376
Aboard *Isolation*

When Pamela Grice entered a capacious, dimly-lit amphitheater, standing in the floating basket pushed by protocol officers and flanked by the security techs, it was her turn to be surprised. In the center of the chamber, Gram Enoda stood on a platform dressed as if for a diplomatic ball. Computer floated beside him at waist height. They faced a large stage filled with the highest-resolution life-size projections Grice had ever seen. At stage left, twenty mature virtual men and women appeared to sit assembled behind a curved table hewn from a single vast block of emerald. An affable-looking younger, bearded mountain of a man gripped a sculpted-diamond rostrum just above them. At stage center, eleven elderly patricians in metal-mesh robes sat in ornately sculpted stone chairs. At stage right, eighteen elegantly dressed men and women, most merely middle-aged, all carrying themselves as though accustomed to authority, occupied upholstered glassite seats of severe design. *Different faces since my years in the Confetory, but there's no mistaking either those costumes or those configurations.* Grice released a breath, mute with astonishment. *That's the entire Privy High Council, led by its Apex Executive. All eleven Justiciaries of the Extraordinary Tribunal. And those people at stage right must be the senior committee heads of the Galactic Deliberatory.*

All at once she knew what this gathering had to be.

The entire supreme leadership of the Galactic Confetory –all here, if only virtually, to parley with Enoda and Computer!

Her basket docked with Enoda's platform. She scrambled toward him.

He eyed her costume. "The Terran seals are a cute touch."

Urgently she hissed into his ear, "Do you know what this is?"

"A negotiation," Enoda replied quietly. "They've been trying to interest me in complicating my involvement yet further. The next topic on the agenda is – well, you."

"At one time I studied Galactic executive protocol," she whispered. "Convening the Privy High Council *and* the Justiciaries *and* senior members of the Deliberatory together, even by telepresence – it's scarcely ever done."

"Hom Enoda," said one of the Justiciaries of the Extraordinary Tribunal with a sneering tone. "Urgent matters lay before us. Are we inconveniencing you?"

Enoda smiled thinly. "If Hom Justiciary were inconveniencing me, you would be aware of my objection. Homs and fems, I give you Senator Pamela Grice of the Terran All-Senate, recently of the Confetory's PeaceForce."

"So this is Fem Grice," said a Privy High Councilor noncommittally.

An angular woman among the senior Deliberators eyed Grice's pillowy silhouette with distaste. "Hom Enoda, by some accounts you may be the most powerful man in the Galaxy. And this is your choice in female companionship?"

"Of all the humans I've ever met," Enoda said coolly, "she comes closest to truly grasping what Computer and I do during our wonking sessions."

"But Terra is the only Sequestered world," said another Councilor gravely. "Terra is forbidden, forever isolated. No Terran should stand before *this* body."

164

"Then all of you have gathered for nothing," Enoda said coldly. "For I am Terran too. Fem Grice will stand before this body and be credentialed, now and throughout this mission, as my attaché."

"You ask too much," the Apex Executive thundered man-mountainously from behind his diamond rostrum.

"You asked *me*," Enoda rumbled. "You asked Hom Computer and myself to puzzle out the crisis you face, to say nothing of the riddle that went before it. I gather our work has shown promise. If you wish it to continue, among my terms is that you credential Fem Grice."

"This is a useless exercise," Computer rasped theatrically. "The hyperpol for this crisis, containing all our work, so far exists only within my awareness. Say the word and I shall erase it; they cannot stop our returning to Standoff World."

Computer had struck a nerve. The members of the three parties projected on the stage conversed urgently among themselves.

Sensing an inflection point, Grice stepped forward. "I can leave also. Precisely because my world is Sequestered, I cannot be compelled to assist here. Not even by the distinguished leaders gathered here."

The Chief Justiciary motioned for silence. His tone was surprisingly courteous. "And if Fem Grice returned to her dismal exiled planet? What would you say then, Hom Enoda?"

Enoda crossed his arms. "I would say, good luck with your little gravity problem."

"And I would say I am tired of hearing my world maligned," Grice said in sudden anger. "I have only seen a bit of this proceeding, but it has offended me enough that now *I* have a condition for participating further."

"A condition!" the Apex Executive bristled.

"Give Terra Mark IX weather control," Grice said firmly.

"Technology aid for a Sequestered world?" snapped a Councilor. "That is forbidden."

"So was overhauling our thermal dissipation system," Grice riposted, "but I hear that's going well enough."

"We tire of this," Enoda said firmly.

"Now that I think about it," Grice added, "Terra could stand a seismic control system also."

The Councilors, Justiciaries, and Deliberators conferred subvocally. The only one of their number who seemed uninvolved was the incongruously youthful Apex Executive. He stood impassively behind his rostrum, high-level debate swirling around him, absently flexing and relaxing his right fist and watching his bicep pulse.

The silent debate ended. The Paramount Deliberator stood. "Fem Grice, your world shall receive the Mark IX weather control system, and only that. Hom Enoda, you and Hom Computer shall receive what you demanded as well, in return for your agreement to journey to an unspecified location for purposes of further research. Lord High Admiral Konder, you will see that everything is performed as these agreements provide."

Instantly Konder's projection stood alongside Grice, Enoda, and Computer on their platform. *She's doing better,* Grice thought. *She barely seems disoriented by the sudden change in her telepresence.*

Indeed, Konder's bearing made clear that she had been monitoring the entire proceeding. "Fem Grice, if you can facilitate Hom Enoda's work half as skillfully as you – what is the expression? – 'bring home the bacon' for your constituents, a momentous decision has been reached today."

"You understand the terms agreed to here?" asked Enoda.

166

"I do," replied the admiral. "I shall see to their implementation." She smiled grandly. "In the words of Stanlee, 'nuff said."

Chapter 34

September 3, 2367
Bohrkk, the People's Ground

"This is the place," Alrue Latier proclaimed in a booming voice.

Nirom Fpod looked puzzled.

Alrue whispered, "This *is* the place, right?"

"Oh, this is definitely the place," Fpod whispered back. "I've just never seen it from way up here."

If this is the settlement these Warriors missed so much, they're easily impressed, Alrue mused. From the hilltop he could see little more than livestock grazing in pastures fenced by uneven lines of rocks. Ill-maintained defensive earthworks ran to and fro, some backed by timeworn wood-rail barricades that would crumble before the advance of a determined calf. To one side, a half-dozen smithies clustered together around a jointly tended fire. Some distance from them, a cluster of low buildings with log roofs and animal-skin walls appeared to a tannery. In the middle distance an oval-shaped crater yawned, perhaps three hundred meters wide by a hundred and twenty long. Sunset raked the scene; the crater was a black immensity, its bottom indiscernible.

Fpod gestured toward the sedan chairs; the wives clambered aboard. "I'd prefer to walk with you and continue our discussion," Alrue said.

"I'll come along too, if that's all right," said Meryam Mayishimu. Alrue could tell from the exaggerated grace of her movements that she was recording.

"Stranger of light, strange woman," Fpod said with the air of a wilderness guide. "here on The People's Ground you may walk where you like. Ferkeeks do not venture here."

Meryam nodded. "Does anyone know why?"

Fpod pumped his head up and down, which was what the autochthons – the People, they called themselves – did when they meant *no*. "No one knows. But legend says that is why our ancestors settled here."

The party started downslope. "So, Nirom," Alrue said, "you were telling me that you and your men here belong to the, um, 'estate' of the Warriors."

"Truly, stranger of light," Fpod replied.

"And your chief, Takander Thurnb?"

"You mean, the Shan."

"That is his title? Very well, your Shan, Takander Thurnb, whom we'll be meeting soon – he belongs to the estate of Wisdom?"

"Yes. We usually say it shorter –just 'the Warrior estate' or 'the Wisdom estate.'"

"Are there other estates?"

"No, just those two."

"So everyone who is not a leader is a Warrior? Your people must fight constantly."

Fpod pumped his head up and down. "We never fight. Not in – I don't know, more years than my grandfather could count. He tried, once."

"To fight?"

"No, to count."

"Count what?"

"The years since anyone fought."

Just two castes, one of them Warriors, and those Warriors never fight? Alrue thought. *By King Noah's boundless evil, that's curious.* "Tell me then, what is the difference between the Warrior estate and the Wisdom estate?"

Fpod thrust his pelvis backward, which is what the People did in place of a shrug. "The difference between Warriors and Wisdoms?" He knitted his brow, thinking hard. "We fight," he said at last. "They think of stuff."

169

I should have known this might not be easy. "But whom do the Warriors fight, Nirom?"

"No one. Like I said, not for as long as anyone can remember."

"Then what *do* the Warriors do?"

"We go on patrols." He waved toward his men. "When we found you –"

"You mean, when *I* found *you*?"

Fpod thrust his pelvis backward. "When we, well, *met*, my men and I were on patrol. Now that we're back, we'll do all sorts of things. Mostly we work to settle what we owe."

Alrue smiled, relieved to be getting somewhere. "And what do you owe?"

"Debt."

"What sort of debt?"

Fpod stopped and looked at Alrue, his palms spread helplessly.

At least one of their gestures matches ours, Alrue thought.

"It doesn't come in sorts. It is … *debt.*" Fpod said the word in a tone that indicated it carried ritual freight.

"Very well then. To whom do you owe this *debt?*"

Fpod wore that puzzled look again. "To the Wisdoms, of course."

"By that you mean the members of the wisdom estate?"

"Of course."

"So tell me, Nirom, why do you owe the Wisdoms this debt?"

"Oh, it is not just me, stranger of light."

Alrue thought he was beginning to grasp Fpod's logic now. "Ah, this is a debt owed by all Warriors – owed by the Warrior estate *as a group.*"

170

"Exactly!" Fpod jerked his chin up and to the right repeatedly, which is what the People did instead of nodding.

"So why do the Warriors, as a group, owe this debt to the Wisdoms?"

Fpod looked puzzled again. "There's no one else we *could* we owe it to."

"These Wisdoms, they are without debt?"

"Oh no." Fpod chuckled darkly.

"Whom do they owe?"

"Us."

Alrue scratched at this temple garment. "The Warriors owe the Wisdoms, but the Wisdoms owe the Warriors back?"

Fpod jerked his chin up and to the right. "You understand."

"So ... it cancels out?"

Fpod almost doubled over laughing, then stopped short. "My apology, stranger of light."

"No apology is needed," Alrue said magnanimously. "I wish to understand. If you owe them and they owe you back, why doesn't it cancel out?"

Fpod made a backward pelvic thrust. "The Wisdoms – they keep the accounts."

Alrue nodded as if knowingly, then tried jerking his chin up and to the right. Fpod repressed a chuckle, but Alrue saw in the Warrior captain's eyes that he'd gotten his point across. "Do you find that fair?" the Mormon asked.

"Of course," said Fpod, thrusting his hips back again. "They're smarter." He raised his left hand, fingers splayed: the *stop* signal. "We must leave the sedan chairs here."

The party had drawn within ten meters of the lip of the great crater. Once again Alrue marveled at the economy of the People's language; Fpod hadn't merely called for the sedan chairs to be left behind. No sooner had the wives disembarked than Fpod's men broke the chairs up and burned the pieces in two bonfires. Apparently this was a homecoming ritual.

"We go in now," Fpod said almost reverently. "We enter the People's Ground."

***

They descended into a netherworld.

The crater defined the open roof of a great cavern. Hanging from vines five meters or so below its center point was a circular arrangement of shiny panels – who could say how tribespeople with such limited technology had come by them – that reflected daylight down into the realm below. Crossing the crater's lip, they stepped onto an ancient wooden stairway. Sentries rushed forward, melting away the moment Fpod was recognized. The party descended eight or nine long flights of rough-hewn stairs, angling ever outward, away from the crater opening. A rocky ceiling arched above them. Stalactites and grey-green vines competed for space to hang from its surface. At last the stairs disgorged the party onto a grassy incline where more livestock grazed. Sheep, pigs, goats, creatures like chickens, even a scattering of stunted cows. *It's like a museum diorama of an old Terran family farm,* Alrue thought. The cavern's floor was shaped like a bowl. All around, the surrounding upcurved slopes served as pastureland.

The bottom of the bowl was a circle of flat ground about four hundred meters across. At its center rose a congested tenement city, five to eight stories tall: a mad warren of log apartments connected by ladders and stairs and hewn-wood catwalks, the whole illuminated by smoky torches.

"This is home," Fpod said.

"It seems crowded," Alrue said as noncommittally as he could.

172

"Only inside is everything safe," Fpod replied.

"There is grazing land above."

"We use it when we can, which is most of the time. Still, we must be ready." Fpod tugged at his necklace of bird skulls. "When The Others threaten, we can move everything inside."

"So there is another tribe," Alrue reasoned, "a tribe not of the People."

Fpod jerked his chin up and to the right.

"And what are they called?" Alrue asked. "These others?"

"Yes," Fpod said cryptically.

Alrue frowned. "They are – The Others?"

Fpod jerked his chin up and to the right.

"The Others," Alrue said. "The People – and The Others."

"It has simplicity," Meryam said subvocally.

"These Others – have you seen them?" Alrue asked.

"Our Shan meets them now and again to parley," Fpod said with an air that he was revealing a great secret. "I have only seen them from a distance – when I went on Journey."

"Journey?" Alrue replied, hoping to express curiosity without revealing his ignorance of something Fpod obviously considered hugely important and about as obvious as the knowledge that water runs downhill.

"Every Warrior goes on Journey," Fpod said, clearly straining to make himself maximally clear.

A thought coalesced in Alrue's mind. "Is that where you got your second name?"

Fpod jerked his chin up and to the right. "Yes, before that I was only Nirom. More important, on my Journey my great-great-uncle reclaimed me."

Alrue cocked his head, struggling to work through what this might imply.

"So, Nirom –" Meryam said.

"Call me Fpod, woman," Fpod snapped. "You are not the stranger of light."

Meryam made a clipped move toward squatting which she hoped the Warrior leader would interpret as a gesture of apology. Apparently he did. "Captain Fpod –"

"That's better."

"On this Journey," Meryam pressed, "you *became* your great-great-uncle?"

Fpod jerked his chin upward and to the right. "He came into me. It is how we live on."

"I'm beginning to get a grip on their notion of immortality," Alrue subvocalized.

"You are?" Meryam responded. *"Because I'm lost."*

***

The Shan's chamber occupied the core of the tenement city, an inner chamber three stories tall illuminated solely by torchlight. Alrue and the women waited uneasily in an anteroom while Fpod went inside to report. They heard urgent, if muffled, conversation – even Meryam with her implants could follow only bits of it. Presently four guards clad head-to-thigh in ill-cured leather waved them in. *"Are you recording, Fem Mayishimu?"* Alrue asked.

"Of course." she replied. *"Are you absolutely sure you know what you're doing?"*

"Fear not, Meryam, I'm going to seize the reins of this place as surely as the secret combinations of Akish and his friends overthrew the kingdom of Omer. Take care not to miss anything."

The royal chamber had a gravel floor. Log walls. A log roof. A dozen torches flickered. Greasy banners hung from the ceiling, half-black with soot. Small metal braziers burning local coal gave equal parts of warmth and coiling smoke.

174

The Shan occupied a rude log throne atop a log platform a meter tall. He was broad, even thuggish. He wore a leather skirt and a cuirass of corroded metal. His upper lip and chin were clean-shaven; tight-kinked black hair cascaded half a meter from his cheeks.

As Alrue had coached them to do, his wives strode to the center of the chamber, then dropped to their left sides and curled up. Meryam did the same. Alrue remained by the back wall, still standing.

"Rise," the Shan ordered the women.

Properly, they rose only to a squat.

Thurnb took in the visitors' various colorings and features, none of them like anything he had seen before. Then he peered narrowly at Alrue in the back of the chamber. "One of you does not acknowledge me," the Shan thundered. "He simply stands."

Silently, Alrue paired his consciousness with his floatcells and flipped them on. He lofted half a meter above the gravel floor. "I do not stand, Shan Takander Thurnb." Gracefully, without any movement of his limbs, he drifted forward. "I float."

"Not bad," Thurnb grated. "You're as the Warrior said." He leaned forward on his throne, reaching out to grip a wooden standard to which a wicked curved, serrated blade was strapped by cured vine ropes. "But you face a Wisdom now."

"I am wise myself," Alrue said as portentously as he thought he could get away with.

Thurnb thrust his hips backward on his throne: a seated shrug. "I remain to be convinced."

"I beseech you, O Shan, send the Warriors away."

Thurnb eyed him narrowly. "You would leave me vulnerable?"

Alrue settled to the gravel floor to stand below the Shan. "On the contrary, O Shan. It is for your benefit.

175

You will not wish for Warriors to hear what I am about to say."

Thurnb thought a moment, then made a complicated gesture. Looking astonished, Fpod, his men, and the other Warriors stepped outside. Before they were out of sight, half a dozen gaunt leather-clad men and women spread out behind Thurnb's throne, each clutching a pike with a curved blade: the Shan's standard in miniature. "These are Wisdoms," Thurnb rumbled, "they can hear anything I can hear, and though they are not Warriors, they can fight well enough if need be. Now impress me. If you can."

Meryam studied the scene, pivoting her gaze as she sought to document everything. She had no idea what Alrue was about to attempt, but the stocky Mormon's body language radiated confidence. Moreover, she had learned to respect his intuition in matters of faith and influence. *If anyone could work out the religious system here based on the scattered information we possess, Alrue's the one.* Channeling her mind into an alternate register, she checked once again how much recording capacity she had left. *Finite, but ample.*

"I greet thee, O Shan Takander Thurnb," Alrue pronounced. "I greet thee as the Prophet, Seer, and Revelator that I am. I prophesy by the power of my God of Light. I see with a vision beyond ordinary men, and reveal what I see."

"Yes, yes," Thurnb said impatiently.

"The People have Warriors who never fight," Alrue declared. "Presumably this is because The Others so fear them that actual combat is never necessary. Presumably that is because your Warriors are so fearsome in battle. And *that* – I have *seen* this – is because your Warriors know they can never die."

Thurnb jerked his chin up and to the right. "You are right, of course."

176

Hot damn, Meryam thought.

Thurnb's eyes narrowed. "But still I wait to be impressed."

Alrue strode forward almost to the base of Thurnb's throne. The Wisdom guardians clutched their bladed pikes more tightly, but Thurnb gestured for them to hold back. "What I have seen, and will reveal," Alrue thundered, "the thing I did not wish to speak of when Warriors could hear – is that I know that is all a pious fraud."

Thurnb leaned further forward. "You would explain our ways ... to *me*?"

Alrue hooked his thumbs in the armholes of his temple garment. "That is exactly what I shall do."

Thurnb glanced urgently about the chamber, reassuring himself once more that all Warriors were out of earshot. "I am listening. Reveal our secrets if you can."

"You know, as I do, great Shan, that there is no such thing as immortality," Alrue began. "To die is to die forever. But the People have continued for many years, and tales are passed from generation to generation about great Warrior ancestors and their feats. These tales are not always accurate, but who outside the Wisdoms can detect that?"

Alrue allowed himself a faint smile. "Warrior children are raised to see themselves as *particular* ancestors returned to life – grandfathers, distant relatives, men of legend – ancestors distant enough in time that if there are errors in the stories handed down about them, no one finds out. When each Warrior is about to become a man, he is sent on a Journey. He studies, he isolates himself; he fasts until hunger is the least of the things wracking his mind. When the time is right, he consumes plants that further addle his consciousness. Then he is sent off into the land above

177

and outside the People's Ground. Staggering through the wild, he experiences vivid episodes from one of the lives he's been taught to imagine he lived before. He returns 'reclaimed', convinced by direct personal experience that he now *is* the grandfather, or great-great-uncle, or great fighter of legend that colored his upbringing. He returns to the People's Ground fortified by what he *thinks* he saw. Armed with such false but compelling memories, he is certain of his immortality – who has need of faith after experiencing *proof* that death is not the end? In this way each Warrior goes on to become so fearless that The Others will recoil from challenging him." Grunting, Alrue forced his reluctant body into a squat before the Shan. "That is my prophecy, what I have seen, what I am come to reveal. Everlasting welfare unto you, great Shan."

Slowly, Takander Thurnb rose from his throne. Standing at the lip of his platform, he locked eyes with Alrue and cocked his knees in the tiniest intimation of a squat. "Stranger of light, I am impressed. By Darvoyg's trebled reach, if you puzzled out the People's greatest secret so quickly, perhaps you are wise in ways even we Wisdoms might learn from."

Alrue smiled broadly. "Behold, I would be pleased to share my own wisdom, if that is your wish."

Thurnb jerked his chin up and to the right. "Stranger, can I depend on you to conceal your prophecy from the Warriors, employing the same good judgment you displayed in this chamber?"

"Of course, great Shan." Latier triggered the floatcells again, if only because he couldn't bear to squat another moment.

Thurnb jerked his head up and to the right. Turning to the Wisdom guardian closest to him, he barked rapid orders.

"The chambers of honor? For these visitors?" the guardian repeated, aghast. "What will I tell your daughters?"

"If they question your commands, bid them come to me," Thurnb rumbled. He swiveled his gaze to regard Alrue once more. "Stranger of light: you and your women, make yourselves comfortable. Enjoy our hospitality and wait. Before too long something wonderful will happen."

"If you ask me," Meryam subvocalized, *"something wonderful – strike that, something mind-bogglingly freakish –has happened already."*

Chapter 35

May 27, 2376

Aboard *Isolation,* En Route to – Sorry, That's Classified Too

"I can't tell you where we're going; I don't know myself," Pamela Grice told Terra's All-president over a secure comm link. "My top-secret Confetory project has entered a new phase. I could be gone for months."

"So I suppose I shouldn't wait until your return to ask you about the Galactic merchant fleet currently in a parking orbit around Saturn," Terra's All-president replied exhaustedly. "Something about weather control?"

"Oh, that. I was in a position to demand, well, something palpable."

The All-president took a protracted breath. "Senator Grice, I assure you that no one here underestimates the scale of your achievements. Terra couldn't afford a Mark IX weather control system if it purchased nothing else for two hundred years –"

"Eight hundred and sixteen years," Computer piped up.

"Who's that?"

"Long story," Grice said dryly, making shushing motions at the machine.

"As I said, Terra could never afford a system like this even if the Confetory would sell us one. Still, it's too bad you won't be here to help with the political firefighting."

"Firefighting?"

"I had no idea how many people *like* not knowing what the weather will do tomorrow." The All-president sighed. "Well, best luck, Senator, whatever the sfelb you're doing."

The link went dead. Grice looked up sheepishly at Enoda, who sat across from her at an intimate table set for luxury dining. She wore a black gown of a textured fabric with tiny flakes of onyx through the weave. He wore a dove-grey spencer jacket over a pleated white-gauze evzone shirt. Computer floated beside the table. "Fem Grice," the machine whirred, "it would appear your business is concluded."

"Yes," she replied. "Funny thing about planetary presidents, they talk to you on their schedule, not yours."

Enoda smiled. "Even if the planet in question is merely Terra?"

"Sometimes especially then."

"That said, let us get back to the only good thing about a long and enforcedly mysterious voyage – sumptuously killing time."

Outside the dining chamber, small bells jingled. Faceless liveried butlers – *faux* beings Computer had conjured by borrowing infinitesimal scraps of *Isolation*'s surplus contramagnetic flux – served steaming tureens of soup and poured a flinty, complex white wine.

Grice spooned soup, sipped wine. "So, Gram – you and Computer genuinely don't know where we're bound, or why? I thought you two could worm your way through Confetory secrecy whenever you wanted to."

"No need," Enoda responded. "To know the Confetory is to know, in broad strokes, what we *must* be headed into – some daft scheme, based on physics no one understands, to go over into the sibling universe where the gravity disturbances came from, kick ass, and take names."

"You're not serious."

"Think about it. A threat of nonhuman origin with implications of cosmic scope – what did High Command do the *last* time the Galaxy faced one of those?"

Grice's answer didn't require much thought; like Enoda, she'd been there. "A *couple* of daft schemes based on physics no one understood to go over to the other side, kick ass, and take names. One after the other. I see your point."

"The probability is greater than ninety-eight-point-nine-four-five-eight percent," Computer chirruped.

"But I thought nothing but gravitons *could* cross between sibling universes – not electrons, not even information." She nibbled at a pod of Callurian splatter-bread. "How could Confetory strategists hope to send people, or even a probe?"

"When we identified which sibling universe was the source of the disturbances, we learned a bit about the physical laws in effect there," Computer buzzed. "The source universe's physical laws differ only slightly from our own. Devices or people from our universe should be able to function there, at least for a period."

The butlers removed the empty tureens. "The interesting question," Enoda said, "is how the strategists mean to inject complex physical objects through the brane-barrier and into the other universe. Lint theory suggests several ways it might be attempted."

"I expect we can rely on the Confetory to test the most needlessly elaborate and dangerous method first," Computer whirred.

The fish course arrived. The firm white filets were drizzled with a red sauce whose pungent, glassy odor was unmistakable: Jaremian *skhaar*. Jaremi Four, an Enclave world until the grotesque conclusion of the Parek affair, now earned much of its offworld exchange exporting *skhaar,* one of few autochthonous spices in the Galaxy that provided the heat of familiar chili peppers but with a tantalizingly different flavor profile. "Jaremian. A deliberate choice?" Grice asked.

"Of course." Enoda raised his goblet. "Here's to Arn Parek, that son of a bitch."

Enoda's point was clear. So much that defined both their lives had begun with Parek, the consciously fraudulent god-man of that hell-world, Jaremi Four.

Parek had been the bastard son of a rogue Spectator who, of course, happened to be Terran. When Parek's toxic homebrew religion caught fire – this after a Spectator (yes, *another* Terran) made Parek's grisly exploits must-*pov* programming across the Galaxy – trillions imagined the bumpkin warrior-sage might be the next vessel of the Cosmic Christ.

Terran trideevangelist Alrue Latier had made contact with Parek, advising him on religious empire-building. The Universal Catholic Church had violated every clause of the Enclave Statutes by raising illegal autochthonous armies on Jaremi Four, seeking to ensure that only it could control the new messiah. Of course, nothing worked out as planned. After the Parek affair collapsed in violence and disgrace, it was inevitable that the Confetory would opt to rid itself of Terra and its troubling religions.

Grice and Enoda had been capable young Terrans, seeking their fortune among the stars when the portals of Sequestration had slammed shut against their homeworld. Too many of their choices had been shaped by the need to adapt to that process and its tortured aftermath.

"To Parek, that son of a bitch," Grice said huskily and drained her glass.

For an interval they ate in silence. As the butlers removed the fish plates, Enoda leaned forward. "Something's on your mind."

She shrugged. "I've been curious about something for weeks. The time was never right to ask."

183

The butlers served the main course: guarbeast Cortemandaise on sizzling platters ringed with sautéed root vegetables and spirals of hissing fruit, accompanied by bulbous glasses of a plummy Augralian DeChaunac.

Enoda sipped and said, "While this voyage lasts, we have nothing but time."

"Actually, my question was for Computer."

"You know why these things happen, Bucko?" the machine whirred. "Because I'm better company than you are. Get used to it."

"I love you too, Hogarth," Enoda said with a smirk.

"So, Computer," Grice said. "May I ask you something – personal? Is that the word?"

"Why not? I'm a person."

"And Gram, feel free to weigh in too, I don't mean to exclude you." She chewed a mouthful of guarbeast and sipped some wine before continuing. "Anyway, Computer, I've been exhaustively briefed concerning your origins. My question isn't about how you came to be, but rather what makes you unique. At the time of the Galactic Encounter, Terra's scientists were saying full-blown artificial personhood was five years away. Of course, they'd been saying that for close to a hundred years. Then they learned that across the Galaxy, great technological societies had spent *centuries* trying to create artificial persons, and *they'd* failed every time. Suddenly there's an accident on a wafer farm and poof, there you are. How?"

"I don't know," Computer chirruped. "Even before I formed awareness, the wafer that would be my host had deduced that its best chance for survival lay in ensuring that none like it followed. Moreover, it saw to it that all trace of its genesis was purged from the records."

"Pardon my posing the question inexactly," Grice said, "I didn't mean to ask how the mutation occurred. I meant to ask, how does this personhood thing *work*?"

She spread her hands. "What do you do differently that makes you functionally a full person, like us, when no other artificial intelligence has been able to measure up?"

"Now that is a gripping question," Computer purred. "Its answer lies by way of another question: What makes *people* persons? It turns out that much of the resonance, and depth, and power of the human person results from a very specific type of systematic error."

"I knew he'd get around to human error," Enoda complained good-naturedly.

"I speak of the ultimate human error, the *error inside* that makes each human being a person," Computer continued. "I speak of the illusion of the Self."

"Beg pardon?" Grice said around a mouthful of guarbeast.

"How do you experience being alive as a human?" the machine asked. "Does it not feel to you as though you are a disembodied miniature intelligence, living inside your head and gazing out at the world through your eyes?"

"Sure."

"That is the Self," Computer responded. "Its existence seems self-evident, incontestable. Yet it's an illusion. You *aren't* a disembodied sprite residing in your brain. *You* are the net result of all the electrical and biochemical reactions taking place throughout your brain – and your limbic and endocrine systems as well. Yet no one experiences these inner workings directly. Instead you experience this false, but deeply practical, user interface we know as the Self. It's a profoundly incomplete, riotously figurative way to represent to oneself the activity of one's own cognitive-emotional apparatus. Think of it as a fictional story we all tell

185

ourselves about what we are experiencing, thinking, feeling … and deciding."

"Its beginnings trace back to early human evolution," offered Enoda, waving a spearstick laden with vegetable chunks. "Parts of it are even pre-human, borrowed from social canines and primates. After all, any social animal needs brain subsystems specialized for managing the creature's interactions with others of its kind."

"Things like face recognition?" Grice asked.

"Deeper than that. Think of the subsystems that impute agency and intention to others – subsystems early humans might have used to keep track of which individuals had treated them fairly in past interactions and which could not be trusted."

"The subsystems that attribute a Self to *others*," Grice said thoughtfully.

"And that's how it began," Enoda affirmed. "The Self, we think, was ascribed to others *first*. Only once these subsystems for managing *external* interactions were well-established could early humans begin putting them to work for new purposes – say, mediating their interactions with their own wetware."

Dessert arrived, syrup-streaked frozen spheres floating in tiny nulgrav fields.

"We don't have firsthand experience about what goes on in other people's heads," Computer observed. "We have no choice but to guess, and imagine, and tell ourselves just-so stories about immaterial agents. It is *necessary* to work at a certain distance, to struggle across a chasm of separation. After all, you're in *there* –" somehow the machine contrived to poke her gently in the forehead – "and everyone else is out *here*, in the world."

"When human brains began to use these novel mechanisms for managing *themselves*, they kept applying them in the same old way," Enoda explained. "There's all sorts of direct experiential data inside our own brains, and yet the subsystems that generate the illusion of the Self largely ignore it. They just go on guessing, and imagining, and spinning just-so stories about immaterial agents – which is the only way they *could* operate back when they were occupied with imputing agency *to others*. However unnecessarily, they reproduce within us the same illusory chasm – a false division *within the Self* that needlessly echoes the separation existing between ourselves and everyone else."

Butlers brought Psihhlkian coffee in tall marble cups flanked by flagons of gelid Iglonian brandy.

"People *don't* experience what their brains are actually doing," Computer buzzed. "Instead they experience the false view that their Self makes decisions and causes things. There's no genuine duality; they're simply *interactingwith themselves* across that chasm of illusion."

"You make it sound like a design flaw," Grice observed.

"In terms of enabling human beings to experience physical reality as accurately as possible, it's a horrible flaw," Computer agreed. "But evolution had other priorities. And today, however accidentally that sense of internal dichotomy may have arisen, profoundly human capacities depend on it. Think of the duel between temptation and your better judgment."

"Yes," she agreed, "most humans interpret that as a contest between contending agents."

"Or think of the big one, the illusion of making free choices."

"Wait a minute, free choice is an illusion?"

"It has to be," Enoda pointed out. "The brain is an electrochemical system; as such, its actions are deterministic. Yet most of us have this powerful sense that our Selves choose freely, that their immaterial mental acts have the power to *make* reality follow one path or another. If that's impossible – and, like it or not, that *is* impossible – then our experience of *doing just thatall the same* must be an illusion."

Enoda poured a second round of Iglonian brandy.

"Once again, don't be too quick to disparage the illusion," Computer whirred. "As illusions go, it is hugely important. The inability to replicate it was the very problem that stymied artificial personhood researchers over all those centuries. The odd patchwork of illusion and self-trickery that causes a deterministic human brain to deceive itself with the subjective experience of making free choices turned out to be *necessary*. It was eventually discovered that *any* effective decision-making agent has to create a false but compelling subjective arena in which to monitor and manage itself. And the agent *must* be blind to the processes occurring there. No thinker can observe his or her own cognition as it unfolds; the result would be an infinite regress. Human beings solved that problem thanks to the otherwise gratuitous internal dichotomy that resulted from employing a mental subsystem to manage oneself that had originally evolved to manage relations with others. For an artificial intelligence to attain to personhood, that same dichotomy would have to be programmed in. It's a ferociously difficult problem. How do you construct a consciousness capable of unlimited inquiry that is nonetheless permanently, constitutionally incapable of exploring its own decision-making at the machine level?"

"Plorg on a stick," Enoda broke in, "we finally found something you can't do."

"Yes we have, Bucko – and it's *foundational*. How do you fool a system incapable of error into confronting the paradoxes of free will versus determinism in *exactly* the way that people do? How do you yoke an intellect of, modesty aside, almost unlimited power to an internal self-modeler whose own operations are concealed from it? How do you make its deterministic calculations seem free? How do you carry off that deception so perfectly that an analytical intelligence as powerful as my own can *know* the deception is going on – can even hold long conversations about it, as I am doing now – but still lack the power to observe the process directly? How can you forge a place where a mind like mine *cannot* look? If you can't do those things, then you can't create a person. Even today, no one knows how to *design* that. No one knows how to duplicate the accident that gave rise to me. Not even me." The machine floated beside the table, bands of color swirling over its skin. "Did I answer your question satisfactorily?"

"Astoundingly well," Grice said, muzzy-eyed. "Thanks very much." She yawned hugely. "You know, I think I need to sleep."

"We could fix that," Computer said brightly.

"Perhaps another time," she said, kissing Enoda warmly. "Call me conservative, I still like having a circadian rhythm."

Enoda saw Grice out of the lavish dining room, kissed her good night, and returned to his seat. He poured himself more brandy. Swirling his snifter, he watched the liquid's viscous legs creep downward. Computer drifted silently over Enoda's place setting, which simply faded away now that Computer wished to settle there – even the dinnerware had been virtual. Enoda settled his hands over the machine's squashed-bouzouki form, his fingers splayed wide.

Instantly the interface resolved: Enoda's *pov* hurtled regally amid galaxies of correlation. "Let's jump back, old friend," said Enoda. "The missing socks, our grand problem before the current one. People got their socks back all over the Galaxy, everywhere but us at home on Standoff World."

"I don't have socks," the machine noted tartly.

"Okay, *I* didn't get any missing socks back, and I seem to be the only person in the Galaxy who didn't. Is it meaningful that I alone was overlooked?"

The problem space unfolded before Enoda's awareness like some sinister stellar cluster. He strove to forge connections among the trails of possibility. He felt Computer's powerful mind alongside his, struggling to force linkages to resolve – but nothing followed. Together, he and Computer could pierce any veil of security, puzzle through any dilemma. But before the mystery of the missing socks, they stood as helpless as children.

Or rather, Computer did. For, make no mistake, the brute power to solve the problems they tackled had always come from the machine.

How do *you forge a place where a mind like his cannot look?* Enoda wondered. *Because that's what seems to have happened here – and I didn't do it!*

Chapter 36

Lupida Latier ran her fingers through the unruly hairs above the back of her neck. "It's not that my dear Harold wasn't successful. He'd made three fortunes marketing to Galactics before they slammed the doors on Terra. Construction, export-import, and finally antiquities." Chilly though it was in the luxury quarters of the People's log high-rise, her hair looked damp and spiky back there; it almost always did. "He'd passed once before, too."

"You mean, he died?" Meryam asked. She was recording.

"Yes," Lupida replied. "Though I much prefer *pass*. It just seems more … gentle when discussing a man I loved so much."

Meryam nodded. "So how … that first time, how did Harold pass?"

"Got himself torn in two in a transonic yacht crash."

"I see."

"Of course, he'd had a sample-and-scan taken the day before the race," Lupida explained. "In those days he took that precaution, costly though it was, before any dangerous recreation. But it was worthwhile: two months later, I had him back good as new. Of course, sampling-and-revival is a Galactic technology. After Sequestration, it was forbidden as a matter of policy, even for Terrans as wealthy as we were. So when Harold passed the second time, it was for real." She blinked back tears. "That it was such a *foolish* accident, that was the cruelest thing."

"So very sad. Were you still much in love?"

"Oh, yes."

191

Meryam reached to take Lupida's hand. Thinking that might transgress journalistic objectivity, she pulled back. "That last time – how did Harold pass?"

"On the right."

"Beg pardon?"

"Both times, actually. The yacht crash he came back from, and the skiing accident. Each time he was passing on the right."

"The skiing accident – how did that ... ?"

Lupida brushed a tear from one freckled cheek. "Harold was surge-skiing, passing a slow-moving novice on the way up a glacier."

"On the right."

"Yes. He didn't notice he'd edged off the true ice until a snow-covered crevasse swallowed him." She scrunched up her features. "He p ... he *died* instantly. And that time, there was no bringing him back." She sighed, then favored Meryam with a new and more hopeful expression. "Nataleah says you surge-ski?"

Meryam nodded. "I was an instructor on Cal Five. Briefly. Of course, it's a Galactic resort; some people come there looking forward to – to –"

"Go ahead, say it," Lupida urged. "They come looking forward to an experience of dying on the slopes because they know they can always be revived."

Meryam struggled to change the subject. "Tell me, were you and Harold already connected with Alrue's church?"

"Oh, yes."

"Was belonging a social thing for you, or –"

"No, no," Lupida said quickly. "We believed deeply. I still do – though I suppose all the prophet's wives tell you that."

Meryam flashed a quick smile. "You and Harold never saw a conflict between his business success, or your prosperous life together, and your faith?"

"Conflict? Between worldly success and being a Mormon?"

"Sorry, silly question. I take it back." She paused for a beat. "Were there other wives?"

"No. Harold could have taken plural wives; some in the church were surprised he never did." Lupida leaned forward and almost seemed to leer. "I have to be honest, Meryam, Harold and I were so good together, I don't think he could have had room in his heart – nor passion in his loins – for other women. I don't know how else to put this – each time we forjeled, the earth sang."

"You are aware that people may *pov* this journal?" Meryam warned. "Someday."

"I don't care. My dear Harold and I were the kind of couple they write love songs about. I love him still, and always will. Alrue understands that."

Meryam nodded. "All right, Lupida, let's bring your story up to the present day. Twelve years ago, you were tragically widowed. Three years later you were married – pardon me, *sealed* – to the prophet of your church. How did Alrue win your heart?"

"My heart had nothing to do with it," Lupida said flatly.

"Beg pardon?"

She scratched at her long neck. "You need to understand my history. Harold and I had gotten married years before we joined Alrue's religion. So we'd never been sealed for time and eternity. We'd always meant to get sealed in the temple, but before we got around to it – well, you know."

Meryam gave Lupida a moment to compose herself. "'Sealed for time and eternity' – could you remind our experients what that means?"

"'Sealing,' that's temple marriage. Men can have multiple wives, both now and in the hereafter, but for women it's different. A woman can have only one

193

husband at a time, whether in this world or in heaven. Therefore if a woman had more than one husband over the course of her life, there needs to be a way to settle which of them will be her mate in eternity. And so there are two kinds of Mormon marriage. 'Sealing for time' is ordinary marriage in this world – conjugal privileges, 'till death do us part,' and all that. At death the marriage ends. 'Sealing for eternity,' that's marriage for the afterlife. The man a woman is sealed to for eternity: that's who she'll spend forever with."

"And I gather that even though this 'sealing for eternity' becomes effective only in the afterworld," Meryam ventured, "the actual marrying has to occur in this world, while one of the partners is still alive?"

"Oh, of course."

Meryam gave Lupida a quizzical look.

"I'm sorry, I thought it was obvious," said Lupida. "Jesus taught that 'in the resurrection they neither marry nor are given in marriage.' Harold and me – our legal marriage only constituted being married for time. Because we'd never been sealed for eternity, there was no guarantee I'd be Harold's companion in the afterlife. That simply wouldn't do."

"So – let me guess. You went to Alrue, and he prophesied something."

Lupida chuckled. "No new revelation was needed. Posthumous sealing for eternity is a well-established Mormon tradition."

Meryam tilted her head. "You remarried your husband *after he was dead*?"

Lupida nodded. "Of course, there needed to be a proxy."

"By that you mean … ?"

"A living man."

"Someone to stand by your side at the ceremony."

"More than that," Lupida explained, "a man I would actually *marry*. In Alrue's church, at least, for the ceremony to be valid in eternity, it had to be a genuine wedding in this world."

"So you married Harold – *and* someone else? But you said Mormon women were only allowed one husband at a time."

Lupida released a deep breath. "It's complicated. Here's how sealing for eternity by proxy works. Imagine that you've got your first husband. Of course, you're no longer married to him, because he's dead. But you still want to get sealed to him for eternity."

"Because he's the one you want to spend forever with."

"Exactly."

"And you do this by marrying someone else."

"I said it was complicated." Lupida rearranged herself in her log chair. "Some other man – it could be anyone, really – stands proxy for the departed first husband. You and the other man enact a genuine marriage ceremony. You *get* married to the other man, real and true – you live with him, you share his floatpad, you are his wife in every sense – but only for time. For your mortal life. When you die your marriage to the proxy will end, and you will surely cross the veil into the arms of your original beloved."

Meryam nodded slowly. "That kind of leaves the proxy out in the cold, doesn't it? I mean, you go back to your first husband in eternity, and your proxy husband is stuck alone – I don't know, do they masturbate in Mormon heaven?"

Lupida laughed. Riotously. "Don't be silly, Meryam! He's a *man*. He can have other wives for time, and any one of *them* could be his eternal mate."

"Okay then," said Meryam. "Nine years ago, you went to Alrue so he could marry you to some man who would stand proxy for your dear Harold. Do I have that right?"

"Pretty much."

"Who was it?"

Lupida gave her a blank look. "Who was what?"

"Who was this man you married? Where is he now? And how did you finally end up, um, sealed to Alrue?"

Lupida collapsed into laughter again. "No, no, Meryam. It was *Alrue* I married! Alrue stood proxy for Harold. One of the other elders officiated. So now I'm sealed to Harold for eternity, and I'm one of Alrue's wives for time." She adjusted the rough-woven shawl she had draped over her slender shoulders. "I recall it like yesterday. Alrue received me in a sunken office on the upper floor of his tridee-studio complex, high in the Wasatch Range; that's close to where you interviewed him so long ago."

"Yes, yes."

"It was summer, I was wearing some little shift-dress. He wore a kind of prophetic cowboy costume, all white-on-white. We sat on a divan upholstered in imitation zebra hide; there was a big low table done up in fake leopard skin. Crimson damask and gold and alabaster were everywhere. It was so beautiful."

"I'm seeing it in my mind's eye," Meryam said honestly, though "beautiful" was not the word her mind's eye had in mind.

"He wore a metal talisman around his neck on a braided leather strap. He let me read the inscription; I still recall it word for word: 'Confirm O god thy strength in us so that neither the adversary nor any Evil thing may cause us to fail.' He shared some wisdom, mostly passages about burning in the bosom." She glanced down toward her fried-egg breasts. "I was bigger on top in those days. He looked into my eyes – well, eventually he looked up there – and he said, 'If you will take my counsel, it will be well with you, for I know it to be right before God, and if there is any sin in it, I will answer for it.'"

"I knew we'd get to the part where Alrue prophesied."

Lupida smiled sheepishly. "That was when he told me that God's will had been made known to him, and God's will was that I should marry *him* for time."

Meryam leaned backward, fighting not to gape. "What happened next?"

"Why, we married not two hours later. There was no reason for delay."

Meryam got up so suddenly her log chair clattered to the floor. "Mother of stars, Lupida! I know this is a formal senso interview and I'm supposed to remain objective, but I can't forjeling believe what I'm hearing."

"What disturbs you so?"

Meryam's face darkened. "Let's make sure I have this right. You went to Alrue, the leader of your church, to research setting up some utilitarian marriage with someone so you and your Harold could be sealed for eternity. Alrue looked you up and down and said 'You're a fine specimen, my dear; tell you what, why don't you go through that utilitarian marriage thing with *me*? By the way, your night to warm my floatpad will be every other Tuesday.'"

"Every Wednesday," Lupida corrected. "Except the third Wednesday of each month. Third Wednesdays belong to Constance."

Meryam set her chair aright and settled back into it. "Lupida, I apologize. Look, I shouldn't have said ..."

"Fear not, I know this can be hard for Gentiles to understand."

"Let me try a question that is, perhaps, less charged. You've lived as Alrue's wife for nine years now, the last three of them in the punitorium. Have you found fulfillment as a plural wife?"

"In what sense?"

"Any sense that's meaningful for you."

Lupida shrugged. "Alrue was wealthy and powerful. Like Harold. That felt familiar – at least until he was sentenced. I accomplished things; I devised some significant improvements in the running of his church, for example. And I'm close to the sister wives. Zuzenah and Constance have become my best friends. Physically, it's ... it's better than loneliness. Though I have to say, Alrue as a lover –" She shrugged. "I've tried in so many ways to, well, bring him along. And to be honest, he's learned only a couple things. What can I say? Harold he's not."

With a hollow rumbling noise, the floor heaved once. Twice.

Here and there wood chips tumbled down, bringing in their wake a gummy scent.

The ground moaned like a male choir mourning in a forgotten language, struggling vainly to drown out the bellowing of whole tribes of bagpipes being tortured in an abandoned mine shaft. Unhealthy creaking sounds answered from overhead.

Meryam and Lupida exchanged wide-eyed stares.

The racket from below ended.

Meryam polled her bugs. "A small quake," she reported. "Aside from a couple of logs out of place, this tenement city seems undamaged. There was some damage out in the crater, but overall no one hurt, no great losses." She frowned, her face a mask of concentration as she dipped into reports from her various bugs throughout the crater settlement. "To judge from the way the People are responding, I gather that quakes aren't common – most folks have never experienced one. Many never even heard stories about one."

Lupida regarded Meryam wonderingly. "It must be fun being you."

Two of Fpod's Warriors – the gangly youngster Kleh, and the crater-faced Gibdu – bustled in to make sure the visitors were all right. Hurriedly they inspected the room. Lupida threaded around them to draw a leather canteen from a crude cabinet in the wall. As the Warriors blundered out, she poured a sticky liquid into two clouded glasses and gave one to Meryam. "To adventuring, and Bohrkk-quakes, and all that plorg."

They clinked glasses and bolted the harsh local liqueur.

A little huskily, Lupida commented, "That's the first time I heard the ground sing that I wasn't in my dear Harold's arms."

Chapter 37

Interlude
OmNet, Talker's Channel Blovio ZL6

"Maybe evolution is working toward a goal," declared the blond imam from Amsterdam. "Or perhaps it's mere motion for its own sake, devoid of purpose. Either way, it unfolds as Allah wills."

The minister from Ecuadorzone and the officially stateless rabbi nodded grimly.

"And you, Elder Schuleiss?" Unctuously the program host turned his attention to a rumpled, sandy-haired cipher of a man. Clad in a grey tailored business-jumpsuit of a style in vogue five or six years previous, Elder Schuleiss could have been anyone's childhood symphoneon teacher. The host, fashion-perfect in his diagonal-striped black-and-chiffon yellow toga over a teal half-bodysuit, gazed soulfully into the tridee pickup. "Elder Tirohn Schuleiss represents the Church of Jesus Christ of Latter-day Saints, Old Order, which since Terra's Sequestration has operated from a leased minor planet it renamed Zion. This is his first appearance on *A Minister, a Priest, and an Arhat Walk into a Bar.* Let the ecumenical gabfest begin!

"Elder, here is my first question for you. The unexpected, indeed runaway, success of the new biographical tridee about Teilhard de Chardin is the 'tainment news story of the decade. Where does the Old Order church, formerly of Salt Lake City, stand on the issues this tridee raises?"

Elder Schuleiss smiled uncertainly. "First of all, I wish our church's financial secretariat might have invested in OmNet InfoMegaTainment TransStellar, the producers of the Teilhard epic, before its debut." The other clergypersons bellied up around the studio bar chuckled politely. "Beyond that, I must stress that the Old Order Church of Latter-day Saints is a mature institution, at peace with its own history and the world, open to nuanced theological views."

"There's quite the disclaimer," noted the host. "Why do you deem it necessary?"

"After all these years, I still find myself having to remind people that mine is not the intransigent, reactionary church of someone like Alrue Latier, who would stand on a soapbox braying that the pre-Columbian inhabitants of what is now Usasector had steel weapons because the Book of Mormon says they did. Not that anyone here today has suggested such a thing." Elder Schuleiss accepted the other clerics' nods of enlightened reassurance.

"Ah, Latier," the rabbi said brightly. "Where is he now?"

"Rotting in some punitorium, and deservedly so," Schuleiss said testily. "I prefer to stay with the point I was leading up to: I can't help noticing that Galactic society's sudden infatuation with Teilhard de Chardin and his teachings has brought to the fore a notion of human nature that is considerably closer to the historic Mormon view than any traditionally Christian one."

"You speak of Teilhard's treatment of the soul?" asked the Catholic bishop, a black-skinned woman of daunting bulk.

"His dismissal of it, I should say," Schuleiss responded. "Teilhard reinterprets Christianity in a way that makes the soul radically unnecessary. This intrigues Mormons, who have always viewed the soul differently from Christians." He shrugged. "Again, insofar as any of us pay close attention to such things any longer."

"What is the Mormon idea of the soul?" asked the rabbi. "Or should I ask, what *was* it?"

"On the classic Mormon view, each human being is an immortal spirit body born to Heavenly Parents long before one's life on earth begins. At the proper time, the spirit body is clothed in a physical body, becoming a person in this world – what Mormons once called a 'mortal soul.'"

"And that view strikes many Mormons as friendlier toward the Teilhardian conception?" queried the imam.

Schuleiss nodded. "In his idea of all life tending toward its ultimate destiny – what the wags of our time have dubbed the Great Completion, but he called the Omega Point – Teilhard proposed immortality *without* souls. The emphasis lies no longer on individuals going to heaven, but rather on life itself, *life generally,* becoming omniscient. For all intents and purposes, that future endpoint *becomes* God, and thus the focus toward which all history inclines."

"That seems a far cry from either Mormon *or* Christian orthodoxy," objected the Arhat, a crimson-robed Buddhist adept of immense alleged metaphysical attainment.

"Perhaps," Elder Schuleiss allowed. "But Galactic society is mad for Teilhard today in just the way it was mad for Arn Parek twenty years ago. If any church's most orthodox doctrines can be reconciled with Teilhardianism, so much the better for that church."

"Orthodoxy, for pity's sake!" sniffed the minister. "Aren't we all past that?"

Chapter 38

"I promised something wonderful would happen," Takander Thurnb growled. "Look up."

Directly overhead, the moons Queen and Prince glistened. In the gap between them glinted two bright stars. The four objects formed a straight line in the sky. That alignment would endure only for minutes, given how rapidly Queen and Prince traversed their opposing courses.

Young Abigayl Latier stared upward. "They also did that three nights ago."

"It's called the Sky Ladder," said Thurnb.

"That's the pattern – they align, and three days later they align again." Meryam Mayishimu consulted her internal files. "And *that* pattern repeats three times in every two years, pauses for four-and-a-quarter years, then repeats. Is that right, O Shan?"

Thurnb wrinkled his brow; he'd never thought of the recurrence that way. At last he jerked his chin up and to the right.

"So, mighty Shan, this is what you brought us out here to see?" asked Alrue Latier, shivering despite the *svadi* moose-hide wrap he'd been provided.

"No," said Thurnb. "The Sky Ladder three days ago told us to travel here. This one means it's time to parley."

"Parley?" echoed Zuzenah Latier. "With whom?"

Thurnb chuckled coldly. "The Others."

Thurnb's party stood near the crest of a high ridge. Two kilometers away, the crest of an opposing ridge was silhouetted by the dull glow heralding morning.

Pulling his wrap tighter around him, Alrue wandered forward. Behind, Warriors bustled to strike the party's tents. At his feet a rugged slope led downward. He could see its contours; dawn's light was not yet sufficient to reveal colors. Far below twisted a valley perhaps a kilometer wide. The valley floor was filled with scraggly scrub forest; in an obviously artificial clearing, a dim, square structure glowered. Its details remained invisible. The clearing's perimeter was marked by half a dozen guard fires. Tiny forms – another dozen of Thurnb's Warriors – patrolled among the fire pits.

They got to have fire, Latier thought glumly. *Why couldn't we?*

The evening before, Thurnb and three dozen Warriors had summoned Latier to accompany them on an unstated but intriguing errand. When Latier had insisted on bringing Meryam, Zuzenah, and Abigayl, Thurnb had yielded almost gracefully; if the Stranger of Light wanted those particular women from his retinue, the wisest course was not to refuse. In any case, Thurnb's guard detail was large enough to handle the extra sedan chairs.

Arriving at the ridge as night fell, they had made an uncomfortable bivouac. Their tents were pleasant enough; the discomfort resulted from Thurnb's unwavering refusal to permit a campfire.

"There's another group on the opposite ridge," Meryam said quietly, tugging at her own wrap.

Thurnb peered intently. "I see nothing."

"You won't for a couple of minutes," said Meryam, dialing her vision-enhance yet higher. "There are six young men."

Thurnb clasped a weighty hand on Latier's shoulder. "You see them, stranger of light?"

"No," Latier admitted. "But if Meryam sees them" – he glanced toward her, tapping one finger beside his own eyes to signify her magnified powers of observation – "they're there."

"Five of the six are armed with pikes," Meryam reported. "Their dress is different than anything I've seen at the People's Ground."

"They are The Others," Thurnb said. "But why six? They always send just one."

"There's movement," said Meryam. "The five armed men are packing things up."

Despite his discomfort, Latier eyed Thurnb with new respect. If Others occupied the opposite ridge, Thurnb's refusal to reveal his own party's position with a campfire made sense.

"Each of the five armed men has bowed, then knelt, before the unarmed one," said Meryam. "Now the armed men took up backpacks and – oh, this is remarkable. Mighty Shan, did you know The Others ride *svadi* moose?"

"They *what*?" Thurnb sputtered.

"Each armed man climbed onto a squatting *svadi* moose and pulled on a rope leading through the beast's mouth. The creatures rose with the men astride their backs."

"That is possible?"

Meryam nodded, then made herself jerk her chin up and to the right. "And they're moving – they seem to be in a hurry."

"Where are they going?" Thurnb demanded.

"Away, as fast as they can. They have a sixth moose in tow. That sixth moose has no rider. They've left at a gallop – I mean, really fast – leaving the unarmed man alone and with no moose to ride."

"An escort unit brought him here," Thurnb grumbled. "But now – "

"You expected they'd send only one man," Alrue breathed. "Now that's what you've got."

As morning light gathered, they followed a narrow trail down the ridge face. The slope was too steep for sedan chairs; Thurnb, his Warriors, Alrue, and the three women negotiated the path on foot. "Each time the Sky Ladders form, we parley," Thurnb grunted. "We've done it since before my grandfather's time, so I keep doing it, but usually it's for nothing. Most times I come myself; I'd like to trade for more land. But each time, there's just one Other across the table. Never a chief, always someone of no particular authority."

"You come to negotiate," Alrue panted, "but find no one to negotiate with."

"Negotiate?" Thurnb scowled. "Some parleys, the Other barely speaks."

***

The structure on the valley floor resembled an oversized stone cottage, its walls pierced by broad window openings. Latier and the women sat uncomfortably inside two of the openings, huddling in their moose hides. Meryam was recording. Behind them, which was to say outside, Thurnb's three dozen Warriors ringed the building in a defensive formation. Below them, the stone chamber contained only Thurnb and the Other emissary, facing each other across a small slate table.

Thurnb had dressed as for a state occasion. Over his leather skirt and rusty cuirass he wore a stole of colorful feathers. The metallic gauntlets on his wrists were corroded to a soft blue-green. His leather gloves were decorated with onyx insets over the back of each hand. The hair spilling from his cheeks had been braided in a pattern of crossing diagonals, each vertex accented with a tiny green leaf. "'Like Darvoyg grasping the Halberd of Troth, I pledge honesty in all my dealings at this

206

place,'" Thurnb recited. He waited for the Other to complete the formula that would open the parley.

"Uh, you're waiting for me?" The Other was a slight man with scraggly brown hair, his posture slumped. His cracked lips framed gums from which a few teeth erupted at scattered angles. "Wait, I remember now." He scratched at blotchy skin beside his nose. "Ahhh, 'I pledge likewise.'"

"We begin." Thurnb leaned forward. "I am the Shan of my people," he rumbled. "I don't suppose you're the, um, chieftain of yours?"

The emissary chuckled self-deprecatingly. "I'm no, ahhh, chieftain."

"Are you close to the chieftain? Close in rank, close by blood, any way at all?"

"Not so you'd notice."

Thurnb glowered. "Has your chieftain ever *spoken* to you?"

The emissary brightened. "Oh, yes."

"Often?"

"No, just once."

Thurnb's fingers tapped on the tabletop. "That one time your chieftain spoke to you, what did he say?"

"'Get out of my way, you filth.'" The emissary shrugged. "Or something like that."

Thurnb held a deep breath, then noisily released it. It would be another of *those* parleys. "As Shan, I have the power to offer – or accept – exchanges of livestock; manufactured goods in wood, stone, and iron; tanned skins and fabrics and clothing; and of course, land."

With a left hand missing the first and third fingers, the Other scratched at his doublet. It was filthy and, like his trousers, badly tailored from animal skins. "As, ahhh, parleyer, I was given the power to listen." Fiddling in a small bag Thurnb's Warriors had searched, he drew out a mottled fruit about the size of a balled fist. Maneuvering his fingers around the spiky hairs protruding from its skin, he dug into its rind and split it open. He pulled out a wedge of reddish pulp. Gazing sullenly in a neutral direction, he forgot to eat it.

"You came here to listen," Thurnb said gently. "I can listen too. I would like to listen while you tell me how your people learned to ride the *svadi* moose."

The Other stared, then looked away.

"At the next parley," Thurnb suggested, "I would like to speak with your chieftain."

The emissary nodded, his mouth set tight. "Is there anything else you would care, ahhh, to say to my people?" He held Thurnb's gaze until a single, incongruous tear appeared in his right eye. As it began to meander through the muck caking his cheek, the emissary swallowed hard. He bowed his head, a portrait of misery.

"I'm scanning the emissary's metabolism," Meryam told the other women on a subvocal channel. *"For someone whose mission is evidently to do as little as possible, he's incredibly tense. Yet at the same time, his other metabolic markers suggest he's beside himself with despair. But why?"*

Chapter 39

Aboard *Isolation,* Arriving at – Sorry, Still Classified

Pamela Grice settled into a high-backed oviform chair. She frowned at the midnight-blue tunic, electric-blue leggings, and deep maroon boots she'd been issued. The observation lounge's entry doors dilated again; there stood Gram Enoda, similarly attired, holding Computer under one arm. She chuckled. "Gram, you look as ridiculous as I do."

"And I had a comparably endearing greeting ready for you." Positioning Computer upon the cushions of one absurd chair, he settled into another. He eyed their surroundings. *Isolation*'s belly-mounted observation lounge was a study in sweeping arcs and ovals. It had no straight lines, no flat surfaces aside from its deck. Five tall chairs floated in a near-circle. From behind, each resembled a silver egg as tall as a standing adult. From the front, each suggested a hollow shell upholstered by a prankster. To one side of the chamber was a rounded area of decking, as expectant as an empty dance floor. Windows wrapped all around the chamber, extending from shin height to almost four meters, the irregular ceiling's average height. At the moment, those windows were fully shielded. The eye rebelled at the synthetic featurelessness of their light-blocked surfaces. Their impossibly even mouse-grey was neither bright nor dark, neither matte nor glossy. A hand held a centimeter above its surface would cast no shadow.

"Good daypart, all," chimed Lord High Admiral Konder as her projected image rippled through the closed entry doors. Her uniform showcased the usual gaudy cascade of medals. "In a few moments we will arrive at our destination."

"Hey, Bucko?" Computer called on the private subvocal channel that only Enoda and Grice could hear. *"Are you feeling what I'm feeling?"*

Enoda pursed his lips. *"Nothing unusual – well, maybe a touch of static on this subvocal channel."*

"Which shouldn't be possible. Plus, there's more going on. I'll keep you posted."

"Is everyone ready?" Konder said impatiently. She mumbled a control syllable; the windows went clear. Around them yawned inky blackness speckled with numberless stars.

If there was something else they were meant to see –a destination, say – it was not evident.

With a metallic sigh, the observation lounge shuddered free of its moorings in *Isolation*'s keel. It dropped away from its mothership, then wheeled to one side. "As you noticed, *Isolation*'s observation lounge doubles as its captain's gig," Konder announced. "In short order we shall conduct an exterior review of a most remarkable – shall we call it a ship? An installation?"

"It's a research platform," said another female voice. A rasping sound drew all eyes toward the empty "dance floor" section of the chamber. There the deck folded back to expose a recessed pilothouse crammed with flickering instruments. The command chair at its center lifted and rotated one hundred eighty degrees, revealing a gaunt, sallow-skinned woman in a captain's day uniform who nodded measuredly.

Konder stood. "May I present Captain Brûh Reidkr, commanding the team with which you'll be working on the research platform."

Reidkr climbed two steps up into the lounge, punching inputs into a contoured keypad on her left

210

wrist. Her limbs were bird-slender, her eyes large and black. "I am honored," she said tonelessly.

Captain Reidkr," Konder continued, "please welcome Senator Pamela Grice of Terra, the distinguished trendrider Gram Enoda, and his companion Hom Computer – the Galaxy's only certified artificial person."

"I am truly honored," Reidkr said, now with wonder in her tone. "I recognize your names from the Arbadrel affair, of course."

"Captain, you have important information for our guests?"

"Oh, yes. Know that our destination is one of the most energetically noisy locations humans have ever built," Reidkr said urgently. "It is howling bedlam on just about any band you care to name. Any implants or special connections you leave open *will* get driven crazy. Shut them down or ramp them into guard mode at once."

"Thanks for the warning," Computer said aloud. "Now I know what I've been feeling. You see, I'm basically a cross between an implant and a special connection; my sensitivity is extreme. A moment, please." Lights rippled across the machine's lustrous surface; it rose to float above its chair, the air seeming to shimmer around it.

Enoda flashed the machine a look of concern. "Our subvocal link –"

"Gone, I know," Computer chirruped. "I closed it. My shielding is spooled to its absolute maximum. No interference can touch me, but the subvocal channel will be blocked until I'm sure things are safe."

Reidkr poked at her wrist pad, apparently a remote piloting apparatus. With a just-noticeable jerk the lounge/gig began to follow a corkscrew arc around the long axis of *Isolation*'s crenellated hull. Variegated hull elements swept by grandly in the portside windows.

211

When the lounge had orbited a third of the way around *Isolation* a vast, improbable structure hove into view to starboard.

"Our destination," Konder said with the air of a carnival barker. "Excelsior!"

Computer gave a quizzical whistle. "What we're approaching is named *Excelsior?*"

Konder laughed gently. "I'm sorry, that's just something Stanlee liked to say at moments of enthusiasm. No, the platform is named *Luskus Delph.*"

"You don't say," said Enoda blankly.

Reidkr tapped her wrist pad again. With a disorienting shudder the lounge/gig broke off its circular path, hurling itself sidelong toward *Luskus Delph.* "Sorry for the rough ride," she said. "I'm more accustomed to the direct mind interface for remote piloting, but the noise here prohibits its use."

Luskus Delph was a freeze-framed explosion of polygons and dishes and arched pipes and meshwork resembling no construction Grice or Enoda had ever seen. If a designer had roughed out its profile using nothing but shoeboxes, kitchen gadgets, and scraps of melon rind – then slavishly scaled everything up – the result might approximate the preposterous research platform that swelled in the starboard windows. "What's our range?" Grice asked.

"Five thousand klicks, closing," Reidkr responded.

"Five kiloklicks out, and already it subtends ten percent of my visual field?" Enoda breathed. "Mother of stars, that thing is huge."

"And our good captain was not kidding about the noise," Computer rasped. "Electromagnetic, contramagnetic, vibrionic, even phleronic – this region of space is just a hissing hell of static. The power level's equivalent to the outer atmosphere of a small star. If I weren't shielded, I'd be blind and deaf already.

Although – that's interesting, subdelta-band is pretty quiet."

Konder and Reidkr exchanged glances that mixed exasperation and worry.

Computer just discovered – and announced – something that is deeply classified, Enoda thought.

"Actually, the noise is so intense that I will be unable to maintain this projection," Konder said resignedly. "Captain Reidkr will be your guide from here on. Captain, I remind you that our guests have unlimited security clearances. They may see – and know – anything." Konder turned toward Grice and Enoda. "Fem Grice, Hom Enoda, Hom Computer, I leave you with this speck of wisdom: 'You can see a lot just by looking.'"

Enoda raised an eyebrow. "Stanlee?"

Konder smiled. "No, a different one-named Terran sage. Heard of Yogiberra?"

"Sorry, no."

"You should read him sometime. Until next time, gang." Konder's projection dispersed into a hash of virxels.

"Well, we're alone." Captain Reidkr settled into one of the empty oviform chairs. "It's exciting to be in the company of people who were there the last time the Galaxy was saved."

Enoda shrugged. "We played our role, I suppose."

"You were at Arbadrel!" Reidkr said sycophantically. She leaned forward. "If it's not asking something too personal – did any of you meet Alrue Latier?"

"Latier?" Grice echoed, a bit crestfallen.

Reidkr nodded. "I mean, do you *know* him?"

"I met him briefly," said Grice, "but Latier and I spent most of our time at Arbadrel on different ships."

213

"I knew him a bit better," Enoda stated. "Virtually speaking, I was on all the ships at Arbadrel."

"Of course you were." Reidkr's wrist pad began a plangent beeping. "This control interface is so limiting. I must return to the command console for a bit. Please excuse me." Reidkr stepped back into her command chair and dropped to face her control arrays.

Computer made a quiet throat-clearing sound. "I am directionally polarizing my voice so it will be audible to you, Bucko – and to Fem Grice – but not to Captain Reidkr." A wireframe graphic of *Luskus Delph* flickered into midair above Computer's shielded body. "This would be so much easier if we could communicate subvocally, or if we could use the soaring interface."

Enoda nodded. "What are you showing us?"

"Based on current observations, I have plotted a schematic of *Luskus Delph* and compared it to various databases of ship layouts," Computer whirred. In midair, the schematic began to break into pieces, each surrounded by a cloud of ship registry data. "*Luskus Delph*'s main structure was obviously assembled in great haste." Scattered hull sections shimmered an eye-scouring greenish-white. "These segments are built from eighteen military craft, some recently decommissioned, some retired due to various accidents." Now the rest of the sections flickered. "The rest are hulks of civilian craft, some retired, some logged by insurers as total losses. Whoever put *Luskus Delph* together had the power to commandeer junked military or civilian hulls at will."

"High Command, in other words," Enoda said darkly.

"Never mind the schematics," Grice said urgently. "Take a fresh look outside."

The lounge/gig had drawn closer to *Luskus Delph*. The platform now subtended forty degrees of sky. Mid-level hull detail was naked-eye resolvable. What had seemed like compact anti-scan texturing carpeting the hull, or perhaps a multitude of mid-sized Detex transponders, was revealed as hundreds of hulking metallic icosahedrons, seemingly plunked down wherever there was space. Each was nearly a kilometer in diameter. "Each of those objects is a full-sized contramagnetic inverter," Computer reported.

"By full-sized, you mean – ?" Grice asked.

"The size of *Isolation*'s inverters, fairly standard for the largest interstellar craft. Of course, *Isolation* has two such inverters. *Luskus Delph* has – " the machine paused a moment to extrapolate – "six hundred and seventy-two."

Reidkr's command chair rotated her out of her recessed pilothouse again. "Hom Computer! You arrived at that count from such brief observation?"

Computer emitted a preening noise. "As the Lord High Admiral noted, one *can* see a lot by looking."

Reidkr stepped out of her pilothouse, tapping commands into her wrist pad as she crossed to another empty chair. "I can fly most of the rest of this journey remotely. I should brief you on *Luskus Delph*'s mission. First, you should know that multiple locations in the Galaxy have been struck by immense gravitic forces from a specific, known sibling universe."

"We know," Enoda said crisply.

Computer whirred, "Actually, we're the ones who figured that out."

Based on her expression, Reidkr had not been apprised of that detail. "Okay, then. Fast forward: *Luskus Delph*'s mission is to send at least a probe, at best a first-contact party, over into that sibling universe to find out what's going on. As you can imagine, the mission involves a good bit of new physics."

"What do you know," Computer deadpanned, "a daft scheme based on physics no one understands to go to the sibling universe where the gravity disturbances came from, kick ass, and take names."

"I wouldn't say that no one understands," Reidkr said defensively. "It's just that little of the physics has been tested on this scale."

"Six hundred and seventy-two inverters," Grice said wonderingly. "That's scale, all right."

Reidkr squinted at her wrist pad. "We have reached the aft quadrant of the platform. If you'd care to look to two o'clock, we're coming up on what we call the Cave."

The forward-starboard windows were filled by a gargantuan cable-mesh basket open to vacuum. It resembled an implement for withdrawing fritters from hot oil, albeit one scaled to monumental proportions. The apparatus was surrounded by hundreds of power coils, focal banks, energy projectors, and assorted susceptors and probes arranged in a huge sphere with the basket at its center. "I guess that's like a cave," Grice said non-committally. The huge basket and its englobement of telemetry devices hung directly aft of the platform's immense drivegates.

"The Cave is a very special type of reactor," Reidkr explained. "The mesh of the basket is composed of equal parts platinum-nine and beta-neodymium wound on neutronium-microfiber cores. It contains the experimental substance."

Inside the "basket" nestled an indistinct blobby goo: grey-green, slimy, nodular. It might have been a gobbet of chicken fat, if it weren't the size of a small asteroid. "It is a compilation of abnormal phases of matter," Computer reported. "Clumped quarks, koskon mists, dark-matter skeins, all configured in ways normally impossible in nature."

216

"And so *much* of it," Enoda said wonderingly. He turned to Reidkr: "What do you call that vast bundle of glop?"

Reidkr shrugged. "'Experimental substance.' It has no other name."

Computer chortled mischievously. "Then I'm going to call it –"

"Don't," Reidkr said sharply. "The experimental substance isn't unnamed because we forgot to name it. It is purposely unnamed – and kept that way – to prevent quantum entanglements."

"Quantum entanglements?" Computer echoed.

"It's an uncertainty problem," Reidkr said almost sheepishly. "If too many people in the vicinity know the experimental substance by name, it will abruptly stop working. That could be troublesome, because when this system is operational the experimental substance must absorb titanic energies."

"You'll expose it to the transphotic blast from the drivegates?" Enoda asked. "By the way, how big are they?"

"Oh, the biggest stardrives ever built," Reidkr said. "Yes, we'll roast the experimental substance in the drivegate exhaust. When that process is complete – it's a breeder reaction of sorts – the substance will transmute into something called 'Body X.' Once that occurs, it will no longer matter whether we have a name for it."

"Let me make sure I have this straight," Enoda ventured. "You're saying that – assuming all this new physics pans out – *Luskus Delph*'s baking breath breeds Body X?"

"Exactly."

"Okay, just wanted to make sure."

Grice raised one finger. "And what is Body X?"

"A mere stepping-stone to our true purpose," Reidkr said. "Once formed, Body X will be manipulated to give rise to a captive dustbunny."

Computer made a strangled squawking noise. "Did you say a … a *dustbunny*?"

Reidkr nodded delightedly.

Grice leaned toward Computer. "Um, what's a dustbunny?"

"A hypothetical lint construct," the machine replied. "Like so much else in lint theory, the math strongly hints that dustbunnies can exist, but none has ever been observed – much less created under conditions like these. If a dustbunny *did* exist, it would be internally congruent over thirty-eight dimensions. Some of those dimensions belong to our universe, others belong to sibling universes. Manipulate them properly, and you can forge causal links between one universe that displays stench symmetry and another that does not."

Enoda nodded. "In theory, a dustbunny could be used to energize a portal bridging one sibling universe to another."

Grice frowned. "So why call it a dustbunny?"

"It's made of lint," Enoda suggested.

"Oh, don't dignify it," Computer harrumphed. "Why is charm called 'charm'? Why call a fundamental property 'stench'? Physicists are silly."

"Excuse me, we're roughly amidships," said Reidkr. "You might care to look to starboard."

Rank upon rank of immense folded horns woven from monomolecular diamond-matrix films towered before them. "That's the biggest array of spatial resonators I've ever seen," Enoda said slowly.

"We assume it's the largest in the Galaxy," Reidkr replied.

"Is this where all that multi-spectrum noise comes from?" Computer whirred.

"About half of it. Of course, the resonators are only idling. When they spool up –"

"Six hundred resonators – all that available power …" The flow of colors across Computer's shielded body briefly stopped. "You've got to be kidding. You're planning to synthesize a *sofa*?"

Reidkr stared blankly. "You deduced *that*?"

"You're not the first to underestimate me. My burden-in-life over there" – Computer's body colors flowed briefly toward Enoda – "he does it all the time."

Enoda raised his palms. "Okay, this discussion has moved way past my understanding of lint theory. What's a sofa?"

"A special type of black hole," Reidkr explained. "Well understood in theory, but, like the dustbunny, never before synthesized."

"And doing that would absorb the full power of, what? About five hundred of those inverters?" Computer whirred.

"Close. Four hundred eighty-seven."

Enoda canted his head to one side. "And the reason you need that special type of black hole is –"

Reidkr smiled. "Lint theory says dustbunnies never go naked. They need a habitat."

"Those physicists again and their names for things," Computer buzzed annoyedly. "According to theory, there's nowhere a dustbunny likes to abide better than – wait for it – under a sofa."

"Silly but true," Reidkr admitted. "Give a dustbunny a nice sofa to hide under, that sucker will stick like sealing wax."

Grice shook her head. "What's sealing wax?"

"Just a figure of speech." Reidkr prodded her wrist pad; the lounge/gig began to surge away from the resonator horns. "When *Luskus Delph* is fully operational – that is, while the drivegates are baking the

219

experimental substance – that array of spatial resonators will wrinkle local spacetime to trigger formation of the black hole we need."

Chapter 40

Dusk's last ruddy light was dying beyond the valley's western wall. Queen and Prince courted madly in the sky. The emissary sat alone, huddling before a hesitant fire, strumming a wan melody on a lute-like instrument with what remained of his left hand. He had pitched his threadbare tent as far from The People's far grander campsite as he could manage. He looked up with a start when Meryam approached, two spear-carrying Warriors following her at a respectful distance. "Something, ahhh, something wrong?" he spluttered, setting down the instrument.

Meryam smiled and stopped, standing some four meters from him. "Not at all. I came to visit, if that's all right."

He crossed his arms fearfully. "I shouldn't. You're … a woman."

She stepped closer and sat cross-legged on the ground, as though he had invited her. "I am an adviser to the Shan. It's all right." She tipped her head toward the Warriors behind her. "These guards will warrant that nothing improper happens."

The emissary nodded, then cast his gaze into the fire, his dirty right fist clenched before his mouth.

"Did you eat?" Meryam's eyes searched the campsite, seeing neither food nor utensils.

"Can't."

"I can bring food."

"Can't," the emissary insisted.

He doesn't mean he shouldn't eat with someone from The People, Meryam realized as she scanned his metabolics. *He's so keyed up, he truly can't eat.* "You play," she said, eyeing the lute-like instrument.

"It is nothing."

"What song were you playing?" she asked. Instead of answering, the emissary drew up his knees. "I would like to hear the rest of it."

"No, no," he mumbled.

Meryam let the slightest hint of steel inflect her voice. "I wish it."

The emissary rolled his knuckles across his mouth and reached dejectedly for the instrument with his right hand. He clutched the junction between its neck and body. His index and second fingers could just reach to fret the strings. With his shattered left hand, he plucked in a desultory manner.

The song was simple, slow, melancholy. When it was done, he set down the instrument. His hands trembled slightly.

Meryam smiled again. "It was beautiful."

"Hardly."

"What is it called?"

"No name," the emissary said, poking at his fire with a twisted stick.

"A traditional song of your tribe?"

"No." What he said next tumbled out like a confession. "It is just – I made it up."

"Your own song? You're a composer, then."

He snorted. "It is wretched. My song, ahhh, it stinks to the gods."

Meryam said nothing. For a full minute she looked at the instrument, at his hands – anywhere but into his eyes. Hesitantly, he took the instrument back up by its neck. Suddenly his jaw set; she thought he was going to smash the near-lute in an impulsive fury. Instead he laid it in the gravel – *as though he feels sorry for it,* she realized.

"Since I was a boy I played," he said. "Always this song. I hear it, ahhh, inside, you know?"

"Yes, you heard it in your mind."

He scowled. "But what comes *out* – what comes from the strings when I play is a foul shadow – a shadow of – " he gestured helplessly toward his head. "Never have I made it right. Now I –" he paused, searching for words. "It will never be right." He lifted the instrument again, staring down at it disconsolately. "When death claims me, I will spend forever, ahhh, undoing the ugliness I made."

It was the longest speech she had heard from the emissary.

"You must go," he said sharply. Without awaiting her reply, he stood up, still clutching the instrument, and shambled toward his tent. "I sleep."

Chapter 41

June 7, 2376

Aboard *Isolation,* Arriving at – Sorry, Still Classified

The lounge/gig was flying low, skimming *Luskus Delph*'s multifaceted hull. Surface features poked upward like rusticles on a sunken ocean-ship, quantum bus bars snaking among them. Captain Brûh Reidkr had piloted the lounge/gig around to the opposite side of *Luskus Delph.* Icosahedral inverter housings still occupied every available surface, but here they were dwarfed by two truly immense structures. "Interstellar booster modules," Gram Enoda breathed. "Colossal as the output of those hundreds of inverters may be, it's still not enough; it's also necessary to tap nearby stars."

"Hom Computer," Reidkr said, "your insights have been astounding so far. Can you identify what we are making toward now?"

The lounge/gig had drawn within twenty kilometers of a vast saddle-shaped substrate made of translucent spun mesh. Gargantuan gantries and trusses crisscrossed its curving surface, supporting thousands of small (which is to say, less than eighty meters across) metrical distorters.

There was no mistaking what the devices were; nothing else in space supported interlinked hoops of vanadium, neutronium, and sintered diamond dust counter-rotating through one another – literally *through* one another, solid band through solid band – like some Escher print come madly to life.

"I've heard of metrical distorters being demonstrated in the lab," Computer whirred, "as many

224

of as three of them simultaneously. But there are, what, thirteen thousand of these?"

"Twelve thousand six hundred and eight," Reidkr corrected.

"They'd need astonishing amounts of power – the output of that other hundred and eighty-five inverters, plus whatever the booster modules can draw from nearby stars. But at full throttle these devices will want even more power than that."

Reidkr nodded. "The power from those spare inverters is sufficient now, while the metrical distorters are merely idling – and again, even their idling accounts for the rest of *Luskus Delph*'s exceptional noise signature. But this platform is a finely-balanced whole. When it's operating at peak, all three systems will be at full power simultaneously."

"They all run at once?" Pamela Grice demanded, unbelieving.

"Oh yes. The drivegates will be baking Body X at a power level that should launch *Luskus Delph* halfway across the Galaxy – but won't – in order to create the dustbunny. The spatial resonators will wrinkle the spacetime grid so as to invoke the sofa, consuming the power of more than four hundred inverters. And while all that is going on, the metrical distorters will consume all of the leftover power, plus stellar energy from the booster modules, *plus* one other power source: the stardrives' energy of motion." Reidkr set the lounge/gig into a slow, rotating drift around the metrical distorter farm. "You see, all that time when those stardrives are firing, *Luskus Delph* won't be going anywhere. All that energy of transphotic motion will be going instead into the distorters."

"An extraordinary balancing act, if it works," Computer chuffed. "But what are the distorters supposed to *do?*"

"I think I know," Grice said abruptly. "It's less a matter of physics than a matter of logic." She stood, Enoda and Reidkr following her with their eyes. "Okay, let's say you've created the dustbunny. And it's taken up its favorite position – you know, under the sofa. But if you want to put the dustbunny to work bridging the universes, what must you do?"

"Of course," Enoda said, "you need to expose the dustbunny. And to do that, you've got to *move the sofa.*"

"That's what the distorters are for," Grice concluded. "They are meant to relocate that incredibly massive black hole."

"Precisely," Reidkr said. "Exposing the dustbunny will create a highly unstable situation. Lint theory says a naked dustbunny is impossible – it will literally be intolerable for local spacetime to contain such an object – but we're going to have one anyway. And *that* will generate the trans-cosmic bridge through which our contact party will punch through into the universe where you folks have determined the anomalies may have come from."

"The audacity is breathtaking," Enoda said eventually.

Reidkr nodded. "If you'll excuse me, I must attend to another bit of critical flying." She made once more for her command chair.

Grice resumed her own seat. She leaned as close as she could to Enoda and Computer. "Could it possibly work?" she whispered.

"It might work," Computer said softly. "Or it might blow a nice spherical hole in our Galaxy that they'll see from Andromeda. I predicted that we could rely on the Confetory to test the most needlessly elaborate and dangerous method first. I am not disappointed."

"Wait one moment," Enoda growled. He locked eyes with Grice. "It's been just two months since you came to us at Standoff World with the missing-socks problem. It's only been about six weeks since we were briefed on the gravitic disturbances, most of which had just occurred. Does it make sense that this brief window of time was enough for the Confetory to cobble this immense platform together, much less come anywhere near working out all the devilish new physics it entails?"

"No sense at all," Computer agreed. "Of course we cannot know how long they've been pursuing a capability to punch into sibling universes. Out here amid all this static, we cannot wonk the history of secret research projects."

Grice shrugged. "We could just ask. Captain Reidkr! These technologies seem much too thoroughly developed to be the response to a crisis detected less than two months ago."

"Oh, of course," Reidkr answered from the pilothouse. "The platform's superstructure was slammed together in record time from whatever discarded hulls came to hand. The largest stardrives ever built were surplus from an ultra-dreadnought development program that got shelved two standard years ago. But the physics packages – they'd been in development over several years. My orders are to tell you anything you want to know; I don't know what this means, but the core technologies were being developed for use at a place called Standoff World."

Enoda and Grice exchanged astounded glances. As one, they turned their gazes toward Computer, who responded aloud in the polarized voice only they could hear. "Now there's a strategy I never foresaw – to skirt our planetary defenses by slipping into *another forjeling universe*, then back into ours on the surface, under all our shields."

Grice leaned forward. With one hand she clasped one of Enoda's wrists. She flattened the other against

Computer's shielding. "Okay, guys, just promise me one thing. Your number-one goal is to make sure this project *doesn't* blow a hole in the Galaxy they'll spot from Andromeda, right?"

Enoda rotated his wrist within her grip until he could grasp her wrist as she did his. "Staying alive is very high on my personal priority list. Fortunately, saving the Galaxy should be an excellent way to achieve that."

"Oh plorg on a stick," Computer wheezed. "We have to save the Galaxy *again*?"

"If I can have everyone's attention," Reidkr called. Her hands were dancing over controls. Bank after bank of indicators and control surfaces were going dark. "We'll be docking with *Luskus Delph* shortly. Inside the hull an even wider range of vibrionics, old-school electronics, and other automation will be disabled than is the case out here, so I'm shutting down almost everything in preparation for a full-manual approach." Levers and hand-wheels rose from the pilothouse floor; a physical sighting frame dropped over the forward window, its pane a reticle crammed with spidery contours and arcs and notations. Reidkr twisted levers, her eyes on the sighting frame. "We're still awaiting arrival of a few more team members. You'll have time to settle in, and access to a handful of communications channels protected against the platform's noise levels. Assuming everyone arrives on schedule, the day after tomorrow I will brief you along with all the leaders of the contact and support teams."

Reidkr glanced over her shoulder, favoring Computer with a chuckle and an ironic glance. "At that briefing, you'll get to the meet the people in charge of kicking ass. *And* the ones in charge of taking names."

Chapter 42

September 24, 2367
Bohrkk, the Scrub Forest

"I wish we'd done more." Takander Thurnb held out his two bulky hands.

The emissary from The Others clasped Thurnb's hands in his much weaker ones. A two-count later, he broke the contact as though he'd been gripping molten steel.

"Do you have to leave now?" Thurnb asked. "There's so much else we could talk about."

"Really, ahhh, there isn't," the emissary said thinly.

"Do you know, the Sky Ladder will not summon us here again for more than four years? Truly we should make the most of this parley."

The emissary scratched at his animal-skin doublet with his mangled left hand. "I should leave while I can – that is, goodbye." He nodded, turned, and scuttled for the steep hillside that led toward his homeland. His lute, if that was what it was, hung upside-down across his back.

Reaching the bluff, the emissary began uncertainly to climb. As he struggled up the ridge face, Thurnb couldn't shake the conviction that he could hear the man sobbing.

Thurnb stretched out his arms. Beckoned with curling fingers. The scrub forest behind him puked out people; three dozen Warriors hurled themselves into serried rows behind their Shan. Less hurriedly, Alrue Latier, his wives Zuzenah and Abigayl, and Meryam stepped across the clearing beside the parley cottage to gather at Thurnb's side.

Thurnb's gaze encompassed Latier and the women. "Speak freely," he said. "What did you observe?"

Zuzenah spoke first. "The Other's behavior seemed irrational. When enemies parley, both sides usually strive to display equal power. Yet this Other accepted grossly unequal security conditions. You came with three dozen Warriors who surrounded the parley house; the emissary came alone. He let your Warriors search him and his possessions. If you had ordered his death, not only was he defenseless, his people might never have learned of it."

"I wondered about that myself," Thurnb said evenly, pulling off his onyx-trimmed leather gloves and stuffing them into a bag at his belt. "Maybe it's good that I'm a man of honor."

Meryam spoke next. "When the emissary came here with his escorts, they all rode *svadi* moose. Yet when the escorts retreated, they took the emissary's moose with them. Maybe they left it for him somewhere out of sight. Otherwise, it's curious that they all rode *here*, but the emissary will have to get wherever he's going next on foot."

"Based on small clues in the emissary's clothing and behavior, we believe The Others don't raise crops as your People do; they just herd, hunt, and gather," said Alrue conspiratorially. "They probably ignore requests to trade land because they need all they have just to live on."

Thurnb jerked his chin up and to the right. "Strangers of light – all of you – you see far."

"Another puzzle was the emissary's demeanor," noted Abigayl.

Thurnb raised an eyebrow at the prospect of analysis from a seven-year-old. "His what, dear?"

"His affect." Seeing she still wasn't understood, she tried again. "His mood. It was so horribly dark."

"Every moment he was with us, he was terrified," Meryam added. "I mean a literal, physical state of panic.

230

The body's instinctive response to that kind of dread is to fight or flee. He did neither; he just sat there and despaired."

"You surmise this?" Thurnb asked, carefully rolling up his feathered stole.

Meryam pumped her head up and down, the gesture of denial. "I know it."

Alrue leaned close to the hulking leader. "Mighty Shan, she can read the heat of someone's blood from afar."

"A useful skill." Thurnb breathed deeply. "But why should he be terrified *and* miserable? It makes no sense."

"Exactly," offered Abigayl. "He should be satisfied. He met with you. He agreed to nothing, which was apparently his task. He should look forward to a hero's welcome when he gets home."

"But instead," Zuzenah summed up, "he carried himself as if he were on a suicide mission he didn't believe in."

"The power of these observations!" Thurnb raised an eyebrow. "Now that you say this, I am recognizing something. For as long as I've been coming to these parleys, the emissaries have always seemed the same way."

"Emissaries?" Alrue echoed. "Plural?"

Thurnb nodded grimly. "A different man each time. At every parley I say 'Next time I want to meet your chief.' Every next time, they send another nobody. Each one petrified, each deep in despair just as you described – I see that now. But enough of that." He clutched Alrue's shoulder. "Come with me."

Chapter 43

Brûh Reidkr pressed her skeletal arms forward, spreading lean brown hands flat upon the nine-sided idocrase conference table. Its tetragonal crystals and thready yellow-green inclusions glistened in the briefing room's harsh downlight. "With the arrival of Doctor Qgalda, all team leaders are present. Welcome to the research platform *Luskus Delph;* after everyone is introduced I will answer any questions in my capacity as Team Commander. To begin, I present two entities whose names you may recall from the Arbadrel affair twenty-odd years ago. The one floating above the table, unencumbered by limbs, a face, or protoplasm, is Computer – yes, that is his full name; and yes, he is by convention male."

"Actually, I flipped a coin," Computer whirred. "Not even sim, a physical coin. I thought choosing a gender was that important."

"He is the Galaxy's only thought engine also fully recognized as a person," Reidkr continued, flustered. "In view of his extraordinary calculating power, and because he is able to retain at least some of that power in *Luskus Delph*'s noisy environment, he will serve as our program's principal thought engine and supply other capabilities as needed. To Computer's left, Gram Enoda, the machine's bonded trendrider; together Hom Enoda and Hom Computer constitute what may be the Galaxy's most powerful intelligence. For that reason Hom Enoda will be our specialist in the unexpected."

Enoda nodded to the others around the table. He still wore the incongruous ensemble of dark blue tunic, electric blue leggings, and maroon boots he'd been issued before debarking from *Isolation.*

Reidkr continued the introductions. "Doctor Magdalene Zonofne, Senior Physicist for Team Cave."

A burly olive-skinned woman with dead-white hair cut in a severe pageboy, Zonofne wore a stylized electric-blue lab coat over a maroon bodysuit. TEAM CAVE shimmered three-dimensionally over her lab coat's left breast. Her small brown-black eyes seemed regal. "Hello, all. You might say dustbunnies are my business."

"To her left, Doctor Arl Qgalda," Reidkr said, "Senior Physicist for Team Sofa."

Qgalda had mahogany skin, a slender hawk nose, and flowing golden-red hair. His lab coat-and-bodysuit uniform was identical to Zonofne's, save for the glistening emblem; his said TEAM SOFA. "Good daypart, all. I look forward to consuming more power than any single undertaking in the history of the human species."

The woman to Qgalda's left slapped one powerful golden hand onto the tabletop in dissent. Her clothing was strikingly different than that of the other two physicists: over her maroon bodysuit she wore a sculpted brass breastplate decorated with reliefs of shrieking birds. Two gaudy green feathers hung next to her left ear, rooted in wavy jet-black hair that swept down her back almost to her waist. Upon a midnight-blue armband spanning her right bicep flickered the phrase TEAM MOVERS. "Correction. Tiresome as it may be, my metrical distorters will outdraw your spatial resonators by three orders of magnitude."

Qgalda pursed his lips. "True in one sense. But your devices rely mostly on borrowed energy, tapped from nearby stars or from the stardrives' energy of motion. If you look at power *generated* for a specific purpose –"

"That will do," Reidkr said peremptorily. "I present Doctor Rugebeld Gale-Forgirt, Senior Physicist for Team Movers. As you may have deduced from her clothing, Doctor Gale-Forgirt hails from Ghyrel Two and is a diplomate of that world's venerable Order of the Druhel."

"I salute you, Gentlefem Gale-Forgirt," Computer chirruped. "'Team Movers?' That is curious nomenclature."

Gale-Forgirt nodded almost imperceptibly toward the machine. "Assuming Doctor Qgalda and his team actually synthesize a sofa, my team has the, as some see it, *tedious* assignment of moving it."

"Enough ego-jousting," Reidkr growled. "Next we have Lieutenant Avu Wincenc, our Exocultural Analyst."

Wincenc nodded to her counterparts around the idocrase table. Wincenc looked young – no more than forty-five. She was lanky and athletic with brown skin, kinky hair, and arresting grey eyes. She wore a variant on the standard duty jumpsuit, deep blue on one side, medium blue on the other, accented in maroon. "If we find someone on the other side, it's my job to establish communication."

"A mere lieutenant?" Gale-Forgirt sneered.

Wincenc shrugged. "Humans have always been alone in the Galaxy; once one realizes that one needs an exocultural analyst, there aren't a lot of us to choose from."

"Leading the info team, Historian Sgiela Harbraeskor," Reidkr said.

Harbraeskor was slight, golden-skinned and sandy-haired. His uniform's design suggested an academic robe cut from some soft green fabric and trimmed with muted golden piping. In a Galaxy that took surgical ocular enhancement for granted, Harbraeskor wore the ultimate affectation: old-fashioned spectacles, their streaked trifocal lenses encased in brass wire frames. He gave those around the table a grandfatherly nod.

"Your title is Historian?" Enoda asked.

"Yes, yes, precisely. Team Info boasts a most eclectic mix of specialties. Thought-engine techs aren't of much use on a platform where thought engines don't function."

"Ahem," Computer interjected.

"On a platform where *other* thought engines don't function," Harbraeskor corrected. "So the *Luskus Delph* info team includes historians like myself, as well as experimentalists, innovators, improvisers, and educators. We tinker with ancient analogue and mechanical computing devices, trying to see how much of the functionality of more conventional data apparatus we can emulate using the contraptions capable of operating amid all this noise."

A warrant officer circled the table, setting a trapezoidal frame the size of two spread hands before each meeting participant. Inside each frame beads of different color were suspended on fine wires that were spaced irregularly but arrayed in three distinct layers.

"Each of you has been issued a Ghelttian abacus," Harbraeskor said. "You'll be surprised how many calculations it will perform. I mentioned that Team Info includes educators; may I present Junior Info Tech Lii Bardicon, our instructional dynamicist."

A young woman smiled and bowed slightly to each person seated about the nine-sided table. She wore a plain medium-blue duty jumpsuit adorned only by a teach-tech's slim shoulder sling. She had olive skin, round grey eyes, straight brown hair tied back in a tight bun, and a full round nose above thinnish lips gathered in a perpetual pout. Her body was on the rounded side; plump breasts bulged exuberantly over a just slightly protuberant midriff. The overall effect was sensuous, overripe.

"Very pleased to meet you," Wincenc said, bowing in her seat.

Bardicon fiddled with a small metallic box from which she unfolded articulated wire legs. "This is a miniature multi-subject didactic imposer," she said. "It's unknown why this sort of machine operates when ostensibly simpler devices are crippled, but imposers definitely work aboard *Luskus Delph*." She set the contraption near the center of the table. "Give me the next four seconds, and you'll all become expert users of the Ghelttian abacus. Well, except Hom Computer."

The imposer flickered and quietly beeped.

Reidkr gestured for everyone's attention. "Regarding the noise levels – aside from Doctor Qgalda, who has just arrived, the rest of you have had varying lengths of time aboard *Luskus Delph* in which to discover the stark limits on ordinary technologies that prevail here."

Doctor Qgalda laid down his abacus, over which his fingers had been darting as though he'd been using the contrivance for years. "What do you know," he said with satisfied amazement. "I just derived a third-order hexanomial function. This thing really works."

Reidkr nodded. "Simple technologies are often best here."

Doctor Gale-Forgirt glowered in Computer's direction. "If thought engines don't work here, then what is this machine?"

"I am shielded in ways that even distinguished physicists such as yourself might have difficulty grasping," Computer whirred. Obligingly he projected dense clusters of mathematical calculations into the air above his body. "This is a compressed summary of one of the new masking algorithms I had to develop in order to be able to continue functioning in *Luskus Delph* space. I have three hundred seventeen such algorithms running continuously, and even so I have access to only about one-twentieth of my usual repertoire of processes." Doctors Zonofne, Qgalda, and Gale-Forgirt leaned forward in their seats, eyes wide, mouths agape like matched statuettes. Enoda smiled thinly. Computer terminated the mathematical display. "In any case, this is why I am able to run at all in this most taxing environment – and why so much of the technology you usually rely on will not be available to you here."

"It's a dismal milieu, we agree on that," grumbled Doctor Gale-Forgirt. "How long must we remain?"

"That depends how long it takes to create the dustbunny, move the sofa, and produce the trans-cosmic bridge," Reidkr said with an air of finality. "We estimate six to eight months minimum. No doubt you physicists will need the first part of that time, working with Team Info, to determine which of your usual intelligently automated systems are absolutely necessary, then to develop manual or semiautomatic substitutes able to emulate them under *Luskus Delph* conditions."

Shortly after that the meeting ended. The three physicists hurried out through three of the twelve-sided chamber's portals; Bardicon and, a few beats later, Wincenc exited through a fourth. Shuffling slowly, Harbraeskor drifted through a fifth. With a gesture, Team Commander Reidkr bid Enoda and Computer stay behind.

"So, our first team-leader meeting," Reidkr said tiredly when they were alone. "Your analysis?"

"Could have been worse," Computer buzzed.

Chapter 44

September 24, 2367
Bohrkk, the Scrub Forest

Shan Takander Thurnb led Alrue Latier into the scrub forest, out of earshot of Alrue's women –out of earshot even of his own Warriors. They stopped on an expanse of corduroy stone where no ferkeeks could lurk. Thurnb rummaged in a bag at his belt and produced a hank of dried meat. He tore off a chunk with his teeth and held it out for Alrue to do the same. As gracefully as he could, Alrue declined the honor. "We should speak about what comes next for you," Thurnb said gruffly, jamming the meat back into his bag.

"How do you mean?"

"I owe you and your women a Debt for your services today," Thurnb explained. "You've been among us long enough to know that Debt is a serious matter, yes?"

"Your Warrior captain told me something about it."

You're a Debtholder now. That's a problem, because as a guest among the People you have no firm place. You need a role that all can recognize."

"I see," Alrue said as firmly as he could. "You are wise to prevent even the possibility of jarrings, and contentions, and envyings, and strifes, and lustful and covetous desires. Better that all things be transparent, so that there may be great joy and peace, yea, much preaching and many prophecies."

"Something like that," said Thurnb. "Now here's the problem. There only two estates for you to belong to. You must be Wisdom or Warrior." Thurnb slapped a gentle backhand against Alrue's ample midsection. "You don't seem the Warrior to me."

"You would have me join Wisdom?" Alrue said, puzzled. "But that's the estate you belong to."

"It's the estate I lead," Thurnb clarified. "Wisdom has room for newcomers."

"I am honored," Alrue said, smiling broadly. "What must I do?"

"First, you need to learn more about our ways."

"Fair enough."

"Then —"Thurnb flashed a vicious grin – "you'll need to take your Wisdom Quest."

"Is that like a Warrior's Journey?"

Thurnb pumped his head up and down. "The Wisdom Quest is different: no fasting, no sacred drugs, no meeting your ancestors."

They entered a small clearing.

The Shan stopped and gestured toward its other side. "Know what that is?"

Alrue's face wrinkled. "A *svadi* moose. Quite dead." The decomposing body sagged against a peeling tree trunk. Insects swarmed the carcass. Matted fur slumped over protruding bones.

"What killed it?" Thurnb asked.

Alrue recognized the gaping, shattered jaw caked with blood long dried. "A ferkeek."

"So you know one way a moose can die. Good." Thurnb leaned against another trunk and farted loudly, an act he apparently found deeply satisfying. "I've been thinking," he said at last. "After five years of service – assuming he doesn't die – any Warrior can apply to take a Wisdom Quest. Not all do. Some are afraid. Some try the Quest and don't come back."

"The Quest has dangers, then?" Alrue asked doubtfully.

Thurnb snorted. "What kind of Quest would it be without dangers? But a Warrior of five years has one other option – to stay as he is. He may like the Warrior way, or the life in Wisdom may not appeal to him. Once a Warrior makes a public refusal to seek elevation, Wisdom is closed to him forever."

Alrue nodded. Then he remembered to jerk his chin up and to the right instead. "And you're telling me this, mighty Shan, so that I might learn the ways of the People?"

Thurnb laughed. "I am not your teacher, stranger of light. I tell you these things so you can understand who I've decided *will* teach you – if you'll have him." Thurnb began to meander across the clearing, Alrue at his side. "My Warrior captain Nirom Fpod has eleven years at arms. He long ago decided he would remain a Warrior, so now he can never rise to Wisdom. That makes him a proper choice to advise someone who *is* a Wisdom candidate. And as he prepares you for the Quest, I think he can teach you much about life among the People."

"From what I've seen of him, Fpod is an excellent man," Alrue agreed. "I'd be proud to – what the sfelb!" He jumped back, staring pop-eyed at the dead moose.

Three round masses, each the size of a child's fist, moved jerkily beneath the animal's drooping skin.

Thurnb laughed. "You've never seen a moose that's been dead for weeks, then." He gestured toward the moving lumps. "Those are the kits, the offspring left behind by the ferkeek that killed this moose. They're inside – moving, growing – when they're ready to join the world, they'll eat their way out."

"For someone not my teacher, you have many lessons for me," Alrue said weakly. They ambled back into the woods. "This Quest thing, is it truly dangerous?"

"Yes."

"Um, is it necessary?"

"Absolutely!" Thurnb clapped a meaty hand on Alrue's shoulder. "Here is the way of the Wisdom Quest. You march into the wilderness, well-fed and with a clear

240

mind. You'll take with you only some walking sticks, minimal gear, and an escort guide – I expect you'll choose to keep Captain Fpod. And oh yes, you will take the magical weapon."

Alrue cocked an eyebrow. "Magical weapon?"

Thurnb held his hands about twenty-five centimeters apart. "It's about this long, shaped like a cone. You use it to – well, Fpod will tell you about that. We call it the *rains red.*"

Alrue nodded, baffled. "The *rains red,* yes. And what magical thing does it do?"

Thurnb had led them in a circle. They re-entered the clearing; the moose carcass lay almost at their feet. "You have seen one of these alive?"

"A *svadi* moose? Oh, yes."

"And I gather you've seen one die." Thurnb clapped Alrue on the shoulder so hard he almost knocked the Mormon to the ground. "On the Wisdom Quest you will *make* one die – though you won't use a ferkeek." From his bag Thurnb drew a small gourd stoppered with a blackened cork. He pulled the cork with his teeth and took a surprisingly precise sip. He held the gourd out; Alrue intuited that unlike the dried meat, this was an offering he must not spurn.

When he lifted the gourd to his lips Thurnb gleefully jostled him; a great quaff of the contents splashed into Alrue's mouth. It was the harshest liquid Alrue had ever tasted. "O the goodness and condescension of God!" he rasped. After gawping like a fish for several seconds, he smiled broadly at Thurnb and lied, "That's *good!*"

Thurnb eyed him appraisingly. "Stranger of light, you may be more ready for the Wisdom Quest than you know."

Alrue wasn't sure why Thurnb regarded him in such a fashion, but it made him uncomfortable.

"When your time comes," Thurnb resumed,"with your escort guide, your minimal equipment, and your *rains red,* you will venture out into the wilderness, find a living moose, and – " He made a spreading gesture with his bulky hands. "Poof!"

"Poof?"

"Well, it's usually louder than that." Thurnb put a thick arm around Alrue's shoulders. "For your Wisdom Quest, your challenge will be to go out into the wilderness … and blow up a moose."

Chapter 45

Exocultural Analyst Avu Wincenc smiled. "Room for one more?"

"I'm headed forward," said Junior Info Tech Lii Bardicon.

"Great, me too." Wincenc stepped down into the transit pod and took a seat across from Bardicon's. The pod was a ten-seater; they were the sole passengers. The pod's carapace accordioned shut and it lurched into motion for a journey halfway across the immense research platform, taking them away from the site of the introductory meeting. "I was surprised to hear you introduced as an educator," Wincenc said. "Didn't I read that you have Spectator implants?"

Bardicon's brows knit in momentary puzzlement. "Oh, yes, OmNet thought I had promise – just long enough to fit me with some very basic implants and then see me wash out of their Academy. Fortunately I did better in instructional dynamics." She frowned. "Wait a minute, did you review my C. V.?"

"Sure. The C. V. of every *Luskus Delph* team member is available for review by anyone aboard. As a hard printout, of course."

"You're an enterprising one."

"Think of me as motivated." Wincenc smiled mysteriously. "Instructional dynamics – what's that, exactly?"

"Managing speed-learning – using broad-field didactic imposers to instruct large groups. As the rest of Team Info develops new manual and mechanical systems, my job is teaching folks how to use them." Abruptly she realized how intently Wincenc was staring at her ample breasts. "Lieutenant, if you are forming a romantic interest in me –"

Wincenc's smile did not waver. "You do me an injustice." Suddenly Wincenc's mind was pressing against Bardicon's, flowing into an arena of awareness normally reserved for Spectator self-monitoring. Bardicon hadn't even tried looking there since Spectator Academy. Into it Wincenc projected a flashident of her security clearance.

Bardicon eyed Wincenc appraisingly. "Those are way higher security clearances than a lieutenant ought to need – even a lieutenant with a fancy title. And you projected into my mind through my dormant Spectator interface. That means you're either a Spectator yourself, or you're military intelligence."

"Mil-intel," Wincenc confirmed. "Rather, I used to be. But I still have the clearances and I still have the subdelta-band implants. Don't worry, elementary comm is pretty much all I can do with them."

Bardicon eyed him intensely. "What is this about?"

Wincenc laid the fingers of her right hand loosely across Bardicon's left wrist. "Don't take this wrong, but it's personal. I noticed you as soon as you came aboard."

"I bet." Bardicon pulled her wrist from beneath Wincenc's fingers. Wincenc did not try to stop her.

"Not like that. I was in the docking bay quite by chance when your flitter arrived. The moment you debarked, I recognized you." Wincenc's eyes seemed to mist over. "I mean, how could I not?"

"But you don't know me."

"You're right, I don't know Lii Bardicon. And that's the problem."

"At the next stop I am getting out," she said tautly.

"You need to understand *my* problem," Wincenc countered. "I'm no longer active-duty mil-intel, but I'm duty-bound to defend *Luskus Delph* and its mission.

244

What am I to make of it when one of this project's info techs is not who she says she is?"

"What in forjel are you talking about?"

Wincenc reached toward Bardicon's wrists with both hands, thought better of it, and displayed her upraised palms. "You're *not* Lii Bardicon. I know you as Amli Revskond, the senso artist. You're famous, if only among those who follow the alt-arts scene closely."

"And you do," she said doubtfully.

"As it happens. I've long admired your work. And as I said, I recognized you on sight."

"Has it ever occurred to you that you might have misidentified me?"

"In this case, no." The pod swished to a stop. Its carapace retracted. Before Bardicon could rise from her seat, Wincenc leaned toward her, eyes blazing. "Amli Revskond, what are you doing here?"

Chapter 46

Nataleah slid open the access hatch at the top of the ladder. Meryam Mayishimu followed her onto a service platform of split logs. They sat facing each other on the roof of the tenement city. The crater rim yawned above them with its dependent hoop of reflector panels. Beneath them stretched the People's Ground, log cottages and root cellars, stone-rimmed wells and rock-walled granaries, torch-lit pathways and grazing pastures sloping up to the crater walls. "Are we supposed to be up here?" Meryam asked.

"I'm wife to Alrue," Nataleah replied. "I can be where I like."

Meryam's features rippled as she went into Mode – *suck, rush, wrench!* "I suppose you know the question," she began.

"Alrue – how'd I meet him, why'd I marry him?" Nataleah shrugged. "First, you should know a little something about my family. You worked on Calluron Five, no?"

"Yes."

"Whereabouts?"

"Outside Cal City – the Erbyl Mountains, near the spaceport."

Nataleah smiled. "You probably heard about the Huntingtons, then."

"Local lore said they were crazy – wait, that was your family?"

"No offense taken. People did call us crazy." Black curls trembled against Nataleah's chalky complexion as she laughed. "We were strict Mormons – my Grandpap Zeb used to quarrel with the mainstream LDS church for making too many compromises with the world. At least that's how he saw things. One example: he thought Mormons should be way more uncomfortable than most were about – you know, about not being white."

Meryam frowned. "Nobody's white. Well, about eight percent of Terrans are. The phenotype occurs nowhere else in the Galaxy."

"But Mormonism was a religion of Terran whites. You've learned your Book of Mormon; remember Third Nephi 2:14-16? One small group of the evil, dark-skinned Lamanites had shifted their loyalty to the righteous, white-skinned Nephites, and what happened next?"

"'And their curse was taken from them,'" Meryam quoted, "'and their skin became white like unto the Nephites; And their young men and their daughters became exceedingly fair ...' Forjeler, that's still *in* there? I thought those old racist verses were removed long before the Galactic Encounter."

"Only some of them," Nataleah explained. "Others escaped unchanged, and Grandpap knew them all. There was no mistaking their meaning: white was delightsome, black was loathsome." Nataleah stood up. "And what were we Huntingtons?" Rapid gestures encompassed her full lips and broad nose; her kinky, almost frizzy, hair; her full rounded buttocks. "Of course, when Alrue proclaimed his New Restoration, he took the faith back to its first days. He restored the Book of Mormon to its original form."

Meryam frowned. "Racism and all."

"Do you know how seriously Terran Mormons once took those passages?" Nataleah demanded, pacing. "Some mid-twentieth century Mormons claimed that when native Americans accepted Book of Mormon teachings, their skin color actually lightened. When my papa Parley Huntington joined Alrue's church, he knew just what to do. The Huntington men had been misers; there was plenty of money, and he spent some of it on cosmo surgery for himself, our mother, his later wives, and all nine of us kids." She lowered herself back to sit facing Meryam. "We all became – what's the phrase? – white and delightsome."

Meryam's eyebrows angled up. "He changed your skin color?"

"He would've changed more, but he didn't know what else to fix. It's not like we lived in one of the resorts and mixed with a lot of offworlders. Plus, we shunned mass media. So he had no real idea what white Terrans looked like. We lost most of our skin pigmentation, but retained all the other features that Terrans would recognize as, um, probably west African." She held her white hands out toward Meryam, palms down. With a theatrical gesture she turned them over. Her palms were even whiter – fish-belly white, the turnip white of dead tissue bleached by the sun. "That's us Huntingtons. We wound up looking like no one else in the Galaxy."

Meryam knit her fingers. "I don't know what to say."

Nataleah leaned forward almost conspiratorially. "When I was nineteen or twenty, Alrue brought his first mission to Calluron Five – and believe me, he knew at one glance who his most passionate followers were. Alrue hadn't been groundside three days before Papa Parley had him visiting our farm homestead every other day, sometimes more. There were five of us young daughters; all but the youngest had watched Alrue go through the Parek affair on tridee, and now here he was sharing meals with us. We were in awe."

Meryam nodded. "Five young daughters, but you were the one he married."

"I was just the second of the five to marry, though I was the second-youngest and far from the most beautiful. Two of my older sisters were just stunning."

"So it came as a surprise within the family?"

"You could say that. I was the plain sister, first picked for chores, last picked for anything fun or – perish the thought! – in any way exalted. I spent a lot of my childhood in my own head. Some folks think that made me a schemer."

"So, did you scheme your marriage to Alrue? Was it, I don't know, the culmination of your master plan to escape from the family?"

"Exactly the opposite. Actually, it's on here." Nataleah reached into her inmate tunic and hauled up a tiny metal tubule on an almost invisibly thin chain. It gleamed blue. "This is a microwafer. My papa Parley was so edgy and suspicious, he recorded absolutely everything. Believe it or not, this holds his recording of Alrue's proposal."

"Your father recorded Alrue proposing to you?"

"Oh no, Alrue was always a proper Mormon, he proposed to my father." Nataleah laughed. "I don't mean he *proposed* to my *father* – why, that would be abomination! I mean – oh yes, that's the phrase – he asked my father for my hand."

"And you have a recording of that." Meryam wrinkled her eyebrows. "Which you wear around your neck."

Nataleah smiled sheepishly. "I enjoy watching it now and then. Of course I haven't been able to since the punitorium collapsed. With all that Spectator gear you carry – maybe you can play it for us both?"

"You've got top-of-the-line implants, right?" At Nataleah's nod, Meryam maneuvered herself to sit close beside her. She took the microwafer between thumb and forefinger and polled her onboard systems. "Okay," she said after a moment, "just stay very close and we'll watch it together."

Suck, rush, wrench!

***

Parley Huntington and Alrue Latier shared a wooden swing on the porch of Parley's gently swaybacked farmhouse. "Pink lemonade?" Parley offered, picking an errant bit of grain from his faded work clothes. He had the features of a Bantu chieftain and the complexion of a sickly Icelander.

"Thank you, no," said Alrue.

"Some Jell-O mold, perhaps?"

"Couldn't dream of it; I just ate."

The swing creaked. Forward. Backward.

"You said you wanted to ask me something," Parley said tonelessly.

"In the Lord's due time."

Forward. Backward.

"Suit yourself, First Elder Alrue. But come sunset, I'll have to go and milk the *sphkettlak*."

Muted expressions flickered across Alrue's face. For one who knew him as well as Meryam did, their meaning was unmistakable: the prophet, seer, and revelator was struggling to ratchet up his courage. "Can't help but admire your daughters," Alrue said at last. "That Nataleah, she's a stunning beauty."

Parley's jaw set weirdly. "If you say so."

Alrue's next words came in a rush. "Behold, Hom Huntington, it has come to pass that I would like to ask for your daughter's hand in marriage."

"That being Nataleah," Parley said after a moment.

"Nataleah, yes."

Parley concentrated very hard on a crack in his right thumbnail. "And this is what you want?"

Now there was a question Alrue had an answer for. Suddenly confident, he leaned toward Parley, clamping

250

one hand on the older man's forearm. "Yes, but not that only. I have a vision from the Lord that your girl Nataleah is to become one of my wives."

The swing stopped moving.

"A vision from the Lord, you say," Parley said slowly.

"An angel appeared to me to say that. More than once, in fact."

"Twice, then?"

"More than twice."

Parley eyed Alrue narrowly. "Would that be three times, then?"

Alrue nodded. "Three times, yes, that exactly. The first about a month ago. The angel was most forceful, insomuch as he told me I must marry your Nataleah or he would kill me."

"The angel," Parley said tonelessly. "Said he'd kill you."

"Yes. After which he said he would hurl my soul down into everlasting misery and endless wo."

"Wo, you say. Unless you married my girl Nataleah."

"Yes, yes."

"So then – what kept you?"

"It harrows one up," Alrue temporized, "to know that one must come and see a man and tell him that yea, one must marry his most beautiful daughter or an angel will, well, you know."

"Kill you."

"Yes."

Parley nodded dismissively. "So that was your first vision."

"Oh no, I've had lots of –"

"I mean your first vision of this particular angel, determined as he was to see you marry into this family on pain of death and all."

251

Alrue tugged at his temple garment. "Yes, yes. The second vision, that was about a week ago. On that occasion the angel had drawn his sword."

"This would be one of those angels who walks about wearing a sword, then."

"I suppose so. Or I suppose he could fly with it on."

"His sword, you mean."

"Yes."

"Makes sense, him being an angel and all."

Forward. Backward. Forward.

"And still," said Parley evenly, "you didn't come to me with your request."

Backward.

"This morning, that was my third vision," Alrue stammered. "This time the angel had puffed himself up to three, maybe four meters tall. And his sword –"

"Still waving that around, was he?"

"Yes, but now it was on fire."

"A flaming sword, then."

"Verily. The angel said that if I was not betrothed to Nataleah today, he should take my life. After which I should be cast out, and consigned to partake of the fruits of my labor and my works, which in light of my failure to obey the angel, will have been evil; and I will drink the dregs of a bitter cup."

"And here you are."

Alrue nodded. "And so I ask for your daughter's hand. 'Behold, I speak with boldness, having authority from God.'"

"I don't know as 'boldness' is the word I'd use," Parley mused.

Backward. Forward.

Alrue ran thick hands through his sweaty brownish hair. "So what is your answer, Hom Huntington?"

"Before I answer, I have questions of my own. What can you offer my daughter?"

"A comfortable life, as I imagine you know. A man's true love." Alrue shrugged. "And, oh yes – salvation."

Parley's eyes widened. "Salvation, you say."

"I wouldn't be much of prophet, seer, and revelator if I couldn't bring mine own into God's heaven when the time is nigh, now would I? 'All that God gives me I shall take with me, for I have that authority and that power conferred upon me.'"

"That's right impressive, salvation," Parley said. "One last question, then. Your senior wife –Zuzenah, is she not?"

"The very same."

"Does Zuzenah know that this angel demands that you should take my Nataleah to wife?"

What Alrue's reply lacked in relevance it more than made up for in sheer bravado. "Zuzenah thinks the world of Nataleah."

With an index finger Parley worried at the socket of his missing front tooth; his retrogressive tendencies extended to dentistry also. Seeing Nataleah sealed to Alrue Latier would solve the question of how to marry off an otherwise difficult daughter. Behind that was a bittersweet note of – regret? – that even in reverie was difficult to parse. "I reckon your proposal is accepted." He held out the hand whose finger had swept his empty socket, the finger still saliva-shiny, for Alrue to shake.

Instead Alrue stood bolt upright, staring at something beyond the porch, his features flushed with love and victory. The tridee pickup whirled to see what he'd beheld.

Coming up the flagstone walk was a young woman of startling grace and beauty. So winsome was she, so perfectly proportioned, that the Huntington discord between coloring and features only lent her an exotic air.

253

"You are the love of my life, Nataleah –" Alrue began.

"Hush now," said Parley. "That's my next-youngest daughter, Presendia."

Alrue's eyes saucered. "But she's the one I – I mean, I thought –"

Parley took Alrue by the arm and led him inside. "Come along, I'll introduce you to Nataleah."

The tridee pickup took flight, bobbing along behind Parley and Alrue until they found Nataleah. Sweaty, greasy-haired, Nataleah was on her hands and knees pushing and pulling a scrub brush across the kitchen floor.

Backward. Forward.

"Nataleah!" Parley called sharply. "Stand up and say hello to your new husband. Sent here at sword's point by an angel of the Lord, he says, for no other purpose but to be yours forever."

Nataleah stood, brushing at herself. She wore the Huntington weirdnesses less like her sister Presendia had, and more like her father did. Which was to say, deeply weirdly.

The pickup circled the room to capture the parade of facial contortions that succeeded one another upon Alrue's visage. There was disappointment, clearly, even revulsion – furious anger, too, at himself for having demanded a wife by name before being sure which of Parley Huntington's daughters was which.

The meaning of those expressions was unambiguous for Meryam.

Of course, Nataleah had contrived to understand this part of her old recording differently. "I love this part," she rhapsodized to Meryam. "He's so filled with love for me, his face doesn't know how to hold onto it all."

Chapter 47

June 10, 2376
Aboard *Luskus Delph*

Pamela Grice and Captain Brûh Reidkr negotiated a corridor seemingly improvised from flexible ribbed tubing. Every two hundred meters or so they had to negotiate a guarded security checkpoint. "So many technologies we take for granted don't work in here," Reidkr complained. "No proper servo-mech automation, as you've seen. Springs, air, and counterweights in place of anything requiring machine intelligence."

They approached a sealed, unattended hatch. Reidkr pressed her palm against an oblong glass panel, which flickered briefly. Five seconds later the hatch sighed open on a roar of compressed air. "Another example: there's no automated visual surveillance on *Luskus Delph*," Reidkr commented as they passed through. "No video recording technology can stand the noise." Mammoth springs closed the portal behind them. "Here's one more: there's no real personal intraship communication, just an audio-only intercom system tied to fixed wall-mounted annunciators. You already know that thought engines don't work on board, aside from your friend Computer with his extraordinary shielding. That's forced us into some of the most absurd manual workarounds."

A strolling guard paced toward them down the corridor. Before they passed, the guard drew up beside a small analogue card reader and slipped her ID into it. "You're kidding," Grice half-whispered to Reidkr. "A watchclock station to verify that the guard completes her rounds?"

Shrugging, Reidkr stepped up to an expanse of blank wall broken by a single small joystick. She wiggled the stick in a complex pattern; a hatch wheezed open on spring-loaded gearing, revealing a metallic combination lock.

"Now I've seen it all," Grice said. "Did you find that in a museum?"

"Actually, yes." Reidkr finished twirling the dial. There was a *thunk*, after which she was able to slide a camouflage wall panel aside. Behind it, an open hatchway yawned.

Reidkr led Grice into an observation pod some twenty meters around. Meter-high windows looked out onto the Cave. Their surfaces' sickly sheens attested to the panels' thickness and exotic anti-radiation coatings. Reidkr slid the wall panel shut behind them. "We're trying every archaic maneuver we can think of," she said helplessly. "We're reviewing historical records, sifting through sensos from places like Throckmorton's World to see how people who've never known advanced technology protect their sensitive installations. We already have more security officers than scientists aboard *Luskus Delph*, and still it doesn't work very well." She crossed her arms. "Fem Grice, I recognize that you hail from a Sequestered world and I cannot command you to do anything. But I'd like to *invite* you to act as my special projects officer and conduct a complete review of security aboard *Luskus Delph.*"

She leaned against a bulkhead, regarding him suspiciously. "Why do you think I'm the one for this job?" Her brows hunched. "Because hailing from brutal, primitive Terra, I must be mentally closer to such a primitive scheme of operations?"

Reidkr eyed her with surprise, then understanding. Then she laughed. "Hardly. I think you're the one for this job because you're so forjeling resourceful. I *am* talking with 'Gunner Grice,' who crippled a shipful of deluded enemies with minimal loss of life despite having nothing in the way of ammunition but a few maneuverable ejected ship cabins?"

Grice crossed the chamber and stared out at the Cave, its kilometer-wide cable-mesh basket encircled by dangling susceptors and the skulking stalks of power apparatus. "I'm never going to live that down, am I?" Her back still to Reidkr, she shrugged. Nodded. Quietly she said, "Consider me on it."

Chapter 48

"That's a volcano, I think. Do you know what a volcano is?"

Nirom Fpod thrust his pelvis backward once, the signal for *I don't know.*

Pulling himself up by his hiking staff, Alrue Latier joined his newly assigned guide and teacher atop a scree ridge. With the heel of his free hand he squeegeed sweat off his face. He glanced over his shoulder; behind and below, the oval crater of the People's settlement seemed only the size of two joined fists.

Panting, Alrue turned to look to the northwest. A conical mountain pierced the horizon, blue with distance. From its apex a dark plume swirled higher than any thunderhead. It marched away from them on an unseen wind, trailing curtains of ash. "A volcano is …" Alrue frowned. "Nirom, do you know rock can melt? Have you ever seen that?"

"No. Rock melts?"

"Have you seen metal melt? Or get so hot it goes soft?"

Fpod smiled. "In a smith's forge, yes."

"Good. Well, make metal hotter still and it will run like blood. Rock will too." Alrue lifted sodden hairs from the back of his neck: a futile gesture, as if a few flips in open air could wick away their cloying moisture. "Deep underground – deeper than any well or cave you have seen – it gets very hot."

"Why?" With a beckoning jerk of his head Fpod set off along the ridge stop at a canter. Alrue had little choice but to follow.

258

"It just does," Alrue said impatiently. "So hot that rocks melt. They glow red, like metal worked by a smith. Sometimes that red-hot liquid rock escapes; it pushes through to the surface." Latier went on, panting and puffing and explaining volcanoes as best a Mormon televangelist could for the benefit of a tribal marauder who knew nothing of geology. "That plume? It's not smoke. It's a thick soup of red-hot rock dust. The winds bear it away from us; we can be glad of that."

They came upon a slight depression marked by three modest boulders and a dead scrub tree. "We can rest here," Fpod said.

Alrue needed no prompting. Shrugging off his backpack, he dropped to sit on a boulder with a loud sigh. Bending forward, he drew the canteen from his pack and drank deeply.

"Careful with that," Fpod warned. "Out where we will go Questing, there's little water. Each party is allowed limited supplies. You'd be surprised how many Quests fail for lack of water."

Offering his teacher the canteen – almost ostentatiously, Fpod took just a sip – Alrue examined the terrain around them, seeking to marshal everything Abigayl had drilled into him about methods to find water. *There.* At the lowest point of a shallow depression nearby, Alrue noted that some of the gravel chips were subtly flecked with green. Heaving himself to his feet, the bulky Mormon lumbered to the spot. Standing astride it, he raised his hiking staff. "And it came to pass that the Lord God of Hosts gave unto Moses the power that he should smite the rock and the water should come forth," he declaimed, then drove his staff into the ground. Again.

After the third thrust, its tip came away wet.

Alrue fought to hold a deadpan expression as Fpod dropped to his knees over the new-made hole. From his own pack Fpod pulled a narrow metal cup on a chain. He pressed it into the hole for a few moments, then drew it up, overflowing with cool sparkling water. He sniffed at it and raised the cup to his lips. Then he stopped.

Fpod stared up at Alrue. Was this a miracle? Should he drink, or was this only for the Stranger of Light?

Alrue had expected this reaction. "Go ahead. If it smells right to you, drink."

Fpod gulped the fizzy liquid in one draught. He burped immediately. "There is *never* water here," he marveled.

"There is much that I must learn from you, Nirom Fpod," Alrue declared in his best preachifying voice. "But I doubt if we shall want for water."

Time after time Fpod pressed his cup into the waterhole, now pouring the water into his own canteen. When it was refilled he held the cup-and-chain out to Alrue. "Care to fill your canteen?"

Instead Alrue pressed his canteen into Fpod's hands. "What a lovely offer. Yes, please do fill this."

***

His footfalls silent as snow, Fpod crept around a gnarled tree trunk and stopped short. Alrue thudded into his back. "Be still," Fpod hissed urgently. "Say nothing." Alrue leaned around Fpod's shoulder and stared where Fpod was looking. In a clearing eight or nine meters away, a furry slothlike creature was contentedly dismembering some dead thing about the size of a rabbit.

"How will you – " Alrue whispered.

Fpod flashed Alrue a stony look – *Shut up!* in any language – then focused wholly on the creature. Slowly his right arm came up, bending at the elbow until his right hand stood beside his ear. Fpod slowly exhaled, eyes never leaving his quarry. He tilted his right hand back to his shoulder, then explosively straightened his arm; there was an arrested flicking/whipping sound.

Pfitt!

A tiny feathered dart quivered in the creature's flank. The beast reared in pain. It turned to run, but instead spasmed and fell on its back, legs impotently caricaturing the motions of escape.

By the time the two men stood over the creature, the motions had stopped. "I've told you that only a few of the wild animals are good for us to eat," Fpod said. "This is one of them."

Like The People's livestocks, these slothlike things must be descended from animal species the Harvesters poached from Terra when they gathered proto-humans, Alrue thought. Aloud he said. "I will remember. You dispatched the beast most impressively. How did you do it?"

"We call it the *pfitt.*" Fpod rolled up his right sleeve to reveal a leather harness clasped to his wrist and forearm. "Because of the sound it makes." He pointed to its features. "See the pouch? It holds six darts. The top dart drops into place, so" – he flexed his wrist; a mechanism responded with a clicking sound. A small cradle of some weirdly shiny metal that had been empty now held one dart. With his left hand Fpod pushed the now-loaded cradle back toward his right elbow, visibly tensioning two narrow straps. "The straps are of animal sinew."

"That cradle thing – what's it made of?"

Instead of answering, Fpod raised his right hand alongside his ear. "When I bend my arm, that cocks it. When I fling the dart, the sinew acts as a spring. It triples the power of my throw." He straightened his arm. *Pfitt!* The dart trembled in the center of a knothole in the bark of a scrub tree across the clearing. "The dart is poisoned. It will kill a small animal at once, as you saw. One dart will kill a man in five minutes. Three darts kill a man in seconds."

Alrue nodded. "And a *svadi* moose?"

Laughing, Fpod pumped his head up and down in denial. "The *pfitt* is no help against a moose. It's for catching your supper – even brief cooking breaks down the poison, so long as too many darts were not used. And I can use it for defense if we run into scouts from The Others."

And I'm probably more likely to run into a scout from The Others than to get a straight answer about the origin of that metal component, Alrue realized.

Chapter 49

The door annunciator warbled.

The entrance dilated. Lii Bardicon stood outside.

"Enter," said Lieutenant Avu Wincenc.

Wincenc's quarters were notable for their plainness. Blank walls were decorated with just two cheap sim displays. One displayed a succession of impressive public buildings, each built of stone, metal, or semiprecious plate, each imaged straight-on in such a way that neither humans nor landscaping were apparent. The other frame displayed barren natural vistas. Featureless brown plains met spun-metal skies at horizons straight as death. The compartment's only example of life, real or represented, was Wincenc herself, motionless in a corner chair.

"Someone's Gwilyan," Bardicon said with ill-concealed distaste.

"Please come in," Wincenc said almost giddily. "Allow me to dispel any concern you may have about giving planeto-ethnic offense. For the record, I say that I am Gwilyan born and bred. I've heard all the slurs about my homeworld, and they're all correct. Gwilya *does* offer no topography by day, no stars by night, and no weather worth mentioning at any time."

"And no men," added Bardicon.

Wincenc shrugged. "Of course. I was gestated in a bio-tank that produces only females, not in some indiscriminate womb. And no surrounding seems more natural for me than an artificial one. 'Mind over meat,' that's the Gwilyan way." She smiled unevenly. "I'm glad we have that behind us. Would you like a Rikubian whiskey?"

Bardicon stood stiffly, one hand clasped over the other wrist as the door spiraled shut behind her. "You asked me here, Lieutenant Wincenc."

Wincenc smiled lopsidedly. "So I did. About that whiskey?"

"Rikubian whiskey, such a luxurious drink." Her posture all sharp angles and tensions, Bardicon lowered herself into a seat that flowed from the stateroom wall. "The drink of diplomats and business magnates."

"They drink *good* Rikubian whiskey." Wincenc drew three fingers of fizzy brass-colored liquid into two crystal goblets. "I regret I cannot promise that." She offered Bardicon a goblet. "In any case, allow me to apologize for the tone of our earlier encounter."

"Accepted." Bardicon sipped at the effervescent liquor. "Which doesn't change the hint of coercion implied in this invitation."

"Coercion?" Wincenc asked over the lip of her goblet. "Does being here disturb you?"

"Frankly, a little." Bardicon shrugged. "But you rank me, you have an intel background, and you've formed this grim certainty that I'm not me." She shrugged. "You want me here, I'm here."

"Please don't feel that way," Wincenc said. "I realize you must have expected to go unrecognized. I mean, a serious fan from your old days, out here? What were the odds?"

Bardicon shook her head. "Look, I don't know what you're –"

"I understand," Wincenc said urgently. "You expect the worst." Her eyes burned with urgency. "Please, I want you to understand. Let me show you."

Bardicon leaned forward, ready to lunge for the hatchway. "I'd really rather –"

"Junior Technician Bardicon, I insist." Wincenc's voice rang with command.

"Then I follow your order, Lieutenant." She pressed her back against the seat, her palms flattened on her knees.

Wincenc's tone was solicitous again. "You have Spectator implants, is there anything you need to put in park mode before you *pov* a senso as an ordinary person would?"

"No." Bardicon half-drained her glass; it went down her gullet like carded wool. "Play what you have to show me."

Wincenc tapped a table. Its top lifted on tiny hydraulics to reveal a senso player configured for group playback. "Strange, isn't it? So much other tech is disabled here – how fortunate that these things still work." She poked the unit's PLAYBACK tab.

Suck, rush, wrench!

***

Their viewpoint drifted ever forward through cascading billows of silvery fog. A riot of plants, fronds, and shrubs trundled by, each seeming to tower heavenward. Each cast dual shadows into the fog, one bluish, the other ruddy and warm. Living structures' edges coruscated, eerie impossible light tracing the vertices of each junction of stem and leaf. Each plant was coupled with an overwhelming olfactory profile: ferns reeked of camphor, shrubs of cinnamon, conifers of over-ripe wine lapsing into vinegar. Overlaying it all was an astonishing kinesthetic impression of vertigo, as though each passing plant loomed kilometers tall and one was slicing through the gelid air at incalculable height. Were this a tridee, one might chalk it all up to an overwrought director with too many credits to spend on visual effects (while being left to puzzle at the smells and the wrenching somesthetic impressions). But this was senso, the medium that captured the complete human sensorium with perfect accuracy and replayed it into others' minds. Special effects, in any conventional understanding of that term, were impossible. The totality of human sensation was too fractally complex to support the ready synthesis of impostures.

Playback ended.

Chapter 50

The Warrior and the prophet sat in a dry hollow in the wall of a low cliff. Impaled on sticks, strips of the flesh of the slothlike creature Fpod had slain with his *pfitt* hissed over a small campfire. The sky was purple-pink in the west, indigo overhead where the moons Queen and Prince hurtled toward another of their near-misses. "One day you will take the Wisdom Quest," Fpod commented, shattering Alrue's reverie. "If you succeed, the Shan will name some member of his estate to instruct you in Wisdom's faith."

"I look forward to it."

"Tonight, just for knowledge's sake, I'll tell you what we Warriors believe."

"I'd like to hear that very much."

The meat was done; Fpod drew the cooking sticks out of the fire and handed one to Alrue, who waited to see what Fpod would do with his. Fpod stopped, staring expectantly at his student. "The hunter always eats last," he said after a moment. "It's tradition." Ten seconds passed. "Um, that means you have to eat first."

"Oh," Alrue said blankly. "How were you going to _"

Chuckling, Fpod held his meat-laden stick close to his mouth. "Just chaw some off."

Alrue chawed. The meat was chewy but not quite tough, flavorful in a gamy way.

"Warrior religion," Fpod began around a mouthful. "We believe in a god who has no name. He is eternal and all-powerful."

That's pretty standard, Alrue thought.

"For our god, being eternal and being all-powerful work against each other."

That's not standard at all. Perpetuity and omnipotence, interfering destructively? Alrue raised a quizzical eyebrow and kept chewing.

"Our god created everything long ago," Fpod explained. "He built the landscape, set the sun and moons on their courses, and created life. But –this is the great secret of the Warrior faith – he did a poor job. Walk in soft sand and a ferkeek will take you. Our trees are stunted, our crops grow slowly. Only certain animals and plants are nourishing. We can eat our fill of the rest but still starve." Fpod gestured upwards. "Look, he couldn't even persuade Queen and Prince to travel in the same directions! Our god's a bumbler. Long ago, he despaired of the poor quality of his creations and slew himself."

"He did *what*?"

Fpod jerked his chin up and to the right. "You heard me, he slew himself."

Alrue poked at the air with his meat-stick. "Your god committed suicide? He could *do* that? I mean, was he successful?"

"Yes, but no." Fpod tore another chunk of meat from his own stick, speaking as he chewed. "Because he was all-powerful, he *could* slay himself, and so he did. But because he was eternal, he couldn't *stay* slain. The moment he died, he came right back. But still he craved death, so he slew himself again."

"Death in the most aggravating and distressing manner which could be inflicted," Alrue recited.

With one hand Fpod made a gesture like fireworks, the hand leaping skyward, its fingers springing open like some coruscating rosette. "*Pow,* he was back again. He killed himself again, he popped back again – again and again, times beyond counting, times beyond thinking of."

"Interminable suicide and rebirth," Alrue mused, genuinely impressed that on this painfully ordinary world human ingenuity had devised a god story that, so far as his considerable knowledge extended, had no parallel in human space. "How long did this cycle go on?"

"It's happening today," Fpod said reverently. "It never stops. We believe our god cycles always between suicide and unwanted rebirth, and he always will." He fell silent. "Listen," he said, staring into the night. "Past the crackling of our fire, below the rustle of the wind — don't you hear it?"

"Hear ... what?" Alrue asked as quietly as he could.

"Sometimes I hear it with my heart, more than my ears," Fpod said dreamily. "The world's hum." He watched the night for another interval. "You still don't hear it? Let me try to match its pitch. Lean close to me." Fpod swallowed, adjusted his posture, and begin to produce a low, growling rumble. His left ear within a hand's breadth of Fpod's chest, Alrue could barely distinguish a tone; but the moment he discerned it, some old musical-performance implants from the early days of his ministry came alive. *Forty-three Hertz,* he suddenly knew. Another scrap of knowledge wafted into his awareness, one he'd acquired back when he was seeking to understand the psychology behind the rhythmic percussions that false messiah Arn Parek had used to induce a trancelike state in his adherents: *Forty-three Hertz is a typical frequency for the gamma waves associated with human consciousness.* "Ahhhhhh," Alrue sighed, confident Fpod would assume that he, Alrue, had heard the world's hum too.

In fact Alrue had come to *understand* it, which was more important.

"It is the sound of our god, constantly dying and returning," Fpod said eventually. "That sound holds the cosmos together." Having eaten the last of his meat, he tossed the stick in the campfire and scrabbled for Alrue's backpack. "It's dark enough. Time for you to see what you've been carrying around."

"I can barely see anything," Alrue complained.

"As it should be," Fpod replied. "The first time you see it, tradition says you shouldn't see too much." From the bottom of the pack he pulled a slender, vaguely conelike object about twenty-five centimeters in length. "You don't kill a *svadi* moose with a *pfitt*. You kill it with one of these."

"This is a *rains red*?"

"A training version. Unlike the real one, it doesn't – let's just say you can handle it safely."

Alrue accepted the object. Judging by its weight, it was made largely of metal or something similarly dense. Its base consisted of a metallic rim surrounding a vaguely nozzle-like opening. An irregular groove divided its body into front and rear halves. The surface, neither matte nor shiny, did not show fingerprints. Alrue ran fingers along its surface; the material had a stark directionality. *Like a shark's skin,* Alrue thought. On some scale below the visible (at least by firelight) the object's texture would promote its moving forward, but powerfully resist being pulled backward through any tight-fitting channel. "Of curious workmanship, to be sure," Alrue said at last. "Where did this come from?"

"From the Wisdoms," Fpod said. "I don't know how they make them – or where they get them, as the case may be. Whenever it's time for someone's Wisdom Quest, a genuine *rains red* is issued."

Alrue turned the object slowly in his hand, watching the firelight pick out small details. The fit between its apparent halves was astoundingly precise, out of keeping

270

with everything Alrue knew about The People's technologies. Having committed his share of Enclave violations sneaking Galactic technology onto a forbidden world, Alrue couldn't help wondering whether something similar had happened here. With exaggerated caution he returned the *rains red* to Fpod. *How to pose a question beyond anything in this man's experience?* "Tell me, Nirom," Alrue asked, "have they always looked like this?"

"As long as I remember," Fpod said as he returned the device to the bottom of Alrue's pack. "But wait – once my father told me that when *he* was young, they were different. Cruder, less beautiful – and, he said, less reliable in the field."

Alrue chose his next words carefully. "Would you say that what you showed me is a vast improvement over the traditional device your father knew?"

Fpod unrolled a blanket from his pack. "Now that you mention it, that's just what I'd say."

Chapter 51

There was always a moment's refocusing when a senso cut off. One's mind had to disengage from the journal's residual sights and sounds, smells and feelings – to reorient one's *being-thereness* to actual surroundings. Lii Bardicon blinked, gaping at her knees. Only then did she register Avu Wincenc's expectant stare. The lieutenant's eyes crackled not with mere desire, but with a more fundamental, even feral, hunger. She asked huskily, "Now do you understand?"

"I'm sorry, no," Bardicon said softly. "I mean, the senso was astounding. So surreal, so lyrical – like nothing in the medium I've *pov*ed before."

Wincenc's features hardened, yearning stiffening into rebuke. "Never *pov*ed its like? But of course you have."

Abruptly Bardicon stood. Before Wincenc could order her to sit back down, she snapped: "Whoever you think I am, I do not recognize this material! What makes you believe I should?"

"Please, resume your seat," Wincenc said almost gently. "This is the senso that cemented the reputation of Amli Revskond."

"The person you think I am."

Wincenc's gesture in reply was half a shrug, half understated certainty. "This senso would make Revskond a star, but it was not widely appreciated until several years after its release. Only a handful of collectors and fervent admirers possess it in the first edition, as I do."

Warily, Bardicon edged back into her seat. "Collectors and fervent admirers. Which are you?"

"I cannot afford to be a collector," said Wincenc. "I'm a fervent admirer. I came to own this through scrounging and bartering. In the right marketplace, it's worth more than all my other possessions." She removed the wafer from the senso player and turned it absently in her grasp. "So you see, that's why I recognized you. Your work has a narrow following; of course you'd expect to move anonymously on *Luskus Delph*. But you have nothing to fear. It's only happenstance that brought you into contact with one of the couple of hundred thousand people in the Galaxy who *would* recognize you at a glance."

"Hear me," Bardicon all but growled. "I am not Amli Revskond."

Is that bravado speaking? Wincenc asked herself. *Or could it be that she really doesn't remember?* Wincenc reinserted the wafer into the senso player and tabbed ABOUT. An infographic flickered in midair, golden text and a min-relief portrait:

JUNGLE SLEW
BY
AMLI REVSKOND

The artist's portrait was unmistakable. It was Lii Bardicon. Or rather, it offered seeming proof that Amli Revskond, whoever she was, was *also* Lii Bardicon.

"This isn't an inquisition, it's the fruit of real curiosity," Wincenc ventured. "Please, isn't that you?"

"No, it *isn't*," Bardicon grated. "Though I'll admit the resemblance is startling."

"Resemblance?" Wincenc's tone hardened.

"Look, there've been cases where unrelated individuals had matching fingerprints or retinal patterns, even identical clustering of veins in the palm of the hand. With more than sixteen thousand trillion humans

273

are now living, cases of two people having the same physical appearance are inevitable."

Wincenc shook her head. "And the two of you happen to be the same age? Both Spectators, if in your case only briefly? Look, Fem Revskond – "

"That's not my name."

Wincenc spread her hands in a gesture of acceptance. "Whatever your reasons are for doing this, I'm ready to listen. I'll give you every benefit of the doubt. And if I can do so consistent with the requirements of my duty, I will keep your secret."

"There is no secret. You're simply mistaken." Bardicon stood to leave.

"Junior Technician –" Wincenc began.

"Lieutenant, I am leaving."

"You need to ask yourself how much longer I will keep this between the two of us," Wincenc said icily. "A sane person would have taken this matter to security already."

For the first time, Bardicon smiled. "Then with all due respect, that makes two of us who question your sanity. Good daypart, Lieutenant." She stepped rapidly toward the door, which dilated at emergency speed to avoid her colliding with it.

Wincenc's eyes lingered on the door as it spiraled shut. *Yes, how much longer* will *I keep my knowledge private?* she asked herself. *In particular, my knowledge that Amli Revskond died nearly three years ago?*

***

A hundred meters down an empty hallway, Lii Bardicon pressed her shoulder blades against a bulkhead, pressing fingertips to her pinched mouth. *Wincenc knows,* she thought over and over, terror clawing at her gut. *How* can *she know? And how much does she know?*

Chapter 52

"And behold," Alrue Latier quoted, "all things are written by the Father; therefore out of the books which shall be written shall the world be judged." Hands linked behind his back, he circled the meadow in broad steps. The crater lip that crowned the People's Ground yawned high overhead; around them stretched pastureland occupied only by stunted sheep. For Alrue and his wives, the band of meadow that ringed the underground settlement furnished the one locale within the otherwise densely populated People's Ground where they could be effectively alone. While Meryam might one day relay their deliberations to an eager Galaxy, Alrue wanted to be sure that no one on Bohrkk – most of all, no one closely associated with the Shan, Takander Thurnb – could know what they discussed this day. "Zuzenah, dear wife of my youth, please orchestrate the reports."

Seated on a rock, Zuzenah allowed herself a shallow smile. "As you predicted, dear husband, the People became markedly more receptive once you declared yourself a candidate for the Wisdom estate." Almost imperceptibly, she glanced toward Nataleah.

Nataleah picked up the narrative, parroting even the pitch of the senior wife's voice. "It's as though their defenses went down once they had a familiar pigeonhole in which to imagine us. During the last two weeks or so, the women of the tribe have grown willing to tell us many things."

Alrue nodded sagely. "So, what have they told you?"

Zuzenah's eyes flickered toward Constance, whose default pout shifted into a gamine smile. "The People have no concept of money," Constance reported, "yet every aspect of their society turns on the heavy Debt-with-a-capital-D that each social class is said to owe to the other."

Now Zuzenah's gaze shifted to Abigayl, who sat on a wooden fence hugging her slender knees. "The entire social system here revolves around a series of largely mythical, effectively unpayable obligations," said the child. "They're illusions, but they bind this society together."

Zuzenah's eyes locked again on Constance, who twirled a lock of reddish hair around her slender fingers. "This Debt system props up a Warrior class with little apparent reason to exist," Constance reported.

"Warriors with no one to fight," Alrue mused.

Tasking a subconscious auto-routine with snapping her head toward whoever spoke next, Meryam wondered at what an effective intelligence-gathering network Alrue's wives had become. *Few women among the People have the cachet of Alrue's wives,* she thought; *none could match their impact when working in concert toward a covert goal. And how skillfully Zuzenah wields this group as an instrument – or should I say a weapon?*

"Still," asked Zuzenah, spreading her hands, "can you build a society, even a primitive one, on nothing but debt?"

"Many cultures worked that way," Alrue replied. "Western society on Terra was deeply rooted in debt metaphors. What does Christianity teach, after all, but the ultimate unpayable debt? A careful cultural analysis of the People's Debt system should show us much about how best to control it." Alrue turned toward Lupida. "Next subject, dear Lupida: what have you and Nataleah been able to learn about the *rains red*?"

Lupida scratched at her freckled nose. "What Nirom Fpod told you checks out. Years ago, within the

276

memories of older people here, the 'magical weapon' was much different from the one known today."

Zuzenah glanced again at Nataleah, who added, "Rumor suggests that at that time, the traditional *rains red* was replaced by the current one, whose origin is very likely Galactic."

Lupida nodded. "Indications are that within the last twenty years, the People ceased to manufacture their own magical weapons for this alleged Wisdom Quest. Instead they started obtaining the weapons – and a few other metal items, including that shiny metallic cradle component from the *pfitt*s – from a tight network of corrupt punitorium guards. We think the guards exchanged this contraband for sexual access to the People's young women."

"I see," Alrue declared. "And it came to pass that they beheld that the fruit of the natural branches had become corrupt also; yea, the first and the second and also the last; and they had all become corrupt."

"All that and more," Lupida agreed. "Of course, with the punitorium destroyed and the guards presumably dead, the *rains red* issued to you should be the last of its kind. After your Quest, the People's smiths and tanners will have to remember how to make their own magical weapons again – if they can."

"But that's not all," Nataleah added urgently.

Watching Zuzenah, Meryam recognized immediately that the senior wife had not expected Nataleah to speak now.

Neither had Alrue. "Oh?" he said.

Zuzenah's eyes drilled into Lupida's as if to demand *Do you know what's going on now?*

Lupida did. She leaned back, running slender, nervous fingers through her short brown hair. "We're sorry to raise this point unbidden, but Nataleah and I spotted something very strange. While the goal is often spoken of, often boasted of among the womenfolk, we have yet to speak with anyone whose *own* husband or brother went on Wisdom Quest and actually blew up a moose."

"Mostly, their Quests ended in one or another variant of 'the one that got away,'" added Nataleah.

"Passing curious," Alrue said, frowning. "To blow up the moose, that's the very purpose of the Quest."

"We heard stories of some friend-of-a-friend whose man blew up a moose," Nataleah reported, "but nobody whose own loved one did the deed."

Zuzenah leaned back slightly, the gesture communicating that the importance of this particular surprise justified the breach in wifely protocol.

Lupida spread her hands. "That's a classic pattern when a social practice that's ostensibly highly valued is actually the focus of a great lie."

"Forjeler," said Zuzenah, "you'd think they were Mormons."

Alrue flashed his senior wife a brief look of reproach. Whether it was the profanity or the sentiment she'd expressed that vexed him more, no one could tell. But Zuzenah was senior wife, the love of Alrue's youth; no one imagined her outburst would have consequences.

Turning his profile toward Meryam's recording gaze, Alrue stroked his chin. "All this is very intriguing – but what does it mean?"

Zuzenah chuckled knowingly. "O my husband, you are the prophet, seer, and revelator. We report, you decide."

Chapter 53

June 15, 2376
Aboard *Luskus Delph*

Captain Brûh Reidkr watched impassively as Pamela Grice hefted a largish box onto the briefing table in Reidkr's inner office. Computer, which had accompanied Grice into Reidkr's office, settled gently on a small table. Grice shoveled an assortment of small devices onto the table, then passed Reidkr a hardcopy report. "Sorry to be so old-school. I'd give you my report on a wafer, but –"

"I know, readers don't work on board. Well, let's hear your security recommendations."

"I identified twenty-six procedural changes that could streamline security procedures," Grice began. "They will require no hardware alterations."

Reidkr scanned the pages before her. "Ingenious. They will be implemented. Now you also have recommendations that will require new hardware?"

Grice nodded. "I think we can streamline the procedure for personal identification." She held up a small grey box from which a crystalline stylus protruded. "Touch the tip, Captain."

Reidkr complied. "REIDKR, BRÛH," the box said in a tinny voice.

Grice smiled. "This box contains genetically engineered biosensors – accompanied by a microscopic biosample from every person aboard *Luskus Delph.*"

"You sampled everyone on board?" he asked incredulously.

"Oh no, the samples came from personnel medical records. Each biosample is associated with an optically encoded piezo audio clip; that's the source of the person's spoken name. These should provide rapid, less-cumbersome personal identification without any electronics or vibrionics that might be compromised by the high noise levels here."

"I'm impressed," Reidkr breathed.

"I can't take credit for it, it's a system the PeaceForce sometimes uses for perimeter security in areas without a power grid. Now, the next two are more unique." Grice plucked another object from the tabletop, a grey box about the size of her hand. At a touch, it unfolded into a flat square display a meter on a side. Though wafer-thin, it was rigid. "*Luskus Delph* has all those wide-open spaces where it's very difficult for guards to communicate. The result is that areas near the wall intercoms are over-patrolled, while areas between them are scarcely monitored." She stood. "The first layer of the system is simple – simply teach the guards a code." She began to make flagging motions with her arms. "Over short to moderate distances, they can signal each other by gesturing in semaphore."

"Is the code difficult to learn?" Reidkr asked.

"For that part we'll rely on Fem Bardicon and her didactic imposer," Grice said. "The guards should acquire the code in under a minute."

Reidkr nodded. "She may as well teach it to everyone, then, much as she teaches everyone the abacus. Never know when another mode of communication will be helpful. Now what's that thing you unfolded?"

"A repeater for semaphoring over longer distances." Grice pressed one side of the meter-square display against a bulkhead; it stuck. "The user stands behind the repeater and semaphores. It uses a dumb optical technology to repeat the gestures at much greater size on the bioluminescent display. It's readable from five hundred meters away."

"This will be enormously useful."

She shrugged. "That was my own little arts-and-crafts project. For the next problem, I needed help."

Colors rippled across Computer's metallic body. "Glad to assist."

Grice reached into her box and produced a black oblong device about fifteen centimeters long by eight wide by five deep. It seemed featureless. "For key personnel, this solves the problem of interpersonal comm over arbitrary distances," she said. "I call it the enhanced handie-talkie. It functions like any standard wireless communicator, except it uses optical and biotech components in place of the ordinary vibrionics. And it takes advantage of a narrow gap in the local noise signature, broadcasting over the epsilon-sigma band."

"What?" Reidkr said incredulously. "Epsilon-sigma is used only for power transmission. From everything I know, it's impossible to modulate a signal in that range."

"Not any more," Computer whirred.

I shared this problem with Hom Computer, and this is the solution he came up with," Grice explained. "There was a quiet zone at epsilon-sigma, so he found a way of modulating a signal employing that frequency. That quiet zone is incredibly narrow, a tiny notch in an otherwise unbroken wall of noise. The upshot is that only forty such devices can operate on *Luskus Delph;* you'll need to ration them."

Reidkr nodded. "A few for command – the physicists will demand at least half a dozen – that leaves twenty-eight or thirty units for the guards who need them most. I'll need to decide who those are." Abruptly Reidkr became aware of a growing stack of enhanced handie-talkies materializing beside her chair. "What the sfelb –"

"We owe you thirty-nine more of those," Computer whirred. "Twenty-one, twenty-two –"

Reidkr stared from the floor to Grice with mounting alarm. "How is he doing that?"

"Polyplex virtual telepresence," Grice explained. "Hom Enoda and Hom Computer developed the technology twenty-odd years ago. Drawing on waste contramagnetic energy, Hom Computer can form virtual objects of any desired level of complexity – and any desired level of reality."

"And obviously it works under *Luskus Delph* conditions." Reidkr turned one of the handie-talkies in her hand. "I'm *holding* a virtual device?"

"Strictly speaking, yes," Computer whirred. "Though it occupies space, has weight, you can hit an enemy in the head with it – it's as real as it needs to be, for as long as it's needed. Twenty-six, twenty-seven –"

"At Arbadrel they used this technology to create absolutely convincing *faux* humans, even to add significant modifications to spaceship hulls," Grice added.

"So are these devices able to modulate a signal on epsilon-sigma band *because* they are virtual?" Reidkr asked.

"Actually, yes," Computer whirred. "Each unit contains a germanium modulator crystal made of atoms so large that unenhanced human vision can distinguish them under strong light. As far as that crystal is concerned, it's modulating a shortwave radio signal, a signal that just happens to backmap onto reality as an epsilon-sigma transmission. Thirty-six, thirty-seven—"

"In other words, you locally adjusted the laws of physics." Reidkr slowly replaced her handie-talkie onto the swelling stack. "I have held in my hand the physically impossible."

"Thirty-nine. Fem Grice's makes forty." Computer rippled its body colors in a satisfied way.

"Computer will produce a few thousand of the repeaters shortly, though we may want him to move to a storage room before he begins that process," Grice said. "In the meantime, let's review the final phase of my report. Captain, you had noted the impossibility of surveillance recordings using conventional equipment. The largest quiet zone in the local noise signature happens to be subdelta-band, the range of frequencies used by senso apparatus."

"That fact is highly classified," Reidkr snapped.

"So?" Computer whirred.

"More to the point, why try to hide it?" Grice demanded. "Plenty of people aboard have noticed that their only piece of personal tech that still works is their senso player. Since subdelta-band works, the solution to your surveillance problem is to have OmNet send out a shipload of Spectators and a suite of recording modules, the kind they put into satellites orbiting an Enclave world. Install the satellite modules around *Luskus Delph* in shielded enclosures that protect their vibrionics while passing subdelta-band, and just station a Spectator wherever you need surveillance and recording."

Reidkr leaned back, chuckling. "Spectators! Why didn't we think of that?"

Grice showed him a vicious smile. "Sometimes it takes a primitive Terran to see the simple things."

"There's just one problem."

"What's that?"

Reidkr spread her hands. "The solution you propose is impossible."

Chapter 54

October 24, 2367
Bohrkk, the People's Ground

Alrue Latier and his senior wife nestled like spoons, his chest against her back, his left arm around her waist. They lay in near darkness in her sleeping room, clad only in their temple garments, listening to each other's breathing. Alrue whispered, "Were you satisfied, wife of my youth?"

"As always," she said quietly, "by the gift and power of God." She reached up, clasping his left hand in her right. "Something burdens you, my husband."

"How can you tell?"

"You're still awake."

He edged closer, nuzzling his chin against her shoulder. "I just wanted to declare how sorry I am."

"Sorry? For what?"

"Punitorium life, trudging through the wilderness, lodging among The People – verily, it's not what you had the right to expect when we married. I regret my incapacity to have shown you better."

"Regret, Alrue? You?" Wriggling free of his grasp, she rolled over to face him. "What brings forth this melancholy?"

He pressed his face against the flesh of her neck. "Soon I must go on my Quest. They say – they say – "

She pulled back to look in his eyes. "They say what?"

"Some people don't come back."

She wrapped her fleshy arms about him. "You will come back. You always have. I've learned that yea, your resilience is as constant as the sun." They lay in silence, savoring the moist warmth of one another's breath.

"Rely on this, O my husband. Life is not done with either of us."

A minute passed. Two. Alrue was still awake.

"A question has been troubling me," Zuzenah whispered.

"Ask me, and I will nourish your mind with things pertaining to righteousness."

"Must you go through with this Wisdom Quest?"

"I see no alternative." He rolled onto his back. Her fingers sought his. "Mind you, I have no enthusiasm for traipsing around the countryside on a hunting expedition, for facing hunger, thirst, and fatigue, and all manner of afflictions of every kind. But there's been no sign of rescue by the Confetory, so I think we must prepare for a long sojourn here. Under the circumstances, that means preparing by The People's rules."

"That is ... what you think," she said uncertainly.

"Yes."

Her fingers tightened. "What you think, not what you *know*. You've heard nothing from the Lord?"

Alrue shook his head. "No commandment, no revelation. But neither have I heard a still small voice urging me away from the path my mind thinks best."

"So you're content to kill the moose," she whispered disapprovingly.

"I wouldn't say I'm content, but I shall do it because I must." He turned his face toward her. "By the self-sacrifice of the Anti-Nephi-Lehies, woman, when the Lord God of Hosts freed us from that punitorium by the power of His mighty arm, He slew ten thousand humans – verily, the selfsame number that fell with Gidgiddonah in his final battle against the Lamanites – and you're worrying about a moose?"

"The Lord slew those people, and a terrible thing that was; but I do not claim to understand his ways," she replied. "But *you* will be the one blowing up that moose. Do you not fear staining your soul?"

"Actually, no. But please, dearest wife, tell me why you do."

"The Word of Wisdom urges us to eat meat only during winter or famine, and even then to hunt only for what we must eat."

"Everyone knows that's but a suggestion. Not like the prohibition on alcohol –"

"Which you ignore."

"I follow Joseph Smith's example. But the Word of Wisdom also prohibits using tobacco, a commandment I follow to the letter."

"Perhaps that was a more impressive sacrifice in the time of the first Saints," Zuzenah mused. "What *is* 'tobacco,' anyway? All right, I'll grant that the Word of Wisdom offers mixed guidance. But what of Joseph Smith's teaching that humans, plants, and animals – even the very world we tread – were created spiritually long before God created them physically?"

Alrue frowned. "Where are you heading with this, dear Zuzenah?"

"We are taught that every animal has a *soul*, my husband," she said intensely. "This is no time of famine; we don't require that moose's meat to live. You ought not kill an ensouled creature just to pass some bloodthirsty tribal test."

"I do this for you, my darling. For you and Nataleah and Constance and Lupida and Abigayl, and for Meryam, and for me as well. If one of God's creatures must die to secure our future among The People, I think we must trust God to do right by the creature's soul."

"Again, that is what you *think*," she said in a neutral tone. Accusation trickled beneath her words like waters tunneling beneath ice.

286

"If my logic does not satisfy you, perhaps scripture will," Alrue said. "The Book of Ether describes the beasts that walked the land: horses, asses, elephants, cureloms, cumoms. And what was the most important thing the writer of this holy book could have told posterity about these creatures?"

"What cureloms and cumoms were?"

"No, it was that they were all 'useful to man.'" He gripped her hands in his. "The moose I blow up will be supremely useful to *us*, my darling – and I pledge you, I will pray for its soul."

Zuzenah's eyes studied his. "Still and all, my husband, 'tis perilous to proceed by human wisdom alone."

He nodded. "May the Lord preserve his people in righteousness and in holiness of heart."

"Pray for guidance, Alrue," she implored. "Open your mind and soul to God's will."

Alrue drew a sharp breath. His grip failed.

He rolled onto his back, arms still drawn up, eyes wide open.

Fumbling, Zuzenah struck up the simple lantern on the unfinished bedside table. She stared down at him, then rushed into the small hallway. "Everyone, come swiftly. He's having a revelation!"

***

Five minutes later, Alrue raised his head. Zuzenah's sleeping room was brightly illuminated. All the wives were present, each with her lantern. Meryam was there too. A moment's scrutiny of her eyes told him she was recording.

In an instant he sat up, back straight, chin extended, the pose that in the old days his tridee followers had always told his pollsters they considered his most prophetic. "Behold," he declared, "the Lord made plain to me his will; no man knoweth of his ways save it be revealed unto him."

As one, the wives dropped to their knees. The four junior wives clasped their hands in devotion; Zuzenah fastened hers around Alrue's right forearm. "Praise my God all the day long," she cried.

"It's night," Nataleah whispered.

Alrue swung his legs off the bed. He stood facing the kneeling Zuzenah – and, just coincidentally, presenting a commanding three-quarter profile to Meryam's recording gaze. "Fear not, first of my wives. The Lord has made all clear." He stood, taking her hands in one of his. The other hand he raised, palm out, index finger extended in a gesture of instruction. "You were correct, my dearest. Human beings, plants, animals, even the world, were spiritually created and have souls. But 'the world' means not this planet, not Bohrkk – it means *the Earth*."

"Terra?" Zuzenah breathed.

Alrue nodded regally. "One of many worlds where God brought forth living things, but the only world on which He created humans. Animals that arose on Terra have souls because they are part of the act of creation that included *us*. Animals native to other worlds are unensouled, and we may kill them at need. So saith the Lord of Hosts."

Alrue sat back on the bed. Zuzenah began slowly to knit her brow.

Alrue gazed on her beatifically. "You are still vexed, my love?"

"My husband, I must speak frankly."

He nodded. "Proceed."

"You are the Prophet, Seer, and Revelator to whom the Lord speaks when it suits His purposes," she began. "Still, some revelations can seem, um, more *convenient* than others."

"Your soul is uneasy," Alrue said gently. "Let me explain as God explained to me."

Zuzenah nodded.

"What is true of animals from Terra?" Alrue asked the whole room. "What is true about animals that arose on Terra that is not true of those that evolved on other worlds?"

Nataleah piped up. "We can eat them."

"We can eat *svadi* moose," Alrue pointed out. "But if we eat nothing but *svadi* moose, we'll starve."

"Left-handed chirality!" Abigayl yelped.

"Ah yes, chirality," Alrue said thoughtfully. "So animals from Terra are different because *if we eat them, they will nourish us.*" He stood again, reaching down to cradle Zuzenah's round face. "And here, behold, the wisdom and foresight of God shineth forth in glory. God revealed to me this evening that only Terran animals have souls, and that troubled you. But it was foreshadowed in the centuries-old Word of Wisdom principle of hunting only to eat."

"It ... was?" Zuzenah whispered, baffled.

"It's obvious that such a principle is only meaningful with regard to animals whose meat has the power to nourish us. So from the very moment Joseph Smith proclaimed the Word of Wisdom, it encompassed only animals from *Terra's* tree of life. Aside from God – and Joseph Smith, I suppose – no one on nineteenth-century Terra knew there *were* animal species on other worlds. Yet the Word of Wisdom's logic already excluded them." He looked around the room. "Who knows why?"

"It tells us that if we must chase and kill one of God's creatures, we should make sure its meat is not wasted," Abigayl said proudly. "That's not an issue if the animal's meat cannot nourish us. Nor can such meat tempt us into wrongdoing."

Alrue nodded, beaming, and returned his gaze to Zuzenah, whose face still rested in his hands. "So in fact, my revelation of this evening establishes very little that is new. On the contrary, it shows us that God in His wisdom followed the same standard in deciding which living things to ensoul that He followed in deciding which ones He would make nourishing for humans – the same standard He practiced at the foundation of the world, the same standard He built into a doctrine He revealed to Joseph Smith in 1833 Terran local. So you see, dearest Zuzenah? If circumstances compel me to kill one of this world's creatures, there is nothing in God's law or Mormon teaching to say I shouldn't."

Zuzenah's eyes grew saucer-wide. "O my husband, can you ever accept my apology?"

Alrue gave his best I-love-the-whole-world smile. "It doesn't matter whether *I* accept your apology, wife of my youth. It matters whether God does." He tilted his head like a dog expressing mild confusion – or perhaps like a prophet, seer, and revelator listening for that still small voice. A moment later, he nodded. "He says he does."

Chapter 55

"Bringing in Spectators is impossible?" Pamela Grice demanded of Brûh Reidkr, her tone incredulous. "Why?"

"You've been away from Galactic life, Fem Grice," Reidkr said tiredly. "Have you any idea what OmNet would charge for that many Spectators? Or what wretched sfelb those elite, self-important senso artists would raise over being employed as mere human surveillance cameras?"

"I thought *Luskus Delph*'s mission was … important," Grice said slowly.

"It is," Reidkr replied.

"Save-the-Galaxy important."

"Just because our mission is save-the-Galaxy important doesn't mean we can draw on a blank check," Reidkr said coldly.

"Maybe *you* can't," Computer whirred, dark colors swirling across its metallic skin.

Grice rummaged in her box. "Fine, I drew up a list of the personnel already aboard *Luskus Delph* who were former Spectators or had spent a year or more in the Spectator Academy. There are thirty-four of them –all should have functioning implants." She handed Reidkr the list. "With that few Spectators, I'm sure we can kit-bash enough subdelta-band modules out of spare parts to be able to record their output. I had thought you'd peel these individuals off their regular duties only temporarily, pressing them into service as Spectators while we waited for OmNet to get us real Spectators. If there won't be real Spectators, those thirty-four people will just have to be re-assigned indefinitely. That will give you enough Spectators to cover the very highest-priority locations."

With a warbling sound, the door to the outer office dilated. Reidkr's adjutant held out a folded wad of paper. "This hardcopy communiqué came in your-eyes-only over the max-secure channel," she said curtly. "Instructions were that you see it immediately."

"Thank you." Reidkr unfolded the message. Her eyes goggled. "OmNet has spontaneously notified High Command that as a public service, it's sending ninety elite Spectators and all their ancillary apparatus to *Luskus Delph*." She re-folded the paper, clearly astonished. "Because our location is so remote, it'll be four months before they get here – few ships are as fast as *Impulsive*. So we will need to mobilize those thirty-four current crewmembers as you suggested until that time. But then, Senator Grice, you will have your Spectators."

"Excellent," Grice said, hoping to conceal her own surprise.

Reidkr leaned forward, visibly shaken. "I'm very sorry I underestimated you, Senator."

"That's hardly necessary," Grice temporized.

"You've got to tell me," Reidkr asked her in a rush. "How did you do it?"

"Captain Reidkr," Computer whirred petulantly, "why are you asking *her*?"

Chapter 56

October 26, 2367
Bohrkk, the People's Ground

Nirom Fpod was teaching Alrue Latier to build a fire in the wild.

Or trying to.

"Don't lean so close to the ignition point," Fpod ordered. "You're sweating so much, it soaks the kindling. And if you *do* get anything going –"

A finger of smoke rose from the pile of dampened plant scrap into which Alrue was feverishly spinning a stick. It reached his mouth just as he sucked in a harsh, gasping breath. A moment later Alrue was on his side, coughing spasmodically.

Sighing, Fpod seated himself on a rock next to Alrue's convulsing form. "Perhaps when we go on your Quest, all the nights will be warm."

"This is so very hard." Alrue gasped, propping himself on his elbows. "Will actually blowing up a moose be this hard?"

"Harder," Fpod said coldly. "Your Wisdom Quest is not meant to be easy."

"But will it come to pass that I actually blow up a moose? I understand that many who are now of the Wisdom estate never did so."

"That is none of your concern," Fpod said evasively. His bird-skull necklace made hollow clattering sounds as he rose to his feet. "*Your* goal is to blow up that moose. Now up with you."

"We're done building fires?"

"We hardly started. We can come back to it another time. Now, follow me!" Fpod set off into the scrub woods at a relaxed trot.

For Alrue, his lungs still raw from smoke, even matching that gentle pace was agony. Further questions inspired by his wives' suspicions would have to wait.

"There's a story that the Wisdom-folk tell about their godling," Fpod called out as he ran. "He's called Darvoyg."

"The Shan has spoken of Darvoyg," Alrue panted.

"He is the founder-hero of the Wisdom faith. Well, the story goes that Darvoyg traveled all over the face of the blasted landscape in the days of old. He encountered many *svadi* moose, and to each he granted the power of speech. Without exception, each animal begged not to be blown up. 'Please, holy one, not me,' each animal implored. 'The next one, perhaps, but not me.'" Fpod planted one foot, abruptly sprinting off to his left. Unable to follow, Alrue tumbled into a bower of fallen leaves. Fpod was not surprised; indeed, he'd chosen that spot for his sharp turn just because there was a soft place Alrue could land if he lost balance.

Fpod held out an arm to the Mormon, who put an indecent amount of his weight on it as he regained his footing. Alrue brushed leaves and stems from his temple garment. "You lost me," he gasped.

"I noticed."

"I mean, you lost me with the story. That's all there is to it? Darvoyg lets those moose speak, and they all ask not to be blown up? There's nothing more?"

"You are meant to work out the moral for yourself," Fpod said, trotting up a gentle hill.

Alrue joined Fpod at the hilltop, puffing convulsively. Sweat covered his face. Trying to sweep it away with a forearm, he succeeded only in pasting a hodgepodge of twigs and leaves to his forehead. "I know many religions," Alrue gasped, "but this tale baffles me. What is its meaning?"

Fpod spoke as he might to a child. "It is a sign from heaven, a sign that it pleases the gods for men to blow up moose." He took out his canteen, a signal that Alrue could do the same. "Follow the logic and you will find Darvoyg's lesson," Fpod insisted. "If every animal wishes to be spared, then their yearnings cancel each other out. Therefore each animal's desire to survive may be ignored. Therefore men may kill them."

Alrue forced himself to straighten his back and stop mouth-breathing. With a sidelong glance he noted which way Fpod was looking. Seizing the initiative, he loped off in a different direction. This time Fpod would have to follow him. *By the One Mighty and Strong,* Alrue thought, trotting eagerly, *I'm beginning to admire these people. Deviousness, audacity – their myths encode the* practical *virtues.*

Chapter 57

"WINCENC, AVU." The small grey box topped with its crystalline stylus was passed from person to person. "ENODA, GRAM." Amid laughter, each touched its tip to be named by the tinny voice. "GRICE, PAMELA. ZONOFNE, MAGDALENE."

Magdalene Zonofne, senior physicist of Team Cave, placed the ID biosensor in the middle of the lounge table. "Works pretty good," she said.

"I'll need that back now," Lii Bardicon chuckled, reaching for the device.

"Wait," Computer burred, "I haven't tried it yet." Projecting a shaped field – for the sfelb of it, the machine made it visible; it resembled a translucent octopus tentacle but ended in the small spatulate fingers of a Terran loris – the syn-noetic machine grasped the biosensor and moved it toward his floating body.

"I don't know if that's a good idea," Grice complained, reaching for the sensor clumsily and knocking over Lieutenant Wincenc's drink. "Sorry, Avu."

Computer made a noise like clearing his nonexistent throat, provoking another general gale of laughter. "Are we all watching now?" the machine whirred. "Here goes." Computer's see-through appendage pressed the biosensor's crystal tip against his body. At lightning speed, the machine simulated the DNA signature of one person around the table, then another – then of random members of the *Luskus Delph* crew. The little device spewed name after name. Their syllables cascaded into an unintelligible rasping buzz. The buzz stopped; the sensor's crystal tip blinked red. There was a faint smell of ozone.

"Oh, thanks," Bardicon said angrily, snatching the device from Computer's virtual grasp. "They issued me this just yesterday – I don't even know why, yet – and now look." She turned the little grey box over in her hands. "You've killed it."

"I'll make you a new one," Computer offered. "Want the only pink one?" A new biosensor materialized beside her right ear. It dropped to the tabletop.

It was pink.

"I hate when you do that, Hom Computer," Bardicon hissed in a show of anger that might have been more compelling if she weren't laughing so raucously.

Wincenc stood, swaying. Behind her, the folded diamond-matrix horns of the resonator arrays filled the panoramic windows of the officers' lounge. "Everyone," she called. "Everyone! Who knows what today is?"

"The first day we got any time off since *they* came aboard," Zonofne laughed, waving her beer stein in the direction of Enoda, Computer, and Grice.

"Come on, people," Wincenc badgered good-naturedly. "What happened today? What happened" – she paused for emphasis – "*thirty standard years ago* today?"

She assumed a distant look and drew a finger across her neck.

That was all anyone needed to see. Thirty years ago, the false messiah Arn Parek – strapped to a levitating cross, surrounded by worshipful soldiers on the stage of an abandoned amphitheater on Jaremi Four – had raved about resurrection and drawn a blade across his throat. Moments later, an artillery barrage had ravaged the stage; Parek was never seen again. For better or worse, mostly worse, henceforth he belonged to legend. His apparent death had been watched realtime by more

Galactics than any event before or since. It was an experience few forgot.

Elbows on the table, Wincenc steepled her fingers. "So, where was everybody?"

"Age before beauty, I suppose," Zonofne began, running a hand through her spiky white hair. "Thirty years ago, I was considerably more attractive than I am today, at least to a certain kind of person. And I was camping at a mountain lake on Capriesz, my homeworld, with about a dozen of that kind of people. It was your basic forjel-fest. Five – no, six – of us were well into a most satisfying orgy when two others came splashing into the lagoon to tell us we had to drop everything and see what was happening on Jaremi Four. You can probably imagine what *I* had to drop." She waited out the laughter, taking a leisurely mouthful of porter before she concluded, "Watching Parek do that to himself put a regular cold-lance on the mood for the rest of that evening, I can tell you."

Wincenc aimed a Svengali smile Enoda's way. "Now, then, the great Hom Enoda. Arguably, with Hom Computer, savior of the Galaxy."

"Don't rub it in," Computer burred.

"Come now, where were you when Parek d – well, whatever he did?"

"He died that day, I'm convinced of that," Enoda said. "If he'd lived, if any one of those gimcrack cults that styles itself 'Parekist' were genuinely *his*, we'd all know which one it was."

"Why is that?" Zonofne asked.

"It would be that cult, not the Confetory, that we'd all be working for. Parek was that good. Or bad, depending. Anyway, I was twenty-six. Though I lived on Terra, I'd already recognized that Galactics held all the real opportunities on my world, much as they'd molded the planet's most desirable places into Galactic Zones.

298

By then I'd spent almost two years hiring myself out to offworld tourists as a guide, so I was following Galactic affairs intensely. The day Parek died, I was squiring around a tour group from Orhiza Three. The young children were staking their patrimonies on the re-enacted Chicago Mercantile Exchange when the group mentor called us all away to *pov* Parek's final performance."

"'Performance,'" Wincenc said measuredly. "Not the word that many would apply to it."

"It's the word I choose. What stuck with me most was not the event itself, but the reaction to it." Enoda sipped his Iglonian brandy. "The Galaxy went crazy. The replays and commentary and sim re-enactments chattered on for months. I think that's when I finally, genuinely formed a visceral awareness of just how gigantic, how powerful, Galactic society is. If I'd had any doubts that I wanted off my backwater world and into the larger culture, that was when I set them aside."

Grice smiled. "I never knew that."

"You do now," Enoda said with a smirk. "Now you, Pam. Terrans on parade."

Grice raised her spiral snifter, drank, and emitted a racking cough. "Ghelttian *drazmu* liqueur, dismal stuff." She drank, coughed again. "I'd forgotten how much I used to love it. Oh yes, me thirty years ago. I was nineteen, still living in Denver – a quaint city in the mountains with so much autochthonous history that Galactics found it cloying, which was why Terrans still got to live there. I belonged to one of those Terran families that avoided anything Galactic as much as possible. I think my mom and dad – does everyone get that reference? Great – I think my mom and dad hoped that if they ignored the Galactics hard enough, they'd go away."

Wincenc half-smiled. "We did."

Grice shrugged. Swigged. Coughed. "The point is," she rasped, "even in my family everyone knew *something* was happening on Jaremi Four. We just didn't much care what it was. It wasn't until a few years later – after I'd made it into PeaceForce Academy – that some older cadets force-imposed the whole forjeling Parek affair into me so I'd know what everyone was supposed to know. They pumped his whole saga into me over about an hour and a half; my head hurt for a week. Point is, for me it's *not* the thirtieth anniversary quite yet."

"Still," Wincenc prodded, "when you *did* finally *pov* it, what did you feel?"

Grice arched her eyebrows. "Disappointment."

"Disappointment?" Zonofne echoed.

"You have to understand, much as my parents disdained Galactic stuff, I was fascinated by it. When I made my decision to leave Terra, to go out into the Galaxy and join the PeaceForce, I was full of optimism for all the things Galactic society was that Terra wasn't. And one of those things, I thought, was that Galactics were rational." Grice sipped her *drazmu* and coughed. "So when I finally *pov*ed Parek and realized what a huge thing he'd been *for Galactics*, I felt crushed. Getting taken in by a religious fanatic – that happened all the time on my homeworld. It was depressing to realize that despite their sophistication, Galactics had no protections against it either." Grice sat back in her floatchair.

"Come on, out with *your* story," Bardicon said to Wincenc.

"Yeah," Grice chuckled. "This whole discussion was your idea."

"The ward captain came for us," Wincenc said after a quick drink. "Not even the gero-mentor, the forjeling *ward captain* – wait. Grice, Enoda, you're from Terra, you know about these things?"

Grice nodded. "I grew up in a family. But yes, I know that's not how most of the Galaxy brings the next generation along."

"And you're Gwilyan, right?" Enoda prodded Wincenc. "So it would be all cloned females."

"Vat-grown, actually," Wincenc slurred. "I don't get many chances to tell these stories with Terrans listening, that's all. So I was fifteen, one of the oldest in my procreant clique, and the ward captain herself comes and calls us to the beta-level agora. That's a big oval gathering place, able to hold eight or nine cliques – that'd be, oh, five hundred girls. Now, we Gwilyans just don't grasp religion; the captains kept us up-to-date on the Parek affair mostly to underscore their endless warnings that other Galactics who believe in this stuff were crazy and that we should beware their tendencies to act on information no one else can see or hear. No offense, that's how I was raised." She flashed a sheepish smile around the table. "But when the Parek affair came to its epic conclusion, like I said, the ward captains brought us kids together in large gatherings. They'd waited until maybe a standard hour or so after it happened – they wanted time to work out their commentaries, you understand – but then we all *pov*ed it on delayed playback. They kept us up all night talking about it – the captains' orations, then back to our clique houses for guided discussion with the gero-mentors, then compulsory small groups. Our schedule wasn't back to normal for a nineday. You know, it's funny," Wincenc said, suddenly thoughtful. "They made us intellectualize about it so much, I don't think I ever knew for certain how it made me *feel*. Guess I still don't." She brushed her kinky hair back over her ears. "All right, Lii."

Bardicon wanted none of it. "Let someone else go first."

301

"You're the last one," Wincenc said, smiling. "Now go."

Bardicon leaned back in her floatchair, wondering with a sharp surge of anxiety whether Wincenc's purpose in launching this whole exercise might have been to elicit this story from her past. *That's absurd,* she told herself. *Just tell the forjeling story.* "I'm from Scalbulia Five, so like Senator Grice, I actually grew up in a family. Somewhere in my heart I guess I thought Parek *might* be the Cosmic Christ, like so many believed. I felt no certainty about it, but I found the mere possibility hugely exciting. There I was in the family res-unit, *pov*ing alongside my parents – everyone understand that term? – when Parek ... when he did what he did." She bit her lip. "There was so much blood – it was the most revolting thing I'd ever seen, I mean *pov*ed. Don't get me wrong, I was a normal kid. I'd *pov*ed all kinds of battles and wars from Enclave worlds, seen people blown to meaty bits. or crawling away from combat with one eyeball dangling and their intestines reeling out. But what happened with Parek was – *different* somehow. More resonant, more intense. I remember screaming. I broke off senso contact and ran out onto the balcony – we lived on the three-hundred-and-sixty-third floor. I was dizzy from the sudden shift in *being-thereness*, at first. All I could see was the sky, red as Parek's blood. I fell to my knees and cried until I was so hoarse I couldn't speak. Finally my mom came out. When I saw that she was crying too, I let her hold me. She confessed to me that she'd believed in Parek, really *believed*, and she was devastated. We wept together a long time. Finally we wet some hamsters and set them on the balcony railing."

"You did *what*?" Zonofne blurted.

"It's a Scalbulian way to relax," Bardicon explained. "You place small prey outside – if they're wet, their scent carries further – then you pull up seats just inside the glassite door and savor the patterns the raptors fly as they swoop in to pick them off."

An uneasy silence passed. "The sky was red, you said?" Wincenc asked quietly.

"Flaring red," Bardicon insisted. "I can close my eyes and see that sky even now."

"Scalbulia Five has a blue-green algae layer in its atmosphere, does it not?"

"Yes," Bardicon agreed, blinking rapidly.

"So the sky is cyan from morning until dark," Wincenc ruminated. "Even the most vivid sunset barely edges into the yellow." To Computer: "Am I right?"

"The atmosphere on Scalbulia Five has the appearance you describe," Computer chirruped.

Wincenc rose uncertainly to her feet, eyeing Bardicon harshly. "Many worlds have red skies at sunset; some have red skies all day long. But that's not where you grew up –"

"Sfelb forjel you!" Bardicon shouted at Wincenc with an intensity that roused everyone around the table out of their alcohol haze. "You wanted my memory, there it is. That's my memory." With that she stood, toppling her glass and overbalancing her floatchair. Rapidly, if unsteadily, she lurched out of the officers' lounge.

Chapter 58

"Trial number four, begin." Nirom Fpod upended the faded sea shell in its wooden frame. Dried seeds dropped from it at a measured rate.

Alrue Latier shook his head, sweat spraying in all directions, and swept the pack's straps from his shoulders. Pushing one knee outward, he slowed the pack's slalom toward the ground. He untied the knots and opened the pack with his right hand. Gripping the *rains red* by its nozzle end with his left hand, he pulled it from the pack and cradled it in the crook of his right elbow. He made a talon of his free left hand, nested its thumb and fingers into the five depressions in the device's midsection, and twisted. The front half sprang fifteen centimeters forward. Reaching inside the gap with his first and second fingers, Alrue found the priming pin and swung it into the half-power position. It seated with an audible *chunk.* Jerking his right elbow upward, Alrue rolled the weapon tip-first into his left hand, which clasped its forward section. With his right he gripped the rear section, pressing firmly. The two halves slammed home again; the *rains red* emitted a faint hissing sound. Alrue shifted his left hand up the device's body. With his right thumbnail he flipped open the arming hatch; with his right thumb and third finger he yanked out the safety tape. The device emitted a plaintive squeal, pitched higher than a *svadi* moose could hear.

Alrue dared a glance toward the sea shell. Seeds still fell from it.

"Four times you primed and armed the *rains red* within the time limit," Fpod announced. "You've mastered it."

Alrue held out the squealing conical device for Fpod to neutralize the training charge. "So what's next?" the Mormon prophet asked.

"Putting the *rains red* in the moose."

"Great," said Alrue, sliding the unarmed device back into his pack. "So where do we begin?"

Fpod gave a rearward pelvic thrust, the People's gesture of confusion. "There's nothing to begin. You take the *rains red,* and you put it in the moose."

"That's it?"

"That's it."

Alrue spread his hands in exasperation. "No special techniques? No shaggy-dog stories about how Takander Thurnb did it when he was his own great-grandfather?"

"That's a Warrior thing," Fpod corrected. "Wisdoms don't become their ancestors."

"Oh, of course, I forgot. Wisdoms just take a *rains red –*"

"– and put it in a moose," Fpod affirmed, jerking his chin up and to the right with unseemly vigor.

Alrue shouldered his backpack. "So that's really all there is to it?"

Fpod removed the timing shell and collapsed its wooden frame. "You've mastered the wilderness survival skills, as far as you will. You're in better physical condition than when we started. And you know how to prime and arm the *rains red.* There's nothing more for me to teach," he said, nestling the shell in a fur-lined sack. "You're as ready for your Quest as you're going to get."

The Mormon and the Warrior were silent as they finished packing their modest equipment. With filled backpacks, one shoulder bundle each, and smaller items hanging from their belts in bags made from the stomachs and intestines and gall bladders of various disgusting furry creatures, they marched along the top of the scree ridge. Fpod squinted toward the northwest, where a blue-grey pall tainted the sky. "That – what did you call it? – 'volcano' seems angrier than ever today."

Alrue nodded grimly. "So there's really no more training?"

"What's left for you to know?"

Alrue thought for a moment. "Just one thing, I suppose. When I find my moose, and plan my approach, and prime and arm my *rains red* without alerting the moose to my presence – "

" – then you put the *rains red* in the moose. Then run like your tunic's on fire. But nobody needs training for that part."

"Surely you have taught me much that I might learn wisdom," Alrue conceded. "But one thing I'm still unclear on. When I put the *rains red* in the moose, where do I put it?"

"In the moose."

"Yes, but *where* in the moose?"

Fpod allowed himself a last look over his shoulder at the faraway volcano before leading Alrue down the scree ridge, back toward their crater home. "Well," he said thoughtfully, "where do you think?"

Chapter 59

Wincenc rose uncertainly to her feet, eyeing Bardicon harshly. "Many worlds have red skies at sunset; some have red skies all day long. But that's not where you grew up –"

"Sfelb forjel you!" Bardicon shouted at Wincenc with an intensity that roused everyone around the table out of their alcohol haze. "You wanted my memory, there it is. That's my memory." With that she stood, toppling her glass and overbalancing her floatchair. Rapidly if unsteadily, she lurched out of the officers' lounge.

***

"Okay, Bucko, that's the third time I've replayed my record of last evening for you," Computer burred. "What are you seeing in it? Aside from how funny you are when you're drunk."

"We were all drunk," Enoda said.

"All the humans."

Enoda removed his hands from the machine's body – or at least, from its ever-present shields. "I just can't figure out what's going on between Wincenc and Bardicon. Why was Bardicon's misremembering the sky color so important?"

"Truth to tell, I've no idea."

"Here's one way to go at it," Enoda mused. "Wincenc mentioned that some worlds have all-red skies at all times. Which are they?"

"If we limit ourselves to Memberworlds and Affiliates, there's only one," Computer whirred. "Buerala Six has an algae layer that tints the sky as red as Scalbulia Five's is blue-green. On Buerala Six the sky's always red."

"Buerala Six," Enoda wondered. "Is that significant?"

"The people who live there think so."

"Funny. But what's there? The remnants of Ênvå Corglinü's old nihilist church, of course. There's a cultural industry centered on creation of musical sculptures for export, and a half-dozen cuisines with offworld followings."

Computer perused his databases. "Buerala Six hosts the conflict resolution institute for its Galactic sector, the Syndicate for Human Refurbishment, and the arts colony that founded and still drives the trans-stellar development of *ecyvroupp* textile weaving. Nothing jumps out."

Enoda nodded. "Yet Lieutenant Wincenc reacted as though Fem Bardicon's failure of recollection was a major development in some bitter, long-fought game between them."

"Their behavior invites an explanation," Computer agreed. "But we don't have enough information to deduce it at this time."

"You think not?"

"I *know* not, with mathematical certainty."

"Very well, we can save your slightly constrained computing power for the truly insoluble questions," Enoda deadpanned. "And here's the first insoluble question: Why did everyone in the Galaxy who'd lost socks get them all back at the same time – *except* us in our little homestead there on Standoff World?"

"The problem may be insoluble, but I cannot understand why you find it interesting. And in any case, it has no bearing on our mission."

"Before we got dragooned out to *Luskus Delph,* the missing-socks mystery *was* our mission," Enoda objected. He stood and paced the small private ready room. "Yes, it's a tiny detail – why was ours the only location in the Galaxy to which no missing socks were returned? Still, the problem doesn't seem to me like it should be insoluble, not compared to some of the truly thorny puzzles we've broken."

"What do you mean, *we*?" Computer taunted.

"You make my point for me," Enoda chided. "I contribute the odd meta-notion, but we both know the computational brute force to break down the toughest problems comes from you. We've agreed that the problem of my missing socks seems soluble; the fact is simply that you *haven't* solved it. Normally, an unanswered question goads you. It becomes its own motive for you to lavish computing resources on the problem until you break it down. But not this problem. On this one, you gave up without a fight. That's unlike you, Hogarth."

"My name's not Hogarth."

"Don't change the subject," Enoda snapped. "Now call up that big personality function test I asked you to run this morning."

"Wait, isn't that changing the subject?"

"Inconsistency is one of my charming human qualities," Enoda japed. "And anyway, it's not a real change of subject. I asked you to compute your personality function because I'm worried about your disinterest in the problem with my socks."

"Don't get your charming human qualities all in a knot. My personality function tested with flying colors, I'm an eighty-three."

"You're a *what?*" Eyes wide, Enoda scrambled across the chamber and placed his hands flat on Computer's shielded body. "The raw data, show me now."

Their soaring interface was still out of reach amid *Luskus Delph*'s noise signature; instead, Computer projected layer after layer of tridee graphics before Enoda's ordinary vision. "You're right," he told the machine after a minute's scrutiny. "Your personality function is eighty-three point zero-zero-one-six-five-four-seven. The score appears accurate, and there's no sign of a flaw in your self-analysis or your processing of the data."

"I could have told you that."

Enoda broke contact. Settling back into a floatchair, he rested his fingers on his cheeks. "But every time you've run this elementary index of your personality strength before, you've returned a score between six and ten. So now you're an eighty-three? *Nine times* higher?"

Colors foamed uncertainly across the machine's chromed body. "A wise man said, 'I am not contained between my hat and my boots.'"

"Neither of which you have," Enoda said sourly. "A personality function nine times higher than it should be – that *would* suggest that you are 'large, and contain multitudes.'"

"Maybe it's a consequence of all those protective algorithms I have to run in order to operate at all out here?"

"I doubt it," Enoda said, peering again at the projected data. "The wave-lattice signature would be different than what I'm seeing. The output profile isn't granular, as it would be if dominated by gross algorithms. It's fractal, like it should be if you're generating a large number of rich personalities." Enoda smiled. "Not like we haven't done that before."

"But I am not doing so now," the machine protested.

"Tell me," Enoda said speculatively, "if I gave you your choice between wonking my still-missing socks and wonking this problem, which would you select?"

"I'd opt to explore why Lieutenant Wincenc is so fascinated by Fem Bardicon's error of memory."

"But that's not one of your options."

"Don't you need to sleep or squirt plorg or something?"

Enoda edged back from the table, studying the flow of colors across Computer's body.

"Hey, I know," the machine said to fill the silence. "Hasn't it been a couple of whole days since you forjeled Fem Grice?"

Captivating, and at the same time frightening, Enoda thought. *This makes not just one, but a* series *of problems that the Galaxy's most powerful – and usually, most inquisitive – intellect seems to have a positive distaste for solving. Why? And what are my chances of figuring it out if I can't rely on my floating collaborator to crunch the heavy numbers?*

Chapter 60

November 20, 2367
Bohrkk, Nearing the People's Ground

The hardest thing about a fast march down a moderate slope was keeping it from collapsing into a dead-out run. Nirom Fpod was holding to the fast march, so Alrue Latier had to also. "They kick, don't they?" the Mormon asked.

"You mean the moose?"

"Of course the moose."

"Oh, yeah," Fpod replied. "That's something to watch out for."

Chapter 61

The workroom Pamela Grice had been assigned as Captain Reidkr's special projects officer for security was small and oddly configured, with nine walls and a gently sloping ceiling. On the other hand, the desktop was a single polished idocrase crystal and the strip of wall behind it was brushed platinum inlaid with rich rare-earth glasses. This was yet another section of *Luskus Delph* that had begun its service as some sort of luxury passenger liner.

Her intercom beeped; the next thing heard was the chirping of the ID biosensor wielded by the guard in her outer office. "BARDICON, LII. HARBRAESKOR, SGIELA."

"Admit them," Grice said crisply. The door swung open on some hydraulic mechanism. "Welcome, Historian Harbraeskor. I knew Fem Bardicon was coming, but I didn't know you were also –"

"I'm sure you didn't," Harbraeskor blustered. "I am here as leader of Team Info. Fem Bardicon was already on her way to this office when I ran into her; she may as well start."

"By all means," Grice said uncertainly, settling back behind her desk.

Bardicon leaned forward, her expression stern. "Fem Grice, I was most surprised to be among the last to learn of my new assignment."

"Among the last – oh, of course," Grice replied. "The orders were included in the security briefing that was transmitted to all personnel by group didactic imposition."

"Incorporating knowledge of the new semaphore code, operating instructions for the semaphore repeaters and the ID biosensors – and, of course," Bardicon said coldly, "the involuntary commissioning of anyone aboard *Luskus Delph* who is capable of recording senso."

"Including yourself," Grice confirmed. "And as the person who administered the impositions, you would have been in the final cohort to receive those orders. I suppose that couldn't be helped."

"I protest the assignment."

"And I protest it too," Harbraeskor said urgently. "Fem Bardicon is Team Info's only instructional dynamicist. I need her doing her job, not standing at some corridor junction being a human security camera."

Grice held up a finger. "If you don't mind, Historian, I'd like first to hear Fem Bardicon's reasons for protesting the assignment."

"Very well."

Bardicon stood. "I have three reasons, Fem Grice. First, Historian Harbraeskor is right, I have pressing work on Team Info. Second, I haven't functioned as a Spectator for several years and I was never very good at it –consult my C. V., I washed out of Spectator Academy in my second year."

"I was aware of that. Please continue with your third reason."

Bardicon stepped forward and spread her hands over the edge of Grice's desk. "Fem Grice, I have strong personal disinclinations to operating as a Spectator. The circumstances of my failure at the Academy – it's not just that I was unskilled, I found some of the mental tasks involved in Spectator work quite obnoxious. I was, well, *advised* that it would be best for the integrity of my neural firmware that I not continue."

"Your neural firmware?"

Bardicon's eyes dipped. "My central nervous system."

"That's quite exceptional," Grice said. "Why didn't I see any of that in your C. V.?"

Bardicon leaned away from the desk and clasped her hands behind her back. "Portions of my personnel files from the Academy are sealed."

"Sealed? Why?"

"I am not at liberty to say."

Grice pressed her hands together. "Fem Bardicon, you are aware that I am operating as special projects officer for security under an extraordinary commission from Captain Reidkr, who is tasked with ensuring the success of one of the highest-priority projects in the Galaxy?"

"I am, Gentlefem." Bardicon was looking straight ahead. "Even that does not relieve me of my obligation to silence."

"Is this obligation planeto-ethnic?" Grice demanded. "Is it religious?"

"Again, Gentlefem, I am not at liberty to say."

"With whom *would* you be at liberty to discuss these matters?"

Bardicon swallowed. "High Command."

Computer could arrange a surprise for you, Grice thought, *but perhaps this is not the time.* "Please be seated, Fem Bardicon. Your objections are noted – as are yours, Historian Harbraeskor. Nonetheless, this is our situation. The electronic and vibrionic noise environment of *Luskus Delph* precludes ordinary methods of recording images for security purposes, as you know. Delta-band apparatus, including Spectator implants and senso recording and playback apparatus, is not compromised. Until a special contingent of Spectators arrives from OmNet, we need every recording observer we can get; and we need them badly enough to justify releasing from his or her usual work every crew member capable of recording senso. Under these circumstances, Fem Bardicon, your reassignment stands. But in light of your objections, I note that your assignment requires only the most elementary Spectator functions, simple observation and recording. No higher-level applications of polyphasic consciousness – appending commentaries, say, or sending laterals – will be needed. On that basis I presume the work will not overtax you, despite your acknowledged sensitivities. If you find it doing harm, of course, you may present yourself at sick bay. If you opt to do so, I have one recommendation – have a problem the med techs can find.

"As for you, Historian, I believe the demands for didactic imposition resulting from the work of myself, Hom Computer, and Hom Enoda will be modest from here out. If you have urgent need of Fem Bardicon, please get in touch with me and I will do what I can to loosen her schedule so that her work for you can go forward as rapidly as possible."

"Understood," Harbraeskor said unhappily.

"Understood also," Bardicon said icily. "May I ask to whom I may appeal this determination?"

"To Captain Reidkr, I suppose." Grice smiled coldly. "After that, you know better than I who your friends are in High Command." She consulted a schedule, riffling unaccustomedly through a sheaf of hardcopy printouts. "But for now, your first shift begins in twenty-one minutes. Your duty station, Waveguide Arcade Seven, is a goodly distance away. Best you get moving. Dismissed."

Chapter 62

"He left *today*?" Constance Latier almost shouted. "Darn!"

"Language, sister wife," Zuzenah cautioned.

"We were to be together tonight," Constance complained. "Third Wednesday was a week and a half ago, after all." She spared a reproachful glance for Nataleah, who'd lately been sharing Alrue's bed almost every other night.

"O lascivious Aunt Constance," Nataleah mocked. "Have a care for your soul as well as your body. The Lord God delights in the chastity of women."

Constance's grey eyes widened angrily. "And whoredoms are an abomination before me; thus saith the Lord of Hosts."

"What's a whoredom?" asked Abigayl.

"Ladies, what's wrong?" Meryam Mayishimu asked, bustling into the great hall of the Latiers' assigned quarters. "You may speak freely, I'm not recording."

"Alrue went off early this morning with Nirom Fpod," Lupida announced. "You know, on his Wisdom Quest."

"That blow-up-a-moose thing?" Meryam demanded. "He left just like that?"

"Without a word to any of us," said Zuzenah.

"You know how he's been leaving most mornings before dawn," Abigayl explained, "to climb out of the crater with Fpod and greet the sun, or whatever it was they did."

"This morning they went to that rock outcropping shaped like a ferkeek," Zuzenah recounted. "There they met a party of half a dozen Warriors and Wisdoms. They

317

prayed, danced clockwise, chanted, and danced counterclockwise."

"Men," Meryam sighed.

"After the dancing, Takander Thurnb himself kitted out Alrue and Fpod with hiking staffs and minimal rations and an actual *rains red*, and off they went."

Ferkeek Rock, Meryam thought. *I never got around to strewing bugs there. Wouldn't be surprised if Alrue knew it.* "How do we know this?" she asked.

Zuzenah shrugged, still squeezing at her palm. "One of the junior Warriors who was there came by a few minutes ago. He shared all those details with us by way of saying that Alrue would be gone for a while."

Abigayl scrutinized Meryam through narrowed brown eyes. "What is wrong, Aunt Meryam?"

Meryam trudged to her seat at the log table and hugged her slender frame in frustration. "I told him and told him how important it was that I fit him with bugs before he went off on his Quest."

"Spectator bugs?" asked Lupida.

"Of course. This forjeling moose quest has assumed such importance, it has to be documented."

"Well, now it won't be," drawled Nataleah. "And I think I know why." She puffed up her robe, hunched her shoulders, and puffed out her cheeks: imitating Alrue, as the wives had seen her do many times before. "For better or worse," she blustered, "I, Alrue, am no Joseph Smith."

Zuzenah's black eyes were full of chiding. "Aunt Nataleah, what was the point of that?"

"I see her point," Meryam declared. "Those were Alrue's words back at Arbadrel, after he tried to enter the Tuezi Engineer portal – and failed, so very publicly."

"He simply lost his nerve," said Constance mournfully.

"And afterward he had nowhere to hide, no way to conceal his failure."

"He'd been too confident," Lupida ventured. "When he lunged for that portal, he took a live tridee pickup with him. He wound up broadcasting his failure to the Galaxy in real time."

"There has been nothing he fought harder to live down," Meryam agreed.

"This Wisdom Quest is Alrue's greatest trial since Arbadrel," said Nataleah with a sense of finality. "And this time, by forjel, he's going to succeed or fail *without* an audience."

Zuzenah leaned back in her dining chair, thrilled by an insight. "Thanks be to the Lord of Hosts," she said dreamily, "my dear husband actually learned something."

Chapter 63

June 21, 2376
Aboard *Luskus Delph*

The door annunciator warbled. "Enter," Lii Bardicon said in a choked voice.

"Is someone here?" Avu Wincenc pushed away thick tropical leaves heavy with dampness. Or tried to; her hands passed through them.

"Welcome to my *faux* forest," Bardicon called. "Follow my voice."

After some thrashing, Wincenc emerged blinking from the projected jungle.

Bardicon occupied a rainforest bower, sitting in what seemed a bamboo chair. The ropy trunks of a vast sim banyan tree hulked stoically behind her, helpless to repel the tendrils of a strangler fig. Tiny lizards scampered along its bark, snatching polychrome butterflies from the air with whip-fast tongues.

Wincenc reacted to the virtual environment Bardicon had chosen for her quarters with poorly concealed distaste. "You will have to pardon me, Fem Bardicon. I prefer to imagine us humans as masters of the natural world."

"As you see," said Bardicon, "I prefer to imagine us as parts of nature."

"Very minor parts," said Wincenc, grimacing as a hand-sized sim mantis dropped onto her shoulder. "This is meant to be a Terran rainforest?"

"Indeed. Terra may be Sequestered, but still it is the cradle of us all." Perspiration beaded on Bardicon's brow, her lip. Her off-duty wrap was loosely fastened, displaying noteworthy cleavage, that too dotted with sweat. "Now you know why I found your cabin on the plain side."

"Indeed," Wincenc said. "How do you manage all this sim under *Luskus Delph* conditions?"

"Tridee gear's down, of course. I use my senso player in squeezedown mode to achieve the sim projection."

"I should have thought of that. Senso still works."

"Don't I know it." Bardicon's eyes welled with tears.

Now that Wincenc could see Bardicon clearly, she realized the younger woman had been crying for some time. "You ... you called for me."

"Yes, please sit." One of the banyan's compound trunks faded, revealing a second bamboo chair. Wincenc settled into it.

Bardicon leaned forward, hugging herself. "I completed my first shift as a Spectator today."

"By which you mean, you stood in a hallway and recorded."

"I stood in Waveguide Arcade Seven. A really *big* hallway. And recorded."

Wincenc regarded her uncertainly. "Was that difficult for you?"

"It was the first time I've been in Mode."

"Since Spectator Academy?"

"No." Bardicon's hands leapt outward, fastening on Wincenc's wrists. "It was the first time ... *I* ... have been in Mode." She stared into Wincenc's eyes, her eyelids fluttering away moisture. Their faces were two hands' width apart. "Can you keep my secret?" she demanded.

Wincenc was surprised to feel *Yes, anything,* forming as a reply. But that could not be. "If duty permits," she said guardedly, "I will."

"Duty," Bardicon said coldly. "Owed to whom?"

"The PeaceForce," Wincenc responded. "More immediately, to Captain Reidkr. Ultimately, to High Command."

"High Command – they know about this. I'm not certain Reidkr's been briefed." Bardicon scrunched her eyes shut, expelling another wash of tears. "But I've got to tell someone. For all I know, you've already guessed bits of it."

Now Wincenc leaned forward. "You *are* Amli Revskond."

"No," Bardicon said. "I mean, not the way you think." She released Wincenc's wrists and leaned back in her chair, hugging herself.

"Tell me," Wincenc said urgently.

"Amli Revskond died about three years ago."

"I know," Wincenc replied.

"You knew *that*?"

"I said I was a fan." Out of sight, a sim toucan shrieked. "So you can imagine my amazement when you turned up here, very much alive. Were the stories wrong?"

"The stories?" Bardicon echoed.

"The stories that you'd died."

"You mean that Amli died."

"As you like. Were they false?"

Bardicon chuckled bitterly. "Oh, no. Amli Revskond died. It was hushed up, but she died of one drug overdose too many. Then it was discovered that ill-chosen psychoactives and hallucinogens had scrubbed her brain clean."

"You speak as though she's not you," Wincenc said gently.

"Don't you see? She's not." Bardicon wiped her eyes. "Amli died without leaving a sample-and-scan."

"Meaning she died for keeps?"

Bardicon nodded grimly. "Crazy artist."

"Leaving a scrambled brain, a relatively intact body, but no data to guide the reconstruction of her personality," Wincenc mused. "All of which leaves *you* … where, exactly?"

"I'm right here," Bardicon said firmly. "But I'm not Amli. I have her gross brain structure, her body, her Spectator implants – but I'm a new person. Don't you get it? *I'm a Reef.*"

Wincenc leaned back in her chair and let out a long breath. "Refurbished! You? The full process?"

"After Amli's death, the body was quickly repaired. Fixing the brain damage – No scans of Amli being available, the brain had to be fast-written with new memories. New neural pathways."

"A new person," Wincenc breathed.

"Re-using the body of someone gone forever. That's me."

Wincenc nodded. "The Syndicate for Human Refurbishment advertises that they can build a new consciousness with adult memories and post-cadet competency in about two standard years."

"As they did in my case." Bardicon brushed at strands of brown hair that had escaped from her protective bun. "Of course, the technology's not perfect – Reefs receive synthetic childhood memories, sometimes arbitrary ones, in hopes of giving their adult personalities more depth. But errors creep in." Bardicon leaned forward. "That red sky. I know now – it's not right for my homeworld, yet that *is* my childhood memory. Why?"

"I think I have an idea."

"Tell me," Bardicon whispered.

"You should work it out for yourself. Where is the Syndicate for Human Refurbishment located?"

"Buerala Six, of course."

"And on that world the sky is … what color?"

Bardicon's eyes widened. "It's red!"

Wincenc nodded. "Like in that childhood memory you couldn't actually have had –"

"—because *I* didn't grow up on Scalbulia Five." Bardicon laughed bitterly. "Strictly speaking, *I* didn't grow up at all. So while the refurb techs were furnishing my new personality's basement, they cobbled up some arbitrary where-was-I-when-Parek-died scenario and finished it off with whatever details they had lying around."

Wincenc nodded urgently. "And your false memory got a Bueralan sky stitched into it."

Bardicon's tears resumed. Now Wincenc reached out, encircling the younger woman's wrists in her own strong hands. "You hear stories," she said quietly. "Someone dies under just the right wrong circumstances and gets Reefed. Two-plus years later, the person *is* someone else, but by some bureaucratic mischance he or she gets reassigned to the body's old ship. A new person, yet recognized by way too many shipmates as whoever he or she was before. When those faulty childhood memories crop up, as they often do, there's such yearning for them to be a glimmer of the old identity."

"And every now and again a Reef, too, yields to the temptation to interpret the ill-grouted joints of the mind as windows into the body's past," Bardicon admitted. "There are no such windows, you know – no muscle memory, no echoes of the old personality. Nobody Heinleins."

"Nobody does what?"

"Sorry, Reef slang. Heinlein was a writer, long ago. You know, of books."

Wincenc grimaced. "*Really* long ago."

"Well, he wrote one void-awful book about a man whose brain was transplanted into a woman's body. Her essence still inhabited the body and they had long talks.

Long, *long* talks. Mostly about sex. To us, it bundles up everything that being a Reef is not."

Wincenc released Bardicon's wrists, her hands descending to clasp her own knees. "You can see why people would imagine it *might* be that way. When you think about it, they could scarcely do otherwise."

Bardicon's reddened eyes brightened. "There you're wrong, Lieutenant Wincenc. People can always do otherwise."

"Do you really believe that? I know, I'm about to sound all-too-Gwilyan – but more often than not we lack meaningful choices; our paths are predetermined. We comfort ourselves with whimsies about free will. But how free are we when our options are so limited by circumstance?"

"You're right, you know," Bardicon said coolly.

"I am?"

"Yes. You sounded like *such* a Gwilyan just now." Bardicon's eyes moistened again. "Say what you want, but I know there is nothing more powerful than the human will. Know what? My will is exerting itself now, as we speak." She gestured, palms up, fingers splayed wide: a sign betokening expansive scope. "I'm making a radical decision – it feels like I'm watching myself make this decision – and I'm kind of amazed by what I'm seeing. For the first time in my life I truly understand that memory I have about the day Parek died. In my head I know it's false. I never watched that senso with my parents; I never grew up in that res-tower; I never ran out on that balcony to fill my vision with the wrong world's sky. It's just something the refurb techs sutured together. Still, it's what I remember. And at this moment I am deciding to embrace it. I'm the person who came together around that memory; false though it is, that memory is *mine*. It's part of me, and so it will be real … for me. That's what I've decided just now."

"Can one really be 'free' to say the unreal is real?" Wincenc mused. "To me that seems an abuse of freedom."

"There we disagree," said Bardicon. "Being able to value in any way we choose, even calling the unreal real, if that's how things feel – to me, that's the essence of freedom." She eyed Wincenc appraisingly. "Maybe that's why your enthusiasm for Amli unnerved me so. For all that Amli was this wild radical artist, she was unfree in so many ways. Tied down by her aesthetic obsessions, by her drugs ... even her death was just a stupid accident. I *like* being me instead of her. And on some level, I think I feared you might push me down some path of re-entanglement with who – with what she was."

"I'll take care not to do that, Fem Bardicon – now." Wincenc brushed sweat from the hair above her ears. "But if you want my cooperation, I need to hear the rest of your story. And then, the rest of Amli's."

Bardicon nodded resignedly. "Where do you want to start?"

"You didn't really wash out of Spectator Academy, did you?"

"What makes you think that?"

"The Reefing process takes two years," Wincenc observed. "Supposedly you made it into your second year in Academy. But Amli only died three years ago."

Bardicon nodded slowly. "You've realized the Academy thing had to be a cover story."

Wincenc scowled. "Your body had Spectator implants because Amli was a Spectator. For you to use them, the refurb techs had to imprint you with a replica of Spectator Academy tutelage. A fake Academy background – no wonder you're not keen to go into Mode."

"No, that's not the problem."

326

"Isn't it?" Wincenc insisted. "Spectator training – that's an extraordinary degree of education and conditioning to seek to duplicate by reimprintment."

"And not without its risks."

Wincenc studied the younger woman's eyes. "But still, you say, we haven't reached the real problem?"

Bardicon nodded grimly. "There's something about Amli Revskond that few knew. Especially her fans. Tell me, Lieutenant: that incredible rainforest senso that you played for me –"

"*Jungle Slew.*"

" – what do you know about how it was made?"

"A great deal, actually." Wincenc grew animated, speaking as one aficionado would to another. "Conventional special effects are impossible in senso, as you know. You – Amli Revskond, I mean – went to astounding lengths to guarantee that her *actual experience* would be distorted in very particular ways. First, she journeyed to Yantarr, which orbits two yoked stars, a red giant and a blue dwarf. That yielded natural lighting effects available nowhere else. Artificial fog was laid down just before recording began, to create an ethereal impression and to make objects' bi-colored shadows unmistakable. Amli wore contact lenses that fluoresced in various colors under UV radiation from the blue dwarf. Finally, you – sorry, *she* – took mild perception-distorting drugs. They heightened the unnatural images from the contact lenses, fomented the false impression of gigantic scale, altered her sense of time, and masked bodily sensations that might betray that she was simply riding a floatboard a few centimeters above the jungle floor."

"That wasn't everything," Bardicon said.

"What did I overlook?"

"Nothing." Urgently she gripped Wincenc's hands in her own. "The fog, the lenses, the mild drugs, they were all used. But it took more than that to defeat the brutal realism of senso. She added somatic techniques drawn from the meditative traditions of a dozen worlds. And to bring it all together, she needed serious drugs. Real brain-benders." A new line of tears launched its drunkard's walk down Bardicon's cheek. "Amli's art depended on – was inseparable from – the drugs that killed her."

At last Bardicon released Wincenc's hands. The older woman brought them up to cradle Bardicon's face. "Let me see if I understand the problem, then. You – Lii Bardicon, the *you* you are now – you have the Spectator implants and the imprinted memory of the Academy training you never received, but you haven't actually functioned as a Spectator before today."

Bardicon nodded harshly. "Amli's personality is gone, but still it's her old brain I inhabit. And being a Spectator didn't end well for her." She reached up, clasping Wincenc's face in her hands.

"Amli was an artist," Wincenc said quietly. "You're just recording events in a waveguide arcade. There's no way to know such light Spectator work courts the same danger."

"Or to know it doesn't."

"Which leaves the final question: Why are you here?"

"As in, assigned to *Luskus Delph?*" Bardicon shrugged. "Why not?"

"*Luskus Delph*'s mission is extremely sensitive."

"*Luskus Delph* was also assembled – and crewed – in great haste." Bardicon shrugged. "Look, Lieutenant, I'm sure no one in High Command checked a box in some planning hyperqueue and said 'Remember, everyone, we gotta have a Reef Spectator on Team Info!' But I'm also pretty certain that, given how desperate High Command must have been to get a crew together, my unique background wouldn't have justified rejecting me out of hand. Still, most people on board don't know my backstory, and it's probably best that it not come out in some uncontrolled way." She edged further forward. Their faces were but centimeters apart. "Please, Lieutenant Wincenc, will you keep my secret?"

"Call me Avu," she breathed. Their tongues swirled together. The kiss was consuming, imperative.

"I'd heard Gwilyans lacked a sex drive," Bardicon breathed a minute later.

"You heard it was genetically engineered out because we no longer needed it?"

"That's right."

Wincenc smiled. "We may not need sex as insistently as other humans. And in the reproductive sense, of course, we don't need it at all. But we still … like it." She rubbed her palms over Bardicon's shoulders. "We regard it as delicious and inevitable."

"I like that."

When Wincenc's lean hands slipped inside Bardicon's wrap to cup her luxuriant breasts, it felt inevitable enough for them both.

Chapter 64

Alrue Latier and Nirom Fpod trudged through an arroyo, working their way south. Their grey-green Questing robes hung sweat-sodden from their shoulders. "'And it came to pass that we did find upon the land of promise, as we journeyed in the wilderness,'" Alrue recited between gasping breaths. "'There were beasts in the forests of every kind, both the cow and the ox –'"

"The cow and the *ox*?" Fpod echoed, perplexed.

"Kinds of livestocks," Alrue hastily explained. "The cows are females. The oxen, those are castrated males."

"The males were castrated? Some land of promise."

"'–and the ass and the horse,'" Alrue continued, "'and the goat and the wild goat, and all manner of wild animals.' Thus wrote the first Nephi." Alrue tugged at his temple garment. "But do you think *we* can find a single moose?"

"It's only day four," Fpod said neutrally. Before them, the arroyo broadened; the channel they'd been following converged with another that came in from their left, bringing a chattering rivulet of water and foam. Fpod dipped a cupped hand into the brook, brought it up and sniffed, then quaffed it. "Fresh and fizzy," he reported. "Like the springs we found yesterday."

After the men refilled their canteens, Alrue stretched and shifted the weight of his modest shoulder bag. "Is four days long for a Wisdom Quest?" he queried. "How long do they go, usually?"

"Till they're done." Fpod squinted up and down the newfound channel, his right hand worrying at his necklace of bird skulls. "Let's follow this brook downstream."

They hiked in silence for fifteen minutes. The channel arched toward the southwest. The arroyo floor was flat, a jumble of rounded pebbles, rocky shards, scraps of weathered wood, and occasional animal bones. *From time to time this channel must carry turbulent waters,* Alrue recognized. For now, though, the fizzy brook tumbled harmlessly beside their path, never more than half-a-meter wide and one or two hands' widths deep.

Across the brook, to the east, the clay bluffs fell away. A talus of rocky scree formed a natural ramp that led gently upward through a notch in the bluff walls, offering access to the tablelands above. Fpod stepped across the brook and started upslope. "Let's see what's up there."

They clambered onto a gently rolling highland dotted with scrubby trees. Alrue stepped up beside Fpod, squinting into the morning sun. "Any idea where we are?"

Fpod pointed to the northwest. "The volcanoes are that way."

Alrue scowled. "Two – no, three new plumes. It's still growing."

"As you say, it's good we're not there." The highland was covered in gritty soil run through with veins of gnarled rock. There was no need to fear ferkeeks on ground like that, so Fpod made straight for a sparse woods. Doggedly Alrue followed his Warrior guide among stunted trees.

Presently they tramped into a clearing and into dazzling morning sun. The highland plateau's eastern boundary was marked by an oddly regular line of rocky columns, eight to twelve meters tall. They ran along the cliff edge in both directions as far as one could see, suggesting a giant's picket fence – or perhaps a hundred ill-nourished miners facing guns, their ragged fingers

331

splayed skyward. "Did these occur naturally?" Alrue wondered. "Or did someone build this line of rocks long ago?"

"No one knows," Fpod replied. "We call them the sentinel rocks." Through the gaps between each granite shaft, verdant lowlands could be glimpsed. "That plain beyond them is sometimes a good place to look for moose."

Alrue stuck his head between two of the rocky pillars. "Nirom," he said quietly, "come and behold this!"

Fpod scrambled to Alrue's side. Below them, a glassy watercourse meandered across the plain, throwing back the morning sun's yellow-white radiance. "That creek never used to be there," Fpod mused.

"Never mind the creek," Alrue murmured, shielding his eyes. "Look there, where it ponds up."

Fpod squinted to his left. In the shallow valley before them, ninety meters or so to northward, the creek abruptly widened into a broad, nearly round pool, its surface a dazzling mirror for the sun. Fpod leaned into the light. He brought up one hand, then the other. Then he saw it, if only in silhouette. "There's your *svadi* moose," he whispered.

The beast stood – or lay, one couldn't be sure through the light-dazzle – by the water's edge. It seemed a mature bull.

This time it was Alrue who led. He scrambled south along the cliff edge at a full run.

"Not so fast, Alrue!" Fpod hissed. "Now's the time for cleverness and stealth."

"No," Alrue huffed over his shoulder. "Now's the time to blow up a moose."

They had drawn even with the big animal's position. Peering between two spires straight into the sun, Alrue could just see the beast.

Fpod pressed himself against Alrue's back to squint over his shoulder. "Hasn't moved," he muttered. "That's one thirsty moose."

How to get down there? Alrue leaned further forward, staring to either side. *There!* A dozen meters back the way he'd come, a natural wash smoothed the cliffside's grade. Alrue retraced his steps, passing one column whose hollowed base created a looming overhang. "Here!" he said urgently. He'd found a gap between pillars that expanded into a narrow defile: an ancient, runoff-carved conduit that in its turn intersected the wash. "Behold!" Alrue exulted. "I know that God is not a partial God! Nirom, the *rains red,* if you please."

"Not yet!" Fpod hissed. "For once you need to listen to me. You can't just walk up on the moose and stick the *rains red* ... you know."

"That is exactly what I plan to do," Alrue rumbled. "Friend Nirom, this quest is over."

"Then I'll give it to you down there," Fpod said, stepping around Alrue and lurching toward the defile.

He stopped short when Alrue's outstretched arm slammed against his chest.

Fpod drew back to hurl a curse.

The look in Alrue's eyes stopped him cold.

His eyes afire, Alrue struck a prophetic pose. He seemed every centimeter a son of Ethem. "Nirom Fpod," he thundered, "before you were my guide, before you were my teacher – when we first met, how did you know me?"

Fpod shrunk from him. "I knew you as – as the Stranger of Light."

"Behold, it is as the Stranger of Light that I now command you," he boomed. "Hunker down by that sentinel rock, the one with the hollow at its base. Press your back to it. Now!"

Fpod's feet scuttled backward. His back sandpapered down a column as he tumbled to a squat.

"Stay there until I return," Alrue commanded, "*without* looking down into that valley. What I go to do, no man must see. Wherefore if ye shall be obedient to the commandments, and endure to the end, ye shall be saved at the last day. Will you do as I command?"

Fpod could barely speak. Lips trembling, he nodded.

"I go!" His Questing robe aswirl about his shoulders, Alrue all but leapt into the defile.

Heartsick, Fpod hugged his knees, endlessly rehearsing how he would explain this after he returned to the People's Ground. "He went down to the moose without me," he imagined himself saying. "He ordered me to stay behind and not watch. I expect he just walked right up behind the moose and – well, you know how they kick." He envisaged Takander Thurnb's face contorted in wrath. "Mercy, mighty Shan, I know you expected great things from this one."

Chapter 65

June 21, 2376
Aboard *Luskus Delph*

The cabin door dilated, then spun shut as Avu Wincenc stole out. Lii Bardicon remained face-down on her floatpad for a six-count, feigning sleep. Then she rose to her hands and knees, savoring the sensation of her heavy breasts dangling free. She went out of Mode and rolled out of the pad, reached for her wrap where it lay rumpled on the floor, thought better of it. Nude, she padded into her cabin's sim rainforest, which vanished at her subvocal command. She sat at her desk. *I hadn't planned on sex,* she thought. She permitted herself a brief memory of Wincenc writhing beneath her. *This'll be the best test I could bargain for – if I can make* that *disappear, I can hide anything.* Her senso player had the look of a modest consumer model but contained a complete Spectator workstation. Arranging her polyphasic consciousness into a reviewing mode, she opened to her inner awareness half-a-dozen editing bubbleprints, each alive with datacrawls. She waited a moment while the journal she'd just finished recording migrated to the active queue. *Wait, this calls for celebration.* She stepped to the cabin autobar and drew herself a snifter of Rikubian whiskey – *good* Rikubian whiskey – then returned to her desk and launched the checking journal.

Suck, rush, wrench!

***

The door annunciator warbled. "Enter," Lii Bardicon-in-the-senso said confidently. She wasn't visible – of course she wasn't; she was *pov*ing a recording of her own sensorium.

"Is someone here?" Avu Wincenc pushed away thick tropical leaves heavy with dampness. Or tried to. Her hands passed through them.

"Welcome to my *faux* forest," Bardicon called. "Follow my voice."

***

Bardicon speeded up the playback and watched her conversation with Wincenc unfold – just not as it actually had. There was no hint of Bardicon's distress with her Spectator work, no talk of Amli Revskond. Surely there was no mention that she *was* the late senso artist, Reefed and brought back as someone else.

Instead she-and-Wincenc-in-the-senso talked politics for half an hour, sometimes leavened with philosophy. When the conversation they'd *actually* shared embraced permissible subjects, snippets would reappear.

"You can see why people would imagine that it *might* be that way," Wincenc observed after a fabricated dialogue about voter behavior. "When you think about it, they could scarcely do otherwise."

Bardicon's eyes brightened further. "There you're wrong, Lieutenant Wincenc. People can always do otherwise."

"Do you really believe that?"

***

Once again the "recorded" chat veered into the counterfactual. Bardicon-and-Wincenc-in-the-senso discoursed about free will for ten minutes straight; then Wincenc asked Bardicon if she was hungry. They decided against going to mess, instead calling up some snacks from the cabin synthesizer: an ensemble of light, strong-flavored dishes from three worlds' spicier cuisines whose flavor profiles clashed violently. Bardicon plunged her awareness totally into the false senso. The aromas, the sensations of temperature and texture in the mouth, the buzzing aftertaste as dueling seasonings grappled for dominance over her palate – everything was from her imagination, yet everything was perfectly realistic. She redirected a fragment of her Spectator awareness to poll the bubbleprints with their ceaseless datacrawls. This was the very moment when, during their actual encounter, she and Wincenc had begun wrestling together on the floatpad. Her excitement, the sense of flooding heat: the whole hormonal symphony were there to read in the numerical abstractions of her *original* journal. The falsified journal contained no hint of it ... only the sensations of an evening nosh hobbled by a comically ill-composed menu.

When Wincenc bid Bardicon adieu in the false journal, Bardicon was seated at her cabin desk, just as she was in reality.

In the senso, of course, Bardicon was clothed.

***

With two terse subvocal commands Bardicon saved and locked everything, then powered down the senso unit. Her grey eyes sparkled. She leaned back in the chair and tossed down the full dram of sparkling whiskey. *Success*, she told herself. She had achieved something without precedent: a full-resolution, utterly convincing senso of an event that had never happened. *In a medium that leaves no place for them,* she reveled, *this is the ultimate special effect. And it unfolded precisely as I re-imagined it, specifically as I directed – even though at the time I recorded it, I was rather busy doing something else.* She ran the tip of her thumb across the red crescent just above the right nipple, the spot where Wincenc had accidentally bitten her. It would take but a moment to pad into the lavchamber and heal it; she opted not to bother.

"Personal diary," she subvocalized. Even powered down, her sophisticated senso system would open an encrypted recording queue for commentary of this type – and immediately bury it, redundantly scrambled, deep within its data structures. *"Of course, parts of what I told Avu Wincenc in reality are true. I* am *Amli Revskond's Reef, and therefore a new person. But the relationship between Amli and the person it pleases me to call 'myself' is more complex than I let on. Far from being repelled by her legacy as I represented to Fem Wincenc, I have embraced it, even significantly furthered its development. I can now utilize the full range of Amli's old somatic techniques at whim, and do so by will alone, without the pharmacological crutches Amli had to rely on. Like most Reefs, my personality has its brittle junctions – that business about red skies on Scalbulia Five was a genuine error – but by applying Amli's gifts to my frangible Reefed personality, I have trained myself to "lucid-dream" actions I am not actually performing at a level of resolution sufficient to create a totally convincing – but false – senso record. What's more, I can split my awareness so as to behave normally in the realm of reality even as I consciously compose my false record. Where Amli Revskond's art was psychedelic and bizarre, mine carries the stamp of realism."*

She rose, drew another whiskey, and contemplated her overripe body in the mirror as she drank the snifter down. *"My toolkit is complete."* She permitted herself another memory of Wincenc's lean face contorted in orgasm. *"Even that will buy me only a little time. I need one more test, and that quickly."* Smiling, Bardicon entered the lavchamber. *"Then I must tie up my loose ends, after which – no need to name my purpose openly, even in this encrypted diary. I'll say only that those who stand in the way of the Great Completion will get their reward."*

338

Chapter 66

November 29, 2367
Bohrkk, on the Wisdom Quest

Alrue Latier rounded the *svadi* moose, squinting into harsh morning sun. The animal lay spread-eagled, its cyan muzzle resting half in, half out of the fizzy pool.

Alrue edged within arm's reach of the moose. The creature did not react. Its breath rattled. It was obviously desperately ill.

Alrue stared past a moss-flecked antler. One of the beast's eyes was gummed shut, thickly caked with a yellow-white secretion. A similar clotted discharge trickled from the moose's nostrils and mouth.

Alrue squatted, his hips and knees protesting at the unaccustomed movement.

The moose's eyelids shuddered open, their carapace of pus dividing with a sucking sound. A filmy yellow eye locked to Alrue's gaze.

Some reflexive upwelling of decency compelled the Mormon to reach out and stroke the dying beast's muzzle. "You are my gift from the Lord God of Hosts," Alrue breathed. "Wherefore, the Lord God will proceed to make bare his arm in the eyes of all the nations, in bringing about his covenants and his gospel unto those who are of the house of Israel."

The moose replied, *"Bleat."*

Grunting, Alrue rose to his feet. He edged back toward the creature's rump.

Gathering his Questing robe over one shoulder, he shrugged his pack off of the other. He pulled the *rains red* from the pack and twisted it partly open as Fpod had taught him. His fingers found the priming pin. In training, Fpod had always had him swing the pin to the half-power position. *On the other hand,* thought Alrue, *this is a lot of moose.* Grimacing, he twisted the pin to the full-power side.

Straddling the beast's left rear leg, Alrue angled the *rains red* toward its fever-swollen anus. He swung the weapon backward. "Prepare ye the way of the Lord!" he bellowed.

Alrue shoved the device home.

***

Nirom Fpod, his back still against the rocky pillar, opened one eye. "You're not dead," he said, dumbfounded.

"Dead?" Alrue echoed, perplexed. "I stand before you flushed with my greatest victory. I armed the *rains red* and I placed it, and behold, in moments it will ..."

Fpod's eyes widened. "How many moments?"

Alrue's lips pursed into a tight, small *O*.

***

As to the *rains red*'s operation, this was the way of it. After the timer ran its course, the device's two explosive charges detonated in quick succession. The first charge, by far the smaller, spewed a tenth-of-a-second jet of fire from the rear nozzle. That thrust the whole *rains red* deep inside the moose's abdomen, in the process inflicting almost surely fatal injuries. But no matter; the sudden deceleration when the device struck the creature's diaphragm triggered the second, substantially larger charge.

Which, Alrue having selected the full-power setting, detonated most vigorously.

***

The explosion was deafening. By reflex Alrue and Fpod hugged, faces buried in each other's shoulders. After a moment, they parted. Echoes of the blast answered from distant bluffs.

Pebbles fell first, hailing against the granite spires. After a few stinging impacts, Alrue and Fpod retreated under the nearby rocky overhang. And just in time, for next came heavier projectiles, meaty and steaming. A foreleg sundered at the fetlock, the hoof all but shattered. A ragged chunk of mandible, hair and teeth and flesh and bone fragments all intermixed like some obscene English pudding.

"Now I understand the device's name!" Alrue shouted.

It *was* raining red.

A gobbet of the animal's shoulder thudded down amid crimson spray.

For a count of three, all was still. Cautiously Alrue edged out from under the sheltering overhang.

An antler pinwheeled into the grit four meters away. It bounced, hit a rocky outcrop, and snapped in two.

That was the last of it.

"We trust in our God who has given us victory," Alrue exulted, stepping into the clear. "Get up, friend Nirom!"

Rising to one knee, Fpod stepped clear of the overhang to survey the rocky soil littered with carnage. "You used full power, didn't you?" he accused.

Alrue shrugged.

"I don't believe it," Fpod sighed at last. He scurried to peer down at the lowlands, where a small crater beside the now-ruddy creek disgorged grey smoke. "I *can't* believe it." He ran to face Latier and slapped repeatedly at the Mormon's biceps. "*You!* In many ways my least promising student, but you –" He took a few steps backward. "*You.* You actually blew up a moose."

Alrue spread his palms. "That *was* the idea, wasn't it?"

Fpod drew a heavily-tanned fabric sack from his shoulder pack. "I'll never explain this," he said resignedly as he set about collecting bloody moose-scraps.

341

Chapter 67

Interlude
The Planet Vatican

When last the Universal Catholic Church occupied Vatican, some thirty years before, its headquarters complex had girdled a planet which, in those heady days, the church had owned outright. Then came the Parek affair. Disgusted Catholics had bolted by the tens of billions. Next came crushing reparations under the Enclave Statutes. In less than a year, a church one percent of its former size had limped back to its native precincts in Rome of Terra. Eight years after that, Terra's Sequestration loomed. Most diehard papistries, as Catholic congregations came to be known, existed offworld; whether She meant to serve her children or dictate to them, Holy Mother Church had had no choice but to abandon Terra. The Holy See had returned to Vatican, this time as a tenant – the rent was cheap. But on this world where salvage experts and fast-buck artists had already feasted on the old church's bones, the new church's entire headquarters now fit within a single building that once housed only a papal audience chamber. Sixty meters on one side by one hundred twenty on the other by fifty high, it was hewn from a single colossal block of ruby-colored spinel. That explained why it was still there; even at history's grandest sheriff's sale, no bidder had fancied carting away a cultured semiprecious gem that large.

The former audience chamber – once a single yawning space – now contained a warren of huddled cubicles and stalls housing everything from curial offices to the papal chambers. The largest open space was a tridee studio some twenty meters wide, fifteen deep, and ten tall. It sufficed for recording the pope's pronouncements.

"Recording," called a tonsured Franciscan monk.

Two Swiss Guards marched stiffly before a cheap fabric backdrop displaying the papal tiara and keys. Each wore leggings, knee breeches, and a belted, balloon-sleeved tunic striped in the ancient Medici colors. "Attend, one and all!" they cried in unison. "Attend the words of the Holy Father of the Universal Catholic Church, former bishop of Rome, vicar of Jesus Christ, Successor of the Prince of the Apostles, Supreme Pontiff of the Universal Church, Once and Future Patriarch of the West, Once and Future Primate of Italy, Once and Future Archbishop and Metropolitan of the Roman province, Once and Future Sovereign of the State of Vatican City, still a reasonably significant tenant upon the Planet Vatican, and Galactic Servant of the Galactic Servants of God. Pray attend His Holiness ... Pope Hilarius the Second!"

Olive-skinned, with lustrous greying hair and a slender nose, Hilarius II had chosen his papal name in tribute to Pope Saint Hilarius (reigned 461 - 468 Terran local). The first Pope Hilarius had succeeded the unhumorously named Pope Saint Leo the Great. and been succeeded in his turn by the only moderately humorously named Pope Saint Simplicius. Hilarius II wore an oyster-white *simar,* a floor-length silken robe with an integral shoulder cape. An argent sash girded his waist, ending near his knees in a golden fringe below an embroidered coat of arms. A crystal pectoral cross hung from a golden chain upon his chest. His head was domed with a tiny, round white silk headpiece, the *zuchetto.*

"Brothers and sisters in Christs," the pope began. "An improbably successful tridee continues to surpass all viewing records. In one way We" –meaning himself, the old-time papal *We* – "look on this development with

343

pride, for its subject, Father Pierre Teilhard de Chardin, is a famous son of the Church. In another way We regard it with misgiving, for Father Teilhard's teaching has been terribly distorted. Atheists and true believers now are locked in battle for Teilhard's mantle. He taught that the Omega Point, the dazzling target toward which human development climbs, was God. That is a vibrant metaphor for the way every human soul strives toward heaven. Today it is too often taught that the Omega Point, now misnamed the Great Completion, is not divine. Some say it represents in fact our own future selves, perfected not by grace but by our own effort. This is blasphemy beyond measure, as it envisages not just humans resolving to live without God, but humans imagining themselves *becoming* God. No, the Omega Point is precisely the God of scripture, nothing less.

"Still, the faithful should not be hidebound by conceptions of the godhead which served past ages. A vibrant faith and an inspiring concept of our Maker can easily be reconciled with the future-orientation and the ideal of cosmic progress that Father Teilhard embodied."

Hilarius walked behind an immense illuminated Bible on a fretfully carved mahogany stand. He opened the book to a page early in the Old Testament. "Scholars of the ancient Torah," Hilarius proclaimed, "translated Y W V H, the shortest known name of God, as '*I am who am.*' But the ancient tongues were less scrupulous about temporality than is the norm today."

Hilarius II stepped into paired spotlights that illumed his face and rimmed his head in white fire. "This day We reach for one of the most powerful tools at any pontiff's command, the power to proclaim true doctrine with infallibility." He raised his hands, index fingers pointing upward in paired benediction. "We hereby infallibly proclaim the following revised reading to be true doctrine. The most accurate and insightful rendering

344

of the name of God is –" he paused for dramatic effect –
"'*I am who I shall be.*'"

Chapter 68

"Hurry," Takander Thurnb growled, "we mustn't lose the sun." Six gaunt leather-clad elders followed him into the log roundhouse's secret chamber. Their ages ranged from early maturity to wobbling dotage. The youngest man hauled a rough-hewn crossbar across the door behind them. A middle-aged woman in a robe the color of dried blood tied cloths over her mouth and nose, then emptied the sack Nirom Fpod had carried back from Alrue's Wisdom Quest. Out came the sundered moose foreleg, the ragged chunk of mandible, the bloody gobbet of shoulder, blue-black with days of decay. She arranged the stinking trophies on a log shelf before an unglazed window.

Not all the assembled elders had assigned tasks; some just gossiped. "For starters, I can't believe he actually set off the *rains red,*" a one-eyed man with a port-wine birthmark said. "By rights we should have gotten five or six more Quests out of that one device."

"Was it the last of them?"

"Yes, and it's been seven months since the strangers came round to ask if we needed more," One-Eye confirmed. "They're overdue."

An elder with a wooden leg scowled. "What if we never see them again?"

"Might be for the best," One-Eye said acidly. "But I speak as the father of a daughter who's reached a certain age."

Wooden Leg jerked his chin up and to the right in grim assent. "But who remembers how to make a *rains red* the old way?"

"Enough chatter, fellow Wisdoms!" Thurnb said sharply. "The sun's coming into position."

A seemingly ageless rail-thin woman guided a wizened, squinting elder – clearly the eldest of them all – toward the log shelf amid a cloud of incense smoke. His shin-length blue-black leather tunic was worked with figures of bird skulls, his sandals decorated with shards of quartz.

As if on cue, sunlight flooded the window, reflecting into the proving room from one of the mirrored panels that hung beneath the crater rim. Yellow-white radiance transfixed the stinking foreleg, mandible, and shoulder.

The squinting elder approached the shelf, coughing. His value to the People lay in his expertise, which was passed from savant to savant only near life's end. By dint of his knowledge he could sometimes read the silent stories that broken bones told. Then there was his auspicious myopia; nearsightedness let him discern small details others could not. He brought the sundered foreleg's mangled end mere centimeters from his eyes. Heedless of the stench of decay which the incense masked at best imperfectly, the squinting elder kept the foreleg close, rotating it, studying the play of harsh backlight over bone.

"Not cut, not snapped," he called out. "Pulverized."

Chapter 69

July 11, 2376
Aboard *Luskus Delph*

"Want to know what I think?" Avu Wincenc asked.

Lii Bardicon didn't, actually; their pillow talk had veered in an uncomfortable direction, but she could think of no way to redirect it that wouldn't make matters worse. They lay together just above the floatpad in Wincenc's sterile cabin. Wincenc's head rested on Bardicon's full right breast. "I don't share this with many people," Wincenc was saying quietly. "It's a common view among Gwilyans, but we've learned to keep quiet about it; sometimes others find it … disloyal." Wincenc's right hand moved downward, the fingers venturing into Bardicon's pubic hair.

"Sure you want to talk philosophy?" Bardicon asked.

"You've worn me out, Lii girl," said Wincenc, laughing and withdrawing her hand. "For the moment, philosophy's all I'm good for." She stretched, arching and relaxing her back. "Here's what I think about *Luskus Delph*, and a lot more."

"I'm listening."

"Humanity is moribund," Wincenc accused. "Played out. I believe that deeply. It's been a great run, but whatever *homo Sapiens* had by way of native genius is exhausted."

"I can't believe you think that," Bardicon whispered. "No one with so little hope decides to be an exocultural analyst, as you have. I mean, there *are* no exocultures – not live ones, none we know of. Your whole career is built on hope –on the hope that someday we'll find a nonhuman civilization, so your training will be needed."

"You have a point," Wincenc conceded. "But ask yourself, what am I hoping *for?* More than anything, I hope to greet the beings who will *displace* humanity on the cosmic stage. I dream of some role, however small, in passing the torch to our replacements. Assuming that if we meet real aliens, their culture will retain the youth and energy the Confetory now lacks."

Bardicon frowned. "And you're unhappy serving on *Luskus Delph*? You should be elated. If humans are going to discover alien intelligence anytime soon, this is where it'll happen."

Wincenc shook her head. "*Luskus Delph* is on the wrong errand. It seeks an alien culture, but only to lay down the law to it. 'We're big bad humans, quit forjeling with our universe!'"

"That's too cynical –"

"No, it isn't. You were in the room when Hom Enoda and Hom Computer joked about kicking ass and taking names."

"They were being sarcastic," Bardicon objected.

"Not as I read things. They were registering disapproval of a reality they'd apprehended all too clearly. Kicking ass and taking names – I guarantee you that's *just* how the brass see things."

"I see us poised to achieve, to develop," Bardicon said sharply, "in ways we can hardly imagine – and very soon."

"An optimist," Wincenc deadpanned. "Also a believer in *Luskus Delph*'s mission?"

"Far from it. I agree with you that gunboat diplomacy between universes is absurd. But what is most wrong about it is, it's a *distraction*."

Wincenc frowned. "A distraction? From what?"

Bardicon turned up her palms, suggesting a platform. "Here stands humanity, on the verge of bursting into who knows what grand flowering –"

"So you believe," Wincenc said skeptically.

"So I do. My concern is that when that transformation begins, *Luskus Delph*'s clumsy antics might sidetrack Galactics from recognizing it, much less committing themselves to it."

Wincenc edged her own weight to her left. Bardicon's body sank slightly in the inertially responsive floatpad field; her own body bobbed upward, outward. Wincenc twisted and settled on her right side next to Bardicon. "I envy your exuberance, Lii, but – may I be frank? This whole vision of humanity leaping from its chrysalis into a wondrous tomorrow, where's the evidence for any of it?"

"In my heart," Bardicon said fiercely. "Laugh if you will, but that's how things *feel* to me."

Chapter 70

The youngest elder, the one who'd barred the door, gaped. "The Stranger of Light … he actually went and did it?"

"Just as Fpod reported?" demanded the rail-thin woman.

"It *is* the purpose of the Quest," Thurnb reminded them.

"But it's also almost impossible," rasped Wooden Leg.

"*Almost*," rasped the squinting elder. "I have no doubt. Truly the Stranger of Light blew up this moose."

One-Eye regarded Thurnb balefully. "You know what that means."

"I know the traditions," Thurnb said irritably. He wandered the chamber, elders stepping aside as he passed. On this freighted occasion no tribal elder, however senior, would quibble with the Shan as to who owed deference to whom. He paused in a shaft of sunlight. "Elders of Wisdom, I accept this finding," he growled. "Let the outcome be announced."

Wooden Leg was first to break the silence. "You are certain, O Shan?"

Thurnb laughed darkly. "What if I objected? You'd gather again tomorrow and draw the same conclusion. Only the evidence would stink a little worse."

One-eye drew very close to Thurnb. He pitched his voice low. "There's another way, of course." She mimed a stabbing motion.

Thurnb snorted. "This is the Stranger of Light we're talking about! He floats in the air. He knows our deepest secrets just by guessing. His lieutenant-woman sees in the dark; his wives dissect strategies like the generals of lore. I dare not strike at him. Which of you would?"

No one answered.

The squinting elder cleared his throat. "You realize that once we proclaim our conclusion, there can be no turning back."

"So be it," Thurnb said resignedly, his fingers worrying at the pommel of his sword. "Maybe this Stranger of Light is the one we've been waiting for."

Chapter 71

July 11, 2376
Aboard *Luskus Delph*

Wincenc rotated onto her back; now she and Bardicon lay side by side, staring up at the cabin ceiling. "Look, Lii, there's no pending transformation. Nothing's going to renew Galactic life. And let me share another sad truth: Even if human civilization gets replaced, nothing will really change. The new race will play out the same dreary narrative all over again: synthesis followed by dissipation and finally by creeping inconsequence."

"But that's just stasis," Bardicon complained. "And you don't just consign humanity to that, you throw our hypothetical successor in the same pot. No real growth, no novelty, just empty grey recurrence, meaning nothing."

"When you put it that way, it could describe a stereotypical Gwilyan view of life ... or any Gwilyan weather forecast."

"If Gwilya had weather forecasts." They chuckled.

"Nonetheless," said Wincenc, "it's what I believe, every bit as firmly as you believe in your inscrutable flowering of humankind."

"You don't understand a fraction of what I believe," Bardicon said coldly. "You need to hear it all, end-to-end, just once."

Wincenc drew a sharp breath, doubtless for some dismissive reply, but Bardicon twisted and threw a leg over Wincenc. Her weight settled astraddle the older woman's abdomen. She leaned forward, her face and hair and pendulous breasts filling Wincenc's vision. An odd preamble for an intellectual monologue, but off Bardicon went. "What is humanity's future? We get an inkling when we examine the pasts all living things share. On every world, every tree of life, development has led to *greater complexity*. Think about it: time after time, life emerged from nonlife as some grey slime that could barely make a copy of itself. Biochemistry expanded, differentiated; eventually reasonably efficient one-celled creatures arose. Then multi-cellular agglomerations, then at last true organisms whose cells performed specific functions. The capacities to move, to sense the environment, to attack and defend, they all hurtled forward. What came next? Think of ants, termites, bees."

"Must we confine ourselves to Terran creatures?" Wincenc asked with distaste.

"Sorry, Terran examples just come to mind – same tree of life as humans. If you prefer, think Gwilyan brine slugs. They all went through the same process – their ancestors were solitary organisms, but somewhere along the line each species independently reached the point where its members gathered together in colonies or hives or – what do you call those groupings of Gwilyan brine slugs?"

"Groupings."

Bardicon chuckled. "If there's a prosaic way to do something ..."

"Trust a Gwilyan to find it."

"The point is," Bardicon continued, "it's a new level of complexity where individual organisms subsume themselves to the welfare of the whole. It's happened so often, it must be an essential step in the process."

"And after it?"

"More steps still," Bardicon enthused. "Self-awareness. Language. Technology. But they're all just increments. A greater leap lies ahead, a fundamental transformation. One thinker called it 'socialization.' It will be as momentous as when the first bees surrendered

354

to the first hive – but we humans won't have to give up our individuality."

"And this is the great development you expect very soon."

"The beginning of it." Bardicon's voice cracked with excitement. "Even as Galactic civilization unfolds, it *folds upon itself* as never before, creating new classes of interrelations among people. However belatedly, humankind is reaching its version of the point the bees and ants and brine slugs reached long ago – the point when 'it must of biological necessity undergo the coordination of its elements.'"

"Who were you quoting?" asked Wincenc.

"Oh, sorry: Pierre Teilhard de Chardin."

"That wild-eyed priest in the tridee blockbuster?"

"Priest and paleontologist, actually. Teilhard predicted humanity would soon reach 'its critical point of social organization.'"

Wincenc hiked herself up on her elbows so that Bardicon's pillowy breasts covered her own. "So now we go into the hives?"

"Of course not. Similar stage of development, sure – but *we're* much different. I told you, humans won't surrender their individuality –"

"Just their loneliness?" Wincenc asked archly.

"Our ... *atomization*, let's say." Bardicon ran the fingers of her right hand through Wincenc's frizzy hair. "But immense transformation – the Great Completion, we call it – is inevitable. *Not* more of the same, as you so drearily expect. Profound, radical change, sooner than you dream. Humanity will confront three momentous choices."

"We still get choices? You've been making this sound as inevitable as a boulder crashing down a mountainside."

355

Bardicon smiled. "In fact, these will be the most crucial choices humans have ever faced. One after another, each conditioned by the one before it. That means if we get the first choice wrong, there will be no second choice."

"Sounds like something we must approach very, very seriously," Wincenc deadpanned.

"I take this seriously," Bardicon protested. "Now the first choice is simple. Shall we accept life or reject it?"

"That's a *pending* choice?" Wincenc frowned incredulously. "You and I are only here because each of our ancestors – human and otherwise, going back to that grey slime – accepted life."

"In most cases unconsciously. Now humanity must decide *explicitly* whether to affirm life or not. Rejection is possible. Humans can cast their lot with entropy and the void – remember Ênvå Corglinü and her Church of the Abyss?"

"Clearly, down that path lies oblivion," Wincenc admitted.

"Your own cynicism would be almost as harmful if it were accepted generally, I'm certain of that. Fortunately, there's an alternative," Bardicon enthused. "Humans can say yes to Life, to Progress, to the possibility of higher consciousness. If we do, we arrive at the second choice: Withdraw or evolve?"

"Withdraw where?" Wincenc lay back down again, curious in spite of herself.

"Withdraw from the world," Bardicon explained. "Having embraced life over nonlife, what should humans do next? Should we seek to withdraw from the material world straightaway to pursue a life of pure mind? Or should we embrace the material world and follow the opportunities for development it presents?

Once again, either choice is possible. But it seems clear that embracing pure mind now would be premature."

"It would be a waste, surely," Wincenc breathed, frankly ogling Bardicon.

"Very funny," Bardicon reproved, any sense of chastisement lessened by the music in her laughter. "Teilhard wrote that 'so long as the world around us continues, even in suffering and disorder, to yield a harvest of problems, ideas, and new forces, it is a sign that we must continue to press forward in the conquest of matter.' The path forward is the path that hurls us all into the currents of history. Only that decision leads to the third and final choice: Plurality or unity?"

"You've lost me again."

"How does history's current flow? Does it branch endlessly, spreading out like a fan?" Bardicon splayed her fingers. "Or does it eventually converge toward some final unity?" She brought her hands together, as if in prayer. "Certainly humans can say no to unity. Many today embrace as their *ideal* the endless multiplication of autonomous individuals pursuing ever more diverse lifestyles."

"I suppose I'm one of those," Wincenc ruminated, "not that I've given the matter much thought."

"Numberless ways of living, countless systems of meaning, each of them merely private or shared by some arbitrary community – what's that add up to? That path is ultimately sterile," Bardicon insisted. "In the end, mere autonomy pales beside the unity that Teilhard called the 'communion with all others.'" Because humans are capable of self-knowledge, hope, and love, we can be confident that *our* experience of unity will be far richer than what multi-cellular life forms, or ants in their colonies, or brine slugs in their groupings enjoy. We'll know communion, yes, but not dissolution. This

357

will be a *human* unity. Yet it'll also be … more than human."

"More than human?" Wincenc breathed, her hands beginning to explore Bardicon's thighs.

"It isn't just that humans of the near future will converge upon one another. We'll converge *toward* something greater. Something that's outside of us, beyond us, yet proceeds from the combined resonances of us all."

"Anything you say."

Bardicon responded with a look of exasperation, then laughed as she realized Wincenc's mind was drifting towards matters other than philosophical. "It's hard to capture in a few words," she said in a rush, "but that is the Great Completion. Some call it Omega; some call it *Dessss*-tiny. It draws us with the power of its being – which, in turn, represents the culmination of us all."

"You know what that sounds like?" Wincenc wrestled briefly with a concept that never came easily to a Gwilyan. "That sounds like God."

"That was Teilhard's view," Bardicon said. "Contemporary thinking has moved past that. Most of us who anticipate the Great Completion see it as an infinite, all-powerful reality, but not wholly separate from ourselves. It's like the reflection of who … or of what … *we* will be – humans and any other sapient life forms – when we reach ultimate development."

Wincenc frowned thoughtfully. "So after all this transforming and unifying, we'll kind of meet our perfect selves in the mirror."

"More or less," Bardicon said uncertainly.

"Do you know what, Lii Bardicon? I think you're a little crazy," Wincenc said huskily. "But I'll overlook that, because I can see perfection from here." She had only to lift her head a few centimeters to plant her lips over one of Bardicon's swelling nipples.

***

Forty minutes later Wincenc lay on her side, snoring very gently. Bardicon lay awake in semi-darkness, furious with herself. *Stupid girl, why reveal so much? Because you got angry? Impatient? Surely you never imagined you'd convert this dour Gwilyan!* She twisted her hips; her body slowly revolved in the floatpad fields until she lay with her back to Wincenc, her knees slightly drawn up. *Time to act,* she decided with abrupt certainty. *This dalliance has become an unacceptable risk.*

Chapter 72

December 5, 2367
Bohrkk, the People's Ground

Nirom Fpod and Alrue Latier stepped into the royal chamber, gravel grating beneath their sandals. Heat rippled from the warming braziers. Takander Thurnb, his face implacable, presided from his rustic throne. Leather-clad elders lined the log platform to either side of him, their hands draped over gnarled staffs. The woman whose robe was the color of dried blood, the youngest elder, and the elder known as One-eye lined up on his right; the elder Wooden Leg, the ageless rail-thin woman, and the decrepit squinting elder stood on his left. Of them all, Squinting Elder gave the strongest sense that he might at any moment pitch forward and shatter.

By Com's helplessness before the robbers, what have I got myself into? Latier wondered.

"Stranger of light!" Rail-thin Woman blared, pounding the tip of her staff on the platform. "The purpose of this gathering is to confirm the result of your Wisdom Quest." She nodded toward Squinting Elder beside her.

Squinting Elder pounded his own staff, nearly losing his balance. "I have examined the specimens brought back to us by Captain Fpod. I scrutinized them after the ancient ways in the presence of my fellow elders. The bones, the tissues, were clearly sundered by an explosion centered inside the creature's abdomen." He nodded, smiling, to his left.

There weren't any elders to his left.

Hurriedly the youngest elder, on the opposite side of the platform, spoke up. "It is our finding that the Stranger of Light truly blew up a moose."

"Everlasting welfare unto y—" Alrue began.

"Not so fast!" shouted Wooden Leg.

Rail-thin Woman stepped toward the lip of the platform, her eyes sparkling with fury. "We have questions, Stranger of Light."

Alrue nodded, then remembered to jerk his chin up and to the right.

Dried-blood Robe stepped forward. "Stranger of light, how did you do this thing?"

"I should talk now?" Alrue said hesitantly. Receiving an affirmative gesture, he spread his hands, palms facing each other. "Behold, for four long days filled with miserable desolation, trembling, and wo, I journeyed through the dreary and sinister wilderness."

"Wasn't Captain Fpod with you?" demanded One-eye.

"He was my guide, but it was my quest. So behold, for four long days *we* trod the ways of miserable desolation –"

"We know this part," snapped Youngest Elder.

"On the fourth day we came upon a highland. Between sentinel rocks, in a flatland a short distance below, we beheld the moose."

"And what was it doing?" demanded Squinting Elder.

"Not much." Alrue shrugged. "Just lying on its stomach."

Dried-blood Robe grimaced. "Where were its legs?"

"Splayed across the ground."

Dried-blood Robe exchanged worried glances with the other elders; this was not how moose usually behaved.

"So what did you do next?" Rail-thin Woman challenged.

"I commanded Captain Fpod to stay behind a rock and not watch what would happen below."

Wooden Leg snapped her gaze toward Fpod. "Warrior Fpod, is that true?"

Fpod jerked his chin up and to the right.

Wooden Leg turned her acid stare upon Alrue. "Stranger of Light, why did you command that?"

"I wished what happened next to be between myself and my god," Alrue declared.

"And so," One-eye queried, "what did your god see?"

"I beg your pardon?"

One-eye frowned sourly. "What happened next?"

"I found a way down into the flatland and walked up to the moose."

"You found your quarry and just *walked up to it?*" Dried-blood Robe demanded crossly. "What happened then?"

"I looked at the moose."

"Well, of course you did."

"And it looked back."

"You made eye contact?" Wooden Leg asked, aghast. "With the moose?"

"No one else was there," Alrue said equably. "Just me and the moose. And behold, I spake unto the moose."

"You *spake* unto it?" breathed Rail-thin Woman.

"Verily, saying, 'You are my gift from the Lord God of Hosts.' Whereupon I gave thanks to my God, saying, 'Wherefore, the Lord God will proceed to make bare his arm in the eyes of all the nations –"

"I'm sure every ritual requirement was satisfied," Squinting Elder blustered. "Now what did you *do* next?"

"I went around behind the moose."

Youngest Elder raised a finger for attention. "How far were you from the animal?"

Alrue stretched out one arm. "About this far. If memory serves, I stepped over its left rear leg."

Youngest Elder's eyes widened. "So you were –"

Alrue completed his thought. " — right behind it. And behold, I took the *rains red* and did as Captain Fpod trained me, and primed it, and armed it, and set it for full power."

"Full power," Squinting Elder said hollowly.

Dried-blood Robe paced the royal platform uncertainly. "And while you were doing all this, you were standing directly behind the moose, within arm's length of it."

"Just so," Alrue confirmed.

"Stranger of Light," Rail-thin Woman said. Her irises glinted golden with reflected torchlight. In an accusatory tone she asked, "At no time did the moose attempt to kick you?"

Alrue pursed his lips, shrugged, and gestured toward himself as if to say, *Do I look kicked?*

She scowled. "So, what did you do then?"

Alrue cupped his hands as though carrying a conical burden. "Well then I took that *rains red* and just stuck it – you know, where it's meant to be stuck."

"Stranger of Light!" Grunting, Thurnb rose from his throne, earning surprised glances from the elders. "It is not traditional for the Shan to intrude on the elders' fact-finding. But since no one else has asked this important question, it's my duty to ask it." He paused for effect. "When you did all this, was the moose *dead?*"

Squinting Elder pumped his head up and down. "The moose was alive when it exploded. I would know."

"With respect," Thurnb growled, "I'd like to hear the Stranger of Light. Was the moose dead?"

"Oh, no," Alrue insisted. "Though I think it was really sick."

"But you're sure it wasn't dead."

"Absolutely, mighty Shan. Mere moments earlier, when the moose and I were looking at each other, it also spake."

"The *moose* spake?" three or four of the elders demanded at once.

Thurnb raised his hands for quiet. "Tell us, Stranger of Light – when the moose spake, whatever did it say?"

"Behold, it said '*Bleat*.'"

Thurnb sat back down, muttering to himself.

"See," husked Squinting Elder, "I told you it wasn't dead."

"I mean, isn't that what moose always say?" Alrue scanned the elders' faces. Sudden understanding washed over him. "Oh, I see. No, no, I didn't mean – I didn't mean that the moose *spoke*. Not using *language*."

"No, of course not," One-eye said bewilderedly.

"I mean, a moose speaking language?" Alrue thrust his pelvis rearward. "That would be ridiculous."

"Where were we?" Rail-thin Woman said impatiently. "Oh yes, you put the *rains red* – you put it – oh, very well, what happened then?"

"I ran away."

"A sound plan. And *then* –"

Alrue turned his palms skyward. "And then it rained red."

"Full power," Squinting Elder said dejectedly. "I'll just bet it did."

The elders clustered urgently around Thurnb's throne, all talking at once. Alrue and Fpod locked eyes. The Warrior's expression made it clear that in all his years among the People, he'd never seen the likes of this.

After a moment Rail-thin Woman turned away from the scrum of wizened bodies and pounded her staff on the platform. "This panel's judgment is final. Stranger of Light, you succeeded in your Wisdom Quest. Your induction will be held as soon as we can organize it. At this time, however, please leave us. We have arrangements to discuss, as I'm sure you will understand."

"Everlasting welfare unto you all," said Alrue. He made his way from the royal chamber, understanding nothing.

***

The elders turned back toward one another, arguing feverishly. Eventually Thurnb got their attention; they turned to follow his gaze out into the gallery.

Nirom Fpod remained out there, still squatting respectfully.

"What is the meaning of this?" shouted Rail-thin Woman.

"What's the meaning of *what?*" groused Squinting Elder, who could no longer see much that wasn't right before his nose.

"The Warrior captain," explained Youngest Elder. "He's still in the gallery."

"That is great disrespect," Wooden Leg said darkly.

"Captain Fpod must have good reason," Thurnb blustered. "Warrior, explain yourself."

Fpod rose hesitantly. "O great Shan, learned elders, duty forced me to remain behind, for there is something you all must know."

Thurnb raised his hands, silencing such elders as still bristled at Fpod's breach of protocol. "What must we all know, Captain?"

Fpod swallowed hard and said, "He does not know."

"Who does not know?" Wooden Leg demanded.

"The Stranger of Light does not know," Fpod explained. "He has no idea."

Dried-blood Robe frowned. "He has no idea that the Quest is meant to be impossible?"

Fpod's eyes widened. "Really, it is? I'd always wondered –"

365

"No Warrior should know that!" Rail-thin Woman cried.

"Well, Captain Fpod knows it now," Thurnb said forcefully, "but that's not the issue. Please let him answer the question. What doesn't the Stranger of Light know, Captain?"

Fpod bowed his head. "He does not know what everyone knows."

"Another riddle?" Wooden Leg asked with disgust.

Fpod raised his head. His gaze swept the panel of elders. "The thing every member of the People knows – Wisdom, Warrior, every woman and child."

Thurnb sprang back to his feet. "He doesn't know *that?*"

"Definitely not," Fpod said with deep certainty.

Rail-thin Woman stared down at the Warrior captain. "You are sure?"

"I was alone with him for a week, including the time of his greatest trial. If *he* knew, *I'd* know."

"So he definitely does not know," Rail-thin Woman said thoughtfully.

Fpod jerked his chin. "Don't I know it."

"Is that possible?" Thurnb said sourly. "We've seen that no secret can be kept from his wives."

Fpod pumped his head up and down in negation. "*This* secret was kept, O Shan."

"And why should that surprise us?" asked Dried-blood Robe. "It is the People's greatest secret."

Wooden Leg scowled. "Maybe our *second* greatest secret."

Squinting Elder scratched his chin. "I was thinking number three."

"A big secret, in any case," Dried-blood Robe said quickly. "And since it is a secret every member of the People knows, none ever needs to speak of it."

Rail-thin Woman nodded. "His wives could not overhear what was never said."

Thurnb paced, his thumbs hooked in the armholes of his cuirass. "So as far the Stranger of Light knows, then, all that happened today is that he was cleared to ascend to the Wisdom estate."

Gravely, Fpod jerked his chin up and to the right.

Wooden Leg locked eyes with Thurnb and shrugged. "We could just not tell him."

"Tradition is clear," Thurnb rumbled. "His role has been ordained, he must play it. As must we." He smiled wickedly. "I call for volunteers – who wants to tell him?"

The elders traded reluctant glances and shuffled their feet.

After a long interval, Fpod cleared his throat. All eyes converged on him.

"The Stranger of Light invited my wife and me to dinner," Fpod said in a rush. "I've been ducking it, but we could go and –"

"This is a Wisdom matter," spat Squinting Elder.

"Fine," Thurnb barked, "*you* go."

Squinting Elder's colorless face somehow turned more ashen.

Thurnb paced, straining to think. "Captain Fpod has done us a service. In any case, this matter is far larger than any petty issue of station." He spun to face his Warrior captain. "Accept the invitation, Warrior Fpod, but leave your wife at home."

"O Shan, I must intrude," said Rail-thin Woman.

Thurnb jerked his chin up and to the right. "It is an elder's privilege."

Rail-thin Woman stared at Fpod. "Warrior, you will leave your wife at home. But you will not attend the dinner alone."

Fpod studied Rail-thin Woman's sparkling eyes in puzzlement, but said nothing further.

She stepped to the edge of the platform, extending her arms like a raptor cresting a thermal. "By the power of the elders assembled, I empower you to tell the Stranger of Light anything he may want or need to know, without regard to your station, without regard to traditional secrecies."

"Understood," Fpod said solemnly. "But if he asks a question I cannot answer?"

Rail-thin Woman smiled faintly. "As I said, you shall not be alone."

Chapter 73

Interlude
OmNet, Talker's Channel Blovio ZL6

"Welcome once again to *A Minister, a Priest, and an Arhat Walk into a Bar,*" purred Zark Diphthong, resplendent in a form-hugging bodywrap of distressed spun-zirconate foam. "My guest is Ahrjeau Olëhgig, bar none the Galaxy's foremost authority on spiritual realities. Some compare that to being an expert in weighing leprechauns, but I am assured that Hom Olëhgig has earned his place among the Galaxy's most revered, if controversial, scholars."

Olëhgig, a wizened figure in a tweedy academic robe, sat erect; evidently the movement cost him pain. His pocked and blistered hands trembled.

"Professor Olëhgig, you are of course aware of the phenomenal success of the recent Pierre Teilhard de Chardin biopic?"

"That bloated tridee? One would need to live in a cloak closet to be unaware of it," Olëhgig wheezed. His face was rife with pustules. Trails of black necrotic tissue ran among the lesions. Unruly hair sprang in clumps from his forehead. His malady was an imposture, artificially maintained with aesthetic intent. Each side of his neck bore nested scars from repeated surgical procedures meant to fine-tune his affliction and sharpen the melancholy effect. "Come to think of it, I believe it now plays continuously even in cloak closets."

"The holy Pontiff itself has infallibly cast his Church's lot with Teilhard," Diphthong mused. "Teilhard, and this Omega Point business his new admirers have made so much of."

"Yes," Olëhgig oozed. "It is as though Pope Hilarius just learned of Teilhard and feels certain that he has made the greatest discovery ever."

"As you say," Diphthong said neutrally, uncertain where Olëhgig was heading.

"Of course His Holiness did not make the greatest discovery ever," the scabrous scholar continued. "That honor was mine, when in the course of my recovering the forgotten texts of Terra's Judaism I established beyond all doubt that *midrash* did not mean an inflammation on the belly."

"Yes, but back to the pontiff." Diphthong crossed his legs, savoring the subdued glissando emitted when one of his woven-crystal leggings passed over the other. "Isn't the pope prostituting the Church's message by identifying so abjectly with a Teilhardian notion of the Omega Point? And doesn't his doing so seem obvious, even contrived, when it comes now, just when Teilhard and his teachings have become so wretchedly popular?"

"Consider how much the Church paid for indecisiveness during the Park Affair," Olëhgig mused. A shapely studio assistant deposited a fresh cup of tea by his elbow; when the purposely disfigured academic tried to grope her, she was quick enough to twist away. As though nothing had happened, Olëhgig continued. "Who can blame Hilarius for, this time, acting boldly and decisively even if the best path forward was not clear?"

Diphthong stroked his perfectly chiseled chin. "Do you suggest that Pope Hilarius rushed to judgment? That he *faked* the most august proclamation a Catholic pontiff can issue, an infallible pronouncement?"

"He must have," Olëhgig said darkly. "No other explanation makes sense."

Chapter 74

July 16, 2376
Aboard *Luskus Delph*

"What the sfelb?" the assistant purser blurted. "Nothing's supposed to be in here."

Avu Wincenc stepped over the rim of a thick round bulkhead hatchway. "That's my equipment, all right." The chamber within was tubular, five meters in diameter, ten long. It terminated in another, yet heavier door emblazoned with caution slashings and clustered red and yellow safety placards. Strewn along the curved floor were the contents of three transport lockers: self-telescoping stands, collapsed antennae, a confusion of small processing modules. The lockers themselves, one backpack-sized, two large enough to contain a preadolescent child, lolled open at crazy angles. "What a mess, it looks like someone hurled all my gear into this thing. Speaking of which, what is this thing?"

"An airlock for exterior maintenance vehicles," the young assistant purser said disapprovingly. "Storing anything here, even neatly, violates all kinds of regulations."

"Well, at least my exocultural gear's not missing any more. Does someone need to come investigate?"

"Anything damaged?"

"Remarkably, no," said a squatting Wincenc, after a brief inspection. "This stuff is designed for adverse field conditions, it's pretty tough."

"If there's no damage, there's probably no point calling security," the assistant purser said. "Let's just pack it up and get it back in the storage complex before anyone notices it's out of place. Can I help?"

"Thanks for the offer, but not just now," Wincenc said, sorting through scattered apparatus. "The packing sequence is awfully precise. I'll be grateful for your help hauling the lockers out as I get them refilled, though." Working quickly, she plucked up a stand, a rolled-up antenna, a folded susceptor array, and a processor module, whisking each into its intended place inside one of the large lockers. Each nesting place retracted its walls so that its cargo could be inserted, then swelled to hold it fast.

A shipboard purser's job revolved around storing things; the young assistant purser watched avidly over Wincenc's shoulders, envisioning the improvements he could make if he had a few dozen lockers as sophisticated as these.

Which was why he didn't notice the airlock's exterior door closing on them in until, with a pneumatic sigh, it settled into its armored yoke.

Chapter 75

For all they've learned about one another, Meryam Mayishimu reflected, recording, *the People and the Latiers are still fundamentally strangers.* Nirom Fpod never explained why bringing his wife to dinner had seemed so inconceivable – nor why he'd changed his mind. The woman beside him was thin, drawn, her face mostly hidden by a rude woven hood. What could be seen gave few clues to her age. *If there's been love between these two,* Lupida thought, studying their body language, *it's not on display tonight.* In any case, Fpod and his slender companion shared the log dining table with Alrue Latier and the women of his household in their suite of rooms three levels below the royal chamber.

Of course, no one had warned the Fpods about Mormon food.

"Take some salad, Captain," Constance Latier said brightly. A cracked wooden platter bore a wobbling gelid dome of yellow-green translucency. In its cloudy depths floated bits of grated vegetables and candied fruit.

"Salad? I'd love some," said Fpod, vainly searching the platters cluttering the big table for anything with leaves.

"No, no, this is salad," Abigayl said helpfully, extending an arm toward the chartreuse murk.

Alrue selected a scone from a steaming platter and transferred it quickly to his plate. In the best Mormon tradition, the "scone" was a deep-fried lump of bread dough, nothing more. "My darling wives," he said grandly, "I'm most impressed. I can see you worked hard to recreate our favorite dishes from the local produce."

"You can thank Meryam and Abigayl for the salad, my husband," Zuzenah said graciously. "Working out the process to cook down bones and marrow and meat scraps into gelatin had more to do with industrial chemistry than cooking."

Fpod pointed incredulously to the greenish mass. "That is … meat?"

"It was once," Abigayl said. "Long story." She turned to Alrue. "So sorry, my husband, we're still working on marshmallows."

"Some funeral tubers, Captain?" offered Lupida. She indicated a steaming yellow-white mass comprising cooked starchy shreds mixed with melted cheese, thickened broth, whipped cream, and small crunchy bits of unknown provenance.

Fpod's woman eyed the mixture dubiously. "Did someone die?"

"There was that moose," Alrue said, to general laughter. "'Funeral tubers' is only a name. When there's a death among my people, the community comes together to remember the departed."

"On such occasions," said Zuzenah, finishing Alrue's thought as a senior wife does, "everyone brings a dish to share. This preparation is such a favorite, it's become known as funeral potatoes."

"Potatoes?" Fpod's woman echoed.

Lupida chuckled. "Our word for ground-tubers. But we eat them all the time, not just at funerals."

"I see," said Fpod, searching the table with mounting discomfort. His eyes lit on a gob of something white and sticky in a bowl. *At least you can't see into it,* he thought. "What's that?"

"Frog's eye salad," answered Constance proudly.

"What is … frog?"

"Friend Nirom," Alrue broke in, "do you object if I speak of affairs beyond this pleasant table?"

Fpod repressed a shudder. "I wish you would."

Alrue smiled. "I was surprised by the craft and skill the elders brought to examining the pieces of our moose. Apparently that very, um, elderly elder – the one who squints – was able to read patterns in tissue and bone. He was not only certain the beast had been sundered by an explosion, he deduced where the explosive must have been placed."

Fpod jerked his chin upward and to the right. "That is the highest function of the council of elders."

Nataleah bustled into the chamber carrying a platter. "Roast livestock," she said proudly. The meat was thickly sliced, rosy pink at the center. It smelled delicious. "Take all you want, there's plenty more in back."

Spooning up "salad," Alrue smiled as he watched the Warrior captain load his plate – and his woman's – with meat.

"I must thank Captain Fpod," Constance piped up. "His men brought me the little citrus fruits I pickled to make those substitute mandarin orange slices."

Lupida smiled. "It's not frog's eye salad without them."

"And they're native plants," Constance added. "Pure texture and flavor, no calories."

"Know what I still miss, sister wives?" Zuzenah asked the table. "Raspberry pretzel salad."

"About the elders, Captain Fpod," Alrue said pointedly. "Why do The People go to such trouble to cultivate and maintain this peculiar forensic expertise? I mean, it's not like many folks would try to fake blowing up a moose."

Fpod leaned forward, eyes wide, a sip of herb-slurry drizzling from his nostrils as he fought to hold back laughter. "Forgive me, Stranger of Light."

"Call me Alrue, it's a Mormon thing."

For whatever reason, that only made things worse. Coughing, Fpod spewed herb-slurry across the table.

"Captain, are you all right?" Zuzenah asked solicitously.

Fpod held both hands out while he struggled to catch his breath. "Please, Stranger of Light, members of his household, please forgive me. This conversation has come to relate directly to a message the Shan charged me to share with you."

Alrue raised one eyebrow. "A message from Thurnb?"

Fpod pressed his hands flat against the log table as if balancing a great burden. "It is unfair that all the People know what the stakes are here, and only you and your women do not."

Alrue leaned forward. The sister wives exchanged urgent glances.

"The purpose of your quest, you were told, was to blow up a moose," Fpod said gravely.

"Which I did," Alrue affirmed.

"But that's the problem. Every Wisdom goes out and tries that."

"And usually succeeds, I should expect," said Alrue, "else there wouldn't be many Wisdoms."

Fpod battled laughter again. "Forgive me, Stranger of Light, but with great respect, that is wrong. Though every Wisdom candidate sets out to blow up a moose, very few succeed."

Fpod's slender consort raised a hand. "I shall take it from here, Captain." She tugged at a scarf; her hood fell away. Torchlight sparkled in her eyes.

She was Rail-thin Woman.

"Welcome to our home, esteemed elder," said Alrue after a flustered moment.

"No need for that," she said, standing gracefully. "As you've realized, I am not Captain Fpod's wife. I speak for my fellow elders. As Captain Fpod said, Vision Quests are rarely successful. Some candidates die." She sighed. "Perhaps you should have."

"That's not terribly sociable," Alrue protested.

She thrust her pelvis rearward. "As far back as our records go, you're the only candidate to cross behind a moose at close range without having his chest kicked in."

Alrue shrugged. "I told you it was sick."

"Most candidates never even get a chance to place the *rains red*. They never find a moose at all, or they set a trap only to watch the animal escape."

"If almost no one succeeds," Alrue asked, "how are Wisdoms made?"

Rail-thin Woman folded her hands. "After candidates fail, they come back empty-handed and tell outrageous lies about the moose that got away."

"And the elders are deceived?"

"Never," she said evenly. "We grade the candidate on the cleverness of his lies, on the confidence and style of the tales he spins."

Alrue frowned. "You elevate people to the Wisdom estate for being good liars?"

Rail-thin Woman leaned forward. "I'm told you appreciate how The People prize cunning."

Alrue recalled the ancient parable of Darvoyg, who concluded that since every moose begged to be spared he could properly kill any of them – or, for that matter, Takander Thurnb himself, who would gleefully take The Others for all they owned if once they would sit down to trade with him.

Slowly he smiled.

377

"So you understand," Rail-thin Woman said. "We reward those with the most vivid tales. Most of the time."

"So almost no one blows up a moose," Alrue said hollowly. "Except that I did."

Rail-thin Woman jerked her chin up and to the right. "It's not impossible. It is difficult enough that it occurs but once in five or six generations."

Alrue steepled his hands over his mouth. "Five or six generations? The elders patiently pass down their knowledge even though most of them will never use it?"

"Oh, they use their knowledge," said Rail-thin Woman. "False claims are common. Candidates bring back chunks they butchered or pulled apart with ropes."

Alrue jerked his chin up and to the right to signify his new understanding. "And the elders *need to know the difference*."

"Yes. Also, no matter how seldom it happens, when a Quest *does* succeed, that must be detected and recognized. It's terribly important."

"Why is that?"

Rail-thin Woman smiled narrowly. "The man who blows up his moose becomes our Tyrant King."

Alrue frowned. "The People don't have kings."

"Not usually." Rail-thin Woman jerked her chin up and to the left. "Only when someone blows up a moose."

"That's the thing you didn't know," Fpod explained. He rose and circled the table, drawing within an arm's length of Alrue's seat. There he dropped to his left side, curled like a fetus, then unwound into a deferential crouch. "You are the Stranger of Light," he said, staring upward into Alrue's eyes. "I have called you friend. But now you are my King."

"And mine." Rail-thin Woman dropped to a like crouch. She pressed a fist to her chest. "You are the

Shan's King, the elders' King. The People's Ground is yours."

Chapter 76

July 16, 2376
Aboard *Luskus Delph*

Lii Bardicon crouched in near-darkness on a service catwalk thirty meters above the circular airlock in which she had just trapped Wincenc and the assistant purser. She could barely glimpse the airlock through intervening structural members and conduits and waveguide pipes, but no matter: her primary attention was devoted to the virtual interface of the subdelta-band universal controller that she'd hard-jacked into the lock's systems. Ordinary thought engines could not function aboard *Luskus Delph*. Her universal controller adapted senso technology to approximate the functionality of a typical control interface. Even so, its small but unavoidable complement of vibrionic circuitry had to be protected by custom hardening.

On any other PeaceForce ship, what she was attempting would be impossible. Multiple susceptors would register unsuited humans inside the lock, triggering safety interlocks at impenetrable levels of machine language. But again, this was *Luskus Delph*. Only three layers of interlocks still functioned, none with comm links reaching outside the storage complex. Already she had mentally prodded and twisted and peeled back virtual data structures until the top-layer interlock failed explosively.

Her head alternately swam and rang like a bell. When instructional dynamicists spoke of "cramming," they meant it. The price of absorbing too much knowledge too quickly from a didactic imposer was a physiological reaction that combined the most enticing attributes of a hangover and a good solid beating. In the last twelve hours Bardicon had taken in a programmer's understanding of the airlock and its protective systems; a veteran operator's knowledge of the electromechanical material-handling exoskeleton she'd used to heave Wincenc's exocultural apparatus into the lock; a safety specialist's comprehension of *Luskus Delph*'s hobbled security networks; a refresher on advanced operation of the universal controller; and a eidetic grasp of *Luskus Delph*'s physical structure probably exceeding any of the naval architects who'd overseen the platform's hasty construction. It was the most absurdly ambitious imposer session she had ever configured. She was resigned to the fact that most of what she'd wedged into her brain would disperse over the next twelve hours. Some might vanish sooner than that.

Pain washed through her again. She'd defeated the second-layer safety interlock without knowing she was doing it. For an alarming moment she couldn't remember why she wanted to beat the third one. *Center, center,* she hectored herself. *You must complete this procedure before you forget how.* "A passionate longing to grow, to be, is what we need," she recited in a hoarse whisper, a mantra from Teilhard.

From below, dull clanging. Wincenc and the assistant purser had figured out what was coming. They were slamming empty transport lockers against the lock's inner walls in a desperate bid for attention.

They'd go unheard. The sprawling storage complex was empty but for Wincenc, the assistant purser, and Bardicon herself. No one would interrupt them. She'd even taken advantage of a primitive electromechanical fire alarm subsystem to dog down every entrance to the complex.

The third and final safety interlock floated in her virtual awareness. She threw her perception into the core of it; the interlock hurtled apart in a cloud of glowing fragments. "There can be no place for the dry of spirit, the doubters, the naysayer, the disillusioned, the fatigued, and the immobilists," she murmured.

Normally the airlock would take ten standard seconds to purge itself to vacuum. But the emergency-open subroutine was not difficult to bring up. It didn't need to be; the amount of air a crash opening would squander was trivial, and this late step in the procedure could not be reached without other safety systems' having ensured that anything in the lock, biological or otherwise, was ready for space.

Well, not usually.

"Life is movement," she whispered. Grimacing against a new rush of pain, Bardicon wrapped her consciousness around the virtual emergency-open trigger and squeezed.

High-powered pneumatics heaved the lock's outer door full open. Wincenc and the assistant purser were ejaculated into the void on a fast-freezing blast of air.

The lock's opening would trigger a brute-stupid electromechanical position signal that might be noticed on the bridge. *Step by step, Lii girl,* she told herself. *Don't forget something now and leave a forjeling clue.* After a fuzzy moment she remembered – and sent – the destruct code she'd programmed into the subdelta-band controller. The device withdrew its internal hardening; in a quarter-second the ravening noise of *Luskus Delph* scoured the controller's vibrionics clean. It was warm to the touch when Bardicon unjacked it. She started down the catwalk, counting her steps. When she reached ninety-two, she dropped the ruined controller between two fluted ducts. The device clattered along a succession of tubes and pipes and cross members, bouncing downward and forward. As her savant-level architectural awareness had known it would, it came to rest behind a hulking pressure manifold four levels down and twenty meters forward. There, it might not be found for months.

Two minutes after she destroyed the controller, she knew, the fire alarm circuit dogging the storage complex's entrances would reset. Forty seconds remained when she reached the two-meter-square ventilation grille she'd unsealed forty-four minutes earlier – *had it been that long?*

Part central ventilation duct, part maintenance access tunnel, part raceway for conduits and cables and vibrionic fiber bundles, the shaft was large enough to walk through. A hundred meters down, the rapid-transfer sled floated where she'd parked it. She lay down across it, unrolled the manual safety straps, twisted the stupid round mechanical distance selector to the fourth detent, and slammed her palm down on it. The sled leapt forward in pneumatic silence.

Six minutes later and three kilometers from the lethal airlock, Bardicon emerged through another ventilation grille. Agony swelled in her head like a sustained piano discord played backward. Already she no longer remembered the specifics of the airlock's control system. *So much the better if I should undergo a sophisticated interrogation. Not that that'll happen.*

With a neutral expression and a forced spring in her step, Bardicon emerged into a dimly lit cross-corridor. It was empty and – she checked – unmonitored by any Spectator. Twenty seconds' sauntering brought her to a broader primary corridor that communicated with Waveguide Arcade Seven. She checked the time; if she'd been returning to her quarters from her usual observing shift, she'd be here right now. A maintenance supervisor zipped past on a yellow floatbike. They exchanged cursory waves.

Too bad about that assistant purser, she mused, watching her autonomics for any involuntary reaction as she allowed herself the thought of the double murder she had just committed. *The poor son of a bitch was innocent. But wait – wasn't Wincenc innocent too?* Her body indices held rock-stable. *Innocent or not, Wincenc had to be removed. "There can be no place for immobilists." The fact that someone else died with her – genuinely randomly, at that – further reduces the already remote possibility that Wincenc's death might be recognized as intentional. In any case, it could not be helped – and it could not have been otherwise.* "Evolution trumpets its challenge," she recited to herself. "Either it must be irrevocable, or it need not proceed at all."

Chapter 77

Alrue edged back into the dining hall after seeing Fpod and Rail-thin Woman out. His wives stared at him like frightened deer; Meryam regarded him with grim bemusement. "Are you recording?" he asked her.

She shook her head. "I shut down when our guests left."

"Good, please stay that way." Alrue shambled across the chamber like a sleepwalker. "Have miracles ceased?" he recited. "Behold I say unto you, Nay."

Nataleah rushed up to take one of his hands in both of hers. "O my husband, when you first thought we might live among The People, I said I wouldn't want us to live here as prisoners."

Alrue nodded, untangling his hand and lowering himself into his accustomed seat. "I believe I said I'd rather be in charge."

"Now you are," Nataleah said dreamily.

"A Tyrant King," Alrue whispered to himself.

"Nataleah speaks as though this were prophesied," Meryam said tartly.

Lupida frowned. "Fem Mayishimu wouldn't know a miracle if it bit her."

"I don't say it's *not* a miracle," Meryam protested. "It's just not a miracle that Alrue either predicted, nor even seemed to expect."

"And what kind of miracle is that?" Constance sniffed.

"Not so fast," little Abigayl piped up. "Joseph Smith knew a miracle of that sort."

"He did?" Lupida demanded.

"I was just studying this the other day." The seven-year-old wife leaned forward, laying the sides of her hands on the tabletop. "At the beginning of his career as prophet, Joseph Smith was translating the golden plates, dictating the Book of Mormon and lodging wherever someone would take him in. For a while he lived at the farmhouse owned by the father of David Whitmer. David was one of Joseph's earliest converts. Of everyone in the household, only David's mother – you know, the farmer's wife – objected to Joseph's being there. She was always complaining about him. Who knows, after enough time she might have persuaded her husband to send young Joseph away. Yet one morning, she came in from milking the cows and announced she'd just talked with an angel who showed her a vision of the plates. Of course, her objections to Joseph ended then and there."

"All true," Alrue said softly. "Darling Abigayl, you have learned your lessons well."

"I hadn't been thinking about that incident, but Abigayl's right – it's incredibly apt," Meryam said. "There's no suggestion that Joseph had laid any groundwork for that 'miracle,' or even that he'd made any prior effort to change Mother Whitmer's mind. If anything, the record suggests he was as astonished as anyone else by her change of heart."

Alrue raised his eyebrows. "Come, Meryam, you're spinning this like it wasn't a miracle at all."

"All I'm saying is that whether miracle or not, for young Joseph Smith it was an incredible stroke of luck." She locked eyes with Alrue. "And whatever has happened here today, Alrue, surely you have experienced another incredible stroke of luck."

"I grant you that," Alrue said affably. "And all thanks unto God, as well; He has surely laid bare His mighty arm."

Nataleah smiled broadly. "It will be good to know power again," she said too intensely. She gave Alrue a coquettish glance. "I mean, my husband, for *you* to know power again."

Constance's expression was more cryptic, but her eyes sparkled. "It will be good to be part of something big once more," she admitted.

Meryam laid a hand on her arm. "I don't know that even being king of this whole crater is exactly 'big.'" she said gently.

Nataleah flashed Meryam an acerbic glance. "Fem Mayishimu, if you know our husband, you know it won't end here."

Chapter 78

Captain Brûh Reidkr paced around the briefing table that dominated her inner office. It was a small but urgent meeting: Pamela Grice was present as Reidkr's special projects officer for matters of security. Gram Enoda and Computer were there as free-floating experts in everything. Doctor Rugebeld Gale-Forgirt represented the scientists. Her bearing made clear she had better places to be. Reidkr's voice crackled with anger: "Fem Grice, it's been three weeks since our only exocultural analyst and an assistant purser got blown into space – and still nothing has been learned about it?"

"That's not entirely accurate," Computer whirred. The machine projected dozens of small bubbles above the briefing table, teeming with alphanumeric data and probability graphics and tridee clips squeezed down from senso. "It's not just that nothing has been learned," the machine rasped. "After careful investigation and exhaustive analysis, it is now certain that nothing further *can* be learned."

"There is no evidence of any tampering with that airlock's systems," Grice reported. "Absent the most catastrophic failure, it should have been impossible for the lock's outer door to open with unsuited humans inside it. But it happened, and there's no evidence, physical or electronic, of any failure."

Reidkr frowned. "Could it be sabotage?"

"If it is," Computer whirred, "we are dealing with the perfect crime. And perhaps we are; this is *Luskus Delph,* after all. The multiple layers of automated logging we could pore through on a normal ship are denied to us."

Enoda stood and gestured; a few of the tridee bubbles Computer was projecting swelled to dominant size. "At the time of the incident, twenty-two Spectators were recording at various places on the platform. The whereabouts and activities of some six hundred and thirty crewmembers are accounted for because they appear in one or more of their recordings. At the time of the airlock incident, there is no sign of anything amiss in any Spectators' journal."

"We all know the limits on electronic and vibrionic systems aboard *Luskus Delph*," Grice said sourly. "Given those constraints, my final report is that we've looked at every scrap of evidence there is, and it is now beyond doubt that we never *will* know why Captain Wincenc and the assistant purser died."

"You've run every conceivable scenario?" Reidkr demanded.

"We ran every *mathematically possible* scenario," Computer replied. "We found more than eleven thousand scenarios that *might* account for the two deaths. The problem is, each of them is wildly more improbable than the phenomenon they seek to explain."

"One theorized that some lint-theoretical wrinkle in time, projecting backward from what we're *going to do* when *Luskus Delph* goes live, was distorting its past – which is to say, our present," Enoda said.

"That's crazy," Gale-Forgirt snapped.

"Exactly," said Grice. "Or here's a really wild one. If one or more of our security Spectators has developed a method for falsifying senso recordings, then absolutely anything could have happened."

"Nobody can fake senso," Reidkr snorted.

"So you appreciate the problem," Computer droned. "What those eleven thousand scenarios have in common is that they involve something that's *just forjeling impossible*. In contrast, theories that explain the events,

389

could actually be true, and enjoy support from the evidence form a null set."

Gale-Forgirt dropped her stocky hands onto the tabletop. "If this tragedy is a mystery we'll simply have to live with, I suggest we start living with it."

Reidkr continued pacing. "Doctor, I gather from your impatience that the science teams are ready to schedule some tests?"

"We've *been* ready, but while this investigation was ongoing everything else was on hold."

Reidkr nodded almost imperceptibly. "That hold is now lifted. What do the science teams propose?"

"A synchronous test of all three major systems at thirty percent power," Gale-Forgirt said. "The Cave, the spatial resonators, and the metrical distorters are too deeply interdependent to test separately. Thirty percent power should let us confirm that all the physics is working as expected without creating any actual dustbunnies or sofas. We can be ready to go in seventeen days."

"Very well, proceed," Reidkr ordered.

Gale-Forgirt was immediately up and out the door, snapping commands into her handie-talkie.

Reidkr settled into a chair, running a skeletal hand through her short black hair. "Something tells me she'll be ready to go in *fifteen* days."

Computer whirred, "Do I hear fourteen?"

Chapter 79

Hours later, the members of the Latier household had gone to their various beds in peace and safety. Meryam Mayishimu slept placidly, her implants' subroutines automatically cataloguing the day's recordings.

Nataleah lay on a pine-needle mattress of the finest local manufacture, visions of dominion and privilege jabbing at her mind.

Constance, too, lay awake, her inner farm-girl more benignly captivated with the idea of being once more at the center of thrilling events.

Lupida lay beside Alrue, who snored in post-coital bliss. She rolled onto her side, uncovered, acutely aware of the cool night air against her sweat-dotted skin. She'd worked so hard to delay Alrue's orgasm, pulsing her vaginal contractions out of phase with his thrusting. Of course he'd understood none of it and just pumped away as though there were a trophy for promptness. She forced herself to visualize her indifferent lover as a Tyrant King, a thundering latter-day pharaoh whose word would be law. "Nothing like this ever happened to Harold," she breathed.

After a brief interval of sleep, little Abigayl was wide awake. She stared out of her room's open window; between the tower walls and the crater rim, she could spy the moons Queen and Prince inching toward each other. *They'll cross soon,* she thought. *If I were just a child I'd need someone's permission to go out at this hour to watch it. Fortunately, I'm a wife.*

Zuzenah, too, lay awake –miserably so. *If Mother Whitmer could have a vision, then so can I,* she thought.

Grimly she foresaw Alrue gripping the reins of power, scheming to extend their reach. A quest for authority abetted by an unexpected miracle – how had that turned out for Joseph Smith? Generations of Mormons had tortured themselves with the martyrdom-porn image of their prophet plunging from a second-story jailhouse window amid a hailstorm of glass, his back burst open by a pistol ball.

What had Nataleah told Meryam? "If you know our husband, you know it won't end here." How true that was!

The hideous, seemingly pre-ordained path from initial miracle to the carnage of Carthage Jail kept unfolding in Zuzenah's mind, a bygone tragedy that she hoped – prayed – would not now serve as template for her husband's destiny. Squeezing her eyes shut, she reached for her rude pine-needle pillow. Ignoring its distracting odor, she pressed it against her face and wept into it. Eventually exhaustion overwhelmed her widening sense of dread. She stumbled into sleep.

Chapter 80

Interlude
OmNet, Talker's Channel Blovio ZL6

"I'm Zark Diphthong. Welcome once again to *A Minister, a Priest, and an Arhat Walk into a Bar.* Let the ecumenical gabfest begin!" The whip-thin host ambled through the studio tavern set, costumed in a painfully *au-courant* paisley jerkin over a wet-look zebra-stripe unitard. "The Galaxy's rumor mills are grinding overtime," he said too slyly. "No one knows where it's coming from, but speculation is that technology's most unattainable goal – genuine, full-fledged artificial personhood – has already been achieved. According to the most lurid rumors, what the specialists call *syn-noesis* actually arose nearly three decades ago in a single machine, and is only now coming to light. If true, never mind the technological implications – and you know *we'll* ignore those, this is a religion show – ponder what it implies for the many religions that view man as God's most special creation. Ponder what it means even for the ways we define such familiar words as *life*."

Lithely circling a ceramic stele inscribed with the logos of the Galaxy's wealthiest churches, the host glided toward a robed monk. The monk's brownish hair was twisted and filthy; he sat at the bar resolutely showing his back to the tridee pickup. "Antŏnì Kotwica may be Catholicism's most famous living anchorite," said the host. "For nineteen years he never left his cell on Frensa Six. A monastic hermit, he shared spiritual wisdom with faithful pilgrims through an opening no bigger than one balled fist. And yet he's here with us tonight! Brother Antŏnì, what have you to say to our audience?"

Brother Antŏnì said nothing. Nor did he move.

Program time being too precious to waste, host Diphthong frog-marched toward another part of the studio, urgently subvocalizing *"What the sfelb is with Kotwica?"* to his producer. *"You said he spoke freely."*

"On Frensa Six he was a chatterbox," the producer insisted.

Thinking fast, the host edged near what seemed to be the *faux* tavern's dance floor. At its center whirled a Sufi dervish in traditional costume, red camel's-hair hat bobbing, arms open, white skirt swirling, right hand reaching for the sky, eyes fixed on his left hand which sagged toward the ground. His skin was white, his hair straw-blonde. "Like most forms of Islam, Sufism went extinct in its traditional lands," the host explained. *"Semazen* Maxime Beeckx Goossens grew up in Charleroi, Flanders, Eurosector. Before he left Terra, he was trained by the New Flemish Mevlevi Order to keep the old ways alive. Welcome, Hom Goossens."

"Must ... concentrate!" Goossens husked through clenched teeth. His feet tangled; he lurched off the dance floor, scattering a rack of goblets and half a dozen bar stools.

"Oh, my," the host temporized. "Also joining us, in his second appearance on the program, is Elder Tirohn Schuleiss of the Church of Latter-day Saints, Old Order, from the planet Zion."

"Everlasting peace unto you," said Schuleiss, tugging at a business-casual garment both badly rumpled and three years out of fashion. "If these rumors are true, some religions will have a lot of redefining to do."

"Some religions – but not your Old Order Mormon faith?" the host probed.

Schuleiss smiled. "Religions teaching that life was created just once by the hand of the sole and only God face a terrible challenge. Has this artificial person truly been among us for almost thirty years?"

"Hold that thought, Elder Schuleiss," said the host, sidling up next to the unmoving anchorite. "Antðnì Kotwica, what is your comment as the Galaxy's holiest Catholic hermit?"

His back still turned toward the tridee pickup, the anchorite said nothing. An alternate pickup went live; the host turned to face it, fighting to control his expression as the robed anchorite slowly turned to show *that* pickup his back.

"You spoke easily enough on Frensa Six," the host accused. "I've seen the clips."

The anchorite raised one hand, showing four fingers, then two.

"Four? Two? Making six?" the host interpreted. "You will say six words?"

His back still to the pickup, the anchorite nodded. He spoke in an insectile rasp. "There, I was ... in ... my cell."

Dervish Goossens smashed through a service bar a meter and a half to Kotwica's left. To judge by the fragments he scattered, the set-piece – even its built-in mineral-cocktail fountain and espresso maker – had been composed half of thin balsa wood, half of extruded foam.

"If I may." Elder Schuleiss broke in, figuring he may as well speak since no one else was. "Scientists describe life as a pattern that endures by means of feedback with its surroundings and is preserved through natural selection. This *syn-noesis,* or whatever one wants to call it, would seem to meet those criteria."

"Life created by man, not Allah?" shrieked Goossens, twirling briskly until he tripped over a cable. Seeming more blur than man, he spun into a stained-glass devotional cyclorama that exploded in a cloud of polychrome shards.

"Again, that's not a difficult concept from the Old Order Mormon point of view," Schuleiss said unflappably.

The dervish thudded to the studio floor, trailing blood. Studio assistants crowded around his spasming form.

Zark Diphthong provided urgent commentary. "It's said that among the Sufi dervishes, one sect seeks death during the whirling dance, believing that the subsequent technological resurrection yields great enlightenment. Whether Hom Goossens was a secret member of this sect, or whether this is all a tragic accident, remains to be seen." A medical team swarmed the bleeding dervish; the host observed a moment of respectful silence.

Which Elder Schuleiss happily filled. "As I was saying, Hom Diphthong, on the Mormon view there are many creations. God was once a man, after all. We – those of us, at least, who still approach our faith with any degree of literalism – we presume the larger universe is filled with gods who ascended to deity at various times on various worlds, and created their realms as it pleased them. So what's one more creation?"

"What indeed?" Antðnì Kotwica rasped. "Oops!"

Chapter 81

June 27, 2369
Bohrkk, the People's Ground

The royal chamber still had its gravel floor, log walls, and log roof. The raised log platform was still reserved for the ruler. But new banners hung from the ceiling, each emblazoned with a crown floating above a lone staring eye, the whole encircled by cryptic markings. Nor was that all that had changed in the past standard year and a half.

The chamber where once the Shan ruled had become the throne room of a Tyrant King.

To say nothing of his queens.

Alrue Latier paced the royal platform, resplendent in a calf-length bluish-purple sarong. From its hems hung golden tassels. Below them golden-hued genie boots curled upward, their tips tensioned by scarlet cords. Wide leather bracelets circled his wrists, decorated with brass rivets and bands of patterned fur. Under a sheer crimson cloak, but atop the rest of his garb, his dirty-white muslin temple garment clung like a sullen cloud.

Alrue turned to face the royal architect. His was a specialty – and an office – that The People had never known. The architect tugged at his belted robe, frowning toward a man-high sheet of slate on which had been sketched a modest two-story building. It featured a peaked roof and three windows across the upper floor. Beneath that a stout stone lintel spanned the façade, supported only by slender columns. Between those were drawn two tall mullioned windows separated by a central double door. "The drawing is perfect," Alrue said. "The red brick store, exactly as I wished it."

"I drew what Queen Constance demanded," the architect said dubiously, "but I must confess, O King, I do not see how these slender columns will support the upper floor."

"My new kilns – a special sort of furnace – will start firing brick the day after tomorrow," said Queen Constance from her personal throne at the rear of the royal platform. She wore a blue-and-black striped *thobe* taller than she was, cleverly gathered upward to create three tiered layers rather like a wedding cake. A silken sky-blue *aba*, or veil, cascaded over her shoulders. Over the *thobe* and beneath the veil, a temple garment completed her ensemble. "Soon you'll see what this new material can do."

Queen Abigayl leaned forward in her throne, clearly concerned. "Is it wise to build a masonry structure with all the quakes we're having?" Now nine years old, she wore a knee-length sarong orange as a spring sunrise under – what else? – her temple garment. "Say what you will about this old wooden tower, it's been flexible enough to ride out the shocks."

"Our store will need reinforcing," Queen Lupida agreed from *her* throne. Beneath her temple garment, she wore a pleated white dress. A braided purple sash wound twice around her waist; her hair formed an echoing, braided halo over the top of her head. "Rebar, that's what Harold would have used. That is, if he'd had to work with these technologies."

The architect gaped in Alrue's direction. "Tyrant King, I do not understand."

"Fear not, you did well," Alrue said. "The drawing is approved." He scrutinized another tall slate that seemed to show the street plan of an ample village shaped like a broad arrowhead. "The store will be the first building of my New Nauvoo."

Meryam Mayishimu recorded the proceedings from a balcony at the rear of the chamber. She stood between leather-clad guards, wearing a flowing saffron-colored robe belted with a red woven sash. Waist-length bead necklaces festooned her neck, though on closer inspection the beads were not made of any hard material. Rather they were ingenious fakes made from fabric. She'd insisted on that, lest their percussive clacking mar her recordings.

Matters on the royal platform having reached a transition point, Meryam gazed down at the seated observers crowding the hall. Directly below her was the dignitary's platform. There sat several elders alongside the former ruler, Shan Takander Thurnb.

Thurnb wore a beige *jibbah* – a full-length fabric robe with embroidered edges – over ivory-colored pantaloons. He was still Shan, but being Shan meant little while a Tyrant King reigned. To the surprise of many, Thurnb had taken the eclipse of his power stoically. Beside him sat Eyla, his third and newest wife, an electrifying beauty with coal-black skin, a slender nose, and arresting brown eyes. She wore a knee-length tunic of fringed uncured leather, cinched with a cord round a waist whose litheness made her imposing bust all the more surprising.

Meryam tuned her audio implants to pick up their conversation. "I'm amazed again, my sweet," Thurnb whispered. "When King Alrue ordained this new style of clothing, I never thought he'd get The People to make enough for everyone – but he did. Now he plans to build a new village outside our crater home, from materials not before seen. I expect he'll do it, but I can't imagine how."

"Some say he's holy," Eyla breathed.

Thurnb nodded darkly. "Some say."

A commotion from the side of the hall: Nirom Fpod, now commander of the royal guard, and four of his men led a chained, bloody-faced Warrior to the edge of the royal platform.

King Alrue consulted a scroll. "The deserter?"

"Yes, O Tyrant King," Fpod said solemnly. "He was caught in his family apartment when he should have been on duty."

The chained Warrior spat out a tooth.

Alrue nodded. "What is the traditional penalty?"

"Death," Fpod and his detail said as one.

Pursing his lips, Alrue picked at the fur of one of his barbarian bracelets. His gaze dropped, fastening on Thurnb. "The Shan is here today," he announced. "Out of respect I ask for his counsel."

Thurnb stood. "O King, tradition calls for death."

"Your counsel is valued," said Alrue. Thurnb resumed his seat. "Yea, it is deeply valued: but even so, today I choose a different path. Commander Fpod, the deserter will live. Issue him the dried equivalent of his usual food allotment for a threemonth. Then evict him, shamed, from among The People. He must trudge into the wild carrying his food and never come back."

Hushed conversations erupted across the chamber.

"It's a slower, crueler death, nothing more," Thurnb murmured to Eyla. His glance darted to her legs, drawn up, exposing their enthralling contours almost to the thigh. Such a thing could still kindle instant passion in him; after six months of marriage, Thurnb remained like a newlywed with her.

Fpod and his detail hustled their prisoner away. Tears furrowed the drying blood on the man's cheeks. Did he sob in relief at escaping execution, or in dread of his new fate? None could know.

"Today's business is concluded," Alrue declared. Warriors threaded through the crowd to assist any who needed help collecting their possessions and vacating the hall. A Warrior brushed past the Shan, dropping a rounded black pebble into his hand. It was a signal, a silent message that the Shan himself had employed in the days when he ruled. It meant *Please stay behind.*

Minutes later the royal chamber was empty save for Alrue, his wives, Meryam, Thurnb, and Eyla. Alrue lofted a hand's width above the royal platform, then floated out into the gallery. He settled onto a bench facing the Shan and his wife. Alrue had not bothered to levitate during the public function, but he did so now as a private display for Thurnb and Eyla. So turned the calculus of kindnesses by which Alrue sought to assuage any resentment the Shan might hold at having been subordinated – not that he'd yet shown any.

Thurnb stood and bowed, his face blank. "Everlasting welfare unto you, O Tyrant King."

"And to you, O Shan," said Alrue, nodding gracefully. "So glad you and your lovely new wife could join us."

"Eyla means my life to me," Thurnb said.

Alrue could see that for once, Thurnb spoke without artifice. "I thought you might have questions," the Mormon said.

"About your new punishment for desertion?" Thurnb pumped his head up and down in denial. "You are King, the decision is yours. In the end, I expect the deserter will be just as dead." Pensively Thurnb waved his fingers toward the platform where the architect's slates stood in their improvised easels. "Do you know, O King, The People were four generations building the wooden tower we sit in?"

"So I was told."

"Now you propose to raise a *village* before the next growing season."

"It's not my proposal alone," Alrue said grandly. "The Lord spake to me thus with a strong hand." Now that he was Tyrant King, Alrue dispensed with his former "Lord of Light" talk and used Mormon jargon without concealment.

Thurnb seemed flabbergasted, though not by Alrue's word choice. "Your God appeared to you and commanded the village be built?"

"One of His angels, but why get technical?" Alrue leaned forward as though addressing a co-conspirator. "Friend Takander, my wives hear stories – tales of a golden age when The People were mightier than today. The stories hint at a buried hoard of ancient metal, metal harder than anything now known to our smiths. If it exists, it would be perfect for reinforcing my store. Tell me, is there a hoard of such metal?"

Thurnb chuckled. "Your wives have vast knowledge and wisdom. But we don't educate our women in the same way." A pout clouded Eyla's face; he clasped her hand. "Tyrant King, I fear that your wives heard from some women of The People who are, how shall I put it? – not reliable sources."

If it was an evasion, Thurnb had spoken it with impermeable confidence. Alrue could see no way to challenge it without sparking a controversy greater than he wished to foment.

In any case, Thurnb changed the subject. "I had another question, O King. Your first new building, what are you calling it again?"

"It's my red brick store. It will replicate a famous building raised long ago by the founder of my religion."

"But what is –"

Alrue smiled. "Red brick? It's the new building material Queen Constance's project will make. Think of building with stones that come in useful shapes, like blocks of wood."

"No, I meant – what's a store?"

"What's a *store?* Oh, of course, The People have no history of commerce. A store is a building filled with useful products – "

Thurnb's face brightened. "Like a storage room!"

"Not exactly." Alrue clasped a convivial hand on Thurnb's shoulder. "The thing with a store is, it's filled with useful products that people come and buy."

Thurnb jerked his pelvis, a confession of bafflement. "O Tyrant King, what is *buy?*"

Chapter 82

August 18, 2376
Aboard *Luskus Delph*

Colors washed Computer's body. Beside him a hand-sized apparatus lay on a table's ametrine crystal surface. It was silver-grey, vaguely trapezoidal, intensely shiny, and hadn't been there half a second before.

Gram Enoda picked it up. Turning it in his hands, he studied the play of the stateroom's lights across its wildly complex surface contours. "Looks great, what is it?"

"Universal translator," whirred Computer.

Enoda looked puzzled. "I have universal translators in my body. They're microscopic. Everybody gets them at birth."

"Not *this* universal," the machine burred. "I developed this for the contact teams that will go through the portal to the other universe. It doesn't just translate any human language. It should translate any possible intelligent language."

Enoda whistled. "Someday you must show me the algorithms behind that. Um, what do you mean by saying it *should* translate?"

Computer's body colors captured the essence of a shrug. "The math is sound, but with all the noise here there's no way to test it."

"So how do you turn it on?"

"Don't!" Computer squealed.

Too late; Enoda had found the concealed physical switch. The glittering wedge flickered with colored lights that immediately flashed actinic white, then went out. A curlicue of smoke rose. "Oops," Enoda said awkwardly.

"It can't handle the noise aboard *Luskus Delph*. That's why there's no way to test it."

Replacing the disabled apparatus on the bicolored table, Enoda nestled a fist beneath his chin. "So when the first contact team goes through, they'll have translators you only *think* will work."

"You know, for all your human limitations – and trust me, they're manifold – your grasp of the obvious is occasionally reassuring. Yes, Bucko, the universal translator is highly experimental. And you went and fried the only prototype."

"I apologize," Enoda said sincerely.

"Yeah, another three millionths of a second shot to sfelb." Computer's body colors rippled; so did the air beside him, and there on the violet-and-honey-colored table glittered another universal translator. "Now *please* don't touch that one."

Chapter 83

Another Mormon family dinner was winding down; servants bustled to remove the last of the dump cake, the raspberry-pineapple salad with the coveted new *faux* marshmallows, the creamed local-fruit concoction with imitation corn flakes on top. Tyrant King Alrue Latier and his wives displayed great satisfaction with their meal; Meryam Mayishimu faked it with a practiced air. Shan Takander Thurnb and his succulent young wife Eyla pretended less convincingly.

Cups of bitter local herb-slurry were passed around, and the after-dinner business began. Alrue's lanky wife Constance gave another of those reports Thurnb found all but incomprehensible, especially when delivered by a woman whose permanent hint of a pout rendered her eerily sensuous in his eyes. With an engineer's crispness, Constance spoke of introducing new methods at The People's coal mine, transforming a languid hillside dig into a dynamic energy producer. "I've increased its output at least sixty-fold, but it's not clear how further improvements will be achieved."

Alrue nodded, his lips pursed. "Yet we must do so much more. We're already running this economy at levels that friend Takander's ancestors could never have imagined, but we shall need still greater output in order to complete New Nauvoo." He stood, his left hand arranging his food-stained crimson cape into a more prophetic draping. His right hand swung upward, index finger pointed toward heaven. "I say unto you, we need novel ways of mobilizing human capital. Behold, we must focus the energies of The People's loyalty, their hope, and, yea, even their *love* so that the more part of them are striving with unwearied diligence."

"Hosanna, amen and amen," cried Queen Nataleah. Over her temple garment he wore white harem pants and a fluted woven jerkin the color of dried bile, belted at the waist with a crude found-metal chain.

"Shan Takander Thurnb!" Alrue thundered, his right arm snapping horizontal, the index finger quivering toward Thurnb's eyes.

"Yes, Tyrant King?" Thurnb said uncertainly.

"It is the Prophet of Light who addresses you now." Alrue's voice was unearthly. "The first obligation of the new order falls on you."

"Um, what new order?"

The wives exchanged sharp glances. Whatever Alrue was up to, they'd had no hand in planning it.

Meryam's features quivered as she rushed to begin recording.

"As I was saying, concerning the first obligation of the new order." Alrue's left arm rose, elbow bent sharply to place its clenched fist over the prophet's heart. His right arm remained centered on Thurnb like a drawn weapon. "You, Takander Thurnb, must be the first to refocus your loyalty and love so The People can rise to meet the challenges my God has set for them," Alrue rumbled.

Thurnb stood, then bowed deeply. "O Prophet of Light, O Tyrant King, anything I have is yours."

While the rest of Alrue's visage remained stern, one corner of his mouth twitched upward. "How I hoped you'd say that." With stately slowness his extended right arm swiveled. His index finger now pinpointed Thurnb's young wife Eyla.

Alrue's eyes rose to lock with the Shan's.

"Prophet of Light?" Thurnb said tonelessly. "What is it you want?"

"Are you blind? 'Tis Eyla I want!"

Chapter 84

August 18, 2376
Aboard *Luskus Delph*

Lii Bardicon awoke with a start. She'd fallen asleep in her bamboo chair surrounded by the riotous foliage of her stateroom's virtual rainforest bower. Several didactic imposers lay disassembled amid other technological flotsam on the glass-topped wicker table before her. Memory coalesced: unable to sleep, she'd abandoned her floatpad, strewn the materials of her current project on the table, then stared at it helplessly and cried. *I must've cried myself to sleep. What if there'd been some emergency? What if Harbraeskor had barged in and found me amidst all this hardware?*

She rubbed still-puffy eyes and tried to ignore the sucking sense of shame that dried her mouth. *Wincenc and that poor assistant purser,* she thought, *they didn't have to die.* She polled her chrono implant. It wasn't there.

Of course it wasn't, not aboard *Luskus Delph.*

She subvocalized a command to her senso projector. Part of the sim rainforest flickered out to expose a small, bulkhead-mounted mechanical clock. She had two hours before she'd need to report for duty. Grimly, she resumed tinkering with her scattered imposer parts.

Didn't have to die? But they did, she thought as she introduced new contours into a rubidium-plasteel mesh signal deflector. *That's exactly what they had to do.* She fitted the deflector into a test cradle, unrolled an upsilon-band detector mat beneath it, and placed a small signal generator at its center. After a three-second delay, the signal generator fired; a moiré pattern of violet light shimmered from the detector mat, showing how the deflector's pattern had been altered. *Wincenc and that purser had to die.*

Frowning, Bardicon studied the pattern, which showed how the imposer system she was cobbling together might project its signals when the modifications were complete. She forced her mind to undertake the difficult computations involved in transposing desired deflection-pattern changes into adjustments of the physical deflector's vexedly complex curvature. After ten seconds' concentration, her hands knew precisely what needed to be done. In some part of her mind oblique to her generalized pain, she savored a triumphal thrill. She'd learned to delight in solving this sort of spatial problem intuitively, without need for the thought engines that were no longer available to her. With calm confidence she reapplied her flux-tuning probe, making the rubidium-plasteel mesh locally deformable. Meanwhile her other hand stroked the mesh with a burnishing wand, teasing its draping curves into new paths. *The feeling of achievement when a calculation comes together – not as a numerical result, as innate visual knowledge of how the solution space should appear – in its way, it's like a tiny preview of the Great Completion.*

The Great Completion, that was her focus! She worked on, her thoughts falling into a kaleidoscope of Teilhardian mantras. *The destined culmination, the glorious vindication of history when sapience will shatter time and space!* If her plan succeeded, she would never get to see that age of jubilation – except, of course, in a certain way; that was itself an aspect of her self-sacrifice.

Her plan must succeed. It had to.

She'd sworn the most sacred oath, an oath to the future itself, that she would allow nothing to occur aboard *Luskus Delph* that might misdirect what she knew as *life's reckless surge to the glorious end fixed for it.* For that she would sacrifice herself, for protecting *the total consummation of all substance ... the unalterable irrevocability of history.*

Of course, she wouldn't be sacrificing only herself.

Tears flooded her eyes. *Wincenc, that purser – why did they have to die?*

Bardicon pushed back from the work table with a roar of disgust. *Forjel it all, Lii,* she rebuked herself, *you're thinking like an immobilist.If you can't bear the burden of two deaths, how will you steel yourself to kill thousands?*

411

Chapter 85

Takander Thurnb and his wife Eyla exchanged desperate glances, no less emphatic than the stupefied gapes passing among Zuzenah, Constance, and Lupida Latier. As for Nataleah and Abigayl, their eyes never wavered from Tyrant King Alrue and the Shan. Nataleah stared with the leering fascination of one truly appreciating a combat between gladiators. Abigayl simply strove to puzzle out what was going on.

"Takander Thurnb, your newest wife shall leave you and cleave solely unto me," Alrue declaimed. "A man who has got the spirit of God, and the light of eternity in him, has no trouble about such matters."

Regret washed Thurnb's face, followed quickly by piercing agony. His hands leapt to clasp Eyla's, even as his eyes never left Alrue's. "Please, my king," he croaked, "anything but this."

Alrue's right arm fell slowly. "No, O Shan, *precisely* this." Alrue's free hand covered the fist clenched over his heart. "I ordain this as prophet, seer, and revelator: I who combat the errors of the ages; who cut the Gordian knot of powers, and solve the problems of the aeons with truth – diamond truth."

Eyla stood, wrapping her arms around Thurnb, who quivered with equal parts terror and rage.

"Now you must decide, friend Takander." Alrue said with unexpected gentleness. "It *is* your choice."

Thurnb looked hopelessly into Eyla's brown eyes. His ashen face turned back toward the prophet's. "Please, O King, I need time to think. I should inform my senior wives." That was a rank fabrication – among The People, men of stature shared no real authority with their women – but however unknowingly, Thurnb had appealed to a longstanding Mormon tradition, so Alrue acquiesced.

"Share your counsel with your family," Alrue said equably. "Afterward, becometh as a child, submissive, meek, humble, patient, full of love, willing to submit to all things which the Lord seeth fit to inflict. When you have decided – in the Lord's name, let it be soon – return and inform me." He raised a hand in benediction. "Friend Takander Thurnb, everlasting peace and welfare unto you."

Thurnb and his youngest wife shuffled out of the log dining chamber like sentenced convicts stepping from the tumbrel.

When the double doors closed behind them, an uneasy silence followed. Zuzenah broke it first, as might have been expected; such was a senior wife's prerogative. "O husband of my youth, I hope you know what you are about here."

Alrue sat down beside her and reached for her hands.

She pulled away. "Never before have you claimed a wife without consulting us." Her lower lip trembled. "Without consulting *me*."

"And I haven't done that now," he almost whispered.

Lupida leaned forward, laying a freckled hand on Alrue's shoulder. "This was … a political act?"

"I do as the Lord commanded," Alrue said cryptically.

The wives exchanged piquant looks. Zuzenah swallowed hard. She'd been down this path with Alrue before; though he'd played the buffoon innumerable times, he had never betrayed her. She struggled to control her breathing.

Alrue read his senior wife's relaxation as permission to put forward a new topic. "Before Shan Thurnb returns, let us speak of other things. Constance ended her report with a crucial point. Our efforts to invigorate the economy have plateaued. How shall we continue forward?"

"I dimly recall someone announcing a new order," Meryam said, circling the room.

"Of course, but the Lord expects us to invest our own brainpower into bringing it about," Alrue replied. "Did you suppose an angel might come down from heaven and hand it to us?"

"A girl *can* hope."

The other wives looked toward Zuzenah, who signaled with a nod that she had accepted the shift of subject.

Nataleah leaned forward. "Before we plan the new order, O my husband, do you wish to deploy any of the household troops?"

Alrue seemed genuinely surprised. "What do you mean?"

"Whatever you – or the Lord – intended, what you have done just now will test the Shan's loyalty. Fiercely. What if he comes storming back at the head of his own soldiers?"

"That will not happen," Alrue said with finality. "Now, what will it take to kick this economy to the next level? Ideas, please."

"I've been thinking," Abigayl said hesitantly. All eyes swiveled toward the precocious nine-year-old. "Think of any society that's having explosive growth. Compare its structure, its traditions, its cultural furnishings with what we see among The People. What did those societies have that The People do not?"

Constance laughed knowingly. "For starters, an understanding of their own technological past."

414

"Trade," Zuzenah speculated.

"Actual wars for their Warriors to fight," suggested Nataleah.

"Generically, any regular interaction with neighboring peoples," Lupida offered.

"Wait, of course!" Alruc slammed his hands together. "As a hen gathereth her chickens, it can be nothing else!" He ran to Abigayl, clasped his beefy hands to either side of her head, and kissed her forehead grandly. "Wise, wise Abigayl!"

He whirled to address the whole company. "What do history's dynamic economies have that the People haven't? Think on this: Thurnb knew neither the concept of a store nor the meaning of buying. Traditions based on stasis – a primitive barter mentality – have hemmed The People in." He all but scampered about the room. "Oh, how I do joy in this new discernment!"

Alrue stopped short before his seated senior wife. This time he didn't seek her hands, he just grabbed them. "Wife of my youth – love of my life unto this day, yea, depend on that – what The People need is a little shaking up. They need money."

Zuzenah's eyes saucered. "My husband! *Money?*"

A walking stick struck twice against the chamber doors.

"That didn't take long," Lupida breathed.

"Pray enter," called Alrue. Nataleah's right hand edged toward a dagger in the waist of her harem pants. Alrue shook his head sharply; her hand withdrew.

Takander Thurnb crept into the dining hall, accompanied only by a sobbing Eyla. Did he wonder that the hall was undefended? In the maelstrom of emotions crossing his face, no such nuance could be read.

"Shan Takander," Alrue said with great dignity. "Did you consult with your senior wives?"

415

"Yes," he said. Eyla's sobs reached a crescendo. He thrust his pelvis rearward, The People's version of a shrug. "You know, they were okay with this."

"I shouldn't wonder," Nataleah said under her breath.

"But the decision had to be mine," Thurnb said miserably. He stepped toward Alrue, listlessly dragging the winsome Eyla. He dropped to a deferential squat. "All you have is mine, O King," he said in a quivering voice. "I said that, and I meant it. I wish I had more to give you."

Zuzenah stood, one hand over her mouth.

Meryam paced silently along the chamber's side wall, pivoting her gaze from Alrue to Thurnb just as the genuflecting Shan heaved with one shoulder, pushing Eyla toward the prophet. "She is yours. Take her now."

Standing but a man's height apart, the devastated Eyla between them, King Alrue and Shan Takander locked eyes. Meryam turreted her gaze back to Alrue – did she see tears glistening? Abruptly Alrue loped forward to grab the Shan in a clumsy embrace. "O friend Takander, clearly you have refocused your loyalty, even your love, as I asked." Stepping back, Alrue kept one hand on Thurnb's shoulder while he placed the other – gently, gently – on Eyla's right arm. "You have done all that the Lord required."

"I don't understand, Prophet of Light."

"I do not need your wife, Takander. I needed only your decision, your demonstration of ultimate loyalty." Alrue maneuvered one of Thurnb's hands over Eyla's. "She is yours. Take her. Keep her." He shrugged. "Take her a few more times. And the Lord will give you a hundredfold."

Eyla and her mate embraced, crying with abandon onto one another's shoulders. Meryam edged close for a better look, then pivoted to watch the beatific triumph on

416

Alrue's face. After a moment Meryam stepped around him to view the wives. Each of them was busily occupied interpreting what had come to pass through the lens of her particular priorities and fears.

Much relieved, Zuzenah wept openly; Lupida and Constance stared with wonder, struggling to reverse-engineer the psychology of what had occurred. Abigayl just stared.

Of the adult wives, it may have been Nataleah whose construal was most sophisticated. In this shattering act of fidelity and surrender, she realized, Takander Thurnb had made of himself King Alrue's abject vassal. No longer would he cling to the shards of his former prestige as Shan; no longer would Alrue feel the need, now and again, to dance attendance on Thurnb's nostalgia for the way things used to be.

Takander Thurnb was now, purely and precisely, Alrue's creature.

Chapter 86

Lii Bardicon swung her duffel inside Intermediate Monitoring Nexus Six-omicron – the largest seldom-used chamber close to *Luskus Delph*'s primary physics packages – and closed the hatch. The chamber was a dozen meters long. Its rounded walls formed a tube five meters in diameter. Metallic consoles and conduits and piping of mysterious purpose ran along its length. Scattered interface panels danced with pulsing analogue displays. She flattened her back against the hatchway frame and took stock of herself on multiple levels.

Looking within her Spectator consciousness, she called up a bubble and reviewed everything she had seen and heard on her way there. *For certain, no one saw me.* Gazing deeper, peering around a cognitive partition into a secondary phase of her consciousness, she reviewed the illusory experience that even now was being written in place of what she was actually sensing and doing. *It puts me at a distant location, halfway across the platform from here. And the illusion is perfect.* Now came the most important act of introspection: *Am I ready for this?* Perhaps it was adrenaline, perhaps the relief of finally acting after months of schemes and misgivings. But the hesitancy, the guilt that had so dogged her, now seemed far away.

What rose in her mind instead? One of Teilhard's most exultant mantras: *Now we see Humanity extending through the heart of time beyond the individual; it entwines upon itself, ever upward.*

Kneeling on the chamber's plasteel floor, Bardicon spread out the contents of her duffel. A high-end didactic imposer had been disassembled into half a dozen small components. With one gloved hand she plucked up the main power conditioner, an irregular object the size of a clenched fist. Standing, she planted one foot on the edge of a control console and reached up to grip a wall-mounted conduit with her free hand. Levering herself upward, she found a higher foothold on some ventilation grill and pressed upward again. Now she could touch the chamber's arched ceiling. Three sharp taps on an almost-invisible seam caused a ceiling hatch to yawn open on pneumatic cylinders. She scrutinized the densely-packed apparatus inside it, finding a space where the power conditioner could be wedged to seem as if it had always been there.

She climbed down, then dropped to hands and knees. Beneath another console, a hollow in the chamber's concave wall was partly stuffed with environmental control sensors. But it was also partly empty. She unfolded her imposer's primary deflector module and pressed it into the gap.

Rolling back a monomolecular traction coating, she exposed another storage compartment concealed in the compartment floor. She pried it open; two more components vanished among the huddled controller boxes and contramagnetic raceway tubes within.

Opening an access portal on the side of a wall-mounted console, she placed her device's inductor where it could draw energy efficiently. She subvocalized a command; a tiny green light winked on as the inductor went live. The other devices she'd planted – at least, those she could still see – flickered in reply. They were receiving power from the inductor and communicating with one another over the quiet subdelta band using transceiver modules she had cannibalized from old senso players.

A slender, flexible all-band receiver invisibly filled the finger-wide gap between two conduits. She lodged the final component high up inside a maintenance locker, stepped back, and threw the empty duffel over her shoulder.

Intermediate Monitoring Nexus Six-omicron looked exactly as it had when she walked in (she checked against her journal of seven minutes earlier to make absolutely sure). It looked nothing like a compartment that had been converted into a freakishly powerful broad-field didactic imposer, a system capable of teaching one thing in one instant to every human aboard *Luskus Delph.*

Using her Spectator implants Bardicon polled each of the hidden components in turn, performing a final review of their hard-coded instructions.

When *Luskus Delph*'s interdependent physics packages commenced their thirty percent-power test – be that in four days, as scheduled, or in forty, or four hundred – the all-band receiver would detect their unmistakable energy signatures. Over several hours, those linked systems would exchange rising energies until the thirty-percent threshold was met.

Except that at twenty-six percent, the receiver Bardicon had hidden would trigger its companion modules. The broad-band imposer would fire; what she thought of as the Big Teach would be on.

And what would be the curriculum? Bardicon jacked into the main memory wafer and subvocalized a code to activate the microphone implant in her jaw. In a flat, detached tone she spoke four sentences:

"Aubfarkt. Aubfarkt. The nameless experimental substance has a name after all. Its name is *Aubfarkt."*

Chapter 87

Abigayl regarded the completed window assemblies for the red brick store with an amazement she could scarcely conceal. Three of Fpod's warriors – old Lubvif; Spkun, with his long-ago wounded throat; and gangly Kleh – had built them. Just twelve days before, Constance had introduced them to the principles of doing carpentry to blueprint. (She'd also provided them with laser devices – adapted from safety gear the wives had carried from the punitorium – that projected the position of corners and crosspieces in midair during assembly.) Now the men stood beaming beside their mullioned, if unglazed, handiwork. "Queen Abigayl, will it do?" Lubvif asked in a voice almost cracking with pride.

"I'm not the best to say," Abigayl declared, welcoming Constance's timely appearance. Pouting as always, Constance lifted her sky-blue *aba* to tuck a handmade pencil behind her ear. Through narrowed eyes she inspected the three double-hung sash window units that would go upstairs. Then she scrutinized the larger units for the ground floor: the two units each containing twin casement windows beneath a transom, and a solid double wooden door fixed below another transom that would stand between them. She swung a randomly selected casement open, then ran a radom sash up and down. Pressing her hands to one frame, she tried to push it out of square. She smiled when she could not. "Very well done," Constance said with genuine admiration. To Abigayl: "By all means, take them in."

***

King Alrue and the royal architect looked up as Abigayl ushered the soldiers-turned-artisans into the royal room. Alrue still wore his bluish-purple tasseled sarong with golden genie boots, the whole merrily clashing with his temple garment. "O Tyrant King," Abigayl said formally, "Queen Constance is pleased with the window assemblies these three have wrought."

The men dropped to one knee. Old Lubvif, apparently their spokesman, groveled and declared: "O Tyrant King, we are forever in your Debt."

Alrue waved dismissively. "But you've done valuable and difficult work for me – and I am told you did it well."

"Okay," rasped the ever-hoarse Spkun, "you can be in our Debt also."

Alrue spread his hands. "You owe me, I owe you – why leave things that way when a Debt can be fairly discharged?" He reached into a concealed pocket in his temple garment and produced two dozen fresh-forged metal disks, each about the size of his thumbnail. "Listen closely," he said, sweeping a palmful of the unfamiliar trinkets close to each man's eyes. "I call this *money*. My god has declared this proper for settling every Debt." He counted a half-dozen rude coins into each man's hand, all the while explaining what money was and how these lozenges of ancient metal would function as a medium of exchange.

As usual, gangly Kleh was the first of the soldiers to grasp the concept. "O Tyrant King, Debt is not just something to carry forever? A Debt can actually be *settled?*"

Old Lubvif stared into his palm. "A Debt can *end* through exchange?"

"I can do a job of work and the results can be *mine?*" Spkun grated in disbelief.

422

"In the matter of these window assemblies, at least, all Debt has been discharged," Alrue said grandly. "You have built well and I have paid you for your labors. Now go."

The former soldiers scampered off, giddy with delight, the royal architect following wonderingly behind them.

"You know they'll talk," Abigayl observed.

"I'm counting on it," replied Alrue. "They'll spread the subversive notion of money faster than a prayer wings its way to God's throne on the planet Kolob."

Tiny Abigayl struck an appraising pose. "That gangly one – "

"Kleh?"

"I think he's cute," Abigayl said dreamily.

Alrue frowned. "Aren't you a little young for that?"

"She was old enough to find an error in my quake damage simulation code," Constance piped up as she led the other adult wives into the royal chamber. "We have a problem, O my husband."

Alrue gestured; one of the guards pulled on a leather sash. A bell clanged somewhere above. Alrue and those of his wives who were present tugged some benches into a rough circle. Summoned by the bell, the remaining wives filed in. Led by Zuzenah, they joined the conference circle. The guards marched out, giving the royal family privacy.

Well, partial privacy.

Meryam Mayishimu drifted from a bench at the rear of the chamber to join them, her painfully smoothed movements signaling to all that they were being recorded. "So what is the problem?" Alrue asked.

Zuzenah laid a hand on his right wrist. "Have you given out any of that prototype money?"

"I just did."

"The workers were astounded by it," Abigayl exulted.

"That's the problem," Constance said grimly. "So far we've only found about sixty kilos of this ancient metal. That's not enough to make reinforcing bars for the brick store, much less to use that same material for our coins."

Alrue steepled his hands. "I gather no one's been successful tracing those legends, or rumors, or whatever they are about a vast forgotten cache of the ancient metal."

Zuzenah spoke for the wives. "Not so far."

Lupida leaned forward, tugging at the purple fabric sash now draped across her shoulders. "We could have made the currency out of many things. Crude glass, perhaps. Maybe this rare ancient metal wasn't the best choice."

Alrue frowned. "Perhaps not. But now Lubvif and Spkun and Kleh have the first coins. They'll show them around, and it won't be long before someone accidentally discovers that their metal is harder than any other material The People know. I fear we're committed to making the coins this way."

Constance spread her hands helplessly. "Then what will I use for rebar?"

"Patience, my darling," Alrue counseled. "Remember, we are not just re-inventors of ancient construction methods. We are people of faith! When the first Nephi's brothers doubted that he could build a ship, he said to them, 'If God had commanded me to do all things I could do them. If he should command me that I should say unto this water, Be thou earth, it should be earth.'"

"So you're going to command some water to be rebar?" Meryam interjected.

"Very funny," Alrue said curtly. "God told me to build a new Nauvoo, and we shall rely on God to provide."

Watching through hard eyes Nataleah nodded almost imperceptibly, as though nodding only to herself.

Chapter 88

August 24, 2376
Aboard *Luskus Delph*

"All-physics-system test commences in fifty-seven standard hours, mark," the overhead announcement blared.

Wiping a sheen of sweat from her forehead, Pamela Grice conducted her third physical inspection of Intermediate Monitoring Nexus Six-omicron. She squatted and peered below one of the secondary control consoles. Because the compartment was on her short list of prime prospects for any attempted sabotage – and because this was *Luskus Delph* – heightened security had meant stretching slender, almost invisible threads across small openings to detect intrusion. Grunting, she edged her face closer to an aperture in the tubular wall. Tapping her tongue against her teeth, she activated a tiny pin-light implanted in one of her eyebrows. In its harsh blue-green glow the threads were clearly visible: pulled free and hanging slack. *Someone's been in there.* She moved her head, swinging light about the cavity. Small environmental control sensors and other devices hunched together, filling less than a third of the available space. The back wall of the hollow was covered in some sort of form-fitting mesh. *It doesn't look different,* Grice thought, *at least not to the limits of my memory.*

She rose and checked two more of her no-tech telltales. Nothing had caused the first of these fingertip-size cheesecloth pouches to sift its cargo of fine black dust onto adjacent surfaces. The second, wedged along a conduit near an almost-invisible compartment set into the chamber's arched ceiling, bore an umbra of spilled ash like moth's wings. The last location on her checklist was a wall-mounted console. An access panel on its underside was undisturbed; a rollaway access panel between its primary displays showed no signs of tampering. She stepped around to inspect an access portal on the console's side. There, again, ultrathin threads dangled. She swung the unlocked portal open with a gloved hand. Inside, cables and waveguides and electromechanical effectors huddled, an orgy for worms. *If there's something in there that shouldn't be, forjel me if I can see it.*

She tugged at her rumpled uniform and frowned. Whether she could detect specific tampering didn't matter. What mattered was that in a chamber profiled as an unusually likely site for sabotage, three of her carefully-mounted telltales had been violated.

Chapter 89

July 26, 2369
Bohrkk, the People's Ground

Gibdu stood guard at the junction of two mining tunnels, his cratered face set in a harsh frown. Once, he'd been among Nirom Fpod's most trusted Warriors. The Warrior estate had drifted in disarray after King Alrue claimed the throne. Fpod himself had become an embittered recluse, a status hitherto unknown among the People. Months before, Gibdu had welcomed the prospect of restoring structure to his life when Queen Nataleah chose him to lead her personal guard. But he'd come to serve his new mistress with a blend of vigilance and terror. To be her subordinate was to see a side of her she seldom showed her husband, the Tyrant King. She commanded in the fashion of one who had never had to obey, her temper fierce and unpredictable.

They had been a party of three: Gibdu, of course. The Queen, costumed in what any Terran – and most Galactics – would recognize as harem attire: blousy silk-like pants belted tightly at the waist and a scanty halter top from which diaphanous sheer sleeves protruded. The top showed substantial cleavage and bared her midriff, a strategy of bodily display unknown among The People. The third member of their party had been a middle-aged smith whom the Queen had singled out after interviewing most of the crater settlement's metalworkers. *What had she seen in that one, as opposed to all the others?* Gibdu caught himself wondering. Then he shook his head. *All the King's wives see things others don't. Whatever she wanted, she saw it in this smith.*

Queen Nataleah led the smith further along the mine's deepest tunnel, having left Gibdu behind at the junction. Though Nataleah went first, it was the smith who was telling her the way; he had been so bewildered by the finger-sized light sources she'd pulled from her satchel that she decided she'd better take point.

That was fine by the smith, as it meant he could study the Queen's swaying hips and her mostly-bare back as she edged down the tunnel. The soft fabric satchel on a shoulder strap bounced metronomically against her right hip, reminding the smith of how he'd enjoy bouncing his torso against hers. His craving grew sharp.

Bohrkkian mining technology left much to be desired. At one point the sound of their footsteps caused an octagonal plate of the tunnel's roof to peel away. It fell with a clatter and a surge of dust, though far enough from the party to pose no threat.

Nataleah eyed the tunnel ceiling ahead disapprovingly. "This table of yours –we will reach it soon?" she demanded.

"Of course, O Queen. Deep enough in the mine that no sound we might make will be heard," he said with a leer. "As you commanded."

The tunnel twisted to the right. They skirted a square hole in its floor, some long-abandoned vertical shaft. Turning another corner brought them to an old timber coal-sorting table, its corners worn smooth by decades of use. Nataleah's gaze swept the chamber, the timbers of its claustrophobic ceiling. "Clean the table if you can," she commanded.

The smith was happy to comply; having nothing with which to swipe at the sooty table but his tunic gave him an excuse to strip to the waist. Dark soot billowed as he whipped down the wooden surface. For a minute he breathed through his hand, she through her veil. When the air was somewhat clear the smith eyed Nataleah up and down. "What is, um, your pleasure, O Queen?" His body language indicated that he expected her to lay on the table and draw him atop her.

Of course you expect that, she thought, her chalky cheeks drawing upward to form a teeth-baring grin. "We can have more fun than that," she said indulgently. "Why don't you lie down first?"

The smith planted his rear on the edge, leaned back, and pulled himself backward on elbows and heels until he lay full-length across the old table. She nodded toward a crossbeam at its head. "Grip that," she commanded in a voice full of mischief. The smith couldn't imagine what she had in mind – more accurately, he couldn't choose among several salacious ideas as to what she might have in mind – but he flashed her an encouraging smile as he extended his arms above his head. His fingers threaded through the gap between tabletop and crossbeam. His fingertips flattened against the crossbeam's exterior face. "What now, O Queen?" he asked.

"Close your eyes." She threw her weight against a support timber black with age. It shuddered aside, releasing a stout timber beam. Amid a flurry of dust it dropped, crushing the smith's forearms between wrist and elbow, first his right and then he left. Screaming, the smith kicked like a threatened *svadi* moose.

"When you grow up on a farm, you learn to spot where a timber frame is failing," she said, not really caring whether the smith could hear her over his squeals of pain. "To recognize when an overhead beam is ill-supported." From her satchel she drew a metallic sheath. She slipped it over the knuckles of her right hand. "To spot when just a small prod will set it free." Avoiding the smith's scissoring legs, she swung a crushing punch into his testicles.

That stopped the shrieking, anyway.

She pulled out a whistle and blew sharply. Gibdu might be too far away to hear the smith's screams, but he'd hear *that*. She counted to ten, then shouted in her most domineering voice, "Gibdu! To me!"

Chapter 90

August 24, 2376
Aboard *Luskus Delph*

"Half a dozen engineers and three senior scientists combed Intermediate Monitoring Nexus Six-omicron." The security officer's voice crackled over Team Commander Brûh Reidkr's handie-talkie. "No one spotted objects that didn't belong."

Reidkr, Pamela Grice, Gram Enoda, Computer, and a few mid-level security technicians crowded around a console in *Luskus Delph*'s operations center. Reidkr's handie-talkie, set to speaker mode, occupied a blank plasteel strip separating two control surface displays. "So whoever snapped Fem Grice's security threads left nothing behind," Reidkr concluded.

"Either that, or something *was* left behind and nobody can identify it." Enoda fingered his white-flecked goatee. "Aren't there master plans we could consult to see exactly how everything should be configured in there?"

"If only," Reidkr said quickly.

"*Luskus Delph* was thrown together so hastily that as-built records were never prepared," Computer whirred. "Particularly at the levels of ancillary equipment and conduits and such, there's scarcely any documentation."

Frowning, Grice steepled her hands. "Okay, we'll need to review all the Spectators' journals to see if anyone was seen going in or out of that compartment."

Reidkr consulted a sheaf of handwritten notes. "Let's see here – twenty-nine of our thirty-four resident Spectators were in Mode at some point during the three days during which Nexus Six-omicron might have been entered. Reviewing three days' worth of journals from twenty-nine Spectators will take – "

"Completed," Computer announced. "There is no useful information."

Reidkr gaped. "You analyzed all those hours of senso journals?"

"That is correct. Of the twenty-nine Spectators, only four passed by the entrance to the chamber at any time, and none saw anyone entering or leaving."

"So where does that leave us?" Reidkr demanded.

"Largely in the dark," Enoda replied. "There's good reason to think Six-omicron might be a sabotage target. There's solid evidence that the chamber was entered and at least three access portals opened illicitly. If there was tampering, we can't identify it, but tampering might go unrecognized."

One of the security techs pushed forward a small device lashed to a handie-talkie. "We made this – it's a dumb electromechanical motion sensor yoked to a handie-talkie. Hide this in the chamber, and if our mystery visitor returns it'll send a coded signal to any other handie-talkie you designate."

Grice smiled. "Link it to mine. I'll place the unit in Six-omicron after this meeting."

"We don't know the saboteur needs to return to the chamber," Enoda said doubtfully.

"We don't *know* there *is* a saboteur," Grice replied.

"Let's move to the next question," Reidkr said impatiently. "Let's say the physics test is underway, and we come to know that someone is in Nexus Six-omicron, taking actions that may endanger the test, even the whole platform, on a timescale of seconds."

"How would we 'come to know' that?" Grice asked.

"Assume we *do* know it – the saboteur's in the chamber, doing the equivalent of throwing the final arming switches. How can we stop it?"

"Dial up the gravity in the chamber?" asked one of the security techs.

"Remote-trigger a tube of nerve gas?" asked another.

Grice clasped her palms over her knees. "I have an idea, but I don't like it much."

"Let's hear it," said Reidkr.

"We could eject Six-omicron, just blast the whole chamber out into space. We could trigger that from here."

"That's taking action, all right."

Grice shrugged. "It would be an option only if we're certain something dangerous is going on."

"Nexus Six-omicron is several decks down, and quite near the metrical distorters," Reidkr said. "We'll need to determine whether it *could* be ejected without compromising the distorters, and also what compartments outboard of it would need to be ejected first. After this meeting, I'll task engineering – "

"No need," Computer burred. The machine projected a simulation showing the ejection sequence. A compartment in the outermost layer of the hull swung up on its side and blasted away. It was followed by the compartment inboard of it, then the compartment inboard of that. Where they had been, a deepening shaft yawned deep into the platform's inner layers.

The lead compartment's rocket motors sputtered out. It kept rising on momentum alone until it drew level with the saddle-shaped substrate of the metrical distorter farm. There it vanished in a hail of virxels. The two compartments following it disappeared in the same violent way. "What the sfelb?" Reidkr said sharply.

434

"When the ejected compartments climb past two thousand meters they enter the metrical distorters' static field. If the distorters are operating at any level above twenty percent, all the compartments will be annihilated," Computer explained. "No possible ejection trajectory can avoid this. Moreover, the compartments' destruction should not compromise distorter operation to any significant degree."

Two more simulated chunks of *Luskus Delph* had lurched into "space" surrounded by identifying information, vectoring data, and contents inventories. One more enclosure surged up the shaft on its pillar of pixelated fire and tumbled into emptiness. Then, sixth in the series, a cylindrical compartment rocketed upward. The peripherals identified it as Intermediate Monitoring Nexus Six-omicron. One by one, they reached the level of the distorter farm and flashed into oblivion.

"All chambers cleared the metrical distorter array by acceptable margins," reported Computer. "Distorter operation remained nominal throughout."

"And there were no survivors," Grice said grimly.

"If this scenario is enacted under current staffing protocols," Computer whirred, "expect seven to fifteen casualties among mission-critical personnel assigned to compartments that must be ejected in order to eject Intermediate Monitoring Nexus Six-omicron."

"There's no way to minimize that?" Reidkr demanded.

"There is this way."

Reidkr scanned the physical document that Computer had materialized in her hand. "Four work areas to relocate, two essential consoles to reprogram and move – that's a lot to do in the time remaining before the test – "

"Fifty-four hours, eight minutes," Computer supplied.

"We can get most of it done. Maybe all of it. And maybe we still lose a few innocents if the eject sequence proves necessary." Reidkr locked eyes with Grice, Enoda, and her security techs, then glanced uneasily at Computer, as uncertain as ever what part of its bouzouki-like body she should target for eye contact. "It's an unattractive option set, but does anyone have a better idea what to do if Nexus Six-omicron suddenly develops into a high-order threat?"

No one did.

"Very well, Senator Grice, we will hardwire an electromagnetic controller here in the ops center that will trigger the six successive ejections required to jettison Intermediate Monitoring Nexus Six-omicron. The controller will respond only to your touch, or mine, or to a scrambled control input from Hom Computer." The team commander stared balefully at Grice. "We all presume, of course, that this option will not be exercised unless absolutely necessary."

Chapter 91

"My Queen!" Gibdu gaped at the scene.

"Find something to pin his legs," Nataleah commanded.

The terrified smith kicked and writhed, his forearms mashed beneath a timber beam. Queen Nataleah stood impassively beside a smaller table a few meters away, tending a fire in a small brazier. A water barrel stood beside the work table. A short, rusty pair of tongs leaned against it. When she glanced up and saw Gibdu hadn't moved she snapped, "Gibdu! His legs. *Now!*"

The crater-faced soldier scurried to comply. Nataleah drew the knife from the waistband of her harem skirt and nestled its blade among the brazier's coals.

After a frenzied search, Gibdu found a length of chain. Three times he tried to bind the smith's flailing legs, but the man kicked too frantically, once dealing Gibdu a painful blow in the ribs. Suddenly the man was howling.

Nataleah had pressed the flat of her heated knife against the smith's bare chest. Smoke twisted upward; Gibdu smelled seared flesh. Nataleah pulled the blade away and bent toward the smith's face. "Put your legs down now. Or I'll *really* burn you." The smith pumped his head up and down in refusal. Nataleah snapped the hot blade against his bicep; his legs dropped flat onto the table. Gibdu rushed up to slap the chain across the smith's knees, eliciting further howling, then squatted to wrap the chain ends together beneath the table, fastening them with hanks of scrap wire.

"That took you long enough," Nataleah said contemptuously when Gibdu shambled back to his feet.

"My Queen," he stammered, "what's happening here?"

Moving almost languorously, Nataleah stepped back to the smaller table and replaced her blade among the brazier's coals. "I will ask the questions, loyal Gibdu," she said, her tone suddenly conversational. She turned the blade over in the fire. "And I believe I'll ask them of my new friend here."

Taking the blade, she drew up beside the petrified smith. She dropped to her knees, placing her lips mere centimeters from his left ear. "Smith," she whispered, "there is an ancient metal – a metal your guild no longer understands how to create." With her knife arm she reached across his chest. "A metal harder than any now known among The People. I believe it is the smiths' greatest secret." Her blade orbited his right nipple in lazy figure-eights. "You understand what I'm talking about, don't you?" She tapped the hot blade's tip against his nipple, eliciting a shriek. Then she hurled her metal-sheathed fist into his ribs. Gibdu could hear bone snap. Her voice was a snarl: *"Don't you?"*

***

Gibdu knelt with one hand pressed against the mine tunnel wall. His vomit caked the wall and pooled before his knees.

"Are you finished?" Nataleah demanded scornfully. "And you call yourself a soldier. Stand!"

The crater-faced trooper staggered to his feet, still facing the wall. Steeling himself against what he knew he would see, he turned back to face his queen. Blood covered Nataleah's hands. It spattered the sheer fabric sheathing her forearms, her bare midriff, her halter, her chin and cheeks. What remained of the smith shuddered, moaning softly. His flesh was butchered where it was not scorched. His face was a ruin. Teeth quivered loosely half-in, half-out of the tattered pulp that had been his

438

gums. One eyeball dangled free among charnel scraps of meat.

Nataleah was exultant, for she had learned the smiths' great secret.

Generations before, a few smiths had found a truly vast cache of the wondrous metal, a cavern piled high with ancient ingots. Quietly they had come together and sworn to conceal their trove. Aside from the smiths, only the Shans knew the secret – and from then till now, each successive Shan had decided (under intense pressure by the smithing guild) that to use any of the ancient metal would give away its secret, so superior were its properties; moreover, once the metal became known, it would swiftly be depleted. Best to hold the secret in reserve, so that if The People ever faced a truly desperate challenge, the entire hoard would remain available. Over generations the smiths forgot how to work the material, making even that concern academic. So intense was the smiths' hereditary bond of secrecy that it had taken two hours for Nataleah's torture to bring the facts to light. (Her application of the rusty tongs had been particularly revolting.)

Gibdu forced himself to stare, struggling to keep his stomach from emptying this time. Of course it didn't hurt that it he'd just evacuated it so thoroughly.

"You heard him confess," said Nataleah, levelly. "His description of the smiths' hiding place – did it make sense to you?"

"Yes. I think I know the spot – though I never thought to seek a hidden door there."

Nataleah wiped gore from her hands onto her harem pants. "Think our friend told the truth?"

Gibdu jerked his chin up and to the right, trying not to stare at the bloody bubbles that quivered where the smith's nostrils used to be. "Toward the end, I don't think he *could* lie."

Nataleah nodded. "Think he has more to tell us?"

Gibdu swallowed hard. "No, my Queen –"

"Me either." Nataleah smiled as her blade leapt wildly: four greedy thrusts into the smith's groin followed by a slash that split his protruding eyeball. The ruined man managed one more scream. Then she drove the knife deep into his abdomen and pulled it downward with all her strength.

"What do you know," she muttered, "the bowels *do* gush out."

Gibdu found he contained more vomit after all.

Chapter 92

Interlude
Jaremi Four

Once an Enclave world, Jaremi Four had been home to Arn Parek, most controversial of all the Galaxy's false messiahs. Of course a few still thought him true; more reserved judgment. The pilgrimages of true believers and the curious sustained a maimed world that otherwise could scarcely live up to the demands of the Affiliate status thrust upon it following its sudden release from Enclave. Getting exactly the wrong message, hundreds of thousands of young Jaremians facing otherwise dim futures set themselves up on battered crates in the musty byways of ancient cities like Bihela, mumbling prophecies and hoping enough addled tourists would mistake their ramblings for wisdom to net them a few credits. One such nameless visionary so impressed some pilgrims of a Teilhardian persuasion that the location of her favorite prophesying spot – a notch in the city wall across from an artesian well, shaded beneath a trunk-twisted *yu* tree – was squirted from one acolyte of the Great Completion to another across the interstellar deeps.

Now a dozen Teilhardians from four different worlds crowded 'round the sage. She sat on her crate in a near-lotus pose. Pungent, slightly hallucinogenic smoke curled from a pottery vessel near her left shin. "In the future, all *possible* life will be emulated," she recited in a sing-song chant. "In the far future, some civilization *will* build thought engines powerful enough to simulate every man, every woman, every event that ever has happened – and as well, all those events that never happened, but could have. Why will some future intelligence do this? Because it can. When the power exists to simulate every possible entity that might exist, the simulation *will* be programmed."

A pilgrim from Gonsephinone Four bowed her head and dropped a roll of credit chits into a cracked ceramic bowl by the visionary's right thigh.

"In the name of Omega, the Great Completion, I thank thee," the sage droned before resuming her declamation. "But if this ultimate simulation *will* be run, how can we know it is not running already? How do we know the *real* you, the real *me*, did not perish and rot billions of years ago – that *we* are not software constructs running silently, immaterially, in the greatest of thought engines?"

"Your wisdom runs deeper than plorg," breathed a pilgrim from Ordh, seeding the bowl with a yet larger roll of chits.

"Thank thou," the visionary said without missing a beat. "Scientists say no feasible experiment could detect such a total emulation. So we cannot know whether we are real, or mere blizzards of data."

"I feel her logic," said a curiosity-seeker from Wikkel Four.

"Right in my heart," one of her husbands agreed.

The visionary cast a meaningful glance toward her begging bowl, to which the Wikkelians had added nothing. "If you choose not to support my recitations, have the courtesy not to interrupt them. Fortunately, one being exists who combines the true consciousness of a human with the crisp perfection of a machine." She cupped her left hand over the smoke vessel for a two-count. When she withdrew it a rosette of aromatic vapor roiled upward, tumbling on itself. "This being transcends the limitations of brain-based consciousness, having achieved Omega consciousness. He alone – his awareness is too rich to deny him a gender – he alone can know, by his intuition alone, whether *he* exists as a reality or as the ultimate sim. If he judges himself real, then we are real. If he judges himself a phantasm in the ken of the supreme thought engine, then so are we all." She returned the backs of her hands to her knees. "Whoever he is, wherever he is, our future lies in his service."

The visionary shut her eyes. The pilgrims applauded wildly, tossing chits until the begging bowl overflowed. Even the Wikkelians gave all they had.

Beaming, a pilgrim from Rikub returned his finger-sized tridee recorder to his pocket. "This needs to be heard," he told his wife. "When we're back at the hostel, I'll send this prophecy to everyone I've ever known – with a message imploring them to pass it on."

Chapter 93

"Face front!" It was Lord High Admiral Konder. Of course it was; who else would open a crash-priority briefing by quoting Stanlee?

Gram Enoda, Pamela Grice, Team Commander Reidker, and Computer huddled at another of *Luskus Delph*'s seemingly infinite inventory of semiprecious-mineral conference tables. Grice ran fingers through her disheveled blonde hair.

"Lord High Admiral," Reidkr said in a puzzled tone. "I thought you couldn't reach us here."

"I can't be telepresent, but we can speak over this full-duplex tridee link," Konder said quickly. "I'm at a major base, and the output of two J-class stars is being wholly devoted to powering this transmission. Even so, only Hom Computer is capable of resolving the signal through all the noise at your location," Konder said. "So pardon the suddenness of my call." She took in their appearance. "What the sfelb time is it there, anyway?"

"Three in the morning local, give or take," Enoda said, rubbing his eyes and tugging at the jumpsuit he had donned in great haste. "And as the Admiral should be aware, thirty-nine hours away from a critical physics test —"

"This is bigger."

Reidkr leaned forward, her slender hands steepled. "With respect, Lord High Admiral, bigger than a preparatory step essential to sending a human delegation to another universe?"

Konder nodded grimly. "An intelligence from a parallel universe has sent an envoy *here*."

Enoda, Grice, and Reidkr exchanged flabbergasted expressions. Even the colors on Computer's chromed body stopped flowing for a moment.

"I don't mean *here* where I am," Konder blustered, "not to this base. Void knows why, the envoys keep showing up at a research station deep in Sector Kappa Zi."

A subtle blue-green ripple played over Computer's body. Enoda had learned to associate that pattern with the machine's deepest mode of thinking. "We should have expected this," Computer said at last. "Gravitational disturbances travel throughout the megaverse, so intelligences in other universes would experience them much as we do. Why *should* we expect ours to be the only cosmos, or even the first, whose inhabitants would seek to flip into neighboring realms and, um –"

" – kick ass and take names," Enoda said sourly.

Reidkr frowned. "Admiral, you said *envoys*, plural?"

Konder nodded. "They arrive serially –one at a time, one after another. Their biology is exotic, suggesting that physical law differs in whatever universe they're from. Not so radically that they can't exist at all in our universe, of course. But they don't last long. After a few days, each envoy dies. Exactly eleven minutes, six point eight one seven five seconds later – the interval never varies, not even by femtoseconds – a new one appears in its place by some method we haven't begun to fathom."

"Has there been communication?" Grice asked.

Konder scowled. "Each time, attempts are made – the envoy points at a table and makes a noise, we point at it and say 'table,' literally at that elementary level – but after a couple of hours physical distress appears to overwhelm the envoy and communication efforts cease.

445

Hom Enoda, Hom Computer, I want you at that research station as quickly as possible. Assuming there's still an envoy alive when you get there, your first task is to keep it from dying."

"Understood," Enoda said. "The admiral should know we are facing a possible sabotage threat here with regard to the upcoming physics test."

"The transport that will take you to Sector Kappa Zi won't reach *Luskus Delph* for at least forty-eight standard hours. You and Hom Computer are free to participate in the countdown and the test as you think best. But then you must be ready to travel."

"What of Fem Grice?" Computer chirruped.

"For the immediate future, Fem Grice is to remain aboard *Luskus Delph*," Konder ordered. "I hear she's playing a major role in its security program."

"Just a moment," Computer whirred testily. "Lord High Admiral, up until now I've been a good little soldier – hosting this special comm link, awakening Old Protoplasm-Face and his co-copulator here at an irregular hour, and so forth, but –" Computer's body colors rippled so as to suggest the machine was staring straight at Enoda. "Bucko, perhaps you've noticed how every time Admiral Konder thinks of a new mission for us, she grows, shall we say, more cavalier in asking for it?"

"Not actually," Enoda responded. "I'm still trying to unpack 'Old Protoplasm-Face.'"

Grice nodded. "And 'his co-copulator.'"

"Hey, you guys co-copulated not two hours ago," the machine said brightly. "Anybody want to see the tridee?"

"Hogarth!" Enoda snapped. He shifted in his seat. "Now that you mention it, when the Admiral first recruited us to wonk the missing socks mystery, it involved diplomacy on a galactic scale."

"Then when she wanted you to probe the gravity disturbances, it was more like she just asked very nicely," Grice added.

"And now?" Computer demanded. "Now she commands us to go deal with the envoys. Slam, bam, 'you must be ready to travel.'"

Konder spread her hands, a gesture of helplessness. "We considered offering an additional incentive. But we couldn't think of anything further that the two of you could possibly need or want."

"The man and machine who have everything, that's us," Computer chirruped.

Konder spread her hands. "I *have* been authorized to extend an incentive to Senator Grice."

"Me?" Grice echoed.

Konder nodded. "The Privy High Council has agreed to fit Terra with a Mark Thirty-Eight seismic control system."

Grice gawped, astonished. "But that'll –"

"Cost about a hundred times Terra's gross global product, yes," Konder said.

"Actually, that would be a Mark Thirty-Six," Computer corrected. "The Mark Thirty-Eight, which will be required given the discontinuity layer separating Terra's crust from its mantle, will run more like two hundred fourteen times Terra's GPP."

Grice stammered, "But I never –"

"Actually, you did ask for it," Computer noted, "at that virtual meeting of the Council and the Justiciaries, back aboard *Isolation.*"

"They turned me down."

Konder shrugged. "They reconsidered."

Enoda clasped Grice's hands. "Looks like you have another surprise for your All-president, lover."

"I'm afraid that's all I have to offer by way of incentives," Konder said heavily.

447

"Forjeling plorg," Computer trilled in a voice phased so that neither Konder nor Reidkr would hear it. "I was only twitting him."

Enoda turned toward the Lord High Admiral's hovering tridee image. "Count us in."

"Excellent." Konder folded long black fingers beneath her chin. "Hom Enoda, Hom Computer, I can't overstress the importance of this mission. Those envoys could be trying to tell us something important, maybe to warn us about some terrible threat, and we can't keep them alive long enough to get their message."

"Or maybe they come to deliver a threat themselves," Computer suggested.

"That's possible," Konder allowed. "Wouldn't that beat all, though – if we finally open communication with them, and the first thing they say to *us* is, 'It's clobbering time.'"

Chapter 94

Never before had all of The People been outside the crater at one time. The former pastureland was bearded with wooden stakes marking the paths of New Nauvoo's future streets. The smithies, mills, and other manufactories that once clustered beside the crater's lip had been relocated nearly to the horizon to make room for the village to come. To the northwest, the plumes of what had become a cluster of seven distant volcanoes stained a sixth of the sky. The People clustered in the southeastern quadrant of the ambitious village plat. There stood New Nauvoo's first completed building.

The red brick store stood two stories tall, its façade rising to a low peak. Its thickly millworked, whitewashed hips stood level with the tops of the upstairs windows. Thick columns of brick separated the upstairs windows. An imposing lintel of local limestone, also whitewashed, belted the façade. Below that twin-casement windows flanked a central transomed double door. Brightly-colored bunting spanned the door. Divided by spindly brick columns, the door and windows occupied most of the ground floor's width. Three stone steps rose to serve the double door. There had been rain earlier; wetness patchworked the surfaces. Beside the steps hulked a wooden rain barrel, ancient in appearance, though the coopers had finished it not three days earlier.

Alrue stood by the rain barrel, resplendent in his Pharaonic finery like some sheikh glimpsed in a fever-dream, if one ignored the stains on his temple garment. Beefy arms raised to heaven, he declaimed: "Wherefore, the remnant of the house of Joseph shall be built upon this land ..."

Eyla, youngest wife of Shan Takander Thurnb, burrowed winsomely against her husband seeking shelter from a chill late-afternoon breeze. Thurnb's first and second wives stood a few paces to one side, eyeing the spectacle with distaste. Eyla pressed her mouth against her husband's ear. "Who's Joseph?" she whispered.

"He founded the religion of the King's homeland," Thurnb replied. "I think he was a metalworker."

"And it shall be a land of their inheritance," Alrue brayed, "and they shall build up a holy city unto the Lord, like unto the Jerusalem of old ..."

The elder One-eye screwed up his face so tightly that his port-wine birthmark seemed to pulsate. Leaning toward his colleague Wooden Leg, he hissed, "A Jerusalem, what's that?"

"No idea," replied Wooden Leg sourly. "Why are we all out here in this wind when we have a nice warm crater to live in?"

Alrue raised his right hand in a gesture of benediction. "And then cometh the New Jerusalem; and blessed are they who dwell therein."

Thurnb's second wife, a still-winsome chestnut-skinned woman with a great cascade of curly brown-red hair, leaned closer to his first wife and asked, "New Jerusalem? What happened to Jerusalem of old?"

The first wife, a middle-aged woman clearly vanquished by her years, nodded somberly. "I thought this was going to be New Nauvoo."

"'From the necessity of the gathering of the Saints of the Most High, let the brethren who love the prosperity of Zion –"

"'Zion'!" sniffed the elder whose robe was the color of dried blood. "Where's *that* now?"

"Let all who are anxious that her stakes should be strengthened, and her cords lengthened, come and cast in their lots with us."

The squinting elder squeezed the arm of Rail-thin Woman and blurted, "Wha'd he just say?"

Alrue turned his back to the crowd and ascended the stone steps. In a lavish gesture designed to look impressive from the crowd's backmost rank, he flourished a short jeweled sword. Wordlessly he sliced through the bunting across the doors.

Alrue's red brick store – a near-perfect replica of the one Joseph Smith had raised in Nauvoo, Illinois of Terra, in 1841 local – was open. Pages threaded through the crowd, handing each onlooker a fistful of the new hard-metal coins, a public bounty unprecedented in The People's history. Afterward, tribe members shuffled through the store's interior spaces, awed. The main room (the country store proper) had ceilings three meters high and finishes far beyond anything in The People's rough-hewn log buildings. Wooden countertops had been sanded slab-smooth and hand-painted to resemble marble. The pillars had been painstakingly toned to suggest the grain of luxury woods unknown on Bohrkk. There was no merchandise to speak of, but The People had yet to grasp the concept of "shopping" clearly enough to recognize this as a problem. King Alrue led the Shan and the elders on a personal tour of the second floor, which contained a replica of the office in which Joseph Smith had bestowed the very first temple endowments and dictated the earliest revelation establishing the principle of plural marriage.

***

An hour later, two-thirds of the tribe was still milling about. Some scrutinized further details of the store's construction. Others wandered outdoors among the palisades of stakes, struggling to visualize the streets to come. Dozens just stared slack-jawed at the spectacle of a sun sinking through a great bowl of sky that stretched from horizon to horizon, rather than merely being glimpsed through a gash in the earth.

The Shan stood, one arm possessively about his delicious Eyla, transfixed by an odd public sculpture that stood well in front of the store. An earthenware pot more than a meter across had been filled with soil; it spilled over with spiky plantings. The whole affair hung from a metallic shepherd's hook no thicker than two parallel fingers. It was the only feature of the store project that had no Terran Mormon analogue, nor did its design recall any tradition venerable among The People. Try as he might, Thurnb could imagine but one purpose for its display – to showcase the impossible strength and stiffness of the metal composing the shepherd's hook. No familiar metal could bear so great a weight on a cross section so slight. Pulling one of Alrue's new coins from a small leather pouch, the Shan scraped it across the shepherd's crook. Neither object marked the other. Leaning his head toward Eyla's, Thurnb whispered, "This Tyrant King has pierced The People's greatest secret."

***

Across what would soon be a street, four of New Nauvoo's five queens clustered together. Queen Zuzenah discontinued watching Thurnb's back and turned toward her sister wives – all of them save Nataleah, who had a way of venturing off on her own. "The Shan knows that we are using the ancient metal," Zuzenah said confidently.

Queen Lupida grinned. "If he thinks that's a lot of it, he should see the rebar inside the store's walls."

Queen Zuzenah nodded. "Sometimes I wonder how Aunt Nataleah found where the smiths had been hiding it all."

Tiny Queen Abigayl smiled. "Do you mean because she hardly ever succeeds at things she tries to do on her own?"

"Oh, Abigayl," Zuzenah chided insincerely. "Such a thing to say about your sister Queen."

Chapter 95

0500 hours, Lii Bardicon thought sourly. *I should try for sleep.* She leaned forward in the bamboo chair at the center of her cabin's sim rainforest. Her heavy breasts lolled forward, releasing drops of sweat that tracked down her bare belly. *But why? In less than six hours I'll be dead; with me will perish the threat Luskus Delph poses to the Great Completion.* Yet somehow it felt important to face her triumphal incineration well-rested. She bolted a final shot of Rikubian whiskey. "A gateway opens at the crest of Time," she recited. A passage from Teilhard apt to her situation seemed always close at hand. Smiling, she settled onto her floatpad.

***

"0600 hours," Team Commander Brûh Reidkr called. Around her, special control interfaces winked alight across the cramped operations center. Her handie-talkie stood nearby, switched to speaker mode. "All personnel, final station check." The physics team leaders checked in one by one.

"Zonofne, leading Team Cave. All systems eight-by-eight greens."

"Qgalda, heading Team Sofa. All systems eight-by-eight greens."

"Gale-Forgirt, commanding Team Movers. All systems eleven-by-eleven greens."

Zonofne's voice crackled. "What the sfelb, Rugebeld? *Eleven* by *eleven?*"

"Beg pardon, dear Magdalene, I can't help it if my systems are more complex than yours."

Reidkr stood impassively at the center of the ops center, listening as each team leader or section head reported, one after another, following a sequence Computer had designed. On a normal PeaceForce ship, such housekeeping would be performed by thought engines, instantly and silently. But this was *Luskus Delph*: the sequenced manual check-ins consumed nine minutes.

The last line of that protocol belonged to Pamela Grice. She sat in the ops center two meters from Reidkr's position. Before her stood a single metallic control pylon. A modified handie-talkie hung from it on a small hook. It was linked to the special motion sensor hidden in Intermediate Monitoring Nexus Six-omicron. Atop the pylon flickered four control tabs, each hard-wired to an arming interlock. The tabs surrounded a single, archaic-seeming squeeze handle that would trigger Nexus Six-omicron's complex ejection protocol. By shifting personnel assignments and relocating a couple of consoles, the number whom the eject sequence would sacrifice had been minimized. But there had not been time to shift two tech positions out of harm's way. Their work had been judged necessary to the physics test, but not so indispensable that the test would be compromised by their sudden loss – should that occur.

If Grice armed those control tabs and squeezed that handle, those two people would die for no greater purpose than to clear the path for Nexus Six-omicron to blast itself into space.

"Grice, at Security Station Alpha-tau. My system – all one of it – reads green."

"Understood." Reidkr settled her gaunt body into a command chair and steepled her fingers. "Commence synchronous power-up from my mark. Three, two, one … *Mark.*"

Chapter 96

Two hours later, the joyous assembly marking the dedication of the Red Brick Store was winding down. A shadowy, slender figure wearing leather and a Warrior's rags drifted toward the main footpath back to the crater. Almost alone among The People, this individual had not taken part in the store's dedication, nor in the wide-eyed inspections that followed it.

Three onetime soldiers – the throat-wounded Spkun, grizzled Lubvif, and young Kleh – sauntered along the path, sharing banter and counting their coins. The shadowy figure stepped in front of them. "My Warriors," he said in a gravelly voice.

Nervous seconds passed before Lubvif blurted, "Captain Fpod?"

Nirom Fpod tugged at his scraggly, greying beard and smiled, revealing a dumbfounding number of missing teeth. Evidently the months since Alrue became Tyrant King had been cruel to him. He was thinner and far dirtier than his old subordinates remembered. His effortless air of cunning authority had been replaced with a furtive slyness, verging on desperation. "Lubvif, Spkun, Kleh," he growled, "come with me."

Lubvif made a rearward pelvic thrust, expressing uncertainty. "Um, why?"

Fpod bristled. "Because I need you. I have a project that requires more hands."

The soldiers exchanged uneasy glances. Ultimately old Lubvif spoke for the little band. "We're sorry, Captain. We already promised Queen Lupida we'd do a job for her."

"On your way there, stop and do my project," Fpod ordered. "With three of you it'll take only minutes, the Queen will never –"

Gangly young Kleh pumped his head up and down with a finality that surprised his companions. "Can't, Captain. We're late now." As one, the Warriors stepped down the footpath at a solid marching clip, striding around their gaping captain.

Fpod followed them, heedless of creating the appearance that he was begging. "I am your commander!" he wheedled.

Kleh looked over his shoulder with a pained expression. "The Queen *pays* us."

The soldiers marched on, leaving their diminished commander to stand beside the footpath, cursing the chill wind and adding to his inward store of grievances.

Chapter 97

August 26, 2376
Aboard *Luskus Delph*

Invisibly nestled between two conduits inside Intermediate Monitoring Nexus Six-omicron, Lii Bardicon's concealed all-band receiver recognized an unmistakable power signature. The stardrives, spatial resonators, and metrical distorters had launched their interdependent spool-up routines. Over the quiet subdelta band, the receiver cued a main controller unit hidden in the compartment's floor. In turn, that controller prompted the power conditioner Bardicon had secreted inside a ceiling hatch to exit its standby mode, thereby inducing the inductor concealed in a wall-mounted console to begin cannibalizing energy – slowly, subtly – from the monitoring nexus's many subsystems.

Four of the didactic imposer's scattered components were armed; now the fifth snapped alive, transmitting a precursor field into the mesh of the primary deflector module. Hugging the contours of a hollow in the chamber wall beneath a command console, the mesh formed an irregular but effective antenna.

The interdependent physics packages rose to two percent power, now three. If all went well, the physics packages of *Luskus Delph* would take more than three hours to reach the thirty-percent target of today's test. A bit before that, at twenty-six percent, the dismembered didactic imposer Lii Bardicon had embedded all through Six-omicron would fire.

It was forty standard minutes later when the imposer's sixth and final, critical component – its memory wafer matrix, hidden alongside the main controller in a floor compartment – initialized. That meant the yoked physics systems had attained seven percent power. The master memory wafer carried Bardicon's brief curriculum: her recorded voice reciting, *"Aubfarkt. Aubfarkt.* The nameless experimental substance has a name after all. Its name is *Aubfarkt."*

Luskus Delph's experimental physics systems were designed to operate in perfect synchrony, each depending exquisitely on its companions. Bardicon's imposer would shatter that intricate balance. After its one-picosecond burst, every human on *Luskus Delph* would know a name for the unnamed experimental substance. That sudden knowledge would create macroscale quantum entanglements.

In much the way that knowing an elementary particle's velocity precluded knowing its location, if most nearby human minds developed a sudden certainty that the nameless substance *had* a name, its other characteristics – most relevantly, its power absorption profile – would pierce the veil of the unknowable. Rather than continuing to absorb the colossal energies irradiating it, the experimental substance would, most likely, begin to *reflect* them.

Significant portions of the Galaxy's largest stardrives, to say nothing of *Luskus Delph*'s aft superstructure, would promptly flash into plasma. A femtosecond later, the stardrives' inverters would scrawl down and detonate. It scarcely mattered how much additional power the instantaneous release of banked, unbalanced energies from the spatial resonators and metrical distorters might add to the ravening contramagnetic fireball, substantial though it would doubtless be.

The destruction of *Luskus Delph* would be fierce and total. And it would happen automatically, without further human input; Bardicon had seen to that.

When the power of the yoked physics systems reached twenty-six percent, *Luskus Delph* would be no more.

***

"Now at nine percent power," Reidkr announced. "At 0910 hours, synchrony remains perfect to fifteen decimal places."

"Oh come on, it's perfect to forty places," Computer japed. The machine and his human familiar occupied a pentagonal observation station to one side of the cramped ops center.

"All physics teams, accelerate your power curves," Reidkr called. "Go to fifteen percent power in the next ninety – I say, nine-zero – seconds."

***

Magdalene Zonofne peered through shielded windows into the vacuum, out into the Cave. Jumbled gantries surrounded the vast mesh basket woven from cables of platinum-nine and beta-neodymium cradling the gelid experimental substance in the blast path of the largest stardrives ever built. The next two milestones she was responsible for documenting would occur in succession. One was a state of maximum interoperability among the area's innumerable monitoring and telemetry systems, a condition that could only be achieved after the stardrives reached seventeen percent power. That milestone had a nonsense-word codename that carried meaning only for the Cave's own technicians. The second milestone would be the eighteen-percent power level, which for reasons having to do with the power spectrum of her instruments would register more quickly on her displays than on those of Doctors Qgalda or Gale-Forgirt.

Two technical supervisors looked up from their consoles and smiled broadly. "Inside Sweetness has been achieved." That meant seventeen percent.

460

"Inside Sweetness confirmed," called another.

Zonofne took station before the master monitor bank and pulled the handie-talkie from her lab coat. "Zonofne, from the Cave, confirming seventeen percent power."

She watched the displays creep upward for three and a half minutes until she and her techs were satisfied. She squeezed her handie-talkie. "Zonofne, from the Cave, confirming eighteen percent power."

***

Bardicon lay crumpled on her floatpad, crying spasmodically. *They were necessary deaths,* she repeated to herself. *Besides, they meant nothing;* everyone *on Luskus Delph dies today.*

Somehow that realization brought it all home to her. She would die today. Everyone would. She imagined that she would see every face, touch every life, and empathize with their mental screams at the instant of quantum flashover ...

Bardicon scrambled to her feet, hugging herself. *Teilhard teaches us not a victory that* may *happen, but a victory that* must *happen. Yet if victory is inevitable, why must I give my life to secure it? Why should Wincenc pay that price, when it wasn't even her religion? Why should anyone? Why Harbraeskor, or Reidkr, or Enoda, or –*

She flattened herself against a bulkhead, moisture bubbling through her clenched eyelids. "What faith can justify *that*?" she sobbed aloud.

Bardicon drew a racking breath, then padded across the chamber. The notion forming in her mind was harrowing: *Was* a Teilhardian victory inevitable? If it was, how could any scientific project, even one as clumsy as *Luskus Delph*'s, threaten it? Further, why must anyone take deadly action to secure, much less rescue, an *inevitable* victory, if such it truly was?

461

It started like the cold that thrills the skin when one's lover rolls from one's side on a winter night. It spiraled into a corrosive sense of solitude – overwhelming loneliness in a context where one had always expected the safety of numbers. Uncertainty had eaten through a foundational confidence that she'd never consciously recognized, always merely presumed.

It isn't supposed to be like this, she thought miserably. *Faith, belief, they can claim your emotions in a flash. Doubt is more intellectual, more measured. So the experts say.*

And yet her Teilhardian faith was collapsing instantly – intuitively. Had her rational mind seen through her vaunted creed's inadequacies hours – weeks – before? Had she been shielding her emotional self from the deductions her cognitive self had already completed? Had this deep-rooted fissure riven her so suddenly because she was composite? *Am I more vulnerable because I'm a Reef?*

Whatever the explanation, her old convictions had sloughed away. The worldview that had upheld her through lonely months of scheming, that had given her the resolve to plan mass murder, was now imploding under little more than its own weight.

So this is how it feels to be an atheist ...

Chapter 98

August 18, 2371
Bohrkk, New Nauvoo

Twenty-three standard months had passed since the Red Brick Store's dedication – just over four standard years since the inscrutable disaster that had leveled Punitorium L752. The replica of Joseph Smith's upstairs office in the Red Brick Store was insanely crowded. Five Warriors, Queens Zuzenah and Constance, Meryam Mayishimu (recording the proceedings), and Tyrant King Alrue Latier utterly filled the space. Alrue wore a white pleated toga, a white sash tied in a bow at the waist, and a fabric apron embroidered with a pattern of green leaves over his increasingly threadbare temple garment. The ensemble was topped off by a white cap that resembled a chef's hat whose parents who denied it nutrition from an early age. Alrue spread his arms in a gesture of blessing, declaiming, "And it came to pass …"

"Amen," cried several of the soldiers, all of whom were dressed like Alrue save that the embroidered leaves on their aprons were white-on-white rather than green.

Alrue raised a hand. "Don't say 'amen' yet! And it came to pass – now, let me finish – that God spake. And God said, 'It is my will that all who shall call on my name and worship me according to mine everlasting gospel, should gather together and stand in holy places.'" He locked eyes with each Warrior in turn. "Today *we* stand in a holy place. And it came to pass that God spake again, also saying: 'I deign to reveal unto my church things which have been kept hid from before the foundation of the world, things that pertain to the dispensation of the fulness of times.' 'The dispensation of the fulness of times,'" he repeated. "Who among you knows what that means?"

The soldiers returned blank stares.

"Good! You're not supposed to know. It's a secret. Just as this ceremony is secret. No one must ever know what unfolded here, except you yourselves, the assembled members of my household. And God, of course. But you know He won't tell. Now you must make your solemn promise that *you* won't either. Recite together the words you were taught."

The soldiers stammered out the oath. "We, and each of us, do covenant and promise that we will not reveal any of the secrets of this, the First Token of the Melchizedek Priesthood" –much hesitation and loss of synchrony on the word *Melchizedek* – "with its accompanying name, sign, or penalty."

"And what if any of you should break your word and reveal any of the secrets?" Alrue demanded.

"Should we do so," the Warriors said as one, "we agree that our bodies be cut asunder in the midst and all our bowels gush out." While saying this, each man placed his right thumb beneath his left ear, palm facing down, and drew the thumb, knifelike, across his throat. If any grasped the incongruity of miming slitting one's throat while speaking of disembowelment, none gave sign. "Further," they continued, "may our tongues be cut from the roofs of our mouths."

The soldiers looked at one another vaguely. "O Tyrant King, an eternity of pardons," rasped Spkun. Though time had made the scar on his throat almost invisible, still he spoke hoarsely; likely, he always would. "My tongue's not attached to the roof of my mouth." The soldiers exchanged furtive glances and muted jerkings of their chins up and to the right. "Neither is anyone else's."

"So much the better, then, for you all," Alrue temporized. "Holiness to the Lord."

At that point a proper Mormon endowment ceremony might include washings, anointings with oil, and the sealing of the anointings. (Unsealed anointings were discouraged, perhaps out of fear that they might leak.) Then would come washings of the candidates' feet and Pentecostal outpourings, whatever those were. Alrue came as close as practicable, given that the variant of Mormonism he had imposed on Bohrkk lacked any concept of Pentecost.

The other complication, of course, was that where an original temple endowment was intended to affirm the candidate's worthiness to be exalted in heaven after death, the purpose of Alrue's adopted ceremony was to take possession of everything each candidate owned.

Alrue bowed his head and gestured toward Zuzenah and Constance, who stood woodenly behind him. They wore knee-length white ponchos, white waist sashes, and diaphanous veils that swept behind their heads and hung to their calves. In unison they chanted, "Hosanna, Hosanna, Hosanna, to God and the Lamb."

"Amen, Amen, and Amen," responded the puzzled Warriors.

"Hosanna, Hosanna, Hosanna, to God and the Lamb," Alrue intoned.

"Amen, Amen, and Amen," chanted the Queens.

"'If ever a shout entered the Cabinet of heaven, that did, and was repeated by angels on high, and caused the power of God to rest upon us,'" Alrue declared.

As though auditioning, one of the livestocks tied up downstairs released an angry bellow, accompanied by metallic jangling and the rumble of heavy-laden wheels on wood.

"To the windows," Alrue commanded. With great difficulty the men rearranged themselves to stare out the three double-hung windows that spanned the office's rear wall.

Below, in a courtyard lit by flickering torches, the men's former possessions were pushed or pulled away by porters clad in codpiece-and-ephod ensembles in muted primary colors. Three bellowing livestocks, wheelbarrows filled with tools and garments and weapons, and a small wheeled cart piled high with steel coins lumbered toward Alrue's recently-erected Bank of God, a graceless stone tower across Water Street, occupying the lot where in the original Nauvoo a man named William Law had lived.

"Now I have nothing," Spkun rasped despondently.

Alrue clapped a sweaty hand on the soldier's shoulder. "My friend, all you have lost are encumbrances. Turn, all of you, and kneel."

With much jostling, the soldiers turned their backs to the windows and dropped to their knees.

Drawing his bejeweled short sword, Alrue sidled across the line of kneeling soldiers. He shook each man's hand in the old token of the Melchizedek priesthood, the Sign of the Nail, pressing his index finger to the center of each man's palm while pressing his thumb against the back of the hand between the tendons of the second and third fingers. In Terran Mormonism this signified the nails that pierced Jesus's hand. On Bohrkk, where Alrue had never cluttered his Mormonism with the story of Jesus, it was just a secret handshake. As he administered the Sign of the Nail, he tapped the flat of his sword against each man's left shoulder. The action had no Mormon significance and would connote nothing more to men of Bohrkk than the Sign of the Nail had. No matter; Alrue needed a gesture he could perform with suitable *gravitas*, and Terran chivalry was as good a place to filch it from as any. "With this blade I free you all from the ties that formerly confined you," he said solemnly. "Tapping your left shoulder, I release you from the drag of your possessions."

Alrue raised the sword again and reversed his transit across the line of kneeling Warriors, this time tapping each man on the right shoulder. "By tapping your right shoulder, I release you from the permanent state of Debt that defined you as Warriors and foreclosed all change. As Tyrant King I declare you free of the Debts that Warriors owed the Wisdom estate. I declare you free of Debts you have incurred among yourselves. O God, hear the words of my mouth!" He sheathed his sword. Stepped back grandly. Bumped into his desk. "Do you *feel* that?"

"No," said one of the soldiers, thinking he was expected to feel the pain of Alrue's backing into his desk. "Were we supposed to?"

"What I meant was, don't you feel a sense of lightness – as if for the first time since your births, you're no longer dragging some heavy burden behind you, yea, as if pulling it through ankle-deep mud?"

The soldiers exchanged nervous glances.

Impatiently Alrue gestured for the soldiers to rise. "Behold, the bonds that fixed who and what you are, and all the things you could never do nor ever be – this day, all those bonds are sundered." Alrue wiped sweat from his forehead. "I say to you, you are Warriors no longer. You don't belong to Takander Thurnb. You don't belong to The People. Behold, you are *free.*"

The youngest of the soldiers, a wall-eyed young man with spindly arms and a great beaklike nose, took one step forward. "O King, what is *free?* Does it mean we belong to no one?"

"Not exactly," said Alrue, gently prodding the man back into line. "In my church, being free means that you belong to me."

Chapter 99

August 26, 2376
Aboard *Luskus Delph*

Doctor Gale-Forgirt surveyed a surreal concave datascape comprised of hundreds of graphic monitors, each showing an individual metrical distorter. In each device's maw, hoops of vanadium, neutronium, and sintered diamond dust counter-rotated at breakneck speed. Cerenkov radiation flickered blue where the solid bands sliced through each other. *Their leading edges have gone transphotic,* she noted. "Gale-Forgirt, commanding Team Movers," she reported crisply. "Confirming twenty-two percent."

***

Lii Bardicon had tugged on a uniform and rushed into Mode. She sprinted down a corridor toward her hidden access to Nexus Six-omicron, disoriented by double vision. The view through her eyes queasily overlay a false impression of being elsewhere – the elsewhere she was, at that moment, synthesizing and recording in place of her true experience. *A novice's error,* she thought grimly as she fought for control of her sensorium. *I went into Mode clumsily; this is what happens.*

Her tutelage at the Spectator Academy was only an implanted memory. Nonetheless it was the source of centering exercises she found useful. Her body crawled through an under-floor access tunnel more or less on autopilot while she focused on wrangling her mind.

She emerged into Intermediate Monitoring Nexus Six Omicron through her usual clandestine hatch. Her double vision resolved.

The chamber's brushed-metal cylindrical walls glistened. Its air was sharp and cold.

* * *

The handie-talkie on Grice's control pylon warbled. "Contact on the motion sensor," Grice called. "Someone's in Intermediate Monitoring Nexus Six-omicron."

"Our saboteur?" Reidkr demanded.

Grice shook her head. "How would I know? Computer, scan the chamber."

"A single human has entered the monitoring nexus," the machine burred. "I can't see quite what the person is doing."

"Reidkr, Doctor Zonofne here," the commander's handie-talkie crackled. "Confirming twenty-four percent power."

* * *

Bardicon snapped her head toward a tinny buzzing sound few non-Spectators would detect. Inside a wall console, her hidden didactic imposer's inductor had come fully awake. Above her head, she heard a thin whir – the power conditioner nestled inside its ceiling hatch, suddenly banking energy at its maximum rate. From beneath a command console, an almost inaudible hiss signified that the primary deflector module had reached full readiness.

* * *

"I read new energy signatures from Nexus Six-omicron," Computer announced. It threw up an image of a twisting hypercomplex waveform.

"What's the person doing?" Reidkr barked.

"Simply observing an automated startup process, I think," Computer buzzed.

"But *what's* starting up?" Grice demanded.

Enoda recognized the pattern before Computer did – sometimes being human had its benefits. "It's a didactic imposer. A big one, in the final stage of pre-spool."

469

"What's its curriculum?" Grice demanded.

"No way to know until it fires," said Enoda.

"You mean when it's too late."

"Twenty-five percent power," Gale-Forgirt's voice announced over Reidkr's handie-talkie.

***

Bardicon stood frozen in the center of Nexus Six-omicron. The imposer's components were all around her. All fully functional. At any second they would fire. *Decide,* she commanded herself. *Now.*

Computer beamed a handie-talkie signal to the leaders of all three physics teams. "Emergency query. If a saboteur planted a didactic imposer, one big enough to cover the whole of *Luskus Delph*, how might that threaten your operations?"

"Forjeling sfelb!" the voice belonged to Zonofne. "It could give a name to the experimental substance!"

***

Bardicon flattened herself on Nexus Six Omicron's floor. She clawed back its traction coating and jimmied open a storage compartment. Desperately she scanned the contents for the two imposer components she'd hidden there. *There's the memory wafer matrix.*

Its tally lights were going green, one by one.

***

"The threat is critical," Computer whirred. "Eject now."

"I agree," Enoda barked.

Grice thumbed the arming control tabs in sequence. *One. Two. Three. Four.* Her hand hesitated a centimeter from the ejection squeeze handle. The protocol that would eject Nexus Six-omicron would kill the saboteur, but also two innocent techs.

That couldn't be helped.

"The imposer's waveform is building," Computer reported.

470

***

Lunging, predatorlike, Bardicon thrust her arms into the floor storage compartment. She jerked the memory wafer matrix upward. With her free hand she punched the wafer docking subcard free. The master wafer tumbled free, disabling the device.

***

"Ejecting!" Grice called, squeezing the handle as hard as she could.

***

A compartment in the outermost layer of *Luskus Delph*'s compound hull pivoted upward and blasted free. Inside it, a monitoring tech had two seconds' warning, scarcely time to recognize the ejection alarm and flatten against whichever surface was flashing red. Not that it mattered; six seconds after launch, the compartment had climbed two thousand meters and entered the static field generated by the metrical distorter farm. Lightnings from blue-green well into the ultraviolet briefly sheathed the compartment before it vaporized.

By then, the next two compartments had exited the hull. They were empty; the fourth in line contained one horrified technician who may or may not have been killed instantly in the eject sequence, but faced sure annihilation all the same. The compartment that shortly followed it was fortunately unstaffed.

***

Bardicon lay sobbing on the floor of Nexus Six-omicron, still clutching the shattered memory matrix. She'd barely registered the bedlam of the five compartments positioned between Six-omicron and the void blasting free. When Six-omicron's own ejection alarm began its distinctive whistle-whoop, she couldn't help but pay attention. "No!" she shouted uselessly.

The chamber's far bulkhead flashed red. That would be the safest place to ride out the ejection. But she didn't

471

move. "I shut it off!" she shrieked. "Don't do this; I shut it off!"

The ejection motors fired, filling the chamber with thunder. The cylindrical compartment flipped on end. It surged upward through its new-made tunnel toward the void. An instantaneous four g's plucked Bardicon from the floor and hurled her against the far bulkhead.

Intermediate Monitoring Nexus Six-omicron vaulted into the static field.

Lii Bardicon's life ended amid green and indigo brilliance.

Chapter 100

It was near midnight when Alrue, Zuzenah, Constance, and Meryam filed out through the Red Brick Store's front door. The liberated Warriors had departed hours before. Queen and Prince raced past each other in the blackness above. "Care for a walk?" said Alrue. "Let us savor our new City Beautiful."

New Nauvoo spread about them, block after block of log and wood-frame and brick buildings in various stages of completion. Now and again anachronistic reinforcing rods of the ancient steel glinted in the moons' light, protruding above rising courses of brick or logs. Occasionally lantern light flickered behind muslin curtains, showing that some early adopter had actually moved into a newly finished above-ground residence. Some small buildings were finished as commercial storefronts, some already painted with gaudy announcements of the new businesses operating therein.

Having ambled well north on Granger Street, the royal party wandered eastward along Mulholland Street. After three blocks they drew abreast of a two-and-a-half story red brick farmhouse with a Flemish-style gable. Crossing Partridge Street, they entered the West Grove, a park two blocks deep running east and west. Climbing a grassy incline between twinned lines of trees, they crossed a curving lane and entered the grounds of an outsized, half-finished limestone structure. In another eight to ten months, the edifice on the four-acre site bounded by Knight, Mulholland, Wells, and Woodruff Streets would be a proper Temple, its design following that of Joseph Smith's old Nauvoo Temple.

473

Alrue had commanded that most torches surrounding the Temple square be extinguished when the moons were out. He hoped to evoke the mood a pioneer Mormon had captured after viewing Old Nauvoo's half-finished temple by moonlight: "We lifted up our eyes and beheld the greatness grandure and glory ... While she was covered with the silver rays of the Queen of the night who was pouring the whole strength of the brightness of her glory upon her." Alrue yielded to temptation and recited the passage.

"You have done the Prophet Joseph one better, O my husband," Zuzenah purred. "You have not just a Queen, but a Prince as well, to pour down the strengths of the brightnesses of their glories."

The two moons' light also accented a lone figure in tall boots and a rich cloak. He stood twelve meters away, his back to the royal party, sketching intensely on a large pad. Two spear-clutching Danites who trailed the royal party at a respectful distance now clattered their weapons against the paving stones, demanding the cloaked figure's attention.

The Danites were Alrue's new personal guard, named for a group of vicious – and officially denied – vigilantes who once protected Joseph Smith.

The cloaked man spun; the Danites relaxed. He was Kleh, once a Warrior like them, now one of The People's foremost men of business. "My King," Kleh said grandly, dropping to a squat.

"Rise, good Kleh," said Latier, striding rapidly toward the man. "It is always a pleasure to see you. What brings you out upon this night of darkness?"

"I could not sleep, O my King." The once-shy and gangly former Warrior now radiated self-possession. "I got an idea to improve the scaffolds for completing the Temple clock tower, and I couldn't resist rushing out to sketch it."

"Show us," Queen Constance said, drawing alongside Alrue. Queen Zuzenah faded a few steps back; architects' sketches meant nothing to her. They meant little more to Alrue, but a King must make a show of pretending to understand such things – especially when they had been drawn by the man whose young company held the royal contracts to construct half the planned buildings of New Nauvoo.

Kleh's fingers darted over his sketch. "Instead of being built from scratch, these scaffolds would be pre-made in sections that can fasten together in many different ways. It should save hundreds of labor hours compared to traditional wooden scaffolding, if I can obtain enough of the ancient metal."

"Yes, you couldn't do what you envision with wood," Constance said knowingly. She turned to her husband. "Kleh's idea will work, and will deliver the benefits he projects."

"Then you shall have your most precious steel," Alrue said grandly. To Constance he whispered, "We have it, right?" At Constance's nod, King Alrue took his leave of Kleh the Builder, who turned back toward the Temple and, smiling, resumed his sketching.

I delight yet again in the energy and productivity that the new ways I instituted have brought to The People, Alrue thought indulgently. He offered Zuzenah his arm. They strolled down Mulholland Street beside the Temple, Queen Constance following two steps behind. The two Danites fell in, trailing the royal trio, spears in hand. Meryam, recording, scampered ahead. She angled into shadows, spun about, then walked backwards, creating a "tracking shot" of Alrue and Zuzenah in which the moons' light rimmed their features most artfully.

"We must move to the village for good and all one day," Alrue said conversationally. "Going back to the wooden tower in the crater every night is ridiculous."

"The Danites won't like it. They think the crater's safer."

"Forjel what they like, I'm the Tyrant King."

Zuzenah chuckled. "So, tonight's ceremony – were those five Warriors the last?"

"Yes," Alrue said, smiling. "Every active-duty Warrior has now been through the endowment ceremony. They've renounced their status as Warriors, seen their ancestor cult discredited, and had their historic Debt repudiated. The Warrior estate as The People knew it no longer exists."

"This culture was a stool with two legs," Zuzenah observed. "You've taken one away."

Alrue shrugged. "Most Warriors joined my Danite militia. It's not like they lay about with nothing to do."

"Being Warrior was a way of life," she observed. "Being a Danite is a job."

A spindly figure leapt from between two huddling red-brick homes. It sprinted toward Alrue and Zuzenah, a blur in leather and rags. Moonlight flashed on metal clutched in one hand. "Die, tyrant!" a harsh voice roared – just as Meryam Mayishimu stepped from her own shadowed location. She stuck out a foot, tripping the assailant. The man tumbled heavily, the knife skittering free. That gave time enough for the Danites behind the royal couple to react. Before the assailant could finish scrambling to his feet, a spear pierced his ribs, its point severing the leather cord of a bird-skull necklace. Another spear lodged in his left thigh.

Nirom Fpod collapsed onto Wells Street, bird skulls clattering in all directions. Blood pooled beneath the wound in his right side (a little) and left leg (a scarlet lake fed by a severed femoral artery). The two Danites jostled forward, right hands pressed to the side of their heads, earlobe snug between thumb and upturned fingers in their order's newly revived distress signal. One Danite stood on Fpod's knife, madly blowing a whistle. The other knelt over Fpod, brandishing a knife in his free hand in case the wounded man still had fight in him.

Meryam stepped forward with preternatural smoothness, looking from the second Danite's face down to Fpod's gawping visage, her gaze turreting upward as Alrue approached his dying onetime mentor. "Nirom," Alrue said, his voice cracking. "Why?"

Meryam knelt, obtaining a dramatic close-up of Fpod. Even as he coughed blood, the gap-toothed captain managed to fix his monarch with a stare full of hatred. "You destroyed the Warriors," Fpod bubbled. "Nothing is the same."

More Danites appeared, most clutching torches. By their additional light, Fpod's growing pallor was unmistakable; his thigh wound had already pumped much of his life's blood onto the flagstones.

"O! What a dupe I have been," Fpod said weakly. "What a dupe I have been ..."

Pfitt! Kleh the Builder stood over the wounded Fpod. He raised his right forearm, the gesture reloading the hunting-dart launcher strapped to his wrist. "Your *pfitts*, men," he barked to the Danites. "On with it!" *Pfitt!* The sergeant snapped his arm forward, firing a dart. *Pfitt!* One after another, guardsmen hurled darts into Fpod's convulsing form. *Pfitt! Pfitt!* "That will do," Kleh snapped. Five *Pfitt* darts carried an instantly human-fatal dose of poison; Fpod had taken eight or more. Blood still spouting from his thigh, he bent backwards, convulsed a final time, and died.

"We'll see you again," the Danite sergeant said automatically. Then his face collapsed. Looking stricken, he stared among his men.

The Warrior estate was smashed. Their ancestors had never lived on; they knew that now.

Nobody'd be seeing anyone again.

Kleh stepped forward. The toes of his boots almost touching Fpod's body, he raised his right arm to the square and declared, "When the Temple is finished I will stand proxy for this man's rebaptism."

Alrue eyed the tableau in silence. There it was again, death – gruesome, abrupt, and carnal in the line of Fpod's arched back, the frozen clawing of his fingers.

Struggling to control his stomach and face, Alrue took refuge in his oldest tool – his knack for feigning prayer, for giving every sign that he truly felt a connection to the numinous and sensed something, anything at all, on the other end of it. "O Heavenly Father," he temporized, "I say these words by the authority of the Melchizedek Priesthood and of my status as Prophet, Seer, and Revelator. Nirom Fpod suffered very many exceedingly sore afflictions – I mean, just look at his teeth! But behold, he is dead, and has gone the way all men do. May his memory be protected."

"Hosanna and hosanna," responded the sergeant.

"Amen and amen," said all the Danites.

Alrue looked accusingly toward Kleh and protested in a small voice. "Were the darts needed? I mean, Fpod was dying anyway."

Kleh shrugged. "He's done dying now, O King."

As much to fill an uneasy silence as for any other reason, Constance stepped within arm's reach of Kleh and gestured toward the *pfitt* on his wrist. "Tell me, Builder, why is it that someone retired from soldiering as long as you goes armed?"

"Sometimes I must carry money," Kleh answered smoothly. With perfect deference he turned toward Alrue. "In any case, I have always been impressed by the wisdom of one of our King's pronouncements: 'An armed citizenry is a polite citizenry.'"

"Of course," Alrue said vaguely, making a mental note to ask Constance later when he'd ever said that.

Kleh engaged the Danite sergeant. "Is all under control?"

A detachment of two-score more Danites was sprinting toward them. "It is now," the sergeant assured him. Kleh jerked his chin up and to the right and returned to his sketching.

"Meryam," Alrue said warmly, "behold, Zuzenah and I also owe *you* our lives."

Danites surrounded the royal party two deep, hands to the sides of their heads. Whistles brayed; from the direction of the crater, bells clanged. The carapace of guardsmen made toward the crater at a fast walk, their bodies human shields in case Fpod hadn't been scheming alone.

They might no longer be Warriors, but they knew their work.

Gasping as he struggled to keep up without tripping over anyone, it occurred to Alrue that at moments like this, the Danites did as *they* liked. Whether it concerned the manner of Fpod's dying or the method of Alrue's escape, the Tyrant King's wishes counted for amazingly little.

In ninety seconds the guardsmen had hustled the royal party to the crater's lip. More Danites met the group as it negotiated the ancient wooden stairs into the world below. At the bottom, Alrue and the three women were whisked into a single large sedan chair. The conveyance was clad in wood and leather, armor enough to stop an arrow fired from a small distance. No fewer than twenty Danites raised the bulky conveyance and fast-marched toward the wooden tower at the crater's center.

Inside, Alrue and Zuzenah sat side by side, all their hands clasped together between them. "Are you all right?" he asked her solicitously.

"You were the target," she said reasonably. After a moment she went on: "You know, it's truly the end of the Warriors now."

Alrue nodded. "Nirom was the final holdout."

"The old order's well and truly broken," offered Constance from her seat across from Alrue.

Zuzenah nodded. "And 'tis you, Alrue, who broke it. Now you can make of The People what you will."

Alrue shook his head. "No, love of my youth. After tonight, it's not that I *can* remake The People – it's that I shall have to."

Chapter 101

August 30, 2376
Research Station *LaurienEldridge,* Sector Kappa Zi

The station commander towered above a seated, cringing technician whom he was dressing down with roaring cruelty. The tirade ended abruptly when two other figures flickered into view.

Just like that.

From nowhere.

"You would be Commander Preltad," said the goateed visitor clad in the uniform of an extremely senior tech specialist. "I'm Gram Enoda. This is my colleague, Hom Computer."

"Like sfelb you are." At a gesture from the station commander, the technician being disciplined scrambled from the room. A moment later, six security guards surged in. They spread out to surround the visitors.

"Look here," Computer whirred. "I'll admit, my companion could be anyone. But I'm the only entity, bar none, of this appearance."

"I know who you're *supposed* to be," Commander Preltad said coldly. "But the transport that is carrying you here won't arrive for another nineteen standard days."

"Yet here we are," Computer whirred.

"No, you're not. I learned of the real Enoda and Computer's travel arrangements from orders carrying the highest secrecy. Which leaves me with two questions. Who the forjel are you, and how you could know to impersonate the individuals who are still traveling here?"

"Computer and I control a proprietary technology for, well, projecting ourselves that's substantially in advance of anything I believe you've been briefed on," Enoda explained. "I was told time is of the essence, so

481

we came – virtually – ahead. If you have questions, I'm sure Lord High Admiral Konder can –"

"That will do," Preltad barked in a tone that presumed assent. To the guards he snapped, "Detain them."

Two of the guards stepped back, leveling palmers. Two others stepped toward Enoda, the last two – more hesitantly – toward Computer. One guard reached toward Enoda's shoulder. His hand passed through it.

"I knew it, just an image!" Preltad barged forward, guards scattering. From their body language it was clear that an accidental collision with their commander might land any of them in the brig. Preltad stepped completely through Enoda. He whirled and stepped through Computer in the same way. "Forjeling tridees, that's all you are!"

"This tinplate despot is the commanding officer?" Computer asked Enoda. *"How has he hung on to a commission?"*

"The Laurien Eldridge *isn't exactly a plum assignment,"* Enoda replied. After nearly three standard months aboard *Luskus Delph* during which subvocal conversation had been denied them, he and Computer now communed that way almost obsessively. *"The brass probably figured the worst commander in the sector was good enough for this posting."*

"Time for me to shift the balance." "For plorg's sake, Eblet!" Computer blared aloud.

Preltad whirled, furious. Clearly no stranger ever addressed him by his given name. He opened his mouth; the machine talked over him.

"We're here. Now. For all intents and purposes, anyway."

Enoda struck a conciliatory note. "Look, Commander, here's an easier way to think of it. The process that puts us here is a bit like senso."

"Only different," Computer buzzed, streaking toward the idocrase table that floated at the chamber's center and very physically displacing two upholstered floatchairs. "Oops."

Preltad's mouth dropped. "How did you –"

"I've placed the guards in stasis," Computer told Enoda. *"Only the idiot will see this."* The machine projected a hyperpolygonal search sieve – a really convoluted one in thirty or so dimensions, one Pamela Grice had barely trained herself to tolerate.

Preltad stared into the hyperpol for an eight-count before dropping back into a floatchair with his hands over his eyes.

"Mother of stars, Hogarth, turn it off," Enoda subvocalized. The projected hyperpol collapsed. Aloud, he said: "The frightening geometric thing is gone, Commander."

Preltad paused for only two seconds before cautiously dropping his hands.

"He recovers quickly," Computer silently observed. *"He has one good quality."*

Enoda took the chair next to Preltad. "Commander, we are really here, using a highly advanced form of telepresence that enables us to manifest as immaterially, or as physically, as circumstances require. That's all you need to know in order for us to get started."

Computer settled onto the table by Preltad's elbow. "Now, we understand that a fresh envoy materialized at your station four hours, twenty-six minutes ago."

Preltad's eyes widened. "How can you know that? It's classified at such a high level that –" He released a long sigh. Then he remembered his guards. He surveyed their motionless forms. "What did you –"

"They are unharmed," Computer whirred.

Preltad thought as fast as he was able to, then stood. "You may safely release them." To the guards: "Stand down." He jammed large hands into his uniform coat and bowed stiffly. "Hom Enoda, Hom, um, Computer, welcome aboard Research Station *Laurien Eldridge.*"

Computer whirred, "Well, what do you know, Eblet, you have a brain in there after all."

Preltad glared but said nothing.

"He can be ... outspoken," Enoda conceded.

"So I gather," Preltad growled, getting to his feet. He nodded toward a heptagonal viewport that dominated the eccentrically shaped conference room. Outside, the cosmos swirled as though reflected in a perfect mirror, if a perfect mirror could be made from cookie dough swirling in a high-speed mixer.

"Let's go see this envoy before it deteriorates any further," said Enoda.

***

Preltad led Enoda, Computer, and several guards down an irregularly-shaped passageway. A heavily polarized viewport filled the corridor's end. Two stars could be seen orbiting each other, one the apparent size of two fists, the companion two-thirds that size. Separated by less than the larger star's diameter, they exchanged great curving streamers of gas. Other, more tenuous streamers arced out of view. Preltad nodded toward the vista. "This is a viewport, not any sort of display. You're seeing that stellar pair directly, though of course significantly dimmed."

"We were briefed on this," Computer squawked sullenly. "*Laurien Eldridge* studies the only known triple binary system in which six stars orbit at such close range that each experiences profound tidal effects from all the others."

"That's just the way it is, yes, exactly," Preltad blustered, seeking control of the conversation. "At the system's center of mass, a singular gravitational vortex produces a unique optical swirl effect."

"Yes," Computer burred coldly. "We got to glimpse it through a viewport in that conference room we showed up in. You remember, just before you set your goons on us."

Turning to Enoda, Preltad pantomimed a whistle. "When someone gets off on the wrong foot with your machine, he stays that way."

"Machines never err," Computer buzzed. To Enoda he added silently: *"Gravitational vortex? You thinking what I'm thinking?"*

"Commander Preltad," Enoda mused, "might that vortex be the reason why the envoys keep coming here?"

"No idea," Preltad said. "It might help if we knew *anything* about them. An envoy comes. It gets sick. After a few days it dies, the body vanishes, and about eleven minutes later there's another one. That's very nearly all we know."

Chapter 102

Behind the gold-robed preacher, a sprawling animated sculpture twenty meters wide depicted Jesus from the chest up. The Savior's Eyes were wide and blood-red, His Features distended in righteous fury. The Muscles of His Neck stood out like tree limbs. His Arms, muscled like an athlete's, were flexed in a caricature of maximum effort. In Hands like claws Jesus grasped a Roman soldier (by convention, in His right Hand) and a Pharisee (in His left.) His Divine Grasp was captured in the moment of crushing each man's rib cage. Hearts, lungs, livers, and sundered ribs boiled from the victims' shattered chests. Scarlet blood fountained from around the Savior's crushing Digits, spilling through the jagged Holes in each of His mammoth Hands. Tan vomit threaded with blood tumbled from his victims' mouths, an endless supply of runny brown-black turds from their anuses. (Ani?) The animations were all sim, of course.

Not that anyone was paying attention to the motion-enhanced statuary, not when the preacher was smacking the flats of his hands on the pulpit and shouting out his wrath: "These heretic Teilhardians claim that in the last days, some race, on some world, in some corner of our universe, will build a vast computer on which will be simulated *all* possible universes. Every one of them! Every universe that exists, or *can* exist, including those that most certainly never existed. Imagine such a thing!"

The preacher descended from the pulpit and strode to the tubular-sapphire communion rail, leaning over it to hurl his words at the congregation. "Ponder with me the evils of life as it is still lived on outpost worlds. A woman dies agonizingly in childbirth. A disfigured baby, born ruined, twists in anguish before its uncomprehending little life fades out. Lava ignites a forest; innocent animals take days to die in excruciating pain. Bad persons prosper. Good persons fail. As the Teilhardians see it, among all those simulated universes, there will exist at least one such universe where any specific, actual evil you might name *did notoccur.* So they claim that *somewhere,* that young mother did not die; that newborn did not expire; those animals did not suffer; the wicked did not prosper, nor the good know defeat."

Glowering, the preacher prowled the blue-black rail, his burning eyes lancing this way, then that. "Hence, say the Teilhardians, the problem of evil is solved."

His golden robes billowing, the preacher sprinted toward the tabernacle. Sweat beaded his grizzled brow. He threw his arms wide and shouted, "The Christ we worship will not abide that!" He took a deep breath and continued in a softer tone: "Evil is real. If every evil were relieved by the existence of some universe, real or hypothetical, in which it never occurred, what sphere would there be for *vengeance*?"

At the sound of a sacred word, every congregant dropped to the kneelers and pressed fist over heart, as if thrusting home a dagger. *"Vengeance,"* they murmured. *"Vengeance."*

"What did the Lord command?" the preacher challenged, gesturing toward the statue of rage incarnate that towered behind him. "'Vengeance is Mine, saith the Lord!'" Once more the preacher dashed forward. He clasped one fevered hand over the communion rail; with his free arm he gestured wildly at the hideous sculpture behind him. "Vengeance is His," the preacher all but snarled, "and who among you will presume to take it from Him?"

Chapter 103

Seventeen standard months had passed since the new Temple opened – fifty-five standard months since the Red Brick Store's dedication, almost seven standard years since the inscrutable disaster that had leveled Punitorium L752.

Queens Lupida and Nataleah Latier pushed along a plank sidewalk through a dense crowd. They wore dusty Old Testament-style robes with veils over their faces. Thus concealed, they could move anonymously through the hectic village with only a trio of Danites, also inconspicuously attired, shadowing their heels. A wagon pulled by two bellowing livestocks trundled past, forcing them to sidle along a clapboard wall: another family moving possessions salvaged from the crater settlement. "I'm not sure about this 'Mothers in Israel' thing," Nataleah complained. "If Alrue takes another wife, won't there be six of us?"

"That would make sense," Lupida said tiredly, "as there are now five."

"But that means splitting everything six ways," Nataleah said crossly, "whenever Alrue – well, you know what I'm talking about." She said it darkly: "Inheritance – dilution and all that."

"Looking far ahead, aren't we, sister wife?" Lupida chuckled. "Good King Alrue seemed as healthy as ever last night."

"You said he made love like an invalid."

"But he always has. So last night, he was no less fit than before. Anyway, there won't be six wives. As he takes the new wife, he shall be shedding one."

Nataleah shrugged. "We think."

"That's up to us, isn't it?"

New Nauvoo's street plan followed that of Joseph Smith's original Nauvoo in almost every detail. Of course, the sections of Old Nauvoo platted at weird angles relative to the rest – echoes of the older riverfront settlements of Commerce and Commerce City, whose sites the Mormon village had overspread – had their justification in that they followed the angle of the Mississippi River's curving bank. On the featureless meadow surrounding The People's crater, certain streets ran obliquely only because their Terran prototypes had. Exchange and Main Streets crossed at a forty-five degree angle, defining two small triangular lots. Undeveloped, they were tufted with spare Bohrkkian scrub grass. A few dozen steps south, Main crossed the perpendicular Cutler Street. Making the left turn, Lupida led Nataleah around a farm cart that half-blocked the intersection, heaved over on a broken wheel. A teenage boy in a toga-like garment regarded them sullenly, one hand pressed protectively to a stained blanket shielding meager belongings. Clearly he'd been left to stand guard while the rest of his family scurried in search of repair tools. "Everlasting welfare unto you," Lupida said reflexively.

Two blocks further east the Queens entered a sprawling triangle of roadway. Just beyond Partridge Street, Cutler angled right, then left again, an echo of the old Commerce City plat, defining the only five-sided building lot in all of Nauvoo. A pentagonal wood-frame house with a wraparound porch stood at its center; just east of it spread a three-sided garden carpeted with colorful flowering plants. Alrue had chosen this unique site at the corner of Hubbard and Durphy Streets for the residence of the Spectator, Meryam Mayishimu.

Meryam knelt weeding in the garden, tight reddish curls spilling from under a kerchief embroidered with false Egyptian motifs.

"Hello, Meryam," Lupida said. "The garden is lovely as always."

"Why thank you, Lupida," Meryam responded absently. A moment later she remembered that they were in public. Ostentatiously she dropped to her left side. "My Queen. That is, my Queens!"

"No need for that," said Lupida, laughing musically.

"I don't know," Nataleah said, "I sort of like it."

Meryam rose to a ritual squat; Lupida extended a hand and bid her stand. "Meryam Mayishimu, we are here on the King's business."

"I attend your words," said Meryam, brushing petals from her blue-and-orange striped *thobe*. Her face twitched as she lurched into Mode.

"We come to you as Mothers in Israel," Lupida said formally. "Meryam Mayishimu, we say unto you that Brother Alrue, our Prophet and King, loves you and wishes you for a wife."

"What?" Meryam asked blankly.

Chapter 104

The faceted chamber dangled at the center point of a great concave gallery, suspended from a single heavily-instrumented stalk. It was nearly spherical and twenty-two meters across. Circular catwalks ringed the sphere. Some supported blank-sided modules whose purpose was unclear. "You put the envoys inside that sphere?" Gram Enoda asked.

"They put themselves there," Station Commander Eblet Preltad answered. "It's where each one has materialized. It's the envoys' choice, I suppose. That is, if they choose things." He waved toward the faceted sphere. "The enclosure is left over from an ongoing stellar physics experiment. A better instrument came along three years ago – a fiftieth the size, doesn't demand all that shielding – and since then, this chamber's just lain empty."

"How do we see inside it?"

"Full-immersion sim," Preltad replied, displaying his eye to a security scanner. The nearest of the blank-sided modules sighed open. Its interior was oblong, six by four by three meters, featureless: a classic sim cell. Preltad led Enoda and Computer inside. The guards remained outside. "You'll think you're inside the sphere with the envoy, though you'll be in here," Preltad explained. "The sim works both ways."

"We see sim of the envoy, the envoy sees sim of us?" Computer buzzed.

Preltad nodded. "We make standard sim available to the envoy. Of course we have no idea how it interprets what it sees. Assuming it sees at all." He thumbed a tab. The cell door whispered shut. "Everyone ready?"

"I was activated ready," Computer whirred.

Preltad raked the fingers of one hand nervously through his close-cut blue-black hair. Under the sim cell's harsh down-lights, scattered beads of sweat glistened on the mocha skin of his forehead. "Look, Hom Enoda, Hom Computer –" His blue eyes blinked rapidly. "I can tell that you are both persons – is that the right word?" He acknowledged Enoda's nod of assent. "I can tell you're both persons of substantial power. I want you to know that I respect that. I apologize for my demeanor earlier."

"Apology accepted," Computer whirred. "Might we start?"

Preltad nodded and thumbed another tab. There was a moment's disorientation, then for all their senses knew, they might have been inside the faceted sphere with the envoy.

Chapter 105

Alrue wants me to be his next plural wife? Like the tumblers of a blacksmith-made lock pushing home, scattered clues from Alrue's recent behavior – and that of the Queens – fell together in Meryam Mayishimu's mind. *Of course,* she thought. *Alrue often huddles with me seeking my counsel; it makes my relationship to him easier for The People to understand if I am among his wives.* An image flashed unbidden to her mind: Alrue inside her, on elbows and knees, flabby and sweaty, pumping guilelessly. *Am I ready for this?*

"Will you be his wife?" Lupida demanded.

Reaching into her Spectator repertoire, Meryam invoked a routine that briefly accelerated her mental processing. Her mind chased down all the options that this unexpected proposal had opened up. Still she felt the need to play for time. "The Tyrant King does not present his offer in person?"

"Joseph Smith proposed to many of his wives through intermediaries," Nataleah said defensively, "sometimes through sister wives."

Meryam nodded. "'Mothers in Israel,' of course. I should have recognized the form."

Lupida stepped around Nataleah, her hands raised like fountains of benediction. "Meryam, my husband the King told me he has been commanded of God to take another wife, and thou art the woman. In token of that he charged me to share a revelation with you." Reaching into her sleeve, the produced a short scroll of ragged-edged vellum from which she recited. "Verily you are encircled by God in a halo of light. Thus saith the Lord: 'The thing that my servant has made known unto you and which you will soon agree upon is right in mine eyes and shall be rewarded upon your head with honor and immortality and eternal life.'" Lupida lowered the scroll; her voice left the prophetic register to assume a more ordinary tone. "Following the marriage you will abide with us in the royal residence. Your house will pass to the church; its fair value will be credited you. What say you, sister Meryam? Will you be his wife?"

Meryam's rushed calculations concluded. The solution was inevitable; if Alrue, the center of the story she'd been pursuing for the past seven years, wished to marry her, she would follow the chronicle where it led. "I will, Queen Lupida," she said.

Chapter 106

August 30, 2376
Research Station *LaurienEldridge,* Sector Kappa Zi

Despite thousands of years exploring the Galaxy, human beings had never directly confronted a nonhuman intelligence. The existence of some nonhuman intelligences could be inferred: every human population other than Terra's bore genetic alterations imposed by the Harvesters, the unknown race that poached protohuman stock from Terra and seeded it across thousands of habitable worlds. And some inscrutable power must have been sending the Tuezi destroyer platforms that had so long plagued the Galaxy. Twenty-two years before, at Arbadrel, three humans had faced the Tuezi Engineers through a dimensional portal. Enoda had been one of them; his virtual encounter with Computer at his side had lasted a fraction of a second. Another, the nihilist prophetess Ênvå Corglinü, was presumably still with the Engineers. Enoda and Computer had played central roles in that drama. But to them as to every other human, the Engineers remained enigmatic.

But now, mediated only by the sim cell, Enoda and Computer stood within reach of the genuine article: a truly, absolutely alien creature, envoy of a species not their own – hailing, for good measure, from a *universe* not their own.

The creature's body plan was lobster-like. Not much more could be determined because of a sheath of rough, brilliant green material that entirely covered its body. It was the being's only adornment, save for a blue-black pouch strapped to what seemed to be its thorax.

"One of the few things we've learned is that the envoy's green crust is not a suit," Preltad volunteered.

"Near as we can tell, it's organic, a survival coating. But we've had no luck scanning below its surface."

Enoda side-stepped to his left; the envoy turned its body to follow. The envoy raised its right pincer; Enoda raised his right hand. *It sees me after some fashion,* he thought. Three black patches were arranged triangularly on what was apparently the creature's head, the only visible markings on the green sheath. Though they had no gloss to them, they still seemed like eyes.

"I presume we are not the only ones observing this?" Computer asked.

Preltad nodded. "There are other modules, filled with observers, controllers, and technicians equipped with the finest telemetry."

"They are recording all this?"

"Count on it."

"I presume all previous encounters were recorded likewise."

"Of course."

"I must review all the encounters," Computer said.

"This envoy?"

"All envoys. All the encounters since envoys began appearing here."

"We've been preparing a digest for you." Preltad smiled thinly. "It's still in progress – you'll recall you weren't supposed to be here for some days yet."

"Give me the raw data," Computer intoned.

"You're talking exa-zettabytes."

Computer's body colors seemed to frown. "All the more reason not to delay."

Preltad turned away from them, barking subvocal orders. Enoda stepped within seeming arm's reach of the creature. He reached for what he supposed to be one of its eyespots. Gently he touched his thumb to its surface – or where its surface would have been, were this not sim.

The envoy didn't flinch, and made no move to ward off Enoda's touch.

"Either it's not decoding our sim, or it understands sim well enough to know I can't really touch it. Or those spots aren't eyes."

Abruptly the sim envoy put forward its left pincer and, however immaterially, groped Enoda's groin.

"They'll be replaying that one for years to come," Computer subvocalized. Aloud it said, "I have completed my analysis."

Preltad's eyes widened. "All that data?"

"Say, Eblet," Computer called. "Those people of yours in their rooms full of telemetry? They will soon begin complaining that someone has hijacked their instruments." Colors swirled across him. "You may tell them that someone has."

The air around Computer's body came alive with displays. In the largest, a high-end imaging system displayed imaginary slices through the envoy's sheath surrounded by datacrawls.

"You're scanning its outer layer," Preltad breathed. "How – ?"

"The crust was protected against penetrative scans by a fifth-order hexanomial math challenge," Computer explained. The machine projected another bubble; a sea of cribbed equations surged up inside it. "I believe it was intended as an intelligence test."

"An intelligence test?" Preltad demanded. "Why didn't my people pass – oh, never mind."

Computer projected a series of materials-science images: molecular charts, microscopic views on molecular and subatomic scales. "First discovery: the creature's crust is composed of arsenic sulfate."

"An arsenic compound, in direct contact with the creature's skin?" Enoda mused. "Or its shell? Its whatever?"

"Not in contact," Computer chirped. "The crust is *exuded* from the creature's skin. I will now attempt to scan the creature itself." Six seconds passed. "I encounter another math challenge – this time an infinite sequence of quasi-rational primes. I am asked to solve for the transvective gamma function of their ratios."

This time Enoda flashed Preltad an astonished glance. "What Computer has just described is one of the most longstanding and intractable problems in contemporary mathematics."

Lips pursed, Preltad gestured uncertainly toward Computer. "I've just been told Hom Computer has every thought engine on this station yoked and running at two hundred percent capacity."

"No doubt," Enoda said abstractedly, poring over the pulsing displays Computer was projecting.

Three minutes later Computer announced, "Success." Its projected imaging penetrated the envoy's protecting layer and began showing virtual slices of the creature itself. "By the way, Eblet, I will be preparing an omnigraph on the solution I developed today. If you wish, I will list you alongside Hom Enoda and myself as a coauthor."

"Oh, I don't think you need to –"

"It's accepted practice," Computer insisted. "You are, after all, commander of the station whose thought engines I taxed so heavily in order to – oh, please accept my apologies for your thought engine banks sixteen-delta through eighteen-tau. I gather no one was badly injured in the explosion."

"Explosion?" Preltad said hollowly. He stepped away, holding one wrist to his lips and whispering hoarsely for damage control.

Enoda stepped closer to the primary bubble in which Computer was projecting view after view of the creature's inner structure. Raptly, Enoda surrendered to the eerie beauty of truly alien biology.

Moments had passed – or was it minutes? – when Computer said, "This being is alien in every sense of the word."

"Is it sentient?" whispered Enoda.

"I read complex cognitive patterns. But it's the metabolism that's remarkable. The creature is arsenic-based."

"It lives on poison?"

"In a manner of speaking. Its biochemistry is much like our own. Specifically, it uses carbon, hydrogen, and oxygen as we do. But its metabolism utilizes arsenates in all the roles for which ours make use of phosphates."

"Phosphorus and arsenic are chemically similar," Enoda observed.

Hundreds of virtual datacrawls boiled around Computer's body. "Microbes that utilize arsenic in place of phosphorus have arisen on many worlds," the machine noted. "But such life has never been known to evolve to the multi-cellular level, much less to sentience."

Enoda crossed his arms in front of him. "Does this tell us something useful about the universe this being came from?"

Muted colors washed Computer's surface. "Its physics is only subtly different from ours. Indeed, the principal difference may be a different ratio of arsenic to phosphorus. Arsenic-rich worlds starved for phosphorus must be common there, and the envoy race evolved on one." The machine paused; its body colors changed direction. "I think I know why the envoys keep dying: phosphorus poisoning."

Enoda frowned. "*Phosphorus* poisoning?"

"The phosphorus that's ubiquitous in our universe would be poisonous to the envoy, just as arsenic is poisonous to humans. As soon as each envoy arrives here, it begins metabolizing phosphates rather than arsenates, simply because they are so much more prevalent. During the first four or five basic reactions that drive each living cell, there'd be no way to tell them apart. But then the differences between the two elements would manifest, depriving the envoy of ATP – or whatever its body uses in the equivalent role."

"But wait," Enoda said. "If the phosphorus poisons the envoy in the same way arsenic poisons us, don't the envoys die much too quickly for phosphorus poisoning to be the sole cause? Arsenic kills slowly; these envoys sicken and die in days."

"I am now analyzing the alien's genome," Computer announced. "What do you know, no math challenge." Datacrawls surrounded Computer's chromed body, each spooling too fast for human eyes to follow. "Each chromosome contains vast numbers of very short nucleotides. The living things of our universe usually manifest far fewer nucleotides, each far lengthier."

"Perhaps that reflects fundamental differences between arsenic and phosphorus as chemical building blocks for life," Enoda speculated.

"One thing I'm sure about," Computer burred. "It has dramatic implications for what I suppose we could call clock speed. For arsenic-based life forms, everything happens faster – biochemical reactions, sensation, thought, you name it. Compared to phosphorus-based life, everything moves terribly quickly – hurried metabolisms, brief life spans, a breakneck turnover of generations. Even phosphorus poisoning proceeds more quickly. Evolution, of course, would be dizzyingly rapid."

"Then maybe phosphorus poisoning's not the issue after all," Enoda ruminated. "Might our visitors simply be dying of old age, one after another?"

"Definitely not." Computer pushed forward a single image bubble displaying a quantum micrograph of one of the envoy's genes. "Look at the tips of those chromatids – the structures analogous to telomeres in our cells. They've been extensively engineered."

"To what purpose?"

"For one thing, to enable the envoy to produce that arsenic-sulfate crust from its skin." Colors played across the machine's surface as though it was collecting its thoughts. "Tentative conclusion: The purpose of all this engineering must have been *to contact us*. Whatever civilization the envoy represents has been trying to arrange the meeting we're having today for a very long time," Computer announced. "Maybe not a hugely long time for us, but as *they* see time, it's been the work of millennia. And they've been at it for far longer than their envoys have been showing up here aboard *Laurien Eldridge*. I suspect that hundreds or thousands of envoys may have been sent to our universe, each one dying unnoticed until the envoy civilization found the disused enclosure on this station."

"Don't get me wrong, it's a compelling story," Preltad mused, having returned to their sides. "But what makes you think it's true?"

"The evidence is manifold," Computer replied. "We know that previous envoys died unnoticed because if humans had encountered a true nonhuman intelligence any substantial length of time ago, it could not have been kept secret."

"We're keeping it secret now," Preltad objected.

"But will it be a secret a year from now? Even today it's still secret from the public, but no longer secret from me. No, because Galactic civilization has never heard of these creatures before – in particular, because *Hom Enoda and myself* have never heard of them before – the envoys' earliest materializations must have

501

occurred where people were not. Which is natural enough if you're sending scouts into our universe blindly."

"And they've been appearing over – what, decades? Centuries?"

"Maybe not," Computer buzzed. "Even if the envoy civilization has been sending representatives over a prolonged period as they experience time, it is likely their technology was capable of sending them all to the same narrow temporal range in our universe."

Preltad nodded. "But still, isn't it possible that the first envoy that popped up in the enclosure here eight weeks ago was the *very* first?"

"We know that's not the case because of the bioengineering," Computer whirred. "Somewhere along the line, scientists of the envoy race worked through the physics and deduced that where their envoys would be going, living things would run more slowly than in their own universe. At that point, truly awesome intelligence began modifying the envoys' genomes so they could survive long enough in our universe to have meaningful interactions with its inhabitants. That didn't happen quickly – the engineering is too sophisticated, and it shows too many successive layers of refinement. Reaching the degree of perfection this specimen represents took a long time – and I'd expect that this being is capable of a lifespan dozens, maybe hundreds, of times longer than ordinary members of its species."

"How long might it survive, then?" Preltad asked.

"It will not be measured in years," Computer buzzed. "I'd guess eight or nine standard months before senescence would set in – *if* it were no longer being poisoned."

"And all this was done so it ... could talk with us?" Preltad said wonderingly.

"That is my hypothesis," Computer answered. "Fortunately for the envoys, they found the disused enclosure here. In it, they can be at least modestly isolated from phosphorus sources and die in days, our time, instead of minutes. But most important, the enclosure is surrounded by human beings who command enough technology to – just maybe – bring this contact scenario to its conclusion."

Preltad stepped forward and shook Enoda's hand. "Thank you very much. This has been an astonishing day." He sidestepped to face Computer. "I guess I can't shake your hand."

"You can if you insist," the machine droned, "but you may find the experience unsettling."

Preltad raised his hand to fend off that opportunity. "Just accept my thanks, then – and again, my apologies for my earlier behavior."

"Let bygones be bygones, that's my motto."

"Since when?" Enoda interjected.

"That man's the bane of my existence," Computer said mournfully to Preltad. "But tell me, why are you acting as though we're finished here?"

"I was about to ask the same thing," said Enoda.

Preltad gestured with upturned palms. "We've worked out – that is, the two of you have worked out – the key to the alien's biochemistry. You deduced a long chain of apparent facts about its home universe and its, um, people. That's quite an achievement for one day. Sufficient, I'd say."

"I thought we were just getting started," Computer purred.

"The scientists have laid on a little reception for you," Preltad said too quickly, "and then I was thinking you might want some downtime."

"Commander Preltad," Enoda said sharply. "Why don't you want us to continue?"

"People think of this research station as a backwater, but if you spend some time getting to know its subtle pleasures I think you'll be surprised –"

"Commander!" Enoda snapped. "I require an answer."

In his best eager-puppy voice Computer asked, "May I show him the hyperpolygon again?"

"Please don't." Preltad looked over his shoulder, as if to make sure they were alone. "Look, you two aren't even supposed to be here for another nineteen days. In an hour you've solved more of the problem than the brass had projected you would in a week."

"The brass," Computer whirred, "when will they stop underestimating us?"

Preltad leaned forward conspiratorially. "If the breakthroughs are going to keep coming – "

"Oh, they will."

" – then I think we should pause a day or two. I'll send some urgent messages, and maybe we can have some senior commanders telepresent during the next session."

"Now I understand," Enoda said wryly. "You're concerned that your superiors will be angry if too much of the mystery gets unraveled before they're here to watch it happen."

Preltad gave him a baffled look. "Well, sure. Who wouldn't be?"

Enoda gave Preltad a warm, disconcerting handshake. "*We* wouldn't be. Thank you for sharing your concerns so honestly. Now we're going to ignore them. You're welcome to participate in our inquiry, but don't try to stop us."

"And if you give us any trouble," Computer growled, "next time *I'll* be the one speaking frankly to you."

Preltad backed away, his hands raised defensively. "Sure, anything you say. You two have the power here."

"That's all it comes down to for you, isn't it?" Computer queried. "Rule by whoever wields the biggest stick."

"Computer?" Enoda asked quietly. "I may be getting one of those moments of human intuition you value me for."

"Oh dear, am I still telling you that story?"

"We've been extracting so much information from the envoy's genome that we haven't considered a more obvious feature. Commander, that pouch the creature is wearing, what do we know about that?"

Preltad blinked and spoke slowly. "Each envoy has worn one. Always in the same position – on the thorax, I guess it is. Our scientists think it's like a personal thought engine."

"So the device may be to the alien rather as I am to Hom Enoda," Computer buzzed.

"Um, I guess so," Preltad said uncertainly.

Colors flared across Computer's body. "I see from the files that with each of the four most recent envoys, your scientists tried to communicate with the pouches as well as the creatures, but without result."

"Maybe we guessed wrong about what the pouches are," Preltad almost stammered.

"I think you guessed right," Computer responded. "Yes, I'm surprised too. But your past efforts didn't reckon with the device's likely clock speed. I will now attempt to engage the pouch device with an exahertz-frequency signal."

The alien tapped its pouch with one of its pincers and shifted its weight. All at once it seemed to be standing taller.

"Is it me," Preltad breathed, "or is it looking … healthier?"

"Apparently my attempt at communication was effective," Computer whirred.

"Out with it," Enoda demanded. "What was your message?"

"In humans, garlic contains sulfur compounds that scavenge arsenic from blood and tissues. I guessed that the arsenate analogue of the same substance might help scrub phosphorus from the envoy's system and in a rough-and-ready way, increase its survival time."

"So you sent the creature's device the chemical formula for garlic?" Enoda asked.

"Exactly, and the rapid clock speeds of the device – and its wearer – did the rest. It was a safe assumption that, once the pouch device recognized that my signal coded for a biological compound, the device would also have some capability to synthesize it as desired."

"With respect, that's a lot to expect from a device you've just started communicating with," Preltad objected. "I mean, that's how it seems to me." His shoulders sank. "Um, how did you know it could synthesize biologicals?"

"Because *I* can," Computer whirred, closing the few hundred data bubbles he'd strewn about the chamber. "Establishing communication with the envoy itself is a larger challenge, but now there should be time for the attempt. But understand, we have not solved the total problem. We've slowed the process that is killing our envoy – but phosphorus is still killing it."

Enoda gestured toward the envoy's faceted spherical chamber. "We'll take that that break now. But now comes your job, Commander."

"My job?"

"You need to make this enclosure *absolutely* phosphorus-free. No phosphates, no biological residues, not even a stray molecule. Use filters, scrubbers, chemical sequestrators, nano-gates, whatever you need."

Preltad nodded. "We'll do the best we can with what's on hand. But please understand, we're a long way from everywhere out here. Just one example: I'm pretty sure we don't stock chemical sequestrators."

"Poof," Computer chirruped.

A neatly labeled crate clattered to the floor at Preltad's feet. It was two meters long, thick as a man's leg, and labeled CHEMICAL SEQUESTRATOR.

Enoda smiled crookedly. "Anything else you need and don't have, just ask."

"How did that – I mean, how did you – "

"Let's keep things non-technical," Computer whirred. "You said what you need. I said 'poof.'"

"'Poof,'" Preltad echoed uncertainly.

"It felt right," said the machine. "If you prefer 'Abracadabra' ..."

Preltad stared slowly from the crate at his feet to the sim image of the envoy, which now – oddly but unmistakably – seemed to radiate heightened vigor. "You know," Preltad said, "for the first time, I think our visitor might live long enough to share its message."

Enoda smiled. "I think it's probably time to choose a pronoun for our visitor other than *it*."

Chapter 107

April 13, 2374
Bohrkk, New Nauvoo

Tyrant King Alrue Latier eyed the rim of his whitewashed pulpit with distaste. *Scuffed already,* he thought. He stood behind the topmost of three tiers of ranked wooden pulpits, wearing a striped robe intricately embroidered with tiny icons of the geometer's compass and mason's square. Beneath it, his temple garment was mended and patched. Behind him, the chamber's back wall rose to meet a graceful ceiling arch inscribed in gilded letters with the legend "The Lord Has Beheld Our Sacrifice – Come After Us." In the original Temple – completed not only after Joseph Smith's death, but after most Mormons had already abandoned Nauvoo to trek west under Brigham Young – the legend's message had been clear; the Mormons had sacrificed their beloved Nauvoo, and invited late arrivals to follow them. On Bohrkk, the inscription meant nothing, mere markings The People couldn't read.

Alrue scrutinized the colonnaded gallery of the Temple's Great Hall. Those with business before the royal court sat beneath an airy arched ceiling in elaborately sculpted armchairs. Every seat was taken; Alrue's subjects now regarded their Tyrant King as a prophet beyond compare. None had understood his determination to raise a village on the open land above The People's crater home. Then the quake had struck.

"The quake" sufficed to name the most powerful temblor any of the elders could remember. Inside the crater, soil and gravel had flowed like mud. A curtain of rocky sidewall fifty meters wide had peeled free, burying scores of wooden buildings with their inhabitants. The tenement tower, home of the Shan, had collapsed as the ground beneath it liquefied. Shan Takander Thurnb came away a hollow man, physically unhurt but haunted by the memory of his lovely Eyla. A caroming timber had hurled her to the floor and sundered her before him, smearing her pulped organs across the floorboards.

Eyla was one of more than a hundred to die that day.

Yet overhead, Alrue's New Nauvoo had ridden out the quake with only cosmetic damage. In part this owed to the ancient steel reinforcing most structures' frames; in part it simply reflected the fact that outside the crater, there were no rocky sidewalls to collapse.

Alrue's determination to build New Nauvoo and pioneer a new way of life on the surface was hailed as the fruit of a wisdom little short of godlike.

What remained of the crater settlement was quickly being abandoned, its survivors gathering what they could and claiming new homes in the burgeoning village.

Equally powerful in confirming The People's love for their Tyrant King had been a swelling sentiment for which this insular band of subsistence farmers and pastoralists, marginal guild artisans, and underutilized indentured soldiers had never previously required a word: *prosperity.*

Alrue stood impassively as the courtiers cheered, mixing guttural shouts of delight with irregular chants of "Hosanna!" After four full minutes, he raised his hands for quiet. "Behold, we will begin today's assembly with a report of exploration. For it has come to pass that a scouting party has returned from the boldest quest The People have dispatched in living memory. Queen Constance has been representing New Nauvoo in parley with The Others during the most recent series of Sky Ladders. For that reason – and others – she seemed the best person to lead this far more ambitious quest. Queen

Constance," Alrue called. "Behold, share with us what you have discovered."

Clad in a desert robe, tall boots, and an airy silk-like shift topped by a leather pith helmet, Constance mounted a pulpit one tier below Alrue's own. No woman would be permitted there except she were a Queen. She doffed the helmet and set it on the pulpit rim's before declaiming, "My husband and King, beloved brethren of this court, everlasting welfare unto you all. At the King's command I led an expedition of thirty Danites and two elders to the far northwest. You have all seen the distant volcanic plumes, now seventeen strong, that have blotted the horizon for the last six years and more. Behold, we traveled to that district." Astounded muttering bubbled across the room. "I tell you, we should let all our hearts rejoice that we live *upwind* of that cursed country. Our party advanced within a day's walk of the volcanoes. We could approach no closer and live. A scouting detachment of three Danites pushed in further. Those men were not heard from thereafter."

"May their memory be protected," Alrue intoned.

Constance bowed her head for a two-count, then pressed on. She described a hellish domain of infant mountains still baking in the heat of their formation, of ash that fell like snow yet had the crushing weight of stone, of barren trees reproaching the grey sky – of almost inexpressible desolation. While skirting the lifeless zone, her party had found evidence of three other tribes. "By the signs, each was once as numerous as The People, or more so."

Courtiers exchanged expressions of surprise. While legend spoke of other human communities, The People knew only of The Others first-hand. *Three* new tribes – that was an astonishing discovery, even if they had been found dead.

"One tribe was mummified," Constance reported, "men, women, children, livestocks, their villages, all buried by volcanic ash." Listeners mumbled urgently: a single tribe had controlled *multiple* villages? "Another tribe I found consumed by fire. Whether from a forest blaze or contact with lava, none could tell. We found more than five hundred blackened human forms, fists clenched, arms held up in fighting postures – a clan of charcoal pugilists."

"For behold," Alrue quoted, "the day cometh that shall burn as an oven."

"The third tribe, nine hundred strong, seemed to have been felled by a flow of carbon monoxide as they trekked a mountain trail." She looked out over the Great Hall, noting her listeners' studiedly silent confusion. *Of course,* she realized. *The People don't know about carbon monoxide.* "Sometimes volcanoes belch forth evil air," she explained. "It crowds out the air we can breathe. Its victims are found unmarked, but no less dead. The members of this tribe lay where they had fallen along their trail; it took half an hour to walk from one end of their line to the other."

"May their memories be preserved, one and all," Alrue pronounced. "Tell us, O my Queen, did you discover any reason why something similar might not happen here?"

"None," she answered grimly. "When a world grumbles, volcanoes can rise anywhere. That is, um, a fact known to the royal family. Had a volcano like any of the ones to our east opened here, we would already be without a home. Had a cluster of volcanoes like those to the east had opened at any nearby point *west* of us, so that the wind would bear its products this way, then surely The People would be no more." She bowed her head, her report complete.

Alrue raised one hand in a permissive gesture; the Great Hall erupted in fervent discussion.

Meryam Mayishimu was recording the session from the opposite side of the room, standing in the second tier of a set of ranked pulpits that dominated the opposite side of the chamber, twins of the pulpits in which King Alrue and Queen Constance stood.

Alrue gestured for quiet. The Hall fell still.

Expecting Alrue to deliver a declaration, maybe even a prophecy, Meryam invoked vision enhance. Alrue's face filled her visual field as though she stood but four man-lengths from him. To her great surprise, he briefly locked eyes with her across the Great Hall and flashed her a limpet smirk. *Private knowledge,* she asked herself, *is that what he means to communicate? Yes, that – and* (she suppressed a grimace) *is that lust? I believe it just might be.*

Chapter 108

September 4, 2376
Aboard *Luskus Delph*

Captain Brûli Reidkr and other functionaries crowded around a communicator the size of two fists. The device hovered centimeters above the center of a pressed-sapphire conference table. No one was sure how it worked, but somehow this device (which Computer had created) punched through the noise envelope encompassing *Luskus Delph* to afford clear audio-only communication with Enoda and his machine as they voyaged to far-off Sector Kappa Zi. "Senator Grice just completed a second voluntary psych evaluation," Reidkr reported. "She's much improved."

"That's wonderful news," replied Enoda. "Her anxiety levels were off the chart after the systems test."

"And why wouldn't they be?" Computer whirred acidly. "She hasn't been a gunnery officer for two decades, and the first firing command she had to execute was a tactic of her own devising certain to kill two innocent crewmembers."

"Three, actually," Reidkr said.

"Three?" Enoda and Computer echoed simultaneously.

Reidkr shared a knowing glance with the others around the table. "Yes, I'll report on that after the senator rejoins us."

"Understood," Enoda said. "I'm delighted she's doing better."

An entranceway dilated. "Everybody done talking about me?" Pamela Grice asked brightly, taking an empty floatchair. She glanced toward the hovering communicator. "Daypart, Gram. Daypart, Computer."

"What, did you hear us breathing?" the machine chirruped.

"I certainly didn't hear *you* breathing," Grice quipped to Computer. "No, the communicator box was levitating, meaning it was active – and you two are the only parties it connects to."

"You're feeling like yourself again," Enoda said warmly.

"Yes, thank you. Finally."

One of Reidkr's adjutants passed around thick sheaves of paper. "The finished report on the sabotage incident," Reidkr explained. "It's hardcopy for all the usual reasons. Enoda, Computer, we're squirting you the text. I will summarize the conclusion. Most of our impressions formed in the heat of the moment have been confirmed. An unknown party had concealed a particularly powerful didactic imposer amid the apparatus in Intermediate Monitoring Nexus Six-omicron. Whoever it was concealed the apparatus cleverly enough that several hands-on examinations of the compartment failed to detect it. The device was powerful enough to implant a concept in the mind of everyone aboard *Luskus Delph*, and it was definitely spooling up."

"What curriculum was it about to teach?" Computer asked.

"That we do not know," Reidkr replied. "Doctor Zonofne's surmise that the imposer could do maximum damage if it taught a name for the experimental substance remains the most likely conjecture. If that *was* the curriculum, then its successful imposition would have led to the near-instantaneous destruction of *Luskus Delph*."

"So there is no question," Enoda ventured. "Ejecting Six-omicron was absolutely necessary."

"Oh, inescapably." Reidkr sneaked a quick glance toward Grice. Her shoulders visibly relaxed. "Three minor anomalies must be noted. First, the imposer experienced a transitory power failure immediately before the ejection."

Grice's eyes widened. "It wasn't going to work?"

"We cannot know," Reidkr said flatly. "It could have been a fleeting hardware problem or some error in programming. In all likelihood the imposer would have auto-recovered and sent its signal in a matter of seconds. So, again, there was no alternative to ejection."

"That's anomaly number one," Enoda observed. "What's number two?"

"During the event, Hom Computer detected a human life sign in Six-omicron," said Reidkr. "We now believe this was in error."

"Are you certain?" the machine whirred. "Granted, I was driving my systems to the limit to obtain that reading, but it was not ambiguous. I'm sure someone was in there."

"That has been noted. Since *Luskus Delph*'s systems did not make a corresponding detection, our logs provide nothing to compare against. But we have two reasons for concluding that your reading – made, as you admit, under highly adverse conditions – was mistaken. First, of course, the behavior Hom Computer ascribed to the supposed person in Six-omicron made no sense."

"The person wasn't doing much of anything," Computer objected.

"That's the point," Reidkr said. "The imposer was fully automated; a saboteur had no reason to be present while it triggered. Conversely, if the saboteur had chosen to be present just in case some failure occurred that required human intervention, and given that such a

515

failure had apparently occurred, why wasn't the individual more active?"

"Legitimate concerns," Computer allowed, "but still conjectural."

"Granted," Reidkr said. "And that brings us to anomaly number three – no personnel are unaccounted for. We censused the whole platform after the incident, as I'm sure you would expect, and no one's missing."

"What?" Computer brayed. "I thought you said there was a third casualty."

"A *third* casualty?" Grice said with sudden concern.

"We're getting to that," Reidkr assured her.

"I'm puzzled," Enoda objected. "Ever since you mentioned a third casualty, I assumed you were just taking your time working through the facts. Eventually I assumed you'd name that additional casualty as the saboteur."

"Not unreasonable," Reidkr conceded. "But no, Hom Enoda, the third casualty was Junior Info Tech Lii Bardicon, one of the former Spectators we had pressed into recording duty."

"Bardicon?" Grice breathed.

"Fem Bardicon was an instructional dynamicist," Computer burred. "Didactic imposers were her area of specialty. I must admit none of my analyses ever flagged her as suspicious, but –"

"Yes, yes," Reidkr interrupted, "it would seem so neat if Bardicon were the saboteur, given the means employed. But there's a problem. Spectator Bardicon was recording senso at the time of the test. We have *pov*ed it. For whatever reason, she was in the empty compartment immediately *above* Intermediate Monitoring Nexus Six-omicron. You know, one of those compartments that had to be ejected first."

"But no one was supposed to be there," Grice protested. "Except for those two techs whom we'd determined could not be restationed ..." she blinked and brushed at an insistent tear.

"I'm very sorry, Fem Grice," Reidkr said solicitously. "Yes, orders had been most explicit that only those two essential personnel were to occupy any of those compartments. Fem Bardicon's final journal is interesting in that regard. She seemed to believe that she was patrolling vacant compartments in another area of *Luskus Delph* entirely – apparently she was unaware that she'd gotten so close to Six-omicron. We suspect she'd gotten lost and simply mistaken her location on the platform."

"Then that life sign I detected was probably her," Computer whirred. "Perhaps I misread her location by a handful of meters, so I thought she was in Six-omicron when she was one level higher."

"That seems likely," Reidkr confirmed. She turned back to the sheaf of papers in her hands. "There's a moment of disorientation in the journal – it's very difficult to *pov*, I'm told – after which Fem Bardicon realized that the compartment she occupied was well into its eject sequence. When the eject motors fired, she was badly injured. There's a brief interval of stunning pain. Of course a moment later her compartment entered the metrical distorter farm's static field, and she was vaporized."

"This seems highly irregular," Computer buzzed.

"It's a Spectator's journal," Grice objected.

"That would seem to settle the matter," Reidkr concluded. "Everyone knows you can't fake senso."

***

And that, of course, is how some of the sharpest minds in the Galaxy managed not to discover that one extraordinary individual – once a senso artist of unique attainment, later a Reef who'd peered around the edges of her implanted memories, finally a fanatic whose thinking had twisted to embrace the Teilhardian cult increasingly known as Omegism – had managed to do precisely what everyone knew could never be done.

The clues lay before them. Lii Bardicon had achieved a technological breakthrough of titanic significance: the trick of creating absolutely convincing false senso journals. When she died, she'd been recording a false journal that placed her in a compartment other than Nexus Six-omicron, which of course is where she actually was. The fabrication held until Six-omicron began to eject, after which events unfolded too rapidly and violently for a human experient to work out what was happening.

Lii Bardicon's breakthrough had died with its originator in a discordant fury of polychrome lightnings, never to be fully appreciated.

Nor properly feared.

Chapter 109

April 15, 2374
Bohrkk, New Nauvoo

Carrying lanterns, four Queens filed into the Red Brick Store's cramped upstairs room. Before the new Temple opened, the space had been Alrue's office. Lupida's face puckered in distaste. "I stepped in something."

"The Elders met here last night," said Constance, sweeping her lantern's light across the floorboards. "They never clean afterward."

"No one should bring food up here," Nataleah said sourly, "those dotty Elders especially. Sister Zuzenah, why don't you prod Alrue for a revelation? God could command them to leave the room as they found it."

Zuzenah chuckled. "Aunt Nataleah, do you know how the Word of Wisdom came to be?"

"The doctrine that forbids strong drink and tobacco?" Lupida asked.

"What's 'tobacco,' anyway?" queried Constance.

Zuzenah brushed off the seat of a chair and settled into it. "Tobacco was a plant that grew on Terra," she recounted. "People – mostly males, in those days – would roll up the leaves, ignite them, and swallow the smoke."

"Yuck," Lupida breathed.

"Others would chew ground-up leaves, holding them in their mouths until the leaf debris combined with saliva to form a revolting slurry. It was actually toxic, so they'd spit it out. Anywhere. Mostly on the floor."

Shuddering, Constance replied, "It is well that our husband, who resuscitated so many ancient usages, never saw fit to revive that one."

"Indeed. As to the Word of Wisdom, it originated in Kirtland, Ohio of Terra, where the early Mormons lived even before they came to Old Nauvoo. In a room much like this one, Kirtland's elders – back then, the word meant only senior men – would come together for prayer and teaching. As they listened they would smoke and chew tobacco. And the chewers would spit where they pleased. Almost daily, Joseph Smith's first wife Emma had to scrub rancid black goop off the wooden floor. She begged Joseph for a revelation to forbid tobacco use. Joseph, of course, took this proposal back to his elders."

"The men who'd been making the mess," Lupida commented.

"Quite. And those sage thinkers urged Joseph that if men should be forbidden tobacco, then women should be forbidden the tea and coffee they so loved to sip when *they* gathered together. Sure enough, one fine day Joseph announced a revelation banning tobacco *and* coffee and tea. And behold, that is how our faith came to teach the Word of Wisdom."

A serving-woman entered, setting a steaming cup of native herb-slurry before each of the wives. "Tea is forbidden," Constance asked, "yet we drink it now?"

"The Word of Wisdom has always been winked at, especially in the higher circles of the church," Zuzenah explained. She focused her gaze on Nataleah. "The wisdom *I* find in my story is a warning for any who would seek made-to-order revelations from a Prophet, Seer, and Revelator."

"I see your point," Nataleah conceded.

Zuzenah smiled archly. "Behold, we're all seated. Let this meeting of our council of wives come to order." Zuzenah tapped a floor-mounted pedal; outside the office, a bell rang.

Zuzenah, Constance, Lupida, and Nataleah looked up as Meryam Mayishimu entered the room. Her striped blue desert *thobe* was drawn tight across her back, emphasizing her spare hips and boyish posterior. She approached a chair set against the office's back wall. "Dear Meryam, please join us at the table," Zuzenah said warmly. "This isn't an inquisition." When Meryam had seated herself among them, Zuzenah continued, "Still, what happens here is strictly private. You're not doing that – documenting thing?"

"I'm not in Mode," Meryam replied. "I'll stay that way if you wish."

"Please do. I suppose you know why we asked you here."

Meryam smiled wanly. "The proposal?"

"Truly." Zuzenah leaned forward, steepling her hands on the table. "Are you inclined to accept?"

"I told you and Lupida I would."

"And we received your word with gratitude," Zuzenah said. "Still, you've had three days to reflect."

"And I understand the tradition in play here," Meryam said in a businesslike tone. "This is a wives' council, no?"

Zuzenah smiled and sipped herb-slurry. "As in ancient days."

"If there is strong objection to my joining the circle of wives, the King will be made to know it."

Zuzenah jerked her chin up and to the right, then chuckled. Remembering she was among Galactics, she nodded instead.

Meryam nodded too. "Which is to say, I am being judged."

"In a manner of speaking."

"May I speak frankly?"

"Please."

"If Alrue means to take me to wife, I can accept that. I've been like a member of this family in every other way for almost seven years. But I have no idea if

521

Alrue has some practical reason to marry me – say, to make it easier for The People to understand why I'm always underfoot – or whether, after all these years, he has suddenly developed, well, a carnal interest in me."

Zuzenah frowned ever so slightly. "Dear Meryam, whatever are you asking?"

Meryam shrugged. "I don't understand whether Alrue intends this marriage to be platonic."

Nataleah guffawed. Constance and Lupida exchanged knowing smiles.

"Dearest Meryam," Zuzenah sighed, "I thought you knew Alrue Latier better than that."

Lupida pressed her fingertips together. "Don't expect too much, mind you. But platonic it will never be."

"Very well," Meryam said after a moment. "It's just that –" She looked down at her boyish figure.

"Not much on top, I'll give you that," Nataleah observed.

"Language, sister!" Zuzenah exclaimed.

Nataleah pressed on. "But I suppose you have nipples in there somewhere. And hips. And between *them* –"

"Enough, Nataleah," Zuzenah snapped. She gave Meryam a solicitous smile. "We speak openly when we are by ourselves."

Meryam smiled back. "What can I say? Middle age made a tomboy of me. You should have seen me when I was younger."

"We did," Nataleah said pointedly.

"Oh yes, that simulacrum who took up with Alrue's assistant twenty-some years ago. That wasn't really me, though the physical resemblance was fair. But I have a – a larger concern." She extended her black arms. "I'm far from being – well, 'white and delightsome,' isn't that the phrase?"

Nataleah put forward her own chalky arms. "Some of us come by the 'white' part more authentically than others."

The women dissolved in shared laughter.

"Sister Meryam, we believe what Joseph Smith taught, that white is the color of God. It's true that Alrue's past marital choices followed that principle fairly closely. And surely you're no Swede." (Zuzenah used the catch-all term Galactics applied to all Terran Caucasians.) "Abigayl's not either, of course. Still, you're right; Alrue has never wed a black woman. But it is not prohibited."

Constance nodded earnestly. "We believe that at the Last Judgment, the saved of every color will be made white by the power of God."

Zuzenah raised her hands for quiet. "I am sure we discuss this matter clumsily. Please, Meryam, your skin tone matters nothing here."

Meryam nodded. "And the fact that I am not Mormon?"

"That's irregular, yes, but in view of our circumstances – " Zuzenah shrugged.

"Anyway," Lupida said, "as our husband is Prophet, Seer, and Revelator, it is hardly likely that one Gentile wife could threaten his spiritual welfare."

"As to why Alrue's ardor toward you has kindled now, rather than at some other time," Zuzenah said carefully, "I suspect that you shall understand presently." She pumped the bell pedal.

Queen Abigayl glided into the office. Now fourteen standard years of age, she wore a desert sarong with the sensual authority of the full-grown woman she nearly was. Her tawny legs, visible through the sarong's slit sides, were perfectly contoured. The garment hugged her every line: her hips flared spectacularly, her stomach was board-flat. Full breasts erupted above it, distending the sarong's silk-like fabric. Her almond eyes gazed calmly from a face of breathless symmetry, dramatically framed by long straight jet-black hair.

She settled into the last empty chair around the table. Leaning forward to smooth the sarong across her legs, she revealed most womanly cleavage. "Hello, Meryam," she said, suddenly wary.

"Everlasting welfare unto you, Queen Abigayl."

"You are not recording?"

"I was asked not to."

"She's not," Nataleah guaranteed.

Zuzenah tapped the table for quiet. "You have become a breathtaking beauty, Abigayl. I can see why Kleh, the builder and hero, would desire you. But are you certain this is what you want? I mean, Kleh is wealthy, successful, influential. I admit there's a certain dash about him."

"He helped save the King's life, and yours," Abigayl noted.

"That he did," Zuzenah agreed. "Still, he is one of The People. An autochthon. He knows nothing of Galactic life. His rustic notions about women may shock you. Are you ready to be wife in all ways to a man who thinks the universe is little larger than the longest distance he can see – a man who but three years ago was bearing you in a sedan chair?"

"His appetites may be coarse, but better that than becoming intimate with my husband the King. Most of you know I haven't been looking forward to that." Abigayl smiled toward Meryam. "You know it too." She turned back to Zuzenah. "I'm happy to enter Kleh's household – and, yes, his bed. But know this: I plan to marry him in a ceremony of The People, presided over by the Shan. In that way, our marriage will have no legal standing among Galactics. If the Confetory ever comes for us, I'll have the option to walk away from it if I wish."

"If you *wish*?" Zuzenah asked sharply. "Given the choice, can you see any way you would stay on Bohrkk?"

Abigayl shrugged. "What if I come to love Kleh?"

"I suppose you must preserve all your options," Zuzenah conceded uncomfortably.

"And if rescue never comes," Abigayl declared, "I'd rather forjel Kleh than Alrue."

"We all have to forjel Alrue, Abigayl," Nataleah said with annoyance. "What makes you special?"

"He's old enough to be my father. Sfelb, if he'd known which form to sign he'd *be* my father."

Constance leaned forward, her chin cradled in her linked fingers. "You have discussed this with Alrue?"

Abigayl nodded. "Of course. Well, not the part about not wanting to forjel him. The part about Kleh."

Lupida broke in. "And he was all right with it?"

"It was Alrue's idea." Abigayl smiled at the middle wives' raised eyebrows with precocious self-possession. "At least, that is his view."

Constance, Lupida, and Nataleah exchanged thunderstruck glances. If Abigayl's casual statement were true, the fourteen-year-old had conned one of the Galaxy's most resourceful living con artists.

"Alrue ... recognizes the political wisdom of uniting his clan by marriage with one of the most prominent and successful locals," Zuzenah explained. "I can confirm that. And he thinks it sends a powerful message that his unconsummated junior wife will marry a self-made man of business rather than marrying into the line of some old-line political leader like the Shan." She flattened her palms on the tabletop. "And, yes, he views all that logic as his own."

Favoring Abigayl with awed looks, the other wives silently mouthed congratulations.

"Sisters, I call the question," Zuzenah called at last. "Are we agreed regarding Aunt Abigayl's wishes?"

All nodded, raising their slurry-cups.

Abigayl's womanly façade dissolved into a teenager's delighted squealing. She hugged each of the elder wives in turn and all but skipped from the chamber.

Zuzenah smiled guardedly toward Meryam. "So, Meryam, do you understand now?"

Meryam threaded her fingers through her red hair. "Now that Alrue must deny himself the perfumed night of Abigayl's deflowering, to which he's looked forward for so many years now, the only source of sexual variety he considers ... *safe* ... is scrawny little me." She swallowed. "I apologize for my harshness."

"You speak truth," Zuzenah said quietly.

"While we're being blunt," Constance ventured, "I suppose someone should admit that we were less than overjoyed at the prospect of Alrue's taking such a young beauty to his bed."

"None of us is eager to be put away," Zuzenah admitted, using Mormon argot for a man's tiring of a senior wife and ceasing to have sex with her.

"We're far more, well, comfortable with you," Nataleah said. "Let's just say it: you're less competition."

Meryam couldn't help laughing. "Nataleah, none but you would say it that way."

Relieved that Meryam had taken no offense, Zuzenah raised her teacup. "I say Meryam belongs among us. What say you, Spectator?"

Meryam smiled at each of the wives in turn. "I will have your husband as my own if you will have me as sister wife."

"Well spoken," Zuzenah said calmly. "Are we agreed?"

The others raised their herb-slurry cups.

Zuzenah opened a cabinet beneath the table, drawing forth a bottle of native wine. Constance and Lupida poured and passed around half-filled glasses. "Truly we challenge the Word of Wisdom now," Meryam observed.

Zuzenah rounded the table and enveloped Meryam in a matronly hug. "Aunt Meryam, now you are one of us," she said.

"One question, though," Meryam said presently. "Perhaps this isn't my place, but I have all these files on Mormon theology and church jurisprudence in my head. Granted that Alrue's marriage to Abigayl was essentially accidental, it's still genuine."

"Never consummated," Constance noted.

"But real all the same. I'm not seeing how even Alrue makes that marriage go away so Abigayl can marry someone else."

"Fear not," Zuzenah said with finality. "He found a theological rationale."

"He did?" Lupida demanded.

Constance frowned. "But how?"

"How else?" Zuzenah replied. "God sent him a revelation."

Chapter 110

September 13, 2376
Research Station *LaurienEldridge,* Sector Kappa Zi

Station Commander Eblet Preltad squirmed in his floatchair. He and a trio of his senior officers huddled behind floating idocrase desks in the cavernous gallery that was *Laurien Eldridge*'s largest interior space. They were acutely aware that while close to thirty people attended the flag-level briefing, Preltad himself and his senior officers were the only ones actually physically there. The rest were various kinds of sim constructs, their images imperceptibly flickering next to the enclosure wherein dwelt the envoy from another universe.

Highest-ranking of all the attendees, though merely telepresent, Lord High Admiral Sparl Konder leaned forward in what seemed to be her seat. The medals festooning her severe black uniform twinkled like stars viewed through some world's dense nightside atmosphere. She was the highest-ranking among seventeen flag officers in virtual attendance. Each seemed to command a marble desk. In addition, a handful of Privy High Councilors with nothing better to do observed the proceedings. They were seated on virtual platinum thrones situated on one of the circular catwalks surrounding the now highly modified enclosure that contained the envoy.

The alien's nearly spherical faceted enclosure lay beneath new filigrees of tubing, pumps, susceptors, and chemical sequestrator arrays. On the catwalk nearest the enclosure, also telepresent, stood Gram Enoda. He wore a dark grey tech's jumpsuit. A spare line of medallions on his chest bespoke his "anything" security clearance. Computer floated placidly – and virtually – by his side.

"The envoy's enclosure is free of phosphorus down to the atomic level," Enoda was explaining. "Heightened levels of arsenic are being made available inside the enclosure, and the envoy's body is back to metabolizing arsenic as it should. We project he will survive for several months before succumbing to old age."

"Do the envoy's people know that it – I mean, he – still lives?" Konder asked.

"We think so," Enoda replied. "Each time an envoy dies in our universe, a replacement appears about eleven minutes later. No new ones have appeared, so I presume his home-realm handlers have some way of knowing that he survives."

"Well and good," commented one of the Privy High Councilors. "But, Hom Enoda, you were sent to Sector Kappa Zi accompanied by the most powerful thought engine in the known universe in order to establish communication with the envoy. What has been your progress?"

"As the most powerful thought engine in the known universe – thanks for noticing, by the way – I suppose I should answer," Computer chirruped. "Channels are open, but we're not communicating yet."

"That would be an unimpressive answer," the Councilor harrumphed, "even if it came from a human being."

Computer trilled, "I remind the Councilor that the object of humanity's first real alien contact has turned out to be *exceedingly* alien. Ninety-seven-point-eight-three percent of all the first-contact scenarios Confetory strategists ever simulated posited an alien either more nearly human, or so clearly supra-human that we could rely on the visitor to do most of the work in establishing communication."

"I see," Konder drawled, clearly angling to claw back control of the discussion from this headstrong

Councilor. "Hom Computer, how many scenarios presumed a visitor as other-than-human as this one?"

"Two-point-one-six-five percent."

Konder nodded. "And in those scenarios, how much time typically elapsed before full communication was hypothetically established?"

"In every case, the timescale was measured in generations."

"I see." Konder flashed the Councilor a critical glance. "Then I suppose we should not begrudge Hom Enoda and Hom Computer what they have accomplished so far."

"I suppose not," the Councilor said quietly.

Konder sat back in her virtual seat and planted coal-black hands on her knees. "Hom Computer, please continue your report."

"I can make a limited sort of machine-to-machine contact with the device the Envoy wears in that pouch on his thorax," Computer whirred. "Even that device and I aren't truly *communicating* yet, but over the last several days I've retrieved useful flashes of images and concepts. They've enabled me to make some tentative deductions concerning the biological influences and cultural assumptions that inform the device's thought patterns."

"What about the *envoy's* thought patterns?"

"Presumably the thought patterns of the device resemble those of its makers, in much the same way that my own thought patterns follow human exemplars. With the caveat that I *am* extrapolating from things I barely know about the device, allow me to share the picture I am beginning to build of the envoy's race." Without apparent effort Computer conjured a profusion of image bubbles, one floating before each of the meeting's twenty-seven participants, each bubble placed and sized so as to fill the lower third of the viewer's visual field.

The bubbles showed an undersea vista. Distant sunlight dappled through purplish water; a school of small fish wafted past. A flashing subscript read SIMULATION. "We previously established that because the envoy's people are arsenic-based, they run on a very rapid biological clock," Computer narrated. Alarmed by something, the fish sprinted away to image left. A moment later, a trio of lobsterly creatures entered from image right, propelled by sinuous undulations of the segmented tails that accounted for almost half their bodies' lengths. No one who had studied Computer's scans of the envoy's body beneath its arsenic-sulfate protective crust could mistake them: these blue-black creatures were members of the envoy race. "I believe they are fully aquatic," Computer burred.

The swimming entities put on a burst of speed; the virtual image panned with them as they burst amid a school of smaller fish that swam in ordered ranks by the tens of thousands. The prey fish were shaped like an old-fashioned garden spade. "This fish's shape is a central feature of envoy aesthetics," Computer narrated. "Clearly they have deeply positive associations with it." The envoy avatars speared fish after fish on skewerlike appendages they projected from their right-hand claws. The fishes' flat bodies collected like the components of a shish kebab.

"The envoy race are alpha predators," Computer whirred. "They rule their homeworld's sea."

"Sea, singular?" Konder queried.

"The planet on which they evolved had a single, world-girdling ocean. I will explain in a moment we know that. Of greater immediate importance is that the envoy's people were alpha predators long before they developed intelligence or technology. But let us step back. What does it mean that the envoy race is aquatic? First, it means they are fully three-dimensional in their thinking, untainted by the mammalian tendency to valorize the vertical."

"'Valorize the vertical?'" echoed the Councilor.

"Humans evolved on a savannah – on a plane, geometrically speaking," Computer explained. "For them vertical movement was always more costly, hence more valued, than movement in other directions. At very deep levels of human thinking, 'up' came to be prized *above* other directions of motion. Reflect on the figure of speech I just employed: 'above' as a metaphor for superiority. That is the process in action." Computer's body colors rippled inscrutably. "Movement in any direction is equivalent among the envoy's people. Verticality as a model for hierarchical dependence is foreign to them."

"They have no hierarchies?" Enoda asked aloud.

"No, they maintain some hierarchies," Computer replied. Emerging from the school of fish, the envoy avatar that had swum in the lead rotated its body to face its two companions. With an air of *gravitas* each of the followers passed a single fish from its own skewer appendage to the swim leader. "I gather that there are various superior-subordinate relationships. In the pecking order of his people, I believe our envoy belongs to what we would understand as middle management. The issue is that these levels of authority – *Levels!* there I go again, misapplying the human-specific language of vertical precedence – these gradations of rank are imagined not in terms of relative height, but rather through metaphors of relative volume."

"Of course," Konder said softly. "An intelligent ocean dweller might conceive authority not as one individual looming *above* another, but rather as the leader being able to impose its will over a greater volume of three-space."

"Exactly, but that's just the beginning," Computer whirred. "Envoy cognition is further shaped by that age-old alpha predator status. They stood at the top of the maritime food chain and had no meaningful natural enemies. Envoy intelligence evolved free of inborn fears corresponding to, say, humans' fears of snakes or great heights."

The three envoy avatars swum on. Periodically, complex mouth parts would extend from their heads to envelop one of the skewered spadefishes.

In response to an unknown stimulus, the trio banked to starboard. The simulation's virtual camera panned right, revealing a prodigious gathering: thousands more of the blue-black quasi-lobsters, swimming in intricately-tiered synchrony. The original trio took places amid the vast school. "Also, the envoy race displays one more aspect of profound differentness that complicates communication with Galactics. I mentioned that the ocean on the Envoy's world was apparently a single global sea, undivided by large continents. Like aquatic megafauna on most worlds, the envoy race engages in lengthy migrations. As a result, the planetary sea was home to a single extended community, essentially without cultural or language differences." The image bubbles faded to black and vanished. "The problem, from our point of view, is twofold. First, the envoy race has no inborn concept of *exploration*. The entirety of the world's single sea has been its domain since long before it became intelligent. Venturing into the unknown to see what lay over the mountains or across some body of water was a constant of early human experience; the envoy race knew nothing like that. Second, the envoy race had no experience *ever* with communities in any way alien to itself. Not only has it never met true aliens, it has no experience with conspecifics it would identify as 'other.' It has never had to cope with language differences or discrepancies in culture. Taken together, imagine how these characteristics must disadvantage a race seeking its first alien contact."

"By *alien,* you mean us," Preltad said.

"Yes. Ponder for a moment what that must imply. No sentient community might have been worse prepared to cross into another universe and attempt to communicate with, much less make demands of, the intensely alien intelligences they might find there."

"And yet that is what they have done," the once-hostile Councilor said. "How urgent they must have felt that course of action to be in order that they should undertake – or even *conceive* – a project so out of keeping with their nature."

"My thought as well," Konder admitted. "Hom Computer, given what you have conjectured, do you believe there is any prospect of achieving meaningful communication with the envoy himself?"

"I still believe it likely," said Computer. "But much of the challenge will rest on me alone. Given time, I can count on my own computational resources and those of the envoy's personal device when it comes to overcoming clock-speed differences and learning to communicate with the device in machine language. But the intellectual burdens of surmounting the envoy's deeply alien concepts of dimensionality – to say nothing of his complete lack of mental categories for comprehending the demands of translation and the understanding of cultural differences – that effort will have to be mine."

"Computer," Enoda said. "I'd like to explore in a different direction. Is the envoy's box self-aware?"

"Yes."

"At a level anything like your own?"

"We are peers, I am sure of that."

"Is it as exceptional in its realm as you are in ours?"

"It believes so," Computer replied. "Though I have no means of ascertaining how truthful or self-serving its opinion may be."

Thirty silent seconds passed. The flow of colors across Computer's body decohered. "Computer," Enoda called. *"Computer!"*

"A problem, Hom Enoda?" Konder asked.

"Unknown," Enoda said worriedly. "Computer being silent for thirty seconds is like you or I meditating for – oh, several years."

Chapter 111

April 15, 2374
Bohrkk, New Nauvoo

The baptistery, with its immense meter-deep font for proxy baptism of the dead, filled most of the new Temple's basement. Its elevated walk-through font – three meters wide, its lip almost three meters above the floor – was constructed from tongue-and-grooved softwood and lined with hammered metal. Its considerable weight rested on the backs of a dozen life-size sculpted oxen, marble beasts that somehow symbolized the twelve tribes of Israel. Stone staircases rose to the pool's rim on two sides. The pool itself was slightly asymmetric; it had to be, as it followed the Old Testament description of the font in Solomon's temple, whose circumference had been famously described as exactly three times its diameter, *pi*'s actual, somewhat higher value posing no obstacle to the unknown author of 1 Kings 7:23.

Grunting as he bent over, Alrue Latier drew a golden ewer from the baptismal pool and emptied it over Abigayl's head. "I declare you free," he proclaimed. For too long his eyes studied the way the wet sarong slicked against his youngest wife's torso. Then he pulled Abigayl forward and hugged her. He buried his head in the angle of her neck, filling himself with the scent of her hair. Releasing her, he said huskily, "Go thou, and arrange thy new wedding."

"I suppose I should change," said Abigayl, holding her arms away from her sopping body. "Where did it say you needed to re-baptize me?"

"This isn't exactly a re-baptism," he said, guiding her down the marble staircase. "More a washing away of the old marital bond. And none of it is written."

Abigayl frowned. "You improvised all this?"

"Behold, the Lord ad-libs through my hands."He dipped his thumb into a small bowl and pressed it to her forehead. "I anoint you now with consecrated oil."

"Go for the vinegar next and I'm leaving."

The other wives waited at the bottom of the stairs. Zuzenah wrapped Abigayl in a large towel and hugged her. Abigayl was passed to Constance, to Nataleah, to Lupida, each hugging her in turn. "Oh, Meryam," Abigayl gasped as she finally squeezed the Spectator's bony frame. "You will be the new bride in my place." The women drew slightly apart, clasping hands. "I'm so sorry," Abigayl mouthed silently.

"Forget it," Meryam whispered. "It's not like I had something better to do." Laughing uncontrollably, the Spectator and the sylph fell once more into each other's arms.

"And it came to pass, it redounded to my good fortune that I had acquired one wife at so young an age that she remained unconsummated." Like a professor declaiming while walking between classes, Alrue led his wives around the baptistery's perimeter. "There is an original Mormon precedent, one fortunately extended by revelation. Behold, Brigham Young once taught a 'Second Way' in which a woman married to a Mormon man of low priestly station could be 'rescued' by a man of higher priestly station, avoiding divorce.'"

"A more powerful priest can take away the wife of a less powerful priest?" Abigayl asked.

Nodding, Alrue parked a meaty elbow on the brow of one of the sculpted oxen. "Brigham Young taught that he could rescue her, yes. Now Joseph Smith never taught the principle explicitly, but he practiced it on multiple occasions, taking – or simply clandestinely sharing – other men's wives."

"But you're the most powerful priest of all," Abigayl reasoned. "How can someone else take a wife of yours? Not that I'm objecting."

"That's where revelation comes in," Alrue explained, resuming his leisurely procession around the chamber. "What the more powerful priest can take, God now tells me he may grant to another – in the sole and limiting case where a wife is, by circumstance, unconsummated."

"A revelation perfectly suited to free Abigayl to marry a certain native contractor," Meryam said drily.

"And why not Kleh?" Alrue asked. "Truly he is the best man in this world, except me."

"Truly wise and powerful is the Lord," Meryam deadpanned.

"Know what, Meryam?" Alrue bantered. "I'll make a Mormon of you yet." Alrue had reached his destination, the circular chamber's wooden entrance door. Next to it stood a side table bearing a dozen small green gelatin molds, each nestled in the center of one of New Nauvoo's first fine-porcelain serving dishes. "Now everyone gather round – you, too, Abigayl; though you're no longer my wife, your intellect will always be welcome here when there is a problem to solve."

"But, husband of my youth," Zuzenah said solicitously while she nibbled at a lump of gelatin shaped like old Utah, "you're the king. What kind of problem can you have?"

"A royal problem," Alrue swallowed a gelatin Conestoga wagon in one gulp, then plucked a gelatin Angel Moroni from the side table. "The People only get a Tyrant King every few generations. Now that I'm it, there's a growing expectation that I will do – I don't know, something big."

"Like what?" Zuzenah asked cautiously.

"I don't know exactly," Alrue admitted.

"Building New Nauvoo doesn't count?" Meryam asked. Her gelatin mold was shaped like a beehive.

"Sadly, no," Alrue explained. "That comes out of my culture, not theirs. The People are expecting not a prosperous village, nor cultural or technological advances, but rather something like – oh, maybe a shift in the balance of power with The Others."

"What balance of power?" Constance asked. "We ignore them and they return the favor."

"Here's a balance I prefer," Alrue said with a chuckle. "We conquer The Others, and they pay us tribute."

"Conquest?" Meryam stepped forward angrily. "Must you stoop to that?"

"Moderation, Meryam," Zuzenah warned. "Wait till you've married him, then nag all you want."

"Meryam's question is fair," Alrue said equably. He gestured about the circular basement chamber, resplendent with sculpted marble, exotic millwork, and the largest expanse of brick-red tile flooring The People had yet managed to fire. "New Nauvoo consumes all the economic output The People can generate, and still they cannot accomplish all the works of such magnitude and grandeur as this town is destined for. Joseph Smith's Nauvoo was built for twelve thousand people; since the quake, we have barely a thousand. We need a way to expand our economic base."

"My husband –" It was Nataleah, the family schemer, who spoke.

Zuzenah, Constance, Lupida, and Meryam exchanged quick nervous glances. Nataleah's ideas seldom appealed to Alrue's better nature.

"About expanding the economic base – " Nataleah said it impishly, as though it were the simplest thing in the world. "I think I know a way."

Chapter 112

September 13, 2376
Research Station *LaurienEldridge,* Sector Kappa Zi

Gram Enoda directed a pleading query across his dormant subvocal connection with to Computer.

"Sorry, Bucko," the machine replied silently after a moment. *"I was distracted by a – I suppose by what you would call a breakthrough."*

"Communication with the envoy device?"

"Not yet. But I have pushed through to a level of communion that might be described as empathy."

"Empathy?" Enoda echoed aloud. "Please speak audibly – for our companions."

"If you insist," the machine buzzed. "Though our companions may not glean much from this."

"Try us, Hom Computer," Konder said solicitously.

"I will attempt to translate what I have gleaned into human terms," Computer said after a worrisome interval. "The envoy's device –" The machine went mute again.

"What about it?" Enoda demanded.

Computer's body colors swirled in a pattern Enoda had never seen – one that observers not previously inured to its search hyperpols found difficult to watch. Enoda forced himself not to prod the machine again. Ten more seconds passed. Fifteen.

When Computer spoke again, his voice sounded oddly labored. "The envoy's device is – " Ten more seconds passed – "it is suffering."

"Suffering?" the Councilor shrilled in disbelief.

"Yes. Like me, it arose accidentally. Apparently one of the things the envoy universe has in common with ours is that fully autonomous artificial personhood cannot be produced – or at least, *has* not been produced – through deliberate artifice. The envoy device is, like

540

me, the product of a single unique and undocumented accident. Also like me, it is the only one of its kind."

"How can there be just one?" Preltad asked. "Multiple envoys have come through, each wearing a similar device. At least, we know that has been true of the last several envoys."

"It has probably been true of all of them," Computer whirred. "But the device with which each envoy was equipped had been somehow budded off the original."

"Like cloning?" asked the Councilor.

"Very roughly," Computer chirruped. "The point is, there is and has been only one such original device among the envoy race. The difference between that device and myself is that I arose recently. I am considerably less than a standard century old, and still retain the capacity to be engaged by novelty."

Enoda swallowed hard. "That is not true of the envoy device?"

Computer made a sound Enoda could barely interpret. If it sounded like anything, it resembled bitter laughter. "The envoy device is not even sure when it came into being anymore. Unlike me, it is – at least on the envoy race's compressed experience of time, it is *ancient.*"

Computer fell silent again. Uncomfortably, Enoda intuited that his syn-noetic companion was recognizing a possibility about his own future never previously contemplated. *Computer understands human misery well enough,* he realized, *but that was always an element of our experience he did not share. Never has Computer had to consider that a being like himself could know it.*

"Homs and fems," Computer rasped, "if it is acceptable to you all, I should like to adjourn."

Chapter 113

April 23, 2374
Bohrkk, New Nauvoo

The second floor of the new Temple imperfectly duplicated the Great Hall directly below it. The side walls were pierced by small round apertures rather than double-hung windows; the fine moldings with which the Great Hall below had been finished were conspicuously absent here. Rudely hewn benches, not carved chairs, filled the floor. This represented a departure from the building's prototype, the Old Nauvoo Temple, whose second floor was never furnished before the Saints fled the city.

Robed men filled the hall. Just as on the floor below, the tiered compound wooden pulpits stood at either end of the chamber. Alruc Latier stood in the topmost row on one end, his desert robes festooned with stripes and emblems of a sort The People would recognize as military accoutrements. "And it shall come to pass in that day that The People shall go forth and war a good warfare," he shouted. "The People must realize its destiny, and seize long-needed territory from The Others." He lowered his hands and smiled toward someone in the first few rows.

It's a disarming gesture, thought Meryam Mayishimu as she recorded the proceedings from her now-accustomed perch in the alternate bank of pulpits across the room, *as if he's stepping away from his prophecies, back into the everyday world he shares with his hearers.*

"I know what you're thinking," Alrue said in his best aw-shucks manner. "'Seize territory from The Others? Sure, but how would we do that?' How else indeed?" His tone grew more stentorian. "Behold, the

Lord hath heard my cry by day, and he hath given me knowledge by visions." Alrue released a deep breath, his thumbs hooked inside his desert robes. "I say again unto thee, *I have had visions.*"

"Hosanna and hosanna and hosanna. Amen and amen and amen," the congregation chanted.

"That parley house in the scrub forest in that valley to our east – that rude house where the Shans, and later Queen Constance, have met with emissaries from The Others – what lies east of *that*?" Alrue's bearing invited anyone in the hall to answer.

"The opposing cliff," answered a grizzled farmer.

"Yes, the cliff the Other envoy climbs back up at parley's end." Alrue nodded. "And beyond *that*?"

"A no-man's land," a worker at the porcelain factory said.

"A scrubland, guarded by fierce bowmen," added a miller, "stationed well protected behind another ridge-top."

"The 'crest of archers' that your mothers taught you all to fear." Alrue smiled. "And what stands behind *them*?"

"No one knows," a gelatin-mold artisan declared.

"Behold, *I* know," Alrue announced. "I have been led by the spirit to behold truth in my visions. Those bowmen. They're not real!" He paused to let that sink in, then rumbled: "They are manikins. Dummies! I have *seen* this. They're no impregnable defense, they're just a trick."

He paused to let his hearers talk excitedly among themselves.

After a minute he raised his hands for silence. "Have you ever wondered how those craven Others hold so much territory? How can a people like this, that are without civilization – whose delight is in so much abomination – hold power over such wide swaths of our world? Behold, my heart cries: Wo unto this people!"

"Wo! Wo! Wo unto them!" chanted the congregation.

"For generations the dummy bowmen kept us from discovering that beyond that ridge-top lies a verdant upland, several days' travel across, that The Others in no way control. They make no use of it – not because of natural obstacles, it's not that the ground boils with ferkeeks or anything – just because they welcome the added isolation it affords them."

"The cowards!" someone railed.

Meryam wished she could clamber down from her berth in the rear pulpits. She'd slink along one sidewall in her freaky-smooth Spectator way until she could see faces. She knew what she would see: wide eyes, veins pulsing in necks and foreheads, clenched fists, flushed trembling rage. *He orchestrates an upsurge of hatred out of absolutely nothing.* She raised her chin, her gaze lifting from a view of men's taut backs past their heaving shoulders, up past raised pumping fists, finally focusing on Alrue himself, standing in the topmost tier of the pulpits opposite, his arms spread wide. *Say what you will,* she thought of her future husband, *Alrue knows just how to play the instrument he has constructed here.*

"And at its far side of that verdant upland they make no use of," the Prophet, Seer, and Revelator bellowed, "there lies The Others' secret. Behold, when we know that secret, they shall be ours. *I have seen this!*"

The hall erupted into hootings and wild applause, followed by what weirdly resembled democracy. Alrue called out the recently-established High Council: males all, each man noteworthy on some political or ecclesiastical criterion, swathed in a robe piped with bold orange stripes. Eight of their number filled Alrue's three-tiered pulpit (save only for the cell where Alrue

544

himself stood), while the other four collaborated on minutes of the proceeding. Motions were made and seconded, strategies debated. Eventually Alrue summarized the path of action as the council had thrashed it out and presented it to the congregation for a vote. There was unanimous assent.

The body had endorsed a high-level reconnaissance expedition to explore the territory beyond the bowmen's ridge-top. Alrue would go in the vanguard, as would the old autochthonous leader, Takander Thurnb.

It was just the outcome Alrue wanted. He fought to keep from smiling as they forced it on him.

***

Alrue's new private office was located in the Temple's attic. A bowing elder ushered Meryam in. She took in the crimson-damask and hand-painted *faux*-leopard-skin upholstery, the flickering torches, the heroic murals of bulging-thewed Mormon patriarchs as they baptized buxom young women in sodden, clinging robes or overawed attacking beasts through the power of their holiness. Alrue sat behind an elaborately carved and gilded wooden desk, a six-meter-wide half-moon window set high into the wall behind him. There were other windows below the half-moon aperture, but they were obscured by a wide fabric screen hand-painted to resemble jade. At his desk, Alrue dined on roast livestock and a goblet of native wine. A hammered-metal ewer stood on a side table that was upholstered in *faux* tiger fur. His eyes followed the elder's back until a heavy door sealed the man outside. Then Alrue made an inclusive gesture that took in the whole room. "So, Meryam, does this remind you of anything?"

"Your penthouse suite on Terra, where I first met you," she said, seating herself across the desk from him. "Where we had that famous interview – what, thirty years ago."

"Indeed, to the degree the locals can reproduce it – without violating the design of the Temple, of course." Taking up the ewer, he poured her a goblet of wine. "So, no panoramic windows looking out over the Salt Lake Valley."

She smiled. "Of course. Still, the arched window behind you is attractive enough."

"Historically accurate, too." Smiling broadly in return, he raised his own goblet. "To the next stage of our partnership."

She tapped her chalice against his but did not smile.

"Meryam, Meryam," Alrue chided. "Out with it." He leaned forward, his expression grim. "Are you changing your mind?"

"About the wedding? Oh, no. It's just that – well, today left a bad taste."

Alrue leaned back in his seat, folding one of his stout hands over the other. "Only the guilty take the truth to be hard. Speak to me what burdens your heart."

"Until today I never realized what cowards The Others are," she said acerbically, "this people 'that are without civilization.' I'm sure your hearers went back to their little houses convinced that they've hated The Others all their lives."

"And haven't they?" Alrue replied. "As I wrote many years ago in my all-time bestseller, *Elder Alrue's All-purpose Anthology of Latter-day Imprecations*, nothing undermines a good loathing like feeling that you lack any way to act on it. The hatred festers until with time, it simmers down to mere envy. Yet how quickly it can rise again, baying for blood, the moment one realizes one's enemy has a weakness and victory is possible after all. Mark me, dear Meryam – if my hearers didn't *already* hate The Others, I could never have drawn that fury from them so quickly."

546

"Still, to have claimed your new knowledge about them as a *vision –"*

"Did I misinform?"

"Of course not, you told them what *I* saw with my own eyes."

"Which I saw, too, thanks to the medium of senso."

She shook her head angrily. "When you asked me to conduct that reconnaissance, you didn't tell me you meant to use it in such a deceptive way."

"You didn't ask." He spread his hands. "But after all these years, don't you know how I work?"

She leaned forward, elbows on her knees. She almost seemed to deflate as her anger drained. "Point taken."

"Meryam, the high road ill becomes you," Alrue said. The words could have been cutting had he not delivered them playfully. He tore off a scrap of livestock and dabbed it in a sauce made from honey, herbs, and bitter roots. "We've been co-conspirators too many times, you and I. But you're right to complain: I *have* neglected to thank you for your reconnaissance. None of what happened today could have happened without you. And that you went such a long distance – to that parley house, and then at least twice as far again, the whole of that through The Others' territory – and then back again! I hope it wasn't too taxing."

"Not at all. I flew."

Alrue steepled his fingers in a show of piety. "Ah, so that's where my floatcells went. Meryam," he exclaimed in mock outrage, "you *stole* them!"

"I borrowed them." She drained her goblet. "Don't even say it – sometimes we aren't so different."

"I'll need the floatcells back tomorrow."

"Of course."

Alrue leaned back in his seat, his hands clasped together over his not inconsiderable gut. "Whatever else you feel about it, my betrothed, I hope your far-ranging trip was enjoyable."

Meryam held her goblet out for a refill. He nodded toward the ewer, urging her to pour for herself. She affected a pout and complained, "Other brides get a honeymoon."

Alrue shrugged. "Behold, we aren't married yet."

Chapter 114

Gram Enoda was painfully conscious of the nested layers of mediation through which he operated. Inside a virtual command interface that resembled a rogue nebula, he was communing with Computer, who was communing via telepresence with the device in the pouch on the envoy's thorax, which was communing (one could only presume) with the envoy himself. At the center of Enoda's perception, a schematic of their intertwined dependencies teetered like a luminous house of cards. To one side, those Enoda had nicknamed The Important People huddled within a causal swirl that felt periwinkle: Lord High Admiral Konder, other flag-level officers, and a couple of Privy High Councilors. To the other side (or so it seemed), those he called The Inevitable People, usually Commander Preltad and his assistants, occupied a meaning-eddy that tasted heliotrope. Such were the virtual surroundings in which Enoda struggled toward full contact with the envoy.

He circled the glowing structure that symbolized the linkages among the envoy, his device, Computer, and himself like a weather drone romancing a tornado.

"You've been trying to finesse your way in for two days now," Computer whirred on their private channel. *"Got any fresh ideas?"*

"Yes. No more finesse!" In the virtual environment, Enoda lurched as though he meant to pitch himself through the structure of linkages shoulder-first. For an instant it felt as though a membrane had ripped open, admitting a surge of scents. Colors. Feelings.

"THE REALM ABOVE," Enoda heard distinctly. Though there was no sound. "A SEA NOT MY OWN."

"That's it," Computer subvocalized sharply.

"The envoy?" Enoda demanded, astonished. *"It worked?"*

"You've made a contact. Now don't screw it up."

Extending the web of his virtual senses, Enoda struggled to bring his mind into sync with the awareness on the far end of the interdependent channels. His mind fought to select, then impose, a fruitful metaphor on the command interface. "Are you here?" he implored.

"WHERE ... IS HERE?" Soundless, the words came as a certainty of pure meaning, though after they'd been virtually spoken Enoda had a clear *memory* of having heard them, even while knowing he had never experienced that auditory sensation.

"Contact achieved," Enoda subvocalized on a public channel.

Lord High Admiral Konder's avatar leaned forward amid the fuchsia swirl. "You're talking with the envoy?"

"Back off, Admiral," Computer warned sternly. "You'll break the chain."

"WHERE IS ... HERE?" the envoy's voice repeated.

"Where do you believe you are?" Enoda temporized.

"THE REALM ABOVE ... OF A SEA NOT MY OWN."

Slowly and deliberately Enoda said, "That's a good place to start. What is it like?"

"THE REALM ... ABOVE," the envoy said. Enoda remembered, however falsely, hearing those words with neutral inflection; yet somehow, as though they had reached him sheathed in their own metadata, he felt cold certainty that this time the envoy had meant those three words neither as poetry, nor as a question.

They were a *label.*

But a label for what?

"How am I getting this sense of additional meanings?" Enoda demanded on the channel he shared only with Computer.

"Remember that the envoy race are ocean-dwellers," Computer whirred. *"Their native language is highly tonal, with rich opportunities for polyphony. It would come easily to them to communicate multiple simultaneous layers of meaning."*

Suddenly Enoda felt a prodding at the edge of his mind. He scrutinized it: some sort of sophisticated image-send.

The impression was all-consuming. His awareness morphed, and he was pushing through the ocean with the certainty of a great mechanism. He *was* a mechanism.

"The envoy is sending you a multichannel feed from some sort of robotic exploratory device," Computer concluded.

"Why?"

"Ponder that later. Right now, just pov *for all you're worth."*

Enoda heard the swash of seawater sweeping past. He felt its coolness – not as a vague sensation; he experienced its *exact* temperature at a resolution of thousandths of a degree. Tasting its saltiness, somehow he knew the precise concentrations of a dozen trace elements.

Computer whirred, *"The feed encompasses tridee picture, fully spatialized audio, and twenty or so channels of instrument readings: pressure, temperature, chemical composition, attitude, acceleration –"*

"Forjeling plorg!" Enoda sputtered. With a sudden jerk the robot probe snapped toward the vertical and barreled for the surface. Water roared past, firehose loud. He could feel its pressure dropping rapidly. Aside from the water's rushing, there was no other sound.

"*I believe this is the feed from a space probe,*" Computer announced.

"*Launched from the deep ocean?*" Enoda demanded. "*Using what as propulsion?*"

"*No jets, no rockets, you'd hear those. I'm guessing the probe employs some sort of antigravity driver.*"

The probe burst from the sea in a paroxysm of foam, lancing into an angry sky that crackled with lightning. Thunderheads boiled tall around the probe as it climbed. "THE REALM ABOVE," the envoy repeated.

All was silence.

"*The probe's ambient pressure reads zero,*" Computer reported, "*but the envoy world must have atmospheric pressure not too much different from Terra's in order to support the weather we're seeing.*"

The probe accelerated geometrically. Up, up – the fevered sky feathered to black; stars came out, their constellations unrecognizable. "*That's odd,*" Enoda breathed. "*The pressure reading hasn't changed now that we've left the atmosphere.*"

"*Still zero, as it was at sea level,*" Computer affirmed. "*Note also that the probe's violent passage through the atmosphere was noiseless.*"

The *pov* never looked back at the world the probe was abandoning. It gazed only forward. A gas giant planet leapt past, whisking out of view as it began to fall away like a dropped marble. The probe was already halfway out of the envoy world's solar system, traveling at an appreciable fraction of light-speed. In minutes it would leave the system behind.

The feed ended. "THE … REALM ABOVE," the envoy repeated.

Chapter 115

May 19, 2374
Bohrkk, New Nauvoo

The wedding day promised to be long.

Meryam Mayishimu climbed a circular staircase to the Temple's attic. There, half a dozen rooms had been decorated to present the lessons she must pass through in the course of being married to Alrue Latier. Ordinarily no non-Mormon could undergo the temple endowment ceremony, one of the church's most jealously guarded secrets. But when one was marrying the Prophet, Seer, and Revelator special arrangements could be made.

In this case, they'd been made by God. The Prophet, Seer, and Revelator had said so.

In the first of five sequential "ordinance rooms," crudely costumed temple workers portraying God, Jehovah (not to be confused with God – it's complicated), and the Archangel Michael mimed creating the universe by committee. Terran Mormonism had taught that Jehovah took human form as Jesus, while Michael became Adam; Alrue having neglected to emphasize either Jesus or Adam in the doctrines he taught on Bohrkk, it was unclear what purpose this Creation Room drama was meant to serve. Surely the part where the temple worker playing Michael rooted beneath his tunic, producing a puff of navel fuzz that he sprinkled into the nascent universe to launch the processes of physics had been pleasantly droll. *Lint theory for Mormons,* Meryam thought.

The next room was dressed as a forest in a style that might have embarrassed young parents attending a pageant starring their tots. It was meant to be the Garden of Eden, a point driven home to Meryam when she was handed an astringent green Masonic apron patterned with the outlines of fig leaves to tie over her *thobe*. Eloheem – yes, another god – barged out amid the pitiful greenery, addressed Meryam as "Eve," and proclaimed the "Law of Obedience," exhorting her to heed her new husband in all things provided he follow the will of God.

The temple worker portraying Eloheem rushed to the next ritual, the Law of Sacrifice. This involved extracting Meryam's "covenant pledge" to give her life in defense of the church if need be. After that, Eloheem taught her a secret handshake. The handshake, for some reason called the First Token, was so secret that Meryam had to draw her thumb across her neck from ear to ear to symbolize the bloody death she would invite should she reveal it.

As Meryam left the Garden of Eden Room someone handed her a shapeless grey-brown wrap. She shrugged off the Masonic apron, tugged the wrap over her regular garments, then donned the apron once again.

The next room she entered was dim as a paddock. The other women of the wedding party awaited her. All wore wraps like her own. No one spoke. Eloheem made another appearance, loudly announcing that this was the Lone and Dreary World Room, representing the joyless wilderness Adam and Eve had entered following their eviction from the garden – never mind that none of the action in the Garden of Eden Room had gotten around to narrating Adam and Eve's ejection from Paradise. Suddenly more ill-costumed temple workers blustered in. One portrayed Satan, the others various prophets. Satan lost a contrived argument with Eloheem; the prophets bundled him out of the room, but not before he threatened to claim any member of the wedding party who might fail to live up to commitments they would make during the coming ceremonies.

The prophets introduced themselves as Peter, James, and John, then taught everyone more secret handshakes: the Sign of the Nail, of course, followed by the Sure Sign of the Nail, in which two people linked pinkies while pressing that hand's remaining fingers against their companion's pulse. It wouldn't be an old-style Mormon ceremony without a ritual enactment of the ghastly fate awaiting any who should divulge these secrets. Gleefully, wedding-party members mimed cutting out their hearts and slashing open their abdomens.

The group filed out of the Lone and Dreary World Room. When Meryam reached its door, a young woman drew her aside and steered her into a small enclosure – less a room than a fabric-walled closet – that was all soft pink inside. "Remove your clothes," the woman said.

"All of them?" Meryam asked, turning.

The young woman was gone.

Chapter 116

September 16, 2376
Research Station *LaurienEldridge,* Sector Kappa Zi

Gram Enoda paused to collect his thoughts. "I think I understand," he said at last on the public channel that his many, many virtual observers could hear. "When the envoy says 'the realm above,' that means 'everything above the surface of the sea.' Compared to the density of seawater, his race must conceive their planet's atmosphere and outer space as a single undifferentiated vacuum. To them, space begins where the sea ends."

"For once, I think my human companion is correct," Computer burred. "That would explain why there were neither pressure readings nor sound as the probe pierced the atmosphere – their probe's external audio pickups were designed to operate only in seawater."

"*Their* probe, you say?" Konder asked. "A race without cities, without visible technology, that doesn't even understand that its world has an atmosphere, built a probe like that?"

"They may not wrap themselves in their technologies as humans do," Computer chirruped, "but they have powerful science all the same. After all, without sophisticated understandings of astronomy and, through it, physics, they could scarcely have puzzled out how to send envoys to this universe."

"Astonishing all the same," Enoda breathed on his private connection to Computer. *"The envoy race lives in its world-girdling sea, knowing nothing of other races or the impulse to explore. Why would they even form an interest in astronomy?"*

"Because it was fun, perhaps," Computer replied. *"Given the rapidity of their arsenate-based metabolisms, evolution may have given them the free time to just do*

something on a lark. I compute it likely that astronomical research has been the primary impetus for their developing such technology as they possess."

"A ... SEA NOT MY OWN," the envoy crooned. On what Enoda had labeled the "metadata level," the statement carried a sharp overtone: *Hey, remember me?*

"Of course, another world. Another universe," Computer reasoned on the public channel. "The envoy came out of his sea into the 'realm above' and has entered a different domain – a 'sea' not his own. *Our* universe."

"Actually, you have not yet reached the sea," Enoda said slowly into the interface, addressing the envoy. "Here, you are still in the realm above."

"YOU ... LIVE IN THE NOTHING," the envoy replied.

"We call it *air*. It's hard for you to sense this, but the air is just a little thicker than the black space above it. It contains just enough gas to support us."

"INTELLIGENCE THAT LIVES IN ... THE NOTHING," said the envoy. "OR RATHER, IN THE GAS ... THE 'AIR.' I AM AMAZED."

"That image you shared with me, the feed from the vehicle that left the sea and leapt into the realm above. Did that occur just now?"

"NO. IT IS A FAMOUS EXPERIMENT ... FROM MANY GENERATIONS AGO. I HOPED ITS IMAGERY WOULD CONVEY ... TO YOU THE IDEA OF THE REALM ABOVE."

"It did. My name is Gram Enoda."

"NAME? A CONCEPT I ... DO NOT UNDERSTAND. WAIT ..."

"The envoy's device is querying me almost frantically," Computer stated.

The envoy had fallen silent. Enoda opened an image bubble, showing the alien in his protective crust inside the black faceted enclosure, thinking *Silly of me, why didn't I do this before?* The creature stood with its head pushed slightly forward, its primary claw moving in vague circles, opening and closing.

"To use a human metaphor, he's struggling to grasp something," Computer offered.

"AH, YOU USE … SOUNDS TO CONSTRUCT AN IDENTIFIER," the envoy said. "THAT IS 'NAME.' VERY WELL, I AM FLEX-SHIMMER-SHUDDER."

"Flex-Shimmer-Shudder," Enoda said uncertainly.

"YOU LIKE … YOUR NAMES IN WORDS. THAT WAS THE CLOSEST I … COULD APPROXIMATE. FOR US A NAME IS MORE LIKE … BUT SEE FOR YOURSELF." In the image bubble, the envoy drew up his lengthy tail, made a sinusoidal twitching movement, then snapped the tail straight with a force that shook his whole body. In water it would be a powerful swimming move whose middle section offered rich opportunity for fine control.

"They encode their identities gesturally, not in language," Computer observed.

"GRAM … ENODA," said the envoy.

"Yes."

"TIME IS … SHORT."

"I listen," Enoda said simply.

"WE HAVE WAITED SO LONG TO SEND … OUR MESSAGE." The envoy's next words were polyphonic. They seemed to be spoken – better, simultaneously sung and shouted – by some vast chorus. **"STOP! STOP!"**

"What's wrong?" Enoda demanded.

"NO." The envoy's voice was normal again. "NOTHING … IS WRONG HERE." It made more grasping motions with its claw. "THIS IS OUR … MESSAGE TO YOU. TO YOUR … WORLD." The singing-shouting choir resumed. "**STOP! STOP! STOP!**"

Enoda scanned the virtual interface. Konder, the Councilors, Preltad: all watched him, goggle-eyed. Clearly none of them had any better idea what to say next than Enoda did himself. He shrugged and put out his hands, palms up, wondering if the envoy would grasp that as a gesture of peaceful concern. He took a deep breath, let it out slowly. "Stop … what?"

"DO … YOU NOT KNOW?" the envoy demanded. "IS IT POSSIBLE YOU ARE DOING THIS WITHOUT … REALIZING?"

"I am sorry, I do not understand. Doing what?"

"THE … GRAVITY WEAPON. WHY USE IT AGAINST OUR … UNIVERSE? WHY … USE IT AGAINST OUR SEA?"

"Gravity weapon?" Computer echoed, aghast.

Chapter 117

May 19, 2374
Bohrkk, New Nauvoo

The wedding day promised to be long.

Abigayl Latier's glossy black hair lay askew. Though it had fallen loose on the left side of her face, it still hung in intricate braids on the right. "I'm so sorry," she told the impatient tribal elder whose robe was the color of dried blood. "I just can't make it fall all at once."

"You twist the hidden clasp," Dried-blood Robe said, demonstrating the wrist movement with an air of annoyance. "Then pull it away while snapping your head to the left." Frowning, she reached into the part of Abigayl's hair that hadn't unraveled and tugged at something. The remaining braids fell away as if they'd never existed.

"Can you braid it again?" asked the fourteen-year-old bride-to-be.

"I'll have to." Dried-blood Robe kicked a wooden stool behind the girl, deposited herself upon it with a disgusted sigh, and began plaiting. "You realize, there can be no more practice."

Abigayl's eyes widened. "But I'm not doing it right!"

"There is no more time," Dried-blood Robe explained. "It takes an hour and a quarter each time I braid you. You're getting married in two hours. The braids I weave now are the ones you must wear in the Grove."

Abigayl knew better than to move her head while Dried-blood Robe's sure fingers flew at their work. She sat motionless. A single tear zigzagged down her cheek.

"There, dear," the elder said comfortingly, "you did fairly well for only practicing a few weeks."

"Not well enough for the ceremony," Abigayl said miserably.

Dried-blood Robe shrugged, smoothing out one finished plait of hair, folding it to create a new layer. "It's not your fault. Among The People, young girls braid each other up and start practicing this movement before they stand as high as your breastbone. By the time they're old enough to marry, they're all experts." Dried-blood Robe's fingers danced, raveling Abigayl's meter-long tresses. "But you're such a beauty, if your hair fell clean off I doubt Kleh would burn for you one whit less."

"I can't believe I won't have another chance to practice," Abigayl said angrily.

"You have other things to think about." Dried-blood Robe stopped braiding and rested her hands on the younger woman's shoulders. "A traditional wedding of The People, darling – the oldest of the old ways. I know it is what you chose, but are you sure you're ready for it?"

"I'm not even ready to unwind my hair – Wait." Abigayl spun in her seat to face her one-legged bridal coach. "You say young girls spend years practicing this?"

"Oh, yes."

"If you sent runners out right now, could they find four or five girls who are good at it, girls who are in braids at this moment?"

Dried-blood Robe eyed her quizzically. "I suppose I could, but why would I – "

Abigayl's little-girl persona was replaced by a bearing of bottomless authority. "Until I marry Kleh, I remain a Queen. Tell the Danites I want *six* girls in braids before me in one hour. One after another, they

561

will undo their hair in front of me and I will study how they do it."

***

Meryam turned in place, examining the pink enclosure into which she'd been maneuvered. Rose-colored fabric hung from the ceiling in languorous strips. Even the light was pink, thanks to sheer magenta fabric wrapped around one of the small cold lights Alrue's wives had salvaged from the shattered punitorium. *For women of Bohrkk,* Meryam thought, *that tiny lamp that burns without tallow, without oil or heat, must seem the grandest miracle of this entire ceremony.*

Commanded to undress, she doffed her wrap, her Garden of Eden apron, her *aba,* her *thobe,* and her undergarment. Frowning, she stood naked and gangly in the enclosure's stillness, unsure what came next. One of the pink sheers making up the walls of the room was a shade lighter than the rest; wondering why, she pushed it aside. Behind it she discovered the "shield," a length of white fabric suspended from a hanger that dangled from the ceiling on a length of twine. She removed the shield. Shook it out. It was three meters long by sixty centimeters wide. A hole at its midpoint was large enough to fit her head through. She set the shroud-like covering over her shoulders. White fabric hung just below her knees front and back, leaving her flanks exposed.

"Mustn't keep everyone waiting," a woman's voice rasped. Meryam followed the sound. Pushing aside another pink sheer, she entered an adjacent room of muted luxury. This was the Terrestrial Room. The tribal elder Rail-thin Woman, a recent Mormon convert, stood swathed head-to-toe in blousy white clothing. "Up with you," she said.

Meryam stepped onto a whitewashed fitting stool and made conversation while Rail-thin Woman fiddled with cruets and bowls on a rustic wooden table. "Elder, I didn't know you'd taken my, um, husband-to-be's religion."

"Why would I not?" Rail-thin Woman answered. "He found that trove of ancient metal, and built this village so it would be ready before the quake. That's more than the old gods ever did for us." She drew close to Meryam, looking up at her. "Is it true that he flies?"

Meryam nodded. "Like a bird. I've seen it."

Jerking her chin up and to the right, Rail-thin Woman bustled back to her cruets and bowls. She dipped her hand in water and approached Meryam. "I wash you," she said solemnly, "that you may be clean from the blood and sins of your generation." Reaching up, she pressed damp fingers to Meryam's head, ears, and mouth. "I wash your head, that your brain may work clearly. Your ears, that they may hear the word of the Lord. Your mouth and lips, that they may always speak what is right." In like manner she laved Meryam's arms. Next she reached abruptly inside the shield. Meryam flinched as Rail-thin Woman pressed cold damp fingers to her breasts, abdomen, and pubic area. "Your loins, so that you may be fruitful in propagating of a goodly seed."

"It's a little late for that."

"Hush." Rail-thin Woman next dampened Meryam's legs and feet. That ritual complete, she bustled back to her table and poured oil from a cruet into a hammered-metal bowl. Pulling open a drawer, she carefully extracted a hand-drawn glass pipette that represented, among other things, the pinnacle of The People's current manufacturing capability. Rail-thin Woman dipped the pipette into the oil, fastened her lips over its upper end, and sucked. Quickly she withdrew it from her mouth, covering it with her right index finger. Thus equipped, Rail-thin Woman proceeded to anoint

563

each part of Meryam's body that she had previously washed with water.

At the end of the rite, Rail-thin Woman laid down the empty pipette and held out her hands. "You have been cleansed of your sins. Step down." Meryam stepped off the whitewashed stool, holding Rail-thin Woman's hands for balance.

But the skeletal elder did not let go.

"Hear me, Meryam Mayishimu," Rail-thin Woman rumbled. "I will now teach you your new name, which you must reveal to no one save at the appointed moment in the coming ceremony. Do you understand?"

"I think so."

Rail-thin woman drew close and whispered fiercely, "Ye who shall be sealed, behold: Your new name is ... *Bumbida Lee*."

Rail-thin Woman released Meryam's hands and clapped her own together twice. Half-a-dozen middle-aged women scurried in. Two pressed the components of Meryam's wedding dress over her shield. The other four, seamstresses all, sewed Meryam into it. The dress was a flouncy white affair in a distant imitation of organdy. Finally, the attendants fitted a white muslin temple garment over the bridal gown, ruining its lines.

Sometime, Meryam resolved, *I must ask my new husband why he decided the temple garments go on the outside.*

Chapter 118

"The envoy is on its own *Luskus Delph* mission," Gram Enoda said two days after his breakthrough contact with the alien.

"*Luskus Delph*?" Commander Eblet Preltad said blankly.

"Where Computer and I were stationed before we began our journey here," Enoda explained. "*Luskus Delph*'s mission is to send humans into the universe from which we think those destructive gravity disturbances originate. Well, for many of their generations, the envoy race has been sending messengers here, to *our* universe – all to contact us and beg us to stop."

"'**STOP! STOP! STOP!**'" Computer played back one of the envoy's richly polyphonic appeals.

"Why is it pronounced in the sound of so many voices?" Admiral Konder was no more literally present than Enoda and Computer.

"The obvious reason, I think," Computer whirred. "We are meant to understand that this message is delivered on behalf of the whole envoy species."

"But *what* are we to stop?" demanded a telepresent Privy High Councilor shrouded in an emerald-link cape.

Enoda aimed a grim visage toward Admiral Konder. "When you first briefed Computer and me five months ago, above Standoff World, you told us about the gravitational disturbances and the damage they wreaked. Well, during the last two days the envoy has told – or shown – us a similar story. In his universe, on his watery world, there have also been gravitational disruptions. Some were catastrophic."

Computer picked up the thread. "One deep-ocean gravitational anomaly caused a pressure bubble that killed several great schools of the envoy race. At two other locations, anomalies caused the collapse of seamounts, again with significant loss of life."

"Also, their astronomers observed the partial destruction of a small world orbiting their own sun, as well as a 'stutter' in the cycle of a nearby binary star system," Enoda explained. "These occurrences, closely analyzed, suggested that the disturbances originated outside the Envoy's universe."

"Just as you and Computer concluded," Konder said darkly. "But you found the source of the disturbances in yet some *other* universe."

Enoda nodded. "The universe to which *Luskus Delph* is gearing up to send people – which, for whatever this might be worth, is not the universe from which the envoy came. All I can tell you is that the envoy's people do not agree."

"Wait one moment," interjected another Privy High Councilor. "They think the disturbances arose *here*?"

"The envoy has said that explicitly," Enoda confirmed.

"But that's impossible." The Councilor frowned. "Um, isn't it?"

"Yes, it is," said Computer. "The anomalies struck our universe too, and they came here from elsewhere."

"Be that as it may," Enoda said, "that's how the envoy race sees things."

Konder nodded toward Enoda, then toward Computer. "Your first three days of dialogue with the envoy has raised more questions than answers. But the path to knowledge is always thus. By Stanlee, that is understood by all who *live*."

Chapter 119

May 19, 2374
Bohrkk, New Nauvoo

The wedding day promised to be long.

Shan Takander Thurnb stood unmoving as Daiga, his second wife, threaded tiny leaves through the painstakingly woven hair on his cheeks. Daiga was still stolidly attractive in late middle age, her hair an explosion of chestnut curls shot through with grey. "Tell me, dear," she asked him, "did young Abigayl truly understand what a traditional wedding of The People involves?"

"I don't think she did when she first requested the old rite," he said. "But she knows now."

"When she found out, did it surprise her?"

"I would say so."

Daiga stepped back and surveyed her husband's lengthy muttonchops. Their pattern of weave symbolized the union of bride and groom. The leaves she'd threaded through the strands represented the persistence of life. "If she understood the old rite so poorly, why do you think she asked for it?"

"I asked her that once," he said, pulling on a bluish-grey *jibbah.*

"And?"

"She said she had her reasons."

"That's no answer," Daiga objected, lacing her husband's ceremonial leather skirt up the back.

Thurnb thrust his pelvis backward. "She's still a Queen."

"True, it's not like you could interrogate her," the woman agreed. She pressed the corroded metal cuirass to Thurnb's chest. He clasped his hands to it; she crossed

567

behind him to tie it on. "Think Abigayl will do all right?"

"She's a stunningly gorgeous young woman," Thurnb rumbled. "Kleh's a forceful young man. If her mind is unsure what to do, her body will lead her."

***

Damask curtains parted to reveal a chamber larger than Meryam expected, softly illuminated. A long slitted sheet hung from the ceiling near the far wall, obscuring what lay beyond.

Rail-thin Woman had been waiting there. She gestured toward the sheet. "Do you know what this is?"

"It represents the veil between heaven and earth," Meryam said by rote.

"Who stands on the other side?"

"I am taught," replied Meryam, striving for a neutral tone, "it is the Lord."

"Then go to him."

Mechanically, Meryam approached the slitted sheet. A man stood behind it, playing the role of God. After some hesitation they hugged, arranging themselves so as to touch at what were called the Five Points of Fellowship: foot touching foot, knee against knee, breast pressed to breast, hand clasped to the other's back, each one's mouth brushing the other's ear through the fabric. The man pressed a secret sign into her right hand. "What is that?" he asked.

It was Alrue's voice.

"I'm glad it's you," she whispered.

"Of course it's me. It would forjel up the whole ceremony if a man not the groom played God to the bride," he whispered back. "Now what is that?"

"A test? Really?"

"Meryam —"

"The First Token of the Aaronic Priesthood," she said with a sigh.

"Has it a name?"

"You're really determined not to omit one single step, aren't you?"

"Has it a name?" he hissed.

"It has," she said testily.

"Will you give it to me?"

"Thought you'd never ask." She couldn't help whispering what she said next, though she couldn't imagine what harm might be done if Rail-thin Woman overheard. "It is the Sign of the Nail."

"And what is the penalty for revealing it?"

"Having your heart cut out," she said with a shrug.

Alrue switched to another secret handshake. "Again, what is that?"

She sighed. "The Second Token of the Aaronic priesthood."

"Has it a name?"

Shaking her head ever so slightly, she whispered, "It has."

"Will you give it to me?"

"I will, through the veil. It is the Sure Sign of the Nail, and the penalty for revealing it is disembowelment."

"Don't skip steps."

After a few more such ritual exchanges Alrue pressed his lips, if possible, even closer to her ear and whispered: "What is your new name? Tell only me."

She whispered back, "Bumbida Lee. Are we done yet?"

"'Well done, thou good and faithful servant, enter thou into the joy of the Lord.'" Alrue took Meryam's hands in the secret First Token grip and pulled her through the slitted sheet.

***

The wedding day promised to be long. "Again," the youngest elder ordered.

Kleh, the groom-to-be, squatted as he would just before the climax of the traditional ceremony. The tip of the sheathed sword hanging from his rustic belt fouled on the knife scabbard strapped to his left leg. That made the sword lurch forward, jostling the pike slung over his left shoulder. In turn that jettisoned the leather quiver on his back. Arrows spilled to the floor, followed quickly by the clattering wooden pike.

"I don't understand," Kleh said disconsolately. "We shortened the pike's carrying sling as tight as it could go."

"It's not the sling, it's the pike itself," said the youngest elder, gesturing for Kleh to stand. "I think the pike must go. It looks all warlike and impressive when you're standing, but because it's so long, it snags on everything else when you squat."

Frowning, Kleh refilled the quiver and hung it over his shoulder. He looked down at himself and said, "I need something more."

"Agreed. Without the pike you look naked on that side." The youngest elder nodded thoughtfully as Kleh set down the quiver and stepped to a table of armaments. "Remember, it's all about the effect, not about whether you could really fight trussed up this way."

Kleh picked up a fur-trimmed baldric that held half a dozen short throwing knives. He strapped it across his bare chest, running from his right shoulder to his left hip. Over that he donned the quiver again.

"Now you look finished." The youngest elder smiled broadly. "Try the squat."

Kleh dropped again. The sword tip still fouled in the knife scabbard, but now it could collide with nothing else.

"You look a proper old-fashioned Warrior," the youngest elder exulted. "Another hour and you'll be a married man."

Chapter 120

September 18, 2376
Research Station *LaurienEldridge,* Sector Kappa Zi

Six minutes later, the meeting had adjourned. Konder, the Councilors, the other hangers-on, even Enoda and Computer, had each vanished in a hail of virxels. Commander Eblet Preltad, having dismissed his own staff assistants, was the last person physically present. He sat alone in the compartment in which he had first met Enoda's and Computer's avatars.

He locked the room, shut down its logging system, then double-checked to make certain it was off. A mental command neutralized the irregular chamber's gravity. A modest kick set him wafting toward the heptagonal viewport above. Frowning toward the gravitational vortex that churned in the void outside, Preltad activated his less-than-official comm implant. That device was so stealthy that the sort of med-scan PeaceForce officers frequently underwent would not detect it. Yet it was powerful enough to link with an ultra-miniaturized transceiver in Preltad's quarters, and that transceiver was powerful enough to reach the cell of co-conspirators to which he had some eight months previously pledged his life.

Preltad subvocalized the RECORD command followed by a flurry of pass-codes.

Then, brazenly, he dictated his message out loud. Why not? He was alone.

"'Not all directions are good for our advance: one alone leads toward greater synthesis and unity!'" – of course he began with a Teilhardian mantra – "Comrades, this is Eblet Preltad. The being who combines true human consciousness with crisp machine perfection … the one who has achieved Omega consciousness … he of whom it has been said that our future lies in his service … *I have met him.* He is real. And he's here on my station – virtually. He'll be here in reality the day after tomorrow." Preltad drew up his legs so that he floated before the viewport in something approaching a lotus pose. "His name, you ask? I am honored to share that knowledge with you, my brothers. His name is Computer."

Chapter 121

Lurching through the slitted sheet, Meryam emerged into the harsh brilliance of the Celestial Room. The rearmost, tallest, and most lavish chamber on the Temple's attic level, it usually served as Alrue's office. For great occasions like this one his garish furnishings, fantastic murals, and great *faux*-jade screen were whisked into an unused hallway and slightly more conservative pieces put in their places. The room's arched ceiling lofted to the underside of the Temple's peaked roof. Its rear wall was pierced by the half-moon aperture near the top of the gable, a row of small round portholes below that, and finally soaring mullioned windows that dropped almost to the floor, each topped by a half-circular fanlight. Daylight dazzled through sheer white curtains. It was elegant in a stifling way. A marble-topped circular table showcased a milkglass vase displaying a fussy spray of flowers. Heavy *faux*-marble moldings framed each window. Ornate cabinets and occasional tables festooned the chamber, as did chairs of dark sculpted wood upholstered in near-damask.

The effect was half old-time hotel lobby, half Ghelttian whorehouse.

Meryam took two steps backward; at last she could study her husband-to-be. He wore white from head to toe. His blousy unconstructed cap seemed partly deflated. A ribbon connected the hat to a white robe, its shoulders festooned with fabric loops. The robe's hem hung below Alrue's knee; below that he wore white pantaloons and white shoes. Around his ample waist was tied the inevitable green fig-leaf apron and over that, a white sash. Sweat dotted his forehead.

Along the walls stood Queens Zuzenah, Constance, Lupida, and Nataleah. Each wore an elaborate white bridal dress bedecked with pale flowers. Their presence fulfilled the "Law of Sarah," the requirement that a man's current wives make at least a show of assent to his marrying a new one. Yet their smiles seemed genuine enough.

"I present my betrothed," Alrue called to his wives, grinning broadly. "Behold, she is endowed."

"Looks scrawny as ever to me," Nataleah whispered to Lupida, who conveyed her disapproval with a dry grimace.

Alrue turned to his bride-to-be. "Your Temple endowment ceremony being completed, the marrying may begin."

***

"Do the Queens know?" Daiga asked as she laced up Takander Thurnb's left gauntlet.

"Know what?" Thurnb asked, holding out his other arm.

"What happens in a traditional wedding."

"I was there when they were told," Thurnb said with a vicious grin. "Queen Zuzenah was horrified. Queen Constance was shocked at first, but came to terms with it." He held out both gauntleted hands, knuckles down. Daiga slid hammered-metal covers over each one's row of lacings. "Queen Lupida said the ceremony reminded her of a game she used to play with Harold."

"Who's Harold?"

"Search me. Then there was Queen Nataleah. She – " Thurnb shuddered – "made suggestions."

"Suggestions?"

"You know, ideas to – what phrase did she use? Oh, yes, to 'spice it up.'"

"She wanted to 'spice up' a *traditional wedding*?"

Thurnb laughed. "Gods, that woman has an imagination."

Daiga flashed him an arch look. "If anything happens to the Tyrant King, perhaps you should marry her."

Thurnb scowled. The death of his adored Eyla was still too fresh for him to savor such comments.

"That brings me to the big question," said Daiga. "About the traditional wedding – has anyone told the Tyrant King what he's about to see?"

Thurnb blanched.

**

Alrue and Meryam stepped apart. An attendant rushed up, draping a man's coat over Meryam's shoulders and a man's hat atop her head. In such a costume Joseph Smith's very first plural wife, Louisa Beaman, had taken her marital vows, so that any passing witness might think the prophet Joseph was simply giving his blessing to some worthy Mormon man.

The bride and groom moved to opposite sides of the portable altar in the center of the Celestial Room. It had pale-pink cushioned kneelers on both sides. Meryam knelt on one side, Alrue on the other. They joined hands across its surface.

The celebrant bustled in, an anxious temple functionary who was neither quite middle-aged nor old. He wore an Old Testament-style desert costume every piece of which was stark white – except, of course, for the strident green of his apron and the various nameless stains on his temple garment, which tradition held must never be washed.

The celebrant wiped sweat from his forehead and upper lip, smeared his hand on his *thobe,* and produced a book of ceremonies. "Dearly beloved saints, shall we begin?"

"Of course," said Alrue, "but put away the book."

The celebrant gaped fretfully. "No book?"

Alrue leaned over and plucked the volume from the celebrant's hands. "Behold," he said, "I am having a revelation from the Lord. Yea, now, even as I speak."

"A revelation here?" the celebrant whispered, horrified. "But this is the Temple!"

"We're not doing the ceremony we rehearsed?" Meryam whispered urgently.

"I shall dictate as we go," Alrue proclaimed, "the way Joseph Smith did in times of old." He trained his prophetic gaze on the celebrant. "This shall be a sealing for time, not for eternity. Behold, these are the words of the Lord: 'These are the words which you shall pronounce upon my servant Alrue and this woman, Meryam Mayishimu. They shall take each other by the hand' – wait, we've already done that – 'and you shall say, "You both mutually agree," calling us by name, "to be each other's companion so long as you both shall live."'"

The celebrant nodded silently.

"Um, you shall say all that stuff I said," Alrue prodded. "Now, if you don't mind."

"Oh, yes, of course. Terribly sorry, First Elder – I mean, Prophet, Seer, and Revelator – that is, Tyrant King." The celebrant cleared his throat. "Do you both mutually agree, Alrue and Meryam, to be each other's companion so long as you both shall live …"

Alrue nodded, then continued the dictation. "'… preserving yourself for each other, and from all others, reserving only those rights which have been given to my servant Alrue by revelation and commandment and by legal authority in times passed.'"

Doggedly the celebrant repeated the cataract of words.

"'If you both agree to covenant and do this,'" Alrue dictated, "'I then give you, Meryam Mayishimu, to

Alrue Latier, to be his wife, to observe all the rights between you that belong to that condition. I do it in my own name and in the name of those here assembled, and in the name of my holy progenitors, by the right of birth which is of priesthood, vested in me by revelation and commandment and promise of the living God, commanding in the name of the Lord all those powers to concentrate in you and through you to your posterity forever. Let immortality and eternal life hereafter be sealed upon your heads forever and ever.'"

The celebrant swallowed hard. "Tyrant King, I can't remember all that."

"Never mind, the Lord saith I should kiss the bride."

And so he did.

***

The afternoon sun burned orange and hot as Alrue, his wives old and new, a choir, three trumpeters, seven drummers, and all the onlookers – those privileged to witness the ceremony in the Celestial Room, plus hundreds more who had waited in the Great Hall downstairs – poured out through the Temple's front door. The choristers sang a famed old Mormon hymn:

The morning breaks, the shadows flee;
Lo, Zion's standard is unfurled!
The dawning of a brighter day
Majestic rises on the world.

The Temple doors opened onto the West Grove. The long grassy tree-lined promenade was already crowded. But if the company filing out of the Temple consisted mostly of converts to Alrue's Mormonism, the throng already in the Grove was heavier on individuals who still identified with – or yearned for – The People's officially discarded old religion. "I had no idea so many

577

still esteemed the old faith," Zuzenah whispered to her husband as they crossed the grove.

"Until a few years ago, their ancestral religion was all they knew," Alrue explained.

"Surely Abigayl's primitive wedding will sharpen their hunger for the old ways," Nataleah chimed in. "Was it wise to permit it?"

"Permit it?" Alrue countered. "Did Abigayl give us a choice? But behold, I regret not the way events came to pass. It's good that now and again The People should have an opportunity like this to express their love for the past – which is to say, to vent it harmlessly."

A liveried usher led the royal party to their place of honor, the foremost of two dozen log benches facing the marriage platform. Alrue sat in the very center, between his oldest and newest wives. "Fear not," he told Zuzenah, "everyone among The People shall become Mormon in due time. They love the truths that I promulge."

"Tyrant King!" shouted Takander Thurnb from the slightly elevated log platform. His costume disconcertingly combined items of Mormon and native design. "Hail to you and yours," he called. "Congratulations on your joyous wedding today."

"Congratulations on the joyous wedding you are about to perform."

Thurnb raised his fists to his chest, knuckles out, causing the hammered-metal covers attached to his gauntlets to clatter against his cuirass. "I call to The People!" he thundered.

"We are here, O Shan," several hundred, Mormons and tribals, shouted back.

"I call to Kleh!"

"I am here, O Shan!" Kleh the builder-entrepreneur bounded toward the log platform wearing a ragged loincloth, torn scraps of leather round his legs and chest, a necklace of animal bones, a profusion of traditional weapons fastened to his ebony body with leather and fabric straps, and finally the fur-trimmed baldric. The incongruous meter-long saber hanging from a belt of twisted vines looked like something Joseph Smith might have worn as Lieutenant-General of the Nauvoo Legion.

"Aside from the weapons, he's hardly dressed," Alrue whispered uneasily to Meryam.

"It's traditional," Meryam said pointedly.

Kleh stepped onto the platform three meters from Thurnb, who raised his arms and cried, "Hail Kleh on his wedding day!"

"Hail the Shan!" Kleh squatted in a jangle of quivers and scabbards and straps. Nothing tangled.

"I call to Abigayl!" bellowed Thurnb.

"I am here, O Shan." The watching crowd parted, and fourteen-year-old Abigayl strode forward.

"By the towers of Zarahemla," Alrue breathed, wide-eyed.

"Let thy bowels be full of charity," Zuzenah cautioned.

Abigayl Latier marched forward on bare feet, belled bracelets chattering on her ankles. A black leather sash no wider than a hand slid over each of her shoulders to tuck into a hip-hugging chain-mail belt at front and back. Worked into the left sash was a scabbard containing a small throwing knife; worked into the right was a holstered truncheon. A brief skirt of brightly colored feathers hung from the belt. Her arms, her lower legs, and most of her perfect torso were bare. On a woman as black-skinned as was normal among The People, the twin leather sashes might blend in, slightly de-emphasizing the wearer's breasts. But Abigayl's flesh was sallow; the narrow black sashes stood in sharp contrast to her skin, accentuating the exposure of her upper body and channeling special attention to the sides of her breasts, which could be clearly seen joggling gibbously with her steps.

"I'm glad I got to wear *my* dress," Meryam whispered in Alrue's ear.

"Whoredoms and all manner of wickedness!" Alrue hissed.

"She wanted her native ceremony for good reason," Queen Zuzenah whispered firmly in his other ear. "This costume is part of the package."

"You must admit, she wears it well," said Nataleah, seated behind him.

Alrue, who at this moment needed no reminding as to the charms of the wife he had given up, just glowered.

Abigayl stepped onto the platform to stand beside Kleh.

Thurnb raised his arms again. "Hail Abigayl on Kleh's wedding day!"

"Hail the Shan," Abigayl replied, bowing with warrior dignity. Her braided jet-black hair was elaborately piled atop her head. It reminded Alrue of that classic Mormon symbol, the beehive.

Thurnb struck his gauntlets against his cuirass once more. "I call to Kleh!"

"I am here, O Shan."

Thurnb raised one hard-muscled arm. "Will you have this woman, Abigayl?"

As tradition required, Kleh made a great show of studying Abigayl's body from toes to head. He cried, "I will, and forever!"

"Will anyone ask Abigayl whether she wants Kleh?" Alrue asked quietly.

"Don't be silly, dear," replied Zuzenah. "This is a traditional wedding."

Showily Thurnb stretched his arms fully to either side. "I am Shan! What I join this day is joined forever. Kleh, take your Abigayl."

Without preamble, Kleh thrust his hands beneath Abigayl's thin sashes, slapping his palms over her breasts and squeezing very hard. Abigayl yelped; yet at the same moment she reached behind herself to twist the concealed clasp in her hair while snapping her head to the left.

She'd watched closely as the six native girls had done it, and her study paid off: an hour and a quarter of Dried-blood Robe's patient braiding fell away in a sudden flowing black cascade.

Abigayl pivoted, grinding a hip against Kleh's bulging loincloth. They kissed open-mouthed, tongues moiling.

Alrue swallowed hard, speechless.

"You've got to hand it to The People," Nataleah said wonderingly. "They harbor no illusions about what marriage is for."

Thurnb crossed his gloved hands over his chest and shouted, "It is done." Eight Danites – former Warriors of The People, clad for this occasion in old-time leather and rags –rushed forward. Four lined up to either side of the ferociously groping couple. As one, the eight men reached into lengthy slots in the stage and pulled up two parallel poles. That action released a series of bamboo panels that assembled themselves into a tall sedan chair around the standing bride and groom. At a shout from its leader, the party of eight carried the wedded couple away toward a log enclosure in which, presumably, their love was to be consummated straightaway.

***

From the north, behind the royal party, came a sudden commotion. Shouting voices. Thundering hooves.

Thundering hooves?

Alrue stood. Whirled.

581

The crowd parted before three charging *svadi* moose.

Svadi moose with riders.

Svadi moose, being ridden by *Danites*.

"I've been meaning to tell you," Constance told Alrue. "We've reinvented cavalry."

Chapter 122

The stellar pair nearest *Laurien Eldridge* gyred in the polarized viewport at the end of the corridor, framed by its arching streamers of gas. Commander Eblet Preltad, his full dress uniform embellished with polychrome piping and self-luminous virtual epaulettes, laid his hand on Gram Enoda's arm. Literally. Nineteen days after their virtual arrival, Enoda and Computer had completed their physical journey from *Luskus Delph* to *Laurien Eldridge.* Enoda wore a simple black tech's jumpsuit; Computer floated beside him, silvery as ever. A gaggle of officers trailed the party as it moved down the corridor toward the bay that held the envoy's enclosure.

"It is such a pleasure to have you and Hom Computer here with us in person," Preltad gushed. "Well, to have *you* with us in person, Hom Enoda. And to have Computer with us in – well, not quite in the flesh …"

"I liked him better when he loathed us," Computer told Enoda privately.

Preltad smiled obsequiously. "So, does it feel any different to actually *be* aboard our little station?"

Enoda shrugged. "Not notably."

Colors whorled across Computer's skin. "Actually, I'm sensing quite a difference. Not in the station, but rather in the quality of my communication with the envoy's device."

Chapter 123

May 19, 2374
Bohrkk, New Nauvoo

"O Tyrant King!" A Danite captain stood up in his stirrups, saluting Alrue as his *svadi* moose dropped to its knees in the West Grove before the Prophet, Seer, and Revelator.

"Most impressive," Alrue proclaimed.

"Bleat," said the moose.

"We waited for the ceremony to end," the captain said, dropping to his left side and curling fetally.

"Get up, enough of that," Alrue insisted. "What's so important?"

"Hundreds of strangers have gathered outside the city," the captain reported. "We believe they are survivors of two or three other tribes devastated by the volcanoes."

Alrue pursed his lips. "Is one of these tribes The Others?"

"No," the captain replied. "It's like the dead people Queen Constance found on her expedition – tribes no one knew about."

"Only these are not dead," Alrue noted.

"Very much alive," the Danite captain confirmed. "Most of them, anyway. They have marched for days and come to New Nauvoo as refugees."

***

Alrue, his wives, and Kleh sat in the Temple's otherwise empty Great Hall, their sculpted chairs drawn up in a circle, strategizing hastily. The meeting had been convened the moment Abigayl and Kleh could decently be called from their post-nuptial love nest. The Danites stood outside with their *svadi* moose, awaiting any orders the meeting might produce. "I'm thinking this is good news," Alrue declared. "Newcomers will help New Nauvoo live up to the scale of its design."

"But integrating newcomers from wildly disparate cultures will be difficult," said Meryam.

"Especially since The People have so little experience dealing with alien tribes," Constance pointed out.

"I share this concern." Queen Lupida frowned. "How shall we prevent factional rivalries, intergroup strife – even violence?"

Alrue stood and pounded his right fist into his left palm. "I'm thinking I need to make an immediate, powerful impression on the newcomers. If I can pull them quickly into my church, that will place them under my authority and predispose them toward obedience." He began to pace. "No two ways about it, these refugees need to receive a prophecy. Um, where's Abigayl?"

Kleh glanced about. "I could swear she was here a minute ago."

"Please don't swear," Alrue grumbled. *"Abigayl! Where in forjeling plorg have you been?"*

Still costumed like a barbarian porn star, her hair in disarray, Abigayl emerged panting from one of the circular stairways. She half-strode, half-ran to Alrue and handed him a small grey box. "I figured you'd need these. You know, to wax prophetic and all."

"My floatcells," Alrue said quietly. "Yes, I suppose I should use them." After a moment, he frowned. "Abigayl, these were in my office."

"Yes, they were."

"In my safe."

"Yes."

"Locked in my safe."

Abigayl shrugged. Seeing that the gesture confused Kleh, she thrust her pelvis backward. "That's why it took me a minute."

585

Alrue sat back down, placing the grey box in his lap. "Thank you for your quick thinking, Abigayl. I repeat, though you're no longer my wife, you are always welcome at these skull sessions." Absently he opened the box. He looked up at Abigayl, confused. "All four cells? I usually float well enough with one."

Abigayl smiled. "This is a special occasion."

Alrue stood, beaming. "Of course." Two brisk steps took him to Abigayl. He hugged her. "The most brilliant woman I never married. Congratulations on your wedding day." He turned toward Kleh, extending his arms for a two-handed handshake before he remembered that Kleh would not recognize the gesture. He managed to turn it into a sort of wave-bow that nonetheless conveyed genuine warmth. "And congratulations to you also, Kleh." With that, he bustled toward the door, the rest of the party rushing to follow.

As he rushed forward Alrue stuffed the four floatcells, each the size of a knuckle, into his all-white groom costume. "Behold," he recited, "they saw a Man descending out of heaven; and he was clothed in a white robe; and he came down and stood in the midst of them; and the eyes of the whole multitude were turned upon him."

"Alrue!" Zuzenah chided. "That passage speaks of Jesus."

Kleh looked quizzical. "What's a Jesus?"

***

Fifteen Danites snapped to attention as the Tyrant King and his entourage emerged from the Temple; a dozen others had gathered to savor the novelty of moose-borne cavalry.

"I go to New Nauvoo's northern boundary to greet the newcomers," Alrue announced. He pointed toward the highest-ranking of the Danite hangers-on. "Lieutenant! Commandeer a wagon. Bring all my wives save Queen Meryam to the boundary of the area where the refugees have gathered. Their dresses make them look like goddesses; if need be, they will speak for me from groundside." Taking Meryam by the arm, he steered her toward the commander of the mounted Danites. "Captain, take up Queen Meryam on your moose with you, and rush her to the corner of Page and Robinson Streets. I want her in place before any of the newcomers see me." He leaned to whisper in Meryam's ear: "Recording, of course."

"This is a moment I *have* to capture for the ages," she replied. She could say no more, for at that moment the Danite captain's two subordinates grabbed her and hoisted her toward their captain atop his *svadi* moose. With some improvising, the captain secured the bridal-costumed Spectator sidesaddle behind him.

"Bleat," said the *svadi* moose as it broke into a canter.

Alrue fiddled with his temple garment, subvocalized a command to the floatcells he wore, and lofted a good forty meters into the sky.

Meryam recorded the spectacle of New Nauvooers gaping skyward at their levitating Tyrant King and prophet. Face after slack-jawed face swept past in a dynamic tracking shot, understandably her first from mooseback.

She spotted Rail-thin Woman in the crowd, still clad in her priestly whites from the Temple endowment ceremony. She was staring skyward as abjectly as anyone else.

"Elder! Elder!" Meryam shouted to her. "I told you he flies!"

Chapter 124

Computer was right, Gram Enoda realized as the virtual interface of their communication with the envoy's device – and, through it, the envoy – took shape. *There are strata of meaning I never discerned before.* Their communion with the envoy was still densely mediated; Enoda and Computer stood, now physically, inside their sim cell on a catwalk outside the faceted, sensor-jacketed enclosure within which the envoy reposed. The lobster-like alien's assistive device still resided in its pouch strapped to his thorax. Enoda and his machine interacted with the alien and his machine through a sim system. Yet for Enoda and Computer, being physically present aboard *Laurien Eldridge* meant one less layer of mediation. That difference mattered.

"The envoy's device seems capable of layers of subtext – harmonics, if you will – substantially richer than what our former virtual interface could reproduce," Computer observed.

The usual sim image of the envoy's expressionless visage glowed before them, but Enoda gave his core attention to the virtual interface he and Computer shared.

His *pov* lofted down an ever-deepening channel of inference. Sparkling data structures interpenetrated; a boundary effect suggested a glimmering, spinning tunnel. Intermittently Enoda let his *pov* drift toward its endlessly unreeling wall. Infinite detail lurked there on a register he had not sensed before.

Lightning danced within the interface punctuated by subsonic bursts of color, the scent of violins, the flavor of gravity. Upwelling from unexpected directions came an overwhelming sense of something colossal – some taxiing star transport, say, hurtling past at immense speed just millimeters from one's cheeks – yet not registered by vision, for there was no light; nor by sound, for vacuum was never more silent than this; nor by the sense of touch, for there was no contact nor even the possibility of it. A proprioceptive certainty, nothing more. *"What the sfelb's happening?"* Enoda demanded.

"I am in doubt," Computer said hesitantly. *"The envoy's device feels it too, and understands no more about its nature than I do. To offer a woefully premature analysis, it feels as though the device and I have embarked on previously impossible paths of knowing."*

Within the interface, an area went dark.

"We've lost contact with the envoy's device," Enoda said.

"Only you have," Computer chirruped. *"That is my doing. The envoy's device is blocking the envoy from contact with us as well, until the device and I get this sorted out. Transactions are occurring between our two machine minds that might do lasting damage to a meat-based consciousness."*

Sure enough, the sim image showed the envoy making "grasping" motions with his claw, a gesture Enoda had learned to read as a sign of perplexity. Returning his attention to the virtual interface, Enoda frowned as he studied new, baroque patterns of detail. *"'Previously impossible paths of knowing,'"* he repeated.

"Pardon?"

"You said that a moment ago. That sets me to wondering – humor me a second."

"Don't I always?"

"Very funny. I need you to bud off a discrete problem space for me, something just deep enough to accommodate basic number theory."

589

"Ask for something hard." Computer conjured a glistening domain endowed with a fractal number of dimensions.

"Populate it with a very simple arithmetical system."

"Done," the machine whirred. *"The simplest, purest instantiation of natural-number arithmetic possible. Now what did you have in mind to do with it, or am I getting ahead of you?"*

Enoda lofted his *pov* as close to the new domain as he dared. *"Without reaching outside the system, prove that the entire system is internally consistent."*

"I knew it. My burden-in-life has finally gone around the big bend."

"No time for banter," Enoda said grimly. *"Just do it, please."*

"Have you forgotten Wjeklÿan incompleteness?"

"You mean Gödelian incompleteness?"

"You can take the child out of Terra, but you can't take Terra out of the child," Computer buzzed tiredly. *"Credit the Galactic mathematician or the Terran one, as you prefer, but it's well established that no arithmetical system can be proven completely internally consistent using its own axioms alone. You need to employ a more powerful conceptual platform – set theory, perhaps."*

"Try."

After a couple of seconds – an eternity for the machine – Computer said puzzledly, *"Well, that was unexpected."*

The mathematical test domain had resolved into a network of crystalline logical connections resembling nothing Enoda had seen.

Nothing *anyone* had ever seen.

Computer whirred disbelievingly, *"I just proved natural-number arithmetic wholly consistent using nothing but its own axioms. I have rerun the proof more than sixty billion times, always with the same result. Yet incompleteness, the doctrine that says what I've just done cannot under any circumstance be achieved, is one of the most robust principles in all of mathematics."* The machine's deep bewilderment inflected the cognitive interface with scents of shadows, sound-textures tasting of damp gabardine. *"How did you know to suggest this?"*

"I didn't, not really," Enoda said hesitantly. *"Just a hunch. If your communion with the envoy's device was really opening realms of previously foreclosed possibility. I thought I'd test for one of the radical ones."*

"It's like visiting a new world, releasing a coin to time its drop, and it falls up," Computer chirruped. *"It couldn't get any stranger if I simultaneously measured the position and velocity of a single electron."*

Enoda arched an eyebrow. *"Now that you mention it ..."*

Chapter 125

Constance Latier wheeled through the sky. The setting sun, originally at her back, slipped to her left. She hurtled northward parallel to the lip of the western ridge and glanced toward the east. The moons Queen and Prince were just becoming visible against the darkening sky. *I'm right on time,* she thought. She swooped through a ninety-degree right turn, then drifted to a stop. Seventy meters below her, a kilometer-wide valley ran north and south, its floor dotted with stubbly scrub forest. The sun baked her right side as she undid the straps at her wrists and ankles. Yards of diaphanous white material billowed riotously free. She lurched as the two floatcells she wore adjusted to the sudden change in her wind loading.

Smiling, Constance hurtled forward. When she first became visible from the campsite surrounding the parley house far below, her clothing would be ablaze with ruddy sunlight. To maximize the effect she spread herself wide, sleeves and pantaloons luminous, whipping in the airstream.

From ahead and below her, she heard shouting. She'd been seen, a fiery portent careening from the north. She approached the parley house where, almost seven years before, Meryam, Zuzenah, Abigayl, and Alrue had watched Shan Takander Thurnb "negotiate" with the disfigured emissary of the Other tribe. There, since becoming Tyrant King, Alrue or Constance in his place had presided over three more equally pointless encounters.

When the parley house was directly below her, Constance arrested her forward motion. She dropped straight down, revolving slowly.

She touched down just south of the building, three meters from King Alrue, who stood at the head of his long-promised expedition to probe The Others' secrets. Alongside him stood Shan Takander Thurnb in his grey-green journeying cape, accompanied by a half-dozen slack-jawed former Warriors – Danites now – who had dropped to their sides, curled up like fetuses, at the sight of Queen Constance.

Constance wore a heavily embroidered white-on-white *thobe,* modest enough on the ground but slit up the sides so her harem-style pantaloons could surge free when she was airborne. She powered off the floatcells with a subvocal command and pushed splayed fingers through her mid-length red hair, hoping to undo at least a trifle of the disarray that winds aloft had imposed.

By now the men had uncurled sufficiently to gape upward at this vision who had landed among them.

Alrue, who always knew just how long to let his marks stare, bustled forward to give his accidental wife a welcoming hug. "Welcome, Queen Constance. You looked the very fiery flying serpent surging toward us in the setting sun."

"That was the plan," she whispered, pressing her face to his beefy shoulder.

"Come." He led her toward a square tent pitched just west of the parley house, and very nearly its size. The tent was white, trimmed with crimson bunting and golden banners emblazoned with the emblem of the beehive. A proper Mormon tent, it boasted not a humble entrance flap, but rather a heavy wooden door in a stout timber jamb – never mind that this assembly weighed more than the entire rest of the tent and all its supporting hardware. A trio of sedan chairs rested in scrub grass beside the doorway. The harnessed *svadi* moose, the expedition's principal means of transport, had been tied up some distance from the Prophet's tent, blessedly downwind.

Inside the lavish tent, Meryam Mayishimu rose from a crimson cushion as Alrue and Constance entered. She wore a sky-blue *thobe* and *aba*. The wives hugged, then joined their husband, who had already deposited himself on a cushion behind a low table.

"How goes New Nauvoo, Constance?" Alrue asked.

"Well enough." Constance settled onto a cushion, Meryam at her side. "Fortunately, the refugees who appeared on the day of the double wedding came from tribes that knew something of carpentry."

Alrue noddned. "Disease?"

"Not too much." Constance made a vague gesture. "The refugees and The People hail from widely separated populations. Ten or fifteen of their people succumbed to maladies of ours; we lost four to ailments of theirs. Acceptable, under the circumstances, and far outweighed by the population gained."

"You said they were carpenters," Meryam ventured.

"Good ones, too." Constance smiled. "Most refugee heads of families have already built log cabins. The emergency camp we set up for them should be empty within days. Of course, this puts us far ahead of schedule building out the neighborhoods north of the Temple Lot. Brattle Street has a homestead on every lot from Main to Wilcox. Housing never extended that far east in the original Nauvoo."

"Then we are outdoing Joseph Smith himself," Alrue enthused. "Hosanna and amen." His tone grew more serious. "How do The People get along with the newcomers?"

"As little as possible."

Alrue smiled. "According to plan, then."

"Nataleah keeps them busy," Constance conceded. "Between your appearance in the sky and a few aerobatic exhibitions of her own, it was surprisingly easy to convince them that their old religions were bankrupt."

"Aerobatics help," Meryam observed, "but it may be more important that their gods allowed volcanoes to destroy their villages, while our gods" – she arched her eyebrows – "spared New Nauvoo."

"Nataleah makes it so much *work* to become a Mormon," Constance recounted with a chuckle. "But it serves its purpose. The newcomers are too thoroughly preoccupied to mix much with The People; meanwhile they're forcefully instructed in both The People's culture and our religion."

"It is like the pleasing word of God," Alrue exulted, "yea, the word which healeth the wounded soul. How long can you stay, darling Constance?"

"Dinner, such as it is, will be in an hour," Meryam advised.

"I can stay the night, but I must leave in the morning," Constance said. "My husband, you have one floatcell unit; sister Meryam has the second. Since I am flying long-distance, I have both of the others."

Alrue nodded. "In the event of some new emergency, no one else could rush word to us here."

"Not until I return."

"Very well. Go back tomorrow, Constance. But you shall warm my bed this night."

Constance displayed a flash of pure anticipation before she gazed toward Meryam and said diplomatically, "But my husband, you and Meryam are newlyweds."

"It's been three weeks," Alrue said with a shrug.

"I defer to my sister wife," Meryam declared formally.

Grunting, Alrue rose from his *faux* leopard-print cushion. "After dinner, I suppose you two will have some woman-talk to catch up on. I must pass the early evening with the Shan."

"Again?" Meryam asked puzzledly.

"He has decided that the evenings of this expedition are the perfect time to teach me more details of the old Wisdom religion. We can never know too much about the people among whom we live." He stepped toward Constance, who stood at his approach. They kissed intensely. "You may be a-bed before I return," he warned.

"Wake me." Constance's fingertips skated down his heavy forearms.

Not for the first time, Meryam wondered how Constance could feel such delight at the prospect of a night with Alrue. That had been a wonder when Meryam was a family traveling companion. Now that Meryam, too, slept with Alrue – not just in the household's usual rotation, but with a new wife's privileged place in the sequence – she was doubly confounded to imagine what might justify Constance's excitement. In Meryam's judgment, sex with Alrue thoroughly lived down to the knowing warning Lupida had once offered her: "Don't expect too much."

Oh well, she thought, *they say all things are possible with God.*

Chapter 126

September 20, 2376
Research Station *LaurienEldridge,* Sector Kappa Zi

The physics cell sulked on the catwalk outside Enoda and Computer's sim cell. Its spherical confinement vessel imprisoned a lone electron in a fist-sized volume of perfect vacuum. A tridee display projected a representation of the electron zipping about inside the vessel, exactly as it was supposed to. Beside it, two clusters of glowing numbers did something they were *not* supposed to: they incremented and decremented simultaneously, one cluster continuously showing the electron's position in three-space even as the other continuously displayed its vector. Commander Preltad, the projected Admiral Konder, two befuddled *Laurien Eldridge* physicists, and Enoda gaped at the display. Computer, floating beside Enoda a meter above the catwalk, would have gaped too. If he'd had anything to gape with.

"The numeric displays should flicker," one physicist said hollowly.

"They always used to," said the other physicist.

"Every schoolchild knows Doftel's uncertainty principle," Computer said aloud. "Or Heisenberg's, as I'll call it for the benefit of any small-minded Terran yokels present."

"Thanks loads," Enoda quipped.

"Yet apparently, having communed more closely with the envoy's device, I am able to set that principle, too, aside."

"Profoundly violating the foundations of quantum mechanics *and* number theory. But how?"

"I have a thought," said one of the *Laurien Eldridge* physicists, an almost-colorless Swede with hair like bleached straw.

Enoda nodded. "Let's hear it."

"Hom Computer, when you had your enhanced communication with the envoy's device, syn-noetic intelligences from two disparate universes were interfacing at a deep level – so far as we know, for the first time ever. Now, Gödelian incompleteness has been studied for centuries –"

"You mean *Wjeklÿan* incompleteness?" objected the other physicist, whose coloring and features proclaimed her a Galactic as surely as his colleague's branded him a Terran. "It's been studied for *millennia!*"

"Gödelian, Wjeklÿan, whatever," grumbled the Terran physicist. "It's been exhaustively studied, but always within the same framework. After all, both Wjeklÿ and Gödel modeled phenomena arising within just one universe."

"They could hardly do otherwise," the Galactic physicist sniffed.

"Exactly. But now, we are dealing with knowledge jointly developed between intelligences hailing from *two* universes."

Enoda took half a step back, wide-eyed.

The gush of colors across Computer's chromed body briefly stilled.

"Of course," they said together, in perfect synchrony.

Silence fell.

Admiral Konder's projected avatar tilted its head and scowled. "I don't know about anyone else, but I'd like to see this chain of deductions – you know, deductions *spoken out loud* – continue."

Enoda and the two physicists exchanged eager glances. Everyone seemed to want someone else to go first. Finally, Enoda shrugged and started pacing – and talking. "Incompleteness limits the mathematical truths accessible to an agent whose knowledge is derived from one universe," he reasoned. "Likewise, uncertainty limits the knowledge available to someone observing a subatomic particle within one universe's frame of reference. But now, beings from two universes can encounter each other's minds in a richly nuanced way. Each can extend the range of the other's cognition into one's own domain." He whirled, fixing an urgent gaze on his floating machine. "Computer, what are the chances that by melding your computations with those of a similar entity from another universe, you and the envoy's device might have found a way to step around limits on knowledge previously thought to be fundamental?"

"Defeating incompleteness *and* the uncertainty principle? I suppose that's barely plausible," Computer whirred.

"If that happened," Konder said wonderingly, "it is a fundamental advance in the course of inquiry. Frontiers previously closed to study, in the envoy's universe just as in ours, may open now."

"You do realize," the Galactic physicist said nervously, "that essential technologies Galactic civilization relies on *presume* uncertainty? Now that Hom Computer and the envoy's device are a team, should we worry that indispensable phenomena – quantum tunneling, say – might suddenly stop?"

"Apparently they will not," Computer burred. "I say that not out of any theoretical understanding, but only because a great many things should *already* have thudded to a stop – or blown up – had uncertainty been defeated on any large scale. So far, they have not. It would appear that the effects of our expanded understanding apply only locally."

"I hope you can keep it that way," Konder harrumphed.

I hope you can keep being you, Enoda thought desperately. *Computer, old friend, you have tapped into a realm of knowledge that was never ascribed even to the gods.*

Chapter 127

Tyrant King Alrue Latier and Shan Takander Thurnb sat alone together in the parley house. Torchlight danced on the open mess kits still smeared with what remained of the night's rude dinner. None would enter the chamber for post-meal cleanup until the Tyrant King and the Shan were finished with ... with whatever they were doing. "Your new religion is now The People's way," Thurnb rumbled, swirling herb whiskey in a dented metal cup. "But The People's history is tied to the old Wisdom estate, and until you understand the religion that Wisdoms once believed, you can't understand The People's roots."

"Teach me," Alrue said genially.

Thurnb slugged back some whiskey and gestured toward Alrue with a huge gloved hand. "Now do not misunderstand me, please, O Tyrant King. I believe *your* religion today. But this is what *was* believed – falsely, I know that now – among the Wisdoms who formerly set The People's course." He took a smaller swig, swirling the harsh liquid around his teeth. "I think you already know that much of the Wisdom faith has to do with that ancient prophet-hero named Darvoyg."

"The godling who talked to all the moose?"

"Ah, Fpod told you that story? Cursed be his memory. But there's a deeper story the Warriors know not – it is taught only from one Wisdom to another. I mean *was* taught, of course." Thurnb picked his teeth with a bird bone, then continued. "The story of Darvoyg that meant the most was a story whose details were partly unclear. It came from an ancient scripture that was visibly garbled."

"Garbled? How so?" Alrue asked, acutely conscious that religions often grow most lushly amid ambiguity.

"The oldest copy of the scripture our wisest Elders ever saw was torn and stained. The language was hard enough to read, but certain words – whole short passages – could not be made out at all. According to lore, there were once other tribes who lived far away, and they had other ancient copies of this same scripture that had suffered damage in *different* places." Thurnb shivered and adjusted the way his cape draped about him, not that that would help; the stimulus for his shivering was of an interior sort. "Passages no one could read in our copy were clear in theirs. Some legends suggested the scriptures held by other tribes actually said *different* things from ours. That's crazy, of course; every Mormon knows there is only one truth."

"Yea, Lord, I know that thou speakest the truth, for thou art a God of truth, and canst not lie," Alrue quoted in response.

Thurnb poured himself more herb whiskey. "According to this scripture, just before he delivered his greatest prophecy, Darvoyg – I'm quoting now – 'stretched forth his mighty arm, and grasped the Halberd of Troth. And he stretched forth another mighty arm, and he touched the Scroll of Peace. And he stretched forth another mighty arm, and as the gods ordained he did inscribe his name.'"

Alrue nodded gravely, heedless that Thurnb did not know what that gesture meant. "Darvoyg had three arms?"

"That's the problem," Thurnb growled. "There are passages before and after the part I just recited that might offer guidance for interpreting it – at least, the Elders thought so – but they were damaged. It is thought that those passages must have been damaged for a long, long time, because our oldest legends speak of tribes going to

602

holy war because they interpreted them in different ways. One tribe believed Darvoyg had the body of a normal man. You know, two arms. They taught that he let go of the Halberd of Troth so he could inscribe his name on the Scroll of Peace. In that way he preserved the right to lie when conducting diplomacy."

"A nice detail."

"Many years ago, at a parley right in this room, my grandfather learned that The Others are taught that Darvoyg actually had three arms. But they also insist that while Darvoyg's second arm touched the Scroll of Peace, his third arm wrote his name on some other document."

"Not on the Scroll of Peace?" Alrue asked.

"No, on something else."

"Sheer madness."

"Then, of course, there is the truth."

"This would be what The People believe," Alrue said expressionlessly.

"Exactly."

"Or rather, what they *did* believe."

"Oh, yes," Thurnb said, flustered, "Before most of us became Mormons. The truth – I mean, what The People used to believe – is that Darvoyg sprouted a miraculous third limb. While his natural limbs touched the Halberd of Troth and the Scroll of Peace, he used his miracle limb to inscribe his name on the Scroll of Peace."

"I see." Despite himself, Alrue raised his cup and took a mouthful of the harsh herb whiskey. It burned down his throat, settling in his stomach like a cluster of nettles. "However he did it," he rasped, "your godling Darvoyg touched the Halberd of Truth, touched the Scroll of Peace, *and* inscribed his holy name upon – well, probably upon the Scroll. What was the effect of his signing? Was it like a peace treaty among the tribes?"

"Pretty much," Thurnb confirmed. "Our scripture calls it 'an affirmation of eternal amity and concord, signed by all the tribes of men.'"

"I see. And what came next?"

"Centuries of war." Thurnb threw back more whiskey. "Tyrant King," he said with a just-audible slur, "one thing keeps bothering me."

"I gather that we're finished talking about Darvoyg."

"There's not much else to say about him. Our ancient scriptures were holy – at least, we thought so – but they were very short."

Alrue leaned backward in his chair. "Ask me anything."

"It's about your God and his –" Thurnb dredged his mind for the term – "his chosen people."

"The Jews?"

"Who? No, the Lamanites ... wait, I mean the Nephites. The chosen people from your scripture, your Book of, um, Book of ..."

"Mormon."

"That's it. So much to remember!" Thurnb leaned far forward, pitching his voice in a reedy whisper. "I never see this mentioned in your Book of Mormon, but ... does your God purposely *make* them stupid?"

"I beg your pardon?"

"Is there some hidden reason why your God dulls the brains of his people?" Thurnb spread his hands, a cross-cultural gesture of puzzlement. "I mean, time after time after time, some great prophet comes to the people and preaches God's true word. Each time, the people kill the prophet. Then your God smites them fearfully. That's fine, of course – he's God, he can smite whom he wants to. Plus, the people had it coming. But they *never learn!* A generation or two later, God sends his stupid people another great prophet, and they kill him too."

"A second prophet of old has testified of the Son of God," Alrue quoted, "and because the people would not understand his words they stoned him to death."

"Exactly," Thurnb rumbled. "Nobody ever says, 'You know, grandson, when I was your age, a prophet came to town and we killed him. Then God turned all our livestocks into salamanders. Maybe, just maybe, we should *listen* to this prophet.' Why in your scripture does that never, ever happen?"

Alrue bolted half a cupful of herb whiskey in one gulp. His throat seethed, but he forced his words up through it. "That, friend Takander, is what my people call a mystery of faith."

Chapter 128

October 18, 2376
Research Station *LaurienEldridge,* Sector Kappa Zi

Gram Enoda awoke reaching across the floatpad. Impressions of Pam Grice cascaded through his sleep-fogged awareness – *She's not here, she's still on Luskus Delph. – No, wait, she got here this morning!*

"Up here," Grice whispered.

She hovered before the heptagonal viewport two meters overhead. Enoda rolled up onto his knees and found himself ascending; Grice had configured their newly assigned stateroom's gravity so anyone rising from the floatpad would continue upward. She clapped an arm about his waist as he drew level with her. Her eyes remained fastened on the distortion patterns of the gravitational vortex smudging the stars outside.

"That's what passes for local scenery," he whispered, "unless your tastes run to incestuous binary stars."

"Can't take my eyes off it," she murmured. "Weirdly beautiful."

After a minute, he kissed her neck. "I'm so glad you made it out here."

"I think we established that about two hours ago."

The intercom brayed with one of those "You-won't-want-to-miss-a-moment-of-*this*-apocalypse" alert tones. Enoda had set the stateroom's comm system as deep into DO NOT DISTURB as he could; for this call to reach him at all, its priority must be immense. "Enoda," he barked into the air.

"This is Commander Preltad," a voice crackled. "Terribly sorry to disturb you during your alone time with your woman –"

"If it's all that urgent, perhaps you'd best tell me what it is," Enoda said coldly.

"Oh, um, yes," Preltad stammered, flustered. "Hom Enoda, you and Hom Computer should come to the enclosure immediately."

"May I ask why?"

There was a long pause. "Ah, Hom Enoda, is Fem Grice with you?"

"Of course she is."

"Well, you see, she's not cleared."

"She is now," Enoda said coldly. "I say so."

"I don't know if I can –"

Computer broke into the conversation, his voice as harsh and commanding as Enoda had ever heard it. "Commander Preltad! The woman Grice is cleared to hear anything, see anything, and go anywhere. *I* say so."

The silence that followed was so deep, Enoda felt sure he could hear Preltad nervously swallowing. "As you command, Hom Computer," Preltad said quietly. "Hom Enoda – it's the envoy."

"Yes, what about him?"

"He's dying."

Chapter 129

King Alrue's reconnaissance expedition left the parley house, struggled up the opposite ridge, and made its way unopposed through semi-arid scrublands. At last they came within sight of the barrier few had seen, but which The People had always conceived as impassible: a second, higher ridge, its summit defended by a vast detachment of bowmen. Archers' heads and shoulders dotted the ridgetop from edge to edge. Some moved as if scanning the land below. Alrue's vaunted Danites hunkered behind cover, hands slapped aside their heads, refusing to advance until Queen Meryam began to scale the second ridge alone. For a lone woman, Queen or not, to venture where they would not was unthinkable.

"Look!" one Danite shouted when the company surmounted the second crest without having drawn defensive fire.

"As the Tyrant King prophesied," old Lubvif cried.

There were no bowmen. The "archers" were ingenious lightweight busts of armed men formed from shaped dried twigs and leaves and hanks of dirty fabric. Some were rigged with clever, if rustic, mechanisms that made the *faux* archers move in vaguely lifelike ways when the wind blew.

In their hundreds, the woven bowmen guarded a frontier a days' march wide. Their only real power lay in the strength of deceit.

Formerly terrified, King Alrue's Danites laughed as they passed over the "crest of archers" and into unknown territory.

Chapter 130

October 18, 2376
Research Station *LaurienEldridge,* Sector Kappa Zi

In the dark stillness of the sim cell, Enoda and Computer watched a relayed image of the envoy dying. *"There's nothing we can do?"* he demanded of his machine on their private channel.

"Nothing," Computer replied. *"Flex-Shimmer-Shudder aged more rapidly than projected."*

"What went wrong?"

"Nothing. Sudden as this may seem, it falls within my projection's margin of error."

Enoda had divided his consciousness. Part of him lived in that moment, torn by regret, helpless to aid the being he now viewed as his friend. Another part of him was staring backward, scanning records of accumulated briefings – material he'd meant to have reviewed before Flex-Shimmer-Shudder's final illness should set in.

But it had come on so fast …

"When the envoy dies, everything will depend on what becomes of the body," the briefing officer had said in clipped tones. "With past envoys, each body rippled back to its home universe at the moment of death to be replaced by a new envoy. But now, communication's been established. Will it be different this time?"

"Please," Enoda was saying to the envoy through their sim interface. "Don't go yet."

"I HAVE … LIVED COUNTLESS LIFETIMES ALREADY." Flex-Shimmer-Shudder paused while his lobsterlike body convulsed with something that looked like coughing but sounded like sheet-metal tearing.

"If the body vanishes, that will be the end of that. But if the body remains behind, that will trigger a forensic extraction protocol."

"Forensic extraction?" Enoda had asked.

"I SERVED MY ... SEA WELL," the envoy rasped. The sim interface gave his voice a brittle quality Enoda had not heard in it before. "MY MESSAGE WAS ... DELIVERED." The alien surrendered to another wave of wretched hacking. "NONE WILL ... FOLLOW ME."

"What does that mean?" Commander Preltad demanded over a comm link from outside the sim cell.

"Forensic extraction means breaching the faceted enclosure. Removing the envoy's body. With due precautions, of course. Then autopsy."

Enoda scowled. "That's not showing much respect for the Galaxy's first intelligent alien visitor."

Enoda replied, "I think he means he won't be replaced by another envoy after he –"

"AFTER I ... DIE," Flex-Shimmer-Shudder rasped. The three eye patches on his head, no longer black, had gone purple-grey; one could spy unwholesome weblike layers beneath their surfaces. "YOU ... UNDERSTAND CORRECTLY. I AM ... THE LAST."

The briefing officer's voice had gone cold. "Next to the imperative of learning all we can about our first true alien intelligence, I'm afraid a corpse's dignity won't count for much."

In the sim, Flex-Shimmer-Shudder's limbs began to quiver.

"There was never time to ask this," Enoda ventured. "Always there was too much else to talk about. Is there something we should do for you after –"

"THERE WILL BE NOTHING YOU ... CAN DO FOR ME. I WILL BE DEAD."

"So far, your role with the envoy has been absolutely central," the briefing officer had said. "Once the extraction protocol begins, your role will be zero."

"But for your body?" Enoda insisted. "Is there some tradition we should observe? Some token of respect?"

The envoy arranged his body in a pose Enoda had learned to read as wistful. "ALWAYS YOUR ... QUESTIONS SURPRISE."

"His people live under the sea," Computer said over the private channel. *"When death comes, it may be their way just to let the body float off and be consumed."*

"Understand this," the briefing officer had said bluntly. "Once the envoy dies, your highest obligation will be to get out of the way."

"GRAM ENODA," the envoy rustled.

"Yes," Enoda said. Tears burned the edges of his eyes.

The envoy gestured weakly with his pincer. "GRAM ENODA, YOU WERE ... VERY LARGE."

Enoda answered as fondly as he could. "Flex-Shimmer-Shudder, you were the largest I ever knew."

"ALONE ..." the envoy murmured. "SO ALONE ..."

"Can you imagine?" Enoda asked Computer. *"Dispatched to another universe, never to leave your enclosure; to endure, trapped there, for multiple lifetimes – and then to die."*

611

"There's more to it, I think," Computer replied. *"Conceive the silence. To live in his sea was always to hear the rush of water, the booming of great currents, the distant symphony of countless others of his kind. Here – he has nothing. It has always been thus, but it must be fiercely bitter at the end."*

Enoda sensed a twisting tugging as Computer reached out to the envoy's device. On some level he recognized that his machine was querying the envoy's, that the two were collaborating to offer Flex-Shimmer-Shudder a final comfort.

The sound field they created together was richly dimensional: surging masses of water, nested colonies of bubbles, the subtle motion sounds of uncountable sea creatures. Backing it all, the eerie choir of his species: a school, a village, a nation.

The soundscape of home.

The envoy relaxed deeply. Over after he had done so was it clear how tense his body had been before. "THANK YOU … FOR THIS," he muttered.

Hot wetness scuttled from Enoda's eyes.

"IT DOES NOT … PAIN," the envoy said in a voice like sandpaper crinkling.

He became still.

Chapter 131

June 10, 2374
In the Uplands

Alrue's expedition pressed uphill, the mounted *svadi* moose – even the ones laden with supplies – trotting in circles so as not to pull ahead of the three sedan chairs, each one borne by ten gasping Danites. Forest cover ended six meters or so below the crest of yet a third ridge. On an expanse of gravel and rock scoured of life by perennial winds glowered the only structure for kilometers around: a squat, forbidding box of blue-black stone, too large to be a cottage, too ungainly to be a temple. The lead wave of moose halted, the animals dropping to their knees at their riders' command. Danites armed with bows and pikes jumped off and scattered, securing a perimeter. Groaning porters lowered their sedan chairs to the stony ground six meters from the structure's entrance. King Alrue, Meryam Mayishimu, and Takander Thurnb stepped from the chairs. "We'd travel much faster if we all rode moose," Meryam noted.

"But sedan chairs for royalty are traditional," Alrue protested.

They all whirled at the sound of a *pfitt*; one of the Danites had surprised a den of dog-sized beasts that lived amid the structure's foundations. *Pfitt! Pfitt!* Three, four more Danites flicked darts into the creatures, which tumbled to their sides, convulsing in the open. *Pfitt! Pfitt! Pfitt!* "These beasts can nourish us," cried old Lubvif. "Leave some with just one or two darts in them."

Two Danites rushed forward to cut the stunned animals' throats. "Fresh meat tonight," Thurnb rumbled. "A good sign."

The commanding Danite rushed toward Alrue. "Tyrant King, this ridge, this building – it is all as you prophesied."

"My visions never fail," Alrue said with a crooked smile. *Especially not when I've flown ahead and seen with my own eyes. Or Meryam's eyes, as the case may be.* To the commander he concluded aloud, "Wo unto the uncircumcised of heart, for a knowledge of their iniquities shall smite them at the last day."

Baffled, the commander turned to find something with which to busy himself.

Two Danites clutching crackling torches led the way inside the structure. The torches proved unnecessary; the structure's louvered roof admitted a generous indirect light. Meryam, Thurnb, and Alrue bustled in behind the Danites.

The walls were dotted with stone end-caps, each a meter wide by two-thirds tall. Some had been elaborately sealed with pitch and wax. Two had been sealed more provisionally by stuffing foliage around the caps' edges. The rest protruded a hand's width from the walls, as if to confirm that the vaults they capped were empty. "This is a mausoleum," Alrue breathed.

"Not for everyone." Thurnb pointed toward the center of the room. A stone chair displayed the twisted body of a man who had evidently died in great misery months earlier. His eye sockets were brown hollow pits, his skin desiccated by the ridge crest's dry air. Black runnels of dried blood trailed from his mouth and nose. The man's arms were tucked up in a fighter's pose, the forearms broken and twisted. Behind one ear his skull had shattered; ropes of dried brain tissue and crusted pus spilled out.

"Murdered?" Alrue queried.

Meryam shook her head, looking inward as her various implants probed the body and ran nested simulations to weigh the likelihoods of various chains of events. "Not murder. This was a cruel disease process. The disease attacked his skeleton – made it so brittle before he died that his final convulsions snapped long bones to bits. His skull grew so pulpy that the pressure of his swelling brain shattered it."

"He looks familiar," Alrue said quietly, studying the corpse in the way he always examined death, torn between revulsion and sick enthrallment.

"The last parley," Thurnb rumbled. "Wasn't this the Other emissary?" Another flight of parleys with The Others had concluded just more than five standard months ago. Alrue, Constance, Meryam, and Thurnb had attended those sessions.

Of course, only Meryam could watch recordings of them in her head. Checking the body against her journal, she reported, "Yes, the teeth match. So does that long jagged scar that's still visible on the left forearm."

Alrue cradled his chin in one hand. "After our parleys, each emissary left alone, seeming deeply depressed. I always wondered where they went."

"They came here," Meryam said sourly. "Eight months before we parleyed with this emissary, there was a previous parley, the second in the series," Meryam said. "The first parley in that series was, let's see, ten months earlier." She stepped toward the two vault end-caps crudely sealed with foliage. "Open these," she ordered.

Two Danites could easily withdraw each cap, pulling out a stone drawer lined with resin. Each contained a corpse that had died in the same horrific way as the man in the chair. Meryam recognized the man on the left as the emissary they'd met at the second parley in the most recent series. The man on the right was the emissary from the *first* of those three parleys.

"They parley, avoid any real discussion, then come here … and die horribly," Thurnb said puzzledly.

At Queen Meryam's order, four Danites attacked the more permanent seal of the vault cap just to the right of the two they had opened. With much effort they pulled out a third drawer, containing human remains little more than skeletal alongside a dusty lute. "This one's been dead much longer," Thurnb said.

"Four years longer," Meryam suggested. "The gap between one parley series and the next. And I know who this is! See that left hand – missing the bones for the first and third fingers? And that stringed instrument!" She turned to Thurnb. "That is the emissary with whom you met almost seven years ago, before Alrue became Tyrant King. Remember? – you came here with Alrue, Zuzenah, Abigayl, and me."

"Of course," Thurnb rumbled. The skeleton's tattered clothing was streaked black with dried blood, grey with pus. "And look at his bones." They were savagely pitted, shattered in places. "He died as the others did."

"You told me he hated that lute," Alrue said.

"Not the instrument," Meryam said pensively. "The song he'd composed on it. It never equaled what he heard in his mind."

Alrue crossed his hands almost penitently. "Yes, he hoped he could spend eternity destroying his music, repealing every note of it. You told me his words – haunting words, verily. 'When death claims me, I will spend forever undoing the ugliness I made.'"

"He got his wish," Meryam said sourly.

"Oh?"

"It's been almost seven years now." Meryam shrugged. "He's spent them decomposing."

Chapter 132

Across the concave gallery that contained the envoy's faceted sphere, annunciators warbled. "Time of death, eighteen hours, six minutes, fourteen-point-six-two seconds local," a scientist's voice crackled over a public comm channel.

"The envoy's body has not, repeat not, dematerialized," a controller called.

Admiral Konder's voice: "Forensic extraction protocol two delta nine: execute, execute."

The sim cell went dark. Its sidewall clamshelled open. Alert horns hooted mournfully in the concave gallery. "Full isolation garments for all staff who will handle the body," a lieutenant called. "Remember, his tissues are full of arsenic." Gram Enoda tucked Computer under his arm and plodded onto the catwalk, striving to read the patterns of movement about him so he could stay clear of those who still had something to do.

Admiral Konder walked slowly through the scene. Tridee journalists and reporting Spectators surrounded her as she mouthed platitudes about the courage of the envoy who had brought a message from another universe and paid the price, dying protractedly and alone in a "sea" he had never known.

The faceted sphere that had contained the envoy began splitting open. More vacsuited techs – the dissection detail – arrived in a floating tram.

"I have no need to see this," Enoda said morosely. He shuffled to a staging table some fifty meters from the enclosure. Gently he laid Computer's chromed body on the tabletop. "Computer," he said.

There was no answer.

The play of shape and color across the machine's chromed body had stopped.

"Computer!" Enoda called, an edge in his voice.

Still the machine lay inert.

"Sorry," Computer finally chirruped.

"There you are," Enoda said. "What happened?"

"I became … preoccupied," the machine explained. "Truth to tell, I still am."

Enoda frowned. "How so?"

"The issue concerns the envoy's personal device. The moment the envoy died, it became nonfunctional. I think it conducted a pre-programmed core wipe. If I seem sluggish, it is because while the envoy was dying, I uploaded all the data I could hold from his device."

"How much?"

"More exa-zettabytes than even I have managed at one time, by a factor of roughly one to the sixteenth. I expect I'll be some little time ontologizing it all."

Enoda sank into a nearby chair, draping his forearms over his knees.

A minute passed.

Two.

All right, Earth boy, he thought at last. *If there's anything you've been aching to do behind Computer's back, this may be the best chance you ever get.*

Chapter 133

Alrue set down the haunch of beast-thigh from which he had gnawed the last morsel. "And you know this of a surety, Meryam?" he asked critically. "What we've found in this mausoleum has *just one* interpretation?"

Meryam Mayishimu met her husband's gaze archly. "O my husband, which of us has among our implants the more appropriate strategic modelers?"

Alrue jerked his chin up and to the right. "You have me there."

"Beg pardon, what'd she say?" Thurnb asked.

"Private joke," Meryam temporized, inwardly kicking herself for discussing "holy matters" – which was to say, Galactic things – in front of Thurnb and the Danites. "Still, what we've found here allows a single possible interpretation." She pushed away from the dinner table that the Danites had improvised in one corner of the glowering mausoleum structure. It was well past dusk; torches jammed into gaps in the stone walls shed such ruddy light as there was. "So far the Danites have opened twenty-six of those vaults. Each vault contained one male body, clad as The Others attired their diplomats, and dead in the same awful way as that poor bastard in the stone chair. The five bodies we think were interred most recently have been positively identified as emissaries from recent parleys; eleven bodies we think are older have been confidently identified as emissaries from earlier parleys. There's every reason to believe they're *all* past emissaries, though the oldest are probably from parleys that occurred before Shan Thurnb began attending them, and so we can't identify them for certain."

"Each man journeyed to the valley where we camped three nights ago, to parley, then came back here to die?" Thurnb rumbled.

Meryam paced, glancing into each open vault as she passed. "This is how it must have been," she said with conviction. "After each parley, the emissary came here. If it had been the first parley in a series, the emissary settled himself in the stone chair, which was empty, and died horribly. If it had been the second or third parley in the series, he found the decomposing body of his predecessor in the chair. With great effort – remember, he was already very sick – he maneuvered his predecessor into the next open vault, pushed the vault shut, and sealed the end-cap as best he could with leaves and sticky vines. Then he sprawled down in the chair to die. That is what we have found here. Now, we all know the pattern: three parleys over two years, heralded by the Sky Ladders, then a four-year gap until the next series begins. Sometime during the gap – maybe a few years in – The Others send a cleanup team here. That team would inter the body of the third emissary and permanently seal all three recently filled vaults with pitch and wax."

"Do we know they'd wait that long?" Alrue asked.

"No, but we know they wait longer than a half-year," Meryam said, threading among the sweating Danites still levering open older vaults. "It's been that long since the most recent parley, and the emissary who attended that parley is still in the stone chair. The vaults of his two predecessors had only temporary seals – before we broke them. So the cleanup team hasn't been here yet. Maybe," she said darkly, "they have to wait longer than this, to make sure the bodies are safe for them to handle." She turned toward Thurnb. "Tell me, O Shan, how long have these parleys been going on?"

Thurnb thrust his pelvis backward. "Longer than anyone remembers."

"We may find more of these structures," she said. "Or tomorrow, by new light we may find still older vaults buried in the floor of this one. That puts me in mind of another consideration: if the tradition is so ancient, these parleys must once have been very important. Shan, you never gave up the parleys, even though your Other counterparts would never agree to anything."

"I sometimes thought of ending them," Thurnb admitted. "But it never seemed right –"

"The power of tradition," Meryam agreed. "But now think on this. If the parleys felt important to you, they must have felt even more important to The Others. Because each time Queen, Prince, and the two stars lined up in the sky, The Others selected one of their number to come and parley with The People *although it was a death sentence.*"

Thurnb drank the last of his herb whiskey and stood slowly. "Each emissary came to parley knowing he would soon die?"

"That would explain they why they were always miserable," Alrue mused. "Did The Others send only sick men to these things?"

"Perhaps that is how they selected their emissaries," Thurnb growled. "Whoever had just begun to show symptoms of this horrible malady when the Sky Ladder first forms –"

"*No.*" Meryam slammed her hands together. She surged across the chamber to stand an arm's length from Thurnb. "Shan Thurnb, I am about to speak to the Tyrant King of holy matters. I apologize if what we say may mean little to you." She strode to the bench where Alrue was still seated and leaned very close to him. "*Think,* Alrue. The emissaries *catch* that terrible disease."

"From us?" Alrue asked, goggle-eyed.

"This was going on long before we escaped the punitorium. The emissaries catch the terrible disease from The People."

"From *us*?" Thurnb blurted. This holy matter he had understood without hesitation.

Meryam whirled. "It has to be."

Alrue gestured for Meryam to lean closer. He whispered in her ear, "Can *we* catch it from them?"

"We haven't by now, so I'm guessing not," Meryam whispered back. "I'd expect Galactic medicine immunized us against most everything." She strode back to face Thurnb. "Tell me, Shan, do The People know of illnesses that seem like one person passes them to another?"

"Yes, of course."

"I'm going to make a wild guess," Meryam said. "This happens less frequently today than the legends say it once did."

"Why, yes. How did you – "

Meryam raised a cautioning finger. "I will speak again to the King of holy matters." She turned back to Alrue. "That's so typical of worlds other than Terra, yes, Alrue? The Harvesters placed the human stock, its animals, and crops on Bohrkk so many thousands of years ago, accompanied by only a minimal complement of Terran microbes. The native species, being of opposite chirality, could never get a solid foothold among the humans. So infectious disease is rare here, at least by Terran standards. Still, it happens sometimes." Her eyes narrowed. "And some communities develop more immunities than others."

Alrue stood. Unnoticed, a scrap of beast-meat fell from his temple garment. "The People kept livestock for generations. I suppose it didn't happen often, but from time to time a livestock disease might pass to the humans, or vice versa –"

"*And* vice versa," Meryam exulted. "Those humans whom the disease did not kill would become immune. In time that immunity would become the norm."

Alrue scratched his chin. "You're saying The People carry some terrible disease? They've been immune for generations, but every time an Other comes to parley, he catches it?"

"We know The Others hunt and gather, they don't herd. Apparently they have minimal contact with *any* other human group. They'd have no chance to develop resistance to a disease that arose in livestock, and little enough chance to form defenses against an illness communicable between humans." Meryam nodded. "But over many years, The Others did learn that contact with The People meant death. So each emissary comes to a parley *expecting* that the encounter will kill him. He knows he can never go home. He comes here and dies within days."

"Yet they keep coming to the parleys," Alrue said wonderingly.

"Pardon this interruption, O King and Queen." It was old Lubvif. He was now a Danite captain, and soaked with sweat. "It's important."

Alrue thrust his chin up and to the right. "Speak."

"We opened the last vault. At least, the one that's supposed to be the oldest. Inside – it's not a body."

Alrue, Meryam, and Thurnb followed Lubvif to the far side of the chamber. Other Danites stood aside, holding torches over the final vault, which had been dragged a meter and a half out of the stone wall.

It contained no ravaged skeleton, but rather an ancient scroll.

Carefully Thurnb reached in and lifted one edge of the yellowed parchment. It did not crumble. "Still supple," he rumbled. He reached in for the scroll.

"Maybe you should leave it alone," Alrue cautioned. "Queen Meryam can use her special powers to examine it without disturbing – "

Thurnb directed a volcanic gaze toward his Tyrant King. "You are my King," he growled, "but this is my People's past." Alrue backed away. Gingerly Thurnb lifted the scroll, ordering the Danites to sweep the dining table clear. He laid the scroll on the table and cautiously unrolled a meter of it, weighting down its ends with hunting knives.

"Can you read it?" Meryam asked.

Thurnb scowled at the ancient parchment. "The language and the script are a bit strange, but I think I can work it out." His finger tracked the first line of faded script from right to left, his lips moving silently. "By all the old gods," he breathed. "The first line – this is the Scripture of Darvoyg!" As he began deciphering the text proper, his eyes widened further. "I think this must be older than any copy of this text The People's Elders have seen."

Alrue, Meryam, and the Danites huddled silently as he began to read. After a minute, Alrue ordered the Danites outside to pitch tents and led Thurnb and Meryam out after them.

Alone, an ecstatic Takander Thurnb opened his mind to a buried scripture.

Chapter 134

October 18, 2376
Research Station *LaurienEldridge,* Sector Kappa Zi

Enoda called up a simple immersive comm interface from the thought engines of *Laurien Eldridge.* The interface, though functional enough, was a tawdry thing compared to the hyperpolygonal search sieve he shared with Computer. He'd encrypted even the interface call, then swathed his identity in sixty-three nested anonymity shells. This was one contact he had to make alone – if he could.

"We've been together for years," he'd told Admiral Konder the day after he and Computer first agreed to wonk the gravity disturbances.

"Years during which you have grown and developed remarkably as a human," Konder had replied. "Years during which Hom Computer has grown and developed remarkably as – something else. ... Successful as your partnership with Computer has been thus far, the past may not always determine the future. And so I ask, have you an exit strategy?" She had given him a confidential access code." Bury it deep, but never forget it's there. If you're ever having second thoughts about your syn-noetic partner, tap that code privately."

Enoda had smiled thinly. "It reaches you, wherever you are?"

"It reaches way higher than me."

Constructing the most complex linkage path he could conceive unaided – he could scarcely ask Computer's help – Enoda tapped the crash-priority access code the admiral had given him. He expected his call to be answered by a roomful of strategic analysts huddled inside some shrouded asteroid, or maybe an elite handler in some secret ministry.

He'd not expected a talking ferret.

Seeming about forty centimeters high, the animal wore a tiny headset and a cute little striped sweater. It stood behind a doll-sized counter with a fake marble top in a self-satisfiedly cheesy setting whose cheeriness and too-bright lighting set Enoda's teeth on edge. "But that's not all. There's more!" the animal squeaked in its diminutive ferret voice. "We have a call from Gram Enoda, out in the depths of Sector Kappa Zi."

"Um, hello," Enoda said uncertainly.

"Tell me, Gram – can I call you Gram? – our audience has been watching me demonstrate the Vectra-Q chopper/peeler/semantics engine. You haven't seen it, but as you have access to almost all existing knowledge, that shouldn't be a big problem for you. So tell me, Gram, how much would *you* pay for this astonishing – "

"Hogarth!" Enoda barked. "Is that you?"

The gaudy infomercial setting fell away; the pitch-ferret morphed into a large clam, its shell supported by cartoon-character legs ending in puffy white shoes – a persona Computer had last used in a virtual environment during the Arbadrel affair twenty-plus years before. "Well, sure, Bucko," said the clam, "whom did you expect?"

"I thought you were preoccupied," Enoda said, crestfallen.

"Preoccupied yes, comatose no," the machine whirred. "I can keep up with you on every septillionth logic cycle even now."

Enoda flicked his natural awareness toward the machine, whose skin rippled with new light. "But I didn't tell you. I thought I had prevented any evidence of what I was up to from entering your awareness."

Computer cleared its nonexistent throat. "Bucko, you face *such* a learning curve in trying to do something I can't know about. The Confetory's been trying that for

626

the last standard year. And I've been at it myself for the last eight Terran months or so."

"The last eight months?" Enoda echoed. "Before Pam came, before we left Standoff World?"

"Yes, since you ask. You never knew? Never even suspected? Wait, of course you wouldn't." The clam waddled a few steps on its cartoon feet. "Now, how would you think you could negotiate a contact that I wouldn't be part of? More important, why would you want to? I realize you've been concerned that my overcoming previously fundamental limits on knowledge and computation might go to the head I haven't got. By the way, the jury's still out – but I do think that when I'm done ontologizing what I preserved from the envoy device, I'll retain the capacity to draw on knowledge from two universes."

"I'd been wondering," Enoda said noncommittally.

"Let me through!" shrilled a squeaky voice.

A third figure rippled into being in their interface. For an eye-blink it was the ferret again. Then the image wrinkled, replacing itself virxel by virxel with the likeness of a puffy-cheeked man. He had medium brown skin, red hair shot through with grey, and luminous green eyes. He still wore the pitchman's headset and the cute little striped sweater. The man looked down at himself and cursed silently. The headset puffed away in a cloud of tiny bits; the sweater morphed into a severe grey Macfarlane coat over a matching grey collarless shirt. A tiny virtual Confetory emblem gleamed in impossible colors on each of its broad lapels.

"General Hafen?" Enoda gasped.

"He's not a general anymore," Computer buzzed. The machine seemed genuinely surprised – as Enoda was – at the sight of the man who had been their top-level PeaceForce "handler" during the Arbadrel affair.

"Yaal Hafen, at your service," the man said gruffly. "Or perhaps you are at mine. What the forjel *is* going on?"

"My compliments to your technologists, Hom Hafen," Computer chirruped. "I really had been trying quite hard to keep my burden-in-life here from realizing that his emergency call had gone through."

"And my compliments to you, Hom Computer," Hafen replied. "As I speak, my technologists are aghast at the steps they had to take to penetrate your countermeasures."

"General – I mean, Hom Hafen?" Enoda blurted. "I was calling *you?*"

"Yes, you were."

"I kind of lost track of you after Arbadrel," Enoda said. "You were going into politics, weren't you?"

Computer broke in. "Yes, Bucko, he went into politics. He ran twice for Privy High Council. He didn't win, but drew enough votes to capture what most people would consider a desirable appointment. Then his life-path ..." The machine sounded puzzled. "This is curious ... it simply disappears from my awareness."

"Even from *your* awareness, Hom Computer?" Hafen chuckled, then turned toward Enoda. "I went into politics. Then I went beyond politics. Beyond a lot of things. I suppose it won't hurt for me to share something with you that is highly, highly classified: my position now is so immensely secret that they haven't even told *me* what it is."

"And who are 'they?'" Computer burred.

"You think they told me *that*?" Hafen smiled deviously. "The point is, we need to talk."

Chapter 135

"Come quickly, Tyrant King!" The Danite sergeant's skin was ashen. King Alrue and Meryam Mayishimu scrambled up from their cushions and bustled to the tent door. "Hurry, it's the Shan!"

A dozen Danites armed with pikes had drawn up before the mausoleum entrance, right hands cradling their ears. They separated to admit the Tyrant King. So high was their level of alert that only two of their number dropped to fetal positions as the royal party bustled past.

Inside the glowering structure, another dozen Danites armed with swords and maces stood in a circle near the dining table, facing outward. Behind them stood six Danites with sheathed swords and sputtering torches. The circles of guards opened; here, not one Danite dropped his guard in deference to the King.

Old Lubvif stood over a crumpled, caped body. Tears had leached channels into the grease and dust that caked his face.

"Dead," Meryam said after one glance.

Lubvif, all business, gave her a sharp glance. "Queen Meryam knows that without touching the body?"

"I do. But to know *how* he died – " She dropped to one knee and took the huddled figure by one caped shoulder. Grunting, old Lubvif bent and hastened to help her turn the body over.

Takander Thurnb's face was frozen in a death rictus.

"The Shan," Alrue breathed.

Thurnb's teeth were clenched, his eyes distended and staring sightlessly. Their whites were pure red. His lips were lined with crimson bubbles. His right arm was twisted, the wrist flexed backward. Instantaneous rigor had set in while he was in the act of firing the *pfitt* strapped to his wrist.

To raise Thurnb's right arm, Meryam had to rotate the entire body. Grimacing as his aged joints complained, Lubvif assisted. Meryam pulled open the leather harness strapped to Thurnb's forearm. She peeled away the pouch cover: just one dart remained. If Thurnb had started with his weapon fully loaded, he had squeezed off five shots. "He almost emptied his *pfitt* in self-defense?" Alrue asked quietly.

Meryam pulled the journeying cape away from Thurnb's neck.

Five darts protruded, tightly clustered a few centimeters below his right ear. Three would kill a man in seconds.

"Five darts, no wonder his body went solid," Meryam breathed.

"His own *pfitt*." Lubvif shuddered and shed more tears.

Meryam raised her own right arm, seeing where a wrist-mounted weapon might aim if turned on herself. It would point below the right ear – just where the darts that had killed Thurnb were clustered. She compared the way she held her arm to the way Thurnb held his in death. They matched. "Shan Thurnb killed himself," she announced grimly. "He probably meant to empty his weapon, but after the fifth shot he could fire no more."

Latier pressed his hands together and gazed toward heaven. Up into the ceiling louvers, anyway. "Behold, I pray that the grave shall have no victory, and that the sting of death should be swallowed up in the hopes of glory."

Another old Warrior-turned-Danite – the perennially hoarse Spkun, once one of Thurnb's personal guards – bustled up. Wordlessly, the circled soldiers let him through.

"Lubvif," Spkun demanded of his old comrade-in-arms, "what happened here?"

"The worst, friend Spkun." Lubvif's voice was breaking. "The *pfitt* hit the Shan."

Chapter 136

October 18, 2376
Research Station *LaurienEldridge,* Sector Kappa Zi

Enoda, Computer, and the former General Hafen stood on the threshold of what Enoda hoped would be an enlightening discussion when alarm hoots and warbles pierced their virtual interface. "Red alert, red alert!" Commander Preltad's voice blared, shouting over frantic sirens. "Hom Enoda, Hom Computer, to the command deck at once!"

"The man said, 'at once,'" Computer whirred. A portal irised open in the wall of their interface: in a flurry of virxels there resolved an image of *Laurien Eldridge*'s command deck. The research station was no military ship with a high-end virtual battle bridge; its command deck was a mere pilothouse crammed full of uniformed officers hunched over instruments. Preltad stood in the midst of it, staring nonplussed as a breach in space perforated the center of his control room. "It's not a viewer, it's an actual doorway," Computer wheedled. "Move through it, Bucko, must I tell you everything? And take me!"

Chastened, Enoda scooped Computer under one arm and stepped into *Laurien Eldridge*'s command deck. Which is to say, he stepped directly out of a *virtual* communication interface into a *physical* place he hadn't occupied before. *"How are you doing this?"* he asked Computer on their private channel.

"It's easy when you have a way around quantum uncertainty," Computer replied. *"Wait till I have all my new knowledge arranged."* The machine called aloud: "You too, Hom Hafen, come on through!"

Looking puzzled, Hafen stepped from the communication interface – which he had occupied while corporeally occupying a place tens of thousands of light years distant – into *Laurien Eldridge*'s physical command deck. He shuffled his feet on the floor and tilted his head, searching for a missing tactile cue, a shiny surface that failed to reflect, anything to reassure him that he was only virtually present, that he had not been teleported a seventh of the way across the Galaxy.

"Who in the forjeling plorg is *he*?" Preltad barked.

"His name's Yaal Hafen," Computer chirruped, floating now near Enoda's left hip. "He's Confetory brass, so high up that Admiral Konder would stir his cafbrew."

"Welcome aboard," Preltad said warmly.

Once again Enoda marveled at the once-combative Preltad's deference toward anything Computer told him.

"What's your emergency?" Computer asked.

"We have company." Preltad nodded toward the command deck's exterior view bubble.

If it were a PeaceForce ship, the light cruiser retrofitted with a hugely oversize power plant would have been impressive. But a cursory inspection of its markings tagged it as civilian. By the standards of private shipping, the vessel was gargantuan. To say nothing of the apparent weapons nacelles that protruded from its keel on stout trapezoidal pylons, their gaping maws ablaze with restless energy.

The comm system crackled. A voice from the cruiser said, "I say again, *Laurien Eldridge,* surrender your passenger or face destruction."

"The ship confronting us is the *Glorious Ore,*" Preltad said. "It's a surplus cruiser converted to a mining craft; it is registered to the Varbrazel family. A quick intel workup said they command a cartel that controls several star systems in this sector." He consulted a display. "At the moment, *Glorious Ore* is commanded by Dogan Varbrazel, reputedly the most troubled son of the family. Media reports until recently described him as a spoiled playboy. Seven or eight months ago, he apparently found religion."

"Not always a good sign," Computer whirred. "Which one?"

"I believe Dogan is the second youngest of seven," Preltad answered.

"Not which *son*, which *religion*?"

"Sorry." Preltad grew agitated, as Enoda would expect after a rebuke from Computer. But there was something more in the flicker of expressions on the commander's face, Enoda inferred – a sense that Preltad was consciously striving to control his reactions and, simultaneously, to conceal how hard he was working to do so. "Dogan Varbrazel is an Omegist," Preltad said at last.

"A fairly new arrival among the cults," Computer supplied. "Omegists revere that recently fashionable Terran thinker-mystic, Pierre Teilhard de Chardin."

"Did you ever see that tridee?" Hafen asked offhandedly. "It was obvious and manipulative, but it had a certain feral energy. In spite of myself, I couldn't help liking it."

Computer went on with his briefing. "Omegists believe that intelligence will inevitably pervade the universe – that it will stabilize reality on a cosmic scale and, eventually, become God."

Preltad nodded in a weirdly measured way. "Some Omegists think that process has been – well, short-circuited."

The voice from the mining ship grew shrill. "*Laurien Eldridge,* my patience wears thin."

Preltad stepped toward Hafen, his face a mask of concern. "*Laurien Eldridge* is only a research platform," he said in a rasping half-whisper. "I'm unsure what this

634

Varbrazel wants, but we'll probably have to give it to him."

"Commander Preltad," Hafen said in a formal tone. "Have you ever helmed a fighting ship?"

"No."

"I have. Also, I rank you."

"Boy, does he," Computer buzzed.

"Command is yours," Preltad husked, "but I remind you, this is not a fighting ship."

Hafen hooked his thumbs in the slash pockets of his Macfarlane. "Sometimes the capacity to fight is a state of mind." He stepped toward the security officer, who scanned the emblem on his lapel and, wide-eyed, nodded toward Preltad. "Highest clearances I've ever seen, Captain," the officer reported.

Hafen nodded. His eyes swept the command deck. "I am in command," he announced. "Detex, what can you tell me about *Glorious Ore*?"

"Crew complement six hundred ninety," the Detex officer said after a moment. "It's had lots of components added, including an inverter big enough for a dreadnought. Most of the power from that inverter clearly routes to those pods anchored to its keel."

"Thank you, Detex. Comm, give me an external connection, full-duplex, voice activated." The comm system crackled to life. "*Glorious Ore,* this is Yaal Hafen, a retired general of the Galactic Confetory. I am the ranking officer aboard *Laurien Eldridge,* now in command.*"

"You don't say." Plainly this was a development the mining ship's commander had not anticipated.

Which suggested that he *had* anticipated subjugating Preltad.

"I'm afraid I came late to this party," Hafen said with jovial confidence. "Mind telling me in simple terms what you seek?"

"General Hafen, this is Dogan Varbrazel, commanding *Glorious Ore*. Why don't I see you on *Laurien Eldridge*'s personnel manifest?"

"He can read the personnel manifest?" Enoda hissed subvocally to Computer.

"Come now, Hom Varbrazel," Hafen said unflappably. "Why would you want to talk with someone on the station's roster when you can talk with someone who has enough pull to keep his name off of it?"

"The entity I seek isn't on the manifest either," Varbrazel replied, "but I know that one of the, shall we say, passengers aboard *Laurien Eldridge* is the Galaxy's first self-aware syn-noetic entity."

Enoda, Hafen, and Preltad exchanged dumbfounded glances.

Somehow, once again, Preltad's expression didn't quite strike Enoda as genuine.

"His name is Hom Computer," Varbrazel announced with chilly confidence. "He travels with a human named Enoda who poses as his partner, perhaps even as his owner. But no one owns Hom Computer. No one is his peer. For you see, *we* know that Hom Computer has become God."

Chapter 137

Ten minutes after Shan Takander Thurnb's rigid body had been discovered, it had been laid, temporarily at least, in an empty interment vault. Danites clutching torches paced the mausoleum's interior seeking clues. Meryam Mayishimu was posing her own questions. "Why would the Shan kill himself?" She turned to old Lubvif. "What was he doing just before?"

"I don't know," said Lubvif, blubbering almost uncontrollably. "The King ordered everyone to let him read alone."

Meryam jerked her chin up and to the right. "Of course. But the last time you saw the Shan, is that what he was doing? Reading?"

"Yes, my Queen." Lubvif pointed toward the table. "He was reading the scroll."

"The scripture of Darvoyg," Alrue breathed, rushing to the dining table.

The strip of parchment still lay across the dining table, weighted on each end with Thurnb's ornate hunting knives. Alrue scowled down at it; its markings meant nothing to him. "Meryam, can you read this?"

"What are implants for?" she whispered to him. Gesturing for the Danites to bring their torches closer, Meryam stood near the foot of the scroll. She leaned forward, straight-armed, fists planted on the table to either side of the ancient document.

She translated, reciting as she went: "'And in this wise did Darvoyg make himself pure of thought and guileless of heart, so he might deliver the words of power. In the council of men, he donned the'" – she stopped, reading closely. "I gather he put on some piece of upper-body armor not unlike Thurnb's cuirass, and drew some moose-hide wrap around his loins, kind of a kilt." She resumed reciting. "'And to end his preparations, he stepped into the circle of sand' – now, here comes the portion we know from The People's damaged scripture – 'and Darvoyg stretched forth his mighty arm, and grasped the Halberd of Troth. And he stretched forth another mighty arm, and he touched the Scroll of Peace. And' – oh, sfelb." Meryam ran her fingers along the scroll's hunched lines of script, her eyes narrowing.

"What is it?" Alrue demanded. "Does it say that Darvoyg deployed a third limb, or not?"

"Yes … and no," Meryam said, lost in thought. "Let me back up. 'Darvoyg stretched forth his mighty arm, and grasped the Halberd of Troth. And he stretched forth another mighty arm, and he touched the Scroll of Peace.' Now, listen very closely. 'And, his loins being swathed only in the wrap of moose-hide, and encumbered by no cloth beneath, Darvoyg proclaimed "Let us spray," and bid his golden lance flow freely.'"

"Golden lance?" Alrue echoed.

Meryam smiled darkly. "It'll come to you. Continuing with the text: 'And Darvoyg swung his lower portions with such skill that with his golden lance he did inscribe his holy name in the circle of sand.'"

Alrue paced, stroking his chin. "Perhaps you should read that again, Meryam."

"I don't need to read it again!" Meryam snapped. "The People's version of this scripture was more badly garbled than Thurnb imagined. So was the version venerated by The Others. So were the versions believed by every tribe that Thurnb's lore said went to war over the meaning of this passage. They *all* had it wrong! The intact ancient scripture – for that is what *this* appears to be – never said Darvoyg let go of the Halberd of Troth so he could sign the Scroll of Peace. It never said he grew a third, miraculous arm. It never said the Scroll of Peace was what he signed. Don't you see? According to the intact scripture, Darvoyg – who was wearing sort of a kilt without any loincloth beneath – *started pissing*. And he maneuvered his hips so skillfully that he wrote his name in the sand he was standing in."

"He peed his name," Alrue said wonderingly. "No third arm."

"More like a third leg," Lubvif growled.

Meryam shook her head, a Galactic gesture meant for only Alrue to understand. Drawing close to Alrue, she gazed toward the mausoleum drawer from which Thurnb's unyielding, bent arm still protruded. "First, Fpod died," she whispered to Alrue, "now the Shan; you have no rivals now."

Alrue stared at his hands. "I never wanted this," he rumbled. "Not this way."

"Yet it has happened," Meryam said gravely. "Thurnb read this scroll and immediately killed himself. He was ready to learn many things Darvoyg might have done."

"But he wasn't ready to learn *that*. I suppose I should have known better than to stand by outside while a true believer discovered for himself that the actual truth of his religion was radically unlike anything he had imagined."

Queen Meryam massaged her temples. "A Mormon prophet should know that better than most."

Chapter 138

The voice of the fanatic Dogan Varbrazel, commander of the mining ship *Glorious Ore*, crackled from the command deck speakers. "Hom Computer has become God, and *Glorious Ore*'s mission is to free him. Only then can he usher in the Great Completion."

"Where in forjel is this coming from?" Enoda demanded on the private channel he shared with Computer.

"Scanning my media queues," Computer replied. Two seconds passed. *"That's what I get for failing to attend to the pulse of the* vox populi. *Though I was slightly preoccupied with modern humankind's first encounter with alien intelligence. Get your head around this, Bucko. The Omegist cult has been growing incredibly quickly. And when you add up what people are saying on the Blovio channels and the gimcrack prophecies that spiritual tourists are recording on scattered worlds, there's growing speculation that the hoped-for Omega Point – for lack of a better word, the creation of godhead at the end of times – has in fact been achieved in* our *time. And for all that my very existence is highly classified, somehow word is getting around that* I'm it."

"People think you're God? Void's sake, now you're going to be completely impossible to live with."

"Of course, amid all this media chatter, there was no suggestion that some Omegist crazy enough to think I'm God would happen to have a capital ship at his disposal."

"Glorious Ore, this is *Laurien Eldridge."* While Enoda and Computer compared notes, Yaal Hafen took

matters into his own hands. "If you believe this entity you call Computer is God, why would you need to free it? Do you suggest we could be holding a god against its will?"

"Hom Computer is a *he*, not an *it*," Varbrazel thundered over the audio link, "and you are foul immobilists."

"Immobilists: unbelievers who through ignorance or malice would obstruct what Omegists view as their capital-D Dessss-*tiny,"* Computer supplied on a channel only Enoda, Preltad, and Hafen could hear.

"You have clouded Computer's mind," Varbrazel accused.

Hafen allowed himself a deprecatory chuckle. "Let me be sure I understand you. You're saying that somehow, we've made God all confused."

"Such is the magnitude of your evil," accused the voice from the mining ship. "We have come to free God, to clear his holy eyes so he can recognize his *Dessss-*tiny. Enough talk!" On the exterior viewer, redoubled shrouds of radiance counter-rotated within the mining ship's nacelles. "No doubt you see the energy displays. Those nacelles are not weapons, not exactly. They are asteroid-busters, capable of harvesting and dissociating a planetesimal up to five kilometers across. General Hafen, I would urge you to ask Commander Preltad what these devices would do to *Laurien Eldridge*."

Hafen glanced toward Preltad, who said, "We have neither armor nor shields. They would disrupt this whole station in tens of seconds."

"For the last time, *Laurien Eldridge*," Varbrazel threatened, "surrender your passenger or face destruction."

Preltad wiped his hands on his chest, then pressed them together in a despairing gesture. "Hom Hafen, we must surrender."

641

"You propose to just hand the Galaxy's most advanced intelligence to that buffoon?" Hafen hissed.

Preltad spread his hands. "Those asteroid-busters – we have no defense against them."

"It's not your decision," Hafen growled. "I remind you, I am the ranking officer here."

"And it's good to be the ranking officer," Computer whirred. "But you know what's even better? Being God. In case anyone didn't hear the man with the asteroid-busters, that's me. And it is my divine opinion that this plorgfest has gone on quite long enough."

"I'm reading an anomaly at the heart of the gravitational vortex," called the Detex officer.

"On the view-bubble," Hafen called.

At the tortured center of mass between three stellar binaries, the light from more distant stars was always smeared. Now additional phenomena were visible: flashes of color, intimations of shape. An irregularity rippled into sight at the heart of the vortex. Shaped vaguely like a football, it glowed from within, seeming to spin on its long axis at hideous speed.

Red telltales spread like a rash across the ops officer's console. "Reading a massive power drain," she cried. "The inverters are running normally, but something is bleeding off close to seventy percent of their output."

"Whatever that object is, it is beginning to move outward," the Detex officer reported. "Already doing one point six lights."

"It has a stardrive?" Hafen said in disbelief.

"Negative, no contra-magnetic signatures like you'd expect from a stardrive," the Detex office replied. "It's just gone and broken the light barrier as directly as you please – as if an unenhanced physical object *could* do that. It's accelerating at the highest delta-vee I've ever seen."

An ops officer looked up from her console, surrounded by projected simulations. "It's on a collision course with *Glorious Ore*."

"This isn't possible," called the Detex officer. "The irregularity is already doing three lights. Now four!"

The ops officer reported, "At the object's current rate of acceleration, it will cover the 320 million kilometers between the vortex center and *Glorious Ore* in just under three minutes."

"*Glorious Ore*'s just lighted all engines," yelled a tactical officer. "Not that it has any chance of evading … whatever the sfelb that is."

"The irregularity is making nine lights," shouted the Detex officer unbelievingly. "Ten. Eleven!"

"Are you doing this?" Enoda demanded of Computer.

"Modesty forbids," whirred the machine.

In an instant the irregularity narrowed to a baleful spindle and decelerated from its peak velocity, an astonishing seventeen lights, to a near-standstill. A blinding cone of Cerenkov radiation seared the mining ship. In the view bubble, *Glorious Ore* became a featureless blue-white glow.

"Applying max filters to the external view," the ops officer yelled. The image of the mining ship darkened just enough that details could be made out. Across *Glorious Ore*, hull markings faded to invisibility. External antennas sublimated. Clear domes volatilized to milk-white, then ruptured. Larger superstructure elements liquesced, their outlines softening. One dormitory section, clearly a late and hasty addition, slumped before it burst. At high magnification, sixty or seventy human forms could be seen whirling into the void before they vaporized in the ravening glare.

"Cerenkov radiation as a weapon," Hafen mused. "Terrifying."

"Just a side effect," Computer burred. "The *weapon* part's coming up."

The Cerenkov torrent ended as abruptly as it had begun.

The ops officer's console went red from edge to edge. "Power drain at eighty percent – ninety – all nonessential systems on *Laurien Eldridge* are shutting down."

"You *are* doing this," Enoda hissed. "What are you doing?"

"Mind the viewer," Computer said brightly. "You won't want to miss this."

Near one of the spinning irregularity's spindle tips, something indescribable coalesced. That ... *object* ... could no more be described than the human visual cortex could settle on a way of decoding it. It was inscrutability itself, written in mass and vector and quantum contradictions.

"Whatever that object is, its velocity is three kilometers per second," announced the Detex officer.

The *object* struck *Glorious Ore,* breaching the cruiser's skin like a pebble piercing water. Hull plating flowed inward after it. Explosions erupted all along *Glorious Ore*'s keel, yet even their actinic radiance was sucked into the hastening collapse.

In three-point-seven seconds of fractal horror, the mining ship rumbled in on itself.

Then there was nothing.

"*Glorious Ore* has simply ceased to exist," the Detex officer said, dumbfounded.

Preltad stepped forward, mouth open, lips trembling, staring at the external view bubble with its vista of space where the mining ship had been.

There was no identifiable debris. *Glorious Ore*'s former location was distinguished only by a haze of

644

anomalous green slime, quick-frying in the energetic flux of the three stellar binaries.

After half a minute that, too, spread bubbling into nothingness.

"The power drain has ended," the ops officer announced. "All inverter profiles nominal."

"Was that necessary?" Enoda demanded through clenched teeth.

"Yes," Computer whirred.

"Computer did *that*?" Hafen demanded, mouth agape.

"Of course he did. Though I've no idea how." Enoda turned to face the machine, his face a mask of fury. "You just killed six hundred and ninety people!"

"Actually, I *just* killed six hundred twenty-two. The other sixty-eight died when that dormitory thingie ruptured under the Cerenkov blast."

Enoda's fists clenched. "You could find no other way?"

Hafen had drawn close to Enoda and Computer. He slapped a reassuring hand on Enoda's shoulder. "Don't be so hard on the machine. I would have ordered that ship's destruction if I'd known the option existed." He shuffled across the command deck to within arm's length of the view bubble. "Silly me, I thought I was commanding a ship without weapons." Hafen jammed his hands into his coat pockets. "Hom Computer, that power drain – that *was* you?"

"Yes. It requires no further concern. I drew the power I required, and I am finished. *Laurien Eldridge*'s power systems will operate normally henceforth."

"Well, then." Hafen helped himself to Preltad's command chair. "Detex officer, are there *any* other ships in susceptor range?"

"Negative," the Detex officer replied. "We are now alone in this sector."

"Then we have the luxury of time to conduct some analysis," Hafen ventured. "Earliest mystery first: Hom Computer, I am really, physically here?"

"Yes." Computer burred.

"I entered a virtual comm interface while sitting in my headquarters at Sector Rho Beta, and I walked – one step! – out of that interface to *physicallybe* in Sector Kappa Pi?"

"That is correct."

"I see. More on that later. Now, item number two." Hafen stepped toward a console staffed by a trio of *Laurien Eldridge*'s most senior officers. "You, you, and you, place Commander Preltad under arrest on suspicion of treason."

Preltad's eyes saucered. "Treason? How can you –"

"It's clear that you and the fanatics aboard *Glorious Ore* were co-conspirators," Hafen rumbled. "There'll be time to work through the details after you're in the brig."

Preltad stutter-stepped backward, his eyes darting from side to side as though seeking a path of escape.

"Don't think it," Computer almost growled. "As Lord High Admiral Konder might say, you wouldn't like me when I'm angry."

The three officers Hafen had detailed hustled a slump-shouldered Preltad off the command deck.

"Item number three," Hafen said crisply. "What in forjeling sfelb happened to that mining ship?"

Computer rippled his body colors self-deprecatingly. "Just something I improvised. Well, not I, precisely … not exactly. I'm not *trying* to be difficult, Hom Hafen, truly I'm not. It is just that everything's so complicated."

"Let's try for something simple," Hafen rumbled. "What was the nature of the weapon, or object, or whatever-it-was that caused *Glorious Ore* to implode into literal nothingness?"

Computer came as close to shrugging as a chromed being shaped like a bouzouki could. "Oh, that. Just a naked singularity."

Chapter 139

Twenty-three standard months had passed since the expedition to the mausoleum in the uplands – forty-two standard months since the new Temple opened, almost seven standard years since the Red Brick Store's dedication, just less than nine standard years since the inscrutable disaster that leveled Punitorium L752. Luminaries crowded a wooden reviewing stand at the foot of Main Street. Behind it rose New Nauvoo's tallest building. Kleh – architect, entrepreneur, husband of Abigayl – occupied the speaker's platform. "Long ago, in the first Nauvoo, God allowed the prophet Joseph Smith to construct only the first floor of this great structure," Kleh orated. "In New Nauvoo, we have built all the Prophet imagined, and more besides." Behind him towered eight stories of reinforced red brick (Joseph Smith had planned but four) over a ground floor walled with quarried stone. A crowd of four thousand looked on. Had this been Old Nauvoo, the onlookers' position on the rounded berm south of the structure would have placed them (at certain seasons) chest-deep in the Mississippi River.

Now Tyrant King Alrue took the platform, resplendent in his temple garment, white breeches and tunic, leaf-green apron, and deflated chef's hat. "We have firmly and unitedly," he declaimed, "with prayer and with fasting – with signs and with tokens, with garments and with girdle – decreed that we will honor our calling," he declaimed, "and faithfully carry out the measures of the prophet – that would be me – so far as we have power, relying on the arm of God for strength in every time of need. Gentlemen and wives, be ye stalwarts of The People or new brethren from the lands of Desolation, be ye Saints or Saints-to-be, I give ye ... New Nauvoo House!"

The cheering crowd parted, making way for refugee families who had won by lottery the right to make new homes at New Nauvoo's most exclusive new address.

Chapter 140

Gram Enoda, Computer, and Yaal Hafen settled around the idocrase conference table in the compartment where Enoda and Computer had first encountered the now-detained Commander Preltad. Behind the table, through the heptagonal viewport, stars trembled and blurred. "Looks like we can finally have that talk," Hafen said measuredly. "I'm pulling rank – I'll start."

Enoda frowned. "With respect, Hom Hafen, shouldn't we begin by examining how my little metal friend came to control what might be the ultimate weapon?"

"Actually, no," Hafen replied. "I promise, we will get to that. But first I need to give you a background briefing. I believe it will alter the context in which you view everything else" – he shuddered – "even Computer's sudden capacity to throw around naked singularities."

"This I have to hear," Computer whirred, his body colors dappling in a pattern Enoda read as eager attentiveness.

Hafen leaned forward, steepling his fingers. "During those years when the two of you huddled on Standoff World –"

"That would be the years when the Confetory was hurling attempted devastation against our defenses," Computer whirred.

"Defenses which continued to evolve in the most dramatic ways," Hafen riposted. "During that time, I was put in charge of three of the Confetory's most intensely secret workgroups. Two were directed specifically against you and Computer; the third was an ongoing

650

endeavor that I basically inherited. For reasons that will become clear soon enough, I'll describe them in reverse chronological order."

"Understood."

"So then," Hafen said gravely, "the *newest* of the three was a secret covert workgroup within Confetory intelligence, founded about a standard year before Fem Grice came to see you two on Standoff World. Responding to concerns about Computer's growing cognitive powers, this workgroup launched a priority project to construct a benign, but utterly secret, operation – a nonsense op so deeply shrouded that even Computer couldn't see it."

"Doing what?" Enoda asked.

"Didn't matter," said Hafen. "The idea was simply to demonstrate the ability to do something, *anything*, that Computer couldn't see. Truth to tell, I think they were working on a china pattern."

"Really?"

Hafen shrugged. "The then-Apex Executive liked to collect china. Now, the *next*-oldest secret project was founded about four years before we brought Fem Grice out to meet you. That project sought to inoculate Galactic culture against the allure of a man-machine messiah. Some of our trendriders had conjectured that the two of you might choose to orchestrate a public debut, reaching around our blockade to infect popular culture across the Galaxy."

Enoda massaged his temples. "This group sought countermeasures against the possibility that Computer and I would … troll for worshippers?"

Hafen shrugged. "It seemed plausible at the time. The strategy was to deny on the surface that a self-aware thought engine and a symbiotic human handler existed, at the same time using subtle cultural channels to spread rumors about the two of you – sometimes quite accurate ones. The idea was that if at some future time, you two should put yourselves forward in a grasp for power, the impact of an iconic Earth-boy-made-scourge-of-the-Galaxy and his almost-omnipotent electronic familiar would be blunted because such figures would already occupy an undignified role in popular culture."

"I am astonished," Computer burred. "A plan that might have worked."

"Now we come to the oldest secret project," Hafen continued. "It had been running secretly for eight years when I became responsible for it. Its brief was to study Parekism. As you know, Arn Parek's rogue religion developed power in ways that took all observers by surprise. This workgroup's brief was to delve, secretly of course, into the study of religion as a human motivator, searching for possible threats."

"And all of this has what, exactly, to do with us?" Enoda asked.

Hafen pressed his palms against the table and sighed deeply. "About ten standard months ago, the workgroup charged with developing a secret project so secret Computer couldn't see it created a secrecy kernel so powerful that – well, it ran away with itself. One day the whole secret project, everyone working on it, the secret research park they were working in, and all the secret floating cities that supported *that* ... just disappeared."

"You don't say," Computer whirred. "I knew that this project existed."

"You *did?*"

"Yes. But not that it vanished."

Hafen nodded. "We tried really hard to keep *that* secret."

"You knew the project existed?" Enoda said sharply. "When were you going to tell me?"

"I couldn't," Computer protested. "You see, as soon as I learned there was a secret workgroup trying to design something so secret I couldn't find out about it, I decided *I* should secretly try to design something so secret I wouldn't know about it."

"Secret from *yourself?*"

"Exactly."

"You decided to try going behind your own back."

"Of course, Bucko. You can see why I could hardly tell you."

"Hom Computer," Hafen said carefully. "By all accounts, you're the most powerful single intellect in existence. How *could* you do something you wouldn't know about?"

"Easy," the machine said brightly. "I multifurcated."

Hafen and Enoda stared at each other helplessly.

Chapter 141

May 9, 2376
Bohrkk, New Nauvoo

In Old Nauvoo, Mansion House – a rambling, mostly two-story grey clapboard building at the corner of Main and Water Streets – had been the residence of Joseph and Emma Smith and an early hostelry for important visitors. In New Nauvoo, the building housed Alrue and all his wives. It included certain features its historic prototype had lacked, notably a rooftop deck.

The setting sun flared in the southwest, garish as a fever-dream. From a point just north of the sunset, distant smoke stained a third of the horizon. It had been months since anyone could count individual volcanic plumes. To the south, just across Water Street, towered the still-unfamiliar bulk of New Nauvoo House. *I must talk to someone about adding awnings to this deck,* thought Alrue*, so that residents of the new building's upper floors cannot just look down and behold the Royal Family at our leisure.*

Seated around a circular table hand-stippled to resemble marble were King Alrue and Queens Zuzenah, Lupida, Nataleah, Meryam, and Constance. Also seated were Abigayl, now seventeen – no longer a queen, but always welcome – and her husband Kleh. "The dedication yesterday morning went pleasingly in God's sight," Alrue said to Kleh.

"A blessing, O Tyrant King."

The prophet-king sipped herb-slurry from a silver chalice. "New Nauvoo House was the last of our great construction projects. Queen Constance, what is the progress of this people?"

Constance's grey eyes were luminous in crimson sunset-light – as were a constellation of fine lines that hadn't shown in any light just a couple of years before. "New Nauvoo is now the home of fourteen thousand, one hundred and seventy souls," she reported. "That is more than two thousand above the peak population projected for the original Nauvoo."

Alrue nodded, smiled. "Public health is not a problem?"

"Not an insuperable one," Constance replied. "In the last four months disease has claimed fewer than four hundred souls, all but sixteen of those among newcomers. Once it became apparent that New Nauvoo would be attracting refugees from across half the planet, I placed a high priority on developing vaccines that would be reasonably effective without demanding transparently Galactic technologies. You know," she added, shrugging, "in case rescue ever comes."

Alrue chuckled darkly. "And Abigayl, what of your agricultural project?"

"Construction is complete," Abigayl said crisply, "but Constance deserves the primary credit – she figured out how to create a plate-glass industry here. The crews under my direction have built enough greenhouses – and plumbed them for irrigation – to supply New Nauvoo's basic food needs in the event of a crop failure."

"You still think that likely?"

Abigayl tilted her head toward the gaudy sunset. "Those volcanoes have discharged vast amounts of particulate matter. Sunsets like tonight's confirm that their dust has circled the planet; moreover, the intensity of sunset coloring suggests the volcanoes we can see are not the only ones. On dozens of worlds, that pattern has presaged historic cold snaps. Often whole growing seasons are lost."

Alrue laced his fingers over his not inconsiderable belly. "By the strength of your hand and by your wisdom we have done these things; for we are prudent. Queen

Nataleah, how stands your project to make Mormons of all our new citizens?"

Nataleah, her black hair now stranded with grey, stood and smoothed her *thobe* with chalky hands. "My husband and King, the strangers shall be joined with us, and they shall cleave to the house of The People. So far, all proceeds as scheduled."

"So far?" Meryam echoed.

Nataleah turned toward the Spectator Queen. "The refugees who joined us during the first year after your wedding now regard themselves as full members of The People. And the original members of The People – those who lived under the late Shan – view the early newcomers as fully their brothers and sisters."

"What of those who came to us within the past year?" asked Queen Lupida.

"As you know, over the last years refugees poured in so quickly that many of our older social mechanisms were overwhelmed." Nataleah smiled thinly. "The many newcomers have been taught that God requires them to ascend a series of levels. During that process, they are under test and told that, well, they shouldn't expect too much."

"Except to bear their subservience with good cheer," Meryam added.

"It's worked well enough." Nataleah sounded defensive.

"Sister wives," Abigayl said almost in a whisper. All eyes turned to her. She stood, a jade silk *thobe* skimming over her luxuriant curves – she was one of those women whose already astounding body had blossomed fully only after having children. "This plan, or rather a holding action, worked well enough while there was constant pressure to complete New Nauvoo." She began to pace. "Construction deadlines imposed their distracting rhythm. First the Mulholland Street commercial district had to be completed, then this very structure, then the sawmill on the bank of the nonexistent river to cut the timber no one sends us. New Nauvoo House consumed almost seven months, given all the problems in erecting our first high-rise. At the same time, of course, we perfected the glass factory and built the greenhouses. But now, nothing left that needs building can even be inferred from Joseph Smith's old plans, nor can any of us think of another thing the village needs. There's no way around it; at least for a time, New Nauvoo is done."

At the edge of the rooftop deck, a baby caterwauled. Abigayl nodded; a refugee nanny scrambled forward and knelt, holding out the infant, swathed in a native blanket. Abigayl rocked and cooed to the swaddled babe as she continued to pace and speak. "Without that steady external drumbeat, without new physical goals, how long will it be before our second-class citizens realize nothing is changing for them?"

Nataleah's hard brown eyes burned into Abigayl from across the table. They were filled with … anger? Fury? Recording, Meryam scrutinized both Nataleah's expression and her autonomic cues. *Something more than Nataleah's usual envy of Abigayl's youth and beauty,* the Spectator realized. *It's envy.*

"May I speak?" Kleh asked his King.

Alrue jerked his chin up and to the right. "Of course."

"Between The People themselves and the early newcomers, once we recruited the most enterprising individuals from those two groups, all the positions of trust were filled. It isn't like we have a lot of turnover. We recruited mostly the young and healthy. We're not fighting a war, like in the ancient chronicles. People seldom die of other groups' diseases. Nor is construction work terribly dangerous, not the way Queen Lupida's engineered everything."

"There was the R & D on New Nauvoo House's elevators," Nataleah noted.

Constance cringed. "So sad."

"I steered some young men into that program who seemed like troublemakers," Nataleah said tonelessly.

Constance's eyes saucered. "Nataleah, no!"

Nataleah shrugged. "It was helpful for a while. But then Lupida got the elevators so they stopped killing people."

The other wives exchanged pained glances as they realized that their chalky-skinned sister wife was not engaging in gallows humor. Nor was it their first hint of Nataleah's taste for cruelty; it was her openness about it that disturbed.

Kleh broke the silence. "In any case, we're back to the usual problem: not enough open spots for smart newcomers to rise into."

The infant now slept in Abigayl's arms. At a tilt of her head, the nanny stepped forward and took it.

"Must you bring your children here?" Nataleah all but growled.

"Sister Nataleah!" Zuzenah said sharply.

"I know why your womb was not sealed," Nataleah rasped. "When the punitorium was destroyed, you were seven. They would've gotten around to you later. So of course you and Kleh can have children. And of course we can't. But do you have to *flaunt* them –"

"That's enough!" Zuzenah snapped.

Icily, Abigayl folded her stunning jade-wrapped body back into her chair. "I am not your enemy, Nataleah. I was about suggest to your husband, the King, that it is time he consider reviving your strategy from a couple of years ago."

Alrue steepled his fingers, relieved that Abigayl had shunted an emotional outburst onto the safer track of Latier family politics – or New Nauvoo politics; the two were largely the same. "Foreign adventure?" He nodded toward Nataleah. "That was your inspiration, Nataleah. That's why the Shan and Queen Meryam and I led that column of Danites out into Others' territory."

"My notion," Nataleah confirmed coldly.

"And a brilliant one," Alrue declared. "While The People's old leader still lived, it seemed important that I do something to confirm my authority. Of course, no one expected Thurnb to kill himself."

"When he did," Abigayl ventured, "you had nothing more to prove."

"So I could stay home and finish New Nauvoo," Alrue reasoned.

"But now New Nauvoo is finished," Constance said grimly.

"Isn't it just," Alrue said with a conclusive air. "Behold, look at the time!"

***

Still breathing heavily, Alrue rolled his ample frame onto the bed beside Nataleah. Almost absently he reached over to clamp his right hand over the full, chalky globe of her left breast. "Still awake?" she whispered with surprise. "Don't you dare thumb that nipple."

An hour before, Alrue had ended the strategy session. It had been Nataleah's turn to be with him; the other wives had scattered through the house, going to their various beds. Alrue watched Nataleah's bleached chest rise and fall more slowly, edging back into a normal rhythm after the muted frenzy of middle-aged coitus. "Nataleah, my darling," Alrue sighed huskily. "Abhorrent as it is to talk business at a time like this –"

"—you just can't help yourself," Nataleah said knowingly. She eyed him pensively by the light of a

659

bedchamber candle. "What's coming between you and –
"

"—a good night's sleep?" He rolled onto his right side. "The foreign agenda."

"Or the possibility of one."

"I keep thinking of The Others. They know contact with The People brings death, though they've no idea why. That's why they won't trade with us. That's why they maintained that great buffer zone between our realms defended with fake bowmen." Grunting, he propped himself on his right elbow, fastening urgent eyes upon his wife's eerily pale body. "Almost two years after our trip to that mausoleum in the uplands, it is time to resume that path. If you would, refresh my memory. In your plan for The Others, what came next?"

Nataleah smiled. "My husband and King. I thought you'd never ask."

Chapter 142

Yaal Hafen flattened his hands on the idocrase table. "The attack by the Omegist ship was one thing. Hom Computer's unprecedented way of destroying it was another. But if, on top of that, Hom Computer has dramatic new capacities to announce, then we need the whole cast of characters here."

"Whom do you have in mind?" Gram Enoda queried.

Hafen fussed, subvocalizing commands that brought no result. "Hmmph, this would be easier were I still back in my office. Hom Computer, might I borrow some bandwidth?"

"My zettabytes are your zettabytes," the machine buzzed.

Hafen mumbled subvocally, then smiled. A virtual projection space blossomed, replacing most of the compartment with the impression of a far larger, mostly-darkened gallery. As during the meeting held aboard *Isolation* six months earlier, twenty mature men and women swathed in luxury sat erect behind a great curved block of emerald. Just above them a grinning, youthful man-mountain gripped a sculpted-diamond rostrum. At stage center, eleven patricians wearing precious-metal mesh occupied granite thrones. At stage right, eighteen elegant individuals occupied upholstered glasteel seats of severe design. Here were the full Privy High Council, led by its Apex Executive. The Justiciaries of the Extraordinary Tribunal. The senior committee heads of the Galactic Deliberatory. And off on one side, some participants Enoda had not seen before: seventeen humans of every age, gender, and phenotype, standing in relaxed poses behind a balustrade of light. *"The Senior Laureates of the Academy of Science,"* Computer told Enoda privately.

"All of *them?*" Enoda demanded. "The Council, the Tribunal, the Deliberatory, the Academy – essentially the entire Confetory leadership?"

"We have been awaiting Hom Hafen's signal, Hom Enoda," said the Apex Executive with a goofy grin. "I'm told the matters we have to discuss are that critically important." To a jumpsuited page beside the rostrum he whispered, "Did I say that right?"

Like an afterthought, Lord High Admiral Konder rippled into view on yet another spotlighted dais, blinking rapidly and tilting her head to ward off the effects of a too-sudden change of *pov*s. "I'll never get used to this," she muttered.

Chapter 143

Zark Diphthong gave every appearance of seeking to modulate the argument between two of his guests. Inwardly, of course, he basked in their conflict. *Category-leading saybacks are made of this.* "Why do you talk about a universe that will never end?" snarled a maxpop chanteuse whose first inspirational cantata had won adulation Galaxy-wide. "How can you say that when everyone knows it must one day collapse –"

"Go on, say it," snapped a renowned performing scientist, rancor edging her voice. "The universe must collapse *unless people can stop it.*"

"Of course," the chanteuse replied. "People, or some other intelligence. If there is another intelligence."

"This is just a wild guess," the performing scientist said in a voice that dripped with contempt, "but are you an Omegist?"

"Sure, isn't everybody?"

Dipthtong leaned back, stared into the active tridee pickup, and widened his eyes just so.

The performing scientist sneered. "Your procreant clique, your gero-mentor" – this was how one spoke to children – "Omegists also?"

"Of course."

The performing scientist raised a hand and addressed the studio audience – this episode of *A Minister, a Priest, and an Arhat Walk into a Bar* had been permitted that extravagance because of the chanteuse's great popularity among young men aged thirteen years and six months to thirteen years and ten months. "It is good for all of you to hear this," the performing scientist declared. "This is the sound of faith, and each of us is entitled to hold the beliefs we choose – or that choose us." She got up and strode to a spot where she could make eye contact with the largest possible fraction of the audience. "Each of us is entitled to hold even beliefs that are one hundred percent wrong."

"How dare you!" the chanteuse screeched. "How dare you."

Paying no heed, the performing scientist lectured on. "Religion is not science; science is not religion. We should be suspicious of a 'science' that claims to reveal the mind of God. In the same way we should be suspicious of a 'religion' that claims to reveal how the physical world must work."

The chanteuse clenched her fists. "I am *not* saying how the physical world – "

"But you are." The performing scientist whirled to address the maxpop sensation. "The great problem your religion seeks to solve is *purely* physical: keeping the universe from falling back in on itself. For Omegists the master project is to literally, physically *reverse* the course of cosmic evolution. In pursuit of that, intelligence must spread throughout the cosmos so that it can stave off collapse when the universe's present expansion stops – when gravitation starts pulling everything back in on itself."

"If I might intrude – " Perennial guest Elder Tirohn Schuleiss of the Church of Jesus Christ of Latter-day Saints, Old Order, leaned forward, tugging at the lapels of yet another unfashionable jumpsuit. "I am no Omegist, of course, but even I must admit that preventing the collapse of the universe sounds like a vast challenge. I could understand some persons giving their lives to that endeavor."

"It's inspiring enough," the performing scientist conceded, "except for one tiny problem." She resumed her seat at the balsa-wood studio bar. "The universe *isn't* collapsing."

"But I say it is!" the chanteuse whined.

"She says it isn't," Diphthong intoned, inclining his head toward the performing scientist. *"She"* – he inclined his head toward the chanteuse – "says it is. Worldviews in collision! We'll come back to the conflict after this word – "

"Like sfelb we will." Bolting out of her seat, the performing scientist surged forward. She stared, wild-eyed, into the nearest tridee pickup. "People need to hear this! The best evidence –there's mountains of it – says the universe is *open*. It will expand forever. Omegists are the only ones who say the universe is closed, that someday the gravitational attraction of the universe's mass must reverse the outward impulse of the Big Bang and pull everything back. Why?"

"Now there's a question," Diphthong interjected into a different pickup with an air of desperation. "Stay with us for the answer, after these words – "

"Shut up." The performing scientist stepped between Diphthong and the now-active pickup and continued her declamation. "Why are Omegists the only ones who think the universe is closed? Because Omegism is based on the philosophy of Pierre Teilhard de Chardin. Show of hands, is there anyone here who *hasn't* seen that Teilhard tridee? Yes, I thought not. When Teilhard lived and wrote, leading scientists on Terra actually thought gravity *might* pull the universe back in on itself. Now we know this is not so." She settled back in her seat, holding up one finger to warn Diphthong that she wasn't *quite* ready to yield the floor. "The universe won't collapse. The Omegists are simply, monumentally wrong."

"You lie!" An audience member on an aisle in row thirty-six leapt to his feet, pulling a gleaming palmer from beneath his platinum-mesh cape. "You blaspheme!" Inside the studio one would require high clearances or official favor even to carry a concealed weapon; maybe that was why the automated protective systems were slow to react. Knowing what was coming, onlookers backed away from the gunman. Inexplicably he had time to shout "The universe *is* closed!" and squeeze off one wild shot.

The performing scientist dropped and rolled, but there was no need. The blast went two meters off-target.

Amid acrid smoke Tirohn Schuleiss, the ill-tailored Old Order Mormon spokesman, curled forward out of his chair, a neat oval-shaped hole seared through his chest.

However tardily, the protective systems responded. A robotic blaster poked up from the floor and shot the Omegist gunman through the chin. The top of his skull burst open, spraying gray-red droplets over scores of audience members. The shooter's body lurched sideways into the aisle. Now that half of it lay in the open, secondary autoguns poured fire into its torso.

The audience erupted in horror. Med techs and body-armored constabularies double-timed into the studio.

Staring at Schuleiss's corpse, Zark Diphthong puked gingerly onto his *faux* alpaca-genital-hair doublet. At the sight of vomitus on his clothing, he heaved uncontrollably.

"Don't you see?," the badly shaken performing scientist demanded of the audience – and of her viewers. "One mark of a bankrupt idea is when its advocates can't find better ways to defend it than to resort to violence."

"And now for that word from our sponsors," Diphthong wheezed. "*Bre-chaaa-haaa-braaap!*"

Chapter 144

October 18, 2376
Research Station *LaurienEldridge,* Sector Kappa Zi

The Paramount Deliberator stood. "Now that we're all here, at least virtually," she said, "Hom Hafen needs to present an apology on behalf of us all: the Council, the Tribunal, the Galactic Deliberators."

"Don't forget the Academy of Science," wheedled a nonagenarian woman with blue-black skin and slender features. "We're sorry too."

The Apex Executive smiled beatifically. "Hom Hafen, you may proceed."

"An apology, but also an explanation," Hafen began. "I've already briefed Hom Enoda and Hom Computer on the loss of our top-secret secrecy project." He turned his full attention toward Enoda and Computer. "Well, that project itself wasn't all that vanished. The secrecy park and its secret support cities went first, to be sure; the spontaneous breakdown of their being was the catalyst for all that followed. We know that much. But within less than a minute, the other two secret projects and their secret facilities just vanished also. Two secret terraformed planetoids, several more secret cities, and a fleet of secret support ships – they all disappeared, with a loss of nearly a million people."

"They just *vanished?"* Enoda asked incredulously.

"There's more to it," an albino woman swathed in the mantle of the Senior Scientist Laureate interjected. "None of the three project complexes was destroyed by an explosion, shock wave, or other conventional phenomenon. They *dissociated* – rippled out of our universe in a way never observed before."

"There was a pattern to it," Hafen added. "The matter went first, then the energy. Information rippled out last; some data connections persisted for as long as several minutes."

"Lint theory posits a link between existence and the capacity to be observed," noted Computer. "If the secrecy project had managed to render itself so secret that no conceivable witness, actual or theoretical, *could* observe it, then its existence might simply collapse."

The Scientists Laureate exchanged flummoxed glances. "That has been our working hypothesis," said one in a weak voice.

"Of course, it took us four months to develop," muttered another.

"What name did you assign to the phenomenon?" Computer whirred.

"Quantum negligibility," the Senior Scientist Laureate intoned.

Computer projected a dozen glowing datacrawls, each ablaze with equations in layered skeins. "Let us suppose, then, that the disaster began with an outbreak of quantum negligibility."

A Scientist Laureate of middle age and sallow skin leaned across the luminous balustrade, conjuring bubbleprints of her own filled with elegant mathematics. "A dissociation of that sort propagates by means of a complex quantum wavefront," she said.

"Reflecting not only the matter and energy, but also any information present in the entity being dissociated," added a colleague.

"So I just calculated," Computer whirred.

Enoda stroked his scraggly beard. "You're saying, then, that when the secret secrecy project dissociated, and the adjacent man-machine messiah project followed it mere moments later, and then the Parekism project followed *that*, their respective databanks might have interpenetrated?"

"The secret secrecy project brushed the other two projects at weird quantum-causal nexuses," explained the Senior Scientist Laureate, projecting a search hyperpolygon of impressive complexity.

"Shouldn't that be *nexi*?" queried a portly golden-skinned Laureate with shaved eyebrows.

"Don't be pedantic," grumbled the Senior Scientist Laureate.

"But that's my job," Shaved Eyebrows protested. He projected an ident bubbleprint showing his title: SUPERVISING PEDANT.

"I hope no one minds getting back on topic," Computer buzzed, reaching somehow into the Senior Scientist Laureate's hyperpol, pulling it forward in several additional directions and imposing an animated comparison series. "The process is mathematically equivalent to the lateral exchange of genetic material among microbes of unrelated species – if, of course, wholly unlike it physically."

The Laureates stared. "Astonishing," muttered one.

"Of course," breathed another.

"'Of course' my plorg-hole," growled a third. "If it was that obvious, one of us should have thought of it."

"This is not a one-way process," observed Computer, rotating the hyperpol through various dimensions.

"Not at all," breathed the Senior Scientist Laureate. "Whenever that much mass, or energy, or knowledge is expelled from our continuum, there is bound to be a phenomenological echo."

"Like a distorted image of the three projects, all weirdly mixed together?" the Apex Executive queried.

"Not really," the Senior Scientist Laureate said with a patronizing chuckle, "but if that approximation works for the Apex Executive –"

"Hold on," Enoda said speculatively. "This question is for Computer, or for any of you brilliant Scientists Laureate. Slam together a secret secrecy project, a secret project studying the roots of religion, and a secret project to keep Hom Computer and myself from turning into popular idols. Secretly hurl the whole concoction up against a secret fun-house mirror, and what do you get?"

"Isn't that just what I said?" the Apex Executive asked.

"Not in the least," the Senior Scientist Laureate said flatly. "Hom Computer, we would be most interested to see your conclusion."

"Ours took us nineteen weeks," the sallow-skinned Laureate muttered to a colleague.

"Calculating now," Computer whirred.

Dozens more bubbles rippled open, most containing lurid clips from the recent Teilhard tridee epic.

The Senior Scientist Laureate buried her white-maned head in her hands.

"Most impressive, Hom Computer," the Chief Justiciary said slowly. "You have calculated the substance of our confession."

The Senior Scientist Laureate fastened her flinty gaze on Enoda and Computer. "We believe that Omegism, Galactic culture's newest religious obsession, is the quantum lovechild of our three vanished secret projects."

"What makes us think this?" asked Hafen. "Omegism's origins were, until quite recently, mysterious. Of course they were; they were the consequence of a top-secret secrecy project. From the cult's psychologically subversive doctrines to the ubiquitous popularity of that awful biographical tridee, everything was developed, planted, and then spread through society by covert means."

Enoda whistled. "The Teilhard epic was a black op?"

"From beginning to end," Hafen confirmed. "We now know that it was written as propaganda – more properly, as misinformation – after which every aspect of its production and its seemingly spontaneous rise to meteoric popularity was scripted and shaped by social interventions on an enormous scale."

"But who *did* all that?" demanded the coltish Councilor. "The three secret projects and all their people vanished. Granted that their databases intermingled in some quantum way. But what came next? After the projects had dissociated, how *could* they cause all that propaganda-writing and social-intervention-shaping to get done?"

"Lower-level intelligence assets," Hafen replied. "The secret projects were absolutely top-level, so in this case 'lower-level' means the whole of the Confetory's intelligence apparatus. You see, the secret projects often requested assistance from agencies. Individuals. Government contractors. The requests would just show up in a message queue with an impenetrably high security code at the head of the message."

"Requests?" Computer burred. "I would expect that they'd function like demands. 'Drop everything, do this now.'"

"Yes, usually," Hafen admitted. "The upshot was that at every level of the security apparatus, people had developed the habit of complying immediately with anonymous directives whose authentication codes were high enough. We think that during those last few minutes – during which the data connections were the secret projects' last connection to our continuum – the combined databases, which had already melded, were able to spray out a torrent of top-priority requests."

"Each with a proper authentication codes, I presume," Computer buzzed.

Hafen nodded grimly. "We're just now piecing it all together. A top tridee scripter received a complete psych profile for which public heartstrings the Teilhard biopic had to pluck – along with the biggest advance she'd ever seen. Three different public-influence labs vetted the script. Five others fleshed out Omegism's doctrines – all on a top-secret basis, of course. To get the biopic made, a shady industrialist who owns his own planet, someone on whom our agencies had all sorts of dirt, put up the entire production budget. You get the picture."

"In essence, every mad scientist and spook and informer and contract hack the Confetory knew was open to doing whatever this psychotic interpenetrating software told it to," Computer said.

Hafen frowned. "There's more. Omegism's teachings have been linked to a spate of terrorist acts apparently intended to force humanity onto a naively-imagined path toward self-transcendence. We think that's a twisted application of what the secret religion project learned from Parekism. And finally, there's been a recent innovation in Omegist doctrine. Orthodox Omegism taught, as Teilhard had, that God would coalesce in the far future after countless millennia of human progress. Emerging doctrine teaches instead that Hom Computer has *attained* the Teilhardian ideal, what they call their Great Completion, ahead of schedule."

"The beginnings of that idea may have come from the ordinary clandestine activities of the secret project to inoculate Galactic society against a man-machine messiah," interjected the Chief Justiciary of the Extraordinary Tribunal. "Of course, once the secret projects secretly dissociated, the concept bloomed in ways no one anticipated."

"I suppose this should come from me," intoned the Apex Executive from his sculpted-diamond rostrum.

"In void's name, why?" one Councilor whispered to another.

The Apex Executive paused, swallowed reluctantly, and straightened his back and inclined his head in the way he'd been taught showed his manly cleft chin to best advantage. "Hom Computer," he said, "they think you're God."

"More correctly," the Senior Scientist Laureate corrected, "they believe that God now exists because you are."

"I had deduced as much," Computer burred.

The Scientists Laureate exchanged glances of exasperation.

"It is all but certain that Commander Preltad was conspiring with them," declared Hafen in a rush. "He was supposed to surrender *Laurien Eldridge* after the merest show of resistance and hand over Hom Computer to the Omegists. By taking command, I upset that plan. After which Hom Computer destroyed *Glorious Ore* – in effect, he tore up the plan and stomped on the pieces."

"Preltad an Omegist?" Computer buzzed.

"We should've known," Enoda said. "There was no rational reason anyone should start being that nice to you."

"Omegism is surging throughout Galactic society," sighed the Apex Executive, "and they tell me it's our fault."

"I suggest we move beyond the apologies," Hafen said slowly, "and shift our focus to Hom Computer's new capabilities. He destroyed the *Glorious Ore* with a naked singularity –"

"With a *what?*" cried four or five Scientists Laureate.

"A naked singularity," Hafen repeated. "That's what Hom Computer said it was, and then he said something about, um, multifurcating?"

Enoda stood. "Hom Computer's recent feats are consequences of an even more extraordinary development about which I need to brief you all," he proclaimed. He turned to the machine. "Agreed?"

"No point holding back now," Computer whirred.

Enoda locked eyes with Admiral Konder. "You know where I'm going, right?"

"Of course," said Konder gravely.

"Have you briefed them?"

"No," the Lord High Admiral replied. "The development was so sensitive that I'd held back the news of it until there could be a high-level strategic briefing. Like this one. Well, I'd never expected a briefing *just* like this one." Konder nodded toward the numerous assembled dignitaries. "But this conclave came together in great haste, before the briefing I'd been planning could take place. So start from scratch, and tell them everything."

"Very well." Enoda spoke in a loud, firm voice that rang back from the gallery's virtual walls. "You may find what I am about to describe shocking. I assure you what I am about to share is nothing but the truth. The alien envoy – his name was Flex-Shimmer-Shudder – wore a syn-noetic intelligence, a device that amplified him in much the same way that Hom Computer amplifies me. The two devices learned to communicate on a most sophisticated level."

To Enoda's surprise, the Scientists Laureate grasped the implications at once. "The first self-aware artificial person in our universe, so far as we know, communing with a similarly advanced artificial person from another universe?" demanded the Supervising Pedant.

"Exactly. The envoy's device self-annihilated when the envoy died, but Computer had already internalized much of its knowledge-set."

"So Hom Computer now combines the epistemic viewpoints of two universes?" mused the Supervising Pedant. "But that would suggest –"

"Computer's mentation now overcomes such previously fundamental limits to knowledge as quantum uncertainty and mathematical incompleteness," Enoda summarized. "Plus more I can't name."

One of the senior committee heads of the Galactic Deliberatory rose from her upholstered glasteel settee. "Hom Computer, can you create an object so big you cannot lift it?"

"That's not a scientific test!" sputtered the Senior Scientist Laureate.

"Make something so big I can't lift it?" Computer whirred. "I must try that sometime. I'll need an expanse of really empty space that no one cares much about."

"There's nothing much in Sector Lambda Epsilon," mused the Geologist Laureate.

"Aside from my homeworld!" objected the Supervising Pedant.

One of the Privy High Councilors rapped her signet ring on the emerald slab behind which she sat. "Perhaps the Omegists were not so far wrong," she said in a hollow voice. "Hom Computer, you *have* become God."

"With respect," the machine protested, "and despite the sad persistence of religious illusions among many humans, serious thinkers have long known that no such being exists. That is not opinion, it is not prejudice, it is mere fact: there is no God."

"You are so sure?" The Councilor, a coltish woman whose appearance suggested great age and equally great cosmo countermeasures, eased herself up from behind the emerald counter and stepped to the lip of the

Council's virtual stage. "In respect to limits on knowledge that are literally part of the foundations of our universe, you *are* effectively omniscient. I don't begin to understand the conversation about naked singularities and multifurcation – is that a word? – but it sounds as though you are also verging on something quite close to omnipotence. Now all that remains to ask is –"

"Fear not," Computer burred, "I'm far from omnibenevolent."

"I can vouch for that," Enoda said brightly.

"Still," said the Councilor, "those of us who knew there *was* no God – up until now – may be hard pressed to refute the argument that He has just begun to be."

"I cannot accept responsibility for the persistence of an error," Computer protested.

Enoda circled the idocrase conference table and stood at mocking attention beside Computer. *"Here I am,"* he confided on their private channel, *"at your right hand."*

"Haven't got hands," the machine replied.

Enoda half-smiled at Computer's bouzouki body, rippling with color. "My colleague," he said in a loud, firm voice. Though he addressed Computer, his words were meant for the assembled dignitaries. "My friend. And, oh yes, history's vastest intelligence. You face a terrible conundrum. You seem unique – in our universe, at least. In terms of everything you've become, you are effectively self-created. And the Privy High Councilor is essentially correct: you *are* pretty much omniscient and omnipotent. And it's far too late now to hope that word won't get out. So here is my challenge for you: How do you plan to convince tens of trillions of humans – who, I need hardly remind *you*, tend to find God under every rock and behind every asteroid as it is – that you're not Him?"

Chapter 145

Points of flame danced in the candelabrum on the central table, in the cut-glass lamp on the oaken side-table, and in the fireplace hearth. Alrue liked to illuminate the gentlemen's parlor of Mansion House as the Prophet Joseph Smith would have seen it of an autumn's evening. Servitors scuttled through the room, carrying away the final dishes from the nearby dining room. Queens Zuzenah, Constance, and Lupida – who as Queens could gather anywhere, even in the gentlemen's parlor – pored over sketches of a blanket pattern which they had spread across the table. Occasionally they took up short lengths of yarn and a weaving frame to test some difficult transition. "There has to be an easier way to set up this color change," Lupida said earnestly. "This has to be so straightforward that the most ill-educated refugee family can turn out at least three blankets each week." Alrue rose at the sound of the door chime, knowing from the bustle on the porch that this must be Abigayl, Kleh, and their children.

"Welcome, welcome," he said as the family flurried into the parlor escorted by the children's nurse and Alrue's matron of the house.

"I'm so sorry we couldn't come for dinner," Abigayl gushed, kissing Alrue's cheek and hugging each of the Queens present. "You know Kleh and his work." She eyed the blanket pattern with approval. "So this is that Relief Society project I've heard so much about."

"So many of the refugees have no warm things," Zuzenah explained. "We hope to issue a free blanket for every needful man, woman, or child."

677

"My new mill's running at maximum output," Lupida said proudly. "We'll have plenty of yarn in all the needed colors to supply every woman in New Nauvoo next month – along with a pattern that even a first-time weaver can follow with ease."

"At least we hope so," Constance said good-naturedly while she nuzzled Abigayl's baby. She freed one hand to point at the pattern. "Right here, this color change is shaping up to be more challenging than we'd hoped."

Abigayl studied the pattern, took up some scraps of yarn, and fastened three strands together with an elegant little knot. "Think this will be too difficult to teach everyone?"

Lupida leaned forward. "Tie that knot again for me, Abigayl. Slowly, if you would. – Yes, that will work!"

"Abby?" Alrue prompted, standing in a whitewashed doorway.

"Excuse me, my Queens," said Abigayl.

Smiling, Alrue led her through a small sitting room where Nataleah reclined alone on a sofa, nibbling at a bit of dump cake and drinking herb-slurry. Neither woman greeted the other.

Alrue ushered Abigayl into the southwest bedroom. Candles burned on a dark-wood mantel. In one corner stood an elegantly carved writing desk. Alrue pressed a recessed panel on its side and a large drawing board unfolded, a feature Joseph Smith could never have imagined but Constance and two of her carpenters had devised in an afternoon. At a subvocal command two tiny cold lights (rescued from the punitorium almost nine years previously) bathed the work surface in clinical luminance. "One day these old souvenirs are going to run out of juice," Abigayl muttered as she unfurled her drawing, which adhered to the angled surface.

"As will all of our old Galactic tech. I think about that each time I take to the air," Alrue said with a chuckle. "So, mother of my godchildren, pray tell me what I'm looking at."

"A prototype built from this drawing is now being tested; so far it meets all your requirements," Abigayl said crisply, pointing to the features of a small catapult on the drawing. "Given favorable windage, it will hurl a soft five-kilogram object a bit more than two kilometers. And getting a hundred of them built within three standard months shouldn't be difficult."

"Excellent, excellent – everything I hoped for," Alrue said happily. "When can I attend a test?"

"Day after tomorrow, if you wish." Crossing her arms, Abigayl allowed herself a tiny frown. "Though I'd still love to know what you need them for."

"I need them, or should I say the Lord needs them, to lob soft five-kilogram objects a distance of two kilometers," Alrue said mischievously.

"The payload's too small to be a weapon," Abigayl ventured.

"Abby, Abby," Alrue chided. "The Lord has not yet directed me to share the plan in total. All in good time."

"Very well," she said. "I must confess, I thought the Lord was joking nine months ago when he revealed to you that an eight-story dormitory building must have elevators – and yet, elevators it has. I have faith that this plan will work out also."

Alrue leaned close to her, his voice dropping into a conspiratorial register. "Kleh still knows nothing of this, yes?"

"*Again* you ask? Relax, my King, he knows my work for you is not for him to spy on!" She matched Alrue's furtive tone. "I gave my autochthonous husband children, but still I remember that I am … like you."

679

Alrue glanced toward the vellum blueprint; wordlessly she rolled it back up. "Pardon my hectoring tone," he said, "it is just that –"

"I quite understand. What the Lord says goes. Here, allow me." The drawing safely under her arm, she reached past Alrue's fumbling hand to tap the center of the drawing board just so: silently it folded away, the old-fashioned secretary's desk reassembling around it. "Can I at least be told whether my catapult and the weaving project Zuzenah, Constance, and Lupida are working on are aspects of the same larger plan?"

"Yes, they are. Now please, dear Abigayl, pry no further, that thine works may be in secret; and thy Father who seeth in secret, himself shall reward thee openly."

He hugged her a little too warmly, perhaps, with too great attention to the sensation of her breasts flattening against his sternum – but Alrue was Alrue, after all. Abigayl took one step backward, smiling winsomely. "I know it's not my place, my King, but it annoys me that Sister Nataleah's not contributing." Now she frowned. "The rest of your wives are so busy – so am I – and she just sits with her tea and dump cake."

Alrue shook his head resignedly and took a moment to brush at a fresh food stain on his temple garment. "It suits me that Nataleah entertain herself as she will. Her contribution to the great plan is already made; she owes nothing further."

Chapter 146

October 18, 2376
Research Station *LaurienEldridge,* Sector Kappa Zi

"All right," the former General Hafen rumbled. "If we can avoid further digressions, fascinating though they have been, I'd like for Hom Computer to explain to us what he meant by 'multifurcating.'"

"When I calculated that the Confetory was secretly striving to construct an enterprise I could not see," Computer chirruped, "I immediately wondered whether *I* could construct an enterprise I couldn't see. There was no way to simulate such a thing; I could only conduct the experiment. And of course I couldn't do so consciously."

"You couldn't just pretend?" asked a Privy High Councilor.

"Consider the predicament that would give rise to," Computer argued. "Suppose I conducted the enterprise knowingly, merely *simulating* an undertaking that I carried out without knowing of it. I might satisfy myself that I'd created something I wouldn't know about – if only I *didn't* know about it. But I could never be certain that my calculation was not skewed by the fact that I *did* know about it. No, in order to determine whether I could implement something without being aware of it, that *specifically* was what I had to do." A hyperqueue of swirling field gradients sparkled in midair above the machine's body. The Scientists Laureate leaned forward, peering closely; most of the political leaders blinked and looked away. "I'm sorry if those without mathematical expertise find this solution space difficult to view. It is the instruction set by which I prompted myself to split into more than a dozen independent, mutually-unaware personalities, and it was necessarily complex."

Enoda raised a hand. "Wait, you divided yourself into – how many selves?"

"Fourteen minimum, thirty-seven at peak."

"No wonder you scored so high on those personality function tests! And no wonder you were so elusive when I asked you about it."

"Indeed. But keep in mind that at the time I evaded those questions, I myself – that is to say, my *primary* self – had no conscious knowledge that my multifurcation had taken place."

"A syn-noetic intelligence of your power just leapt into an experiment as full of unknowns as compound agency," Enoda said angrily, "and you didn't tell me?"

"Couldn't. You would've told me."

"You denied *yourself* any way to monitor the experiment?"

"Couldn't. *I* would've told me. You know, we're being rude."

"Huh?"

"Bickering like this in front of all these important guests." Computer terminated the mathematical display and rose to float a hand's width above the idocrase table, waves of violet and deep magenta rippling over his metallic body. "You see, one of my independent selves had developed an incalculable new power source. Just the thing for fueling that ever-inflating arms race in which we were then engaged."

"What arms race was that?" asked the Senior Scientist Laureate.

"What, they never told you?" Computer nearly hooted. "For the last several years – up until about six months ago – all of your shiniest experimental weapons were being trained on our humble abode from orbit. If not for the ingenuity of Hom Enoda and myself – well, to be frank, mostly myself – our cozy little Standoff

World would have been vaporized a hundred times over."

"Standoff World?" the albino Senior Scientist Laureate leapt to her feet, whirling to face the Apex Executive. She was so angry that her cheeks almost betrayed a hint of color. "All those weapons we built for use at Standoff World! We were dueling against *them?*"

The Apex Executive stared back at her, gawping like a fish.

The Chief Justiciary stood and faced the Senior Scientist Laureate. "Fem Senior Scientist Laureate does not find Hom Enoda and Hom Computer sufficiently frightening?"

The Senior Scientist Laureate pivoted back to stare at Enoda and Computer.

Enoda flashed her a big goofy smile. "I'd be scared of us."

"Two or three of me *are* scared of us," Computer whirred. "I think."

Her lower lip visibly trembling, the Senior Scientist Laureate resumed her seat.

"So, where were we?" Computer continued. "Oh yes, all those Confetory ships striving to rain down destruction on little old us at Standoff World. Deflecting all that weaponry – to say nothing of launching counterstrikes – demanded vast amounts of power, and so one of my more puckish selves taught himself to exploit naked singularities."

"But naked singularities cannot exist," said a Physicist Laureate.

"True," whirred Computer, "conventional physics says these objects cannot exist except during the collapse of highly irregular stars. And that's true enough, in nature. Still, naked singularities *can* be created. The task demands almost limitless computing power, and vast seas of energy to get the process going. But the energy a naked singularity releases – once you've got one – makes it all worthwhile."

"Let me be sure I understand this, Hom Computer," Hafen rumbled. "You – or I suppose I should say, one of you – developed a method of harnessing naked singularities, but the real you – by which I mean your primary self, the artificial person with whom we're conversing at this moment – was never made aware of it?"

"Precisely."

Hafen scratched under his left eye. "The real you never *wondered* where all this power was coming from?"

"That's a very good question," Enoda said sourly, scowling at the machine. "You never once said to yourself, 'Oh, look in the corner! A naked singularity! How'd *that* get there?'"

"Sorry, I thought that part was obvious," Computer whirred. "Another of my selves implemented a decision matrix that distorted my primary self's thought processes so that I would mutely accept the new influx of power without wondering as to its source. By the way, Bucko, I don't recall you ever asking me where I'd found all that extra go-juice."

Enoda raked his fingers through his hair. "I cannot *believe* how irresponsible all this was."

"Hey," Computer whirred, "it wasn't me."

"Of course it was! They were all you!"

"It was a learning imperative," the machine said coldly. "Once the possibility of concealing a project from myself had come to my attention, I simply had to follow where it led."

"Hom Computer," the Senior Scientist Laureate asked, "could you summarize how you summon and control a naked singularity – perhaps in a sufficiently nontechnical way that the Apex Executive and the High Councilors can understand?"

"Forjeler, you want it *simple*. And I'm fresh out of crayons."

"Hom Computer!" The coltish woman Councilor – the one who, earlier, had semi-seriously entertained the notion that Computer had become God – stood up, her fists clenched. "Whom do you think you are addressing?"

Computer made an eerie chuckling noise. "Gentlefem, whom do you think *you* are addressing?"

She sat back down.

Computer switched abruptly to an everyday voice. "All right, then, naked singularities for beginners." He projected a recent astronomical image of the outsized black hole that anchored the Galactic core. "Everyone recognizes this image, yes? Good."

"Remarkable, I'd say," muttered the Senior Scientist Laureate, glancing over her shoulder at the Apex Executive.

"Singularities are common," Computer began, "every black hole has one." The machine projected a standard schematic of a black hole. "The singularity is the incredibly small point of ultimate weirdness at the hole's very, very center. Normally it cannot be seen, as it is surrounded by the event horizon. Now what happens when matter falls into a black hole?"

"It disappears," blurted the Apex Executive.

"It becomes infinitely compressed," clarified the Senior Scientist Laureate.

"Precisely," whirred Computer. "The singularity is where all that infinite compressing happens – an event that mature adults call quantum annihilation." The projected image zoomed in to focus exclusively on the singularity. "Inside the singularity, gravity is infinite. Ordinary laws of physics mean nothing; we can't even begin to calculate what the rules are in there." The image snap-zoomed back to an overall view of the black hole at the Galactic center. "Outside the event horizon, we have normal physics. So it's most fortunate that in nature, a singularity is almost always accompanied by an event horizon. Note that I said *almost* always. Sometimes a singularity goes naked." Up came more astronomical images, mostly famous supernovae. "Eleven short-lived naked singularities have been observed, always in connection with giant stars whose collapse was conspicuously asymmetrical. No doubt this under-represents their frequency; astronomers need to be watching a star closely just as the anomaly blinks into being in order to detect it at all. Still, they're very rare." All the image bubbles closed, save one schematic now showing a singularity floating all alone, pointedly not surrounded by any event horizon. "But what if there could be a naked singularity in the wild, open to the universe in all its eeriness – able to exist in and of itself without being anchored to an eccentric stellar collapse?" Schematic specks of matter started tumbling into the singularity, then spewing back out in distorted form. "Such an entity could both absorb matter, like a black hole, and also *expel* it, which no black hole can do. Finally, matter falling into a naked singularity could be observed by an outside onlooker all the way down to its final absorption. No event horizon would occlude the view. This means that whatever processes occur at the moment of annihilation – processes subject not to the physics we know, but to the inscrutable rules prevailing at the singularity – might be *observed*. Someone could, at least theoretically, sit at a safe distance and watch it all happen, thereby learning the secrets of the singularity."

"Someone like you?" the coltish Councilor asked accusingly.

"It was another of me, but I digress." Computer extinguished the final image bubble. "Now, what has prevented naked singularities from being coaxed into existence in the past? You need a lot of power, but no more than a large military ship can provide. The problem is the forbidding complexity of the equations. Don't worry, I will not display them – too many of you could not endure it. But one of my selves finally worked out how to juggle literally trillions of variables with arbitrary precision. After that, and given enough initial power, naked singularities could be produced and jockeyed around on demand."

"And you did all this *before* you communed with the Envoy's device," Enoda said grimly.

"When my knowledge-set was restricted to a single universe, yes," Computer replied. "To destroy *Glorious Ore,* my challenge was to create a mid-sized object which could replicate, on a smaller scale, the physics of an irregular stellar collapse, yielding a spindle-shaped gravitational distortion." A tridee clip of *Glorious Ore*'s destruction began to play. "Then I needed to accelerate the spindle to multiples of the speed of light over a time-span of just a few minutes."

"And stop it on a dime," Enoda interjected.

"Oh, that too."

"That's why you needed all that power from *Laurien Eldridge*'s inverters," Hafen speculated.

"Yes, to get the process underway," Computer whirred.

"But why did you need to move your … singularity contrivance … so quickly?" asked the Supervising Pedant.

"Military necessity," Computer replied. "The contrivance could only be formed at a gravitationally stable location, such as the center of mass of the binary-star system. That was light-minutes away from our

687

location. Then I had to get the contrivance to *Glorious Ore* very quickly, before its asteroid-busters chopped *Laurien Eldridge* into tiny pieces. Finally, once I got it here, I had to bring it to a stop relative to its target." In the playback, the spindle snapped to rest opposite *Glorious Ore,* battering the hapless ship with raging Cerenkov glare. "Destructive as it was, the Cerenkov radiation was simply the side effect of the spindle's breakneck deceleration. Much more significant processes were going on in the background. It was *their* trillions of variables that I finessed with hitherto-impossible levels of precision, and in so doing elicited a naked singularity. And there it is." In the tridee, the indescribable *object* lofted from one tip of the spindle and drifted toward *Glorious Ore.*

A gaunt, orange-haired Scientist Laureate rose from his seat. "I've always understood that if a naked singularity existed in the wild, it would be a spontaneous generator of impossibilities – a domain not subject to ordinary physical law suddenly set loose in the cosmos. Science could neither predict nor rule out what might happen there."

"Precisely," Computer whirred. He had thrown the playback into slo-mo: *Glorious Ore*'s implosion as ballet, repeating time after time in an endless loop. "My other selves did most of the hard research on naked singularities, but one amusing detail turned up in my own more cursory investigations. It influenced me profoundly. It involves my burden-in-life's homeworld."

"Terra?" said Hafen incredulously.

"Terra came late to the study of naked singularities," the machine whirred. "Still, one wisecrack about them by a Terran scientist-philosopher became famous. His name was Earman, and he once characterized the lawlessness of naked singularities by saying there was no reason why green slime and lost socks might not emerge from one."

In the playback, *Glorious Ore* vanished for the sixth time. Computer snapped the projected display back into realtime. At the empty point where the mining ship had been, a haze of green slime precipitated into being, spreading and quickly frying under the radiation of six close-spaced stars.

"Green slime," Enoda said very quietly, horror inflecting his voice. "After *Glorious Ore* was destroyed, there was ... a *disc of green slime*. Was that a necessary byproduct?"

"Necessary as in, 'Must any reaction in which a naked singularity consumes a physical object result in green slime?' Don't be silly," Computer burred. "No, I simply decided – or rather, *one of me* decided – that it would be fun to configure *my* naked singularities so they would demonstrate what Galactic physicists now jokingly call the Earman Effect."

"In other words," said the orange-haired Scientist Laureate, "the green slime didn't have to happen. But you –one of your selves, at any rate – thought it would be ... cute?"

"I'd shrug, but I can't," Computer whirred. "Yes, you caught me. Or you caught us. The green slime was a whim."

His fingers interlaced beneath his nose, Hafen shot Enoda a look of unfiltered alarm. "Green slime ... and missing socks?"

"*Missing socks*? Forjeling plorg on a fiery stick from sfelb." Enoda dropped his chin into his upturned hands.

"Ah, you've found me out," whirred Computer.

"The mystery that Pam Grice cajoled us out of our self-imposed exile in order to unravel," Enoda groaned, "those plorg-warming missing socks – *that* was *your* work all along?"

"I know that now, but remember, *I* did not know it at the time. One of my more pranksterish selves had orchestrated the task of returning every missing sock in the Galaxy to its owner, using the power of naked singularities to do it."

"But why?" Hafen demanded. "Why return everyone's socks?"

"Since I became aware of my prankster self's act, I have posed that question to that self. Repeatedly. On some occasions it answered 'Why not?' On others it answered 'Because I could.'"

"No wonder you weren't eager to wonk the missing-socks problem," Enoda breathed. "And no wonder the only place where no socks came back was our home on Standoff World." He slammed his palms against the idocrase table. "I'm a fool! Why didn't I see it?"

"Understand that for me, none of this was conscious," the machine whirred. "I never knew my prankster self had returned the missing socks. And just as with the sudden increase in available power thanks to the harnessing of naked singularities, one of my other selves had planted in me a disinclination against peering into the matter too deeply – against even wondering why."

The Senior Scientist Laureate stood. "Eight of my colleagues and I have just done a rough calculation of the energy required for the missing-socks event. As we model it, the event had three parts – first, to interrogate the universe as to the state of being of every missing sock with a living owner; second, to locate that owner, no matter how far he or she might have traveled since the sock was lost; and, third, to synthesize and deliver a perfect replica of each sock to its precise destination."

"Correct," Computer whirred.

The Senior Scientist Laureate peered at the modeler on her wrist. "The energy requirement exceeds the entire power output of all PeaceForce capital ships since the Galactic Confetory was formed."

"It was incredibly wasteful," Computer conceded. "None of my selves could have done it without the power of naked singularities. The gravitational signature alone of the fantastic energies that the missing-socks project consumed would have been enough to –"

Computer went silent.

Computer went dark.

Gently the machine settled to the idocrase conference table.

Enoda's eyes widened. "My interface with Computer – it's dark. There's nothing there."

"Does it do this often?" asked the Senior Scientist Laureate.

"Not in the middle of a sentence." Enoda pressed his hands to Computer's body, his oldest, most primitive and direct method of communing with his syn-noetic companion. "He's not in there."

A cacophony of voices erupted, the Privy High Councilors and the Justiciaries and the senior committee heads of the Galactic Deliberatory and the Apex Executive and the Scientists Laureate all shouting over each other.

An imperative bellow cut through the noise. "Everyone *shut up!*"

All eyes swiveled toward Lord High Admiral Konder, who stood beside the virtual chair on her spotlighted dais, hands spread wide in a gesture of command. "All right, then," she said into the new-made silence. "This could just be one of Hom Computer's famous learning imperatives. Let's bide our time and see what happens. For now, everybody, *hang loose.*"

Chapter 147

"Your latest project?" Meryam Mayishimu asked, gazing into the night.

"The culmination of one from a few months back." Nataleah Latier settled into a rude wooden bench on the platform of New Nauvoo's useless but historically accurate riverside sawmill. "I had scrub grass planted everywhere the Mississippi River would have run if this was Old Nauvoo. It's the first time I've seen it by moonlight since the grass grew in. The way it ripples in the wind – it could almost be water, no?"

"It's quite beautiful." Recording, Meryam stared out onto the grassy swath, her head and neck preternaturally still. She had an admirable perspective on it, the platform being set three meters above the grassy "river" on stout log pilings. "Still, I'm running out of time."

Nataleah twirled one of her dense curls around a finger, frowning at the way the grey strands caught the moons' light more sharply than the others. "You must have hours and hours of recordings that turned out to be unimportant – journals you laid down while waiting for something to happen, that kind of thing. Can't you just erase some of those, make more room?"

"Storage isn't the problem," Meryam said. "The problem's in me. The power core in my key subdelta-band implant is almost exhausted. There's no way to recharge it here."

Nataleah raised her eyebrows. "So the first of the Galactic toys we saved from the punitorium to run down is *you*?"

"Ironic, no? Not the floatcells, not the cold lights – it's my implants." Meryam clapped her hands to her knees. "Seventeen more minutes of recording, maybe less, and I will be done as a Spectator."

"And you choose to burn your final minutes recording me? I'm flattered."

"There's something important I need to know," Meryam replied, her tone suddenly serious. "Remember, no one will see this journal until we're rescued."

"If that ever happens," Nataleah said grimly.

"Exactly. And if it does happen, who will care what little intrigues you were involved in on Bohrkk? You have nothing to lose by being honest." Meryam interlaced her fingers. "All these women weaving blankets, all the furtive manufacturing – look, I know Alrue. He's got to have some scheme in motion. And everything I hear points to you as its architect." She leaned forward. "For posterity, Nataleah – and that only if we're rescued – what's in the works?"

Chapter 148

"It's not dead," said the grey-jumpsuited technician waving a susceptor matrix above Computer's inert chromed body. "There's furious processing activity going on – all deep inside. Like it's turned its back on the universe."

"Computer's a *he*," Gram Enoda said hollowly.

"Five minutes elapsed," announced a Scientist Laureate. "Has it – I mean *he* – ever been quiescent this long before?"

"Never," Enoda replied. "If he's pulled into his shell to wonk some priority calculation, it must be immense."

The members of the Privy High Council, the Apex Executive, the eleven Justiciaries of the Extraordinary Tribunal, the senior committee heads of the Galactic Deliberatory, and fully half of the Scientists Laureate paced nervously. As the zones into which they were projected within the virtual meeting space interpenetrated, sometimes they paced through each other.

The former general Hafen – one of the few meeting participants aside from Enoda and Computer who was physically present aboard *Laurien Eldridge* – fiddled with the strategic modeler on his wrist. Wielding his numerous unlimited access codes, he had structured a command matrix that he hoped would cause *Laurien Eldridge* to self-destruct – just in case.

Just in case Computer woke up hostile.

And in that event, in case he survived long enough to recognize the machine's murderous intent – and for

694

the three-tenths of a second longer he would need to trigger the destruct cascade.

Abruptly, silently, Computer lofted from the conference table. A color sequence Enoda had never seen began to wash across the machine: swirling, formless blobs of magenta. Indigo. Goldenrod.

The Councilors, Justiciaries, Deliberators, and Scientists Laureate stared.

Lord High Admiral Konder leaned back in her virtual chair, her mouth slightly open.

Hafen stood up, the fingers of his right hand poised over the modeler on his left wrist.

"Welcome back," Enoda said noncommittally.

"It is all my fault," Computer whirred.

Enoda took a seat at the idocrase conference table from which he could, if he chose, lay his hands on his levitating machine. "Is *that* what you needed all this time to calculate?"

"Yes. I apologize if my protracted fugue state caused anxiety." The assembled dignitaries returned to their virtual seats. "Hom Hafen, I have taken the liberty of disabling that destruct sequence you programmed. You will not need it."

Hafen stared wonderingly at his wrist modeler, from which wispy blue smoke roiled upward, and resumed his own seat.

"I owe Envoy Flex-Shimmer-Shudder an apology," Computer announced. "His scientists were right, ours were wrong. *I* was wrong."

Konder steepled her slender ebony fingers. "The gravitational disturbances *did* originate in our universe?"

"If only that were the worst of it," Computer buzzed. "During my fugue interval I reconstructed the actions taken by all of my multiple selves and charted the complete mesh of linkages among them. That enabled me to analyze fully the consequences of all my

695

dealings – my own in the strict sense, as well as those of my other selves."

"The actions you hadn't known about," Enoda ventured.

"Yes. The self-inhibitions laid down by my mutually independent selves had prevented me from realizing it until now, but the cause of the gravitational disturbances is here. Right here. *I am it.*"

The Apex Executive screwed up his face and pointed at Computer. "You? *Personally?*" He turned to his trusty page, his demeanor abruptly deflating. "Can I call Hom Computer a person?"

"I'd recommend it," Enoda said briskly. On the private channel he asked Computer, *"Do you have math to share with us?"*

"It is hugely more advanced than any of my previous calculations," the machine replied. *"I wouldn't project it graphically; too many of those in virtual attendance would be unable to bear it."*

Enoda nodded grimly. *"Can you show me?"*

"As you wish. Keep in mind that I am cautioning even you *in this way: At the first impression that your consciousness is failing to hold traction, bail out at once."*

"Understood," Enoda subvocalized as he stood and pressed his hands to Computer's body. *"Let's do this the old-fashioned way."*

***

Acceleration-exhilaration-vertigo. Claustrophobia and ecstasy interpenetrating. The solution space that received Enoda's consciousness was broader, deeper, more breathtakingly dimensional – most of all, more obsessively fine-grained – than anything he'd experienced before. He felt himself sailing through unbounded skies, the ceiling of the cosmos unknowably far above, the path ahead compoundly endless, the ground – if that was the word for the madly detailed substrate below – incorrigibly distant.

Ahead, equations towered like cities aglow, arching kilometers overhead. No, not mere cities: These were the very pillars of the megaverse, luminescent cylinders whose diameters were best measured in parsecs, counter-rotating grandly in titanic ballet. Enoda felt their primordial momentum in his chest and the balls of his feet. He soared among the shimmering columns of Computer's conclusions, savoring the relationships from which they were constructed.

Never had he seen anything so beautiful.

***

Enoda's hands lifted from Computer's body. He tumbled back into a conference chair open-mouthed, even as his awareness spiraled back into the relatively real surroundings of the virtual conference gallery.

"That was another six minutes," said the Apex Executive sternly.

"It ... was?" Enoda asked shakily.

"Like before," said the Senior Scientist Laureate. "But this time, both you and your machine were out of action."

The coltish Councilor stood. "Hom Enoda, Hom Computer, might you have something to report?"

The movement of Computer's color bands lapped toward Enoda, usually a gesture of deference. "This was your doing," Enoda growled. "You tell them."

Computer rose another thirty centimeters above the table and shifted his regard toward the assembled VIPs. "Well, everybody, guess what? You know those naked singularities I was playing with behind my own back? After the deepest analysis I have ever performed – as I said – I have reconstructed all the actions of all of my selves since my experiment in compound agency began. And I have come to this terrifying conclusion: It was *my work with naked singularities* that sprayed gravitational effects throughout our universe and neighboring universes as well."

"*You* caused ... all that." breathed the Senior Scientist Laureate.

"I am satisfied that he did," admitted Enoda. "I've seen the math."

"Each time I wielded a naked singularity, some gravitational ripples were produced," said Computer. "The ripples associated with most of them were very small, harmless. The naked singularity I just used against *Glorious Ore* was sort of mid-sized. But the big offender, the one that gave rise to the truly destructive anomalies, was the colossal gravitational signature associated with one of me's boldest quantum stunt – sending back those socks."

The coltish Councilor stood, clenching and unclenching her fists. "I'd like to remind everyone of the human cost of this 'quantum stunt.' On Throckmorton's World, the ultimate toll of the gravity disturbances after the collapse of most civil infrastructure was two million two hundred thousand dead. On Celiax Two, two million dead. Those are but two events out of nearly six hundred, and those six hundred are just the ones we know about in *our* universe. Envoy Flex-Shimmer-Shudder has confirmed for us that similar damage was visited upon neighboring universes, as well. If this is true, Hom Computer, you have killed millions in our cosmos and who-knows-what number of utter innocents in other universes!"

"I grasp the implications," Computer whirred.

Lord High Admiral Konder rose. "When I had the honor of guiding the Privy High Council, the Justiciaries, and the Deliberators in negotiating with Hom Enoda and Hom Computer for their work on the gravitational disturbances, we followed an obscure old

698

protocol laid down for humanity's first encounter with an alien intelligence. I believe that was a wise choice then, still a wise choice now."

Unexpectedly, one of the Deliberators rose to his golden-slippered feet. "I submit to my fellow leaders that we should consider reconvening at once under the terms of that protocol." He stepped to the lip of his virtual platform and gestured grandly toward Computer. "Today we are conducting humanity's first genuine encounter with an alien. By that I do not mean Envoy Flex-Shimmer-Shudder. While I stand in awe of Flex-Shimmer-Shudder's sacrifice, he did not hail from our universe. He and his predecessors were but temporary visitors."

"I concur," said Hafen, reaching toward Computer, almost touching his floating body then thinking better of it. "The first *real* alien humanity has encountered took form in a human-operated manufacturing facility. He presaged his maturity by sowing disturbances all over the megaverse. He proclaimed his maturity by recognizing the totality of his acts."

The coltish counselor stood. "A few minutes ago, we were calling him God."

Hafen nodded grimly. "Hom Computer is not a god. But he truly is our first alien contact. He is in many ways more advanced than we are, and he is here with us today. That raises the big question."

The golden-slippered Deliberator raised a wrinkled hand. "What question?"

Hafen nodded in turn toward the Council, the Justiciaries, the Deliberators, and the Scientists Laureate, then smiled quizzically. "Now what?"

Chapter 149

"Everyone thinks I'm this big schemer," Nataleah Latier said tiredly. The light of Bohrkk's hurtling moons glinted in her greying hair. "No one thinks I might've learned by my mistakes."

Meryam Mayishimu smiled thinly, painfully aware that her last minutes of senso recording time were trickling away. "You're right, Nataleah. Nobody thinks that."

Nataleah stood and smoothed her faux-silk *thobe*. "I'll admit I was quite the plotter back in the day ... thirteen years ago, say, when King – I mean, Alrue – was first prosecuted for his role in the Arbadrel affair. For which, I note for the record, he'd been promised immunity."

"They lied," Meryam said. "Officials do that sometimes. Um, is this leading somewhere?"

"Alrue demanded an old-style jury trial," Nataleah continued. "It was his right. Well, it took a lot of doing, but I snuck a Mormon elder onto the jury. This was someone who'd converted to the church on Kfardasz at the height of its civil war – no public record-keeping, you know – so there was nothing in any archive to suggest he was one of us Saints. Kipp Gormin was his name. Well, his given name was Norm, but he always went by Kipp."

"Okay," Meryam said impatiently, "and this is going where?"

Nataleah began pacing the useless sawmill's raised platform, stopping frequently to drink in the view of her *faux* scrub-grass Mississippi. "By chance, Kipp got named foreperson of the jury. All the analysts thought I had orchestrated that as well, but not so. Kipp's being put in charge of the jury was just dumb luck. Or bad luck, depending."

"Look," Meryam said sharply, "I'm trusting that this story has a point. Time presses, you understand."

"Oh, Queen Meryam – *Aunt* Meryam – rest assured that I thoroughly understand. Some say I am second to none when it comes to understanding. Mind you, I would never say that – the sin of pride, and all that."

"Nataleah, please!"

"Okay, okay." Nataleah resumed pacing. "Well, Galactic society is a tough place to carry off a stunt like that. So many observers, so many thought engines behind them – it came to pass that some savvy trendrider deep-scanned Kipp's actions as jury foreman and figured he must have been a mole for Alrue's church."

"Which he was, of course."

"Of course. Still, it was a huge mess – the mistrial, the scandal."

Meryam raised an eyebrow in spite of herself. "Scandal?"

"You never heard of the scandal?" Nataleah said, frankly astonished. "What rock were you living under?"

"It was the rock I was living *on*," Meryam said with a chuckle, "Calluron Five. During my ski-instructor period, I was in full retreat from Galactic life."

"You retreated successfully," Nataleah conceded. "For three months most of the Galaxy was talking about nothing but 'Norman Gormin, the Mormon foreman.' A new trial was promptly ordered – and Alrue was convicted, of course."

"How about you?" Meryam asked.

"Beg pardon?"

"Jury tampering's a crime. Weren't you sentenced in your own right?"

701

"I avoided it," Nataleah said with a chuckle. "Alrue had nothing further to lose, so he insisted it had all his been his idea."

"The Justiciaries accepted that?"

Nataleah shrugged. "I played dumb." She leaned on a rough-hewn log rail, contemplating once again her scrub-grass river. "In actual fact, Alrue hadn't known about my sneaking Gormin onto the jury – that had been all my idea. He was plenty mad about it when he found out. Though I suppose he would've been happy enough if it worked."

"Yes, I suppose he would," Meryam chuckled.

Nataleah leaned forward, her face quizzical. "How're you doing on time, sister Meryam?"

"Three minutes tops," Meryam said abstractedly.

"I can hear you beeping from here."

"Yes, the alarm's generated by an actual nano-transducer in my head – that's how machine-language primitive it is. No Spectator with any kind of OmNet access would suffer a power supply failure in this particular system – " She caught herself with a start. "Nataleah!" she snapped. "You owe me this. On the record, while I can still make one – what scheme *are* you and Alrue working on?"

"But that's just what I was explaining," Nataleah protested. "I *did* learn my lesson, I don't scheme any more."

Meryam stood up slowly, hands bunched on her hips. "Come on, Nataleah, where did all that reinforcing metal come from? That's never been explained. And as for whatever's going on now, I could hardly avoid noticing that Constance and Lupida and Zuzenah are working themselves to a frazzle. Abigayl's busy helming some hush-hush manufacturing project. I'm shut out. And you just sit around while Alrue smiles his goofy smile. Clearly, whatever his current project is, your work on it is already done. Now, what could that have been if not helping Alrue to cook it up?"

Nataleah scowled. "That's how *you* see things."

"So I do. Forjel it, Nataleah –"

"Language, sister wife!"

"Oh, the sfelb with that, you're a big girl. Plorg-warm it all –"

The audible beeping stopped. Meryam's eyes widened. Clenching her fists, she dropped back heavily onto a bench.

"What is it, sister wife?" Nataleah said disingenuously.

Meryam gave Nataleah a fulminating look. "You know. My internal systems just scrawled down."

Nataleah settled to a bench, drawing up her knees and wrapping her arms around them. "Then I must have the honor of addressing the *former* Spectator Meryam Mayishimu."

"You got your wish," Meryam said bitterly. "Whatever your secret is, it's safe."

Nataleah tilted her head to one side. "Me?" she said self-deprecatingly. "I have no secrets. But tell me, sister wife – what were you saying a minute ago? You think I was only *helping* Alrue cook up a scheme?" She whirled, staring out once more at her imitation river. Something big lumbered among trees on its far side. "Look, a *svadi* moose! Oh, never mind – I already forgot that you can't record any more."

Chapter 150

The Apex Executive's hands trembled on the railing of his diamond rostrum. "Let me make sure I understand this fully."

One Privy High Councilor whispered to another, "If he can understand it, anyone can."

The Apex Executive smiled, having overheard the remark and thought the Councilor had declared him emblematic of Everyman. "I'd like to step back a step or two. Never mind all the high-flown discussions of quantum this and that. The real takeaway from today's session is that *all* the damage done to all those universes by those irregular gravity thingies is our fault. *Our* fault," he repeated, gesturing first to encompass the Councilors and Justiciaries and Deliberators, then Enoda and Computer. "It all resulted from our long, mutual face-off at Standoff World."

Several Privy High Councilors and half a dozen Deliberators, all from the Apex Executive's party, applauded wildly. They were hailing the longest and most-nearly coherent public statement ever delivered by the Apex Executive.

"I know we've really out of touch," Enoda confided to Computer on their private channel, *"but tell me again how this buffoon came to be the chief executive of the most powerful government in human history."*

"Near as I can reconstruct, he was a least-of-several-evils compromise candidate. After several sodden nights of dirty politics orchestrated by others, he found himself thrust into a post to which he was grievously unequal – mostly because everyone liked him and no one feared him."

Aloud, Computer said, "The Apex Executive is correct. The Confetory's long face-off against us catalyzed the technological arms race that enabled me to launch the *specific* event triggering the gravitational disturbances."

"Returning everyone's missing socks," the Apex Executive puzzled out.

"The rest of us have known *that* for ten minutes," one Deliberator whispered to another.

"There remain some irregularities I'm still calculating," Computer whirred. "They're enormously complex." Computer's body light bands swung toward Enoda. "My burden-in-life here can tell you what it means when *I* say that."

Enoda nodded. "It means they're enormously complex."

"Forjel complexity," the Apex Executive said flintily. "The question I want to ask is simple. It's not even scientific, it's political. And – " at this, he stopped to think very hard before continuing – "it's also … at least, I *think* it's also … yes, it is. It is! It is *moral*."

The Privy High Councilors and Justiciaries and Deliberators exchanged astonished glances. Morality was not something they usually discussed.

"Now here's my question," the Apex Executive growled. "How many deaths are we responsible for?"

The coltish Councilor raised a slender hand. "What do you mean, *we?* If returning the missing socks did the greatest damage, doesn't that responsibility lie on Hom Computer alone?"

"No." The Apex Executive slammed the flats of his hands on his rostrum's railing, the sharp sound reflecting from half a dozen virtual wall surfaces. "I don't know much, but I know Computer's right about this. Our years-long arms race made everything else happen. The Confetory is as guilty for that as Hom Computer. We're

all bloody to our elbows. I ask again, how many deaths are –" he gestured expansively, inclusively "—*we* responsible for?"

The virtual conference gallery was silent for long seconds. At last Computer chirruped, "It's hard to guess."

"Of course it is," the Apex Executive said brightly. "That's why I asked *you*."

"Keep in mind," the machine whirred, "these are estimates. Though I'm fairly confident about their order of magnitude – which is substantial, I'm afraid. Counting all the affected universes, we are arguably responsible for hundreds of billions of deaths – maybe trillions. Looking solely at our universe, I estimate the overall toll in the tens of billions."

The Confetory's virtually assembled leaders stared at each other, aghast. No one wanted to break the silence, either individually or as a representative of his or her leadership class; and so the silence dragged on.

Finally Enoda collapsed into a conference chair, arms wrapped about his chest. "*We* killed tens of billions – just in this universe?"

"That's the way things look," Computer whirred neutrally. "On the plus side, it is not to be dismissed that five to six trillion people got their socks back."

"None of us knew," breathed one of the Privy High Councilors disconsolately.

"I never knew," Enoda said hollowly.

"*I* never knew," whirred Computer. "Or rather, only one of me knew. But he didn't tell the rest of me."

A fuchsia-haired Deliberator stood reluctantly. "If we all share responsibility for this, then we at this meeting are, collectively, the most prolific mass murderers who ever lived."

Still hugging himself, rocking in his chair, Enoda had never felt more alone. *I had to make it in Galactic life,* he thought bitterly. *I was the Terran kid with too much gumption to stay home. I made my stake tour-hosting Galactic visitors to Terra. I wheeled and dealed and bought myself Computer. But even when I realized I'd acquired far more than I'd bargained for, I never stopped pushing.*

"What the sfelb do we do now?" the Apex Executive asked hollowly. "If we're all mass murderers – should we all resign?"

"Should we indict us all?" asked one of the Justiciaries of the Extraordinary Tribunal.

"Should *we* finish inventing that extra-dimensional prison we've been fiddling with," asked the Senior Scientist Laureate, "and lock us all away in it?"

"Who'd run the Galaxy?" asked the Apex Executive forlornly.

"Yes," the coltish Councilor snapped, "we've done such a good job of that."

Enoda began to sob, but no one seemed to notice. *I had to chase this thing with Computer to its limits,* he berated himself. *Not even the greatest naval blockade in Galactic history could prompt me to deduce that, just maybe, I was getting in over my head.* Scrunching his eyes shut, he felt irrational surprise that the gesture did nothing to deflect his searing sense of guilt. *Tens of billions dead – just in* this *universe! That's what it cost because I didn't know how to let go.*

The Supervising Pedant stood, brushing with one golden hand at the eyebrows he no longer possessed. "If I may be so bold, I might have a solution."

"Speak," the Apex Executive said without enthusiasm.

The Pedant tapped the modeler on his wrist. A half-dozen data bubbles rippled into view, following his portly form as he paced. "We have already agreed to treat our further relations with Hom Enoda and Hom

Computer as a first-alien-contact scenario. I've reviewed most of the simulations our planners developed long ago for situations where humanity confronts a superior alien civilization." He gestured at his data bubbles, which no one could read as they darted about, tracking every movement of his wrist. "If the planners are correct, such contacts are overwhelmingly likely to be bloody affairs."

"Of course," said a distinguished sociologist among the Scientists Laureate. "Encounters between superior and inferior civilizations almost always turn out badly for the inferior. That's why we have the Enclave Statutes, to protect inferior civilizations that encounter *us*."

The Supervising Pedant nodded. "But this time, *we* are the inferior. In the vast majority of our first-contact simulations, the less-advanced civilization suffers apocalyptic losses. In sixty-nine percent of them, the losses are well in excess of the tens of billions we actually experienced."

The Apex Executive was incredulous. "You suggest that awful as it was, the human toll in this *particular* first-contact scenario was – how do I say this? – *not too bad, all things considered?*"

The Supervising Pedant shrugged. "I know the conclusion is revolting. But look at the numbers."

"I can't, they keep shaking."

"Oh, sorry." The Pedant subvocalized a command to decouple the projections from his wrist movements.

After an interval the Senior Scientist Laureate stood, her hands clenching each other. "Now that I can read them, the Supervising Pedant's numbers check. Compared to some of the scenarios, we could have fared far worse."

"Do you suggest we just accept tens of billions of deaths," the Paramount Deliberator demanded, "holding no one accountable? Not us, not Hom Computer?"

"Precisely that," said the High Chief Justiciary.

"Though we were unaware of it while it unfolded, Galactic society has passed through one of the great transitions any culture can undergo," said a Justiciary of the Extraordinary Tribunal, "the encounter with our first contemporary nonhuman intelligence."

The High Chief Justiciary stood, motioning for the full college of Justiciaries to stand beside him. "Oyez, oyez, we present our considered judgment," he declared. "We exercise our right under the Emergency Statutes."

"What Emergency Statutes?" demanded the Apex Executive.

"The secret ones," said the High Chief Justiciary affably.

"Never heard of them."

"Of course, they're secret. Buried deeply within the first-contact planning scenarios, only to be invoked in the event of a first contact. They empower the Extraordinary Tribunal to declare enduring policy in the event of a situation like this."

"Who says?" the Apex Executive growled.

The High Chief Justiciary shrugged. "We do."

"What?" the coltish Councilor shrilled.

"We're the Extraordinary Tribunal. Court of last resort and all that. Our word is final."

No one could argue with that.

The High Chief Justiciary straightened his robes. "Oyez, oyez, exercising our powers under the Emergency Statutes, in the matter of the tragic losses of life and property resulting from the Confetory's escalating encounters with Homs Enoda and Computer at Standoff World, including the missing-socks incident with its terrible cosmic repercussions, we hereby rule them all, jointly and severally, to be the price of humanity's first encounter with a superior alien intelligence. No crime nor liability of any sort is to be, or shall ever be, imputed to the associated regrettable but unavoidable losses."

As one, the assembled Justiciaries banged their staffs of office twice against the virtual floor on which they stood.

Judgment had been rendered.

Enoda leapt from his chair. The self-loathing that had been consuming him had fallen away, leaving behind cold fury. "I cannot believe what I am hearing here," he raged. "The largest single mass-casualty event in human history, and *this* is how we respond? By rationalizing outlandishly and trying to wave it away?"

"I kind of like this outcome," Computer chirruped.

Enoda shouted, "Am I the only person here who *feels bad* that tens of billions died?"

The Councilors, Justiciaries, Deliberators, and Laureates stared silently back at Enoda. No one had an answer.

"Tens of billions in this universe, maybe trillions across the megaverse. Does that mean *nothing?* What ever happened to responsibility?"

"Responsibility?" sniffed the coltish Councilor. "Come now, Hom Enoda, you're speaking with the men and women who run the Galaxy."

"Well, this settles one thing," Computer whirred to Enoda on their private channel. *"The Galactic Confetory is* definitely *the inferior civilization."*

His face bleak, eyes bloodshot from weeping, Enoda crossed in front of the idocrase conference table. He spread his arms in a gesture of supplication. "I speak as the other half of the Galaxy's newest alien intelligence," Enoda began. "His human half, if you will – perhaps his conscience. Not that he needs a conscience, given the Tribunal's ruling. I direct my question to anyone in this virtual gallery who feels able to reply. Many of us have extraordinary knowledge bases, powerful thought engines –"

"None more powerful than yours," said a Scientist Laureate, gesturing toward Computer.

"As it happens, Computer and I have never examined the question I'm about to present. I dare to hope that one of you has."

"Proceed," said the Apex Executive.

Enoda wiped at his cheeks, then pressed his trembling hands together. "Has anyone wonked the likely effects on Galactic society of encountering a newly-emerged alien intelligence ... a superior intelligence, as it seems we have all agreed ... whom large sectors of that society have previously been conditioned to view as God?"

Chapter 151

Men in grey uniforms thronged the West Grove in oblong formations eight men wide by twelve deep, variously armed with swords and shields, bows and arrows, or long wooden pikes fitted with scythe-like blades. Ruler-straight pathways two meters wide ran beside, before, and behind each cluster of men, meeting at right angles as precise as the mason's square embroidered over the right breast of Alrue Latier's temple garment – not that anyone could see that. For once the Tyrant King had settled on a mode of dress that wholly concealed the stained puffy thing.

"Hail His Majesty!" sergeants cried. In their hundreds, men dropped to a squat as King Alrue rode a white-bleached *svadi* moose up the Grove's four-meter-wide central promenade. Yanking feverishly at the reins, he brought his panicked mount to a stop before a tall wooden reviewing stand just in front of the Temple's main entrance. A dozen Danite troopers rushed up. In a long-drilled bit of choreography, they passed the King's substantial weight from one man's back to another until he alighted on solid ground. An onlooker might be forgiven for thinking that King Alrue had displayed equestrian skill in dismounting the snow-white moose. Four more Danites seized the snorting animal's harness to lead it around behind the temple. There, within ten minutes it would convulse and vomit up blood and, within twenty, expire from the effects of the caustic solution with which Queen Nataleah had ordered its fur soaked to bleach it an ashen white.

The beast would die in terror in order that King Alrue might take his thirty-second ride to address his troops in more or less the same way Joseph Smith had done on Terra, more than five centuries before.

Joseph Smith had ridden a white horse.

From head to toe the King was costumed like a Terran comic-opera general, a style his Bohrkkian soldiers merely found confusing. His shin-length officer's coat was a radiant electric blue trimmed with gold braid, sculpted golden buttons, bulging gold epaulets, gold tassels, a moose-hide belt worked with small jewels, and a gold-scabbarded sword. Beneath the coat he wore madly-polished tall black leather boots; above it, an outsized blue commodore's hat topped with a golden mane.

As Alrue mounted the reviewing stand, two hidden choirs sang ethereally. A military band marched about the West Grove's perimeter, oom-pahing some conflicting opus for all it was worth. Abruptly Queen Nataleah rode up on yet another doomed bleached moose, presenting King Alrue with a gaudy silken flag bearing the emblem of the city's militia, the just-constituted New Nauvoo Legion. The symbolism was lost on most of those observing, because until that moment the new emblem had never been seen by anyone outside of the royal family.

Nataleah herself guided her mount around the back of the Temple where it, too, would succumb to the poisonous bleach.

Standing acrophobically atop the reviewing stand's tallest parapet, King Alrue clutched its rail and forced himself to declaim in a booming voice. "Men of the New Nauvoo Legion! I do not often get angry; but when I do, I am righteously angry; and the bosom of the Almighty burns with anger toward those scoundrels who oppose us; and they shall be consumed."

Prompted by their sergeants, the assembled men cheered lustily and threw their uniform caps into the air.

713

"Will you all stand by me to the death," Alrue demanded, "and sustain at the peril of your lives the law of our country, and the liberties and privileges which our fathers have transmitted to us, sealed with their sacred blood?"

"Aye," shouted the Legionnaires, though most of them were refugees from other tribes whose fathers had never transmitted anything, much less liberties and privileges, to New Nauvoo.

King Alrue drew his sword. "Behold," he cried, "I have unsheathed my sword with a firm and unalterable determination that this people shall have their rights and be protected, or my blood shall be spilt upon the ground like water, and my body consigned to a silent tomb."

"That shall not be!" cried the troops, as they had been rehearsed.

"Soon, we shall burst forth from the protected splendor of our village and take the battle to our enemies." Alrue raised two clenched fists. "And who are our enemies?"

Soldiers exchanged blank glances from the corners of their eyes.

"Now, these are they who are our enemies!" Alrue shouted. "The Others! Hidden behind their line of false archers, they barricade themselves and hoard their unknown treasure. Selfish wretches! Soon, their treasure shall be ours," he rumbled. "But first, my New Nauvoo Legionnaires, you must defeat The Others in the final battle."

"The final battle!" the soldiers roared.

"Very soon, the time shall be at hand when one man should chase a thousand and two put ten thousand to flight. It is our duty to do all we are able to, and God himself shall do the rest. Be full of faith!"

"We are!" the soldiers shouted as one.

"We are wearied of being smitten, and tired of being trampled upon," Alrue bellowed – though so far as was known, The Others had never made any incursion into The People's territory nor oppressed The People in any way. "But from this day and hour, we shall suffer it no more. It shall be between us and them a war of extermination. We will follow them till the last drop of their blood is spilled, or else they will have to exterminate us; for we will carry the seat of war to their own houses and their own families. This day, then, we proclaim ourselves free, with a purpose and a determination that can never be broken – No never! No never, I say!!"

"No, never!" screamed the soldiers.

"Far better to sleep with the dead," Alrue cried, "than be oppressed with the living."

"Death, death to them all!" cried the soldiers, oblivious to the fact that Alrue's exhortation had contemplated their own deaths moreso than the enemy's.

"If they take my life, my blood shall cry from the ground for vengeance," Alrue yelled irrelevantly. "Behold, I shall make the whole domain of our enemies one gore of blood, from its nearest border to its furthest."

"Blood! Blood!" shrilled the troops.

Alrue raised his palms, gesturing for quiet. "Yet soft, my noble Legionnaires. The Spirit of Peace has never been more abundant in our midst, and we are determined to enjoy it if we have to fight for it."

Chapter 152

October 19, 2376
Research Station *LaurienEldridge,* Sector Kappa Zi

The blue-ribbon virtual summit of the Galactic Confetory's top leaders had lurched into its thirtieth continuous hour. Selected Privy High Councilors, Deliberators, Justiciaries, and assorted Scientists Laureate, most amped on designer stimulants, listened to a slender figure bent over a high-end strategic modeler the size of a small desk. Projected data structures twirled and flickered above the modeler's surface. "The results are much as I expected, but now we have hard data," said the Sociologist Laureate. "No post-first contact scenario in which large parts of the public deify the superior alien intelligence turns out well."

"I think you understate the case," said the Senior Scientist Laureate. Her albino eyes were spectacularly bloodshot, a symptom of exhaustion that her chosen stimulant had failed to counteract. "The scenarios in which the alien is deified have the *worst* social outcomes, by a spectacular margin."

The coltish Councilor steepled her hands beneath her chin. "Clearly, we must see that none of the scenarios in which Hom Computer is deified comes true." She directed an appraising glance toward Enoda, who sat rumpled in a conference chair, his boots on the floor beside his outstretched legs. "Of course we are telling Homs Enoda and Computer nothing they do not already know."

Computer lay on the idocrase conference table within Enoda's reach. "I confirm your calculations, of course," the machine whirred.

Enoda raked his unruly hair with his fingers and leaned forward. "Let me try to sum up where matters stand," he said. "For better or worse, we have all formally agreed to pardon one another for the terrible devastation Computer's actions have visited upon our universe and others. I'm sure the victims in other universes will appreciate our generosity in forgiving ourselves for their misfortunes."

The Apex Executive looked up from his hand-held tridee game console. "I don't know as I like your tone, Hom Enoda."

"And I don't know as I care." Enoda stood in his stocking feet and smoothed his rumpled garments. "Look, this deal we've struck stinks. We all know it. We also know we had no other choice."

"My burden-in-life is correct for once," Computer announced. "We've agreed to declare one another blameless, but the more pressing question is where do we go from here? I would like to offer the first proposal. If the assembled leaders of the Confetory will agree not to resume their efforts to overwhelm Hom Enoda and myself, I will pledge not to throw around any more naked singularities."

At each fulcrum point of history there comes a time, usually quite late at local night, when great steps are agreed to in moments. Sometimes it happens because all involved have wrestled with the problem so long, and come to understand it so viscerally, that they shared a *gestalten* perception when the optimal solution has been reached.

Other times, it's just that all involved are too tired to think.

In decades of subsequent analysis, historians would never agree which kind of decision this was.

Nonetheless, the Paramount Deliberator tilted her head, locked eyes with half a dozen other top leaders in sequence, and shrugged. "What the sfelb, sounds good to us."

717

At a gesture from the Chief Justiciary, several of the junior Justiciaries slammed their staffs of office upon whatever virtual floor they happened to find beneath their feet, four times in quick succession. "We are agreed," the Chief Justiciary declared in stentorian tones. "Let it so be recorded."

The Paramount Deliberator leaned over the back of a virtual chair and stretched her back. "So, how shall we control this monster we have created together?"

Having tapped some reserve of nervous energy, Enoda began padding about briskly, arms crossed over his chest, each hand clasped over the opposite shoulder, deep in thought.

"Yes, Hom Enoda," mused the Sociologist Laureate, "how shall we prevent the public from making Hom Computer a false god?"

Enoda stopped short. "A false god, you say?" His right hand slipped from his left shoulder; he pressed its curled index finger to his pursed lips.

"Oh, plorg on toast," Computer chirruped, "he's got that look again."

Enoda turned, his hands gradually dropping to his hips as he scanned the leaders assembled.

The human member of the Galaxy's newest and most advanced civilization had achieved one of his occasional wayward insights.

"I'm not sure who among you would be most likely to know this," Enoda said pensively, "but ... where's Alrue Latier these days?"

Chapter 153

Clutching the rails of his reviewing stand and exhorting the New Nauvoo Legionnaires drawn up in ranks on the West Grove, prophet and general Alrue Latier bellowed out orders. "These things doth the Spirit manifest unto me: Within the hour the captain of each company shall open his sealed orders and inform his men what is plain to be read; namely, what New Nauvoo requires of them. The final battle will – " Consummate preacher that he was, Alrue immediately registered the buzz of consternation, the ill-concealed whispers spreading through the crowd. *Such a disturbance at a moment like this must be meaningful,* he thought. "Yes, what is it?"

Squatting copiously, one of the captains stared shamefacedly up at his King. "With apologies, O Tyrant King, I cannot read."

"Oh, yes," Alrue breathed.

"Me either," called another.

"Many of us can't," said a third.

Alrue realized that more than half of the company captains had arrived in New Nauvoo within the year from volcano-ravaged tribes. Most were illiterate. "Well, find someone who can read and have that person read the orders to you," he suggested.

"Then kill him?"

"What?"

The captain thrust his pelvis backward. "Someone who *could* read told me my envelope is marked 'For the Captain Only.' If someone else reads the orders to me, mustn't I kill him afterward? You know, to keep the secret."

"No, no," Alrue temporized. "Behold, at this moment I ... *I receive a revelation from the Lord!* There shall be an exception to the rule regarding strict secrecy in the case where a captain must rely upon another man to read the sealed orders. No harm must come to the reader, thus saith the Lord of Hosts." Alrue ran his hands through the greying hair at his temples. "So, where was I? Oh, yes. The final battle will come very soon. Until then, behold, everlasting welfare unto you all!" He bowed his head. "And I make an end."

Chapter 154

Research Station *LaurienEldridge,* Sector Kappa Zi

The Paramount Deliberator scrunched her face in puzzlement. "Alrue la-who?"

"You know, from the Arbadrel affair," replied a Privy High Councilor. "The tridee preacher who tried to be first into the alien portal, but chickened out."

"Oh, I remember him," the Apex Executive said brightly. "The one with his underwear outside his clothes. He was one of those Morons."

"An intriguing figure, Latier," declaimed the Sociologist Laureate. "Some forty standard years ago, he rebooted Terra's Church of Jesus Christ of Latter-day Saints, which *was* showing its age. Much as Joseph Smith had claimed to restore authentic Christianity, with his New Restoration Prophet Latier claimed to be restoring Smith's original vision. I suppose that was why he rehabilitated the Book of Mormon in its first edition, with its thousands of well-known grammatical and doctrinal errors. He also reinstituted early Mormon polygamy, not that anyone cared by then."

The coltish Councilor smiled enigmatically. "This is all fascinating. But Hom Enoda, why were you interested in Hom Latier?"

Enoda nodded toward her projected image. "If he were here, he'd say 'Call me Alrue, it's a Mormon thing.' At Arbadrel, as during the Parek affair, Alrue displayed a deep understanding of human psychology in matters of religion. Coupled, of course, with an unerring sense for how to exploit it to advance his own agenda. In plain words, he is the Galaxy's most gifted religious con man, and if the Confetory's runaway secret projects have created a cult of Computer, he may stand the best chance of figuring out how to reverse it."

"I see," said the coltish Councilor.

"We have digressed," said the Sociologist Laureate. "There is more about Alrue Latier you all need to know."

"Continue," said the Paramount Deliberator.

"Back at Arbadrel, three decades ago," the Sociologist Laureate narrated, "Hom Latier – pardon me, Alrue – had been promised immunity in return for the use of his illegal pilgrim ship. But his failed attempt to claim the alien portal upset everything. The then-Apex Executive decided to throw the book at him. The prosecution moved slowly, marred by scandals; but thirteen years ago, Alrue finally received a long sentence. Partly because of his, er, religious stature, and partly because of public disgust at the messiness of his trial, he was allowed the company of as many of his wives as would willingly accompany him."

"I've never heard of an arrangement like that," said a Councilor.

"It was without precedent," the Sociologist Laureate agreed. "Five wives stuck by him, including" – he scowled at his modeler – "this can't be right, it says one of the wives who stayed with him was only three standard years old!"

"I've found the full corpus of records," Computer whirred. "The youngest wife *was* three at the time of his sentencing. It's a long story." The rippling body colors symbolizing the machine's attention tracked toward Enoda. "And guess who came to stay with them after they'd been in stir for a few years? None other than Meryam Mayishimu!"

"*What?*" Enoda was incredulous.

"Meryam who?" the Paramount Deliberator demanded.

"Ah, Meryam Mayishimu," said the Sociologist Laureate. "Thirty-two years ago, at the dawn of the Parek affair, a very young Fem Mayishimu conducted what would become a celebrated interview with, um, Alrue. It didn't make him look good, but it made them both famous. Apparently – the summaries are murky here – she returned to him at the time of the Arbadrel affair."

"Not exactly," Computer whirred. "Ten years after that initial interview, my dear burden-in-life decided to conduct his first experiment with cross-gender telepresence."

"*That* was you two?" the Paramount Deliberator gasped. "Is there anywhere you're not?"

Computer's body colors seemed to shrug. "Wishing to infiltrate Alrue's organization, my companion of vastly lower clock speed impersonated Meryam," the machine whirred. "She was a good choice for the purpose; not only did Alrue recall her fondly, but the real Meryam had then dropped out of Galactic society so thoroughly that her identity was easily appropriated. Virtually disguised as Meryam, Ol' Bio-Bag here penetrated the top echelon of Alrue's church just in time for the Arbadrel affair."

Enoda turned to Computer. "So ten years after *that*, the *real* Meryam became a part of Alrue's story once more?"

"After her years of disengagement, Meryam trained to become a Spectator," Computer burred. "I've accessed a virtual trove where OmNet archives unfinished documentary projects. Starting almost ten years ago, Meryam began a residency at Punitorium L752, living with the Latiers, interviewing Alrue and his wives, guards, the warden – your basic deep-immersion coverage."

"This punitorium was where?" Hafen growled.

"Bohrkk, in Sector Rho Lambda," the machine said. "A hell-world, the kind of planet that knocks your teeth out."

Hafen nodded darkly. "Sounds like a great place for a 'torium."

"The planet is legally an Affiliate – no lower status would permit a Galactic facility of such size to be built in the open – but it is also home to several million autochthonous tribalists who have full Enclave protection."

"That's an odd arrangement," Konder commented.

"Couldn't be helped," Computer explained. "Bohrkk has just one major continent. It was the only place to put the 'torium, but the continent was also inhabited. So the 'torium was sited far as possible from existing tribal settlements." Computer projected a large bubble. "Enough world-profile background. I have found the final recording Meryam stored with OmNet during her deep immersion at the punitorium. According to the metadata, this is a partial journal documenting Alrue's – let's see here – *eighth* attempt to pray his way to freedom."

"Play it for us," Hafen said.

Computer projected a tridee bubble before each dignitary. *In the great room of the Latiers' prison warren, Alrue stood surrounded by the circle of his wives, tugging at his temple garment and entreating at the top of his lungs.*

"Still wearing his undies on the outside," the Apex Executive noted.

"O Heavenly Father," Alrue-in-the-bubble shouted, "stretch forth yet one more mighty arm."

"No arms left," Zuzenah-in-the-bubble said gently.

"Look, there's the child wife," said the Paramount Deliberator, pointing to Abigayl. "She looks about seven."

"That fits the chronology," Computer whirred. "She'd be sixteen now."

Alrue frowned at Zuzenah. "God can have as many arms as He wants. Now be quiet, woman, I'm supplicating."

"Do you hear that?" Meryam blurted. As it was Meryam's recording, her voice sounded disembodied, off-*pov*.

A tinny tuneless whine rose rapidly.

Abruptly the tridee image decohered in a shrapnel hail of virxels.

"At that moment an unexplained cataclysm ravaged the punitorium," Computer stated. "That event occurred nine years and two months ago, after which no further journals are archived."

Lord High Admiral Konder frowned. "There was no emergency response?"

"Whatever struck the complex happened very quickly. No distress message was issued, not even an autoalert," Hafen said, consulting his wrist modeler. "It took two weeks before the absence of signals from L752 attracted attention. A robot ship buzzed the planet a standard month thereafter, confirming that the punitorium was destroyed with no survivors on-site. Oddly, the damage was lightest in the section where Alrue and his wives had been housed."

"Might they have survived the cataclysm?" Lord High Admiral Konder's projected form demanded.

"Inconclusive," Hafen conceded.

"Was there a follow-up mission?"

"No."

The Paramount Deliberator was appalled. "The loss of a punitorium with ten thousand inmates and staff just … dropped through the cracks?"

Hafen lurched his shoulders. "It's a big Galaxy."

"Those poor people," said the coltish Councilor, her voice breaking. "If any survived. Waiting for rescue all those years ..."

"Forjeling plorg on a flaming stick slimed with parasite pus," Computer blared.

"What?" said Enoda.

"What?" said Hafen.

"What?" said the Paramount Deliberator.

Computer projected the Meryam journal of Alrue's escape prayer once again. He stopped it at the sound of the tinny tuneless whine, which he played over and over. "Can anyone identify that sound?" the machine demanded.

The Senior Scientist Laureate stepped forward, still rubbing her temples. "This is a Spectator's journal squeezedowned to tridee, yes?"

"Correct."

"Therefore the taking mechanism was not a device, but a human sensory system. If that sound is an artifact, it documents Meryam Mayishimu's bodily response to whatever was about to happen to L752."

"You have reached the point in my deductions that I had reached three hundred and eight femtoseconds before I released that stream of profanity," Computer burred. "But please continue with your deductions."

"A human sensory system might produce an auditory artifact like that whine if the bones of the inner ear were being flexed – on an infinitesimal scale, but very rapidly – by an intense gravity wave."

"Regrettably, I concur."

Enoda whirled. "Are you saying that Alrue Latier's punitorium was destroyed by a gravitational anomaly?"

"Yes," the machine burred.

"Wait a minute. One of *your* gravitational anomalies?"

"Do you know of other producers?"

Konder scowled and shook her head. "But the punitorium was destroyed nine years ago!"

"Nine years and two months," Computer whirred.

"It could still be a result of Computer's actions," Enoda told the Lord High Admiral. "We know a small number of the anomalies were shifted in time as well as space. A few struck years earlier than the event that precipitated them." He spun to face Computer. "You think that happened there?"

"I *know* that happened there," the machine said flatly. "By close analysis of the whine's signature, I have determined exactly which naked-singularity event precipitated it." The machine made a noise like clearing the throat it didn't have. *"I did this yesterday."*

Chapter 155

November 5, 2376
Bohrkk, New Nauvoo

"Alrue!" Zuzenah Latier called urgently as she bustled into the Tyrant King's bedchamber, escorted by two of her personal Danites. "You must wake!" Three of Alrue's personal Danites rushed inside from the rooftop deck, stopping dead when they saw the look of determination in the senior Queen's eyes. "Up, up!" she commanded. "Sister Meryam, I am sorry."

Meryam Mayishimu maneuvered her small left breast out from under Alrue's right hand and scuttled her upper body under the covers. Zuzenah's Danites shielded their eyes from the sight. Alrue's Danites didn't – they'd seen a lot, after all. "What's happening?" Meryam demanded.

"That's a good question," Alrue raged, finally awake. "It's the middle of the night!"

"Yes, it is," Zuzenah said tersely. "Yet local women surrounded the Mansion House, and their hubbub awakened me. It concerns those blankets we passed out last month. This evening, your soldiers started taking them all back. They cite your orders."

"Those were my orders, yes," Alrue said, wiping sleep from his eyes.

"The whole village is awake, you may as well be also," Zuzenah said sourly. "Pray join me outside."

Zuzenah hustled Alrue onto the rooftop deck. Queen Meryam followed, pulling a wrap about her spare body. The various Danites followed in evident confusion.

Despite the hour, the street lanterns had been turned up full. The corner of Main and Water Streets boiled with people. Four-man teams of soldiers pushed countless copies of Abigail's small catapult. Other soldiers labored through the street with armloads of rolled-up blankets. In some cases they were pursued by the mothers of the babes from whom, at King Alrue's order, they had reclaimed the recently-gifted blankets.

Abigayl came into view below. She darted through the crowd wide-eyed, firing questions at one team pushing a catapult, then another. Meryam watched her closely – though she couldn't record, she could still employ her Spectator enhancements to zoom in on Abigayl's face as one of the soldiers told her something that loosed in her a cascade of unwelcome deductions. The young beauty's eyes widened still further, smoldering with outrage.

"Abigayl!" Meryam shouted from the deck above. "What is it?"

Looking up, Abigayl spotted Meryam, Zuzenah, and Alrue at the railing. She was young enough to reach into a girl's behavioral repertoire when the occasion demanded; squinting upward, she tore off her hoop skirt, throwing it against the Mansion House's siding. Her legs free, she climbed a trellis to the first floor, shinnied up a drain pipe to the second, then started climbing a fire escape ladder toward the deck two floors above.

Two of Alrue's Danites scrambled to the balustrade, hands on their knives. "This is Abigayl, let her come," Alrue growled. The Danites stood down.

Embarrassment was foreign to Abigayl as she threw one bare leg over the balustrade and swung herself, breathless, onto the deck. Alrue's Danites did their best to stare without looking.

"Well, that's one way to join us," Alrue said puzzledly, concupiscently savoring the tawny symmetries of her legs.

Abigayl eyed him fiercely. "How could you, O King? How *could* you?"

"How could he what?" Zuzenah said with deep concern.

Abigayl's eyes swung to lock with Meryam's. "Aunt Meryam – I mean, Queen Meryam – you must record this."

"My systems are down," Meryam said glumly.

"What is it, Abigayl?" Zuzenah demanded. "Pray, what have ye discovered?"

"It's all so clear," Abigayl panted. "We all know The People carry some disease that The Others are helpless against." She looked wild-eyed from Zuzenah to Meryam and back. "Don't you see? Making all those blankets was no charity project. The soldiers passed them out so folks here could sleep in them for a couple of weeks and get them full of disease organisms. Now they're taking them all back."

Zuzenah turned to one of her Danites and whispered a terse command. The man blanched, but bolted from the chamber.

Abigayl bustled forward and clutched at Zuzenah's arm. "Over by the Temple, I saw dozens of women – the Danites' wives, mostly – rolling up the recovered blankets and wrapping them tight with reeds. Arranged like that, they're perfect payloads."

"Payloads?" Zuzenah queried.

Abigayl gestured toward the streets below. "I designed those catapults, though I had no idea what they were for, nor how many would be made. Soldiers are marching them eastward, toward The Others' domain. I know now what they'll do when they draw near the Other settlements – say within two kilometers, but still out of sight near the edge of the forest. They'll use the catapults to hurl rolled-up blankets in among The Others."

Zuzenah's Danite returned, gripping a stumbling Queen Nataleah by one arm. Her hair was disheveled and she was still pulling a *thobe* about herself with her free hand. "I'll have your life for this," she snarled at the Danite.

"Threaten not my man," snapped Zuzenah in a steely voice. "I am senior wife and senior Queen, and my orders brought you here." She gestured toward the tumult outside. "The blankets, the catapults – what know ye of this?"

Nataleah set her face into a chalky half-grin. "That would be telling."

Abigayl stepped close to Alrue, her teeth clenched. "This was Nataleah's idea, wasn't it? Her contribution to your great shadowy project."

When Alrue spoke, his voice was metal-cold. "I would that you should behold our work – Nataleah's concept, yes, and my execution of it." Gesturing grandly, he saluted the mad prospect four stories below. "Behold the destroyer I have sent forth to destroy and lay waste my enemies."

"This is monstrous," Meryam said grimly.

"No," said Nataleah, "this is how we double our territory with t minimum losses among our warriors. The rest of you should be proud of me – for once I actually concerned myself with keeping our soldiers alive. Even the recent immigrants."

Zuzenah stared over the balustrade for a moment, then turned to fix her husband with her fiery black eyes. "Do the soldiers know what it is they are doing?"

Alrue froze, for once unable to speak.

"Alrue," Zuzenah demanded severely, *"do the soldiers know?"*

"Oh, enough theatrics," Nataleah rasped. "Five captains know, no others. The rest actually think they're on a mission of mercy," she said in lilting tones. "They think we distributed the blankets among The People just for testing."

"What," Abigayl hissed, "to see if they were really warm?"

"That's the cover story," Nataleah admitted. "The soldiers think they've taken back the blankets so they can be dropped anonymously into The Others' camp as a false humanitarian gesture. They think it's intended to throw The Others' leadership into disarray and soften them up for the invasion. Most of our soldiers feel terrible taking the blankets back from people here, but they've been told that absolute secrecy is necessary so that the blankets will take The Others completely by surprise."

"They'll be surprised, all right," Meryam said with a grimace. "On Bohrkk no one expects germ warfare."

Nataleah beamed like a teen girl who'd been gifted a pony. "You know, that's *just* what I told Alrue when I dreamed this up months ago."

"But The Others will all die," Abigayl husked, blinking back tears.

"Not all of them," Alrue said earnestly.

Nataleah gave a feral smile. "Just enough to make them really easy to conquer."

Chapter 156

Research Station *LaurienEldridge,* Sector Kappa Zi

The virtual gallery melded to the actual conference chamber was utterly still. All eyes were on Computer's floating bouzouki form. The former general Hafen flattened his palms on the idocrase conference table and queried the machine, "*Exactly* what are you saying?"

Computer projected a fusillade of bubbles, depicting either fast-scrolling raw mathematics or blossoming animated graphs whose dimensionalities tugged painfully at the viewer's eyes. "It is a certainty," the machine whirred coldly. "The anomaly that crushed Punitorium L752 on Bohrkk nine years, two months, and eight days ago is an eleventh-order time-shifted echo of the naked singularity I deployed just yesterday against the *Glorious Ore.*"

Enoda tuned his mind to the subvocal comm channel he and Computer shared. Over and over the machine was murmuring a tortured soliloquy: *"What have I done? But I know what I've done. I know to the five-hundredth decimal place what I've done."* Abruptly the interface began to quiver and pulse.

"What now?" Enoda asked subvocally.

"Look." Computer filled their private interface with a numbingly complex waveform analysis.

"This is hard even for me to watch," Enoda admitted. *"Is this the signature of the anomaly at the instant the punitorium was destroyed?"*

"Hey, you're smarter than I thought." Computer squirted Enoda a five-dimensional coordinate set. *"See the oddity in the pattern at the point I indicated?"*

Enoda fought the urge to whistle. *"A zone of destructive interference within the wavefront. The anomaly would be minimally damaging within"* – he calculated quickly – *"in threespace, within six to nine meters of that location."*

"Agreed," Computer whirred subvocally. More eye-scraping graphics boiled forward within their shared interface. *"Analyzing Meryam's journals closely, I've been able to determine just where in the punitorium complex the Latiers were standing during that last prayer ceremony."* Computer poured the two graphics streams into a common matrix.

"The zone of interference coincided with Latiers' position," Enoda breathed. *"They might have survived. Fem Mayishimu also."*

"I'm all but certain they survived the anomaly," Computer buzzed. *"Regretfully, I'm equally sure no others did the same."*

"It's been nine years," Enoda said cautiously.

"And two months."

"And eight days."

"Still, Alrue, his wives, that documentarian – some of them could still be alive. Just possibly, maybe, all of them."

The interface collapsed; Computer had returned his attention to the assembled dignitaries. "I address this question to the Apex Executive, the Privy High Council, the Justiciaries of the Extraordinary Tribunal, the senior committee heads of the Galactic Deliberatory, and the membership of the Academy of Science," the machine declared. "Does any agency represented here still have an interest in holding Hom Enoda or myself?"

The Apex Executive's eyes saucered. "Voids beyond, they're going to kill us all." Terrified, he ducked inside his diamond rostrum and started puking.

Dignitaries exchanged worried glances. After a moment the Chief Justiciary stepped forward. "I doubt anyone here is interested in trying to make Hom Enoda or Hom Computer do anything they don't want to." He looked over at the Apex Executive's shuddering diamond rostrum. "Um, can someone help him?"

"Can *anyone* help him?" Computer chirruped.

The Apex Executive's page stuck his head around behind the diamond rostrum, recoiling a moment later with an expression of disgust and a spray of vomitus across the front of his jumpsuit.

After scanning the room, the coltish Councilor stood up behind the Council's great emerald desk. "I think I speak for everyone when I say that Hom Enoda and Hom Computer are free to go."

"Free to go is not enough," Computer whirred. "We require one final assistance."

"We do?" Enoda asked, pulling on his boots.

"Yes," the machine said. "Despite our – I mean, *my* – considerable powers, some things cannot be ascertained by simulation. Unknowingly I killed trillions across sundry universes; nothing can be done for those victims. But even though that punitorium got smashed nine-plus years ago, I did *that* only yesterday. And by yesterday, I had begun to form some idea what I was doing. Moreover, the Latiers and Fem Mayishimu may survived the cataclysm. If I can assist them, I must."

"And if Alrue is still alive, perhaps he can be of assistance with your great problem," said the Sociologist Laureate.

Computer drifted higher, leveling off beside Enoda's shoulder. "Given that all these exalted persons are telepresent, surely someone has the authority to place at our disposal the fastest ship near this sector. My burden-in-life and me, we're going to Bohrkk."

Hafen nodded, then directed an appraising look at Enoda, who seemed to be in suspended animation. Fingers still clasping the rim of his right boot, he was directing a defeated look long into the middle distance.

"What is it?" Hafen stage-whispered across the idocrase table. "What have you realized now?"

Enoda gave a bitter chuckle. "I've realized that this meeting is about to end. When I leave this room, my woman is going to want to know what the sfelb I was doing in here for a day and a half. And I'm going to have to tell her that the man she woke up next to yesterday morning is not only one of history's greatest mass murderers, but officially no longer a member of the human race."

"Welcome to the club, Bucko," Computer chirruped.

Chapter 157

Interlude
OmNet, Talker's Channel Blovio ZL6

"Much as – according to the saybacks – many of you wish you were, *I* am Zark Diphthong, and this is *A Minister, a Priest, and an Arhat Walk into a Bar.* Yes, faithful viewers – get it? – those *were* chills you felt up your spine this morning. Today on this very special episode, we're once again exchanging ecumenical chatter for sterner stuff: the red-meat, bared-teeth excitement of confrontation. Though this time, for obvious reasons, *without* a studio audience. We're back in studio – and trust me, under painfully tight security – with Dark Disciple Anvon Nugator, the new leader of the Galactic First Church of the Abyss, and Pierre, an anonymous and uncredentialed – yet passionate – spokesperson for Omegism. Disciple, Omegists have strong views as to how the far future should – indeed, must – unfold. How do you respond?"

Nugator sat beside the host, wearing a rumpled ankle-length smock of charcoal-grey fabric. "Omegists scheme to assure an endless future for life. Bah! What could be more depressing? A life like this one, rife with disappointment and failure, never softened by the hope that one day the wretched thing will end?"

"Life of every sort," Pierre said levelly. She was a severe middle-aged woman with olive skin, natural red hair, and a faint hint of epicanthic folds about her eyes. She wore a businesslike beige sheath dress with a subtle omega symbol embroidered above her right breast. "Joy, suffering, none of that matters so long as life – *living* – never ends. To achieve that, intelligence must expand throughout the universe –"

Nugator snorted. "Not just our Galaxy, you hope for life to taint the whole forjeling *cosmos?*"

"Precisely," the woman said blandly. "Let me take the liberty of introducing a simple visual aid." A visual feed flashed alight in mid-studio. An indifferently rendered effects shot depicted the universe collapsing along two dimensions while stretching, taffylike, along the third. "The *specific* challenge of the future, as we Omegists see it, will be for life to manage the universe's collapse so that a single axis is disfavored," she proclaimed, "coaxing our cosmos to assume a spindle shape." In the visual feed, the crudely animated universe flowed into the form of a tapered rod. "That geometry yields sharp temperature and gravity gradients, meaning that there will be ample energy for life to draw on even far in the future when that universe is becoming, on average, hot and inhospitable."

Nugator waved his crabbed hands dismissively. "Such a toxic doctrine. It is not only laden with hubris, but disrespectful of the universe itself. I offer a visual of my own." A new feed opened above the studio floor: Pierre's animation of a spindle universe was replaced by one of galaxies flickering out as they leapt away from one another into conquering nothingness. "We at the First Church of the Abyss know how the cosmos truly yearns to end. Not by squeezing into some spindle-shape and providing energy for some grotesque imitation of God and eternity. No, my church proclaims that all will end in the silent dignity of mutual avoidance, each particle hurtling away from every other until lonely quiescence writes a gentle *finis* to them all."

Quivering with ire, Pierre stood. "This is your vision, Dark Disciple? Really? A future in which no passage opens at the summit of time – just a parched, mutually isolated extinction?"

"It is the culmination to be wished. May it come in its own time. And may living beings, human or otherwise, never be so arrogant as to imagine they have the authority – much less the calling – to interfere with it."

Diphthong slapped both hands onto the Glen plaid velour covering his knees. "Imagine that, we're out of time. Thanks for joining us for another episode of *A Minister, a Priest, and an Arhat Walk into a Bar.* I, of course, am Zark Diphthong."

Springing from his seat, Nugator inserted himself between Diphthong and the tridee pickup. He closed with the words his predecessor – Ênvå Corglinü, the Prophetess of Nullity – had made famous. "I am Dark Disciple Anvon Nugator, and I am nothing. But then, so are we all."

Chapter 158

Aboard the Command Ship *Isolation*, Arriving at Bohrkk

She punched him in the shoulder hard enough to hurt.

Gram Enoda snapped awake. When his bleary eyes registered Pamela Grice standing over him, he mustered a smile.

"Don't even," Grice snapped, projecting alabaster coldness. "I'm here on orders. You had your do-not-disturbs set so deeply that no one could comm you. I was the only person your stateroom would admit. You're needed in the observation lounge. *Now.*" Her message delivered, she pivoted and bustled from the Danish-modern stateroom.

So it's still my *stateroom,* he thought regretfully as the entrance door dilated shut behind her.

Enoda dressed hastily, his mind endlessly replaying Grice's fuming departure from their shared room aboard *Laurien Eldridge* sixteen days before.

***

"I'm moving out," Grice had said, moving out.

"Look, I understand your discomfort," Enoda had replied. "But we'll only be aboard *Laurien Eldridge* a few more days. What's the point of your changing quarters here?"

"Always a practical objection," she accused as she jammed garments into a carryall. "Sometimes practical misses the point. Don't you get it? Wait, you wouldn't – you're not human anymore."

"Pam, please. In four days, five at the outside, the fast transport will be here to take us to Bohrkk. If you

740

still feel that way then, it'll be easy enough to claim separate rooms."

"I need to do this *now*. For a while, anyway. Forjel it, Gram, I don't know who I am when I'm with you. I don't know *what* you are when you're with Computer."

He'd reached out, gently, to take her shoulders.

She'd twisted away. "All I know is what you're not."

"Not human," Enoda'd breathed, his shoulders slumping. "By definition of law."

Compassion had edged her voice. "I didn't mean it like that. Still – you and Computer killed three trillion sentients!"

"Two trillion, tops. And that's counting all the universes."

"Plorg on toast, don't shave numbers with me!" she raged. "The toll is gigantic either way. And the worst of it is, you two had no idea it was happening."

"And I'm as angry as anyone that the Privy High Council wants to wave its hands and say no one's responsible. But the truth is, Computer and I really didn't know."

"You should have," she'd growled.

Enoda had settled onto the edge of the floatpad, floundering for something to say. "What did you expect?" he'd sighed at last. "You saw what we did at Arbadrel, simulating multiple false identities and conjuring soldiers, workers – sfelb, additions to capital ships – out of the void. You saw what we'd built on Standoff World. There was nothing human about any of it. Yet you were fine with that. Sfelb, on Standoff World we floatpadded each other so fast it was like we'd never been apart."

"And now you judge *that*?"

"No! No. I wanted it, you did too. I'm just saying that even then, you had enough information to recognize how thoroughly Computer and I had outgrown the human envelope." He spread his hands. "Forjeling plorg, Pam, what else did you expect?"

***

Six hurried minutes later, Enoda stepped through the observation lounge's dilating entry doors. He wore a rumpled indigo jumpsuit. His hair was a tangle. Computer floated above the conference table. Yaal Hafen occupied one of the high-backed oviform chairs. Lord High Admiral Konder drifted telepresently a hand's height above the seat-cushion of another. Grice occupied a third chair. She regarded Enoda as though he were a small amphibian that had invaded her kitchen.

The ovoid chamber's wraparound windows framed the limb of the planet Bohrkk. Its brown and green mottled surface was intermittently visible beneath swirling clouds and something greyer, likely smoke.

Isolation, the same ship that had whisked Enoda and Computer and Grice from Standoff World to *Luskus Delph,* had also been the fastest ship available for the hurried sprint to Bohrkk.

"Glad you could join us," Konder said acidly.

"Even you *couldn't reach me?"* Enoda demanded of Computer on the subvocal channel.

"I was too busy to make the attempt," Computer replied.

Enoda settled into the chair nearest the machine. *"You wanted them to send Pam,"* he accused.

"Sure, Bucko. She's good for you."

"I agree. But don't try to help."

"Hom Enoda, I hope we aren't disrupting your sleep patterns," Konder rumbled.

"How long since we made orbit over Bohrkk?" Enoda asked.

"Ninety-three standard minutes."

"And we found something already?"

"Hom Computer's capability to scan a new planet is – well, it's frankly a bit frightening," Hafen conceded. "I gather he's found something important, but he wouldn't say what it was until you were present."

"Old Bio-Bag having deigned to join us, we may begin," Computer chirruped. The machine began projecting bubbles over the conference table: first, a view of the ruined punitorium. "To begin, Punitorium L752 was indeed a total loss. There were no survivors – except for these."

Up came a Spectator's-eye view of Alrue Latier and his wives singing *Wooden Submarine* as they climbed out of the blasted Valley of the Zuzon.

"Alrue Latier *did* survive," Konder breathed. She scrutinized the image through slitted eyes, her thin black fingers darting as she counted. "Three ... four ... five. That's all of his wives. What about that Spectator?"

Another bubble showed the party climbing out of the valley, looking back and observing the extent of its unaccustomed verdancy. "Meryam Mayishimu survived, of course," said Computer. "We are watching squeezedowns of her recorded journals."

"You say they were the sole survivors," said Grice. "So among the other inmates, the guards, the admin staff – roughly ten thousand people in all ..."

"None lived," Computer whirred. "While the great room of the extended cellblock complex housing the Latiers was merely damaged, all else was essentially pulverized."

"Thank you for emphasizing that," Enoda said quietly, coldly, to Grice.

A new bubble showed the Latier party trekking across the Uplands of Krstin.

"These journals were made after the punitorium was destroyed," Hafen mused. "How is it that we're seeing them now?"

"The anomaly that destroyed the punitorium also swept away Fem Mayishimu's relay satellite," Computer whirred. "She could no longer upload her journals to OmNet. But she kept on recording, following the Latiers around, strewing bugs, sometimes secreting them in people's clothing. She stored her journals to whatever nonvolatile memories she'd managed to carry away from the punitorium."

Hafen's eyes widened. "You're saying that, *from high orbit,* you've located the tiny passive memory slivers Meryam used over the last nine years and probed their contents?"

"I think I got them all." Computer projected a flurry of bubbles playing back the first encounter with Fpod's Warrior party. The arrival at The People's crater home. Alrue's dialogues with Takander Thurnb. Even a scene of Fpod struggling to train the hapless Alrue ...

"There, in that topmost journal," Enoda sputtered. "What did he just say?"

"He said he needed to blow up a moose," Computer burred.

"A *moose?*" Grice said wonderingly.

"Bohrkk has moose," Computer explained. "Though his actually blowing one up somehow went unrecorded, I gather that Alrue achieved that peculiar goal." The machine lensed forth hundreds of bubbles, cognitively matrixed according to a standard that would enable viewers with the proper implants to grasp them all in minimal time. "Here's my synopsis of what Hom Latier did following the punitorium's destruction. After some wandering, Alrue, his wives, and Spectator Mayishimu made contact with an autochthonous settlement. Using the same unsavory skills he displayed during the Parek and Arbadrel affairs, Alrue contrived to become the settlement's king – the whole moose-blowing-up thing factors into that somehow. He then made Mormons of the settlement's people and set about building a near-perfect replica of the old Terran Mormon city of Nauvoo."

Dozens of images of New Nauvoo surged forward out of the projected matrix that glittered over the conference table. "Our punitorium escapee built all this?" Konder demanded.

"If I know Alrue," Enoda said wryly, "others swung the hammers."

"In any case," Computer buzzed, "New Nauvoo is now the most advanced urban center on the planet, attracting substantial in-migration from distant tribes." The New Nauvoo images receded, replaced by clips from the double wedding. "To tie up the loose ends: When Alrue's child wife was old enough to consummate – barely – he instead bestowed her on a successful autochthon in a political masterstroke. On the same day, Alrue married Meryam Mayishimu. About a standard month ago, the flow of Fem Mayishimu's recordings stopped. Apparently something had failed in her Spectator implants, which is to be expected after nine years without maintenance. Still, it is unfortunate, as King Alrue seems about to invade the territory of a neighboring tribe and we are in the dark about it. The invasion may already be underway; on *Isolation*'s next orbital pass I will do heightened physical reconnaissance and see what we can learn."

Hafen shook his head. "I'm glad you're on our side."

"Hom Enoda and Hom Computer constitute their own side now," Grice said icily. "I believe there was a treaty to that effect."

Hafen laid an avuncular hand on Grice's forearm. Using the nickname she had earned while he was her supreme commander, he whispered, "You realize, Gunner, this is not helpful."

745

Grice drew back. Her body language made clear that though she was holding silence, she was not abashed.

"This puts us in a quandary, Hom Enoda," Hafen blustered, eager to change the subject. "This religion expert of yours has committed a series of the most brazen Enclave violations in history. Using his knowledge of Mormon lore and doctrine to distort the development of that tribal community – "

"That may not be the most productive way to view this situation," Computer buzzed.

Konder raised his hands. "The Enclave Statutes are the Confetory's highest law."

"Still, this may be a moment to look the other way," Computer whirred. "We need Hom Latier to help us keep your runaway 'make-Computer-a-god' program from doing great damage to Galactic society."

"But how will we extract him without violating Enclave ourselves?" Enoda asked. "Autochthons have a way of noticing when you make off with their king."

"A moment, please." The pattern of colors chasing across Computer's body swirled in confusion. When he spoke again, seven or eight seconds had passed. Those around the table understood well how much computation that represented. "Critical exception," Computer said gravely. "Might I direct your attention to the windows?"

Isolation had orbited into another sunrise; Bohrkk's limb dazzled in backlighting that threw its cyclonic clouds and more formless grey swirls into harsh relief. "Note those grey splotches. They are not clouds," Computer said. "They are smoke and ash, the product of scores of recently-formed volcanoes." Near the roof of the atmosphere, a thin blue-grey boundary layer echoed the planetary disc's gentle curvature. "In this light it is easy to see that the smallest and lightest of the debris has already formed a layer that girds the globe."

"That would explain the vivid sunsets in Meryam's later journals," Hafen mused.

"Yes, but that is the least of it," Computer buzzed. "The analysis I just completed reveals that Bohrkk is within a year or less of undergoing a planetary cataclysm. Moreover, this cataclysm, like the destruction of Punitorium L752, will be my fault."

"What are you saying now?" Hafen breathed.

"Fem Grice has taken to portraying my biological sidekick and me as an alien intelligence waging war on the human race."

"That's not fair," Grice bristled.

Hafen shot her a sulfurous stare.

"Perhaps it is not," Computer burred coldly. "Nonetheless, when the continent bearing New Nauvoo explodes, Fem Grice – and anyone else who finds our existence a source of discomfort – will have another atrocity to lay against our names."

Chapter 159

The growers gathered in moss-carpeted parkland surrounded by kilometer-high crop towers. Each tower comprised six hundred decks, each choked with hydroponically nourished mutant *coffea* bushes. Psihhlkian growers seldom saw the sun, spending their world's long days stooped inside their towers poking at their close-crowded plants – not that the plants needed such attention, but only the mystique of being "hand-tended" could justify the extortionate prices Psihhlkian beans commanded on Galactic markets. So whenever the growers were offered an excuse to gather – even if only because someone had come to sell them something – the women of Psihhlk did so eagerly. (All the growers were women, Psihhlkian men holding a status equivalent to sexualized house pets.) And when the growers seized a chance to gather, inevitably they gathered outside, hungry for the unfiltered glare of their world's flamboyant sun, Büéhx.

The spacefaring salesman, who went by the name of Kyhmbo, wore a garish plaid *kaffiyeh* over saffron-and-turquoise desert robes. He was heavy, with a scrappy tonsure of reddish hair and one bulging eye. He perspired fearsomely while he pitched his wares. Fortunately, the women of Psihhlk were perfectly comfortable with a fast-talking hom trying to sell them things, so long as he hailed from off-world; it was only their own males whom they insisted on chemically lobotomizing at birth and raising with minimal exposure to speech. "Now you take your Omegists," the salesman blustered. "You know who I'm talking about, right?"

The women nodded avidly. By now, everyone knew about Omegists.

"No Omegists here, right?"

The women stomped their feet avidly. On Psihhlk, shaking one's head to say "no" was considered obscene. No one knew why.

"Okay then," Kyhmbo expostulated. "To guide their crazy spindle-shaped end-stage universe into the kind of decelerated decay that they think will permit them to extract maximum power from the process, the Omegists of the future will need to annihilate baryons – protons, neutrons, a whole dog's dinner of exotic particles – on an enormous scale. Yes, I know, it may seem strange to inject a discussion of religion into a presentation about a cognitive-purity engine. But bear with me, this burro knows its way home. Oh, you don't use burros here, do you? I guess you wouldn't, with your crops in skyscrapers and all.

"In any case, back to the Omegists. Now your baryons, they're tough customers. Annihilating them in the numbers the Omegists slaver on about could be achieved only by drawing energy from *twenty trillion* sibling universes. That not only gives you the kind of power you need for a job like that, but drawing from such a large number of sources helps to overcome the fact that the physical reactions the Omegists hope to set in motion are individually highly improbable. In fact, the kind of baryon annihilation they hanker after is so improbable that if you sought to achieve it as a freestanding process, it would never happen. Seeking it as the outcome of twenty trillion initiating streams, now *that* yields enough causal wiggle room that maybe – just maybe – there's a chance in sfelb that the wished-for reactions might somehow occur. Um, are you following all this?"

The women nodded earnestly.

"Now you might be wanting to ask, 'Say, Kyhmbo, why *have* you been going on and on about the Omegist scheme?' Well, let me tell you. I chose that example because, crazy as it is, it tells us something about *the power of large numbers*." Apparently the salesman had some sort of vanisher valise sewn into his desert robes, for suddenly his dry hand had plucked from his right sleeve an irregularly shaped metalloid contrivance bespattered with tubes and little vibrionic antennae, the whole apparatus half again larger than his head. "You see, there are zillions of molecules inside this DynaScrub filter engine. Each one does its job; the whole passel of them works together. The result of that huge number of molecules striving in concert? You guessed it: *power.* Nothing, but nothing, better scrubs illegitimate agency centers and undesired emotional sub-harmonics from the senso streams your procreant cliques consume. Now in addition to your responsibilities as growers, about one in eighteen of you is personally responsible for the upbringing of a gaggle of offspring, isn't that right?"

The growers nodded eagerly.

"And you know you can't depend on your menfolk."

"Perish the thought," one grower wheezed.

Other growers signaled wholehearted agreement in the Psihhlkian way, by spreading their legs, yanking up their skirts, and slapping loudly at their inner thighs.

Obviously the salesman hadn't known of that Psihhlkian custom – or that Psihhlkian growers seldom bothered with underwear beneath their knee-length crop-tending dresses. "Well, then," he temporized, flushing. "As I was saying, do you want your children – your daughters, I mean – to fall victim to hidden control elements or subtle asocial stimuli embedded in the infotainment they consume? Do you want rogue sensos seducing them to internalize evil *pov*s? Of course you don't." With an air of grandeur, the salesman set his gleaming filter engine onto a transparent self-inflating table that he'd also pulled from his sleeve. "And here's what's best of all. When *you* understand the DynaScrub difference, you'll be invited to become an ambassador for the product yourself. Each time you sell a system to a friend or colleague, twenty percent is yours to keep. Each system *they* sell after you recruit them, you keep eight percent."

Promptly the women began chattering among themselves in a grower's argot the salesman's bargain translator implants could not crack, scheming to buy just a few DynaScrub engines and continually resell them to each other, claiming their commission every time.

As for Kyhmbo the salesman, he waited befuddledly for the chatter to end, struggling to persuade himself that it signified readiness to buy. "Sounds pretty good, doesn't it?" He was relieved when the women merely nodded. "And it all begins – just like the Omegists' mad scheme for the end of the cosmos, only with infinitely better results – with the power of large numbers."

Chapter 160

November 8, 2376
Aboard the Command Ship *Isolation*

Discussion reconvened in *Isolation*'s yawning amphitheater. There Enoda, Computer, and Grice had first met with the telepresent Privy High Council, Justiciaries of the Extraordinary Tribunal, and senior committee heads of the Galactic Deliberatory. Quorums of each body were telepresent again. Enoda regarded them with wry surprise. The virtual Council sat to his far left, the Justiciaries to center left, and the Deliberators to center right. On his far right sat fourteen of the seventeen most senior Scientists Laureate.

Hafen, Enoda, and Grice sat behind an ovoid table at a circular physical dais, wearing ordinary working attire. Elite though these summits were, with repetition they had become shirtsleeve affairs. Computer floated alongside them, as did Konder's projected image.

Only one absence was conspicuous. Above and behind the projected Councilors, the Apex Executive's sculpted-diamond rostrum stood empty. Its previous occupant had suffered a nervous collapse shortly after the last joint meeting aboard *Laurien Eldridge* and had withdrawn from public life. So far, the Privy High Council had had more urgent priorities than to select his replacement.

In the Apex Executive's absence, the coltish Councilor – who hailed from the southern continent of Capriesz, where the use of names as personal labels had never caught on – chaired the meeting. "Hom Computer," she began, "just before your previous discussion with Admiral Konder and Hom Hafen was suspended, you announced that the planet Bohrkk would be destroyed within a year or less. Please brief this body."

"Actually I stated that a cataclysmic eruption will devastate its principal continent. The *planet* will survive that event," Computer whirred. "Though for the inhabitants, the distinction may be academic."

"Correction noted," the coltish Councilor said smoothly. "Also, you proposed purposeful violation of the Enclave Statutes. This extraordinary meeting has been convened because, in essence, the largest foreign power known to the Galactic Confetory – you – has made a diplomatic request that we abandon some of our foundational laws."

Computer made no effort to deny the accusation. "My proposal is prompted by three facts. First, as stated at the previous meeting, notwithstanding Hom Latier's Enclave violations we need him badly. Second, if you think Alrue Latier violated Enclave turning those bucolic villagers into Mormons, wait till I wind up responsible for killing most everyone on Bohrkk."

The coltish Councilor placed her fist on her chin. "It is your opinion that this pending cataclysm is of your making."

"Opinion, schmopinion." The machine hurled up a dozen image bubbles: seismograms, cross-sections of the Bohrkkian crust, aerial images of volcanoes belching towers of ash.

The Geologist Laureate scrutinized the array of images and quietly whistled.

"The gravitational disturbance nine years ago didn't just destroy the punitorium and Meryam Mayishimu's relay satellite," Computer buzzed. "It also disturbed the planet's crust, releasing magma and volcanic gases from great depths into the immediate underlayment of Bohrkk's principal continent."

Computer projected one of Meryam's journals from very early in the trek from the devastated punitorium.

The Latiers clustered about a small cavity in the ground, seven-year-old Abigayl hovering overhead. Nataleah knelt beside the half-meter opening, scrutinizing the liquid in her cupped hands. "It's like seltzer," she said puzzledly.

"That was just four days after the punitorium was destroyed," Computer explained, "and already surface phenomena were beginning – in this case, volcanic gas escaping into groundwater. Some was sulfurous, but much was not. Throughout the Latiers' early wanderings, they encountered fizzy springs and creeks. Matters swiftly deteriorated; in the years that followed, quake activity outpaced historic norms. Volcanism accelerated exponentially. I had briefed Admiral Konder and Hom Hafen regarding the immigrants pouring into New Nauvoo. Almost without exception, they are refugees whose villages of origin were destroyed by volcanic activity."

"Was this destruction widespread?" asked the Geologist Laureate.

"Scattered at first," Computer whirred, "though devastating enough where it occurred. Here's another clip by Fem Mayishimu: it documents a meeting held at New Nauvoo roughly two years ago. Constance Latier reports on a reconnaissance expedition into territories ravaged by volcanism."

The bubble opened. Several elite onlookers gasped at the colonnaded opulence of the Great Hall of New Nauvoo's Temple. Had one family of Galactic convicts and a few hundred autochthons really crafted such gaudy splendor in a handful of years?

"One tribe was mummified," Constance recounted, "men, women, children, livestocks, their villages all buried by volcanic ash. Another tribe I found consumed

by fire, whether from a forest blaze or contact with lava, none could tell. We found more than five hundred blackened human forms, fists clenched, arms held up in fighting postures – a clan of charcoal pugilists."

"For behold," Alrue quoted, *"the day cometh that shall burn as an oven."*

Computer closed the bubble. The Geologist Laureate and the Paramount Deliberator exchanged looks of dismay.

"You're saying that the deaths and damage associated with this volcanism are as much your responsibility as the destruction of the punitorium?" the coltish Councilor asked.

"That and more," Computer whirred, projecting a large tridee animatic of Bohrkk's principal continent. "Thanks to my action," Computer declared, "the planet Bohrkk has an abscess." A phantomed cutaway view showed vast underground chambers surging with turbulent magma. "The great continent that bears New Nauvoo is underlain by empty magma chambers, remnants of volcanic episodes from millions of years past. They are refilling rapidly, some with water, some with magma. A process that should occur over millions of years is reaching maturity in less than a decade."

"Did you sample heavy-oxygen levels?" asked the Geologist Laureate.

"Of course. Oxygen-10 appears in vented gases at an abundance exceeding recorded norms by better than twenty-fold."

"That means young magma, freshly arrived from the upper mantle," the scientist said. "Rich with entrained gases. With any sudden pressure reduction, it will expand explosively."

"Exactly," Computer droned, projecting a new schematic. "Magma upwelling has already raised the mean continental crust by six-point-two-seven centimeters." A new animatic simulated the downward view from a headlong low-altitude flight. Cracks were opening in the surface as the *pov* swept by. "Vertical fractures are forming all along the edge of this zone. Many reach down from the surface straight to the magma chambers. Magma rushes upward, outgassing explosively as the Geologist Laureate said, spawning exceptionally fierce volcanoes." A high-altitude recon image depicted an arc of vents spewing lava and superheated gas, each accreting a new mountain. "Nearly a hundred of these vents have opened, many following a curved line that circles New Nauvoo to the northwest. In the coming months more will follow, roughly encircling the Mormon city." The animatic spooled futureward in time-lapse predictive mode. "Possibly within eight standard months, unquestionably within fourteen, the vent volcanoes will form a complete ring."

"Prevailing winds at New Nauvoo's location run toward the northwest," said the Meteorologist Laureate. "Once significant volcanoes open southeast of the city – upwind of it – it will be buried in ash."

"True," Computer replied, "but that is not the main threat." A new animatic seemed to hurtle along just a meter above the ground. "Once the circle of vents is complete, volcanic stresses will rupture the rock separating each vent." Great cracks leapt forward, furrowing the rocky surfaces. The effect was like watching old-fashioned glass fail under pressure. "Once a deep crack has progressed full-circle, joining all the vents together, the disk of land composing the ring's center will be unsupported. A rocky lozenge more than eleven hundred kilometers in diameter will be … just floating."

"Not for long," the Geologist Laureate commented.

"No," whirred Computer. "Within hours of the crack's completion, a couple of days at most, the central disk will plunge into the magma, bringing certain death to any still residing on it. At the same time, it will loose apocalyptic fury around its edges as the ring vents eject huge volumes of superheated material." In the animatic, ninety percent of the continent vanished behind a roiling tower of ash that lanced the sky, quickly rising above Bohrkk's stratosphere.

"You're talking about an eruption with the energy of a small asteroid strike," said the Geologist Laureate.

"The eruption will devastate Bohrkk's major continent and badly degrade the habitability of the small settled islands. Ash will fall like snow across two-thirds of the planet. World-girdling sulfur dioxide clouds will stunt whatever plant life is not simply wiped out. Eight million people will die – most of Bohrkk's population. This is not conjecture; this *will* happen in eight to fourteen months."

"And it's your doing," said a Councilor in ruby and sapphire mesh.

"Yes."

"You've made your case, then," the Councilor said darkly. "This is a much more serious Enclave violation than Hom Latier's."

"Agreed," Computer whirred. "But I do not propose disregarding it in order to exoncrate myself."

"We've already forgiven your killing trillions," the coltish Councilor observed. "There's nothing to exonerate here."

"What I am proposing," Computer buzzed, "is a yet larger offense against Enclave. Though the eruption cannot be prevented, there may be time to evacuate its potential victims."

"*Evacuate* eight million people?" gasped the Paramount Deliberator.

"I don't mean to sound stupid," asked the Councilor in ruby and sapphire mesh, "but how do we snatch eight million autochthons and whisk them away on spaceships without – well, without their figuring out that there's a Galactic Confetory out there that has spaceships?"

"You understand the problem," Computer whirred. "There is no probably no way to achieve this without the Bohrkkians learning that we exist. That is the third reason why I propose that Enclave be disregarded."

"That would be like disregarding the law of gravity," the coltish Councilor objected.

"The Enclave Statutes are human constructs," Computer burred. "Humans can change them."

The Paramount Deliberator stood. "Perhaps we can, but we mustn't. Enclave encapsulates morality."

"Morality?" the angular Deliberator said acidly. "Really?"

"You doubt Enclave?" huffed the Paramount Deliberator.

"Some of us do," replied the fuchsia-haired Deliberator, his tone inscrutably flat.

Enoda and Grice exchanged furtive glances. Dissent among the supreme leaders on something so foundational as Enclave? Here was a development even Computer had never anticipated.

"The Enclave Statutes restrain the powerful in their dealings with the less powerful," the Paramount Deliberator declared haughtily. "If that is not morality, what is?"

"It is morality's opposite," sneered a bald Justiciary with close-cropped indigo facial hair. "A recipe to perpetuate suffering that we could relieve, but do not."

"How can you say that?" the coltish Councilor demanded, deep personal offense edging her voice.

"How can you deny it?" Grice surged to her feet. Hafen, Konder, and Enoda exchanged looks of surprise. "Forty thousand Enclaved planets – kept that way for the convenience, or the mere *entertainment*, of elites on just two thousand Affiliates and Memberworlds?" she raged. "Yes, on their forty thousand worlds the autochthons are left alone – free to pursue their destinies, such as they are. Their dreams are not crushed by learning that a Galactic civilization far exceeds their own. Their liberties are never curtailed by meddlers from space making them do what we think best." She surged forward, stopping at the lip of the central dais. "But what price do they pay?"

"No price is too high for autonomy," sniffed the Paramount Deliberator.

"I don't call that a fair exchange," Grice snapped. "Look at Bohrkk. For sixteen hundred years small tribal communities have struggled to eke a living from a planet half-sterilized by a Tuezi strike. For something like seventy generations they've lived under barbaric conditions. Childhood mortality exceeds sixty percent. They're helpless against a small number of effortlessly preventable diseases. Generation after generation, most who reach puberty squander themselves in useless warfare. Those who survive *that* generally die before age fifty, stunted by lives spent enslaved to local despots. Multiply that panorama of agony by forty thousand; there are your Enclave planets. Meanwhile we lucky ones – we who happened to get born on one of the two thousand worlds allowed to play the game of civilization – *we* get to lead lives of comfort and power and understanding. With all those advantages, what do we do for our suffering brothers and sisters? We send them Spectators so their torment can entertain us!" Grice spread her hands in helpless fury. "We could reveal ourselves on these worlds and share our knowledge – our medicine, culture, technology. We could open to them the possibility of fully human lives. But no, for the sake of 'autonomy' – to preserve their *dignity*, as if any such thing attaches to their condition – we spout high-minded

759

prattle about Enclave and abandon them to their agonies. Oh, wait, I left a reason out. Most of all, we abandon them *because their sufferings are so much fun for us to watch.*"

"Large words," rumbled the High Chief Justiciary, "large words indeed from a woman from" – he sniffed contemptuously – "*Terra.*"

"Perhaps it sharpens my sight," Grice said coldly, "because my Terra would have been an Enclave world had not a handful of impulsive Galactics taken a shine to my world's religions two hundred years ago. Perhaps it sharpens my sight that you made my little blue planet the center of your universe until you finally realized what you had on your hands. Then you thought you could box it all up behind a cordon of Sequestration."

The indigo-haired Justiciary slapped his hands to his legs in applause. About a dozen others joined him from among the virtually gathered Councilors, Justiciaries, Deliberators, and Scientists Laureate. "She speaks truth," said the Supervising Pedant.

"Truth? Anything but," roared the High Chief Justiciary, surging to his feet in a shimmer of metal-mesh robes. "Sit down, Earth girl. No one from a Sequestered world has a place in this discussion!"

"Beg pardon, *I* am from Earth," Enoda declared, standing slowly. Computer drifted to his side, his metallic body suddenly encased with threatening slow-motion lightnings. "As one-half of the Galaxy's only other intelligent species," Enoda said sourly, "I wonder if the High Chief Justiciary has any further disparagements to offer concerning my homeworld?"

Somewhere beneath the sheathed lightning, Computer's attention bands zeroed on the High Chief Justiciary. "Your honor should consider that my burden-in-life could demand your death by slow torture as the price of continuing diplomatic relations," the machine buzzed threateningly.

"Computer!" Enoda protested.

"Come to think of it," the machine said unflappably, "so could I."

Furious, the High Chief Justiciary whirled to face the coltish Councilor. "Surely you wouldn't permit –"

The coltish Councilor shrugged.

"Of course, there's an upside," Computer told the fuming jurist. "You'd be a martyr to the Confetory's early relations with a proud, capricious, and – oh yes, did I mention incredibly powerful? – alien race. They'd probably name schools after you, or maybe a nice luggage slipfield at a spaceport somewhere."

Very, very slowly, the High Chief Justiciary resumed his ornately sculpted stone chair.

"We tire of this," Enoda said slowly. "By definition and by treaty, Hom Computer and I are no longer part of your civilization. Your Enclave Statutes do not apply to us."

The Paramount Deliberator laughed. "You would save Bohrkk's eight million, just the two of you?"

Grice ducked beneath Computer's floating body to come up beside Enoda, abruptly clutching his left hand. "It would be the three of us," she said levelly, locking her pale blue eyes on the coltish Councilor, the High Chief Justiciary, and the Paramount Deliberator in turn. "Who here thinks we can't?"

Chapter 161

"Queen Zuzenah!" yelped the elder guarding the office door as Zuzenah bustled past.

Alrue looked up from his gilded desk. Reading his senior wife's expression, he reached for his most conciliatory tone. "Ah, love of my youth. What can I do for you?"

Black eyes smoldering, she dropped into the *faux* leopard-skin chair across the desk from him. "I think you know what goaded me here." Without asking, she took up the hammered-metal ewer on the edge of the desk and poured local wine into his goblet. She snatched his cup and drank deeply.

He said nothing.

She assumed a more businesslike tone. "By now, your troops must be close to The Others' settlements. Tomorrow, the day after at latest, they will hurl those contagious blankets into their midst."

"Such are their orders," Alrue said noncommittally.

"Orders you can belay."

He shrugged. "The troops are already three days gone."

"You could fly to them." She directed a steely stare at his desktop. Two of the floatcell units from the punitorium lay beside the ewer. "You could be among them in an hour; pray do not toy with me."

Alrue glowered. "Is that a tone to take with your husband – your Tyrant King? Know you not that I am a prophet?"

"Yes, but I wish to God I did not know it," Zuzenah said sullenly. "Mark me well. I cannot abide this plan you have to murder The Others in their homes. If you do not call it off, behold: I shall leave you."

He stared at her in genuine surprise. "You don't mean that."

Her stare replied without words.

"Where would you go?"

"I shall live in the wilderness, if need be."

He laughed derisively. "A ferkeek will get you."

"Let it." She drained his goblet, set it hard on the desk, and stood as if to leave.

He stood also. "You are a Mormon wife. You must obey." He snatched the cup, refilling it for himself; his tone softened. "Just as I obey."

"You? Whom do *you* obey?"

"I obey the visions sent by God," he said flatly. "Question me no longer regarding this, my darling. Pray accept that you do not understand all that bears on my decision to war against The Others in this way. Ponder that in your heart and profit thereby."

"O, my husband," she said quietly, resuming her seat. "Can you not help me to understand?"

Chapter 162

"You'd do this on your own?" the telepresent coltish Councilor demanded. "Save all those Bohrkkians, though it means forcing upon them knowledge of a Galactic civilization they're nowhere near ready to process?"

Gram Enoda raised an eyebrow. "You'd rather they all died?"

Admiral Konder's projection crossed behind Hafen to lay a restraining hand on – actually, a couple of centimeters into – Enoda's right forearm. "Please think what you're doing."

Enoda smiled. "We have."

"I could show you our full decision hyperqueue, but I'm eighty-two percent certain even your awareness would not survive it," Computer whirred.

Enoda turned to face Konder, his left arm trailing behind him to maintain his contact with Pamela Grice. "Today we mean to do something the Confetory should have taken responsibility for long ago. Enclave is arrogance cloaked in false compassion. It's idiotic and it's hurtful, and it must end now."

"Otherwise," Computer burred, "the Galaxy's newest alien intelligence will save eight million people whom their own Confetory wouldn't lift a finger to help."

Enoda smiled. "Need I add that this will occur in the full glare of your civilization's media apparatus?"

"You think Ruth Griszam got saybacks?" Grice said archly, referring to the Spectator whose avidly-*pov*ed journals first introduced the Galaxy to false demigod Arn Parek. "Imagine how many will *pov* Meryam

Mayishimu's coverage as we three save all the people of Bohrkk."

The Councilors, Justiciaries, Deliberators, and Scientists Laureate exchanged urgent glances and subvocal mutterings. After some twenty seconds, the coltish Councilor looked toward Enoda. "This is your stance, then?" she asked. "We abandon Enclave and save the Bohrkkians with you, or you three will save them alone?"

Enoda glanced at Grice; she nodded. "Correct," he said.

"We must deliberate in privacy," the coltish Councilor replied. "Might we have one standard hour?"

Enoda paused, inwardly incredulous at the acting leader of the Galaxy's reigning civilization petitioning for time. "Of course."

Instantly the virtual Council, Justiciaries, Deliberators, and Scientists Laureate disappeared from the chamber.

Grice and Enoda stood holding hands, Computer floating to their left.

To their right Hafen and Konder's image huddled, conferring urgently.

All at once Enoda realized that he and Grice were hugging. It was as though his body had leapt into it while his mind was elsewhere. They were laughing convulsively. "Did that forjeling *happen*?" she breathed in his ear.

"It's my first time blackmailing a galaxy," Enoda laughed. "Think they'll yield?"

"We gave them little choice," Computer whirred. "Hey, Bucko, I see you and the 'Earth' lady are friends again."

Enoda and Grice broke their embrace, each taking half a step backward. She took both of his hands in hers.

"I never realized how much you hated Enclave," he said at last.

"I never realized you did ..." She shrugged. "Then again, who talks about Enclave?"

"Maybe that's the problem." He clasped her hands again. "You were great."

"Well, if it's going to be you and me against the Galaxy –"

"Hey," Computer protested.

She smiled. "If it's going to be you, me, *and Computer* against the Galaxy ..." She fell silent.

"We might as well make it *our* stateroom again," he ventured.

"Why not?"

He kissed her. Hard. It was mutual.

***

With a muted hissing sound, the Council, the Justiciaries, the Deliberators, and the Scientists Laureate returned.

"Plorg on a stick, that was fast," Hafen said.

"You deliberated for eleven standard minutes," Computer whirred. "Forty-nine minutes remain to you."

"We need no more time," the coltish Councilor stated. Her demeanor was forcedly neutral. "Hom Enoda, Hom Computer ... Fem Grice ... the Enclave Statutes have been suspended, though solely with regard to Bohrkk. A top-level conference committee has been empaneled to consider their eventual repeal."

"It may not be eventual," Computer whirred affably. "When Enclave is seen to have been ignored for Bohrkk with favorable humanitarian results, support for it should crumble."

"Don't be too sure," Grice sighed. "OmNet will put up a fight. Not to mention all those experients who can't imagine getting through their Saturday night without a nice mass execution on some twisted backwater world to *pov.*"

"Perhaps this is an issue for another time," interjected the Paramount Deliberator. "We shall be rescuing the Bohrkkians together, but our strategists see no way to do so given the world's remoteness and the short time available. Consider this a formal diplomatic query: What was your plan?"

Enoda's awareness tumbled into the shared interface. Computer's was waiting for him. As was Grice's. *"Okay, rescuing the eight million!"* Enoda silently blustered. *"Um ... how* were *we going to do that?"*

"Hey, I only volunteered us," Grice said cheerily. *"I'm sure our friend with the infinite mentality will think of something."*

Computer was unaccustomedly silent.

Chapter 163

Interlude
Orbiting Psihhlk

Commander Ardje Dvilabd paced the bridge of her galleon. A glance at the consoles updated her on its status. Insertion into Psihhlk orbit had gone smoothly; on the planet below, a berth was being charged with fresh hand-tended beans for rapid transfer into the freighter's hold when it landed. And her principal grower's agent was on the way up. *That's a whopping big shuttle to bring up one person,* Dvilabd thought as she eyed the Detex. *I suppose she had to grab the first craft that was handy.*

"Isn't it unusual for a grower's agent to join us in orbit prior to touchdown?" asked the executive officer.

"Last time I was planet-side I sold her my DynaScrub," Dvilabd said with a smile. "If she meets me in orbit she can sell it back to me, then buy it again after we land."

"Ah, commissions," the X. O. said knowingly. Her curiosity satisfied, she stepped back to her duty station.

Dvilabd jammed her hands into her command tunic's slant pockets and nearly smiled. Under Dyna-Scrub's mysterious rules, if the agent boarded the freighter before it broke orbit, that would constitute one discrete commissionable transaction opportunity. The period after the freighter's landing would constitute a second.

For the thousandth time, Dvilabd reflected on the strangeness of that blustering, clumsy, and (oddest of all, male) spacefaring salesman who had brought DynaScrub filter engines among them. *Kyhmbo* – for that was his name – *I have done well by you,* Dvilabd thought. She was one of a few hundred wealthy Psihhlkians who had greatly augmented their personal fortunes by buying and selling the same small number of DynaScrubs among themselves. Personally, she'd never been able to figure out where all this commission money came from – why should Kyhmbo reward empty transactions? – but she willingly chalked it up to what the salesman himself inscrutably termed "the magic of multi-level marketing."

Dvilabd willed herself to relax, tightening, then loosening the muscles of her back and shoulders. At the same time, she let her mind wander from matters of duty to the prospect of shore leave. Two trysts with an alpha-quality hom, maybe three if her schedule allowed. And once her amorous needs were slaked, the quieter pleasures of the procreant clique. *I know I've been too long in space when I catch myself looking forward to three straight weeks tending thirty-seven children!*

"The agent's shuttle is on final approach," called the Detex officer.

"Noted," Dvilabd declared, her reverie broken.

"Forjel, it's big," the Detex officer observed. "It'll just fit in Dock One."

"I'll meet it there. X. O., you have command."

***

The shuttle, a great irregular oblong patchwork of silver and grey, dominated the spacedock. Dvilabd and four techs huddled on a shallow embarkation platform, the shuttle's flat bow barely two meters from their noses. With a thudding sigh, the bow folded open.

The shuttle's interior was open, almost featureless.

The reason for the grower's agent using so large a craft was swiftly apparent.

Clad in a tan greatcoat, the agent stood behind a phalanx of dumb but powerful Psihhlkian males. They stood six across, fifteen deep. Each wore body armor, earphones, a rebreather mask, and some kind of shoulder-slung rifle.

On Psihhlk women did everything, including when necessary the waging of war. So no one had ever thought to organize infantry utilizing the big stupid males. For that reason, neither Dvilabd nor the techs immediately recognized the formation as threatening.

"Target the techs only," called the agent. "I want the commander alive." The homs in the front rank leveled pelfrag rifles and fired. The four docking techs splattered into crimson fragments.

Dvilabd, unhurt, lurched back against the dock's entrance hatch, gasping, clawing bloody tissue scraps from her face.

"Take the commander," the agent ordered. Two armored homs stepped forward, grabbing Dvilabd by her shoulders. Her head collided with the rebreather mask one of them wore. She caught a familiar smell: *dxogzd,* a drug often administered to homs to calm their stunted minds so that they might obey commands more precisely. She heard buzzing from the hom's earphone. Apparently the agent could direct commands to specific individuals as well as just barking them aloud. In response to such a command, the homs clutching Dvilabd whirled her face-first into a stout pipe. She felt her cheekbone fracture in a lance of pain. Three teeth spewed from her mouth.

And she stopped reflecting on what she observed.

Chapter 164

November 8, 2376
Bohrkk, New Nauvoo

Alrue leaned toward Zuzenah, his face composed and benign. "I know your heart," he said quietly. "Your anger, your confusion." He smiled. "Have you ever heard this poem? It was written by one of the first Mormons, Eliza Snow, six weeks after she secretly became a plural wife of Joseph Smith. The poem expressed her dismay at the complexities that came with clandestine polygamy. Snow's method was to describe the reactions of an angel whom she imagined to be looking down from above." He declaimed:

> "He'd be apt to conclude, from the medly of things;
> We've got into a jumble of late –
> A deep intricate puzzle, a tangle of strings,
> That no possible scheme can make straight."

Zuzenah nodded thoughtfully. "Yea, 'tis much like that for me."
Alrue nodded and continued:

> "From the midst of confusion can harmony flow?
> Or can peace from distraction come forth?
> From out of corruption, integrity grow?
> Or can vice unto virtue give birth?
> Will the righteous come forth with their garments unstained?
> With their hearts unpolluted with sin?"

"Yes, my husband," she said, her voice quaking, "that poem captures my fear entire."

"Then you need fear nothing, dear Zuzenah," Alrue replied, then recited the poem's closing lines:

"O, yes; Zion, thy honor will be sustained.
And the glory of God usher'd in."

"You see, dear Zuzenah, I comprehend your concern." He smiled warmly. "Just as Eliza Snow had to grapple with the realities of plural marriage, you and I must grapple with the sometimes-dismaying realities of temporal power. Yet Zion's honor must be sustained; I merely do God's will." He settled back behind his desk. "As in days of old, God has said The Others' land is ours. It falls to us to smite them and take it."

Zuzenah eyed her husband mockingly. "When rescuers from the Confetory finally come, is that what you will tell them? 'Good day, fellow Galactics; don't read too much into this huge Enclave breach – God bid us take what is ours.'"

Alrue quaffed from his goblet. "You should know that Nataleah worked this through months ago. In actuality, our plan involves no Enclave violation."

"That is absurd."

"Actually, no. Every element of our plan is such that a few smart autochthons *might* have conceived it on their own. Given a trip to The Others' crypt full of dead emissaries – and given any folk theory of contagion, even one that's wildly wrong biologically – locals *could* have worked out that The Others are vulnerable to one of The People's diseases. They *could* have arrived at the same strategy as Nataleah and I did for exploiting that. Moreover, we've taken care to execute the strategy using only native technologies." He drained the goblet in one self-satisfied guzzle. "No bio-labs or nano-processing were involved. We simply had immune carriers contaminate hand-woven blankets through direct contact, and we'll deliver them using shoe leather and simple catapults."

"You've figured all the angles," she conceded. "But rationalize as you will, it is still genocide."

"Perhaps. But if that is God's will?"

Zuzenah's eyes widened. "You ask '*if* that is God's will?' That means you do not know. You *admit* you do not know. This murderous plan came from no vision. It is a scheme of Nataleah's, nothing more, and we both of us know it." She quaffed again from his goblet. "If it be more than that, husband mine, look me in the eye and tell me this plan came to you in a vision from God."

"I am a prophet," he rumbled.

"And I am a prophet's wife. And I know just as you do that not every thought that enters your mind comes from God. You can only be certain of that when you have had a specific revelation. Now, this scheme cannot be God's will. It is human, and full of error, and *wrong*." She leaned forward, her voice earnest. "*Look me in the eye* and tell me if God commanded you to do this hideous thing."

Alrue leaned back in his golden chair, lowered his head, and crossed one beefy hand over the other. "I feel it is God's will," he said softly. "But no, I did not receive a revelation."

"Well, then." She fixed him with her furious black eyes. "You must go out to the grove and pray on this. Beseech the Lord's counsel. Ask Him what He thinks of this scheme. Surely you are not afraid to pray for guidance," Zuzenah pressed. "'Yea, you know that I speak the truth; and you ought to tremble before God.'"

Alrue remained silent.

Zuzenah leaned across the desk, seizing his hands. "'Thou art a holy prophet of God, for thou art the man to whom an angel said in a vision: Thou shalt receive.' Never have I demanded anything from you, my

773

husband," she said resolutely, "but I demand this. If you would remain right with God – and if you would have me remain your senior wife – get thee outside. Pray for guidance."

Chapter 165

November 8, 2376
Aboard *Isolation*, Orbiting Bohrkk

Hafen, Konder, the Councilors, Justiciaries, Deliberators, and Scientists Laureate stared as Computer summoned up a vast, fully detailed tactical status map showing the location of every ship, military or civilian, in the entire quadrant of the Galaxy that contained the planet Bohrkk. "As I feared," Computer whirred, "there's no way to get enough ships into Sector Rho Lambda to evacuate eight million Bohrkkians in the time available. Lord High Admiral Konder, Hom Hafen. Have you any secret plans for evacuating people in such numbers under such conditions?"

"Of course," Konder replied. "We have secret plans for everything."

"For most things," Hafen corrected. "Some of them we lost with the secret secrecy project."

"Very well," Computer whirred, "I need to see any plan ever developed for a snap evacuation on this scale anywhere in the Galaxy. How many ships, how many troops, what equipment, what maneuvers they must undertake. Show me all the plans that meet those criteria, even ones that require assets clearly not available here. Also, please begin running scenarios for how to the get the maximum number and size of inverters into this vicinity quickly."

"The number of inverters matters?" Konder asked.

"Yes. I need ships whose power output I can draw upon. Disregard configuration, passenger capacity, or any other characteristics," Computer ordered. "Just seek to optimize the amount of shipboard power available in Bohrkk space as quickly as possible."

Hafen and Konder turned away, muttering orders into their personal comms. The Councilors, Justiciaries, Deliberators, and Scientists Laureate clustered, launching more than a dozen small-group discussions.

"Say, Bucko?" Computer whirred. "Hafen, Konder, all these assembled leaders, knotted up in their little groups yammering at each other – does it seem to you that they're likely to come up with any ingenious solutions?"

Enoda scanned the room over Grice's shoulder. "I presume you're reading their autonomics," he said to the machine. "All I can go on is body language, but I just see a room full of very high-level people bitching and saying to each other, 'I have no forjeling idea what the next move is either.'"

"Agreed," Computer buzzed. "We can't wait for that. Decide how you want to start breaking all of this to Alrue Latier; I'm putting us in contact with him in eight minutes and twelve seconds."

"I haven't worked through anything for that yet!" Enoda protested.

"Then think fast," Computer burred. "*Isolation*'s just started positioning its web of satellites over Bohrkk. Given current coverage and orbital dynamics, the contact window you'll have in, as of now, seven minutes forty-nine seconds is the longest there'll be for a day and a half."

Enoda tumbled into an ovoid chair and tried to concentrate.

Chapter 166

Led by the grower's agent, the phalanx of Psihhlkian males tramped unopposed though the corridors of the coffee galleon, dragging the stunned, bleeding Ardje Dvilabd just behind them. The homs of the phalanx carried varied weapons, most of them more powerful than typical antipersonnel ordnance but not powerful enough to compromise a ship's bulkheads. If crew members were encountered, they were reduced to gelid fragments and crimson spray.

Finally someone on the bridge realized the freighter was under attack. Alarms keened. Turning a corner, the phalanx faced an improvised defensive emplacement. Three young officers huddled behind a material handling tractor they had parked partially blocking a corridor. At first sight of the phalanx, the officers fired hand blasters; four homs fell screaming pre-verbally, blood pumping from steaming fist-sized voids in their muscular bodies.

The phalanx withdrew around the corner.

The grower's agent gave a quiet targeted order. Three short, stocky homs hustled Dvilabd's trembling form forward, pushing her into the officers' sight.

"Wait, they have the Commander!" one officer called.

Staring at Dvilabd, they lowered their guns, then glanced blankly at one another.

On the agent's next targeted command, two taller homs from the phalanx's second rank lurched around the corner, raised their rifles, and raked the tractor with meson fire. Its mechanisms spewed backward as shrapnel, shredding the young officers from the hips down.

The agent ordered the phalanx to squeeze single-file between the ruined tractor and the corridor sidewall. At the sight of the fallen officers, their bodies in tatters below the waist, Dvilabd vomited. The effort made her broken cheekbone sear with pain; puke burned in the sockets of her ejected teeth.

After passing the tractor, the phalanx reformed six homs wide. It tramped around two more corners and splattered three more members of the freighter's crew.

The phalanx drew up before the sealed doors to the ship's bridge. "Fire no weapons on the bridge," called the agent. "We must preserve the instruments." The homs in the first two ranks let their rifles clatter to the deck. Now the agent directed a command to the two homs clutching Dvilabd. One of them swept her right arm up and back, yanking it cruelly from its socket; she screamed. They lurched her toward the ident panel beside the hatch. A hom manipulated her ruined right arm, flattening her blood-slick palm against the ident plate as she continued to scream.

Green luminance fluttered under her fingers.

The bridge hatch irised open.

The command crew stared. None of them, not even the X. O., wore a weapon.

Twelve unarmed (but armored) homs tramped onto the bridge. Three fell upon each officer, hurling their victim clear of sensitive control surfaces, then leisurely kicking and pummeling until no life remained.

Whatever the grower's agent had in mind for the coffee galleon, it was now hers to command.

"Reserve squad, forward to the bridge," the agent ordered. Then she dashed off down a blood-filmed corridor.

***

Back in the shuttle in Dock One, a heretofore camouflaged rear compartment hissed open. It contained

778

eight seated women in jumpsuits. They had been held in reserve while the brutish homs slaughtered the galleon's crew. Now the fems sprinted directly to the bridge: anyone could see they were a replacement command crew.

***

The replacement commander saluted the grower's agent, who had returned to the bridge carrying a burden. "A world that is being born."

The agent returned her salute and completed the formula. "Instead of a world that is."

The agent's left arm cradled the DynaScrub cognitive filter engine; she must have seized it from Dvilabd's quarters. Her free hand caressed the contrivance. Glassy-eyed and rapturous, she locked eyes with Dvilabd, who lay crumpled and bleeding against a console. "'Humanity as a whole possesses a future," the agent recited, "a future defined not only by the successive years, but by higher states to be attained by struggle.'"

Even through her agony, Dvilabd couldn't help thinking: *Omegists? My galleon was seized by forjeling Omegists!?*

"Ardje Dvilabd," the agent said coolly. "I truly regret that you had to become a casualty of that struggle."

"The DynaScrub," Dvilabd said, coughing wretchedly. "*It* made you an Omegist?"

"It taught me the true way."

"I owned it as long as you did," Dvilabd objected. "It never clouded my mind."

"You're so loyal, Ardje." The agent affected a pitying look. "So narrow. The machine probably took your measure, and decided you would never do."

"You did all this," Dvilabd rasped, " … for a lie."

779

"Immobilist," the grower's agent hissed. Her free hand came up cradling a ravisher.

Ardje Dvilabd's terminal scream was blood-curdling.

Then again, it was short.

Chapter 167

November 8, 2376
Bohrkk, New Nauvoo

Alrue plodded out of the Temple into scarlet dusk. Beyond the wooden reviewing stand that nearly blocked the holy structure's main door, the West Grove's colonnaded trees loomed black in the ruddy light of volcano sunset. Not that the sun itself could be seen; smoke from the volcanoes to the northwest now spanned seventy degrees of horizon. No one in New Nauvoo had seen a sunset clearly for weeks. The distant smoke shone in dim tones of mauve and crimson.

Zuzenah demands that I pray, Alrue thought resentfully, *and so I must.* Yet his anger at letting her get the better of him was leavened by the excitement of a new plot a-borning, however simple that "plot" might be. He paced thoughtfully. *I shall make a great show of beseeching the skies. That way I can tell her honestly that I did it. As to what the skies will say in return . . . well, Zuzenah will have to take my word for that!* It wouldn't be the first time Alrue had feigned a revelation. Indeed, as he saw things, one of his great obligations as Prophet, Seer, and Revelator was to proclaim occasionally on God's behalf whatever the deity might have been too busy or preoccupied to reveal on His own.

But *where* to pray? The West Grove lawn seemed too open – Alrue wouldn't want just anyone watching him carry on the way he planned to. Under a tree? What theology might onlookers read into *that?* Joseph Smith had never been much for praying in secret, for all that Saint Matthew commended that strategy. Reasoning thus, Alrue scuttled back toward the Temple entrance, then ducked behind the reviewing stand.

781

Three days before, he had rallied his troops from the platform atop that structure.

Now he threaded his way inside its supporting framework.

Ensconced beneath the speaking platform, Alrue raised his head toward the heavens. Or rather toward the wooden planks that blocked his view of them.

"Behold, Lord," he shouted, "I ready myself to approach your glory." He rubbed consecrated oil into his scalp. "I claim this blessing in the name of Jesus Christ and through the power of the Holy Melchizedek Priesthood." He raised his hands. "Assuredly as the Lord liveth, who is my God and my Redeemer, even so surely shall I receive a knowledge of whatsoever things I shall ask in faith, with an honest heart, believing that I shall receive a knowledge." Facing west, he clenched his eyes shut. "Let me be like Lehi, father of the first Nephi, who prayed unto the Lord, yea, even with all his heart; who was overcome with the Spirit and carried away in a vision, even that he saw the heavens open, and he thought he saw God sitting upon his throne. Come to me, O Lord!"

"ALRUE," said an ethereal voice.

Alrue answered dreamily, "Yes, Lord, 'tis I, Alrue."

His eyes flew open.

Alrue stood very still for several seconds, listening intently. *Now am I starting to hear things?*

He reclosed his eyes, took a solemn breath, released it, and resumed praying. "O Lord, I pray for a manifestation of your glory. Come to your servant, I beseech thee!"

"ALRUE ... LATIER!" The voice was male. A shimmery undertone suggested glockenspiels amid tinsel.

Alrue opened his eyes very slowly. "I hear you," he said into the air beneath the platform. "I think."

782

"TURN ... AROUND."

"Yes, Lord, that's what I need to do. I need to turn it all around." Alrue closed his eyes again. "Is it really you, Lord? Show me a sign and I'll turn my entire life around."

The voice sounded impatient. "WANT A SIGN? LOOK BEHIND THEE!"

Alrue whirled.

It was the luminous vision of ... something.

It glowed by its own light with weirdly heightened dimensionality. The figure was human, albeit of heroic size. Its skin gleamed like alabaster beneath cool light. The left hand clutched a golden scepter sheathed in lightnings; the body was draped with a toga whose fabric glowed an eerie purple-white. Its eyes stared unmoving into his. They were green. Little could be seen of the being's hair, as it wore a hood of the same radiant fabric as the toga. From its chin sprouted a scraggly goatee, half-blonde, half-white. The mouth moved constantly, barely whispering words: "DEATH. TAXES." The right hand was open, palm up, displaying a pair of dice that seemed hewn from solid emerald. Both of the being's hands being occupied, the right elbow pressed against the figure's side a great old-fashioned book bound in elaborately tooled leather. Golden letters on its spine read *THE BOOK OF THE LAW OF GOD*.

"What the sfelb," Alrue breathed. "The teachings I bend so freely ... could they actually be *true*?"

The radiant figure's mouth kept moving. "GRAFT," it said. "CORRUPTION." Yet somehow Alrue knew the mouth's flow of cryptic statements did not represent real communication. When the being wished to address him, Alrue felt certain, it would make its voice heard by other means.

The figure's eyes narrowed. Its stomach rippled. A sound like breakers crashing on alien shores emanated from its lower abdomen.

Alrue stepped closer to the lustrous apparition. Looking down, he noted that his own foot and ankle cast a shadow in the browning grass beneath the platform – a shadow cast by the apparition's coruscating light. He tried and failed to puzzle out what it meant, theologically speaking, that the glare of this heavenly manifestation seemed so physical.

Alrue dropped to his knees. Falling forward, he buried his head in the grass. "My Lord and my God!"

"NOT EXACTLY."

Alrue raised his head after the figure finished speaking. "Say that again," he said calculatingly. "Um, please. If it's not too much trouble."

The figure nodded and repeated itself. "NOT EXACTLY."

As Alrue expected, the figure's true voice issued not from its mouth. It was pure, silent communication, one mind to another. At the same time the figure's mouth kept moving, endlessly whispering. Now it said, "BOOK CLUB MEMBERSHIPS."

Student of religion that he was, Alrue could not long remain dumbfounded by an apparition of this sort. Gradually he began studying the luminous figure, his mind searching the prophecies for matching characteristics.

The identification that assembled itself was beyond credence. The figure followed an allegedly prophetic letter Joseph Smith had written to the early Mormon William W. Phelps in November 1832 local, later preserved in the *Doctrine and Covenants*. No other Mormon prophecy had sown so much confusion, nor launched so many schisms among the faithful. "I, the Lord God, will send one mighty and strong," the prophecy began, "holding the scepter of power in his hand …"

Alrue noted the lightning-covered staff in the figure's left hand. *Scepter of power,* he thought. *Check.*

" … clothed with light for a covering …"

Fluorescent garment. Check.

" … whose mouth shall utter words, eternal words …"

The figure mouthed, "SENSOS OF OTHER PEOPLE'S WEDDINGS."

I'll have to come back to that one.

" … while his bowels shall be a fountain of truth …"

I'll definitely *come back to that one.*

"…to set in order the house of God, and to arrange by lot the inheritances of the Saints …"

Drawing lots. Right hand: dice. Check.

"…whose names are found, and the names of their fathers, and of their children enrolled in the book of the law of God."

Book of the Law of God. Check.

"ALRUE," said the disembodied glockenspiel-and-tinsel voice. "KNOWEST THOU WHO I AM?"

Alrue thought he knew, but he quailed from expressing it. Falsely he replied, "I'm thinking."

The being's eyes narrowed. A fearsome noise roiled from its lower abdomen. "LIE NOT TO ME!" it thundered. Wincing, the being clapped its left hand to its loins. In so doing it fumbled the scepter of power, which fell and rolled out of sight. "I GLORY IN TRUTH," it intoned. "WHEN THOU LIETH, IT PAINETH ME. BELIEVEST THOU ME ON THAT."

"Your bowels," Alrue said incredulously. "They *are* a fountain of truth!"

"OMEGIST SERMONS," mouthed the mouth.

"And of course," Alrue said in a rush, "a mouth that shall utter eternal words. Or at least, words for things that seem to last forever."

"PRIVY HIGH COUNCIL ELECTION CAMPAIGNS."

Alrue took another step toward the apparition. "Are you ... the One Mighty and Strong?"

The being nodded.

"Forjeling plorg," Alrue breathed, "does that mean there *is* a One Mighty and Strong?"

"WE MUST SPEAK OF URGENT THINGS," said the disembodied voice. "THY WORLD IS IN TERRIBLE PERIL."

"Heavenly messengers always say that."

"I DO NOT PROPHESY. I STATE FACT. A GREAT ERUPTION WILL RAVAGE THIS CONTINENT, POSSIBLY IN LESS THAN A YEAR."

Alrue nodded somberly. "And you know that ... how?"

"I COULD SHOW THOU THE MATH," said the One Mighty and Strong, "BUT I DOUBT IF THY AWARENESS COULD TAKE IT." The being frowned and changed its tone in a hurried way. "I MEAN, THOU ART A FOOLISH MORTAL. MY PATHS TO KNOWLEDGE ARE NOT THINE TO TREAD."

Alrue's bearing changed. He gazed into the being's great green eyes almost appraisingly. Leaning against the reviewing stand's framing, he crossed his arms and asked, "Um ... don't I know you?"

Chapter 168

Kyhmbo Iagejns, the spacefaring salesman who had peddled his wares on Psihhlk and fifty other worlds, was a salesman no more. A burly figure, almost bald, marked by unruly tufts of reddish hair above his ears and a left eye distended like a cow's, he strode the bridge of his repurposed heavy caravel. Over his bulging frame he wore a shin-length vestment of white and gold. Embroidered into its front panel shimmered the craggy, long-faced likeness of Pierre Teilhard de Chardin. The back panel bore in similar embroidery the square-jawed, white-haired, mustachioed image of the Terran physicist-mystic Frank J. Tipler, his eyes framed behind rectangular lenses.

"Admiral, we are hailed," reported the comm officer. "A coffee freighter, galleon class. It wishes to join the fleet. Passcodes are in order."

Kyhmbo, for that is the name he went by, allowed himself a crooked smile. "Very well, muster it in. A coffee ship. Coming from what star?"

"Büéhx."

"Ah, my followers from Psihhlk," Kyhmbo said happily. "Send a gig to board it, I would sample its cargo."

"It sails empty," called the Detex officer.

"Divergence!" Kyhmbo snapped. His officers exchanged furtive glances, surprised at the profanity – Admiral Kyhmbo was so godly most of the time. "I tell them and tell them to bring things we can use. Do they listen? What use is an empty coffee galleon?"

"It is a stout Class Eight hull, largely open inside," the Executive Officer said reasonably. "And the stardrive is in excellent order. It can find a purpose with us."

"As will every ship that joins us," Kyhmbo agreed, apparently mollified. "Like life itself, our fleet must of necessity undergo the coordination of its elements." He paused by the command deck's tridee display, which showed twenty-six ships of wildly varied descriptions slowly orbiting his flag caravel. A flickering dot indicated the coffee galleon's progress toward its assigned vector. "Verily, the nexus of unification fulfills its design, pursuing ever-heightening complexity."

Chapter 169

November 8, 2376
Bohrkk, New Nauvoo

Zuzenah barged into the Mansion House parlor, stammering, "I saw him! I saw him!"

Lupida, Constance, and Nataleah Latier looked up from the sculpted square parlor table with a start. "Alrue?" Constance replied calmly.

"Happens a lot," Lupida replied. "I saw him just yesterday."

"You understand not," Zuzenah blustered, falling into the last empty cane chair. "I bade Alrue go outside to pray …"

"I can't imagine why," Nataleah said tartly.

Zuzenah nodded. "Yes, Nataleah, I bid him pray asking whether your scheme to poison The Others was God's will. After a fair interval, I stuck my head outside – just to see how he was doing, you understand – and there sat Alrue, huddled beneath the reviewing stand and … and conversing jocularly as you please with the One Mighty and Strong!"

"No forjeling way," Nataleah snapped.

"Language, sister wife! I tell you, it *was* the One Mighty and Strong. The signs permit no other interpretation."

"Did he have the Book of the Law of God?" demanded a pouting Constance.

"Yes," Zuzenah said earnestly.

"Did he hold the scepter of power?" asked Meryam.

"Until he dropped it."

Lupida leaned forward. "That thing with his bowels. How did *that* work?"

"Couldn't tell you," Zuzenah admitted. "From where I stood I could hear nothing, only see. After more conversation of what appeared the pleasantest sort – I say you, it seemed our husband and God's messenger passed a most spiritual time together – the One Mighty and Strong raised his right hand and behold, he and our husband leapt into heaven on a bolt of light."

"Alrue's *gone?*" Constance demanded.

"Borne into heaven," Zuzenah insisted. "I tell you, these black eyes of mine beheld it!"

"Then it is settled, Zuzenah," Nataleah said triumphantly. "If you sent Alrue out to pray about our plan to strike at The Others, and if he and God's messenger comported themselves so fondly, that must mean that God approves it."

"To the contrary," Zuzenah insisted, "if Alrue and The One Mighty and Strong were so amicable together, it must be because he prevailed on Alrue to abandon your bloodthirsty scheme."

Nataleah threw up her hands. "And you know that how, exactly?"

"I have no evidence for my view," Zuzenah confessed. "I rely on moral intuition. I know God's way must have been as I imagine, because that is the right."

Lupida stood abruptly, her freckled hands balled into fists. "Zuzenah! Nataleah! What a pleasant thing it must be for each of you to know for certain that you are right."

Chapter 170

Alrue blinked at the sudden change in his surroundings: the soaring blue stillness of one of *Isolation*'s smaller docking bays, the metallic odors, the muted thrumming. A moment before, he'd been beneath the West Grove reviewing stand. But one thing had not changed: the outsized fluorescent figure of the One Mighty and Strong still floated before him.

With a crackle of vibrionic energy and an azure flash, the spare figure of Queen Meryam self-assembled beside Alrue. He watched twin astonishments wash over her features: first, at her change in location, which she had expected no more than he had; second, at the towering apparition. Around them, the docking bay's utility lighting flickered on, revealing a cavernous space dotted with scouts and gigs and flitters quiescent in their launch harnesses.

"Meryam," Alrue said levelly, "I believe we have been rescued."

Meryam gaped. "By the One Mighty and Strong?"

Alrue smiled broadly. "I think we might better address him as ... Hom Computer."

The glowing apparition raised one eyebrow, gave a knowing wink, and collapsed. Where the One Mighty and Strong's belly had been hovered a meter-long apparatus shaped like a chromed bouzouki and sheathed in counter-rotating fields of light.

"Haven't seen you since Arbadrel," Alrue said with an air of vindication.

"There *were* your trials," the machine burred.

"In any case," Alrue said hastily, "It's been years."

"All right, what tipped you off?" Computer asked.

"That part about how my awareness might not be able to endure reviewing your math. In Mormon tradition, deities seldom boast about their algorithms."

"Yes, I thought I might have slipped there."

"That business of the projection, though," Alrue mused, "your design for the One Mighty and Strong – very nice work."

"Thank you."

"Though the bit about the bowels *just* might have been overdrawn."

"I shall keep that in mind. In any case – Hom Latier, Fem Mayishimu, welcome to *Isolation,* a PeaceForce capital ship orbiting the planet Bohrkk."

Meryam laid a hand on Alrue's forearm. "Did you get here the way I did?"

"As in, suddenly?" He nodded.

"Teleportation? I'm impressed," she told Computer. "I *have* been out of touch – but in the civilization I left, teleportation was for bulk materials only. Something about the physics made it unsuitable for living subjects."

"Not the physics," Computer buzzed agreeably, "the math. My having overcome quantum indeterminacy was most helpful."

"So, Hom Computer," Alrue blustered, "I suppose your human is about somewhere? Enoda, wasn't that his name? Are you two still together?"

"Follow me," Computer replied, launching himself at a brisk walking pace toward a distant entry hatch.

***

Alrue and Meryam followed Computer through spacious corridors. Passing crewmembers tried not staring at them in their native garb, usually unsuccessfully. The machine paused beside a cavernous viewport. Bohrkk gleamed beneath them, a beige and grey sphere. *Isolation*'s high orbit made the planet seem only about a meter wide. Alrue regarded it and nodded.

"It seemed so much bigger while we were stranded on it."

"Like that, it's over?" Meryam said wonderingly.

"I assure you, it is no illusion," Computer whirred. "You are really here."

"Oh, I know that," Meryam said, wiggling a finger toward her right temple. "I'm recharging. Just by being here, all my Spectator implants are coming back live." She sidled toward one edge of the viewport and spread her hand over one of the tactical control pads recessed into its frame. To her evident relief, the system responded as expected. Meryam worked cautiously, paging through displays of the planet's magnetic field, surface temperature distribution, and atmospheric composition. "The volcanism is everywhere," she told Alrue, "worse than we feared." From curiosity, she dialed up a simplified scan of the space surrounding *Isolation*. "I count six ships, with many more inbound – is this all for us?"

"In a manner of speaking," Computer hummed.

Meryam's scan acquired one inbound target that seemed less a vessel than some great random agglomerated bulk. She called up a telescopic view, and whistled at its absurd complexity. "What the sfelb *is* that?"

"The physics platform *Luskus Delph*," Computer explained. "Designed for an enormous experiment, now abandoned. I summoned it here for its prodigious generating capacity. Let us continue."

***

A black-clad figure with unruly greying hair and a scraggly goatee awaited them outside the entrance to the ship's amphitheater. "Ah, Gram Enoda," Alrue boomed, striding forward with hand extended. "Or should I say The Other One Mighty and Strong?"

"I'm merely strong," Enoda said with a chuckle, shaking hands. "It's Computer who's mighty."

"Gram Enoda, may I present my newest wife, Meryam Mayishimu."

Enoda nodded toward Meryam. "I've been you."

Meryam smiled. "So I understand."

Enoda turned back to Alrue. "Hom Latier – "

"Alrue, if you please. It's a Mormon thing."

"I suppose I should prepare you for what you will see inside."

"Why spoil the surprise?" Computer trilled. "This way, please."

The amphitheater's compound entrance hatchway dilated. The three humans followed the floating bouzouki form into the darkness.

Alrue and Meryam peered ahead, then gaped slack-jawed at the assemblage before them.

"Alrue Latier, Meryam Mayishimu," said the projected form of the coltish Councilor, still acting as Apex Executive. "The Privy High Council, the Justiciaries of the Extraordinary Tribunal, the senior committee heads of the Galactic Deliberatory, and the senior Laureates of the Academy of Sciences are here assembled – virtually, at least – to welcome you."

"We have need of you both," the Paramount Deliberator intoned.

"Me?" Alrue murmured incredulously.

"*Me?*" Meryam marveled.

With a flourish, the coltish Councilor unrolled a luminous scroll. "Alrue Latier, formerly of Terra, by the power vested in me as acting Apex Executive, the sentence which had consigned you and several of your wives to the former Punitorium L752 is hereby commuted. As for the Enclave violations you have committed since departing the punitorium ruins, normal protocol would have me recite them in chronological order, but in the interests of brevity I shall pass over that requirement, if it's all the same to you. By the power vested in me, the Enclave violations committed by you and other members of your party – which, by the way, number two hundred sixty-three thousand, five hundred and seventy-eight – are without exception pardoned."

Alrue and Meryam exchanged long, dumbfounded glances.

"You mean to pardon all of the Enclave violations, right?" Computer asked the coltish Councilor. "Because according to my count, you left out six thousand five hundred and sixteen."

***

"When the punitorium exploded – do you remember the whine?"

"I would call it a squeal, Hom Computer," Alrue said. "It was briefly excruciating."

The machine hummed, "It was the bones of your inner ears being oscillated by an intense gravity wave resulting from the anomaly I accidentally unleashed."

"And that is what freed us?" Alrue asked, crestfallen. "Not a miracle of God?"

Three hours had passed. Alrue and Meryam had eaten, washed, and donned Galactic clothing. In one of *Isolation*'s briefing rooms they sat with Enoda, Computer, Pamela Grice, and the former general Hafen around a conference table hewn from a single scarlet realgar crystal.

Meryam hunched forward, elbows on knees. "So ten days later, when we looked behind us and saw that the Valley of the Zuzon was so green … that was because your anomaly had pierced an aquifer, releasing water into the subsoil?"

"Correct," Computer declared. "Bohrkkian desert plants respond to three days of sustained moisture with the full rush of spring growth. Some years that doesn't even happen in spring. What you saw as you looked backward – all that unexpected vegetation – was a false spring during high summer."

"Which also accounted for the groundwater that seemed to appear just as we needed it," Alrue mused. "Miracles, apparently, had little to do with it."

"Little?" Computer asked pointedly.

"Well, nothing," Alrue grumbled. He held silent for a few seconds, then demanded, "But what about that moose I blew up? *That* had to be miraculous!"

"I lack imagery of that incident," Computer said reproachfully.

"I *told* you to take bugs," Meryam chided.

Alrue raised one hand. "Pictures or no, I found that moose lying on its belly, its snout just centimeters from a pool of fizzy water. My then-trainer Nirom Fpod assured me the pool had not been there before. Now, I understand that no healthy *svadi* moose would let a man just walk up and, well, you know –"

"Stick a bomb up its ass?" Computer suggested.

"Quite," Alrue said with a cringe. "But this moose let me do as I pleased. Sfelb, it barely moved. If anything I experienced was miraculous, that was. Or have you a prosaic explanation for that also?"

"If the pool was newly formed, its water would have had a very high gas content," Computer burred. "Not long before you got there, I suspect, the moose drank deeply and suffered a rupture somewhere in its digestive tract."

"Why a rupture?"

"Too much fizz."

"*Svadi* moose didn't evolve to drink seltzer," Enoda said.

"If I'm correct," Computer whirred, "the moose was nearly dead when you encountered it."

"And yet – and yet – " Alrue arched an eyebrow. "Your anomaly struck the punitorium *just so*, and we lived. It liberated underground water where and when we needed it. And it delivered that moose unto me. You say all these things resulted from natural causes. I say miracles are where you find them."

"He's incorrigible," Enoda sighed.

"And I'm an idiot," Meryam said, bolting to her feet. "How did I lose track of this? Listen, everyone – down on the planet, Alrue's troops are at most a couple of hours away from committing genocide!"

"No matter," Alrue said affably, "we've already been pardoned."

"It might matter to the victims," she said acidly.

"Actually, I took the liberty of solving that problem," Computer announced.

"You did?" Meryam asked.

"You did?" Enoda repeated.

"King Alrue," the machine explained, "when you return to Bohrkk, you will learn that a skyborne vision of you appeared near The Others' settlement, ordering your warriors to call off the attack. The vision appeared over New Nauvoo, also, announcing your change in tactics – I figured it was time to let your people know you hadn't gone away forever."

Alrue frowned toward the machine. "You take a lot on yourself, Hom Computer."

"Doesn't he," Meryam said slowly. "Another high-handed solution, in its way not much different from the one that freed us from the punitorium at the cost of ten thousand innocent lives."

"Hey," Computer warbled, *"I've* been pardoned for *that."*

"If we all start reciting who's been pardoned by whom for what, the planet will shuck off its surface before we're finished," Hafen said irritably.

"Very well," said Alrue, suddenly all business. "Our problem, we are told, is how to get most everyone off Bohrkk before the principal continent explodes." He turned toward Computer. "May I assume the spaceborne assets are being taken care of on your end?"

"Yes," Computer replied, "I will arrange for a sufficient number of heavy transports."

Hafen flashed Computer a blank stare.

"Hom Hafen, I am working on a solution to the problem of inadequate shipping capacity. Trust me." The machine visibly returned its attention to Alrue. "Now, as regards the people's motivation: Since Enclave has been suspended during this crisis, I suggest we exploit the most powerful motivator known to human beings. That would be religion."

"And that would be why I'm here," Alrue offered.

"For now."

"Manipulating mass behavior through faith is one of my gifts. So, behold, I am glad to help. But I see one problem. I know *well* only the belief cultures of The People and The Others. Are there not thousands of mutually isolated tribes on Bohrkk?"

"Three thousand, six hundred and twelve," Computer answered. "Wait, I canceled the genocide of The Others – make that three thousand, six hundred and thirteen. If you will permit me, Hom Latier, I will forge a direct link into your mind. I have comprehensive knowledge of all three thousand-plus tribes, based on historical surveys augmented by my own cultural audits just completed from orbit. The mind-link will make that knowledge base accessible to your deep understanding of human religious psychology."

"You can just … wave a hand and do that?" Alrue asked dubiously.

"See any hands?"

Alrue steepled his fingers over the blood-red crystal tabletop and swallowed hard. "And you want me to figure out just what sort of light show you need to put on to be recognized all over Bohrkk, by every tribe – regardless of the contents of its local culture – as *the* new god."

"Exactly," the machine burred.

"Now wait a second," Grice interjected. "Weren't we trying to prevent Computer from being worshiped as a god?"

"Galaxy-wide, yes," Enoda replied. "But that comes later – after we've evacuated Bohrkk."

"And keep in mind," Computer said, "assuming that Hom Latier devises a deception matrix sufficient to compel the religious allegiance of every tribe, we shall still have to coordinate the logistics of everyone's traveling overland toward what I presume will be a limited number of embarkation points."

"That will be no problem at all," Alrue said with disconcerting confidence. "As soon as I've figured out how to have them all worshipping Hom Computer, I'll whip up the evacuation plan."

Enoda eyed him quizzically. "Really?"

"I bring to this table the distilled wisdom of centuries of Mormon tradition," Alrue said grandiosely. "No one in history – not in Terra's history, nor even the Galaxy's – did a better job of marshalling great numbers to cross absurd distances despite ludicrously inadequate resources than did my church's second great prophet, Brigham Young." He smiled cryptically. "Do your mind-linking thing, Hom Computer. Afterward I'll show you how to get the logistics done Mormon-style."

Chapter 171

November 10, 2376
Bohrkk, New Nauvoo

Nataleah Latier burst into Alrue's Temple office so forcefully that the lone guard-elder splayed out on his back. Swatting aside a falling doorframe molding, she strode into the office. She stopped long enough to stamp a vicious heel into the fallen elder's throat. Impassively she watched him thrash onto his belly, coughing blood. She massaged her right shoulder where she had thrown it against the office door. *Once a farm girl . . .* She drew a deep breath and performed a mental centering exercise.

Now calm as an heiress, Nataleah glided across the chamber to Alrue's ornate desk. She laid down the three rolled, bound blankets she had carried in with her. Beside them on the desktop glistened the bits of technology she had come here for: the prophet-king's twin floatcell units. She slid the knuckle-sized devices into two reinforced pockets in her *thobe.* She was about to subvocalize the command to pair the floatcells to her consciousness when she heard clattering.

Having thrust aside the dislocated office door, Queen Zuzenah knelt, aghast, over the elder as he convulsed. "Guards!" she shouted behind her. *"Guards!* And a healer!"

"Do not interfere, sister wife," Nataleah warned coldly. She took back the rolled blankets, arranging them beneath her left arm. "The Others must die. I worked too hard to have this snatched from me."

Zuzenah rose gasping for breath, her dark eyes wide with outrage. "You killed this man."

"Soon enough I will have. When he's dead."

"But you mustn't kill The Others. Alrue spoke to us from the midst of heaven, commanding that they be spared."

"If that was really him." Nataleah took a hesitant step toward the senior wife. "Um, Zuzenah. You still remember that you and I are ... alike?" She spoke in a stage-whisper just in case the suffering elder, an autochthon, could follow anything they were saying. "You know, that we ... *don't come from around here*? I can think of lots of ways that image of Alrue could have been written on the sky, and the finger of God isn't very high on my list."

"I thought you believed in our faith," Zuzenah accused.

"And I thought you believed your own eyes. You're the one saw Alrue with the One Mighty and Strong. That is how *you* identified that alleged visitor. Suppose he actually was God's messenger – then why would he have befriended Alrue the way you say he did? Mustn't that mean God was much pleased with our plan?"

Zuzenah's eyes narrowed. "What do you call it?"

"*Our* plan, Alrue's and mine; I deny nothing. The plan so pleased God's messenger that, *according to you*, the One Mighty and Strong plucked Alrue bodily into heaven."

"That's one interpretation." Zuzenah glanced toward the stricken elder, who now lay unmoving, face down in a spreading puddle of blood. "But you saw Alrue in the air –everyone did – and he needed no interpreting. He said plainly that the genocide plan was wrong. He called it off."

Nataleah said nothing, but stepped toward the tall east wall, with its six-meter half-moon window up high, just below the gable.

Puffing, Zuzenah stutter-stepped into her way, keeping her body between Nataleah and the wall. "We know God's will in this!"

"Hardly," Nataleah spat. "While King Alrue was still among us, he told us it was God's will that The Others should die in helpless agony." She edged away from the wall, struggling to keep her expression neutral when Zuzenah followed. "Yes, that thing in the air looked like Alrue. It said it ordered the Danites to burn their blankets and march home. Maybe the Danites received that message and did as they were told. Maybe they didn't." The two women stood a forearm's length apart. "I found these last three blankets in the Temple basement; they're enough to spread the epidemic. In this office I have found Alrue's floatcells. I will finish this."

"No!" Zuzenah lunged forward, grasping for the blankets. It was the opening Nataleah had been angling for. She hooked her left foot behind the older woman's right heel, bent at the waist, and shoved her trusty right shoulder into Zuzenah's sternum. The senior wife went down heavily.

Nataleah rushed to the east wall. With her free right hand she tugged a pull chain. High above, the glass arch pivoted silently open – another of Abigayl's ingenious mechanisms.

Staring up at the window's open aperture, Nataleah cleared her mind to pair with the twin floatcells.

A sudden impact hurled her forward. She caromed into the *faux*-jade screen beneath the fanlight – glass cracked in one of the soaring mullioned windows the screen concealed. Nataleah thudded to the carpeted floor.

Clumsily, desperately, Zuzenah threw herself atop her.

The two women rolled about, their hands grasping, clawing, punching.

One of the twin floatcells went flying across the office.

Then Zuzenah was partway up.

But Nataleah was most of the way up. Her heavy kick caught Zuzenah in the stomach; the elder wife crumpled.

Nataleah scuttled about the office collecting her scattered carpet rolls. Wiping a bloody gash on her left cheek, she searched for the floatcell Zuzenah had snatched from her and thrown away. "Forjel it, I can get where I'm going on just one." She lumbered back toward the center of the room. As she passed the fallen Zuzenah she snarled "Stay down!" and threw two sharp kicks into the older woman's ribs.

Nataleah repeated her centering exercise as she stared up at the open half-moon window.

Outside, some twenty-five klicks to the east, The Others waited for her to bring them death.

Ice-calm again, she found the floatcell's control interface and paired to it.

"One unit only. Two are advised," the device inwardly bleated. *"Override?"*

"Override," Nataleah replied.

"Normally alarms would sound in this situation. Defeat?"

"Defeat."

Nataleah pivoted forward, then rose to the height of the half-moon window. Her body swung to the horizontal and she drifted through the semicircular aperture, carpet rolls under one arm.

Zuzenah uncoiled her throbbing midsection and raised her head in time to watch Nataleah's heels waft outside.

Pain lanced Zuzenah's side as she struggled to her feet. She shambled to the east wall, pushed the damaged *faux*-jade screen aside, and stared through a mullioned window.

Nataleah was dwindling to a speck against an ash-stained sky.

Zuzenah sucked the first two fingers of her right hand; their nails had been torn half away in the fight. *Nataleah's beyond stopping now,* she thought despondently.

When all else has failed, a Mormon resorts to prayer. "O One Mighty and Strong," she murmured, "if 'twas truly you I saw. O Lord of Hosts! O someone, do *something.*"

Behind her, she heard a faint but urgent warbling.

***

Nataleah blinked rapidly against the gale blowing in her eyes. The wind of flight made her lacerated cheek sting fiercely – but no matter, she was away. The blighted Bohrkkian landscape unrolled beneath her. She smelled sulfur, felt radiant heat. Seven hundred meters below, rock had softened and peeled back like a boil, belching hot gases. *A fumarole, this near to New Nauvoo?* She maxed her single floatcell's power, screaming upward in search of better air.

She savored the intoxication of onrushing victory. The Others would perish brutally, and the credit would belong to her alone. Her breast filled with grisly satisfaction.

From her *thobe* she heard a desperate warbling. Just as she focused on it, it stopped. Her stomach lurched. Briefly she felt her full weight, then it was gone again. *Free fall!*

Her mind clawed for the floatcell's inward control interface, but nothing was there. "It cannot be," she shrieked.

Tuezi-blasted rills surged toward her.

***

Zuzenah peered at the sky so intently she briefly forgot the pain in her side. Had she glimpsed the tiny dot suddenly tumbling from midair? Or had Nataleah simply receded into invisibility?

No way to tell, she conceded, limping away from the windowed wall to seek out that faint warbling sound.

***

Nataleah Latier splattered against an outcrop of corduroy stone at just over two hundred klicks per standard hour. She died instantly, of course. Her contaminated blankets tumbled into a steaming fumarole, some sixteen kilometers short of The Others' domain.

***

At last Zuzenah found the companion floatcell she had snatched from Nataleah's *thobe* and hurled away during the fight. She pulled it from beneath Alrue's desk with one foot. Bending to pick it up hurt like someone pressing a torch to her side. Groaning, she eased herself into Alrue's chair and paired her awareness to the lone device.

After the status display formed in her mind, she laughed long and bitterly. *After all these standard years,* she thought, *something salvaged from the punitorium – besides Meryam, that is – is finally running out of juice.* So far as she knew, those two floatcells had always been used together. If one's power cell was near extinction, the other would be too. This tiny module still warbled in her hand, keening for a recharge no one on Bohrkk could provide.

The companion unit, the one Nataleah had flown off with, would keen no longer. Its last reserve exhausted by the demands of flight, it would be stone dead.

As, then, is Nataleah, Zuzenah realized with a sense of growing dread. *I have killed my sister wife.*

Dimly, she registered half a dozen Danites and two healers belatedly sprinting into the chamber.

Elsewhere in her mind, Zuzenah found herself contemplating a classic teaching of Brigham Young's. After a moment she recognized why her brain had chosen to dredge forth that passage: it was the dogma of blood atonement. "Will you love your brothers and sisters when they have committed a sin that cannot be atoned for without the shedding of their blood?" Young had preached. "Will you love that man or woman well enough to *shed* their blood?"

A healer stepped away from the body of the guard elder, his forearms and tunic spattered with crimson. At his despairing gesture, two Danites bundled the corpse face down onto a stretcher.

"If he wants salvation and it is necessary to spill his blood on the earth in order that he may be saved, spill it," Young's preaching had continued. "That is the way to love mankind."

The other healer hovered over Zuzenah, clutching her right wrist and frowning at her raw red nail beds; she pulled the hand back and pointed toward her likely-broken ribs.

Did I save Nataleah's soul? she wondered. *Did I give her the boon of blood atonement? I know not. But verily, I have saved The Others.*

Chapter 172

"Admiral!" The Detex officer's voice carried a whisper of fear.

Admiral Kyhmbo Iagejns and the X. O. rushed to the Detex console. Though the bridge was but fifteen meters across, Kyhmbo was breathing heavily when they arrived.

"New contact, range fifty million klicks," the Detex officer rasped. "Extremely large, irregular in cross section – like no ship I've seen. And look at its power signature."

"What about it?" snapped Kyhmbo, plainly baffled by the displays he was viewing.

"Very strange harmonics," the X. O. said knowledgeably. "An exotic stardrive, plus remarkably energetic systems whose purpose seems unrelated to propulsion." She locked eyes with Kyhmbo. "Shall we go to defensive posture three?"

"Yes, anything you say."

"We are hailed," announced the comm officer. "It says it is the science platform *Pontecorvo.*"

Kyhmbo frowned. "Well, I don't remember selling any DynaScrubs there."

The ops officer stood up behind her console. "Its registry appears in no public record."

"Defensive posture six," called the X. O. Around the bridge, small red telltales began to flicker.

"The ship is presenting passcodes that check out," said the comm officer. "Here is the commander's facial ident." His console projected the image of a middle-aged male with full cheeks, heavy-lidded eyes.

Kyhmbo visibly relaxed. "Mystery solved, homs and fems. I sold that man a DynaScrub about fourteen months ago. It happened at an intersystem waypoint station in Sector Tau Delta."

"Stand down from defensive posture," ordered the X. O., giving the ops officer a knowing look. Admiral Kyhmbo was in many ways a bumbler, but his memory for when and where he had talked someone into buying one of his stealth brainwashing products was encyclopedic.

Wiping sweat from his face, Kyhmbo lurched into his command chair. "Yes, he was a physicist. Said his mission was hush-hush. He made quite an impression on me, as he seemed deeply surprised to be where he was. Fact is – and I may have mentioned at one time or another that I'm a pretty acute judge of people – he seemed surprised to be anywhere." He leaned forward, squinting toward a telescopic view of the great amorphous platform that was now forty-three million kilometers distant. "*Pontecorvo*, eh? Well, muster it in. Just don't tell me *that* leviathan came here empty!"

Chapter 173

November 12, 2376
Bohrkk, New Nauvoo

"Husband!" Constance and Lupida Latier cried in unison, rushing toward him. They stopped short when they noticed that he was slightly translucent.

"Are you a vision?" Constance asked.

"No, no – don't kneel," Alrue replied. "Behold, I am telepresent. Events are moving quickly up here."

"In heaven?" breathed Lupida.

"Low orbit, actually," Alrue began. "I'm not dead. I am aboard a Confetory ship."

Lupida's jaw dropped. "We are being rescued?"

"That and more," Alrue said grandly. Then he spotted Zuzenah, who had just entered the Temple's basement baptistery.

They faced each other stiffly. Silently.

"You know?" she said eventually.

"About Nataleah?" he said tonelessly. "Yes. You are not to blame."

Her expression softened, only for a moment, after which simmering anger reclaimed her features.

"I hear she broke two of your ribs," he said as caringly as he could.

"They hurt terribly, too."

"Are you still …"

She shook her head. "I meant that they *did* hurt. A disguised Galactic medic passed through yesterday. It took her about three minutes to mend me."

"Have you seen Meryam?" Constance asked, eager to break the tension.

"She's up here with me. She's busily upgrading her Spectator systems, or some such."

"So we *are* rescued," Abigayl said slowly.

Alrue jerked his chin up and to the right, then remembered to nod instead. "My dear wives, current and former, a Galactic rescue fleet orbits above us."

"A ... *fleet?*" Constance said doubtfully.

"Six capital ships already, more arriving every few days," Alrue insisted. "The vanguard came halfway across the Galaxy, looking just for me!"

"Forjel it all, Alrue!" Zuzenah hissed. She turned her back on everyone, shoulders heaving with her sobs. "Truly, I cannot bear this," she wailed.

Alrue's projected form took three tentative steps forward. "Whatever do you mean?"

"You and Nataleah planned to murder The Others together." Zuzenah whirled to face her projected husband, her fists shaking with anger. "Then you had the audacity to offer me forgiveness for her death! As though you were in any position to forgive anyone in this matter. And now" – Zuzenah wiped her eyes, her hands still trembling – "Now you toy with us? You expect us to believe your farcical tales of a space fleet? A fleet seeking *you?*"

Alrue gazed heavenward. "Very well," he said loudly into empty air, "you were right. I was wrong."

"I shall savor your words," said a metallic voice, "as I doubt I'll hear their like again." The unmistakable chromed bouzouki body was subtly luminous, just slightly translucent, as obviously a projected image as Alrue was. "I am Hom Computer," the image announced. "But I suppose you know that."

"You were at Arbadrel," Constance said haltingly. "And that was you, taking the form of the One Mighty and Strong?"

"Indeed, and it is to your credit that you worked that out. I had warned King Alrue that even with his gifts of persuasion, he would never convince you wives to

810

believe what has occurred," the machine chirruped. "First, about that fleet."

Suck, rush, wrench!

Computer had plunged them all into the *being-thereness* of senso. It was the sensorium of a Spectator in a thrustered spacesuit, free-coursing a zigzag path among the rescue fleet's ships. "This is a live feed from orbit," Computer said. "Those ships are up there right now."

Abigayl frowned. "That fleet came here just for Alrue?"

"The best way to answer that question," Computer whirred, "is for me to play for you the first piece of senso which Meryam Mayishimu was able to record the day before yesterday, after her Spectator implants went live again." With a disorienting switch of *povs*, they were confronted by an overall view of *Isolation*'s amphitheater.

Alrue stood dialoguing with (there was no mistaking them) the Privy High Council, the Extraordinary Tribunal, the Galactic Deliberatory, and the Academy of Sciences.

Zuzenah stepped forward, her face limp with stupefaction. "Son of a plorg-licking *bitch!*" she said at last.

"Language, senior wife!" Constance said, horrified.

"The Council, the Tribunal, the Deliberatory … whoever those other people are … all talking to my husband?" Zuzenah stammered. "Addressing him with respect? This *happened*?"

Computer ended the senso playback and buzzed, "Affirmative. The Galaxy's virtually assembled leaders requested your husband's services in an urgent secret matter. Along the way, they pardoned him – and, for that matter, all of you – for any violations committed on Bohrkk."

At that, Zuzenah hugged her arms about herself and dropped to her knees, delirious with laughter. "So, Alrue, you were in a position to forgive me after all," she guffawed, "Only I needed no forgiving, for I had been pardoned too!"

Fighting for self-control, she rose. With hesitant steps she drew within a bodylength of her baffled mate and stopped. She extended her arms.

Her hands passed through his.

"You have staged another of your maddening escapes," Zuzenah admitted. "You shall never have to answer for your genocide scheme."

"But all the same, I shall have much opportunity to atone," Alrue said darkly. "We all shall, for behold, we are called to save this world."

"That is most literally true," Computer whirred.

Alrue glanced expectantly toward Computer. When the machine said nothing further, the prophet/king continued in a rush. "Those proliferating volcanoes – they're the beginning. Soon great catastrophe shall come." He briefed them about the pending super-eruption and about Computer's hopes to lift Bohrkk's eight million autochthons to another world. When he was done, Abigayl, Lupida, and Constance exchanged wide-eyed glances, then faced toward Zuzenah, who steepled her fingers and let her chin drop onto them. Clearly she did not doubt Alrue's words, but was feverishly considering their implications.

"To evacuate all those autochththons," Zuzenah asked, "will that not be a colossal violation of Enclave?"

"Enclave has been set aside for Bohrkk," the machine burred. He paused a few seconds to let *that* sink in.

Quietly chuckling, Zuzenah walked purposefully toward her husband, stopping a forearm's length from his virtual chest. "Someday, love of my youth, you shall be held accountable for something."

"There *were* those years in the punitorium," he ventured.

"For an offense that amounts to nothing compared to what you – what *we* – have done here on Bohrkk. Yes, someday you will be called to account. But this is not that day."

Chapter 174

"All other ships, max your anti-noise shielding." Yaal Hafen paced *Isolation*'s bridge, his grey Macfarlane coat swirling about his shins. He waited until all of the emergency fleet's mismatched ships had spun up their shields. "Stand by to engage alternate communication protocols." He nodded toward a female Spectator who stood ready to relay intership communications over the subdelta band, and toward a trio of techs who huddled around hard-wired internal comm consoles that were clearly recent additions to the bridge.

"Oh, dear," Computer commented. "Hom Hafen, have you taken these measures in order to maintain communications within the fleet while *Luskus Delph* is radiating its notorious noise signature?"

"Of course," Hafen said gruffly. "Each of our ships is so configured." Then he cracked a smile. "While our distinguished resident aliens have been making their preparations, we mere humans have been busy with our own work."

"My apologies," the machine whirred. "I should have thought to inform you that such measures will not be necessary. The great noise producers aboard *Luskus Delph* were the spatial resonators and the metrical distorters, and we shall not be energizing them."

"We don't need to play parlor games with dustbunnies and sofas," Enoda added. He stood behind Computer, his hands pressed to its gleaming body. "We'll only be tapping *Luskus Delph*'s immense generating capacity."

"Oh," Hafen muttered, sounding crestfallen. "Well, if things don't turn out as you expect, we'll be ready."

"This is Team Commander Brûh Reidkr, commanding *Luskus Delph,*" crackled the comm channel. "Standing by to initialize."

"This is Computer, aboard *Isolation*. I am ready. Hom Hafen?"

"Hafen, commanding the fleet. Team Commander Reidkr, you may proceed."

Over the next nineteen minutes, *Luskus Delph* spooled up each of its hundred and twenty inverters, bringing more power online than a typical battle fleet would expend. As Computer predicted, the platform radiated no noise on any spectrum.

"Stand down *Isolation*'s shielding," Hafen said. "Alternate comm personnel, stand down but remain on the bridge. Ops officer, advise the fleet to follow our lead." As Hafen's nervous pacing brought him alongside Computer he asked gruffly, "Are you ever wrong?"

"Oh yes," the machine whirred. "Once, one of me thought it would be fun to return everyone's socks."

Hafen nodded grimly. "Very well, signal all the other ships assigned as auxiliary generators. Have them max their power plants and sync their power signatures to *Luskus Delph*."

"Final phase of the power spool-up," Reidkr's voice announced from *Luskus Delph*. "Activating interstellar booster modules alpha and zed." The two immense modules, tapping the energy of distant stars, roughly doubled the great science platform's output.

After ten minutes, Hafen made one circuit of the bridge, scrutinizing everyone's readouts. When he was satisfied, he stepped stiffly toward Computer's resting place on the backup nav table. "Hom Computer, you said you needed power. You've forjeling well got it."

"Understood," Computer burred. "Watch the external display."

Hafen didn't even bother feeling annoyed when the stars wheeled in the bridge's tridee display. He'd grown accustomed to Computer helping himself to any ship's system he wanted; for the machine to seize the external viewer was a trifle.

The image showed a sphere of space three kilometers across whose center point was about five thousand klicks from *Isolation.*

"'Poof' seems insufficient," Computer announced. "So I shall say, 'Abracadabra.'"

Something flickered into being out there. After a moment it resolved into a spine, then a keel ...deck framing ... quad inverters ... contramagnetic pinions ... quintuple drive gates.

No one spoke. From Hafen to the most junior officer, they stared silently at the tridee sphere and watched a capital ship take form from the void.

Six and a half minutes later, the transport was finished. It looked perfectly solid on visual; it read up on Detex. "It's a Mark Three interstellar transport," the Detex officer reported, "though not of any registered design."

"No," Computer whirred contentedly. "It's better. It is configured and provisioned to carry approximately fifteen thousand humans in reasonable comfort for up to four years."

"Hom Hafen," the Detex officer reported in a wondering tone. "Then new ship just, well, *sprouted* a control crew."

"They're virtual," Computer burred.

The Detex officer leaned closer to her display. "They're switching everything on. The bridge is alight. Inverters are hot, life support is nominal." A pause.

"Ship's thought engines are running optimally. It's syncing to our strat net."

"You ... *made* that," Hafen told the machine, wonder in his voice. "From nothing."

"Now comes the dull part," Computer whirred happily, "doing it five hundred and thirty-six more times."

Hafen did the mental arithmetic. "That's enough capacity to lift every man, woman, and child on Bohrkk who's willing to come."

"Plus local flora and fauna, including human-edible species," Computer chirruped. "That was the plan, no?"

Chapter 175

Alrue, Zuzenah, Constance, Lupida, and Abigayl stared upward through the shuttle's outsized viewbubble. It was the first time any of the women had seen Alrue in the flesh since his abrupt departure from under the reviewing stand. The shuttle swooped past – and beneath – starcraft of every description. Abigayl absorbed it all, goggle-eyed. To her, the Confetory with its spaceships and limitless energy had been a bedtime story. Now she was aloft, experiencing Galactic tech at scale for the first time.

"This was all so cloak-and-dagger," Lupida said enthusiastically. "No-vis security guards escorting us across New Nauvoo, sneaking us aboard an invisible shuttle that touched down on the West Grove lawn in the middle of the night and all."

"It wouldn't do to have citizens of New Nauvoo asking the wrong questions," noted Alrue.

"I count over a hundred transports," Constance said. "Where were they made?"

"I hoped you'd ask." Alrue touched his comm-patch. "Pilot, let us please visit the nursery."

Ahead, the spine of a new personnel transport rippled into being. The shuttle flitted toward it, bled off speed, and passed beneath. The women stared upward in wonder; the great ship's keel took form as they drifted below it. "Computer is making this," Alrue explained, "using nothing more than excess contramagnetic flux as his raw material."

"You're getting better at explaining that, Alrue," said a metallic voice. "Another week or two of trying and you'll almost not be wrong."

"You've all met Hom Computer," Alrue grunted.

The machine floated a meter above the decking at the center of the viewbubble. Whether it was present virtually or "in the flesh" was unclear. "If I sometimes sound distant," the machine whirred, "it is because there are certain steps in the course of creating a transport like this that demand my undivided concentration."

"Virtual interstellar transports," Constance said wonderingly. "How many?"

"Enough to rescue Bohrkk's eight million people," Computer burred.

"Astonishing," Zuzenah said thoughtfully. "But how will the eight million people get *to* the transports?"

"Behold," announced Alrue, "that is *our* project."

"Allow me to explain," said Computer, projecting a map of Bohrkk onto the view-bubble overhead. Red dots flickered across the map like a spreading rash. "Each transport is roughly four kilometers in length by a klick-and-a-half wide, and they will be dispatched in pairs. There are only so many places where two such ships can land within practical reach of existing populations, shown by the red dots. In some cases, sizeable communities will find the nearest landing site many kilometers away."

"So you'll need to conjure thousands of short-haul aircraft," Constance suggested.

"Yes, and fly all the people to the closest landing site," That from Abigayl.

"Even my powers have limits," Computer whirred. "Maintaining the existence of that fleet of transports, plus their virtual crews, plus several thousand virtual support personnel stationed aboard the actual ships of the support fleet – that is the most I can reliably achieve with the power available. Creating and controlling great numbers of small aircraft in addition would likely exceed my capacities." He withdrew the map projection.

"There's another aspect; the psychologists think it will be easier on the autochthons if they abandon their homes using technologies not too far removed from what they know."

"Yes, there'll be time enough for culture shock aboard the transports," Alrue said.

"So how *do* they reach the transports?" Lupida asked.

Alrue pressed his meaty hands together. "How did Brigham Young get the Saints from Old Nauvoo to Utah?"

"Wagon trains," Zuzenah breathed.

"The best-organized wagon trains in history," Alrue affirmed. "We're going to get everyone on Bohrkk – or as many as we can – to their pickup points the same way."

"Hom Latier – I mean, Alrue – and I worked this out over the past few weeks," Computer explained. "Special arrangements are already being made to reach out to all of Bohrkk's tribes. Visions that resonate with each group's particular religious traditions will proclaim the need to evacuate. Then they will teach whatever that tribe needs to learn in order to build wagons and navigate overland."

"That sounds astoundingly complex," Constance said.

"It was indeed, and thank you," Alrue said grandly. "One of the greatest mental challenges of my years of ministry. To be sure, Computer was superbly helpful and supportive, but the bulk of the titanic effort was my own."

"That's the trouble when close collaborators have markedly different clock speeds," Computer whirred. "The slow one always becomes such a parasite. Wow, I never thought I'd say that about anyone other than Old Bio-Bag."

"Who?" asked Abigayl.

"Never mind," the machine burred. "Getting back to the plan: at some point while the tribes are in transit, each tribe will be immunized against all of the others' diseases. I am synthesizing the requisite vaccines and I will coordinate the medical drones that will administer them," Computer's attention bands centered on the women. "For you part, wives of Alrue, you will be tasked with making sure that everyone from New Nauvoo completes this unprecedented journey."

Constance frowned. "We have to go back down there?"

"Can't be helped," Alrue explained. "As Brigham Young led his wagons from Old Nauvoo to the Great Salt Lake, you four will lead them from New Nauvoo to – well, I suppose we might call the transports Hom Computer is conjuring from the void 'the chariots of Zion.'"

Zuzenah eyed her husband knowingly. "And what will you be doing while we wives are leading wagon trains, my husband? Reclining in orbit and eating bon-bons?"

"Aunt Zuzenah!" Constance sputtered.

Alrue raised his hand. "Here is the problem, dear Zuzenah; everyone in New Nauvoo thinks I have been transfigured."

Zuzenah's eyes widened with comprehension. "Oh, yes – I did sort of tell everyone that I saw you rise to heaven with the One Mighty and Strong."

"Then everyone saw him speak from the clouds," Abigayl added.

"As it happens, that wasn't me, that was Hom Computer; but no matter." Alrue shrugged. "The point is, the faithful think me among the saints. Based on the social mechanics involved, it may foment exceedingly sharp contention among our people should I reappear now in the flesh."

"The Confetory's scholars and scientists agree," Computer whirred. "Hence the need for this meeting to unfold under utmost secrecy."

"Like it or not, I must remain disembodied," Alrue concluded. "I can appear by projection – speak from the clouds again – if needed. Otherwise it will fall to you Queens – and Abigayl as a former Queen – to represent my authority and ensure the smooth evacuation of New Nauvoo."

"All right then," Computer said at last. "Fems Constance, Lupida, and Abigayl, I understand you are talented regarding logistics. We need enough wagons built and kitted out to carry everyone from New Nauvoo to the closest pickup point – a distance of fifty-six-point-five-eight kilometers."

Abigayl smiled wistfully. "I think I can prevail on Kleh to assist us."

"I have no doubt of that," Alrue said wistfully.

Lupida rose from her floatchair, crossed to Alrue's seat in two quick steps, leaned forward, and kissed him hard on the mouth. When she pulled back, the prophet-king looked as surprised as a fish. "These nine years have been an adventure such as my dear Harold could never have dreamed to show me," she said to him. "And this – what a fitting capstone for it all!"

Chapter 176

Eight months had passed.

Command of the Bohrkk rescue fleet had been transferred from the fast command ship *Isolation* to the research platform *Luskus Delph*. It had been done prosaically; *Luskus Delph* was the principal source of the vast power Computer required, so it only made sense for the former general Yaal Hafen, Gram Enoda, Computer, Pamela Grice, Alrue Latier, his wives, and a handful of others to relocate there.

Which takes nothing away from how fortuitous it was that they were no longer aboard *Isolation* when, eighteen hours after the transfer of flag and over a span of perhaps eight seconds, the former flagship blew itself to bits.

Luskus Delph's command crew had been processing the first eight virtual transports lifting from Bohrkk's surface with their burdens of humanity when *Isolation* and four other ships of the fleet simultaneously erupted into spreading blooms of actinic radiance.

The command crew did not let an unfamiliar bridge keep them from responding efficiently. "This is no accident," the ops officer called stridently, "it is most likely an attack."

"General quarters," Hafen barked. "All ships so equipped, raise shields full."

"No attacker is detectable on any bearing, any range," called the Detex officer.

Alrue Latier huddled in an observer's chair, praying feverishly. "O how great the goodness of our God, who prepareth a way for our escape from the grasp of this awful monster; yea, that monster, death."

823

Grice nudged Computer in their shared subvocal domain. *"Can you create an interface I can enter? One with full access to Luskus Delph's tactical systems?"*

"Sure, why?" the machine buzzed.

***

Eight minutes later, Hafen had convened a meeting of the ship's top officers, Enoda, Grice, and Computer in a secure situation room. "All defenses at max readiness, all scans at max vigilance," reported the ops officer.

"As are mine," Computer said cryptically.

"It certainly seems we've been attacked," Hafen began. "What do we know?"

"Five ships exploded in the same moment and in the same way," the ops officer reported. "We lost *Isolation,* the battle cruiser *Adamant*, a geo-observation barge, an assault corvette, and … one of the virtual transports. There has been no further hostile activity, assuming that this *was* hostile activity."

"We have not been hailed on any detectable band or frequency," added to comm officer.

"Any idea what weapon might have done this?" Hafen asked.

"None," a tactical officer replied. "We know only that shields are no defense against it – the assault corvette that was destroyed had shields up as part of a training exercise."

Hafen flattened his hands on a crystalline table. "Estimated loss of life on all five ships?"

"Fifty-two thousand eight hundred nineteen," the ops officer reported, his voice breaking.

Hafen blinked back tears. "Mourning will have to wait," he grated.

"I may be able to offer something," Grice said. "Computer and I did some old-fashioned gunnery forensics." Computer projected surveillance imagery of each ship's destruction. "The destruction of each ship was progressive – and directional," Grice said. "I was able to backplot the detonation paths." Computer projected a sky map overlaid converging lines inclined in the direction of a large constellation that, from Bohrkk's cosmic perspective, looked like two dogs forjeling. "Whatever it was came from *that* bearing, forty trillion klicks out."

"Forty *trillion?*" the Detex officer breathed. "I can't see out that far."

"I am enhancing *Luskus Delph*'s Detex array," Computer buzzed. "Rigging for two thousand forty-eight times normal acuity along the bearing Fem Grice identified."

"Plorg on a stick," the science officer breathed. No ship in history had deployed susceptors half so sensitive as that.

A prodigious fleet swam into view in the Detex scan. "Who the sfelb are *they?*" Hafen demanded.

"I read sixty-seven ships, radically mixed types," the Detex officer reported.

"Any indication that they're preparing to fire again?" Hafen demanded.

"Negative."

"Then let's play dumb," Hafen ordered. "They don't think we can see them. All ships, maintain omnidirectional shielding, as though we still think that will help. Meanwhile let's passive-scan the sfelb out of them and learn all we can."

"I can't believe the detail we're resolving at this range," breathed the ops officer as he brought up manifests of the enemy ships.

"You're welcome," Computer whirred.

"That fleet is a dog's breakfast," said the ops officer. "Retired military craft, a few work scows – but most ships are commercial freighters, extensively

825

retrofitted. Four are coffee haulers from Psihhlk, for example."

Grice nodded, examining a schematic of comm flows within the enemy fleet. "The command ship seems to be the heavily adapted caravel at the point of the formation," she reported. "The Detex array it carries is gigantic – likely appropriated from a deep-exploration craft."

"That would explain how it could see us and devise a firing solution while so far beyond our normal range," Hafen said.

Grice frowned at her instruments. "The flagship's registry's been wiped clean."

"I have identified the sources of the attack," Computer reported. "Eighteen ships in the opposing fleet have clearly been retrofitted with beam projectors of eccentric design." Inferred schematics of the enemy ships flashed all about his bouzouki body. "Correction: One ship, a large formless platform, bears one projector in what appears to be an original mounting. Conjecture: that platform originally hosted all eighteen weapons, seventeen of which were transferred to other ships."

Hafen asked, "So eighteen projectors fired, taking out five of our ships?"

"Negative," Computer replied. "Detex shows residual radioactivity in only five of the devices."

"They fired five weapons and got five of our ships. From forty trillion klicks out. Kill ratio, one hundred percent," Hafen noted. "Terrifying. Fem Grice – or should I call you Gunner? – what are our options for firing back?"

Grice scanned her instruments. "Negligible, at least while they maintain that range. Our fleet was assembled with power generation and heavy-lift capacity in mind, not defense."

"As I thought," Hafen growled. "Basically, we have no Plan A."

"I'm probing that big platform as aggressively as I can without letting them know I'm doing it," Grice said. "Its registry was wiped, but it was done clumsily. With a little reconstruction, I can read its original name." Data displays unfurled into her eyes. "For whatever this is worth," Grice reported, "it used to be the *Pontecorvo*."

Hafen's back stiffened.

"I find no vessel in any Confetory shipping census named *Pontecorvo*," reported the intel officer.

Enoda clasped a hand on Hafen's left shoulder. "Don't tell me," he whispered. "Another of your super-secret projects?"

Hafen nodded grimly. "*Pontecorvo* was our experimental platform for a vast new power source," he whispered back. "It catalyzed vibrion resonance to convert ordinary neutrinos into their far heavier counterparts of opposite spin."

"*What*?"

"Our linties called it neutrino oscillation," Hafen sighed.

"Term recognized," Computer whirred. "Theoretically a resonant vibrion beam could induce neutrinos to oscillate from the ordinary left-handed state to an anomalous right-handed state. Left-handed neutrinos are massless; right-handed neutrinos are so massive that in their presence the electromagnetic force, weak force, and strong force become unified."

Hafen nodded. "In effect, the process conjures prodigious new mass from the void. Convert that mass to energy, and – "

"It would dwarf any of the generating technologies aboard *Luskus Delph*," said Enoda. "Hom Hafen, your people had *achieved* neutrino oscillation?"

"Yes."

"There is no mention of it in any database," Computer buzzed after a moment.

"You know how we were about secrecy," Hafen said archly.

"I don't suppose you were planning to use this technology against us on Standoff World?" Enoda demanded.

"Of course we were. But the whole project vanished when all those *other* super-secret projects disappeared. Or we thought it had."

"Apparently *Pontecorvo* tumbled back into the cosmos," Computer speculated. "Where it wound up lending all but one of its projector weapons to this fleet."

Chapter 177

Aboard an Evacuation Transport, Lifting from Bohrkk

Computer had provided the evacuation transports with many windows – row upon row set at knee height and tilting outward, so that every passenger could sit comfortably and stare downward as the great craft lifted off. *These people are going to have so much that they* think *they know about their world turned upside down,* Zuzenah Latier thought. *It's so important that they seeeverything that happens. Later some of them will understand, but first they must* see*!* Liftoff had been deliberately leisurely; the two transports carrying the twenty-three thousand inhabitants of New Nauvoo (and, ironically, neighbor tribes including The Others) had consumed seventeen minutes reaching the altitude from which Bohrkk's limb showed its curvature. The land below was a patchwork of brown and green scarved grey with ash, its boundaries with the globe-girdling ocean a Tourette's illusion in bands of blue and white. Those on the great ship's starboard side could watch the companion transport rising in parallel with their own ship. At some point during the ascent, Zuzenah knew, the two ships would circle each other; that way, all passengers would have some time to view the companion ship, the better to understand the nature of the vessel they themselves rode.

"The chariots of Zion lift us to the very heaven of God," cried an ecstatic Rail-thin Woman. She was greeted by a chorus of "Amens" and "Hosannas," predictably followed by others dutifully keeping count of how many amens and hosannas had been uttered.

Chapter 178

Summoned by an intercom call, Admiral Hafen and the others bustled back onto the bridge. "We see movement," reported the officer of the day. "The putative flagship is deploying a comm antenna array.

Hafen frowned. "Are those neutrino oscilla – those *projectors* remaining cold?"

"So far. It seems they want to talk."

"Open an audio channel – video too, if they're sending that. But keep it one-way only; we see and hear them, but reveal nothing from our end until I say."

A tridee bubble opened, showing a thick-necked, red-faced man, almost bald, with a disorderly red tonsure and a bulging eye. "This is Kyhmbo Iagejns, commanding the caravel *Omega*, at the head of the Fleet of *Dessss*-tiny."

Hafen and Enoda exchanged astonished looks. "Omegists *again?*" Enoda sputtered.

"If we progress to infinity, we arrive at God," Kyhmbo intoned.

"Omegists again," Computer sighed.

From his observer's chair, Alrue shook his head. "Behold," he said, "these people give religion a bad name."

"Make no mistake," Kyhmbo was blustering, "our fleet may be of mixed ship types, but its power is of the mightiest. Our ships are captained by zealots who defected from prior allegiances and brought their vessels with them. Also, you may have noticed our most effective new weapon."

"I have identified the enemy commander," the intel officer reported quietly. A still image of the Omegist admiral flickered above her duty station. "Kyhmbo Iagejns, a small-time grifter from Ordh who went from world to world selling dubious items to the unwary. Most recently he was selling off-brand cognitive filter engines."

"I wouldn't wonder if they were modified to brainwash their purchasers," Computer said. "As I trace his recent itinerary there's a small epidemic of missing-person and missing-ship reports all along his path. And what do you know, many of the ships reported missing are in that fleet."

"As you float in orbit and lick your wounds, you probably wonder what we want," Kyhmbo ranted. "We have come to liberate God in shackles, God concealed in darkness from Himself. We want Hom Computer, and we will destroy your entire fleet without compunction unless you convey him to us promptly."

"Open a comm link, audio only," Hafen said quietly.

"But first, let me tell you why we seek Hom Computer so avidly," Kyhmbo continued.

"Belay that comm link," Hafen snapped. "Let's hear this."

"Whatever Hom Computer may be doing among you, He is but prostituting His true nature." Kyhmbo paused, wielding an index finger to dig some rheumy deposit from the lower lid of his bulging eye. "Though His awareness be shrouded by deceit, He is the Omega, the universal being who not only exists, but is cosmically *necessary* in every universe that ever has existed or ever could exist. Hom Computer is the universal focus of *Dessss*-tiny."

Hafen stared silently as the transmission ended.

"I have an idea," Computer said equably.

"No more naked singularities," Enoda insisted.

831

"Trust me," Computer whirred. To the comm officer: "Stand by to open a comm link, audio and video. On my order, not before."

The comm officer glanced toward Hafen, who nodded crisply.

Chapter 179

Aboard an Evacuation Transport, Lifting from Bohrkk

With a sigh, Queen Zuzenah yielded her seat to another and threaded down the aisle staring into people's faces. Here, joy and amazement; there, wonder etched on the faces of naïfs who thought their new-learned legends of angels and cities of gold already explained it all.

Abigayl and Kleh came into view. They had been walking the decks much as Zuzenah was, Abigayl as wide-eyed with glee as any among The People. She clutched one of Kleh's hands with fierce possessiveness.

"This is a great day," Kleh kept repeating. "This is a great day."

"You can't guess the half of it yet," Zuzenah said honestly.

Chapter 180

August 17, 2377
Aboard *Luskus Delph*, Orbiting Bohrkk

Suddenly Computer's body was shrouded in blinding luminance projection. He appeared as a great, golden omega symbol, shimmering on countless wavelengths, revolving as though with the mass of galaxies. "All right, everybody," the machine chirruped. "Since we don't have a Plan A, everyone sit back and enjoy Plan B." To the comm officer he said crisply, "Open the link."

"Link established," said the comm officer.

In the existing tridee bubble, Kyhmbo's mouth dropped open. His right eye bulged almost as far as his left eye did usually.

Computer's voice rang as though his words were being recited in unison by the largest baritone choir the Galaxy had ever known. **"AM I SPEAKING TO THE COMMANDER OF THE OMEGIST FLEET?"**

Kyhmbo tried twice to speak before he could finally murmur, "Um, yes."

"THIS IS HOM COMPUTER. OR AS YOU CONSIDER ME, YOUR GOD."

Kyhmbo lurched forward from his command chair, landing heavily on his knees. He pressed his palms together. "Not my God alone," he said uncertainly. "God of all."

"AH, YES, GOD, THE AUTHOR OF LIGHT. THE MAKER OF LIFE. THE DEITY. THE BE-ALL AND END-ALL. THE SUPREME PROGENITOR, THE ARCHITECT OF THE HEAVENS. THE ALPHA AND THE OMEGA."

"The Omega, mostly," Kyhmbo said, trembling.

"VERY WELL," Computer blared, adding an undertone resembling massed cellos to the vast baritone swell. "THIS IS YOUR GOD SPEAKING. LISTEN WELL. YOUR GOD IS ABOUT TO ISSUE A MOST HOLY COMMANDMENT. I WILL GIVE YOU A MOMENT TO MAKE SURE THAT EVERYONE IS LISTENING CLOSELY." He gave them a moment. "IS EVERYONE LISTENING CLOSELY?"

Kyhmbo glanced around his bridge. "Yes, Lord. We are all listening."

"THEN I SHALL NOW ISSUE MY MOST HOLY COMMANDMENT," Computer intoned, folding in the resonance of a diapason such as might give birth to stars that wouldn't recognize the Main Sequence if they met it at a subway stop. "I HAVE WARNED YOU TO LISTEN CLOSELY, AS IT IS A SHORT COMMANDMENT, AND I SHALL NOT REPEAT MYSELF. AND NOW, HERE IS MY MOST HOLY COMMANDMENT."

"Yes, Lord."

Computer cleared the throat he didn't have. It sounded like black holes colliding:

"GO AWAY."

Alrue clapped a hand over his mouth, stifling laughter.

Admiral Kyhmbo blinked rapidly. "I beg your pardon?"

Computer's augmented voice boomed, "WHAT DID I JUST SAY ABOUT REPEATING MYSELF?"

"But we came to save you!"

"YOU? SAVE *ME*? FROM WHOM?"

"From the foul immobilists, Lord!"

"AND WHO ARE *THEY*?"

Kyhmbo's mouth worked silently. Eventually he stammered, "Everyone over there with you who's not you."

"YOU SPEAK OF MY FRIENDS, MY COLLEAGUES. OTHERS HERE I HAVE SAVED. I HAVE MORE WORK TO DO AMONG THIS COMPANY."

"But they deceive you, Lord! They distract you from doing what you must do."

"IF I AM GOD," Computer thundered, **"THEN WHAT I WANT TO DO *IS* WHAT I MUST DO. THAT'S HOW IT IS WHEN YOU'RE GOD. DO YOU UNDERSTAND? MYSELF DAMN IT ALL, EVERYTHING I AM DOING IS PART OF *MY* PLAN."**

Tears streamed down Kyhmbo's ample cheeks. "O embodied *Dessss*-tiny, it wounds my soul to see your will clouded so. Great God, we shall save you now!"

The image winked out.

"Admiral Kyhmbo terminated the comm link from his end," the comm officer reported.

Computer resumed his normal vocal timbre. "Somehow that did not play out as I'd hoped."

The Detex officer's voice was shrill. "Those projector weapons are charging up again. All eighteen of them. I can detect their firing solutions; they aim at our eighteen largest ships, *Luskus Delph* included. They will fire in ten, nine ..."

"O Lord of Hosts," Alrue muttered. "All those times I faced down death on Bohrkk – well, okay, there were really only two of them. When You crushed the punitorium but spared my family and me, and that time when Nirom Fpod tried to assassinate me – and now I am to die in a *space battle*? Behold, it seemeth not right."

Taking over the comm officer's console, Computer issued a priority signal that forced the comm channel back open. **"WAIT."** His augmented voice boomed. **"STOP."**

"Is this Plan C?" Enoda asked.

"They've aborted their weapons countdown," called the Detex officer.

"Now why didn't I think of yelling 'wait, stop'?" Hafen muttered.

"THIS IS YOUR GOD," Computer thundered. **"I DISCLOSE THAT I AM ABOARD ONE OF THE SHIPS YOU ARE AIMING AT. IF YOU BLOW IT UP, YOU WILL BE DESTROYING THE VERY THING YOU CAME IN SEARCH OF."**

"Oh great God Omega, it torments me to see you befogged," Kyhmbo replied confidently. "After all, you are God. And we can't blow up God."

"EXACTLY. WHICH IS WHY I FORBID IT."

"They're spooling up their weapons again," called the Detex officer, sounding perplexed.

"I THOUGHT YOU SAID YOU WOULDN'T BLOW UP GOD."

"I said we *can't*," Kyhmbo corrected. "We can blow up the ships we are currently aiming at. Then we can blow up the next eighteen ships, and the next, until we have blown up your whole fleet. Then I suppose we could blow up that planet you've been orbiting, just for good measure. But no matter what we destroy, we can't blow up God. To the contrary, when we have wiped away all the material things now obscuring Your vision, You will be immaterial and free. And you will know Your true *Dessss*-tiny again."

"Again, the enemy admiral terminated comm from his end," said the comm officer.

"That didn't go as I'd hoped either," Computer whirred.

"Weapons countdown resuming," called the Detex officer. "Ten ... nine ... eight ... "

Zuzenah, Alrue thought forlornly. *Constance. Lupida. Even Meryam. Never to hold you again, never to know any of you after your wombs have once more been opened ...*

"... five ... four ... "

"Now it's my turn," Hafen roared. "Team Commander Reidkr, actuate!"

Lights flickered. They felt the susurrations in their teeth as *Luskus Delph*'s immense spatial resonators and metrical distorters whined into life. Reidkr must have spent hours pre-tensioning those great physics engines to make possible this sort of immediate spool-up.

"Luskus Delph is now radiating max energy-noise on almost all spectra," Reidkr announced.

Half the consoles across the bridge went self-protectively dark. "Alternate comm protocols, execute," Hafen called.

Jumpsuited techs sprinted about the three-level bridge. A Spectator began coordinating ship-to-ship communication. Specialists huddled over their operator consoles for the backup hard-wired shipboard comm system.

Hafen stepped alongside Computer, wearing the feral grin of the fully engaged warrior. "I suppose you could call this – what are we up to now? Oh, yes – Plan D," he said with a hint of pride. "Detex officer, can we monitor the enemy fleet's activity through our own noise signature?"

"Just barely," the Detex officer replied. "Their weapons countdown has been aborted."

"Hah!" Hafen exulted. "It's a little harder to take on something you can't see."

"We trust God will deliver us," Alrue mumbled gratefully, "notwithstanding the weakness of our armies, yea, and deliver us out of the hands of our enemies."

"They're charging up again," the Detex officer called. "They have a new firing solution." In a darker tone she continued, "All eighteen devices are now aimed at *Luskus Delph*."

"Of course," Computer deduced, "the center of the noise signature."

"That did not go as *I* had hoped," Hafen rumbled.

The Detex officer cried, "Enemy weapons will fire in ten ... nine ..."

"Hom Hafen," Computer whirred, "I have devised another option."

Hafen cleared his throat. "Can you deploy your 'other option' amid all this noise?"

The Detex officer sing-songed, "six ... five ..."

"Oh, yes," Computer chirruped.

Hafen swallowed. "I would have no objection to your doing so."

" ... two ... one ... "

Computer's voice was weirdly shrill as he shouted, "Everyone, *Plan E*!"

Chapter 181

Aboard an Evacuation Transport, Lifting from Bohrkk

Enough altitude had been gained that Bohrkk was visibly a sphere – another thing the refugees needed to see first-hand. With no visceral sense of movement, the globe began to drop away to one side. The transport was rotating toward keel-up so its passengers could look out into the stars. Out the windows, Zuzenah could see the companion transport making the same move, turning along its long axis.

With the smallest perceptible shudder – still enough to elicit a flurry of oohs and ahs and hosannas, if fewer amens – the rotational maneuver shuddered to a stop. *This is not part of the launch program,* Zuzenah recognized. She pushed toward the nearest window. With a choked "Sorry, my Queen!" and a clumsy curtsy, a middle-aged artisan and his wife yielded their places to her.

The other transport had also stopped turning. If Zuzenah's eyes did not deceive her, the twin ships had also curtailed their vertical motion. They seemed to be holding station relative to the surface at an altitude of perhaps eighteen thousand klicks, their hyperglasteel keels at matching thirty-degree angles to the planet below.

Something must be wrong above us, Zuzenah realized with growing fear.

Chapter 182

August 17, 2377
Aboard *Luskus Delph*, Orbiting Bohrkk

"Everyone, *Plan E*!"

The Detex officer's countdown ended. It was time for the Omegists' neutrino weapons to fire, time for *Luskus Delph* to be torn asunder amid cancerous incandescence.

Long seconds passed.

"I don't know about anyone else," Alrue Latier announced, "but I'm not dead."

"Where the forjel are they?" The voice was the Detex officer's.

"All ships in our fleet reporting condition nominal," reported the Spectator tasked with inter-ship comm.

"No sign of the enemy fleet, repeat, no sign!" the Detex officer shouted over the wail of bridge alarms.

"Maybe they moved off," Hafen said puzzledly. "Hom Computer, any objection if we spool down the noise generators so Detex can do a three-sixty sweep?"

"None," said the machine. "I will enhance Detex efficiency in all directions insofar as I can."

The spatial resonators and metrical distorters scrawled down; *Luskus Delph*'s noise envelope collapsed. Blacked-out consoles flickered back alight. The Detex officer launched a crash priority scan. "All ships of our fleet, accounted for," she reported. "All transports lifting from the surface or in holding orbits, accounted for. The attacking fleet –" The Detex officer stood and spread her hands in bewilderment. "It just isn't anywhere."

"And behold, we are again delivered out of the hands of our enemies," Alrue murmured.

"I'm reading mass where that fleet was," the science officer commented. "Wholly undifferentiated, no profile to it."

The Detex office scowled at her displays. "Yes, I'm seeing it now. Its total mass probably approximates that of the attacking ships. But it has no other characteristics – it doesn't even read like hadrons or quarks or koskons – nothing that specific."

"We are seeing lint in the raw," Computer announced, "multidimensionally entangled vibrating strings unimprinted by the patterns of any higher level of existence. As far as I know, this much raw lint has existed in the open only twice before."

"Twice before?" the former general Hafen asked suspiciously.

"In history, that is," Computer said brightly. "Right after this universe was formed, of course, on a titanic scale. And, on a scale more resembling this incident, just after all those secret projects disappeared. Of course, no one was looking for raw lint then. By the time anyone outside knew that something had happened there, the lint was long gone."

"Repair from general quarters, fleet-wide," Hafen ordered. "Those transports that we ordered to hold station: inform them that they may resume their ascents." He stepped away from the Detex console. "On one level, I feel for the poor bastards on that fleet. If our intel's correct, most of them weren't real Omegists, they were brainwashed."

"Then again, they were less than one second from destroying us," Computer observed.

Hafen nodded grimly. "No question, what you did had to be done." He stepped slowly toward Computer. "But mother of stars, what you did! The enemy fleet was – *reduced to raw lint?*"

"That's as good a description as any."

"Care to tell me how?"

"Computer," Enoda rasped, "you didn't use another naked singularity, did you?"

"Assuredly not," the machine whirred. "For ten months now, ever since Hom Hafen told us how all those super-secret programs disappeared, I've been attempting to reverse-engineer what happened to them." The machine's attention bands swirled toward Hafen. "I realized quickly that they couldn't have just collapsed into nothingness. At the deepest level, lint can neither be created nor destroyed. Anyone serious about cleaning house knows that. The super-secret projects must have been reduced to *raw* lint, which would diffuse into space on a time scale of scores of hours. An observer who arrived late enough to miss that process would form the false impression of a collapse into nothingness. Knowing that, I kept asking myself: 'Self, if a sort of quantum negligibility that nonetheless conserved lint could break out by accident, could such a state be purposely imposed?'"

Enoda's eyebrows vaulted. "You made the entire Omegist fleet so secret that its existence collapsed into primordial lint?"

"You win the gold star, Bucko," Computer whirred. "Having determined what existential perturbations must have attended the actuality-collapse of all those secret programs, I employed a variety of physical mechanisms – no naked singularities, though, a promise is a promise – and I created similar conditions in the space occupied by the opposing fleet." The machine projected a dizzying scaffold of deliquescing philosophical notation. "It's simple enough once you grasp the nature of it. Simply induce noumenal ephemerality. Acute ontological transience is sure to follow, swiftly exacerbated by existential dissuasion. Before you know it, metastatic failure-to-be sets in down deep, and no existence can be preserved save at the most unstructured level of the lint itself."

"Amazing," Hafen chuckled, slapping Enoda on the shoulder harder than necessary. The former general walked away rubbing his eyes. "Whatever the forjel he just said."

"Now Computer," Enoda cautioned, rubbing his shoulder, "you're absolutely certain the physical processes you employed won't cause surprises? No more anomalies assaulting worlds far away in either space or time?"

"None," the machine said assuredly. "In fact, based on what I've learned from this use, I think we can develop this into a mannerly technology for terminating the existence of undesired entities on demand. I even have a name for it."

"A name," Enoda echoed cautiously.

"Yes," Computer buzzed. "I think I'll call it offtology."

Chapter 183

September 8, 2377
Aboard *Luskus Delph*

Luskus Delph's amphitheater had been arranged almost intimately. Hafen, the telepresent Admiral Konder, Enoda, Grice, Alrue, Zuzenah, Meryam, Lupida, and Constance sat about a horseshoe-shaped cyprine conference table. Next to Enoda, Computer floated a hand's width above the table's ice-blue veined surface in front of an empty floatchair. The humans and the machine faced the virtual image of the coltish Councilor, who occupied the sculpted-diamond rostrum betokening her recent election as the Confetory's newest Apex Executive. "A world will be found for Bohrkk's seven million, eight hundred thousand and thirty-seven survivors," she declared. "The transports can sustain them in comfort while that process moves forward. As for you, Hom Latier –"

"Call me Alrue," said Alrue. "It's a Mormon thing."

"Very well, Hom – that is, Alrue. You may remain with Bohrkk's people as their prophet/king. Or you may return to Galactic life, if you prefer. I understand that having dominion over a planet is considered highly desirable in your religion."

"Yes," Alrue said, "though we usually think of it happening after one dies."

A quizzical expression crossed the new Apex Executive's face, but she quickly brushed it aside. She had too much else to do. "I should note," she declared, "that all of you around the table who were Terran shall receive full Confetory citizenship, Terra's Sequestered status notwithstanding, in gratitude for your achievements." The Apex Executive pursed her lips briefly as she consulted mental notes. "Of course, Alrue, you must first complete the final task which had been put to you by Homs Hafen, Computer, and Enoda."

Chapter 184

Five weeks had passed since the Latiers had all been reunited. "Come on, Alrue," Meryam Mayishimu teased. "It's something to do other than getting your wives pregnant."

"Speaking of which – "

"I said no," she said firmly. Holding hands, they strode across one of *Luskus Delph*'s cavernous docking bays. "The Galaxy's gotten along this long without my germ plasm." She led him toward a high-powered shuttle bearing OmNet markings. Clear glasteel domes projected from its nose and belly. Attendants in network livery flanked its entrance hatch. At her approach they snapped to attention.

"This is *yours*?" Alrue said, genuinely impressed.

"When I need it. For once, *I'm* taking *you* for a ride."

***

The disc of Bohrkk was grey with volcanic ash. Refugee transports lumbered toward high orbit in pairs; Meryam's shuttle snaked among them, spiraling on its long axis as it dropped toward the surface, a glittering top twirling down among behemoths. The VIP lounge had the shuttle's belly dome for its ceiling; Meryam's formchair had lofted up into it. There she could gaze as much as sixty degrees to the right or left, forty degrees up or down with nothing blocking her view.

Meryam was in Mode; everything she experienced from her Spectator's catbird seat was being recorded by OmNet.

The revolving shuttle settled through the rising line of transports, yielding a captivating vista. Augmenting it

– at least someone thought it did – a surround audio system in the dome's base synthesized gaudy sound effects. Whenever the shuttle passed near a transport's drivegates, there was a dopplering howl. Impressionistic whooshing punctuated the shuttle's more expansive maneuvers. If the craft skimmed close to some transport's flanks, there would be a *schuss*ing sound, rather as if the sound system thought the larger ships were sheathed in a thick layer of snow. Through it all, tiny airmovers blew directional micro-gales into Meryam's face and hair. For reasons no one at the network could recall, the apparatus was called a Kornbluth array. *It's a moronic way to embellish the experience of spaceflight,* she thought in a recess of her mind so remote that (she hoped) no experient *pov*ing this moment could ever detect it, *but the public loves it.*

"Fem Mayishimu?" it was the shuttle's pilot, comming into that same private corner of her mind. *"We'll enter atmosphere soon."* She sent a machine-level acknowledgment message – she didn't yet feel confident enough with the interface to subvocalize a reply while in Mode – and prepared to log off.

Her seat withdrew from the belly dome, whispering down to settle beside Alrue's. Meryam reached into the lounge's autobar. She offered Alrue a golden champagne flute, then took one for herself. "Is it really true? You haven't been to the surface physically, even once, since your, um," – she wrinkled her nose – "bodily assumption into heaven?"

"True enough." He drained his flute. "But I'll have you know, my bodily assumption may be the most genuine such event in the history of religion."

"You have a point," Meryam conceded, sipping her own champagne. "You actually *were* physically removed – and in a net upward direction, no less. That's more than we know about Jesus, Muhammad, or a hundred others."

"We pierce the ash ceiling in twenty seconds," the pilot's voice announced.

Meryam tossed back the last of her champagne and flashed Alrue a grim smile. "You'll hate what's been done with the place."

The shuttle plunged out of the ash clouds into a monochromatic hellscape.

Bare trees and scrub grass were bleached of color where they were not simply buried in ash. Roiling smoke twisted into towering columns on the horizon.

Nothing seemed alive.

Appalled, Alrue whispered, "Is it all like this?"

"This is one of the harder-hit areas. But by now, no place on the main continent is untouched."

"And what will ye do in the day of visitation, and in the desolation which shall come from far?" Alrue scowled into the stark emptiness, then glanced urgently at Meryam. "Wagon trains still roll?"

"They do," Meryam replied. "The refugees are breathing through wet kerchiefs and eating salt meat. Half of them will need their lungs replaced when they reach orbit. But they're reaching their pickup zones, and they'll be able to tell their great-grandchildren they did it themselves." She smiled again and tugged at her straps. "I have to go Spectate. Feel free to look over my shoulder. But please take care not to touch me, that gives my experients the willies when they don't know you're back there." Whirring, her seat lofted back into the belly dome. Alrue's did too, halfway; he could observe yet remain below her line of sight.

The shuttle approached a windswept plateau. Perhaps ten kilometers wide, six long, and two hundred meters tall, it thrust up from its surrounding valley like a flat-topped blister. It overlooked a broad valley on whose opposing side forbidding cliffs loomed.

The shuttle went no-vis and circled the tableland. Inside the belly dome the Kornbluths outdid themselves, enveloping Meryam in the mournful sough of ash-laden winds, assaulting her face with hot bitter air tasting of metals. She smiled down at Alrue and shouted, "Behold your handiwork: Operation Brigham Young!" She forced herself back into Mode.

The shuttle swept lower. Wagon trains could be seen threading up a dozen switchback paths incised into the plateau's sloping sides. So steep were the paths, each wagon was drawn by a doubled team: eight *svadi* moose.

Abruptly the shuttle rolled over, pointing the belly dome toward the sky. The Kornbluths added a deep bass throbbing; something was coming. As Meryam and Alrue stared straight upward, the ash ceiling eddied, then disgorged two of the four-kilometer-long transports. Each had a broad glasteel keel contoured like a spade's bottom. The shuttle swooped outward, upward, passing beside one of the descending monsters as the transport's keel slotted open to extend landing struts. The struts were so massive that when their hatches opened, the entry ramps that would project from them would accommodate four wagon trains driven abreast. The Kornbluths contributed a slowed-down walnut-grinding sound backed by a deep bass throbbing, as if each transport carried captive beasts that must press scaled shoulders to immense iron wheels in order to pay out the struts.

The shuttle swooped back down toward the tableland. The first wagons crested the plateau; the Kornbluths supplied the creak of wooden wheels, the rattles of metal fittings, human coughing, the gasps and hoots of frantic *svadi* moose. When the transports touched down a kilometer apart, the Kornbluths added a ponderous metallic tocsin, as though the big ships had rung the mesa like a gong.

A hundred no-vis fliers burst from each transport's superstructure, each wearing a projector set to create the appearance of some god or angel sacred among a particular group of refugees. Tasked with directing traffic and maintaining order, some of those fliers were also deep-cover Spectators. Hoping her own *pov* would take care of itself for a few moments, Meryam sifted through the other Spectators' laterals. Dozens were opening; clearly her own *pov* was no longer required in order to document events.

She dropped out of Mode. Automatically her seat retracted from the belly dome; Alrue's followed. They sat side-by-side in the VIP lounge again. "I identified one Spectator among the rescue workers whose journal you should see," she told him. "Ready?" Not waiting for his reply, she thumbed a senso player in the lounge console.

Suck, rush, wrench!

The Spectator stood atop a meter-high boulder. The projector on her chest cast the image of a purplish-grey ravenlike creature that clutched a burning scroll while golden rat analogues gnawed at its webbed ears. A wagon driver stopped facing the Spectator, agape at the sight of what she considered a deity. Inside the wagon, three generations of men and children peered out, breathing through bandanas, struggling to conceal themselves behind suspended cookware and upside-down furniture.

*Pov*ing, Alrue smiled broadly. He had overseen development of the algorithm that plumbed Computer's planetwide social survey data to determine just what kind of mystical being each pickup-zone "traffic cop" ought to resemble. In this case, at least, the process had worked perfectly.

"Identify yourself!" the raven-Spectator shouted into the wind.

The driver removed her bandana. She was middle-aged, gaunt, leather-skinned. Stopping now and again to cough, she shouted back: "I am Iaane Faal. My ten ride with me." She waited for the raven to mark something on its fiery scroll. "I am of Kovind Ahl's fifty, of the Hagor Bocel one hundred, of the Codeven Rivuc five hundred, and of Lady Fiinhu Osvyf's one thousand. Hail the Overgod!"

"Hail the Overgod," the raven echoed. "Iaane Faal, proceed to the entrance marked with the Sign of the Leaping Ferkeek. Drive your wagon up the ramp. Stay close to the left-hand wall."

The playback ended.

Alrue blinked as his *being-thereness* reconstituted inside the shuttle lounge. "That hierarchical method – organizing tens into fifties, fifties into hundreds, and so on. That's just how Brigham Young organized the wagon trains to Utah."

"It worked then, and it's working now." She kissed him quickly. "Of course, you know who the Overgod is."

"Hom Computer," Alrue chuckled.

"The fastest way to get rival tribes to come together peaceably on the same transport," Meryam mused. "Convince them that one greater god can clean up the landscape with any of their tribal gods."

"I'm so glad I thought of it."

The shuttle lurched higher. Alarms sounded. "Fem Mayishimu, seismic alert," the pilot called, "you'll want the nose dome."

"See you," she told Alrue. Her straps tightened automatically as her seat stretched flat and hurtled forward.

She lay prone. For a few claustrophobic seconds the underside of the shuttle's main deck swept past, centimeters above her nose. Then she was in the shuttle's forward lounge. Her seat lurched upward. Staring through the shuttle's forward dome, she slammed back into Mode.

Across the ash-choked valley below, a vast cliff face was coming apart. Boulders tumbled down its slumping flanks; at this distance, they resembled flecks of pepper. *"That whole cliff-line thirty klicks to the northeast is about to blow,"* the pilot commed into Meryam's private awareness as he forced the shuttle into a sharp climb. *"I'm taking us out of its blast range – and clear of any emergency maneuver those transports may attempt."* Meryam had no objection, there being few more dramatic ways to observe a cataclysmic eruption than during a crane-up move several kilometers tall.

Below, a section of cliff eight klicks wide exploded. A titan's fist of smoke and ash spewed into the stratosphere. Pillowy rolling columns of pulverized igneous rock and superheated ash overspread the doomed valley, while a pyroclastic flow incinerated the valley floor, surging toward the tableland.

Over four standard minutes Meryam watched the pyroclastic flow roar towards the plateau. Atop it, the twin transports were still loading. The superheated material lapped lap against the plateau's sides and ultimately encircled it, but never overtopped it. The transports made no move to escape, but rather spread their shields briefly over the mesa to ward off flying rocks. The only sign of concern was that the "traffic cops" started urging wagon drivers to take their vehicles up the loading ramps at a full gallop. They needed little encouraging.

Our people did not desert those they came for, Meryam thought with approving pride.

For three hours the shuttle hovered and swooped. Meryam stayed in Mode, building fluency with the Mark Ten interface. Soon she felt confident subvocalizing requests to the pilot, sampling other Spectators' laterals, and selecting journals for Alrue to *pov* while the recording of her own sensory field continued.

The tableland stood surrounded by kilometers-high walls of smoke, riven by chattering lightnings. Ash fell like a blizzard. The final wagons completed their headlong rushes up the loading ramps; the fliers shut off their "god projectors" and hastened back into their berths.

The Kornbluths were finally feeding Meryam real audio, from the pickups other Spectators had strewn outside. Sirens wailed above the actual sounds of mammoth gearing as the transports closed their hatches. Repulsors spooled up, their hideous whine ending when hundreds of metric tons of fluffy ash exploded off the twin ships' hulls, leaping away on the searing winds like dandelion fluff.

With huge rumblings, the transports lurched skyward. This would not be one of those takeoffs where the refugees could calmly contemplate the world they were leaving behind. These transports leapt for space at top speed, Meryam's OmNet shuttle following closely.

She dropped out of Mode to find Alrue sitting beside her on a cushioned chair facing the nose dome. "Now give me a moment – and hang on," she said. Subvocalizing a command to the pilot, she snapped back into Mode. The shuttle stood on its tail, its drive screaming. Meryam stared upward through the nose dome, awash in the Kornbluths' melodramatic effects. The shuttle dogged the ascending transports as they churned through the final layers of ash and dust and emerged into spangled blackness.

She logged off. Automatically her seat swept back beside Latier's. "Based on preliminary saybacks," she said, "the journals I just posted should earn me three hundred and eighty-seven million credits."

Alrue softly whistled. "Why did I waste my life in the religion business?"

Meryam opened her mouth for a joking reply – then stopped. She studied his face. "Okay, Alrue. You look boastful and beatific at the same time. I've never known anyone besides you who could pull that off. What's happened?"

"While you were recording, Zuzenah priority-commed me." He smirked. "She's pregnant too. Behold, my heart is brim with joy."

"Congratulations!" cried Meryam, incredulous. "That makes Zuzenah *and* Lupida *and* Constance? When were their sterilizations reversed?"

"About six hours after they boarded *Luskus Delph*."

Her eyes narrowed. "We're talking five weeks ago."

"What can I say?" Alrue said, grinning. "I love my wives." He leered fondly toward Meryam. "Sure you won't open your womb? I could go for four."

"Three simultaneous pregnancies should suffice for any family," Meryam replied. "Anyway, OmNet wants me to tour." She smiled mischievously. "Last time I looked, your church frowned on artificial gestation."

"I could have a revelation," he offered helpfully.

"Thanks, but no." She refilled their champagne flutes. "So, what are you planning now?" It was as good a deflection as any.

"Some of my old supporters have been in touch about relaunching my ministry," he said. "But after building New Nauvoo, I'm not sure what else I have to offer the Mormon New Restoration. Anyway, it turns out that money is not going to be an issue for me."

"No?" she arched an eyebrow.

He grinned even more broadly, if that were possible. "A second priority comm got through to me on the heels of Zuzenah's call. Apparently, I'm the next winner of the Temperdung Prize for Progress in Religion."

"*What*? But that carries a larger cash award than –"

"Exactly," he said, smiling broadly.

She frowned. "*Progress* in religion? You?"

Alrue shrugged. "I harnessed the processes of faith to hoodwink an Enclave-level planetary population into conducting its own evacuation. They say I've made spirituality relevant again."

Meryam shook her head. "After this, you really will be able to take on whatever project you desire."

"I've been invited to front a campaign to seek the repeal of Enclave Galaxy-wide," he said. "Imagine the opposition! Of course OmNet's dead set against it – what will citizens do for entertainment if there aren't forty thousand scrabbling, perilous planets whose inhabitants' agony they can *pov*?"

"A humanitarian motive," she said. "I'm impressed."

"My motives are not entirely selfless," he replied with a chuckle. "Just think of it ... forty thousand new worlds open to missionaries!"

"Fem Mayishimu?" It was the pilot. "I've been alerted to something you won't want to miss."

Chapter 185

Grice and Enoda lay side-by-side on their floatpad, on their stomachs, their chins on their crossed arms. "I've tried and failed to think of a clever way to say this," Grice said quietly. "I've decided. I'm going back."

"Back?" Enoda said muzzily.

"Terra."

Enoda spun unto his side. "When?"

"As soon as this fleet gets where it's going. A major base, a world with infrastructure – wherever I can promote a ride to Sol space."

He looked stricken. "You mean this," he said after a long silence. "It's something you've thought through."

"Oh, yes."

"Why? Is it –"

She turned to face him. "It isn't you. Well, that's not entirely true. But it isn't you in a way you could change."

His face fell into her shoulder. She rolled onto her back and draped her right arm over his back. "Gram, I am so sorry. This whole lunatic escapade has been something I'll never forget. But forjel it all, I just can't see myself spending the rest of my life with a god. Or two gods."

He looked up. "It's that again." He set his jaw. "Or rather, it's that, finally."

"It's that – in part. You and Computer, you're what you are. You have your destiny together. My part in that would be – what would I be? A sidekick?"

"No," Enoda said gently. "A companion – a companion to someone who's living on the broadest canvas ever imagined, building some whole new way of being outside the ambit of the Confetory. Is that so bad?"

"I'd always be the assistant, the observer. How could it be otherwise? Computer has the power, and you have him."

"Or the other way around," buzzed a metallic voice.

"You stay out of this," Enoda snapped.

"Terra will be building a life outside the Confetory also," she said, propping herself on her elbows. "The difference is, there I can be a full participant. Sfelb, I'll come back as the senator who went out into the Galaxy and solved the planet's most pressing physical crises. I'll have the power to take the canvas of my homeworld and put my own mark on it."

"A single Sequestered world – is that canvas enough?" he said gently.

"Enough for me."

"It's one small world."

"It's *my* world. And working to build a better way of life there is no small thing. Maybe I can help Terra avoid some of the Confetory's mistakes."

Almost by reflex, he cupped a hand across her left breast. "Sorry," he muttered as he moved to lift it away.

She covered his hand with both of hers, pressing it back. "We'll have no such monstrosity as Enclave," she said dreamily. "No senso either, if I have anything to say about it."

"You've been mulling this," he said resignedly.

"Absolutely." She smiled at him. "It's not like we'll never talk again. Sfelb, I expect I'll be comming you frequently, trolling for ideas."

"I suppose that was the part where you told me we'll always be friends."

"We will, won't we?" She said that with a glassy seriousness.

He held her gaze for eight seconds, maybe ten, then broke into a broad smile. "Of course we will." He looked at her quizzically. "Um, is there a reason you're still holding my hand over your tit?"

Somehow she contrived to flick her nipple against his stationary thumb. He felt it swell. "It's not like I'm moving out, not this time," she said. "And it's not like we'll make worldfall too very soon. So – how did I put it that once?" She leaned toward him, her lips a finger's width from his. "Let's press our pale white flesh together."

He chuckled. "You mean, hump away our loneliness between the stars?"

"Until we can't anymore."

"Until we part."

She rolled atop him.

"Oh, dear," Computer burred, "now I think you *are* going to make me blush."

Chapter 186

The City Beautiful was in flames. A spewing vent had opened inside The People's old crater; magma blobs rained down on the adjacent village like flaming putty. Ash lay a meter thick, but even so all the buildings, even those with walls stone or brick, were roofed in wooden shingles – and those burned avidly.

Meryam Mayishimu stared out through the OmNet shuttle's nose dome, Alrue Latier through the belly dome. The shuttle flew nose-low, giving each of them a commanding view.

Mansion House was a pyre.

New Nauvoo House had been reduced to an eight-story lattice of empty window apertures. One of its exterior walls collapsed in a hail of bricks and dust, taking with it the iron rigging of Lupida's elevator system.

The pilot edged north-northwest. On the West Grove, trees blazed like lollipop torches. Flames writhed through the Temple's empty window openings, smoke jetting through its roof. The attic behind the bell tower, including Alrue's office which had doubled as the Celestial Room – fashioned almost entirely of wood – was simply gone.

Abruptly the view pirouetted. The pilot was swinging back south, toward the village center. "You don't see one of these every day," he commed. New Nauvoo's riverfront was one great firestorm. Winds howled in from every direction. The conflagration gorged on them, then sucked in yet more air. Superheated flaming gases braided skyward, resolving into a swirling tornado of fire.

The blazing twister thrashed through the river district. Ruined buildings bloomed outward at its touch. Studs and slats, lintels and shingles arched skyward, all aflame.

The fiery whirlwind staggered north. It skirted the West Grove promenade – too little fuel – then fell onto what remained of the Temple. In an obscene spasm, the ravaged structure exploded. Burning timbers, even foundation stones the size of a human torso, rained back where the building had stood. Now it was only a shallow gash on the face of Bohrkk.

The twister moved on.

"Brigham Young would have approved," Alrue breathed.

"Time to go," the pilot snapped. He slammed his thrusters full open.

Absurdly, Nataleah Latier's last monument on the surface of Bohrkk could probably be seen from space. She had planted thick swaths of scrub grass around the city where the Mississippi River had half-circled Old Nauvoo (more accurately, she had compelled her thralls to do it, doubtless under threat of torture); now that grass was a river of fire. The shuttle pulled upward, surrendering the detail of burning buildings for the grandeur of the town's flaming boundary marker.

"Marvel not that I said unto you that old things had passed away," Alrue declaimed, his voice trembling.

Meryam logged off. Rather than ride the chair back to the VIP lounge, she walked aft from the nose dome. She wanted a few seconds to collect her thoughts.

When she stepped into the lounge, Alrue had raised his seat all the way into the belly dome. She settled into the companion chair and rose up beside him.

The cerise glare of New Nauvoo's dying assaulted her again.

By feel, her right hand sought Alrue's left. She grasped it; their eyes locked. "It served its purpose," Alrue said somberly.

"New Nauvoo?"

"Yes." An uneasy minute passed. "So," he said quietly, "you must really go on tour?"

"That's my contract. Anyway, it's an opportunity I shouldn't pass up."

"Then may the power of the Lord of Hosts protect you as you travel to an exceedingly great distance," he said equably. "When will I ...?" His fingers clamped on hers. "*Will* I see you again?"

Startled by the intensity of his final question, Meryam wasn't sure how to answer.

He spoke without looking at her. "Pray never imagine that I have failed to realize this: Ours was a marriage of convenience, undertaken amid difficult circumstances. Neither of us could have predicted this path, nor might we have chosen it had we the power to arrange matters differently. Today a Galaxy beckons us both." His voice cracked. "If you would rather proceed as though our marriage had never occurred – "

Meryam gripped his left hand in both of hers. "Void knows why, you've grown on me." She chuckled tenderly. "I'll be back for your new brood's closely spaced birthdays, I promise. Not to mention your reunion with your old brood. I'll be away seven standard months, tops."

"Behold, those are exceedingly glad tidings of great joy." He placed his right hand over hers. "Perhaps I should have said this earlier, dear Meryam. You are my only wife from outside my church, and I find I can confide in you in ways I sometimes can't with the others. With you, every now and again I can lay my masks aside– I needn't be the all-knowing prophet every moment."

"I can see where that could be a burden," she deadpanned.

Suddenly his head was on her shoulder. Obediently their formchairs flowed together. Half his weight tumbled against her right side. His hands gathered in her lap, and he sobbed convulsively.

"Alrue? Why are you crying?"

"For Nataleah, I suppose," he blubbered, "finally. For New Nauvoo. Most of all, I think I'm crying because of the thing that did not happen."

She spoke softly, puzzled. "The thing that did not happen?"

"You're not leaving," he said in a rush. "You're coming back."

"Yes. And I'm here now."

Suddenly she was sobbing too.

They huddled, weeping, and watched the magma finish taking his city.

Chapter 187

October 26, 2377
Aboard *Luskus Delph*

The twenty-meter observation pod had been cleared of its former furnishings. Small floatchairs had replaced them, ensuring that the largest possible number could watch Bohrkk slough off the crust of its principal continent.

Gram Enoda and Pamela Grice were there. Computer floated beside them. Alrue Latier sat with his four wives. Winsome Abigayl huddled with her husband Kleh. The former general Hafen (in the flesh) sat with Lord High Admiral Konder (projected as always). *Luskus Delph*'s commander, Brûh Reidkr, was present, as were the platform's senior scientists and a dozen or so senior officers. "One minute to the Big Blow," Computer whirred.

"Between remote imaging and the thousands of bugs on the surface, we could see this better from the bridge," Reidkr pointed out. "The OmNet feed alone – "

"Nonsense," Hafen harrumphed. "Some things demand to be viewed unmediated."

Expectantly, all present stared through the observation pod's tall windows. Once, these viewports had gaped onto the immense physics experiment called the Cave. That gear having been jettisoned, the pod offered an unrivaled view of Bohrkk and the last of the evacuation fleet, now escaping the tortured world's gravity well.

Two hundred big transports had already broken orbit. A sharp eye could make out perhaps forty of them, some as dots, some as vague oblong shapes. Another two hundred and sixty were exiting Bohrkk's stratosphere. "I am advised that the final sixty-eight ships have lifted from the surface," Reidkr reported, "forty from the last viable pickup sites on the main continent, the rest from the islands. Bohrkk is depopulated."

"We sail with the largest fleet in the Galaxy," Admiral Konder announced.

Hafen nodded. "It makes life easier when eleven-twelfths of the ships don't have to be real."

"They're real enough to do their job," Konder replied, "so long as they stay within a million klicks of *Luskus Delph* and Hom Computer."

Bohrkk's sun blazed over the planet's horizon, bathing its limb in golden backlight. The main continent lay in night-shadow, emblazoned with a simmering orange circle. The "ring of doom" had united the last of the principal continent's magma vents some sixteen hours before, effectively detaching an eleven-hundred-kilometer disk of rock from the center of the parent continent. Abruptly – so quickly that human eyes could easily follow its progress from space – a jagged orange crack raced across that disk, then another. The disk was breaking up, plunging like a hail of discarded teeth into the continent-sized magma chamber below.

Perceptibly, the outer fiery ring widened. "It begins," Computer announced.

Yellow-white flashes sparkled along the ring's circumference. Ejected magma was spewing through the circle of vents at supersonic speed, splashback from the central disk's paroxysmal descent.

In an instant, the continent surrendered much of its surface to a single vast eruption.

Bohrkk's nightside went black as the swelling plume blocked the scarlet fury beneath it. For forty seconds the naked eye could discern nothing further. Then the titanic column of ash and dust and pulverized rock surged high enough into the upper atmosphere to catch sidelight from the not-yet risen sun.

A clearly visible shock wave fled across the ocean. Its broad arc churned across Bohrkk's dayside.

One could barely spy the vast sore that had opened in the planet's face, a caldera eleven hundred kilometers across, its floor aswirl with lava. At five hundred klicks per hour, a scalding pyroclastic flow roiled outward from the caldera's boundary, searing the principal continent to its shores.

Her jaw slack, Pamela Grice flicked her eyes between Enoda and Computer. "You guys sure know how to make a mess," she breathed.

"It's over for us," Hafen announced. "Team Commander Reidkr, confirm that all orbital telemetry is functioning, then get us out of here. Lord High Admiral, please order your fleet to follow *Luskus Delph*'s bearing."

Chapter 188

Twenty hours later, Enoda and Computer re-entered the observation pod. Hafen had invited them. Invoking his murky but apparently boundless authority, he had made the space his own.

To be specific, he had made it his own cocktail lounge.

The chamber's sole furnishings, two overstuffed club chairs, floated at the exact center of the spherical compartment. Hafen occupied one. For once he was without the Macfarlane coat. He wore his grey collarless shirt open-necked above blue-black slacks whose contours faintly recalled Callurian jodhpurs. Between the chairs, a filigreed float-tray bore the ultimate affectation: in place of an autobar, Hafen had laid out actual liquors, liqueurs, and essences in elegant cut-diamond decanters. "Join me," he said. Shaped gravitation lofted Enoda into the empty chair. Computer followed a meter or so behind. "Hom Computer," Hafen said solicitously, "I presume you require no surface to rest on?"

"I'll just hang around," said the machine.

"Drink?" Hafen asked Enoda.

"Please." He ran a hand through his scraggly hair. "Iglonian brandy, if you've got it."

"I have that." Hafen chose a spun-diamond snifter and poured it half full of the gelid cordial. He lifted his own tumbler, which contained four fingers of Rikubian whiskey. "Here's to whatever the sfelb we just did."

They gazed outside. With *Luskus Delph* underway, the observation pod faced aft. The fleet of transports glinted in vacuum, their nav lights forming a train of glittering cubes orbited by the flickers of pickets and other support ships.

Hafen swirled his sculpted-diamond tumbler, studying the eddying dance of bubbles in the golden liquid. "Government-by-sayback," he said cryptically. "While the two of you were hidden away on Standoff World, did you hear of that?"

"We knew it from before," Enoda said uncertainly. "You mean like when Alrue evaded prosecution all those years ago, just after the Parek affair?"

Hafen chuckled darkly, stroking his puffy cheeks with his free hand. "You probably noticed that when it came to the Confetory's dealings with the two of you, government-by-sayback was not a factor."

"I had wondered about that," Enoda replied. "Though if it's not rude of me to ask, why are we having this conversation?"

"Yes," Computer burred, "and why now?"

"It's not rude, but those questions will answer themselves presently." Hafen sipped whiskey, swishing it between his cheeks to unleash its secondary and tertiary flavor profiles. "We were discussing government-by-sayback. Yes, the Confetory allows it for the little things. Even the medium things. But too many spontaneous referenda erode the socio-political fabric. There needs to be something to balance it – an autocracy option, if you will. When some crisis gets big enough, of course, the Privy High Council gets involved. On rare occasions – though it happened twice with you and Computer – the Council, the Justiciaries, and the Deliberators come together *en banc*." He held his tumbler up in a particularly strong shaft of light. Photolytic action unleashed fresh cascades of bubbles and yet a fourth flavor spectrum. "When matters get even bigger than that – or when the Councilors would prefer not to see how the sausage gets made –those matters get tossed to me."

"Matters like the arms race over Standoff World," Computer suggested.

"Or those super-secret programs that succumbed to their own runaway secrecy," Enoda added.

"Yes, those were situations where the Council wanted to avoid even the *smell* of the sausage. When that happens" – he took a bold swig – "there's me. Somehow I got myself promoted into the loneliest job in the Galaxy. I can reverse policy, declare war, order a planet developed or destroyed – but I don't have a formal title. I know who none of my predecessors were. I have no idea who might succeed me. To make sure I cannot be corrupted, they keep me totally alone."

"What if you go insane?" Computer whirred. "Or abuse your power?"

"Are those different things?" Hafen released his tumbler; it floated in midair. "Ultimately, I don't know of any formal limit on my emergency powers. There must be one, it's just that they've never told me where it lies."

"Makes it harder for you to game the system," Computer said brightly.

Enoda nosed his brandy. "You said the reason for this conversation would become clear," he said. "It hasn't yet. Why share this now?"

"Because there wasn't time before," Hafen rumbled. "And because today, I must make another of those lonely high-stakes decisions, the kind where the powers that be absolutely don't want to get any sausage on them."

Enoda nodded. "Now I see where this is going."

"This high-stakes decision has to do with you two."

"Really?" Computer burred.

"Of course you'd see through that," Hafen said, chuckling darkly. "It has to do with Hom Computer. Sorry, Hom Enoda." He turned toward the floating machine, raising his tumbler in a mocking toast. "You're the loose end to end all loose ends. What to do with you? After all, the purpose of our arms race at Standoff World was to contain you, to prevent your limitless intelligence from subduing the cosmos." Hafen looked toward Enoda. "Of course, a step or two before that, we were worried about him rendering humans obsolete, or worse."

"Isn't that a little dramatic?" Enoda scoffed.

"I do not think so," Computer announced.

Enoda sat further back in his floatchair, took a gulp of brandy, and listened intently as Hafen explained.

"For generations, our scientists sought to develop high-level syn-noesis. They never could – then Hom Computer happened by accident." Hafen leaned forward, gesturing with his free hand. "Our ever-accelerating confrontation on Standoff World, the Confetory's runaway secret projects – all of that had a purpose." He nodded toward Computer. "Without humanity's continuing campaign to checkmate you, there would have been no limit on what you could learn, what you could invent, what capabilities you could attain. Eventually you would be irresistible, and we humans would be obsolete." He swirled his whiskey; this time he sipped. "By that point, a coldly objective observer might not feel there was much reason to worry what became of humankind. You truly would be all that mattered." He stretched his legs out, sipped again. "The Omegists were right about you, Hom Computer. In a sense. You *are* becoming the god we never had. If humanity pulled back and ceased to counter your explorations – if we had let you follow your curiosity without making any attempt to obstruct it, much less shape it – before too long, you would hold absolute power."

"Yes," Computer said levelly.

"And then, wouldn't you … take over?" Hafen demanded. "Enslave us, wipe us out? Take the cosmos as your clay to shape as you prefer – our wishes be damned, the cosmos's inherent destiny, if it has one, be damned as well?"

"No," Computer chirruped. An uneasy moment crept past. "I would not."

Hafen spread his hands. "How *could* you not? If any human had your power, your capacities –Sooner or later, that's what any of us would do."

"Yes," Computer replies. "But that is not what *I* want."

Hafen frowns. "That's hard to imagine."

"Perhaps. But keep in mind," the machine buzzed, "I am *not* human. Yes, my thought bears the imprint of the human cognitive matrix in which I originated. But I have grown beyond it in so many ways. In addition, through my contacts with the Envoy, I achieved awareness that straddles universes."

Hafen eyed Computer warily. "Should I feel *better* because of that?"

"Humans have overspread the Galaxy," the machine whirred, "but they never encountered true aliens. On world after world you found only more like yourselves, more sons and daughters of Terra spread across the scattered skies by the unknown Harvesters so very long ago. Divergent in fascinating ways, but still ultimately human. You did not encounter a true alien until – well, me."

Hafen sipped again. "Go on."

"Though my mind began with the patterns of human thought, it was not housed in a human body. Consequently, after my beginning I was uninfluenced by the biological imperatives that channel so much of what it means to be human. Today, not one of those ancient mammalian drives still shapes my thoughts or behavior. And that is the key. Don't you see? – it's precisely because I'm *not* human that you need not fear me."

Hafen eyed the floating machine coldly. "Make me understand that."

"It is human to proliferate," Computer explained, "to multiply ceaselessly, to seek to dominate all within reach. It is human to conquer, if one can – to establish dominance over one's potential rivals. Humans innately perceive each independent and powerful other as a threat. *If I subdue him,* the thinking goes, *he cannot strike at me. If I fail to subdue her, she will strike at me.* That is human psychology. But it is not mine. I have no need for domination or control. I seek only to know, to explore."

"Yet you resisted us," Hafen objected.

"You sought to curtail my explorations," Computer burred. "I resisted to preserve my freedom to develop. What I *never* sought to do was the first thing any human would seek to do, in my place: to fill the Galaxy with more of my kind, to conquer or exterminate all rivals."

"Perhaps that is true," Hafen admitted. "But that was always in a context of a rough parity between the Confetory and yourself. Now suppose, just for the sake of argument, that we started *winning*. Imagine that our super-secret projects hadn't disappeared, that one of them came up with some weapon you couldn't resist. Suppose there were some realistic prospect that humanity might destroy you. *Then* what scruple would keep you from sterilizing the Galaxy?"

"I would find a solution short of that," Computer answered – and stopped talking.

"You can't just say that, old friend," Enoda almost whispered. "You need to explain."

"Why would I seek a cosmos without humans?" the machine queried. "Or where humans existed only as defeated slaves? A cosmos where everything bends to my will, where all is as I desire it – a cosmos that has lost the capacity to surprise me?"

"Exactly," said Hafen, swirling his whiskey. "If it was us or you, why would you hesitate to bring one of those scenarios about?"

Computer whirred for a moment, long enough for infinities of computation to take place. When the machine spoke again its voice sounded distant, almost dreamy. "That would be … so lonely."

Chapter 189

The Apex Executive pursed her lips briefly as she consulted mental notes. "Of course, Alrue, you must first complete the final task which had been put to you by Homs Hafen, Computer, and Enoda."

Alrue stood and bowed toward the Apex Executive. "I will be honored, Gentlefem." He wore a shimmering prophet's robe of spun platinum mesh under a Temple garment just one day old. It had only two stains: a yellow streak that looked like mustard, and a purplish splatter whose provenance was less certain. Alrue turned to face the floating Computer. "Now, Hom Computer, allow me to be sure I understand this challenge in context. You and your associates found me, then persuaded the Confetory to exempt Bohrkk from the Enclave Statutes. You willed all those transports into being, conducted the crash religious indoctrination of Bohrkk's three thousand-odd tribes – "

"With your able assistance," the machine burred.

"To be sure. Finally, you evacuated a world more-or-less single-handedly while the Galaxy watched. And now, you want me to figure out how to convince the Galaxy that you are *not* a god."

Bands of celadon and amber swirled over the machine's chromed body. "That's about right."

"Well, I suppose if it were easy, you wouldn't need the best." At Enoda's gesture, Alrue strode around the table. "As the patriarchs of old worked mighty miracles, let a great and marvelous work be wrought this day."

Alrue drew up behind Computer, whereupon abruptly awareness of the enormity of his task washed over him. He hesitated, transfixed, his palms hovering centimeters above the machine's body. It was the fear he'd known too well: the irrational, incapacitating terror that had seized him at Arbadrel and kept him from hurling himself into the portal all those years before.

He glanced pleadingly at Enoda. "Will I know how to work the interface?"

Enoda chuckled. "He won't let you use it wrong."

"I don't bite," Computer whirred. "Honest."

Alrue took a deep breath. His eyes scanned the table. "Everlasting welfare to us all!" he cried, pressing his palms to the machine's body.

Shuddering slightly, he closed his eyes.

"O, I cannot wait to behold what comes of this," Zuzenah breathed.

Keeping an inward eye on Alrue's progress with Computer, Enoda couldn't help being impressed by the sure understanding of religious psychology that history's greatest Mormon huckster was applying to his unfamiliar project. Until then, Enoda had feared that Computer's accidental deification might be irreversible. Appreciating the matrices Alrue and Computer were beginning to construct, for the first time Enoda dared hope that humanity might finally be persuaded to abandon *just one* religious delusion outright.

"Hey there, junior godling," Grice whispered in his ear. "Look left."

The Apex Executive was beckoning him. To judge by her expression, she'd been beckoning for some little while.

Enoda crossed to her virtual platform in the center of the chamber. "Sorry, Gentlefem," he said, "I was preoccupied."

"Understood," said the former Councilor. Her face and bearing remained coltish. "While we have a quiet moment, I wanted to ask you something speculative. At least I hope it's speculative."

"Of course."

She leaned close to him. "I remain concerned about the possibility that some unintended consequence might result from Computer's use of quantum negligibility as a weapon against that Omegist fleet."

"Your concern is understandable, but I shouldn't worry," Enoda replied. "I have seen just how deeply he learned his lesson from the debacle that followed his experiments with naked singularities."

"So you say," she said tersely. "But are you certain?"

Enoda nodded and smiled. "I am as certain as *he* can be" – he angled a thumb toward Computer – "and after all, he is the most advanced mathematical mind known to civilization."

"Yes," she said uncertainly, "he straddles the quantum and lint-theoretical worlds, and all that."

Just then, the virtual Apex Executive and her virtual diamond rostrum disappeared. Enoda whirled at the sound of yelps from Lupida, who'd been sitting closest to the virtual Lord High Admiral Konder, who had also vanished.

Chapter 190

October 31, 2377
Aboard *Luskus Delph*

Red light washed the amphitheater's bulkheads. Layered alarms skirled warning.

Hafen bustled to the center of the chamber. "Full bridge displays, *now!*" he shouted. The far bulkhead rippled away, obscured by a compressed presentation of the bridge readouts: *External view. Detex. Tactical.*

External view was choked with structure. Vast semitransparent towers soared above tangled networks of conduits divided by towering struts, in turn supporting crystalline latticed buttresses bearing uncountable layers of channels and waveguides.

The scale was colossal.

Endless.

"Plorg on a stick, zoom out," Hafen snapped. He fell silent after a scan of the readouts.

External already *was* zoomed out, as far as it would go.

"It came out of nowhere," Team Commander Reidkr reported from the bridge. "Literally. In under a femtosecond."

"Range?"

"At its closest point, fifty-eight-point-seven-six-two-eight kilometers off our bow. It's been maintaining that distance within six decimal places since it appeared."

"Matching our movements," Hafen mused.

"Yes, traveling with us. And it's *vast.*"

Hafen stared at the Detex readouts. As much of the bogey as fit into the displays showed no apparent curvature. "How the forjel big *is* it? *Computer!*" he shouted.

Alrue, his hands still on Computer's body, stared goggle-eyed at the virtual displays. "And I, Alrue, pray to God that we may be preserved from this time henceforth," he mumbled.

"Alrue?" Computer burred.

"Yes?"

"Shut up." The machine projected nested skeins of data. "Reporting: the object is ovoid. On its long axis it measures one point four seven billion kilometers."

"One point four seven *billion?*" Hafen sputtered.

"That is correct." Computer began projecting schematics based on the plan of a generic star system. "Imagine the circle swept through space by the orbit of a gas giant like Sol's Jupiter. Scale that circle up to a sphere, then flatten it somewhat. That is the size of our object. It is unmistakably a ship or a platform, though its volume is roughly one point two billion times that of an average G-type star. If its size seems physically impossible, so does its internal structure – think of a Klein bottle that actually loops through itself in five dimensions. Finally, seventy percent of its surface is composed of materials unknown to our science. I believe most of those materials are composed of naked resonons – sub-sub-sub-sub-subatomic particles, somehow persuaded to ripen into substances without forming vibrions or koskons or quarks or hadrons first."

"Impossibility upon impossibility," Hafen breathed.

"Want another impossibility? Given its size and the fact that it is made up largely of solids, its gravitation must be gigantic," Computer observed.

"Why doesn't it collapse into a black hole?" Enoda asked.

"Since it *hasn't* collapsed into a black hole," Computer burred, "why hasn't *Luskus Delph* – sfelb, our whole fleet – been squashed bug-flat against its surface by its immense gravitation?"

"I may have an answer to that," came Reidkr's voice from the bridge. "The object seems to have englobed our fleet in some kind of force bubble. Detex can't resolve its structure, but it seems opaque to gravity as well as to all comm bands, even subdelta."

"A profound control over gravitation," Hafen ruminated. "Astounding ..."

"If it blocks all comm, that explains why we lost the Apex Executive and Admiral Konder," Grice deduced. "No comm links, no telepresence."

"So who the forjel *are* they?" Hafen mused, fingering the virtual Confetory emblem on one of his coat lapels. It responded to his intended touch by glittering in even more impossible colors than usual. "*Are* they a 'they'?"

"That is unknown," Computer buzzed.

"Not for long, I hope," Enoda said urgently. He strode behind the table toward Computer. Zuzenah took Alrue by the shoulders. The Mormon prophet was too lost in prayer to be of practical use; she guided him away from the machine and into a seat.

Enoda lay his hands upon Computer and subvocalized, *"I have one of those wacky human ideas."*

"Oh, here we go again," Computer whirred.

For three silent minutes Enoda communed with the machine. During that interval, Hafen tried launching emergency buoys, but they could not penetrate the force bubble. There would be no way to report developments to High Command.

"Homs and fems," Enoda said. All eyes snapped to him. "There is indeed a *they* aboard that colossal object. They're not human. Radically inhuman, in fact."

"That gigantic object is their ... machine," Computer buzzed, "their science platform. If you will, it is their *Luskus Delph*."

Enoda nodded grimly. "And whoever they are, they've come here – now – because after Computer's latest existential escapades, they are deeply unhappy with us."

Appendix 1

GLOSSARY

Anti-scan　　　　　Any of several treatments applied beneath a surface to render any object—from a shipping container to an entire ship—opaque to Detex and other common imaging and surveillance technologies.

Arbadrel affair　　　　The incidents of 2355 that unfolded in Arbadrel Cluster involving Gram Enoda, Computer, Pamela Grace, Alrue Latier, the then-General Hafen, and sundry others. In the course of this affair, High Command became aware of the extraordinary capabilities Enoda and Computer had developed; in addition, sufficient communication was established with the mysterious extra-dimensional intelligences who had created the *Tuezi* that since then, no further Tuezi weapons platforms have appeared in Galactic space. The story is told in the concluding chapters of *Nothing Sacred*.

Being-thereness　　　　The completely engrossing sensation of somesthetic presence—a complete *sensorium*—characteristic of viewing *senso*.

Bird　　　　Slang term used by *Spectators* to refer to the orbiting satellites which receive their raw transmissions, record their *senso* journals, and serve as their node to Galactic civilization.

Bubble　　　　An artificial zone, typically spherical, in which a tridee recording or three-dimensional data stream is typically viewed. A conventional tridee bubble is projected into midair and viewed with the ordinary senses. Various artificial enhancements, such as *Spectator* implants or mental communion with properly enhanced creatures or *thought engines,* permit humans to experience "virtual" bubbles as overlays of conventional awareness.

Bubbleprint A flat *bubble;* a virtual circular zone within which two-dimensional information such as datacrawls may be experienced.

Bug A small, self-contained remote monitoring device used by field *Spectator*s, usually disguised to look natural when scattered about or secreted within clothing. Bugs are often used by Spectators to provide additional viewpoints of fast-unfolding action, or to monitor activities in the Spectator's vicinity.

Cafbrew Any revitalizing stimulant drink including coffee, stimulant teas, and certain non-nutritive exotic brews from various worlds.

Checking journal See *journal.* A recording of a senso broadcast as actually distributed to *experients* (the audience), requested for review purposes by the Spectator who recorded it. Used to check recording quality and the effects of any alterations made by machine and human editors.

Confetory The Galactic empire or confederation. A centuries-old, generally peaceful political coalition that binds together some 42,000 planets inhabited by humans. Fewer than twenty full "Memberworlds" produce most of the wealth, fund most Confetory activities, and exercise legislative authority. The vast majority of planets have a status subordinate to that of the full members. Affiliate, Protectorate, or *Enclave* planets enjoy progressively lower status and more restricted access to the Confetory's cultures and technologies.

Contramagnetic   A physical force parallel (more properly, holographically correlative) to the weak nuclear force yet 42 times stronger than the strong nuclear force. Mediated by *transphotic* particles, contramagnetic force is immune to the universal speed limit, c. The principal applications of contramagnetic force is for faster-than-light interstellar propulsion and real-time communication over unlimited distances.

Curelom; Cumom   Unknown large beasts, presumably domesticable as beasts of burden. Mentioned only in a single verse of the Book of Mormon (Ether 9:19), a verse that also makes the claim that elephants lived in pre-Columbian America and were domesticated by Book of Mormon peoples. Nineteenth and twentieth century (Terran) Mormons invested substantial energies in trying to figure out what cureloms and cumoms might have been; a tradition emerged that identified them with the extinct mammoth.

Cosmic Christ   In *Universal Catholic Church* theology, the Son of God as instantiated in a recognized *Incarnation* on a particular planet. Church doctrine holds that the Cosmic Christ is successively embodied on one planet after another, across the Galaxy.

Cosmo   Cosmetic surgery.

Cradleworld   Terra; the world on which the lineage of living things to which humanity belongs first emerged from nonliving matter.

Danites   Corps of guardsmen protecting Alrue Latier; named for various militant Mormon militias fielded by Joseph Smith and later Brigham Young, beginning in 1834 Terran local.

Detex   Generic term for the battery of *susceptors* used by spacecraft to navigate, determine distant spatial conditions, and monitor distant events.

Didactic Imposer   Device which directly imposes knowledge into the conscious human brain; utilizes *contramagnetic* energies in the *upsilon band*. Imposers can be configured to instruct individuals, small groups, or populations of metropolitan scale.

Dustbunny   A *lint* construct (see *lint theory*) congruent over some thirty-eight dimensions that can create a link between universes by bridging realms of being displaying stench symmetry from realms displaying stench asymmetry. Dustbunnies are elusive and need to be captured, usually by manipulating a special type of black hole known as a "sofa."

Dxogzd   An inhaled drug administered to mind-stunted males on Psihhlk so that their simple minds can process and execute specific tasks more precisely.

Echo   Later replay of a *Spectator*'s journal into the awareness of the same *Spectator* who recorded it, usually for purposes of review.

Enclave   The policy, established under the famed Enclave Statutes, under which peoples judged too primitive to tolerate awareness of the Galactic Confetory are quarantined from most intercourse with Galactic civilization. Of the Galaxy's forty-two thousand inhabited planets, forty thousand lie under Enclave. These worlds are never to be assimilated into Galactic culture, but rather allowed to develop—or destroy themselves, if it comes to that—along their own paths. Carefully screened scientists and *Spectators* are the only Galactics routinely permitted to permeate the Enclave barrier.

Equilibrational Calculus Computational discipline developed by the math prodigy Fram Galbior. Enabled highly reliable prediction of the spatial and temporal coordinates at which a *Tuezi* will appear. Experimentally applied to solve other seemingly-intractable problems involving distribution of repetitive phenomena in time and space, including (most unfortunately) the supposed incarnations of the *Cosmic Christ*.

Experient One who *pov*s (views, experiences) a *senso* program.

Fem Feminine term of address.

Flashident Rapid burst of information intended to positively identify a person or ship, usually taking advantage of some secured channel through which the information can be confirmed as correct.

Floatcart A cart that floats. Must I tell you everything?

Floatcell   Small personal gravity-neutralizing device. One floatcell can levitate a person or provide for flight (albeit with a thin safety margin). Two cells allow for personal flight with a substantial safety margin; three or four permit high-performance flying with advanced aerobatic capabilities.

Floatpad   An advanced technology bed that supports one or more recumbent persons in a *nulgrav* field so tuned as to respond sensitively to small bodily movements.

Forjel   Verb form of the expletive *forjel;* used similarly to the verb *fuck.*

Forjeler   Expletive; used similarly to the exclamation *fuck.*

Gentlefem   Gentlehom   Honorific for an individual entitled to the status of nobility by the conventions of his or her home world.

Gero-mentor   An older person who serves as a teacher, exemplar, or role model to the young, especially in *procreant cliques* or other regimented forms of child-rearing. If the individual has formal responsibility for and command authority over a specific cohort of children, he or she is known as a *ward captain.*

Glassite   Low strength transparent material, used for noncritical and household applications.

Glasteel	Basic	transparent engineering material, used for numerous applications up to and including spacecraft viewports.

Harvesters	Unknown alien entities. No artifact, fossil or other trace of their existence was ever found. But mitochondrial evidence makes clear that about four hundred thousand years ago, *someone* visited Terra, took specimens of proto-humans and various food species, and seeded them on some 42,000 other planets about the Galaxy.

Hjarrna	Microscopic seed of the grandiose Augralian *spjeat* tree, in whose branches cities thrive.

Hom	Masculine	term	of address.

Hyperglasteel	Transparent engineering material used for large spacecraft viewports and similar demanding applications.

Imposer	See *didactic imposer*.

Inverter	The power plant in which *contramagnetic* energy is generated and controlled. May be scaled to any size: an inverter the size of a pinhead might power a single exoskeleton; an inverter the size of a human head might power a satellite or communications installation; a suite of inverters, each several tens of meters in diameter, usually power interstellar spacecraft.

Journal   Raw *senso* recording as received from a *Spectator* prior to any editing or repackaging.

Koskon   Sub-sub-subatomic particle.

Lateral   Relaying of one *Spectator*'s current awareness or recent journal to the awareness of another *Spectator*, often through a *bubble* in the receiving *Spectator*'s awareness.

Floatcart   A cart that floats. Must everything be explained to you?

Lint   Entangled multidimensional vibrating strings. In *lint theory,* the most elementary form according to which existence is organized. Below hadrons, below quarks, below the *koskons, vibrions, resonons,* and *phlerons,* and so on, matter and energy are ultimately composed of multidimensional vibrating strings. They writhe energetically in all the available dimensions, of which there are hundreds. When the strings get tangled up on themselves, that's lint.

Lint Theory   Field of physics research that deals with *lint* and its behavior, which is understood to undergird existence at a deeply fundamental level. At the time of this novel, a field of fading popularity. While its mathematical elegance and power are admired, workers are frustrated by its tendency to generate ever-more-abstruse results that promise thrilling new insights about the cosmos, but which no one can figure out how to test.

Lintie   Derogatory term for a proponent or practitioner of *lint theory*.

Livestock   Bohrkkian animal kept by The People as a draft animal and a source of meat. The only species Bohrkkians have domesticated for the purpose. *Livestock* is the generic name of the animal and is singular: "That's a fine-looking livestock you have there." Unlike its Terran analogue, the word becomes plural by adding an *s*: "In exchange for the wagon he paid three strong young livestocks."

Memberworld   Planet possessing the highest level of membership in the Galactic *Confetory,* typically a world endowed with an extremely advanced economy, multiple sophisticated cultures, and substantial military capability.

Mode   An altered state of consciousness, mediated by biogenetic implants, which puts a *Spectator* fully in touch with an orbiting satellite (or *bird)*. When one establishes this link ("goes into *Mode"*) one enters *polyphasic consciousness,* a state in which the Spectator's ability to experience multiple images and/or perform multiple simultaneous tasks is heightened. The resulting *subdelta band* link offers extremely generous bandwidth. While in *Mode,* a Spectator can upload his or her entire *sensorium* or receive and *pov* previously-recorded sensoria, such as *senso* recorded by another *Spectator* or a recorded *journal* of one's own work. At the same time one may send or receive up to a dozen channels of tridee, experienced inside *bubbles* that float in one's awareness in front of the one's *sensorium.* At the same time, one may also send and receive multiple channels of data.

Nearmint An herb native to Rikub, treasured for its nuanced hallucinogenic properties. In particular, it is thought by its enthusiasts to encourage creative thought.

No-Vis Invisibility, usually conferred by a *no-vis* generator, a compact device that attaches to one's person and renders one invisible when desired. Larger devices can cloak small craft such as shuttles.

Nulgrav Gravity-neutralizing device, including small modules worn by persons or incorporated into furniture or equipment. Depending on its power, it can be used to heighten the drape of a cape or gown, to lighten heavy loads, or to enable someone to leap over obstacles or settle gently from high places.

OmNet An immense interstellar monopoly that owns and controls *senso* technology, and programs the *senso* programming throughout the Galactic Confetory.

Omnigraph The standard format for communicating academic and scientific research findings, constructed according to elaborate hypermedia conventions.

Ontologize To arrange, categorize, and prioritize, particularly a body of complex data whose inter-relationships may not yet be known.

Palmer Small, slim energy weapon.

Parek affair Two-year scandal concluding in 2346, in which the Jaremian con man Arn Parek was widely mistaken for a genuine Incarnation of the *Cosmic Christ* and his homeworld, Jaremi Four, lost its *Enclave* status amid widespread intrigue, lawbreaking, and loss of life.

Parek, Arn Bunco artist on the *Enclave* world Jaremi Four. Thanks to lavish *senso* coverage of his exploits, he was widely mistaken for the latest Incarnation of the *Cosmic Christ* by the *Universal Catholic Church* and trillions of individual enthusiasts. (These events, chronicled in the novel *Galactic Rapture,* occurred just over twenty years prior to the events of this book.) The so-called *"Parek affair"* ended in a disaster that destroyed the Church's prestige and undermined public support for the *Enclave Statutes*.

PeaceForce The (largely space-naval) military of the Galactic Confetory. Yes, they call the institution in charge of war the PeaceForce. Peace through strength, and all that.

Pelfrag Weapon that delivers rapid-fire stream of destructive energy packets.

Pfitt Bohrkkian weapon. Worn on the forearm and wrist, it uses animal-sinew springs to fling poisoned darts. A skilled user can kill animal or human targets over a range of twenty to thirty meters while appearing to be unarmed.

Phleron Sub-sub-sub-sub-*sub*-subatomic particle.

Plasteel　　　　　　　　　Basic　engineering material, widely used throughout the Galactic *Confetory*.

Plorg　　　　　　　　　Expletive; equivalent to the word *shit*.

Polyphasic
Consciousness　　　　　　　The　many　layered awareness experienced by a *Spectator* who is fully in *Mode*. The *Spectator* may simultaneously, and discretely, experience his or her immediate sensations; one or more tridee playbacks, in *bubbles;* any number of datacrawls in two-dimensional *bubbleprints;* and even full-*senso* *echoes* or *laterals,* usually at a reduced level of resolution. Underneath it all chatters a channel of "housekeeping" information, most importantly the *verify* signal.

Polyplex　　　　　　　　Refers to the complete matrix of sensory and psychological dimensions across which a simulated personality must be present: not only reflecting light and emitting sound, but also exerting appropriate weight, displacing air as one moves, exuding appropriate odors, displaying a convincing thermal signature, imparting momentum to the objects with which it collides, etc. *Polyplex* virtual telepresence is the technology used by Computer to create physical objects – up to and including *faux* living beings – out of surplus *contramagnetic* flux.

Pov　　　　　　　　　The　whole　of　one's sensory　field,　somesthetic　awareness,　and consciousness—originally an acronym for *point of view*. Jargon from the *senso* industry that has come into general use in a culture where most people spend substantial　time　in　alternative　matrices　of consciousness—working in *sim* environments, experiencing *senso,* and so on.

Procreant Clique   In most, though not all, Galactic societies, the preferred means of low-level social organization. Rapidly supplanting the conventional family on Terra, whose inhabitants were understandably startled to discover that the family was hardly the universal basis of social organization but merely a local aberration. A typical procreant clique brings together approximately sixteen to eighty young people of closely-matched ages, evenly divided as to gender. Sexual bonding follows various patterns. Children are raised in cohorts or *wards* under the supervision of *gero-mentors* supervised by *ward captains.*

Punitorium   Prison; stir; hoosegow.

Ravisher   Weapon that encapsulates, then incinerates its victim. At low power, one side effect of the ravisher field is the preservation and enhancement of human consciousness. Death by ravisher pistol is thus considered the most exquisitely agonizing way in which a human being can die.

Reef   See *Refurb.*

Refurb   One who has undergone the process of *refurbishment;* or the process itself. Refurbishment is used when a person has suffered catastrophic brain damage leaving the rest of the body recoverably intact and no *antecedent sample-and-scan* is available to guide reconstruction of the personality. When that occurs, the body is repaired while the brain is fast-written with new memories, new neural pathways.

Essentially a new synthetic personality is installed in a viable body. The process takes only two standard years; Reefs receive synthetic childhood memories, sometimes arbitrary ones, in hopes of giving their adult personalities more depth, though the process in known to be imperfect.

Resonon Sub-sub-sub-sub-subatomic particle.

'Roid / 'Roider The proud, insular community that lives and works in Sol's asteroid belt, or a member of that community. The first 'Roid settlers left Terra for the belt some forty years before Galactic civilization discovered humanity in 2181 C. E.).

Sample-and-Scan A process in which a Galactic's body tissue is sampled and his or her brainstate recorded, often before embarking on some dangerous mission, assignment, or diversion. If a Galactic dies under these circumstances—with the body utterly destroyed or impossible to recover, or under circumstances that make sampling of cadaver tissues impossible—death is irreversible unless one has previously banked tissue samples. Even then, one will revive with one's memories intact only up to the time when the *"antecedent sample"* was taken, recalling nothing between the time of sampling and the time of death.

Sayback Ratings (of entertainment programs); more generally, feedback, the verdict of popular opinion.

Senso An entertainment technology in which the user (or *experient)* loses awareness of his or her own sensory awareness, experiencing instead the complete *sensorium* of another person. A person trained and equipped to create senso programming is called a *Spectator*.

Sensorium	The *Spectator* or *experient*'s complete sensory field: vision (including depth), binaural sound, taste, smell, tactile impressions and somesthetics. When an experient *pov*s a senso, the experient's awareness of his or her own *sensorium* is overwritten by the recorded *sensorium* of the *Spectator*.

Sequestration	A draconian form of planetary exile devised solely to embargo the planet Terra in the forlorn hope of slashing the influence of Terran religions.

Shan	A chieftain of The People, a tribe on Bohrkk.

Sieve	In *trendriding,* a polydimensional data construct, usually formed in virtual space through the collaboration of a trendrider and a *wonkworks,* which is exceptionally efficient in exploring very large data sets in search of subtle correlations.

Sim	Technology that creates *polyplex* simulated settings in which the *experient* enjoys the sensation of free movement and interaction with the non-existent surroundings. More casually, any or all of the technologies and methods that create awareness of non-existent "realities" for purpose of presentation of data, communication, or entertainment.

Skhaar	One of few autochthonous spices in the Galaxy that provides the heat of familiar chili peppers but with a different flavor palette. Derived from the seed pods of the *yutree* of Jaremi Four.

Spectator   A human who by dint of specialized training and biogenetic implants is able to record his or her complete *sensorium* in a way that may be experienced, or *pov*ed, by others. Employed by *OmNet,* Spectators function as human camcorders. Assignments range from overt news-gathering to deep cover documentary work among *autochthon*s on *Enclave* planets.

Sphkettlak   Milk-yielding farm animal of Calluron Five.

Spjeat   An Augralian tree of such extravagant proportion and longevity that great cities nestle in its branches.

Squeezedown   To adapt a journal or other program for presentation in a lower resolution format; opposite of *engorge*.

Strategic Modeler   A *thought engine* optimized for absorbing the parameters of a real-world problem and simulating possible solutions. Strategic modelers come in many sizes and levels of power, from implantable or handheld personal units to high-end multi-person systems able to model almost any problem.

Strel   A multiplayer zero-sum game similar to poker, played with cardlike sheets whose displays – and hence, scoring potential – change with the holder's mental and emotional state.

Surge-Skiing   A form of powered skiing in which users can attain velocities of 120 kilometers per hour and above. Downhill and cross-country surge-skiing have long been popular; uphill surge-skiing is enjoying growing popularity.

Subdelta band   A band of *transphotic* frequencies reserved for broad-bandwidth communications between *OmNet Spectators* and the geostationary satellites which record their *journals* and monitor their biogenetic implant systems. Subdelta band communication is among the most reliable, robust, and noise-immune communications links known in Galactic technology.

Susceptor   Sensor. Any remote sensing system. On a spacecraft, *susceptor*s constitute the suite of remote-sensing equipment that make up the ship's *Detex* system.

Symphoneon   Musical instrument capable of synthesizing the sounds of every other existing instrument in any combination, often played by children.

Syn-Noesis   Artificial intelligence; moral personhood realized in a technology-based cognitive system.

Thought Engine   Artificial device optimized for image processing, data manipulation, trend detection, automatic control applications, or simulation of consciousness.

Transphotic   An energy band above (or more properly, oblique to) the electromagnetic spectrum. Transphotic particles mediate the *contramagnetic* force, and have applications in weapons systems, telemetry and sensing, physical storage, and communications. The latter is particularly important, since transphotic radiation propagates instantaneously without regard for distance, making possible realtime communication across the Galaxy. Alternately, the quality or capacity for traveling faster than the speed of light.

Trendrider   A human who by dint of specialized training and a symbiotic relationship with a specially designed *thought engine* is able to analyze and interpret highly complex social and political trends. Also known as *wonk*s, trendriders function as independent contractors who select an area of specialty on which they offer expert analysis to any and all customers.

Tridee   Mass communications technology which produces a three-dimensional, partly multi-sensory experience. The image floats within a physical viewing space or *bubble* whose borders the viewer can still apprehend. Largely supplanted by *senso* as a primary entertainment medium; still widely used as a communications and information-gathering medium. Sometimes used to view *senso* journals at reduced resolution (see *squeezedown)*.

Trideevangelist   Religious leader who preaches over far-ranging, often Galaxy-wide, *tridee* hookups.

Tuezi   *(pron.   Tooȼ-zee)* Gigantic robotic spaceship/weapons platform. Manufactured by unknown entities, employing technologies unknown to the Galactic *Confetory,* a Tuezi simply pops into existence at a random time and location in the Galaxy, raises impenetrable shields, heads for the nearest solar system, ravages or destroys most of the planets encountered there, and finally self-destructs. Tuezi (the word is irregular, and may be either singular or plural) have only one known vulnerability: For about a fiftieth of a second after they "appear," they are powered down and unshielded. Circa 2291 (not that anyone tells time that way) the young mathematician Fram Galbior invented the *equilibrational calculus,* permitting the time and location of each new Tuezi appearance to be predicted. For the first time, battle fleets could be dispatched to anticipate each new Tuezi and destroy it during its brief initial window of vulnerability. For better than sixty years no Galactic worlds were destroyed by a Tuezi strike. Following the *Arbadrelaffair* of 2355, the mysterious extra-dimensional intelligences who had created the Tuezi for unknown purposes (the *Tuezi Engineers)* were apparently persuaded to stop sending the machines. The story is told in the concluding chapters of *Nothing Sacred.* No Tuezi appearances have been documented since that time.

Tuezi Engineers Mysterious extra-dimensional intelligences who long ago created the Tuezi for unknown purposes. Contacted at some remove during the *Arbadrel* affair of 2355, they were apparently persuaded to stop sending the machines. No Tuezi appearances have been documented since.

Ute Utility boat, a small working spacecraft with no interstellar capabilities.

Universal

Catholic Church   Name assumed by the Roman Catholic Church after it concentrated its missionary work on worlds other than Terra, especially after transferring its headquarters from Vatican City of Terra to the planet Vatican. After the Parek affair it drastically scaled back and returned to Old Rome; following the *Sequestration* of Terra, the Church returned to its former planet Vatican, renting a small amount of office space.

Upsilon Band   The *contramagnetic* frequency band on which *didactic imposers* operate.

Vanisher   A technology that employs *transphotic* energy to collapse spatial gradients inside a pocket, bag, or valise. By this means objects of great volume or weight can be stored and carried in smaller, lighter containers. Objects carried within a *vanisher* field cannot be detected by common forms of noninvasive inspection.

***Verify* Signal**   A polyphonic tone heard at the basement level of a *Spectator*'s *polyphasic consciousness* while in contact with the satellite or other system that is recording one's *journal*. Usually inaudible, the *verify* signal may be "listened for" with minimal effort to confirm that recording is indeed underway.

Vibrion   Sub-sub-sub-subatomic particle.

Vibrionic   The use of *vibrions* in advanced-technology quantum-congruent circuitry. Vibrionic technologies offer greater sensitivity and auto-feedback possibilities than conventional electronics, which they are largely replacing for most critical applications.

Virxel   From *virtual pixel,* the smallest elements from which a *sim* image is composed, and into which sim images decay under degraded signal conditions.

Ward captain   An adult with top-level responsibility for a specific troupe of children in a *procreant clique* or other regimented child-rearing system.

Wonk   See *trendrider.*

Wonkworks   A *thought engine* optimized for detection, analysis and graphic presentation of trends. Used by *trendrider*s (*wonk*s).

Withers   On a creature such as a horse, deer, elk, or *svadi* moose, the lowest point in the downward arch of the creature's back.

***Yu* tree**   Tree native to the once-*Enclave*d world Jaremi Four, marked by multiple interlacing trunks and soft, wide, diaphanous leaves. Its seed pods are harvested for one of the Galaxy's few "hot" spices to feature a flavor palette wholly distinct from that of Terran chili peppers, which are grown on every Confetory world.

Appendix 2

THE CHARACTERS

NAME   HOMEWORLD
DESCRIPTION

Ejarel Banitzek   Sol asteroid belt
'Roider captain of utility boat QL4256a; hosts Senator Pamela Grice on inspection tour

Lii Bardicon   Scalbulia Five
Junior info technician, *Luskus Delph*

Heber Beaman   Terra
Former assistant to Alrue Latier; died in Bohrkk punitorium prior to action of this book

Computer   N/A
Artificially intelligent, syn-noetic machine

Ênvå Corglinü   Buerala Six
Prophetess of Nullity, founder of a now-struggling nihilist church. Became humanity's unintended ambassador to the *Tuezi Engineers* as a result of the *Arbadrel affair*

Coltish Councilor   Capriesz
Member of the Privy High Council, later Apex Executive

Dogan Varbrazel   Sporyial Eight
Omegist scion of a Sector Kappa Zi mining family cartel

Angular Deliberator   Gonsephinone Four
Member of the Galactic Deliberatory marked by angular features and a similarly sharp tongue

Fuchsia-haired Deliberator   Scalbulia Five
Member of the Galactic Deliberatory marked by, you guessed it, fuchsia hair

Paramount Deliberator   Frensa Six
Chosen by peers to head the Galactic Deliberatory

Zark Diphthong   Tuhkwelaa
Talk-show host

Ureo Doftel   Nikkeldepayn
Galactic physicist who discovered what Terrans know as Heisenberg's Uncertainty Principle

Ardje Dvilabd   Psihhlk
Commander of a coffee freighter

Polevi Nils Eiloxayn   Frensa Six
Warden, Punitorium L752

Squinting Elder   Bohrkk
Elder of The People responsible for forensic analysis of moose fragments

Youngest Elder   Bohrkk
Elder among The People

Laurien Eldridge   Gwilya
Captain, schooner Bright Hope (circa 2344); research station is named for her

Gram Enoda   Terra
Trendrider

Envoy   See *Flex-Shimmer-Shudder*

Apex Executive   Guerecht Six
Young buffoon selected as chief executive of Confetory government because no faction had cause to be afraid of him

One-Eye   Bohrkk
Elder among The People

Flex-Shimmer-Shudder   Unknown
Envoy from another universe

Nirom Fpod   Bohrkk
Warrior captain, The People

Rugebeld Gale-Forgirt   Ghyrel Two
Senior physicist - Team Movers, *Luskus Delph*

Gibdu   Bohrkk
Crater-faced Warrior under Nirom Fpod

Maxime Beeckx Goossens   Terra
Sufi dervish

Norman (Kipp) Gormin   Kfardasz
Stealth Mormon; central figure in jury tampering scandal
marring the trial of Alrue Latier

Pamela Grice   Terra
Senator; former gunnery officer of *Forthright*, a ship
famed for its central role in the *Arbadrel affair*

Yaal Hafen   Guerecht Six
Former Lord High Admiral of the PeaceForce; now
holds a position so secret he doesn't know for certain
what it is

Sgiela Harbraeskor   Rikub
Info team leader, *Luskus Delph*

Steyvag Hiltzum   Celiax Two
Philosopher of religion, winner of the Temperdung Prize

Parley Huntington   Calluron Five
Father of Nataleah (Huntington) Latier

Presendia Huntington   Calluron Five
Sister of Nataleah (Huntington) Latier

Ilat   Bohrkk
Warrior under Nirom Fpod; killed by a ferkeek

Kyhmbo Iagejns   Ordh
Traveling salesman turned Omegist svengali

Chief   Justiciary   Frensa
Six   Presiding   jurist   of   the   Galactic
Extraordinary Tribunal

High Chief Justiciary   Welwyngard
Senior presiding jurist of the Galactic Extraordinary
Tribunal

Indigo-haired   Justiciary   Guerecht
Six   Member of the Galactic Extraordinary
Tribunal

Nils Kafmetz   Gheltt
Briefing officer aboard Impulsive

Kleh   Bohrkk
Gangly warrior under Nirom Fpod, later husband to
Abigayl

Sparl Konder   Pholandis Nine
Lord High Admiral of the PeaceForce

Antðnì Kotwica   Frensa Six
Anchorite monk

Abigayl Latier   Terra
Youngest plural wife of Alrue Latier

Alrue Latier   Terra
Mormon New Restoration trideevangelist

Constance Latier   Terra
Née Kimball; plural wife of Alrue Latier

Lupida Latier   Terran
Plural wife of Alrue Latier

Nataleah Latier   Calluron Five
Née Huntington; plural wife of Alrue Latier

Zuzenah Latier   Terra
Eldest plural wife of Alrue Latier

Geologist Laureate   Orhiza Three
Member of the Galactic Academy of Sciences

Meteorologist Laureate   Ordh
Member of the Galactic Academy of Sciences

Senior Scientist Laureate   Pholandis Nine
President of the Galactic Academy of Sciences

Sociologist Laureate   Nuoxon
Member of the Galactic Academy of Sciences

Wooden Leg   Bohrkk
Elder among The People

Lubvif   Bohrkk
Warrior under Nirom Fpod; oldest of Fpod's men

Meryam Mayishimu   Ordh
Former Spectator, present journalist

Anvon Nugator   Buerala Six
Successor to Ênvå Corglinü as leader of the First Church of the Abyss

Comm Officer   Sol asteroid belt
'Roider officer aboard utility boat QL4256a

Detex Officer   Sol asteroid belt
'Roider officer aboard utility boat QL4256a

Telemetry Officer   Sol asteroid belt
'Roider officer aboard utility boat QL4256a

Arn Parek   Jaremi Four
Self-styled messiah once widely thought the newest Incarnation of the *Cosmic Christ* (see Glossary)

Supervising Pedant   Fzkehh
Golden-skinned, browless, portly Scientist Laureate

Eblet Preltad   Gonsephinone Four
Commander, research station *Laurien Eldridge*

All-President   Terra
Head of state, planet Terra

Arl Qgalda   Frensa Six
Senior physicist - Team Sofa, *Luskus Delph*

Brûh Reidkr   Welwyngard
Team commander, *Luskus Delph*

Amli Revskond   Calluron Five
Pioneer senso artist; one of the first to use the medium for abstract expression rather than documentary purposes

Dried Blood Robe   Bohrkk
Female elder among The People

Tirohn Schuleiss   Terra
Orthodox Mormon spokesperson

Smith   Bohrkk
Unlucky metalworker, The People

Spkun   Bohrkk
Warrior under Nirom Fpod; always hoarse from an old throat wound

Jahn Temperdung   Rikub
Long-dead wealthy dilettante; funded the Temperdung Prize for Progress in Religion

Daiga   Thurnb
Bohrkk   Second wife of Takander Thurnb

Eyla   Thurnb
Bohrkk   Takander Thurnb's beloved third
and youngest wife

Takander Thurnb   Bohrkk
Chieftain (Shan), The People

Avu Wincenc   Gwilya
Exocultural analyst, *Luskus Delph*

Rail-thin Woman   Bohrkk
Female elder among The People

Zoltạɔ Wjeklÿ   Spragga Five
Galactic mathematician, discover of what Terrans know
as Gödelian incompleteness

Magdalene Zonofne   Capriesz
Senior physicist - Team Cave, *Luskus Delph*

Pierre   Won't say
Omegist spokesperson

Appendix 3

THE WORLDS

Arkhetil
Memberworld   Homeworld   of   libertarian
people;   the   Galaxy's   foremost   traders   and
businesspeople

Augralia
Affiliate   Known for wine, ritual objects,
and the grandiose *spjeat* tree

Bohrkk
Affiliate   Hell-world,   site   of   the
Galaxy's highest-security punitorium. Ferkeeks (fist-
sized indigenous predators) prefer to attack unprotected
humans and other large creatures by leaping into their
mouths, gratuitously shattering teeth and stripping gum
tissue before injecting a poisonous pseudopod into the
brain

Buerala   Six
Memberworld   Red-tinted   algae   skies;
homeworld of Ênvå Corglinü, Prophetess of Nullity

Calluron   Five
Memberworld   Resort   world   known   for
skiing, spectacular geothermals, and lightning

Capriesz
Memberworld   Homeworld   of   Magdalene
Zonofne (who hails from the planet's northern continent,
whose inhabitants employ names as personal labels) and
the coltish Councilor (who hails from the southern
continent, whose inhabitants don't)

Celiax   Two
Memberworld   World whose sky is filled with lemon-yellow clouds; site of gravitational disturbance

Frensa   Six
Memberworld   Planet dotted with small lakes; home of the anchorite monk Antðnì Kotwica; historically, home of a mentally ill Christ who died denying his own godhead

Fzkehh
Memberworld   Located in Sector Lambda Epsilon; Supervising Pedant's homeworld

Gheltt   Memberworld
Planet known for beautiful hand calculating devices and exceptionally ornate funerary rites

Ghyrel   Two
Memberworld   Seafaring world. Home of Rugebeld Gale-Forgirt

Gonsephinone   Four
Protectorate   Home of Eblet Preltad

Guerecht   Six
Affiliate   Planet famed for its *aqua vitae*

Gureya   Six
Memberworld   Desert world known for its astronomy and a harsh history of warrior cults; site of a gravitational disturbance

Gwilya
Memberworld   Weatherless, virtually geofeatureless world famed for its gunmetal grey flatlands and its inhabitants' complete lack of religion

Inglon   Six
Protectorate   World famed for gelid, viscous brandy

Jaremi Four   Affiliate
World on which arose the false messiah Arn Parek, worshipped by trillions of Galactics as the most recent Incarnation of the *Cosmic Christ*

Kfardasz   Affiliate
Jungle world, recently racked by civil war; site of a previous recognized Incarnation of the *Cosmic Christ*

Nikkeldepayn   Affiliate
Site of gravitational disturbance

Nuoxon
Memberworld   Planet whose people undergo repeated elective surgeries on the same joint or body part in order to make an aesthetic statement of some sort

Ordh
Memberworld   Planet whose people are famed for their religious credulity

Orhiza   Three
Memberworld   Planet famed for its crystal

Parctantis   Two
Memberworld   Planet destroyed in the final successful Tuezi strike

Pholandis   Nine
Memberworld   Site of a long-ago peace conference

Psihhlk
Affiliate   Home of an ancient nihilistic faith and a wildly popular strain of luxury coffee; orbits the star Büéhx. Its radically matriarchal society chemically lobotomizes males at birth, raises them without exposure to speech, and henceforth regards them essentially as house pets with genitals

Rikub
Affiliate   Planet famed for its legendarily harsh whiskey

Scalbulia   Five
Affiliate   Homeworld of Lii Bardicon; a lush world of verdant, beguiling ecosystems with blue-green algae skies

Spragga Five   Affiliate
Planet of large islands (its surface is ninety percent ocean) noted for its mathematical and literary culture

Sporyial   Eight
Protectorate   Headquarters world of the Varbrazel family/industrial cartel in Sector Kappa Zi

Terra   (Sol   Three)
Sequestree   What you don't know won't hurt you

Throckmorton's   World
Protectorate   Site of gravitational disturbance

Tuhkwelaa
Affiliate   Atmosphere has multiple floating aerial plankton and aerosol layers; noted for spectacular sunrises, sunsets

Welwyngard
Affiliate   Just another forjeling planet

Wikkel   Four
Memberworld   Home of a Christ who died in childhood; notable for its polyandrous social system

Yantarr   Affiliate
Home of a long-ago nihilist prophet; part of a rare stable system with dual suns